# *The*

# LOST

# TREASURE

# *of the*

# SILK ROAD

A Novel

*by*

# Saeed

# Derakhshani

*and*

# Shirin

# Derakhshani

**The Lost Treasure of the Silk Road**
Copyright © 2014 by Saeed Derakhshani & Shirin Derakhshani

This book is a work of fiction. Names, characters, businesses, organiza- tions, places, events and incidents either are the product of the author's imagination or are used fictitiously. Any resemblance to actual persons, living or dead, events, or locales is entirely coincidental.

For information visit: www.Facebook.com/LostTreasureOfTheSilkRoad/
Book and Cover design by Derek Murphy

ISBN: ISBN-10: 0990921700
ISBN-13: 978-0-9909217-0-7

First Edition: December 2014

Parthian Shot Press

10 9 8 7 6 5 4 3 2 1

# Contents

We dedicate this book to Dorothy Derakhshani, our wonderful wife and mother. This book wouldn't be what it is without her.

And
To our beloved
Lady

We hope you enjoy reading our book. As new authors, your voice is very important to us. Please favor us with a review on Amazon, Goodreads, or Facebook to help spread the word!
Visit us on Facebook for updates, Sales, and fascinating info on Ancient Persia.

A portion of every sale will support
Ovarian Cancer research

THE QANAT IS A WATER DELIVERY
SYSTEM WHICH BRINGS WATER FROM
THE DISTANT MOUNTAINS TO THE
CITIES AND VILLAGES, DATING BACK TO
THE FIRST CENTURY B.C. IN ANCIENT
PERSIA.

QANAT ENGINEERS BUILT AND
MAINTAINED THESE TUNNELS, DEEP
WITHIN THE MOUNTAINS, ENSURING A
CONSTANT FLOW OF WATER FOR THEIR
COMMUNITIES.

THESE BRAVE MEN FACED EXTREME
DANGERS EVERY TIME THE SET FOOT
INTO A QANAT.

# *1*

# THE QANAT

**The Steppes of Central Asia, 9th Century**

Fumbling his flint out from his pocket in the absolute darkness, he struck the flint once, twice, three times, and the tunnel lit up with the golden glow from the oil lamp. He prayed it would not go out again. Holding his lamp up high, the light revealed a landslide inside the tunnel, blocking the flow of water from the mountain to the town.

The flow of water to the town of Abrisham had slowed to a trickle and then stopped altogether. The town elders called upon him to investigate and fix the problem within the qanat. Since he was the only qanat engineer around, the only person who dared to venture into the dark, narrow channels deep within the mountain, he accepted this duty.

Persicus entered the tunnel the afternoon before and crawled all night, hunched over on his hands and knees. He held his oil lamp in one hand; a pickaxe, tied to a rope connected to his belt, trailing behind him; and an inflated goatskin on his chest, tied around his back. His leather kneepads gave little protection from the rocks he had to crawl over. Not knowing where the problem was, he had to start at the entrance of the qanat and work his way inward, towards the master shaft in the belly of the mountain. He had worked in many qanats over the years, some stretching over twenty-five miles. Thankfully, this one, which served his hometown, was only fifteen miles long. The last few miles were above ground, where the water flowed through a network of stone-lined courses into the fountain in the courtyard of the town.

He began having problems as soon as he entered the qanat. His oil lamp kept going out for no apparent reason, as if some phantom kept blowing out the flame. Each time it went out, he had to stop and relight it—a difficult task under normal conditions and almost impossible in the complete darkness. He had slowed his pace, creeping along, careful to keep the oil lamp as still as possible, hoping that this would help the lamp stay lit. As luck would have it, the lamp would never blow out anywhere near the thin beams of sunlight that streamed in from the vertical airshafts, which were placed at regular intervals throughout the tunnel.

He inched his way to the obstruction, set the lamp on the ground, and ran his hands along the base of the landslide. It felt dry. He inspected the obstruction from top to bottom. With caution, he removed a small rock from the top of the mound, placing it on the ground behind him. The dirt behind the rock felt wet, saturated with water. "That is not good," he said aloud, fearing the water could be building up behind the blocked area. He swallowed hard and took a few deep, reassuring breaths. He brushed off a layer of dirt from the top of the mound.

This was always the risky part. He needed to find out if it was a small blockage — a few feet of dirt and rocks blocking the tunnel — or if a large portion of the tunnel had caved in. As the dirt was soaking wet behind the first layer of rocks, he felt hopeful it wasn't a huge blockage, but a large amount of pressurized water could be building up behind the mound.

Persicus dislodged another small rock from the top of the landside. A rumble sounded from behind the mound, and he felt a vibration through the ground, up into his knees. Persicus said a soft, "Uh oh," as a small stream of water squirted out from where he had removed the last small stone, shooting straight into his mouth. He jerked back, coughing, as the vibration grew stronger. One moment he was taking in a deep breath and the next, water burst through, making a hole a foot wide, shooting straight into his face, and knocking him flat on his back. His oil lamp went out again, and he struggled to get back up on his hands and knees in the darkness. The rumble intensified into a deep thunderous sound that grew louder by the second, emanating from behind the landslide, and echoing off the tunnel walls.

"Damn!" Persicus cried out as a wall of water, rocks, and mud gripped him, knocking him over onto his back, and sweeping him away backwards, towards the tunnel's entrance. He fought to turn over onto his stomach so that the inflated goatskin would help keep him above water. Being swept away headfirst on his back with debris slamming into him was his worst fear at that moment. He managed to turn over onto his stomach; the goatskin pulled him up, keeping his head above the water, as he rushed forward in a whirlpool of sharp, jagged rocks, and ice-cold, muddy water swarming around him.

The torrent of rushing water threw him into the side of the rock wall, his shoulder taking most of the impact, but his head hit the wall, causing a moment of panic at the thought of blacking out as a bright starburst lit up his vision. Trying to protect his head, he took a deep breath, tucked his chin down towards his chest, and stretched both arms straight out in front of him, blocking the rocks that bashed into him. This was the safest position he could think of for streaming headfirst into the dangerous darkness. Every few moments he turned his head to the side to take a deep breath.

Persicus knew the severity of the situation. He knew that he could hit his head hard enough that he would lose consciousness and drown in moments. At times like these, he always told himself that if he survived, he would never set foot inside a qanat again. Even as he thought it, he knew that he was lying to himself. Every time they called upon him, he always went. Who else nearby would do this?

Each time he passed one of the vertical airshafts, a brief flash of light penetrated the roaring darkness. He counted them as he passed them by, holding his breath. *I'll be out of here in no time*, he thought as he rushed by another brief flash of light.

Something stung his face and he spared a second to wonder if the cut was deep. Only nine more flashes of light to go before he reached the entrance.

Eight ... Seven ...

Suddenly the back of his head slammed into the top of the tunnel. Water completely filled the tunnel and now he had no more air to breathe. He held on, desperate for air.

Six ... Five...

His lungs burned with the need to breathe. He felt himself going lightheaded and the next flash of light from the airshaft seemed dimmer than the last.

Four ...

Unable to hold his breath any longer, he unintentionally inhaled a small amount of muddy water, causing him to gag and cough, which made him suck in more muddy water.

*Drowning!* he thought.

Three ... Two ...

He braced himself, still coughing, gagging, and choking. After what seemed like an eternity, he saw daylight. He shot out of the tunnel, expelled with enough velocity that he landed yards away from the qanat entrance in a shallow pool of water.

On hands and knees, he coughed up the water stuck in his lungs and relearned how to breathe. He turned his head from side to side and moved his arms and legs. "Great, nothing is broken."

Stiff and sore, Persicus dragged himself upright. He washed the mud out of his eyes, face, and clothes.

Tandiz, his horse, walked to the edge of the shallow pool, peered down his long nose with a look of disdain, and gave Persicus a sardonic snicker.

"Are you laughing at me?" Persicus asked Tandiz in mock astonishment. "Keep it up and I'll give you away to the widest man I know."

Tandiz lowered his head, pleading with his big brown eyes, nudging Persicus on the shoulder with his long snout.

Persicus sighed. Dripping wet, bruised, and battered, he mounted his horse and headed back to the caravanserai on the outskirts of the town                                          of                                          Abrisham.

# 2

# CARAVANSERAI

Persicus arrived at Abrisham's caravanserai early that morning. The rising sun had dried the morning dew, warming the cool spring air. He guided Tandiz through the open gate into the large courtyard. Caravanserais, often located just outside of most cities, are fortresses constructed for the safety of merchants and travelers. They are generally spaced every twenty to twenty-five miles, about a day's journey apart. This caravanserai was one of the largest on this trade route.

Shops filled the courtyard for the convenience of the traveling merchants and other adventurous souls who frequented this route. Blacksmiths, carpenters, shoemakers, tailors, and inns offering food, tea, and a safe place to sleep lined the courtyard, all within the tall fortress walls of the caravanserai.

A large, rectangular water fountain sat in the center of the courtyard, surrounded by a shallow water basin. From the qanat, the water travels through an underground canal, along the stone-lined courses, and into the fountain's basin. From there, the water is distributed through a network of underground canals and aboveground stone-lined courses to the individual homes and businesses within the city. The basin sat at ground level, edged by a short stone barrier, with four steps leading down three feet below ground level, where the water collects.

Persicus stopped by the fountain, inspecting the flow. Thick, brown water oozed into the basin. He dismounted his horse and tethered him to an iron hitching ring impaled into the ground in front of the inn, rather than trying to find room for him in one of the stables this early in the morning.

"I'll bring you back some barley," Persicus said, rubbing the horse's neck.

Weary from the day's events, he made his way to the chaikhana — an open-air tearoom. He sat at a table beneath a tall birch tree in the shade. The caravanserai remained blessedly quiet; all of the travelers still fast asleep on their rented carpet-covered platforms — the safest place to sleep while traveling the trade routes. He had always disliked sleeping side by side amongst so many strangers, but it did protect you from wild animals and bandits who would slit your throat while you slept. He was happy that part of his life was behind him and that he had a home he could go to every night.

The innkeeper looked out from the kitchen window and bid Persicus good morning. Moments later, the innkeeper appeared with a platter of food and set it on the table in front of Persicus: a bowl of hearty lamb and barley stew, sesame-crusted flatbread, and a steaming hot cup of tea on a small saucer, with lumps of crystallized sugar on the side. Steam from the stew and tea heated his face and hands, making his mouth water. He wrapped his hands around the teacup and brought it to his lips. He took a small sip, letting out a sigh of contentment as the warmth traveled down his throat and into his chest. He tasted cardamom — a spice he had always loved in tea, regardless if the tea was Persian, Indian, or Chinese.

"I see you got the water running." The innkeeper looked from the brown running water to the thoroughly disheveled man before him. "But what in God's name happened to you? You look as though you've been fighting in a battle."

"I was." Persicus set the teacup on the table. "It was me or the mountain. I may be wrong, but I think the mountain won."

"Indeed." The innkeeper smiled and raised his eyebrows, waiting for an explanation.

"A landslide blocked the tunnel. Unfortunately, there was no way of knowing how much water had built up behind it. I only removed a small rock, but a wall of water burst through, sweeping me all the way back to the qanat's entrance. The bright side is that while it took me half a day to reach the blockage, it only took a few minutes to come back out." Persicus gave a half-hearted smile, trying to make light of the event. "Anyway, the water should run clear by lunchtime."

A sudden loud rattle came from the fountain. Alarmed, Persicus jumped to his feet and looked towards the fountain. The muddy water slowed to a trickle. Persicus groaned, dreading the thought of returning to those hellish underground tunnels. They walked over to the basin and stood, watching for a long moment, hoping the flow of water would pick up again. Another jarring rattle screeched from inside. Persicus narrowed his eyes and bit down on his lower lip, puzzled.

Muddy water squirted out through the water canal in a burst, pushing out a broken and battered oil lamp. The lamp plopped down onto the first step, right side up, toppled over, and tumbled down the last three steps with a loud clang and splash at each landing. It settled into the basin on its side.

Piran, the innkeeper, turned to Persicus with an amused grin. "Did you lose something?"

Persicus shook his head and burst out in laughter. "Thank God! For a second I thought I might have to go back in there."

"I don't know how you can stand to work in those giant ant holes in the belly of the earth. How did you ever end up working in the qanats?" Piran asked, as they walked back to the table.

Persicus' uncle had been a traveling merchant. He had spent his childhood and teens on the road with his uncle. When his uncle passed away, he inherited all his mules and Bactrian camels. He had no home and he was tired of the life on the road. After several successful, but unpleasant and unrewarding months of taking over his uncle's business, he sold all the mules and camels for a good price, and bought an apple orchard on the outskirts of Abrisham, where he could settle down.

"Well, I kind of fell into it. A few months after I bought the orchard, an old man named Bahman came pounding on my door, pleading for my help. He had been working in a nearby qanat and his assistant took a nasty fall down one of the narrow, vertical airshafts. The old man couldn't get him out on his own. Too weak and hurt to pull himself free, Bahman had to leave him there to come find help. So, I went with Bahman to help the assistant. The poor guy had been there all day, wedged in tight in a small space, one of his legs broken, and his ribs cracked and bruised."

They sat down at the table. Piran poured tea from a silver teapot, refilling Persicus' cup.

Persicus had entered the qanat that day for the first time and crawled almost two miles before he reached the vertical airshaft where he saw a pair of legs dangling down in front of him. Being careful not to hurt the trapped assistant any more than necessary, he widened the shaft, removing the dirt and stones from around his legs a handful at a time, until he could tie a rope around his waist. After he crawled out, he and Bahman were able to lift the assistant free of the crevice.

"Well, that explains why you went the first time, but not why you went back again and again."

Persicus shrugged. "The old man asked if I could help him finish the project. I accepted after he pointed out that he couldn't finish the job by himself and that I needed water for my orchard."

"That's why you did it?" Piran asked in disbelief.

Persicus chuckled. "Well, no, not exactly. The money he offered me finally convinced me."

Persicus had been hesitant to accept the job, but Bahman, impressed by him, had tried every means of persuasion. Bahman had tried to convince him that it was a noble profession, in high demand, and that he would be helping create villages and jobs. Which were all good things, but the money had sealed the deal. He was broke, having put everything he had into the purchase of the apple orchard. Since the trees were still young and not producing enough fruit yet, Persicus accepted the job. Bahman took him under his wing, teaching him all he needed to know about where to look for underground water, and how to get to it. His apprenticeship had lasted a little more than a year, until Bahman had died working on an altogether different project in Cattula Land. He wasn't certain, but he suspected that Bahman — who was not known for holding his tongue — had most likely fallen victim to the Cattulas after some witty remark.

Piran stood and slapped Persicus on the back. "We all thank God that you are here. Without this qanat, there would be no Abrisham. Enjoy your breakfast. It's on the house. I'll let you know if the fountain returns any more of your belongings." He walked backed to the kitchen, whistling, to prepare for the morning rush.

Persicus finished his stew and savored the hot, aromatic tea. He watched the crisp morning breeze stirring the young leaves of the birch tree. The rising sun warmed the morning air and the birds began singing melodically. He was exhausted, but also content.

Persicus was in his mid-twenties and quite accomplished for his age. It had been six years since he bought his apple orchard and had only been producing good quality fruit for the last two years.

Persicus stood six feet tall with a well-built, lean body. The color of his eyes matched the color of the evening sky, a striking deep blue, which stood out in startling contrast to his midnight black hair and fair olive skin. He had a well-proportioned face, with high cheekbones and full lips. Thick, wavy, black hair fell down around his shoulders and a day's worth of stubble covered his usually clean-shaven face. Three scars marred his face: one beginning above his left eye and three striking down his right cheek. He was a Tajik and still spoke with a slight accent, even though he left Tajikistan as a young boy. As always, Persicus wore a simple tunic, a warm caftan, thick cotton pants, and leather boots.

A group of Chinese merchants arrived in the caravanserai. They fed and watered their camels, and settled down in the courtyard to play a game on a gridded board with colored stones. Persicus had seen the game, called Go, many times. When he was young, he had always asked his uncle to teach him how to play, but there was never time. His uncle had always put it off, promising to teach him after they finished their journey, but as soon as one trip ended, another began. It was a never-ending venture. He made a vow to himself, at that moment, to make time to learn the game at the first opportunity. Well, after he got some sleep.

Another group of merchants arrived and settled in by the fountain. He noticed they were Arabs by the long, loose, striped garments, and sandals they wore, but they could have been from anywhere: Egyptians or Western Sahara Berbers. Most of them came bearing bolts of bright colored silks, Chinese medicinal herbs, or colorful ceramics, which they traded for the highly valued Egyptian cotton.

Persicus' eyes grew heavy as thoughts of the game Go and his uncle drifted through his mind. Exhausted, he fell asleep while sitting at the table. He was still holding the cup of tea in his hand when a loud "Ahhhem" jarred him awake. His eyes flew open in alarm and he jerked, spilling the cooling tea all over his hands and table. He grabbed the cloth napkin from the tray and looked up to see an elderly man smiling down at him.

The man, dressed in fine, tasteful clothing, was covered in a layer of dust. Everything but the dust seemed out of place here in the caravanserai. He had a well-trimmed white beard, thinning white hair, and thin lips set on a narrow face with bushy, white eyebrows. Sharp cheekbones jutted out from underneath his small, dark brown, almost black eyes. The whites of his eyes had dulled with age and his cheeks were hollow. Persicus looked down and noticed his left arm was missing from the elbow down.

Persicus dried his hands and blotted the spilt tea off the table.

"Oh, I am so sorry." The old man shook out a handkerchief and helped Persicus dry the spilt tea. "I didn't mean to startle you."

"It's all right." Persicus was glad he had been woken up. This was the last place he would want to sleep. He dropped the napkin onto the table and looked up at the old man. "Is there something you need? I can get the innkeeper for you."

"No, I do not need the innkeeper." The old man cleared his throat. "Are you Persicus, the famous qanat engineer and traveler of the Silk Road?" the old man asked, leaning forward, hovering over Persicus.

Persicus blinked the sleepiness from his eyes. "Yes, I am."

"Excellent! May I sit here? I have been seeking you for a while now," the old man exclaimed in delight and gestured to the empty seat across from Persicus.

Persicus raised an eyebrow. "Yes, please do. You look as though you have been traveling a bit yourself." Persicus chuckled. "I didn't know I was famous."

The old man leaned into the table, resting his arm across the wooden surface. "I have heard many great things about you. Your travels. Your bravery facing the cruel bandits that stalk the trade routes. The amazing feats and dangers you face in the qanats. All say you are far braver than any silk or silver merchant traveling with a full load of precious cargo."

Persicus frowned, perplexed. "I'm sorry; I don't know what you mean."

The old man gave a tsk, shaking his head. "Such modesty, after all I have heard about you."

Persicus' eyes narrowed in suspicion. He was a simple man and did the best he could. He shook his head. Persicus decided the man must be trying to ingratiate him for some unknown purpose.

The old man gave him a look that said he wasn't fooled by the humble facade. "You must know what is said about you and I won't believe otherwise."

Persicus gestured around the courtyard to the various merchants milling about. "All of these people, who have left the safety of their homeland to venture through these harsh and unforgiving steppes, have faced the terrors of the ruthless bandits out there, and survived. Each of us have faced untold perils and have nothing, but our strength and wit to rely on. Many never make it home." Persicus returned his gaze from the scattered merchants to the old man. "We are all humbled by our travels. You said you have been seeking me. What can I do for you?"

"My name is Hakim." Hakim reached across the table, offering his hand.

"Good to meet you, Hakim. Now, what can I do for you?" Persicus asked again, shaking his hand. This was the third time he asked Hakim what he wanted. He was tired and wanted to go home.

Hakim smiled, looking up at the taller man. His smile stretched the skin across his weathered face. "It's not what you can do for me, but what we can do for each other. I have a proposition for you, which will make us both very wealthy, if all goes according to plan. I would have gone through with it by myself, if I could have, but as you can see, I am not all there." He laughed at his own joke, raising his missing forearm, then his tone became serious. "I need an experienced guide who knows how to travel the dangerous Silk Road and who is also an expert navigator of the world beneath the earth's surface. After asking around, your name is the only one that keeps coming up."

"Well, I'm listening. What is your proposition?" Persicus leaned back in his chair, crossed his arms over his stomach, and got comfortable, thinking this might take a while.

Hakim looked to his left and right before he leaned over the table. "Have you heard of the lost treasure of the Silk Road?" he asked in a hushed voice.

"Hasn't everybody? It's the oldest myth on the Silk Road, maybe as old as the road itself."

"What if I can prove to you that the story is true and only I know where the Mother Earth is hiding it?" Hakim's thin lips spread ear to ear with a smile.

Persicus stared at him for a moment, wondering if this man had lost his mind. "Go on."

Hakim reached under his shirt and pulled out a greasy, old leather pouch with a cord drawn around it. He loosened the cord and tilted out the contents. Four shiny gold coins spilled out and rolled onto the table. Persicus picked them up one-by-one, examining them.

Persicus leaned forward in his chair and held the coins up to the sunlight to see the inscriptions and markings. As he inspected them, his interest grew. "I haven't seen coins like these before."

"I know. Where do you think these coins are from?"

"Well," Persicus paused while he studied the markings, "these two have Chinese characters, and I have seen all of the Chinese coins in circulation, but I must admit these are new to me." The writing seemed similar, but they were altogether different from the modern Chinese coins. Persicus picked up a third coin. "This one has Latin characters, probably Roman." He picked up the last one and studied it. "And this last one ... I couldn't say."

"You are quite right." Hakim nodded, clearly impressed. "The first two are Chinese. This one is a Roman coin, minted in Phoenicia when they were under Roman occupation. The last one has an old Persian script that doesn't exist anymore since the Arab invasion. But note that all of these coins have one thing in common: they are all from the same era, centuries ago."

Persicus thought about the implications. "Are you suggesting that these four coins are a part of the missing treasure?"

Hakim smiled and nodded.

"Hmm." Persicus picked up the Persian coin and turned it over in his hand while examining it. "If that's true, how did you come to possess them?"

"Well, that's a long story and you look exhausted." Hakim leaned back in his chair, thinking he had him hooked. "Perhaps you should get some rest and we can continue this conversation later."

"You are right, I am quite tired. I've been up all night working in the qanat, but please continue. You have aroused my curiosity."

"Have you ever heard the real story behind the myth?"

"Well, I know the bedtime stories I heard as a child. Are you suggesting that there is another story that people do not know?" Persicus asked, intrigued.

Hakim smiled again. The smile began to bug Persicus. It reminded him, in a vague way, of how a reptile would smile if it could. It was unnerving to see on a human face and he wished he would stop smiling, but he could not hold an unfortunate smile against someone—at least, he tried not to. Besides, he really did want to hear this alleged true story of the lost treasure of the Silk Road, one of his favorite bedtime stories as a child.

"Yes, that is exactly what I am saying." Hakim sat up straight in his chair. His eyes lit up in excitement. "Centuries ago, when this region belonged to the Persian Empire, there was a tribe who owned some land between Persia and China. They did not give their allegiance to either China or Persia and considered their land sovereign. A part of the Silk Road went right through their territory. They had allowed travelers access to their road for a small tax. Those who would not pay, well, they were slaughtered. One day, a caravan led by a courtier of the Chinese Emperor tried to pass without paying the tax. They were ambushed and killed. Every last Chinese merchant perished and the tax was collected. Several bags of gold coins were taken, along with the rest of the cargo.

"Now, the Persians had a treaty with the Chinese. The Persians had ensured the land was safe to travel. Neither the Chinese nor the Persians acknowledged this sovereign land. When the Persian officials heard of the death of the Chinese caravan, via their pony express, they honored their treaty with the Chinese, and the tribesmen of the sovereign land were declared bandits. The Persian armored cavalry set out to capture these bandits and bring them to justice, by either public hanging or crucifixion. This, the Persian King would do to discourage the rest of the bandits along the many trade routes."

Hakim paused and took a deep breath. "Are you familiar with the Forbidden Land of Fire and Dragons?"

"Yes, I am." Persicus shivered at the thought of the place. "I had to pass through that land twice because of extensive flooding in the lower lands."

The Land of Fire and Dragons was not a place that he would go, given a choice. No place else in the entire known world could match its sinister atmosphere. Thick, black clouds, of a sort not seen anywhere else, covered the sky as far as the eye could see. The first time Persicus had traveled through there, it had been late afternoon, but somehow it was darker than the desert on a moonless night. In the middle of the day, the only light to penetrate the smothering darkness were the frequent flashes of unnatural lightning. The ground rumbled with as much intensity as the sky rumbled with thunder. Persicus remembered the obnoxious, pungent odor of sulfur, so strong it burned his nose, made his eyes water, and felt as if it crawled down his throat to nest in his stomach. *If there is a hell on earth, that is it,* he thought. Persicus rubbed his arms, trying to rid himself of the lingering goose bumps.

"Yes," Hakim said solemnly. "That is the place where the bandits went to hide. The poor fools, they never had a chance. The Persian cavalry, close on their tail, tracked them to the Forbidden Land. A fierce battle took place. Of course, the bandits were no match for the Persian cavalry. The bandits were slaughtered and their leader deserted them. Desperate to escape, he made a run for it up a steep hill, but the weight of the heavy sacks of gold slowed him down."

"How have you come upon such a tale?" Persicus asked. This story was not even similar to the story he had been told as a child.

"Patience, I will tell you all," Hakim assured. "Now, eh, where was I?"

"The leader was making a run for it up a hill."

"Ah, yes. Large boulders covered this hill. The Persian cavalry dismounted their horses and chased him up the hill on foot, with their swords drawn, but when they got to the top of the hill, they couldn't find the bandit anywhere. They searched the area, only finding a small crater at their feet, with hot steam billowing out of it. Figuring the bandit must have fallen into the crater, they retreated down the hill.

"At the bottom of the hill, they saw an entrance to a cave. Now thinking the bandit might be hiding in the cave, they went to investigate. As they approached, an inexplicable force began pulling them towards the cave. They braced themselves, but the soldier closest to the hill lost the battle, and got sucked into the mouth of the cave. The others, seeing this, turned, and tried to flee, but the invisible force overwhelmed them. They struggled to the point of exhaustion until, one by one, they too, were sucked into its gaping mouth."

"And if the entire cavalry and the bandit were all sucked into the cave, how has this story emerged?" Persicus tried not to sound derisive.

"Patience. Let me finish and all will be explained. I was also skeptical when I first heard the tale, but rest assured—I am a highly educated man. I examined all the facts and I know what I am telling you is true."

Persicus waved his hand, gesturing for him to continue.

"Now, where was I?" Hakim mumbled.

"They were all sucked into the cave." Persicus leaned back in his chair, amused.

"Ah, yes. So, hiding behind a rock, a single bandit survived and he saw everything. Later, the reinforcement cavalry, sent to search for the missing regiment, found him. He was ranting and raving. His captors thought him mad. He told them a dragon within the cave had inhaled everyone into its gaping mouth and would eat all who passed by. He warned the cavalry to stay away and begged them to keep him safe from the dragon.

"His mutterings were dismissed as nonsensical. They extradited him to China, where the Emperor also dismissed his traumatized palaver. In the end, they put him to death and that was the end of that."

"Fascinating. Where did you hear this story?" Persicus asked.

Hakim smiled that reptilian-like smile that stretched across his weathered face. "Ah, that is the interesting part. It is all improbable up to this point, yes? That is what I believed, too."

"So you do believe a dragon sucked the cavalry into the cave?" Persicus couldn't manage to rein in his sarcasm this time. Hakim responded with a look of impatience. Persicus smirked. "Sorry, go on. I am interested."

Hakim continued, "About six months ago, I happened to be passing through an abandoned village, not far from the city of Astana, when I heard a man screaming. A sudden sound of vicious wolves, snarling and growling, drowned out his panicked voice. I followed the sounds until I found a withered man sitting on the ground, surrounded by a pack of snarling beasts. He fought them desperately, waving and stabbing his staff at the wolves in desperation, trying with his failing strength to keep them at bay. His swollen, black hands clutched the stick. He was too weak to stand. I chased the wolves off and they reluctantly left their easy meal.

"As I leaned over to help the man up, he threw himself backwards, pushing his arms straight out to ward me off. 'Stop! Don't come any closer,' the man yelled.

"I asked him what was wrong and he said, 'Plague! I have the Black Plague. Damn curse! They kicked me out of the city and I came here to pass what's left of my short life in peace. Then those damned wolves showed up.'

"I thanked him for warning me. The man was on the verge of death. He struggled to speak, breathless and gasping for air after every few words. 'No, thank you for chasing the wolves away. I no longer fear death, but I cannot bear the thought of being eaten alive. I am not long for this world. If you would promise to bury me so the wolves cannot get to my body, I will reward you with a map.'

"I told the man that I already had a map. The man shook his head,

14

gasping. 'No, not an ordinary map. This map leads to the lost treasure of the Silk Road. It's within a dark, blackened mountain. Listen! I have been there. Look!' The dying man pulled out the pouch that you have in your hand and threw it to me."

Persicus dropped the pouch onto the table, drew his hands in, keeping them hovering before him, not touching anything. A look of shocked panic on his face. "You let me touch something infected with the Plague?" Persicus shouted.

"Relax, my young friend. I would not do that to you, would I? I washed it. It's safe. I've had it for months and I'm fine. The dying man, Sumat, the poor sick fellow, had overheard an old Chinese man recounting the legend—that I just told you—to a rapt audience in a teahouse in China. The old man told the story in such vivid detail that Sumat thought there had to be some truth to it. By the end of the story, he knew that this was the real story, the true story behind the myth, and that the treasure does exist. Sumat approached the old Chinese man and questioned him about the location of the treasure. Sure enough, the old man knew the location. Sumat drew out the description on an animal skin. When the old man realized Sumat was going to seek out the treasure, he warned him that the gold is cursed. He said a dragon protects the treasure and that many have gone seeking it, but none have ever returned."

"And all this, the dying, plague-riddled man told you, gasping for breath between every few words?" Persicus asked.

Hakim nodded solemnly. "Yes, I spoke with him at length, waiting for him to die so I could do the decent thing, and bury him before the wolves got to him. What else could I do? Now, eh, where was I?"

Hakim pondered for a moment and Persicus did not say a word, waiting to see if the old man would remember where he left off. Persicus thought he might be as crazy as the bandit, sputtering about dragons inhaling people into a cave. But then again, maybe only some of it was crazy. There are the gold coins to consider. Persicus knew how people embellished stories as they passed them along, although he couldn't help but think that Hakim had meticulously rehearsed telling this story before coming here.

"Oh, yes. Sumat rushed home to his wife to tell her about his plan, paying no heed to the incessant warnings of the curse and the dragon by the old Chinese storyteller. He left the next day, searched for a length of time, and finally he found a hill that matched the description, complete with the steam-bellowing crater at the top of the hill. Having difficulty seeing past the steam, he went down the hill in search of the cave entrance, but he never found it. Instead, he only found a stream. When he went to freshen up and have a drink, he saw a gold coin glittering in the sandy riverbed. Excited, he retrieved the coin from the water and waded into the stream in search for more. He found three more. He was elated. But alas, we are all skeptics at heart. He didn't know for certain where these four coins came from. Perhaps some poor fellow had dropped them while stopping for a drink, the same as he had done.

"He returned to the city in haste and found a scholar who confirmed the dates and dynasties of the coins. And now ... now he knew he had found a part of the lost treasure of the Silk Road. He headed home to his wife to tell her of their great fortune and that they would soon be as wealthy as kings. He planned to return better equipped to find the rest of the gold, but on his way home, he fell ill. He made it to his doorstep and his wife, a superstitious woman, took one look at him, and denied him entrance into his own home. She had warned him not to go out seeking cursed treasure and this is what he got. No way would she allow the curse to spread to herself and their children."

"And you want to go after the cursed treasure now? And with my help?" Persicus asked.

"Ah, you don't really believe in curses or dragons! It's just a myth. You know how people can get carried away with these stories. I think this way they don't feel bad about not seeking the treasure. Besides, anyone can get the Plague, even those who have never heard of cursed treasures." Hakim watched Persicus with unveiled anticipation, waiting for that sparkling gleam of greed to enter his eyes. "He gave me the map. He told me everything, warned me to take care, and seek it at my own risk. Well, I have decided. I want it. And you do, too. You are lucky I have chosen you, since I need to partner with someone who is knowledgeable about mountains, how to get inside them, and who is experienced traveling the trade routes. It's very fortunate for you, if you agree to help me. We can split the treasure fifty-fifty."

Hakim knew he had him. He saw the spark in this qanat digger's eyes.

"It sounds tempting." Persicus paused as he studied Hakim. Something about Hakim made him uneasy. There was a definite lack of trust. Persicus thought about saying no and going home to his orchard. Then he thought about all the adventures he used to have while traveling the Silk Road, before he had settled down, and bought the orchard. Now, he had a chance for another adventure. With a sudden jolt, he realized that he wanted to do this. That he had been longing for another adventure for some time now. "It's a deal."

Hakim's face lit up and he reached out, shaking Persicus' hand. "Excellent! Excellent!"

Persicus stood, stretching his arms. "I am going home to get some rest. I'll bring all the supplies we should need."

"Shall we meet here tomorrow at sun up?"

"No. Is sun up three days from now all right? I have some things I need to take care of first."

"Yes! Yes! Thank you! You won't regret your decision," Hakim said joyously, getting up as well.

𝕪𝕪𝕪

Persicus headed to a vendor in the corner of the courtyard to buy some barley for his horse, Tandiz. After some brief small talk about the qanat, the grain vendor slid a scoop of barley into his feedbag. The caravanserai was busy now; people scurried to and fro, oblivious of each other. Persicus made his way back to his horse, attaching the feedbag around his neck. Persicus stood by his horse, eyes scanning the courtyard while Tandiz ate his barley. He saw Hakim standing across the courtyard, petting a brown horse while gazing absently into the distance. He seemed to be talking to himself. Persicus took a moment to observe his new partner. He did indeed seem to be talking to himself. Other people also watched him curiously as they passed him by. Only a short, bald man talking to a tall, lanky man stood near Hakim. They leaned against the wall, behind the horse Hakim was petting, oblivious to Hakim's presence.

A pistachio vendor stopped in front of Hakim, pointing to the bags of nuts draped across the donkey's back. Hakim waved him off dismissively. He looked up and saw Persicus watching him. Hakim gave a sheepish smile, waved at Persicus, and walked off, leaving the horse behind. Persicus watched Hakim leave the courtyard.

"Unusual man," Persicus said to himself. He mounted his horse and rode home.

# 3

## THE JOURNEY

Three days later, Hakim waited for Persicus, sitting on the edge of the fountain.

Persicus arrived on horseback, riding into the courtyard with a mule trotting alongside him. He had loaded the mule with two goatskins filled with water, plenty of rope, a shovel, a small pickaxe, two shiny new oil lamps, a bag filled with food, and other necessary supplies. A large bow and a quiver filled with his special arrows were strapped to his saddle. Persicus' neighbor, an arrowsmith, had designed a new arrowhead he hoped would take off in the marketplace. The arrows were a brilliant modification of traditional arrows; Persicus always filled his quiver with these preferable weapons before he left on any journey. A sword, sturdy and unadorned, was sheathed on his left hip, attached to a belt. The dagger he wore had been a gift from his uncle for his twelfth birthday — a beautiful, handcrafted masterpiece, which never left his side. He always kept it hidden under the folds of his caftan, as he saw no reason to show it off, and tempt thieves who might try to kill him for the gold and silver of the dagger.

His belt was made of overlapping bronze plates with an inlaid silver geometric design. The rectangular buckle, made of silver, had a large, round onyx stone in the center, surrounded by smaller turquoise stones. The belt overlapped a dark blue waist shawl that wrapped around his usual cream-colored tunic. His long caftan covered the belt, stopping just above his knees. He wore his usual black pants and leather boots.

"Are you ready?" Persicus asked, riding up to the fountain.

Hakim got up, stretched, and mounted his horse. "Looks like you are ready for battle."

"This is how I always travel, ready for anything." Persicus angled his horse towards the gate. "Once, a couple lions were stalking me not far from here. A couple arrows did the trick."

"It's good to be well prepared." Hakim had brought with him a goatskin filled with water, draped over his horse's back, and a blanket in his saddlebag. He had dressed in thick pants, a long tunic, a warm black caftan, and leather boots—much more suitable for travel than the expensive clothing Persicus had first seen him in. "I don't think we will have many problems. Isn't the sword and all those arrows a bit much to scare off some lions? Are you sure you want to carry all that around?"

Persicus just smiled at him.

He rode through the gate with Hakim at his side and the mule following close behind. They headed north, taking a shortcut to get to the main trade route.

The Silk Road stretches across the Asian continent into Africa, in a network of highways connecting many small and large cities throughout the mountains, deserts, and valleys along the way.

Shortly after leaving Abrisham, they crossed the vast, vibrant green, flat grasslands that stretched on for miles. A sea of tender grass rippled in the gentle spring breeze. Patches of red poppies accented the greenery for as far as the eye could see, delighting their senses, and lifting their spirits. A mountain range loomed in the distance, its rocky peaks still covered in a blanket of winter white. Persicus veered off the main road, leading Hakim towards the imposing, jagged mountain range.

"We're not going to climb over that, are we?" Hakim asked.

"Well, how else do you propose we get to the other side?" Persicus mused.

"Are you out of your mind?" Hakim's voice rose in fear. "That's impossible!"

Persicus thought about tormenting Hakim with the prospect of climbing the mountain range; he smiled at the thought of it. He always had to battle with his mischievousness, but he decided not to torment the old man. He didn't know him well enough yet. *Maybe tomorrow*, he thought. "One does not go over these mountains. You have to go around them; however, there is a shortcut that not many know about, which will save us several days. Up ahead, there is a narrow chasm that is hidden from view, unless you know where it is." Persicus pointed to a specific spot in the mountain range. "When we get there, you'll see it better. It looks as if a giant has taken a sword and cut the mountain clean in half."

Hakim sighed, relieved.

19

𓏤𓏤𓏤

Several hours later, they were nearing the mountain range. Hakim silently watched Persicus, who stared at the ground with uncanny interest. The narrow passage at the foot of the mountain stood a hundred yards ahead. Persicus stopped, pulling back on the reins. He leaned over, inspecting the ground.

"Is something wrong?" Hakim stopped his own horse. The horse pulled back on the reins, shaking his head, almost yanking the reins out of Hakim's hand. The horse turned to the side of the road and began eating the grass that lined the road.

"I don't know. I see fresh tracks of two horses going in our direction." Persicus pointed to the hoofprints on the ground.

Hakim craned his neck to see. "So, what's the problem? They are probably travelers, same as us."

Persicus looked up from the hoofprints, meeting Hakim's eyes. "Maybe they are, maybe they are." He nudged his horse with his foot and took off at a trot.

Hakim pulled at his horse's reins, trying to get him moving. His horse shook his head and stubbornly kept eating. "Damn stupid horse, get going!" He gave him a good, solid kick. The horse neighed as if offended and trotted after Persicus.

They rode up a small incline in silence. A huge wall of rock loomed in front of them, protruding out from the main mountain. From a distance, it created an illusion of a solid mountain, but behind the protruding rock, a narrow passage opened up, creating the shortcut through the mountain. On either side of the chasm, the mountain walls shot straight up, the space just wide enough for a mounted man to squeeze through.

Persicus stopped outside the passageway. "Guardian of the Steppes. It is as I suspected." Persicus sighed and looked up, examining the mountain.

Hakim stopped short, his horse jerking the reins from his hand. "What's the problem now?" he asked, grabbing at the reins. He looked up to the top of the mountain, following Persicus' gaze. A wave of dizziness overcame him; he closed his eyes and grabbed the saddle horn.

"Look down here." Persicus pointed at the ground. A trail of hoofprints led off the passageway, onto a narrow overgrown footpath, up the mountain. "See these hoofprints?"

"Yes. What about them?" Hakim asked.

"They are going the wrong way."

"They are going the wrong way? What do you mean?"

Persicus looked at the old man, wondering how he could have survived the perils, all too obvious to himself, traveling alone on the Silk Road. "Don't you see these hoofprints are going up this path? This path would put them above us while we cross below them. Travelers come this way to go through this passage, not to climb the mountain."

Hakim's eyes widened. "I don't like this. We have only just begun the journey and something's wrong." His voice dropped to a whisper. "If you think we are in danger, maybe we should go back, and take the main route."

"I'm going to go check it out. Keep quiet down here." Persicus jumped down from his horse, grabbed his bow, and a couple of arrows. "If I'm not back soon, I suggest you head back the way we came."

"Listen, we don't have to do this, we can find another way," Hakim whispered. A series of rapid twitches fluttered his right eye.

"It is not a matter of this way or that way. I am not going to allow some bandits to stop me from traveling through God's land." Persicus squinted at Hakim. "What's wrong with your eye?"

"What are you talking about? There's nothing wrong with my eye." Hakim slapped his hand over his eye. "All right, go. Go."

Persicus headed up the steep, narrow, and overgrown path on foot. Halfway up the incline, he came upon two horses tethered to a dead tree branch. He crouched behind a cluster of tall brush, looked around, but didn't see anyone. He crept up to the horses. Two sets of human footprints continued up the hill. The horses wore crude nomadic saddles on their backs. Persicus untethered the horses, slapped them on their rumps, and watched them trot down the path.

Having dealt with opportunistic nomads, he knew what to expect, and was grateful there were only two of them. Most opportunists wouldn't want to put themselves in harm's way; they preferred to ambush oblivious merchants who traveled unaware and unprepared along the trade routes. Regardless of their preferences to ambush, they would no doubt be armed and dangerous if confronted.

When the path ended, he climbed the rest of the way grabbing hold of rocks and weeds, pulling himself up to the top. He crouched down behind a boulder and peeked over the top. Fifty feet from him, two men knelt at the edge of the cliff, peering down, with a pile of rocks between them. They each held a large rock in their hands, patiently awaiting the next unfortunate person to ride through the passage below. By himself, Hakim would have made an excellent target for them.

"They should have been here by now. Where are they?" whispered the smaller man.

"I don't know. Let's wait a little longer," said a big brute of a man with long, greasy hair, balding on the crown. He spoke in a deep, slow voice.

The smaller man shook his head. "Something must have happened."

Persicus climbed on top of a flat boulder soundlessly, raising himself an additional foot off the ground, giving him a clear shot of both men. He swung his bow around and placed an arrow against the bowstring. Down below, his mule gave a loud bray. The nomads looked at each other, grinning wide, raising the rocks above their heads, ready to pummel down onto the heads of their victims.

Persicus took another step forward, trying to secure his footing on the uneven surface. His boot knocked over a small pebble, sending it tumbling down the boulder. Both men spun around, jumping to their feet, their mouths opened wide in surprise. The smaller man let out a yelp and fumbled to draw his sword, while his partner — the big, greasy brute — whipped out his sword in a quick, practiced motion.

Persicus pulled back on the bowstring, preparing to shoot. He aimed at the space between the two nomads.

Built as big as a bull, tall and muscular with a large, square head set on top of a wide, thick neck and a barrel chest, the big brute pointed his sword at Persicus. His nostrils flared, furious that anyone had snuck up on him.

Persicus maintained his calm composure and spoke in a loud, clear voice. "If either of you moves so much as an inch, you will feel the agony of this arrow tearing through your heart!"

The smaller nomad looked from Persicus, to his partner, and back. He appeared to be a teenager who hadn't filled in yet — delicate and child-like. His nose, mouth, and eyes seemed too small and scrunched together in the center of his face. Nervous and fidgeting, he shifted his balance back and forth, from leg to leg. He reminded Persicus of a ferret — fidgety and annoying.

Bull stared at Persicus, rage radiating from his eyes, breaths huffing from his flaring nostrils, his hand balled into a tight fist. "Who are you? What the hell are you doing up here?"

"Shouldn't that be my question?" Persicus asked. "What are you two doing up here with a mound of rocks between you?"

Ferret glanced at his partner. "What do you want?" he asked in a faltering voice.

Bull snorted. "Who are you to question us? There are two of us" — he took a step forward — "and only one of you."

Getting courage from his partner, the younger one nodded in

agreement. "And even if your arrow hit one of us" —he pointed at his partner—"the other will surely kill you!"

Persicus shifted his arrow towards the ferret. "That raises another question. Which one of you wants to be first in line? Which of you wants to suffer the agony of this arrow? For this is no ordinary arrow. It is called The Plower. If you haven't heard of it, it is because no man has ever survived it."

Worried, Ferret's legs began their nervous shifting again.

Bull laughed. A deep, masculine chuckle. "The Plower. What nonsense. You would say anything to save yourself right now. You made a grave mistake coming up here." He took another step towards Persicus. "You should have gone through the passage. Your odds of survival would have been better."

Persicus' lips curled into a cold smile. He shifted his aim to the bigger man. "If you look close, you genius you, you will see that the ends of the arrowhead are curved outward, towards the tip. This creates a much wider wound and rips to shreds whatever it penetrates. Keep coming closer, I'll give you a once in a lifetime view." His voice came out flat, devoid of emotion.

The boy paled and glanced at his partner again. Watching his friend, he realized that it would be every man for himself. His sword began to waver as if too heavy for him; a fine tremble ran through his arms, down to his knees.

"Looks like we may have a mis-misunderstanding," the boy sputtered. "We mean you no ha-harm. Ya-ya-you can go in peace."

The larger man cast an angry, contemptuous glare at his small companion.

"My only intention is to cross this passage in one piece. Throw your swords down, head down the path, and I will let you go."

The two men looked at each other, weighing their options. If they gave up their swords, they could both easily be killed. If they kept them, The Plower would definitely pierce one of them.

Persicus saw their reluctance. He pointed his arrow at the ferret, certain of his surrender. "I won't ask again!"

Ferret dropped his sword without hesitation. It clattered down at his feet.

Persicus nodded to his right. "Kick it over there."

Still trembling, sweat trickling down his brow, the boy kicked the handle of the sword with the bottom of his worn sandal. The sword spun in a rapid circle, the blade slicing through his big toe, bone deep. Howling in pain, he fell to the ground, tore off his sandal, and gripped his bleeding toe. Though he pressed his lips together to stop from crying out, whimpering sounds still escaped from deep in his throat.

Persicus shook his head. The ferret was a disgrace to bandits everywhere. He turned his attention to the bigger man, aiming at his chest.

The big brute stared at his fallen cohort before shifting his blazing eyes to the man bearing the lethal arrow at his chest. He fumed, chest heaving with each breath. Defiantly, he held onto his sword and took another step forward.

Persicus yelled, "Don't be a fool!"

With a barbaric cry, Bull charged towards Persicus, barreling forward, dodging left and right, making himself difficult to target. Persicus tracked him with his arrow. He waited calmly, aiming as best as he could at the vacillating target. He was almost on top of him. He let out his breath and released the arrow.

Bull saw the bow release; he hesitated for only an instant and then veered, desperate to get out of the arrow's path. The arrow tore through his right arm, severing it completely at the elbow. The force spun him around. He staggered forward, screaming. Reaching out with his left arm, he tried to grab Persicus.

Persicus didn't know if the nomad was reacting in blind panic or if he was still trying to fight, and he didn't wait to find out. He drew his sword in a quick, fluid motion, and kicked the nomad in the stomach at the same time. The nomad flew backwards, the air knocked out of him, his left arm flailing, too shocked, and in too much agony to brace himself. He landed on his back with a solid thud. Persicus jumped down from the boulder, ran forward, raising his sword overhead, the blade pointed down, driving the sword towards the nomad's neck.

An anguished cry tore from the throat of the young nomad.

That cry, that anguished cry, resonated deep within Persicus, bringing back a flood of unwelcome memories. He drove the sword down into the ground at the last second, inches from Bull's head. Persicus stood still for a frozen moment, adrenaline pumping through him, hearing only his deep, fast breaths, and blood pumping through his veins. Then he heard the boy's choked sobs. He yanked the sword free and backed away from the injured nomad, staring down at him.

Bull lay on his back, staring up at Persicus with wide, terror-filled eyes. Blood gushed out in tandem with his rapid pulse, creating a dark red puddle growing at his side. Shocked, he shifted his eyes to his severed limb lying on the ground, the hand still clasped tight around the sword's handle in a death grip. As if he hadn't realized he had lost his arm and only the sight of it lying there, gripping his sword, confirmed the loss, reality dawned on him; he raised the remnants of his arm up before his eyes. He screamed. One loud, ragged shriek after another, as fast as he could draw air.

Persicus stepped over to the still-bleeding arm and sword. He picked up Bull's sword, the large, filthy forearm dangling grotesquely from the handle, and flung it over the edge of the cliff.

The boy's face turned from pale to green and his jaw dropped in disbelief. "But why?" he asked over his friend's screaming.

Persicus looked at the young man. "Out of sight, out of mind." He walked over to Ferret's sword, laying where he had dropped it, and threw it over the edge, as well. Persicus turned towards the two injured men.

The boy crawled to his friend and tried to stop the bleeding. Uncertain what to do, he grabbed the injured arm with one hand and covered the wound with the other. Worry, fear, and revulsion painted across his face. He looked at Persicus, young eyes pleading for help.

Persicus sighed. The boy was too young and inexperienced to be thieving on the Silk Road. Why the older man had brought him was a mystery. He turned and started down the path.

After a moment, he stopped and looked back. He stood, thinking, staring absently at the hill.

Persicus returned minutes later with some wood and dead brush. Pulling a flint from his pocket, he started a small fire. He couldn't leave them here in this condition.

Bull had mercifully passed out from the pain and shock. The young nomad looked at Persicus, suspicious. "You're helping us?"

"I don't need another death on my conscience. Put more pressure on the wound and try to slow the bleeding." Persicus drew his sword and placed the blade in the fire. When it was glowing red, he picked it up with a piece of leather, and walked over to the prone man.

The boy looked on with wide eyes. "What are you doing?"

"Hold up the arm, let me see the wound," Persicus ordered.

The boy took his hand off the wound; blood squirted out onto his face. He looked away, swaying, blood dripping off his chin. He swallowed back the urge to vomit, putting one hand to the ground to steady himself.

"I am going to sear his arm to stop the bleeding. He will probably wake up. You'll need to hold him down." Persicus got into position, kneeling by the unconscious man's head, red-hot blade in hand. The boy had his hands on his partner's chest. Persicus hesitated, looking at the young nomad, who couldn't have weighed more than a hundred and thirty pounds, opposed to his friend, who appeared well over three hundred pounds. "I think you had better sit on his chest and be ready to

25

hold on tight."

The boy nodded too fast and crawled on top of his friend, bearing all his weight onto his chest.

Persicus shoved the searing-hot blade onto the wound. The skin sizzled and smoked, the bleeding slowed. The rancid smell of burning flesh filled the air, clinging to the back of Persicus' throat.

Bull's eyes flew open and he screeched, loud and anguished. He bucked, writhed, and cursed. The boy bounced feet into the air with each buck, trying to hold on, landing with a solid thump back onto his chest. "I'm sorry! I'm sorry!" the boy cried out frantically.

Persicus jumped to his feet and planted his boot firmly against his shoulder, holding him in place while he pressed the red-hot blade onto the wound a second time. The wound cauterized and the squirting blood ceased to flow.

Bull passed out again.

"All right, the bleeding has stopped." Persicus stepped away from them. "That is all I can do. When he comes around, tell him he's lucky he only lost an arm. Anyone else would have just killed him."

Persicus held his sword down at his side. The boy sat on the ground by his friend, catching his breath, his face beginning to return to its normal color. Blood seeped from the gash in his toe. It had already begun to swell.

Persicus glanced at his sword, still glowing red. He cocked an eyebrow and asked in a serious tone, "You want me to do your toe?"

Blood drained from the boy's face, turning him as white as fresh cotton. He shook his head. "No … no …" He wrapped his arms around his knees and began to rock himself.

Persicus tried not to smile, but a sly grin broke out on his face anyway. He reminded himself not to tease the injured and feeble. *After all, the poor boy is having a terrible day.*

*Poor boy,* Persicus thought. *He would have killed and robbed us.* He turned to leave and remembered he had set their horses free. He sighed and turned back to the young nomad. "Do you have any supplies up here?"

He shook his head. "Everything is down with our horses."

*Not anymore.* "I'll put some food and water at the bottom of the hill. When you're able to walk, go find your horses, hopefully they haven't wandered too far."

Hakim sat on a rock, his face creased with worry when he saw Persicus coming down the mountain. "What happened? I heard screaming."

Persicus went to the mule and grabbed some dried apples, bread, and a pouch of water. "As I suspected, they were waiting for us to cross the passage." He set the food and water on a large rock by the path. "Come on, let's go. We're behind schedule now."

"What's with the food? Why are you leaving it here?" Hakim asked, following Persicus from the mule, to the rock, and back to the horses. Persicus mounted his horse, but Hakim stood in front of him, his arms crossed, waiting for an explanation. Persicus knew that he wouldn't understand, he couldn't explain it to a man like Hakim.

It was the scream. The boy's scream that jarred his memory. The scream that reminded him to do only what was necessary, not to let his anger control him.

At fourteen, Persicus and his uncle were heading back from India, where they had purchased a load of sandalwood for the new governor of Antioch's Palace. To get to the Mediterranean Coast, they had to go through a passage in the Hindu Kush Mountains. A treacherous landscape, made impossible by a winter storm. They must have missed the passage and decided to backtrack when the storm turned into a blizzard. Unable to travel in the harsh winds and blinding snow, they sought shelter under a concave niche at the base of a mountain, deep enough to protect them from the elements. On that first night, Persicus lay awake, unable to sleep. The howling wind tore at their shelter. After several hours, he heard a noise that had nothing to do with the storm—the clanging of metal outside. His uncle had finally fallen asleep and he didn't want to wake him. Instead, he grabbed his sword and snuck out of the shelter.

Through the heavy veil of snow, he saw a dark figure hunched over in front of their supply bags. Persicus rushed forward, sword raised over his shoulder, confident that his footsteps crunching in the snow would be masked by the wind. The man turned, fear in his eyes, and fell backwards as Persicus loomed over him. The man tried to crawl away. Then, seeing it was useless, raised his arm in front of his face to block the blow.

Persicus' sword was already driving down when a scream tore through the air. The man fell onto his back, turning away at the same time, which was the only reason Persicus didn't kill him then and there. Persicus put the sword point to the man's neck before he looked around for the source of the scream. Standing yards away, he saw a young woman with a baby in her arms and a boy, no more than five years old, holding her hand. The boy cried, wailing for his father, snow sticking to the trail of tears. The woman handed the infant to the boy and came towards him. Her face held a look of resigned anguish. Persicus looked back down at the thief, who pulled a piece of bread out of his caftan, offering it up to him. He spoke in a language Persicus couldn't understand, his eyes wide, scared.

Persicus looked towards the shelter and saw his uncle standing there, watching him. He threw down his sword and held out his hand to the man.

Later that night, with the family well fed, Persicus' uncle translated that foreign tongue. They had been robbed two days before. All their food, clothing, money, and horses, taken in the middle of the night. The wife and child were starving. They couldn't go any farther without food.

This is what Persicus couldn't explain to Hakim. Since that day, he couldn't help wonder what the reasons were when people decided to steal. He knew that not every bandit was starving, many were simply rotten and lazy—as, no doubt, those two up on the hill were. However, he had sworn to himself long ago to kill only when necessary, lest he mistakenly kill someone not rotten or lazy, someone thrown into a deplorable circumstance, with deplorable choices—steal or die.

Persicus realized Hakim was still asking about the food, standing before him. He had been lost in his memory for a moment. He decided the truth was none of Hakim's business and would no doubt lead to more explanations and debate. "It is an offering to the Guardian of the Steppes. I always leave an offering when I come out of a dangerous situation unharmed."

Hakim gave him a cockeyed, dubious look. "Guardian of the Steppes? I've never heard of it. What is that, some kind of obscure religion?"

Persicus smiled to himself. Of course, Hakim had never heard of it. He had made his own religion; borne of his disdain for many religions that forced people to fight Holy Wars, killing anyone who refused to convert. He gave Hakim a noncommittal answer. "Well, it's a little of this and a little of that." To Persicus, all religions he knew of had good and bad aspects. He had taken what he liked from each and combined them into his own belief system. What had started out as a personal joke—the Guardian of the Steppes—had, in time, turned into something much more real to him than any other belief.

"Well, I can tell you, no Guardians need our food. We need our food. What if we run out before we make it back?" Hakim mounted his horse; he and Persicus headed through the passage. The passage narrowed enough in places that their legs grazed the sides of the mountain.

*And that is the problem with lying,* Persicus thought. *You have to keep on doing it.* "We won't run out of food. I always bring extra, just in case." He didn't think they would run out of food, unless something unexpected delayed them, but Hakim rattled on, complaining, and finally declaring that if they did run out of food, that he would get the last of it, as Persicus had left his share for the Guardians.

Persicus ignored him. He thought about that day in the Hindu Kush Mountains. They had parted ways with the family the next day after the storm had cleared. His uncle had given them a mule, which they could take turns riding. It was all they could spare, as the rest of their animals were laden with their goods. They had also given them enough food to make it through the mountain range, back to civilization, and an extra blanket.

Then they headed back towards the passage that would take them towards the coast. They walked for miles before they found a passage, but the snow having piled up over a foot high, blanketing every surface, made it impossible to know if it was the right one. His uncle declared that it must be the passage, for they had come across no others.

Days later, now completely lost, another blizzard rampaged through the mountains. They had run out of food. The water in their goatskin pouches was frozen. When they couldn't make a fire, they used the freezing snow for water, letting it melt in their mouths, freezing their gums and tongues. For two days, without food, they searched through deep, icy gorges, trying to find their way. The snow had piled up high, making it difficult to walk. Each step, their legs penetrated the snow to their knees. They wore leathers and furs, which helped immensely, but the bitter cold still ate at their hands and faces.

On the third day, they were startled to hear the sound of a beautiful song echoing through the mountains: strange doleful voices mingling with some sort of resonant instrument. After searching for some time, they found a group of robed men—Buddhists. The Buddhists took them to their village to wait out the storm.

Persicus hadn't thought of that long ago time in many years and now he recalled everything in clear detail, as if it happened days ago.

The Buddhists led them to their village in the Bamiyan Valley. Shimmering blue streams weaved through the land. Gardens, orchards, cows, and goats were scattered throughout the valley.

On the side of a sandstone cliff that shot straight up hundreds of feet, stood two colossal statues, sculpted in a relief, within a deep recessed niche in the mountainside. One stood over one hundred and fifty feet tall. Persicus had stopped in awe of the gigantic figure. It glittered with gold and precious jewels; a brilliant red robe flowing with graceful ripples hung past its knees. When he asked, they told him the statue was of Buddha — The Enlightened One.

Persicus and his uncle followed the monks through the village. Some buildings remained in ruins, appearing as though someone had taken an axe to the beautiful columns. In one building, only a few columns remained, keeping the building standing. Persicus glimpsed another statue of a figure lounging inside that building, his head resting on the palm of his hand, reclining on his side, sculpted with the same impressive detail and care as the first Buddha.

Later, Persicus learned that an army of iconoclastic barefoot barbarians had stormed their peaceful village, intent on destroying their false god. But the statue still stood, undeterred, impervious — not so fragile, after all.

Persicus and his uncle spent a week in the village. He became good friends with a young monk named Ashoka, who embraced him into their culture, and taught him about their way of life. Ashoka was young when the barbarians attacked and found it impossible to forgive their savagery, as his teacher taught him to do. Vinzeh, the monastery teacher, had told Ashoka that forgive he must, as holding anger only hurts yourself, and prevents you from achieving enlightenment.

This proved difficult for Ashoka, because at a young age, these barbarians held him down while making him watch the brutal murder of his father and mother. Tormenting him further, they promised him they would be back when he grew up to kill him and the rest of his clansman, if they didn't renounce their false god.

Ashoka tried to forgive these savages, but regardless of all his prayers and meditations, he could never forgive them the destruction of his family.

The monastery, saved from the barbarian's savagery, as it remained hidden behind the relief of Buddha on the mountainside, had a main large, cavernous room, and many connecting tunnels and caves. Persicus remembered exploring the monastery with Ashoka, wandering through the many tunnels and enormous caves. Beautiful paintings adorned the walls, paintings that Ashoka's ancestors had painted centuries before.

Persicus remembered his time there with great fondness. Everything he had longed for as a child on the road with his uncle, he had found there in his brief friendship with Ashoka. A friendship that stayed with him long after their paths had parted ways.

While Persicus was fond of the Buddhist way of life, he also thought that if they had not been pacifist, the barbarians wouldn't have been able to overcome them with such ease. But regardless of its pacifism, he had incorporated many Buddhist principles into his own beliefs — though he would always defend himself. He believed, above all, in a balance.

Persicus suddenly recalled the last day that he had spent there, something he had all but forgotten. Vinzeh, the monastery's teacher, asked him to accompany him before he and his uncle left that morning. He followed Vinzeh into the monastery behind the relief statue and sat down facing the old, fading paintings on the wall.

With his eyes closed, Vinzeh sat cross-legged in undisturbed silence for a long moment, while Persicus waited, trying to quell his brimming curiosity. Persicus had exchanged nothing more than a few greetings with Vinzeh the entire week and had no idea what this unexpected invitation was about.

When Vinzeh spoke, it was nothing that he could have anticipated. "You have a special destiny ahead of you. Many years from now, you will embark on a quest for something seemingly very valuable, but you will find something so much more precious beyond the lost dark river. Do not give up hope, even when it appears all hope is lost. Reach high and you will find a way."

Persicus remembered a chill had gone down his spine as Vinzeh spoke those words, but mostly he felt puzzled. Before he left, he asked Ashoka what this meant.

Ashoka had smiled and said, "No one will know, perhaps not even Vinzeh, until destiny brings you to that moment. But never forget what he told you, because he has never been wrong yet. Now, my good friend, go enjoy your life, and its many grand adventures. Some day in the future, I'm sure we will meet again."

As Persicus recalled these events with the clarity of a vision, he felt something deep inside him stir with the memory. An eerie feeling came over him, but he shrugged it off, and concentrated on the road.

# 4

# THE DEADLY PATH

There it is." Persicus pointed to a busy road ahead. The road was buzzing with a steady flow of caravans. They waited for a gap between horses and camels, and eased their way onto the eastbound road. Getting too close to the unpredictable camels could be dangerous, as they are known to kick, stomp, or spit on unwary travelers.

They continued east until they reached a fork in the road. At the junction, a group of Chinese merchants sat, resting in the shade. They eyed Persicus and Hakim suspiciously, and stopped talking altogether as they drew near.

Persicus nodded and smiled, bidding them hello in their native tongue with a warm, "Ni Hao."

The merchants smiled in delight and returned the greeting.

Hakim looked at Persicus, surprised. "You speak their tongue?"

"Yes. Well, just enough to get me into trouble." Persicus pulled his reins to the left, heading for the northern road, the mule trailing alongside.

One of the Chinese merchants jumped up, his smile replaced with concern when he saw these two men veer onto the northern road, towards The Forbidden Land. He yelled out in Chinese, "Hey, stop! Where are you going? No one goes that way!"

Persicus and Hakim stopped, turning to look back at the Chinese men. Hakim's horse danced in place, stomping his hooves.

"What are they saying?" Hakim's horse turned around in a circle in search for food, lowering his head to tear off some shrubs.

Persicus gave the Chinese men a kind smile. "They are warning us not to go this way," he told Hakim.

"What the hell does it matter to them?" Hakim said, exasperated. "Tell them not to worry. Tell them that we are going only a short way up the path to retrieve a bag of supplies that our dimwit servant dropped when his horse got spooked; he realized he took the wrong fork in the road and raced out of there."

Persicus raised a questioning eyebrow at Hakim and then translated it to the merchants. He thanked them for their concern and assured them they would be fine.

"Time taken to select your help is time well spent," said one of the older merchants in Chinese, shaking his head in sympathy.

"I know, but my partner here hired him without consulting me," Persicus replied in their tongue with a sly smile. Persicus waved goodbye to the sound of their laughter and they headed up the northern road.

Persicus looked over his shoulder at Hakim. "Quite a good lie for such short notice."

"Time taken to tell a good lie is time well spent." Hakim laughed and trotted off ahead of Persicus.

Persicus frowned, staring at Hakim with an uneasy feeling. He shrugged it off as jitters about nearing the Land and Fire and Dragon again, but he couldn't shake the feeling. Why would Hakim pretend he didn't understand Chinese, when he obviously did? In his short time with Hakim, he had come to the conclusion that Hakim thought of himself as brilliant, but in constant need to reassure himself of his own brilliance, he questioned and tested other's knowledge whenever he could. He figured Hakim must be insecure of his intelligence. It was annoying, but not in any way an untrustworthy trait.

Persicus sped up to catch up with Hakim. He wanted to be ahead of Hakim going up the road, as it would become dangerous from here on out. The mule, attached by a length of rope to Tandiz' saddle, struggled to keep up. This northern road travels up a hill to the rocky sandstone mountains beyond. As they climbed uphill at a steep angle, the road narrowed to a mere uneven, rocky path, about four feet wide, edged by a jagged sandstone cliff to their right, and a sheer wall of rock to their left. They rode single file, the mule in the middle, and Hakim bringing up the rear. The width of the path waxed and waned, barely wide enough for the horses in many places. Persicus' uneasy feeling kept him alert and watchful. Stones and dead tree branches protruded from the sheer mountain wall, forcing them to duck under them, or come much too close to the cliff's edge. For a couple of hours, they rode in complete silence, concentrating on the treacherous path, as the height grew greater, and the valley below grew smaller with each passing minute.

Persicus came to an abrupt stop. "Guardian of the Steppes!"

"What is it? What's wrong?"

Persicus stared for a full minute, unwilling to believe his eyes. This was going to create a problem.

"A part of the path has collapsed." Persicus got off his horse, careful of the edge. He scarcely had room to plant his feet alongside the horse. "Stay where you are, I'll check it out."

Rocks tumbled down the edge of the massive cliff as he inched his way around his horse. He whispered a quick prayer, "Oh, Guardians, do not let me fall."

Once around his horse, he walked to the gap and inspected the ground around it. It seemed stable enough. The gap itself stretched only about two and a half feet across. It would be no problem for him to jump the small gap, but he wasn't sure about Hakim, or the mule. Jumping a gap this small wouldn't normally be an issue for any horse, but the pathway was narrow enough on the other side, the landing had to be exact, or they would fall off the side of the cliff. He jumped up and down on the ground. It didn't collapse.

"What are you doing? Are you crazy?" Hakim yelled, his voice echoing off the mountain walls.

"Testing to see if it is stable." Persicus walked back and inched around his horse to the mule. "We are going to have to jump it. It's only about two and a half feet to the other side."

"Oh, no. I can't jump that. Look how narrow it is. This horse will never make it."

"Not with you on top of him, no. We're going to jump on foot and bring the animals over one at a time." Persicus began unloading the supplies and set them in front of the mule.

"Let me rephrase that. I'll never make it. We need to find another way."

"There is no other way. There is no room to turn around and the horses can't walk backwards down this narrow, winding path." Persicus looked into Hakim's worried eyes. "Don't worry, I won't let you fall. We'll tie a rope around you. That way, if you don't make it, I'll pull you up from the other side. Besides, it's only a hop away. You'll make it, no problem."

"All right, all right. But if you let me die and go get the treasure without me, I will haunt for the rest of your days!"

34

"Well, if I have traveled all this way, why not finish the journey? Do you want me to have done all this for nothing … partner?"

Hakim frowned — wondering, worrying. His eye began twitching again.

Persicus finished unloading the mule, untied him from the horse, and inched his way back to the front.

He looked into Tandiz' big, brown eyes, rubbing him along his long snout. "All right, buddy, you are up first." Tandiz shook his head, sending his mane flying. Persicus secured all the reins and straps, inched his way behind his horse, and gave him a hard smack on the rump.

Tandiz took off at a run and jumped at the edge. One second he was in the air and the next second he landed. Three legs landed on solid ground. His rear right leg missed, falling off the side of the cliff. Tandiz pulled his leg up with a loud cry and walked forward, secure on the other side. A few rocks had dislodged and fallen from the side of the cliff, where Tandiz' leg had struck.

Persicus jumped the gap, led his horse down to the widest area on the path, about twenty yards ahead, where the horse had enough room to turn around. He jumped back over and brought the supplies across, an arm-full at a time. It took him five trips to move everything.

Persicus pulled the mule forward and gave him a short pep talk, gently rubbing his head. Persicus had always been fond of this mule — a magnificent, gentle creature — whereas most were stubborn and ornery. After he secured the mule's straps, he smacked him as hard as he could on the rump and the mule took off at a run.

As soon as the mule jumped, Persicus knew he wouldn't make it. The mule landed with his front legs on the ledge and the rest of his body hanging off the side of the fissure. His hind legs kicked out, rapid and frantic, and he cried out in shrill, terrified brays, echoing horribly off the mountains.

Tandiz trotted to the struggling mule, bit down on the rope around the mule's neck, and backed up, trying to pull to mule to safety. The mule made one rapid cry for help after another. Tandiz stomped his front legs on the ground, trying to get enough traction.

The ground crumbled under the weight of the mule's front legs. Tandiz let go of the rope and backed up along the narrow path, hugging the rock wall as the ground collapsed.

Persicus watched, horrified, as the ground fell out from under the mule. His loud cries reverberating throughout the mountain range. He watched as the mule tumbled down, hundreds of feet, hitting the jagged mountainside. About halfway down, the mule's heart wrenching screams cut off with startling abruptness, leaving its mournful echoes to fade away at its own pace.

Persicus turned away in the deathly silence that followed, praying the mule had died before he hit the bottom.

After a long moment, Persicus turned back towards the path and examined the gap, now two feet wider. "This is not good," he whispered. He looked at Hakim, who stared at the empty space where the mule had fallen, his pale face full of dismay. "Come on. Let's get your horse across."

"You still want to go through with this?" Hakim asked, his tone incredulous. "Listen, get my horse across, he'll have room to turn around on that side. Then the horses can jump back over here. We can go back down and find another way around the mountain."

Persicus shook his head. He realized that Hakim probably never travelled these dangerous trade routes. You go one way, something bad happens. The next time, you choose another way and something worse happens. There was no easy way.

"It doesn't make any sense to go back. We are halfway there. If we go back, it will take days more to go around this mountain. And we would still have to climb another mountain. Besides, it's too risky. Every time the horses jump, a little more land will fall off the edge. Chances are they wouldn't make it back. You'll have a rope tied around you, so don't worry. Even if you don't make it, you'll be fine."

Hakim wanted to argue. He wanted to talk some sense into him. But he had hired Persicus for his knowledge; perhaps he was right. He wondered if Persicus would let him fall so he could go off and collect all the treasure, but he had the map, and he had not shown it to Persicus. I've given him enough information that he can find the treasure without the map. His eye twitched again.

Hakim sighed in defeat and dismounted his horse. He clung to the animal as he inched his way around to the rear. He gave him a solid smack on the rump. The horse neighed, sounding offended, and walked a couple feet forward. Hakim tried again, smacking him harder. "Go! You worthless hide! Go!" He punctuated each "Go" with another smack on the rump.

The horse turned his head to look Hakim square in the eye and turned forward again. He lifted his tail and dropped a steaming-hot load of manure onto Hakim's boots. Hakim's face turned red. "You! You are done! I'm sick of this shit!"

Persicus burst into laughter. "Why don't you let me handle this?"

"Fine," Hakim barked.

Persicus led the horse a few feet forward. "All right buddy. You're up next. I know you can do it." He inched his way behind the horse and gave him a solid whap on the back.

The horse took off running, jumped, and landed with his rear legs

36

on the edge of the cliff. Rocks dislodged and tumbled down the mountain, widening the gap by inches.

Persicus turned to Hakim with a confident smile. "Well, this is it." He tied the rope around Hakim's chest, under his arms. He pulled it tight and handed the length to Hakim. "Throw me the rope when I get across."

Hakim nodded. His vision blurred as his eye twitched again. He smacked his eye, cursing under his breath.

Persicus took a few deep breaths, focused on where he wanted to land. He got a running start and jumped. His foot leapt off at the edge. He flew through the air, airborne for a brief moment before landing at the edge on the other side.

"Throw me the rope."

Hakim tossed the rope across and Persicus caught it with ease. Persicus looked around for something to tie it to. He thought about tying it to the dead tree stump protruding out of the side of the rock, but it crumbled in his hands as if it was dirt. He walked towards the horses and found a thick hook-shaped stone protruding out of the rock wall. It seemed secure, imbedded deep into the mountain. He wrapped the rope around the stone twice, tied it, and leaned back against the rope with his full weight. He nodded in approval and turned towards Hakim.

Persicus stood several yards back from the edge, not wanting to impede Hakim's landing in case he made it. He held the rope tight in his hands in case he didn't make it.

"All ready. Now, all you have to do is run and jump," Persicus said cheerfully. Hakim looked doubtful. "I'll catch you. Don't worry."

Hakim walked to the edge and looked down. He could see a vague outline of the mule lying in a crumpled heap at the end of the long drop.

"Oh, for goodness sake. Just do it," Persicus yelled. "It's really not that far. Only four and a half feet."

Hakim stood there, uncertain.

"Come on, Hakim. I won't leave here without you, but if you don't jump now, we'll be spending the night up here."

Hakim decided he was being distrustful. Persicus won't let me fall to my death. Persicus won't let me fall to my death. "All right." Hakim took a shaking breath. He backed up again and ran as fast as he could. He jumped, but his feet left off much too soon.

Persicus knew he wouldn't make it. He held tight to the rope and pulled, leaning his whole body backwards. The roped tightened and he jerked forward with Hakim's weight.

Hakim yelled, "Pull me up! Pull me up!"

Once Persicus felt confident the anchor would hold, he released the rope, and jogged to the edge. He peered down and saw Hakim hanging about ten feet down.

"Hang on!"

Hakim looked up and said, "As opposed to what?" His one full arm desperately held the rope, the other half-arm waved in the air above his head, trying to keep balanced.

Persicus gave a half-laughing sound and began pulling Hakim up. Halfway up his arms began to feel the strain and shook with the effort. Hakim's head came into view and then his shoulders. Persicus paused, resting his head on his arm, catching his breath. Sweat trickled down his temples. His muscles burned from the exertion.

Hakim panted hard, gulping his breaths, sweat dripping off his nose. "Hurry up." He looked down and a wave of dizziness overcame him. He closed his eyes to keep from swaying.

Persicus stared at him, chest heaving with each breath, and let the rope slip through his fingers, only an inch, before he tightened his grip.

Hakim yelped. His eyes flew open and he glared at Persicus. He swallowed back his rapid pulse. "That is not funny!"

Persicus grinned. Flexing his fingers had relieved the burning in his muscles a little. He pulled the rope up until Hakim could swing his knee onto the ledge. He let go of the rope with one hand, grabbed Hakim by the shoulder, and pulled him the rest of the way up. Hakim fell on all threes, catching his breath. Persicus stood over him, bent at the waist with his hands on his knees, when he saw a fissure appear under Hakim. He grabbed Hakim by the neck of his tunic and dragged him backwards.

"What are you doing? Let me go!"

Persicus kept dragging him as the ground at the edge collapsed.

The mountain settled and quieted, leaving a gap ten feet wide.

Hakim stared at the empty space where the ground had been. "We better get moving."

Persicus hurried to the horses and reloaded the supplies, dividing them between the two horses. Up ahead, the path narrowed further, winding around the mountainside. Persicus couldn't see beyond the first bend, but knew that it continued at the same unsettlingly narrow width. "We'll need to walk the rest of the way on foot. It will be too dangerous to go farther on horseback." He tied Hakim's horse to his own with a long rope. "You walk ahead of me and I'll lead the horses."

"Do you think it will get narrower from here?" Hakim asked.

"Maybe. We'll be fine. Stay as close to the rock wall as possible and try to watch your step, but don't look down. You may get dizzy."

"That makes no sense. This is impossible. How are we to know if there isn't another collapse up ahead? Then what are we to do? We'll be stuck up here. We shouldn't have come across. We should have gone back. This is madness." Hakim was working himself into a state, as if he hadn't thought this trip would be this dangerous. His eye twitched.

Persicus looked over his shoulder at him. "There's something wrong with your eye again."

"There's nothing wrong with my eye," Hakim snapped.

"You're not afraid of heights now, are you?"

"Don't be ridiculous."

They walked down the path in silence, concentrating on their footing. Hakim kept glancing off to the right, at the long drop. The path narrowed and widened. Then the mountain wall to their left opened up, sloping away from them instead of shooting straight up, giving the horses more room for their bodies, as the path narrowed to the point where they had to walk on the edge of the drop. Persicus worried about having tied them together. If one of them fell, it would drag both of them off the cliff. Each time the path narrowed, Persicus could hear an audible gulp ahead of him. The path wound around the barren, rocky mountainside. The silence was broken only by their soft footsteps and the ominous sound of loose rocks tumbling over the side of the cliff when they stepped too close to the unstable edge. Hakim tried to focus on the reward at the end of this venture, but it was too nerve-racking.

Hakim stopped and looked from Persicus to the edge of the mountain. Persicus could almost feel his fear. Feeling a brief bout of sympathy for him, he decided to try to distract him.

"We don't have much farther to go today. We should try to make it to the river by sundown and we'll camp there. We will need to start before sunup tomorrow if we are to cross the sea of sand before tomorrow night. We lost a lot of time today."

Hakim mumbled something indiscernible.

As they crept past a sharp curve, an unobstructed view of the expansive desert appeared before them. Pale yellow sand, for as far as the eye could see, stretching to the distant horizon, where a dark mountain range stood. They stood for several minutes, in awe of the breathtaking view.

"Do you see that dark ridge on the horizon?"

"That little thing over there?" Hakim asked.

Persicus nodded. "That is The Forbidden Land," he said in a mock whisper.

They began their descent down the serpentine path. When they got to the bottom of the mountain, they settled down on a smooth rock, guzzling down the cool water from their goatskin pouches. After ten minutes, Persicus mounted his horse.

"Let's rest a while longer." Hakim lounged on a rock on his back with his head resting on his arm.

"Come on, we are almost to the river. We'll camp there, but I want to make it before dark."

Hakim groaned and got up grunting.

An hour later, they reached the river.

Hakim whistled. "Look at that! It looks completely different on the other side of the river. Nothing but sand for as far as the eye can see. I think God is trying to tell us something here."

"And what's that?"

"That we should have gone the other way."

"If anything, God created this challenge for his amusement, and will reward us if we are worthy. On the other hand, if we are not worthy, we will likely perish there in the golden sand." Persicus waved his hand through the air, dismissing the thought. "Enough of this colloquy. Why don't you feed and water the horses while I'll gather some wood."

By sundown, with the animals fed and watered, Persicus made a fire, and spread out the blankets on the ground. He handed Hakim a handful of dried apples and nuts, with unleavened flat bread. Hakim looked at Persicus in disbelief.

"This is dinner?" Hakim asked, taking a bite of the hard, dried apple. "This is tasteless, hard, and dry."

"It is what it is."

When Persicus finished his meal, he stretched out on his back beside the glow of the fire, staring up at the stars. The clear indigo blue sky shimmered with billions of stars. The Milky Way scintillated across the heavens above. "I haven't seen so many stars in the night sky in a long time. I haven't even slept out-of-doors since I bought the orchard."

"What's the big deal about stars? They can't light your path, as the moon can." Hakim sat by the fire, in a cantankerous mood, eating his dried apples, and muttering under his breath.

"When I used to travel with my uncle—may he walk with the Guardians above—he taught me how to identify the constellations. He said that as long as you have a clear sky, you could never lose your way. He said astronomy is how the Magi found the Messiah."

"Who found the what?"

"Not what. Who. According to the legend, three Persian, Zoroastrian Priests followed a bright star to Bethlehem, where they say the Messiah was born. They traveled a great distance to pay their respects, bringing with them gifts from the east." Persicus rubbed his eyes, growing sleepy.

"Ah, Zoroastrians, those are the silly fools who worship fire." Hakim stretched out on his blanket. "Do you know what you want to do with your share of the gold?"

"Hmm, I haven't thought about it yet. Let's see. I already have a good stone home and a plentiful orchard. I don't have a wife. Maybe I'll put some money into finding a good wife. My neighbor's house needs some major repairs, maybe I'll give him some money for that. He helped me a lot when I bought my land. How about you? What will you do with your money?"

"Well, I've given it a lot more thought than you. I plan to use my money to make much more money. But that is all I can tell you for now. I am exhausted. Good night."

"Good night." Persicus' eyes grew heavy. As he drifted off to sleep, he thought of his uncle and saw his smiling face.

𐎛

The next morning Persicus awoke in the pre-dawn hour and shook Hakim awake. Stiff from the hard, unforgiving ground, Hakim spent five minutes moaning and stretching, and moaning some more, before he finally got up.

Persicus took the goatskins to the river, filled them with ice-cold water, heaved the heavy skins over his shoulder, and made his way back to camp, where Hakim stood by his horse, packing up the blankets. Persicus wondered how he managed to fold them into neat squares without the aid of a second hand.

"We should be able to cross the desert by sundown if we keep up a good pace," Persicus said, mounting his horse. "The problem is the horses will have a difficult time in the sand. I wish I had my Bactrian camels now."

"I hope this part of the journey will be easier than the last." Hakim stood staring across the endless pale, undulating sea of soft sand, void of any living thing. As the sun rose, the heat would become unbearable. "Are you sure we have to go through the desert? Is there any way around it? Another shortcut?"

"Yes, there is another way." Persicus tried to keep the impatience out of his voice. Hakim wanted everything to come easy, with no hard work, an utterly unrealistic expectation. "You could follow this river for five days, cross a snow-covered mountain, and pass through Cattula Land. I don't know about you, but I would rather not set foot in Cattula Land. I have heard disturbing stories about the Cattulas using magic on anyone they find crossing their path. Our chances of surviving unharmed are better through this desert. This here, is No Man's Land."

Hakim spat on the ground. "I don't like this. No sir, I don't like it one bit."

They rode down the bank of the river, searching for a good place to cross. Even in the dim light, they could see the smooth river rocks on the sandy bottom, and small fish darting around. They found the shallowest point of the river and made their way across on horseback.

The landscape completely shifted on the other side of the river. No rocks, trees, or shrubs littered the ground. Only mound after mound of sand stretching to the horizon. They dismounted the horses when they began to struggle with each step in the fine sand. The eastern sky took on a crimson glow as the morning sun peeked over the horizon.

They passed one sand dune after another. They all looked the same. By ten in the morning, the sun blazed, scorching the land. Their sweat dried almost instantly against their parched skin. The hours ticked by as they slowly made their way, sometimes sinking knee deep into the sand, as difficult as wading through mucky, muddy water.

The sun became blinding against the sand. Heat waves shimmered. Some inexplicable force cast the illusion of water in the distance—the desert's famous mirage—everywhere Hakim looked. Hakim became disoriented. He stopped, turning around, wondering if they were going in circles. He gazed out over the quiet sand dunes, shielding the sun with his hand raised above his brow. "How do we know if we are on the right course when all we can see are hills of sand in every direction?"

The question almost shocked Persicus. "It is quite simple. We need to keep due north. That means keeping the sun to our right during the morning and to our left in the afternoon—as the sailors do on high sea with no landmarks in sight."

Thinking about water made him thirsty. By noon, the sun burned hotter than inside a brick oven, pounding down wave after wave of scorching heat rays. They stopped, got out their goatskin water pouches, took a long drink, and watered the horses.

Persicus looked into the distance and noticed the western horizon had taken on a reddish tint. "Do you hear anything?"

Hakim shook his head. "No, nothing."

Persicus' forehead creased in concern. He squinted, trying to see past the blinding glare of the sun. "Guardian of the Steppes!"

"What? What is wrong? What do you hear?" Hakim raised his hand over his eyes, shielding the sun, scanning the distant horizon.

"Nothing. That is the problem. Not even the wind."

"What is wrong with silence?" His left eye began to twitch again. He muttered a curse, squeezing his eyes shut. "Isn't silence good thing?"

"There is a time for all things. In the desert, this eerie quiet means

the calm before the storm. When the sky turns the color of blood ..."
Persicus stopped mid-sentence.

"Calm before the storm? Color of blood? What are you talking about?" Hakim asked, panic creeping into his voice.

"Wait here." Persicus ran, stumbling, and crawling up the tallest sand dune to get a better view, his hands and feet sinking into the sand with each step, slowing him down. He prayed he was wrong as he crawled. He reached the top and stood, staring straight ahead, his hands shading his eyes. What he saw dropped him to his knees.

A wall of red sand as wide as the desert itself, as high as the soaring clouds, was quickly encroaching upon them. Persicus knew there was no way to escape it, nowhere to hide. "Oh, Father of Thunder, Mother of Lightning ..." Persicus sat on his heels, head bowed.

Having experienced the terror of sandstorms twice before—once in the Gobi desert and once in the desert between Mesopotamia and Antioch—he couldn't know if it would last for minutes, hours, or for days. This wall of sand had to be the widest, the highest, the largest that he had seen so far, covering the entire western horizon.

"Hey!" Hakim called. "What do you see up there?"

Persicus slid down the dune as fast as he could. Half way down, he lost his balance in the soft sand, tumbled down sideways, landing at Hakim's feet with an avalanche of sand settling down around him.

"Quit horsing around! What did you see up there?" Hakim reached down to help Persicus up.

Persicus ignored his hand, getting to his feet on his own. He ran to the horses and began unloading the supplies.

"It's not good." Persicus didn't want Hakim to panic. He would need him to stay calm and follow his instructions to survive this storm. "I'm afraid there is a big sandstorm heading our way. There is nowhere to take shelter. We have to make do right here and we don't have much time."

Hakim's face fell. "You're joking ... right?"

"No. But don't worry. I have been through this before. Quick, do as I tell you and we will make it through this together. Help me unload the horses and pile everything right here." Persicus pointed to the pile he started making. "Get out your blanket and unwrap your waist shawl. We'll make the horses lie down around us."

Hakim helped unload the supplies as best as he could with one arm, fumbling and dropping them in his anxious haste. When they had everything in a pile, they each grabbed their blankets, and unwound their waist shawls. Persicus took the water pouch, guzzled down some warm water, and handed it to Hakim, who drank from it in long, greedy gulps. Persicus took the water pouch back from him, soaked Hakim's shawl, and wrapped it around his head, covering his face.

"You must try to keep the sand out of your mouth, eyes, and ears. Breathe through your nose and keep your eyes shut." He pushed Hakim to his knees.

The wind picked up, making a thunderous sound as it whipped against their shawls and clothes. The sun vanished under a veil of red sand. The wind and sand began swirling violently around them, clawing at their clothes, and slashing Persicus' hair against his face, stinging his eyes.

Persicus shouted over the howling wind. "Stay down! Put your blanket over your head, now, and keep it tight around you, like a tent, with the ends underneath you." Persicus wrapped his own wet shawl around his head. He pulled the horses down to the ground. "When it feels heavy with sand, stand up, and shake it off, or you will end up buried in the sand! And no matter how long this lasts, you mustn't fall asleep! Entire cities have been buried alive in sandstorms!"

The wind grew stronger, blowing loud, and ferocious. Hakim couldn't hear the last thing Persicus said. Persicus sat down, pulling the blanket over himself, wedged in between his horse and Hakim.

Even covered in the blanket and the wet shawl wrapped over his head, fine grains of sand still found their way through the layers of cloth. Tiny, hot needles that stung and stabbed his skin.

The relentless wailing wind filled their ears, as though the roar of a thousand war drums pounded just beyond his blanket. The sound became hypnotic. The merciless heat quickly became suffocating under their blankets. The moisture from the water-soaked shawls dried in the heat after only a few minutes.

Time ticked on painfully slow, breathing in stale air, the drumming, thunderous wind beating at their ears, and the hot sand pounding through their blankets.

Hakim nodded out within the first hour. Persicus had no way of telling time. He had no idea how long he had been under there, but still, the scalding wind beat down on him. The overwhelming heat became a drug, trying to pull him into death's sleep. Desperate to stay alert—to stay awake—Persicus dug his fingernails into his arm. The blanket felt heavy. He struggled to stand up against the wind, shook the blanket, and sat back down, tucking the ends of the blanket under his knees. He would have yelled out to Hakim, but he wouldn't have been heard. He dared not lift his blanket to check on Hakim. It would only be torn away from him and he would be left exposed to the elements.

The sound grew increasingly mesmerizing. Accompanied by the heat, it became strangely soothing. He felt as if he was basking in the heat of the sun by the riverside, watching the clouds drift by as he had done as a child. He kept his eyes opened to slits, with his head bowed down against the wind, as closing your eyes during a sandstorm invited sleep. If he had had more time, he would have told this to Hakim, but better to have them closed than dried out, damaged, or even blinded by the heat and sand.

His eyes closed, intending only to blink.

Persicus saw a thousand horses running through a green field. Their hooves pounding against the ground, creating a rhythmic thunder. The ground shook with their power as they ran and ran. That image dissolved. He felt the earth shifting and reforming under his feet. The devastating rumble of an earthquake. The earthquake that had taken his family and changed his life forever. He stood at the river in the village of his childhood.

He realized he had drifted off. The heat had increased, now insufferable, sweat dripped down from every surface of his body, drying against his face with the sand and dust, leaving him sticky, dirty, and grimy. The air was steamy and thick; he couldn't get a full breath. The hypnotic sound pursued him relentlessly, luring him back into that comfortable place.

He saw his mother standing in a green field. She looked worried. An instant later, his sister appeared, holding his mother's hand. Her mouth moved, but he couldn't hear her over the sound of the rumbling and shaking earth. His mother held out her other hand towards him, reaching. He wanted to reach out to them, but he couldn't move. Out of the hypnotic fog, a voice rose over all the other thunderous, quaking sounds—his uncle's voice. "Get up!"

Persicus jerked awake, eyes flying open. He realized he had dozed off. His muscles ached from sitting in the same position for an unknown length of time; he wondered how long it had been. The blanket felt heavy on top of him. He wondered if he had dreamed getting up to shake off the sand earlier. His ears were ringing, a high-pitched whine. He could no longer hear the howling wind. He realized he didn't feel it either. He sat for a moment longer straining to hear past the sharp ringing in his ears.

It was over. Persicus struggled to raise the blanket. He wasn't sure how much sand had piled up against him, but he knew his head wasn't buried, because he could still breathe; hot, stuffy air flowed through the blanket. Unable to move his hands more than an inch or two, he began wiggling himself free. Clawing at the sand, pushing it aside, away from his knees until he could get a grip on his blanket, and pull it out from under his knees. After pulling the blanket up, sand cascaded down around his knees, up to his chest. He inched his way out, scraping away at the mound of sand that kept him trapped, shoveling it away from his body. At last, he crawled free, leaned back on his heels, gasping in his first full breath of fresh air. His mouth felt as dry as sand and breathing the hot, dry air only made it worse. He looked at the landscape.

Nothing looked the same. The whole landscaped had changed. The horses were gone and so was Hakim. He began digging where Hakim should have been, throwing the sand aside as fast as possible. He felt the top of the blanket and starting digging around it. The sand was loose and easy to move, but more slid back into the hole with every movement. After several long, strenuous minutes of frantic digging, he pulled the blanket off Hakim, and shook him awake.

Hakim took a deep, gasping breath. "What? What? I was having a good dream. What's happening?" Hakim asked, spitting sand from his mouth, his disorientation fading.

"That was the dream of death coming to take you." Persicus leaned on hands and knees catching his breath.

Hakim crawled out of the hole. "Where are the horses? Are they buried?"

"No, they ran off. Maybe we'll catch up with them later. Help me dig out the supplies." Persicus crawled over to where he had piled the supplies. They dug with their hands through several feet of sand.

They found the saddles first, then the bag of food, Persicus' weapons, the lamps, and pickaxe. Last, they found the goatskin water pouches, which were empty; the weight of the sand having pushed the water out through the leather cinches.

By the time they had dug everything out, the dust had settled, and the sun was a big, orange ring of fire setting in the western sky. Hues of red, orange, and pink streaked across the sky, surrounded by fading blue. They had maybe three hours until dark, then the unbearable heat would start to cool.

"We have no horses or water. We'll have to cross the rest of the desert tonight. We'll never make it during the heat of the day. We'll find water when we make it through this wasteland by morning." Persicus licked his parched lips. "Let's get some rest and we'll leave after sunset."

Hakim nodded, relieved that they would get a couple hours to rest. After Persicus propped up one of the blankets to provide shade and spread the other blanket over the sand, they sank into the soft, comfortable sand.

They both fell quiet, thinking, with their eyes closed.

Hakim thought that the last of their troubles were over. Surely, there would be no more disasters. He pictured the piles of gold awaiting him. At last, he would get what was long overdue.

Persicus covered his face with his waist shawl, blocking out the last of the glaring sun, and thought about his uncle's voice jarring him awake. Was it only his internal alarm forcing him awake before he suffocated? No, he didn't think that was the case. Since his uncle's death, he had often felt protected, watched over. He thanked his uncle for saving him, yet again. Several times during his life, he had felt something guiding him in the right direction, always when life-threatening danger was close at hand. He heard his sister's giggling laughter as he drifted to sleep.

Persicus and Hakim awoke in the evening. The sun had set hours before and the temperature had rapidly cooled. Persicus divided the supplies up between them. He gave Hakim the bag of food, the empty water pouches, and one of the oil lamps to carry. Persicus rolled the blankets up, wrapping the rope around it several times, and tied them around his shoulders, cradling the back of his neck. He carried his bow and arrows swung over his shoulder, tied the second oil lamp and his pickaxe to his quiver of arrows, and swung the shovel over his other shoulder. His sword and dagger remained sheathed on his hips. Only the saddles were left behind.

They began their journey through the nighttime desert. Persicus frequently stopped to examine the stars, making sure they stayed on course.

Around midnight, the temperature dropped close to freezing. Hakim's pace had been slowing over the last hour. He stopped to rub his arms and exhale hot air onto his cold hand. Persicus unraveled one of the blankets and draped it over Hakim's shoulders.

"Ah, thank you," Hakim said through chattering teeth. "I'm too old for this madness. My bones don't want to work when it's this cold."

They continued through the desert, stopping to rest a few minutes every hour. The blowing wind felt like ice-cold daggers stabbing through their sunburnt skin.

Dawn came, spilling the sun over the horizon, bringing with it a sense of relief. They pushed on with renewed avidity. The rising sun warmed the frigid air, heating their skin, as would a growing fire. Their thirst was insufferable, their throats scratchy, burning, drier than the saltpans of the Sahara. Their lips were parched and cracked.

The Forbidden Land of Fire and Dragons came into view, appearing out of nowhere, as if it were yet another merciless mirage.

Hakim smiled ear to ear. "We've made it!"

"Yes. There it is. We should be there in no time."

Drawing closer, differentiating between the dark hills and the dark clouds that loomed over them was nearly impossible. Incessant flashes of lightning struck, with a crash of thunder, illuminating the morbid landscape for an instant. Charred, ancient trees with gnarled branches cast ominous silhouettes against the blackened sky. The land remained eerily reticent, but for the thunder, as if the land held its breath, waiting. Waiting for something. No birds or insects sang. No snakes, scorpions, or beetles crawled along the dark, crusted surface of the earth. No sign of life revealed itself, anywhere. The ceaseless lightning caused an illusion of movement, casting down scintillating silver-white flashes that made the shadows shift and dance after each strike. Thick, dark clouds slid overhead, but no wind seemed to move them. The clouds cast them in a deeper gloom. They stood watching the bleak and dreary landscape.

Persicus shivered at the unnerving thought of going to this place.

Two bolts of lightning tore through the darkened sky, appearing to emanate from the ground up.

Hakim jumped. "Well, here we are," he whispered, as if afraid to awaken something sleeping in the bare trees surrounding them.

A foreboding feeling clawed at Persicus' gut. He turned around and scanned the desert behind him. He had a feeling someone was watching, stalking him through this eerie land, waiting, as a predator bides his time, waiting for the opportune moment to pounce, and kill his prey.

"Is something wrong? I get nervous when you look around like that. Something bad always happens." Hakim looked around, still whispering

"I don't know. I have a feeling that we are being followed." Hair rose along his arms and he rubbed away the goose bumps.

Hakim smiled. "Ah, I know what you mean. I have kept an eye out, making sure those nosey Chinese merchants didn't follow us, but they couldn't have followed us after the path up in the mountain collapsed. I think this place is what is making us nervous. I feel it, too."

"Come on, standing here is making me anxious." Persicus put his hand on Hakim's shoulder, smiling warmly for the first time in over a day. "We are close to our fortune. God has tried us and now will reward us for our endurance."

Hakim smiled that lizard-ish smile and nodded. "Yes, yes. I am ready for my reward."

They walked in silence until they reached a tall hill, keeping a watchful eye on their surroundings, glancing around, nerves on edge. Hakim withdrew his animal skin map. He studied it for a long moment. He looked at the hill, back to the map, and to the hill again.

"I think this is it! It's an exact match, down to the rock formations on that steep hill. There should be a stream on the other side, where he found the gold coins," Hakim exclaimed, no longer whispering in his excitement.

Persicus looked over Hakim's shoulder, examining the map, and nodded in agreement. "Maybe. Come on, let's check it out."

Walking around the hill, they heard the trickle of the stream before they saw it. Thirst overwhelmed them and they hurried to the water.

After dropping his supplies by the stream, Persicus shoved his face into the cold water, drinking, slurping, gulping, and spitting cold water. Hakim jumped into the stream, drinking, splashing, and laughing in the water. After Persicus drank his fill, he sloshed into the stream, and floated in the chilled water, enjoying the goose bumps dancing along his body.

Once clean, they crawled ashore, collapsed onto their backs, ecstatic and weary, dripping wet, and delightfully cold, under the dark ominous clouds.

Persicus convinced Hakim to take a rest for a few hours, as they had been walking all night. Hakim agreed with some reluctance, eager to search out the treasure that was close, almost within reach.

When Persicus went to gather firewood, curiosity required him to investigate the crater to ensure they had come to the right hill. He returned fifteen minutes later. "Sumat was right. You can't see inside the crater through the steam." Persicus made a fire and sat on the blanket that Hakim had set down.

Hakim passed Persicus some dried fruit. "Ah, excellent. You found the crater. We are on track." Hakim devoured his fruit without a complaint, washing it down with fresh, cold water from the stream. "By tomorrow, my friend, I will be a very happy man." Hakim stretched out on the blanket and looked up into the smoldering, dark sky.

They both lay awake for a long time. The relentless, jarring thunder and lightning made it impossible to sleep for more than a few minutes before the thunder shook them awake again. After a while, Persicus hid his head under the blanket, trying to block out the noise and flashing light. Hakim stared at the rocky formations glowing in the lightning flashes, appearing more and more like demonic beings leering down upon him as the minutes ticked by. For an hour, he tried to convince himself that it was his exhausted, sleep deprived mind, playing tricks on him that made horns and red glowing eyes appear within the mangled tree limbs. After a while, unable to focus any longer, he drifted off to sleep.

# THE WALL

Persicus awoke in the early evening under a darkened sky. The lightning and thunder had somewhat subsided while they slept. The ominous clouds had turned a lighter shade of gray. They had made camp by the stream; surrounded by dark, rolling hills; dark boulders; and black, dead trees.

Hakim slept on his side, his blanket pulled up to his chin, snoring lightly. Persicus considered waking him, but decided to let him sleep while he tended to the fire, so he could enjoy a few more whine-free moments. He found a dead, gnarled tree limb and dropped it onto the dwindling embers; they sizzled and caught, whooshing into a large flame. He rummaged through his supply bag, pulled out some dried fruit and bread, and put a small kettle on the fire for tea.

Hakim woke up groaning, stretched his stiff body, and sat across from Persicus.

Persicus handed him a cup of tea.

Hakim picked at the dried fruit, eating it in distaste. "Great. Dried fruit and bread, again."

"Anything else you want to complain about?"

"Yes, as a matter of fact. It's too damn cold and —"

"Sorry, it's God's day off today. I will fill Him in on your list of complaints tomorrow."

"Well, you asked."

Persicus finished his food and dusted the crumbs from his hands. "Let me see the map."

Hakim fished the map out from under his caftan and tossed it to him. Persicus studied the map and stood. He followed the stream to the hillside, where water poured in a steady trickle out from a small crack at the base of the hill.

"Didn't you say that the soldiers were sucked into the cave on the side of a hill?"

Hakim nodded, his mouth full of food.

Persicus walked back to Hakim, putting his belt on, fastening his sword and dagger to his belt.

"Come on. Let's go find the cave."

Persicus walked along the bottom of the hill, Hakim following at his heels. Black stones and boulders covered the hillside, spilling down to the ground.

Persicus picked up a melon-size black stone. The underside was shiny black, almost translucent. He tossed it to the ground.

Halfway around the hill they stopped to consult the map, comparing it to their surroundings. It all seemed strikingly similar to where they had camped, but from here they could see steam rising from the top of the hill.

As Persicus continued along, he felt a tap on his thigh. He spread his caftan wide, looked down, and saw the tip of his sword lifting inches away from his leg. He took another step forward. His sword and dagger rose higher, pointing towards the hill. When he took two steps back, the sword and dagger fell back against his thighs. He stepped forward, the sword and dagger rose again.

"Guardian of the Steppes …" Persicus frowned, looking from his sword to the spot where his sword was pointing.

Hakim stood at his side, staring dumbfounded at the levitating sword.

Persicus took a few more steps forward. His sword and dagger rose horizontally, pointing to the hill, where a patch of black sand lay in a large mound against the hillside.

"What's happening?" Hakim asked. "What does this mean?"

"It means that I have to dig where my magic sword is pointing," Persicus answered sarcastically. He pointed to the mound of black sand. "The answer is there."

Whatever it is, good or bad, we're about to find out, Persicus added in his mind.

After careful consideration, Persicus removed his belt with the sword and dagger, set them on a smooth, black boulder, outside the reach of the curious force. With the trepidation of a lone bandit sneaking into a palace, he approached the mound, and stood by the black sand. Nothing happened, though he wasn't sure what he expected to happen.

The sand was in a heap, the result of a landslide. He knelt down and dug away layers of sand. Under the sand was a tall pile of rocks. Hakim helped toss aside the small rocks while Persicus cleared away the larger ones.

While clearing the mound, Persicus heard something coming from inside the hill. He stopped and pressed his ear against the dark earth. There came a tinny, distant sound of rushing water and a faint, almost inaudible, low-pitch hum. As he threw more rocks aside, the sounds grew louder.

"Do you hear that?" Persicus asked, his voice a touch higher with enthusiasm.

"Yes. It sounds like a river." Hakim stood staring down at the remaining rocks sitting against the hillside.

Dirt shifted above them and trickled down on their heads. Persicus paused, rock in hand, and looked up. He dropped the black stone, grabbed Hakim's arm, pulling him back, away from the hill. A massive boulder sat fifty feet above their heads, teetering on the hillside.

"I don't think that's very stable. Keep an eye on it while I finish moving the rocks." Persicus took one more look at the boulder before he cautiously walked back to the mound.

The last of the black rocks were larger and heavy. He struggled, pushing the rocks on top to the side, to fall off the mound. Removing the rocks from the top revealed a small, tapered opening. Persicus peered into the small, dark hole in silence. He turned and looked at Hakim, a smile spread across his face.

"I think this is it," Persicus said.

Hakim paced, unable to stand still.

As he cleared the last of the black rocks away, a cave entrance appeared. One last large rock blocked the hole. Too heavy to lift, Persicus pushed at it, using all his strength. The progress was painfully slow, moving an inch at a time.

"Push harder," Hakim instructed. "Use your strength. Push with your legs. You got it. A little more. You got it."

The rock moved, inch by inch, until it revealed a wide hole, which tapered closed at the top, leading into a darkened cave. Persicus collapsed against the rock, bent at the waist, catching his breath, peering into the pitch-black hole.

The setting sun disappeared behind the hills. Darkness crept in, deepening the sinister atmosphere. A flash of lightning struck with a clash of thunder.

The opening, large enough to walk through, absorbed the ambient light from outside, as if sucking the light into its consuming darkness, reflecting nothing, but the palpable darkness within. Persicus turned and walked away.

"Where are you going?"

"To get my weapons. I don't think we'll encounter anything in there, but I want to be prepared." Persicus strapped on his belt and headed back to the cave, prepared for his sword and dagger to begin dancing in the air again, confident that he could handle it—whatever it was. With each step towards the cave, the mysterious force grew stronger, pulling at his sword and dagger.

Thirty feet from the cave, Persicus felt a strong jerk, pulling at his hips; he stumbled and fell forward onto his knees. He tried to get up, but the invisible force kept pulling and pulling. He slid forward a couple feet and fell forward on his hands, trying to stop. In a futile effort, he pushed his hands against the ground. He knew that he couldn't lift his hands, as that was the only thing stopping the powerful force, which would suck him into the mouth of the cave, into dangers unknown, and there wasn't a damn thing he could do to stop it. The scabbards of his sword and dagger ran along his chest, brushing his chin. He tried to back up, but the force was overwhelming, overpowering him. He had to do something. He decided.

He threw himself onto his side. Before his body even hit the ground, the force caught him, and pulled him through the air. He flew through the open space, pulled with such force he could do nothing to resist, with his hips thrust forward, led by his sword and dagger. It seemed the cave was a gaping mouth that would swallow him whole. He stretched out his arms, trying to grab hold of anything, but there was nothing to grab. Finally, he did the only thing he could do—he screamed.

Hakim stood rooted to the spot. His mouth dropped open, eyes wide, frozen in fear.

The invisible force grew stronger the closer Persicus got to the cave, pulling him faster. Within an instant, he was at the gaping mouth of the cave. He stretched out his arms, grabbed the edge with both hands, and kicked out at the last second, catching his boots on the other side of the cave's entrance. His weapons pulled at his hips with violent ferocity.

Persicus yelled, "Hakim!"

Hakim stood far back, still rooted to the ground. He did not want to be sucked into the cave.

Persicus yelled again, his voice frantic, "It's the sword! The metal! Take it off me! Hakim!" Terrified, staring into the despairing darkness with wide eyes, he felt his fingers slip a little as the overwhelming invisible force grew stronger. He looked where his hands were struggling to maintain their hold. His heart froze for an instant, eyes widening further when he saw deep scratches embedded in the stone. He stared at it, trying to understand this ghastly image before his eyes.

*Oh, Guardians!* he thought. Old, dried fingernails were embedded in the cracks of the stone.

"Hakim!"

Hakim stared in disbelief. The fear had temporarily paralyzed him. In his mind's eye, he saw a dragon sucking Persicus into the cursed cave and once done with Persicus, it would inhale him next. *The story is true*, Hakim thought. *Impossible.* When Persicus yelled for the third time, he broke free of the terror that had consumed him.

"I don't want to get sucked in."

"It's the metal," Persicus yelled. "My belt, unbuckle it!"

Hakim walked closer, hesitant at first. When he felt nothing pulling him, he came to Persicus' side, reached tentatively over his body, and pulled on the buckle. The buckle came loose and the whole belt, with sword and dagger attached, whipped away from them, and flew into the cave, crashing into something with a loud clang of metal against metal. Persicus collapsed to the ground the moment the belt had left his body. He rolled onto his back, stunned for a moment.

"Are you all right? What in the world happened?"

"Guardian of the Sss-Steppes! No one has ever managed to take a weapon from me!"

"Calm down. You're all right."

"A lifeless cave at that! I can't believe it."

"Let's hope it's lifeless," Hakim mumbled.

Persicus got to his feet. "Wait here." He turned and didn't take more than half a step before Hakim's stupefied voice called out after him.

"What? Wait here? Where are you going?"

"To get the oil lamps. We will see if the cave tries to eat them, too," Persicus called back without turning.

"Are you sure it's still a good idea to go in there? It seems that the story is true."

Persicus turned like a storm to face Hakim "That was no dragon. It was pulling the metal." Persicus' frustration grew. "We have come all this way. You don't expect us to quit now, do you? Go back empty handed, after all we have already lost on this journey. No. We are going in there. We will figure out what the cause of this madness is, get the treasure, and go celebrate. There is no other option!" He turned his back on Hakim before he could reply and went to retrieve the lamps.

Hakim sat on a boulder next to the cave, scanning the landscape. A bolt of lightning tore across the sky, accompanied by a jarring roar of thunder. Hakim jumped, his eyes wide. Seconds ticked by slowly. About to head for the stream, Hakim sighed in relief when Persicus came into view, oil lamps in hand.

As Persicus drew near, the oil lamps swayed only with the rhythm of Persicus' stride, but he felt the familiar pull on his pickaxe. He backtracked a safe distance and set the tool down behind a boulder.

"The oil lamps are copper. Perhaps It only likes iron." Persicus handed Hakim one of the lamps.

They stood at the entrance, peering in. Persicus held his lamp above his head and took a step inside the cave. Hakim followed one step behind.

A narrow passageway sloped down and opened up into a huge cavern. A low hum reverberated off the cave's walls. A soft, fiery, pulsing, red glow illuminated the cave, intensifying as the hum grew louder, and diminishing as the hum grew softer.

At the back of the cave, a river rushed by, flowing out from behind a wall on the far left side. It flowed past a tall archway, into a dark tunnel in front of the entrance, going deeper into the cave. Limestone formations melted down from the cave's walls, creating odd shapes in the cool, damp darkness. Stalactites hung from the ceiling, like large, creamy gray icicles ready to fall, and bane whoever walked under at the wrong time. By the far left wall, in front of the river, high up in the ceiling, the crater vented steam fed by some unknown source.

They turned to their left, towards the red glow, and low humming noise. Hakim drew in a sharp, gasping breath and stepped back. Persicus tried to make sense of the sight before him. His eyes moved over a massive black wall at the far left end of the cave.

A web of glowing, red fissures covered the blackened wall, as if a spider had thrown its silk in an intricate design over the entire wall. Hot steam hissed as it seeped through the glowing cracks, filtering up through the crater to the surface of the hill. Something else stuck to the wall, large and bulging, masked by the darkness.

Persicus moved closer.

"Don't." Hakim reached out to stop him.

Persicus stepped around Hakim, without taking his eyes off the wall. Hakim hesitated and then followed, staying close by his side. They held out their oil lamps, driving back the darkness. The light fell on the objects upon the wall. Gasping, they stepped back in unison.

Hakim turned and tried to make a run for it. Persicus grabbed him by the neck of his caftan and pulled him back to his side.

"Where do you think you are going? This was your idea." Persicus turned back to the black wall, dragging Hakim with him.

"But don't you see them?"

"I see them. They can't hurt you."

Persicus stepped closer to the wall, illuminating a cluster of shining suites of armor, their owners' dull-white skeletons protruding out of them. Skeletons, everywhere, covering the entire wall. All of them wore armor, most still clutching their swords and lances in their boney hands. Some of the skulls seemed to be staring right at them through their armored hoods, but most of them had flown face first into the wall. Steam seeped out around the soldiers' armor, the red glow emanating from their hollowed eye sockets. Some must have died on impact. Persicus wondered how many had starved to death, or died from thirst, hanging there until death took them, stuck to this black, morbid wall by some invisible force with their companions decaying beside them, unable to free themselves, water visible, but out of reach, unable to move their armor-covered hands to get out of their full-body armor suits.

Hakim shivered and looked away.

In the middle of all the skeletal remains, remnants of a chariot stuck to the wall as if it was a relief sculpted into the stone. The lower half of charioteer remained wedged tightly inside the chariot. His armor-covered torso and head, severed from the rest of his body long ago, stuck obscenely against the wall. Persicus didn't want to think about how the charioteer had died, but the thought came anyway, even as he tried to suppress it. *Guardian of the Steppes! He must have crashed into the wall and then something cut him in two!* Persicus' all too vivid imagination was at work, running rampant. *He probably watched as ...* He cut off the thought and tried to focus on the mass as a whole.

Persicus spotted his sword amongst the many sticking out of and onto the black wall. His sword had impaled the ancient armor of an unfortunate soldier's chest. His eyes searched the wall for his dagger in vain. Swords, lances, daggers, and other bits of undefinable metals, too many to pick out a single object, scattered all over.

"So this is what happened to the Persian Cavalry," Persicus said. His voice held a hint of awe. "What a way to die!"

Horrified, Hakim backed away from the wall. Fear consuming him, bubbling up to the point where he wanted to run out of the cave screaming, and never return. He stepped backwards in the darkness and his foot tangled on something heavy. Losing his footing, he stumbled, and fell on his back. His head connected with something brittle that snapped under his weight. Turning, he saw that he had landed on top of a skeleton, his head in the grasp of a boney rib cage. His lamp extinguished when it fell to the ground, but he could still make out the dull-white bones of the ribs, bits of dried tissue, and disintegrated cloth still clinging to the old bones. He scrambled, hysterical, shrieking, trying to get away from the skeleton.

Hakim rolled over, brittle bones cracking under him. The skeleton's left hand hooked into the neck of his caftan. He shrieked again, desperately trying to crawl away, but he couldn't move any farther. The skeleton had a firm grip, refusing to let go. Frantic, Hakim kicked out wildly with both legs, still shrieking, bone fragments skidding across the ground.

Persicus rushed over to Hakim and saw him battling with the crumbling skeleton. He stood over him, shaking his head, and set the oil lamp on the ground. "Hold still a second. The hand is just caught on your caftan."

"It won't let me go!"

Persicus got a hold on Hakim and pulled him closer to the skeleton so he could unhook the hand. Hakim resisted, jerking away. "Calm down, let me unhook you." Persicus yanked him again, harder this time. Hakim fell back, landing beside the skeleton. He caught himself on one hand, looking down at a sack underneath him that he had not noticed until now. An old leather sack, gripped in the skeleton's right hand.

Persicus untangled the skeleton from Hakim's clothing, but Hakim made no move to get up. His eyes remained fixed on the sack. After a breathless moment, he got up on his knees and reached for the sack. Persicus followed Hakim's gaze and saw a sack—the sack. He sank down to his knees at Hakim's side.

Hakim tried to lift the sack, tugging on it, but the skeletal hand, clasped tight around the neck of the bag, and tangled with the drawstring, held on as if even in death, it refused to let go.

Persicus stood and stepped on the skeleton's wrist. "Try now."

"That's morbid," Hakim said, as he yanked the sack again. The hand separated from its owner and plopped onto the ground, its fingers curled and claw-like. He pulled open the leather drawstring.

Persicus moved back to his side. They knelt, eyes wide, and leaned forward to look inside the sack.

Hakim squealed with glee, "Yes! Persicus! I have found it!"

Persicus retrieved his oil lamp and brought it closer to the shattered skeleton, illuminating the area. The golden glow revealed three more bags of gold.

"This must be the leader of the bandits," Persicus said, reflecting on the story Hakim told him the day they met. Looking up, he saw the crater directly above them. "So he did fall through the crater."

Hakim looked down at the skeleton. It was an odd look, almost sympathetic. "Well, the treasure is where it belongs now." To the skeleton, he said, "Sorry, buddy."

Persicus knelt down, set his oil lamp beside him, and opened a second bag. Hakim knelt beside him and scooped up a handful of the ancient gold coins, laughing, letting them spill through his fingers, back into the bag. Persicus laughed with him, grabbing a coin, and holding it in the lamp's glow.

A strange reverberation came from the river behind them, accompanied with the sound of something large racing through the water. Jumping to their feet, they turned towards the sound, and gasped. They froze for a fraction of a second, staring into the cold eyes of a large reptilian creature perched on the bank of the river. It was enormous, dark, and glistening. It made a hissing noise and charged out of the water towards them.

Persicus shoved Hakim towards the exit and ran as fast as he could, leaving the gold behind.

Hakim felt hot breath on his back and heard the clink of dagger-like claws on the ground behind him. Persicus sensed Hakim several paces behind, could hear his labored breaths wheezing in and out in rapid huffs. Sparing a glance over his shoulder, Persicus saw the creature close on Hakim's tail. He whipped around, grabbed Hakim's arm, and pulled him forward, faster than Hakim could have run on his own. He saw the glint of outdoor light a few feet ahead. He exited the cave, pulling Hakim through, almost dragging him along.

They stopped several yards away from the cave. Only their panicked, gasping breaths broke the silence. They watched the entrance. It was large enough for them to pass through, but Persicus couldn't tell how large the creature was, and wasn't certain if it could squeeze through.

Silence. They waited. Their eyes locked onto the darkness within the cave. The eerie semi-darkness of the cloud-covered sky seemed bright in comparison with the pitch-black of the cave from which they had emerged.

"Was that a dragon? It couldn't be. They are not real. They're only stories. Fairy tales. I don't believe it," Hakim said, his voice growing frantic.

"It wasn't a dragon."

"It was a dragon."

"No," Persicus persisted, only half believing.

"Yes. A dragon ... A drag—"

"Whatever it is, it is in there with our gold."

"Did you see the size of that thing?"

"Yes, it's enormous."

"It almost got me. God, it was fast."

"But it didn't."

"What are we going to do? We can't leave without the gold."

"Shh ... Let me think ... let me think." Persicus walked in a tight circle. "Let's go back to the stream and come up with a plan."

## ͷ

Persicus knelt on a rock by the stream, splashing cold water on his face. He sat, thinking furiously. He bit down on his lower lip in concentration, his eyebrows creased. Hakim paced back and forth, stopping to glance at Persicus from time to time.

"This place is cursed. Definitely cursed. Did you see that wall? Black and gruesome, with all those bodies. An entire cavalry." Hakim shivered. "The dragon must suck its victims into the cave and sticks them up there like … like a fly on a spider's web. I've never seen such a thing."

"I think there's a much simpler explanation," Persicus said.

"Oh, really? Well, I think it's perfectly obvious that the story was true."

Persicus shook his head. "The wall has nothing to do with the creature. There's a legend about a black stone, called lodestone, sucking the nails right out of peoples shoes when they walk over it. The stone is attracted to certain metals."

"A legend? Most legends aren't true. They're made up, nonsense."

"When I was a boy one of my uncle's business partners, a Chinese man, told me they have used lodestones for centuries to tell fortunes and for a compass at sea. They use a small piece of this stone, a needle, and some water, and the needle would point north and south." Persicus turned to face the stream. "But I've never heard of an entire wall of lodestone. If I hadn't seen it, I wouldn't believe it. It's no wonder the force is strong enough to pull a full grown man to it."

Hakim stopped and gave him a bewildered look. He waved his hand in a dismissive gesture and resumed his pacing.

Persicus stared into the water for almost twenty minutes, formulating a plan. Finally, he stood. "I've got an idea."

Hakim looked at him, hopeful.

Persicus retrieved his bow and arrows, and a length of rope from the pile of supplies.

"You are not thinking of shooting that monstrous beast with a few arrows are you?" Hakim asked. "That's absurd."

"There are forty-nine arrows in here."

"You think that creature will let you shoot it with arrows forty-nine times? That he'll just stand there, one blow after another?"

"No. I doubt that, but I do not intend to shoot him forty-nine times. I only need to shoot him once with forty-nine arrows," Persicus said, as if it made perfect sense.

Hakim looked at him skeptically. "How?"

"Here's the plan." Persicus picked up a stick and drew a diagram in the black sand as he explained.

# 6

# A HANDFUL OF GOLD

A re you crazy?" Hakim yelled when Persicus finished explaining. "How could you want to go through with this ... this dangerous plan, when we can go back to town, and get some better supplies? I mean, going up against a dragon with some arrows!" He waved his hand as if dismissing the entire idea.

Persicus gave Hakim a stern look. Determined as he was to see this through, he needed Hakim for the plan to work. "There was a saying I heard often as a child: A brave man dies only once, but a coward dies time after time. How do you want to be remembered? A coward, too scared to try, or a brave man who fought? If you have to die, die as a hero who fought the dragon of the Forbidden Land!"

"That's exactly my point! We don't have to die. We need to come up with a plan that does not include suicide, or using me as bait."

Persicus picked up the arrows, bundled them together, looped the rope around the arrows' shaft, and tied it in a tight knot. He stood, holding the bundle under one arm, and the length of rope with the other. "If you are done whining, I need you for this to work. This whole journey I have heard nothing but 'there has to be another way' as if things worthwhile come easy. They don't. This was your idea. Your plan to come here." Persicus looked into Hakim's worried eyes and couldn't help but feel sorry for him. He was old and couldn't move fast, and here Persicus was asking him to put his life in danger, trusting that he would keep him safe. "Listen, arrows are perfect for what we need to do. Going back to get better weapons won't help us. One of us will still need to distract the creature. And it has to be you because of your ... handicap."

Hakim stared out into the distance, not seeing anything in particular. He took a shaky breath and nodded. "All right, let's do it."

As they drew near, Persicus felt the familiar pull. With each step, he felt the invisible, magnetic force increasing with the pulsing hum from within the cave. Holding tight to the rope, he let go of the bundle of arrows, and let the rope slip through his fingers, a little at a time, until the bundle floated about ten feet in front of him, just outside the entrance to the cave.

As Persicus began to slide forward, Hakim reluctantly jumped in front of Persicus, holding onto the rope as best as he could with one hand. He leaned back, adding his body weight to counter the invisible force pulling at the metal arrowheads. Between the two of them they managed, one strenuous, trembling step at a time, to cross the threshold of the cave without being sucked into the black, lodestone wall.

They shuffled inside, opposite the black wall, struggling to hold onto the rope.

Persicus' muscles were burning from the constant strain. He wedged himself between the cave wall and a small boulder that sat low to the ground, across from the morbid tableau. Hakim stood in front of Persicus, hand wrapped around the rope, just behind the bundle of arrows. Persicus leaned his back against the wall behind him and put his feet on the boulder in front of him, anchoring himself in place. Closing his eyes, he took a deep, reassuring breath, steadying himself.

"Now, Hakim! Now!" Persicus said through clenched teeth.

Terrified, his vision blurring, Hakim let go of the rope, and he felt his left eye twitch twice. He hated his eye twitch. He walked into the middle of the cave on shaking knees.

Hakim tried twice before the words would form. "Here I am … Come and get me, you ugly, oversized lizzar—" All coherency left him as the creature raised its huge head from the river in the eerie darkness. Hakim stood frozen in place, not daring to breathe, as it emitted an ear-piercing shriek, and charged out of the dark water, heading straight for him.

Hakim tried to run, but he stood staring, helpless, paralyzed. In his mind, he had already turned, and fled to safety. Aghast at the speed and ferocity of this creature as it closed the distance between them in an instant, something screamed at him from deep within—Run! His eye twitched again. It jolted him from his paralyzing terror. He ran on quaking legs towards the exit. His legs gave out from underneath him and he fell flat on his face within an arm's length of the exit.

Hakim glanced over his shoulder, anguish of his impending doom whipped across his face as he saw the dragon bearing down on him.

ᛏᛏᛏ

Persicus cursed. Hakim had run the wrong way. He yelled, his voice massive, echoing off the cave's walls, "Here! Over here, you damned lizard!"

The dragon paused only five feet from Hakim, turned its long neck, and fixed its cold, reptilian eyes on Persicus. Persicus struggled to hold onto the rope, the arrows still fiercely pulling towards the black, magnetic wall.

If this failed, they would die in here.

Afraid to move, fearing the most miniscule movement would draw the creature's vicious attention back to him, Hakim cowered face down on the ground, face buried in his hand, whimpering helplessly.

Persicus yelled again, daring the creature to charge him. The gruesome creature raised his head, looking Persicus up and down, forked tongue slithering out between its lipless mouth, but all Persicus could see in the dim light was its rough, jagged, spiked head, its glowing red and white eyes with black pupils, and its huge form. It held neither warmth, nor sanity in its steady, hungry gaze. Persicus understood that look; he had seen it before in a wolf. The look of a predator who knew nothing, but hunting and killing—the perfect predator.

The creature reared. The dark form towered above Hakim, at least ten feet tall standing on its hind legs. Its tail lashed through the air, whipping back and forth fast enough that Persicus felt the vibration of it in his eardrums. The cave amplified every sound.

The creature dropped down onto all fours, emitted a heart-shattering roar, and charged towards Persicus.

The angle wasn't right; Persicus had to wait until the creature moved directly in front of the arrows.

It opened its mouth to let out another deafening roar as it charged. Persicus saw rows of razor-sharp teeth lining its massive jaw. As it charged forward, looming, almost on top of Persicus, it reared up to strike. As it brought its head down towards its prey, Persicus let go of the rope. He couldn't wait any longer.

The bundle of arrows shot straight out, pulled by the invisible force of the lodestone wall, into the creature's mouth. It reared back, feeling a sting at the back of its throat. It scrambled backwards on all fours, shaking its head in confusion. It paused, working its jaws, trying to rid itself of this stinging object in its throat. It tried to charge again, but the fierce force of the wall pulled hard at the arrowheads.

The dragon stumbled, its front legs collapsing to the ground. As it brought its front leg up to claw at the rope hanging from its mouth, the magnetic force overpowered the creature. It flew backwards, coughing out a terrified shriek. It smashed into the lodestone, crashing into the long dead soldiers with a thunderous bang. Bones and armor shattered away from the wall with explosive force. Fragments of arms, legs, and ribs rained down all over the ground. The creature curled up and flailed out its legs rapidly, kicking with all its might. Its long, scaly, spike-covered tail whipped back and forth in a rapid, frantic frenzy. The tail smashed into the suits of armor, swords, and skeletons on either side, sending more bone fragments flying through the air. The armored suits projected through the air about fifteen feet before the magnetic force overcame the forward motion and sucked them back to the wall. Along with the armor, a great, ancient curved sword, and Persicus' dagger dislodged from the wall, flew halfway across the cave, before the wall pulled them back.

The curved sword impaled the dragon's head, lodging into the wall behind, and the dagger pierced the dragon's heart. It let out one last piteous shriek and slowly went limp.

Persicus had ducked behind the boulder as the armor, swords, and bones flew through the air. Several swords and pieces of bone struck the rock wall over his head. Persicus peeked over the top of the boulder. He looked at the dragon and saw it pierced against the wall. A wave of relief flooded through him. He thought he saw his dagger piercing the dragon's heart. He smiled, feeling victorious, and went to help Hakim, still on the ground by the exit, curled up in a fetal position, whimpering, "No ... No ... Oh, no ... No."

"Get up. It's dead." Persicus grabbed his arm and pulled him to his feet. Hakim's wide eyes darted around in his deathly pale face. Persicus led Hakim out of the cave, took him to the stream, and splashed cold water on his face.

"Is it really dead?" Hakim asked, his color returning to normal.

"Yes." Persicus reassured him. "Wait here. I'll go back and get the gold."

Hakim watched as Persicus walked around the hill.

As soon as Persicus disappeared around the hill, two men appeared from behind a large rock.

Hakim immediately perked up.

"Where the hell have you two been all this time?" Hakim asked.

"We've been hiding behind those rocks," one of the brothers said, pointing to a huge boulder.

The two men studied Hakim. They could tell he was shaken. His eye would twitch every now and then when he was at his worst.

"What happened?" asked the other brother.

"I almost died!" Hakim said. "But we found the gold. I'll tell you everything later. Now get out of sight, he should be back soon."

"Where did he go?" Asif asked, glancing over his shoulder.

Asif stood a foot taller than Hakim and about twenty years younger. He had a slim, lanky build, and had similar features to Hakim. His hair was graying and receding, thin on the top, but still full around the edges.

"To get the gold. Now get out of sight!"

"Great! After he brings the gold here, we'll take care of him. Send him back to the cave. We'll be waiting behind some boulders and we'll ambush him. He'll never know what's coming," Asif said with a sly smile.

A sudden pang of conscience overcame Hakim. His eyebrows furrowed with concern. "What are you going to do to him? You aren't going to hurt him, are you?"

Hamzeh looked astounded. "What's wrong with you? This was your idea! Your plan, remember? That whole speech you gave us, 'He's just a stupid Tajik. A hole digger. He will probably try to double-cross us anyway, so he'll get what's coming to him. And now you act concerned!"

Hamzeh was thirteen years younger than Hakim and the exact opposite of his two brothers. He was the same height as Hakim, but had a thick, muscled body, and a large round belly. He had deep brown eyes and a round, clean shaved head.

Hakim relented. "All right, all right. As long as it is not too painful a death."

Hamzeh gave Hakim an impatient look. "You remember what we did to the old 'diseased' man that we got the map from? He didn't even see it coming when I snuck up behind him and bashed his head in. Will that make you feel better? When we take care of your stupid Tajik, it will be quick and painless."

That didn't make Hakim feel better, Hamzeh may have surprised Sumat—the man they found in Astana—but it wasn't quick and painless. He looked from Hamzeh to Asif. "I don't know. Do not underestimate Persicus. He has turned out to be much smarter and stronger than I expected. He is always aware of his surroundings. I don't know if you would be able to surprise him."

"You think he'd be able to take both of us?" Asif asked in disbelief.

Hamzeh chuckled.

"I would rather not find out," Hakim snapped.

Hakim brooded over this, trying to overcome his guilt. He had known this moment would come eventually, but he had not planned on Persicus having saved his life, nor had he thought he would grow fond of him. As he stared at the scattered black boulders, a thought formed in his mind. "No, here is what you will do." He looked over his shoulder in the direction Persicus had gone and then huddled with his brothers, devising a new plan.

Persicus slung the bags over his shoulders, two on each side. They were heavy, but manageable. He would have to come back for his sword and dagger. He had no idea how he would pull them away from the wall, but he would think of something.

He walked back to camp and saw Hakim sitting on a boulder. Hakim looked better, but still nervous. Persicus wondered if he was in a state of shock. He set the gold down. Hakim got to his feet and walked over to him.

Hakim avoided looking Persicus in the eyes. "Where are your weapons and the rope? Did you leave them in the cave? We may need them later."

Persicus nodded, exhausted after trudging around the hill with the heavy bags. "Give me a minute to catch my breath. I have to figure out a way to get my weapons."

Persicus sat on a flat boulder and drank from his water pouch. After five minutes, he got to his feet, stretching out his sore arms. "Wait here. Maybe you could fetch some more wood for the fire."

"Yes, yes. Of course."

Persicus headed back to the cave.

In the meantime, Asif and Hamzeh climbed the hill, following Hakim's instructions.

Hakim waited until Persicus disappeared from view again and then joined his brothers.

Persicus walked back to the wall, looking at the pinned dragon. He saw his dagger sticking out from the dragon's chest. He looked around for his sword and spotted it wedged between a limestone formation and the wall, close to where he had hid.

𝗧𝗧𝗧

At the top of the hill, Hamzeh shoved a piece of petrified wood under the precariously balanced boulder above the cave's entrance. Hamzeh pulled down on the wood while Asif pushed the boulder from behind, trying to pry it loose.

𝗧𝗧𝗧

Inside the cave, Persicus unsuccessfully tried to pull the rope from the dragon's mouth. He knew what he must do, but the thought of it made him shiver.

He placed his hands on the dragon's ridged and spiked tail, and climbed up to its mouth. He pulled the jaw down, opening the mouth wide. Grimacing, he reached into the mouth, trying to avoid the razor-sharp teeth, and began untying the rope from the arrows. The rope was slimy, thick tendrils of saliva and bloody mucus hung from the back of its throat, dripping down onto Persicus' arm. Persicus swallowed hard. He leaned in further, trying to get a better grip, his cheek pressed against its lower jaw. The smell was nauseating. It smelled as if something large and furry was rotting inside its mouth. He inched his hand over to the right, where the rope had snagged on one of its rear teeth, submerging his entire arm deep into the creature's mouth. He felt along the rope. It felt smaller, ribbed, and far too firm. He turned his head to look inside the mouth and repressed the urge to gag when he saw he was trying to free a rat's tail that was wedged between two teeth. He turned his head, took a few shallow breaths, and concentrated on untying the rope. A thick glob of mucus oozed down his arm. He tried to ignore it as it trickled down, pooling in the shallow spot between his collarbone and shoulder.

𝗧𝗧𝗧

Above, on the hilltop, the boulder teetered as Asif and Hamzeh heaved and pushed, and gravity took its hold. The boulder crashed down in front of the cave's entrance.

A thunderous boom echoed off the cave's walls, followed by the unmistakable rumbling sound of a landslide, as a portion of the unstable earth from above slid down, sealing off the cave's exit, and sending a cloud of black dust into the air.

The ground shook, startling Persicus. He lost his footing and fell flat on his back, his head landing on the edge of the dragon's tail. The oil lamp toppled over and everything went dark. He lay there for a moment, stunned, with the wind knocked out of him.

A cloud of fine black dust hung in the air inside the dark cave. Persicus took a shallow, ragged breath, inhaling a lung full of thick, foul air. He coughed, covering his mouth with one hand, while he fumbled to untie his waist shawl. He wrapped it around his head, covering his nose and mouth.

Persicus had worked underground long enough to know what had happened, but he couldn't gauge how bad it was until he checked the exit to see how much it was blocked.

He waited until the dust settled and let his eyes adjust to the darkness. He found his oil lamp on the ground and lit it with his flint. He saw at once that the large boulder from above had completely blocked the exit. He knew he wouldn't be able to move it without a lot of help.

"Hakim! Can you hear me? Hey, Hakim!" He hoped Hakim had heard the rumble from the other side of the hill and was rushing over to see what happened.

After a moment's hesitation, the reply came, echoing down to him from the crater above the cave. "I can hear you," Hakim said, his voice calm and sure.

"I can't believe I made such a careless mistake, not securing the exit, but what's done is done. The problem is the two of us won't be able to move this boulder by ourselves. You have to go to Abrisham and tell them what has happened here. They will send help. Tell them we'll need at least six mules."

"I'm afraid your problem is slightly more severe than this rock," came an unfamiliar voice.

"Who are you?" Persicus asked, as little bells of alarm sounded in his head.

"I am Hamzeh, Hakim's brother."

"Brother? Hakim? What's going on?"

Another unfamiliar voice said, "This is an unfortunate predicament, don't you think? Just when you thought you would be a very, very wealthy man. Life has many ups and downs, why only a month ago—"

"Let me talk to Hakim!" Persicus demanded.

"Yes, I am still here."

"What's going on up there? Who are those men?"

"Not much going on up here. What's going on down there?" Hakim said, sounding almost happy.

"Who are those men?"

"They are my brothers. If you would be quiet a moment, what Asif is trying to tell you is that we are not going to your Abrisham. We have made other plans. Maybe I'll send a message to your people when I get a chance. Let them know of your unfortunate choice to go the Forbidden

Land and your ultimate demise inside a cave after a terrible accident. You have been extremely resourceful throughout this journey. Maybe you can save yourself, though I doubt it. But it is all right, as you said, since you will die a brave man, yes?"

"We made a deal! You gave your word!" Persicus could no longer hold in his disbelief and outrage. His voice boomed off the walls.

"No, I said, 'We *can* split the gold fifty-fifty,' not we *will*. This just goes to show how inferior minds don't think the same as superior minds do. However, you are right that you deserve some compensation. You worked for me for three days, yes? Here are your wages." Hakim threw a handful of gold coins down the shaft from the crater. "Consider yourself paid. This is more than I usually pay the help and more than you could make in a year, so be a little grateful."

"*Grateful!*" Persicus yelled.

"Are you mad? Throwing our gold down that hole when he's just going to die in there!" Asif barked.

"No, I am not mad. On Judgment Day, when God and all his prophets and angels are sitting up there, Persicus will no doubt be waiting for me to show up, and will demand his wages. How will I be able to pay him up there? I will pay him now, so my soul won't be cast down into the everlasting fires of Hell."

Persicus was speechless.

"With this, I have paid my debt, and you and God himself have witnessed it. Now, I will worry myself no longer. Persicus has been paid for his services. Let's get out of this hellish place."

Persicus stood rooted to the ground below the crater, flabbergasted. He could not believe what had happened. He listened as their footsteps faded, until the ominous hum of the wall and the incessant sound of rushing water drowned out the horses' clatter.

# 7

# THE LOST DARK RIVER

**P**ersicus wasted no time. He needed to find a way out of this cave, but first, he needed his weapons. He walked back over to the dragon, with oil lamp in hand. He could see it much better now; the sight of it revolted him. It had multi-colored scales: green, yellow, and black. Each scale was the size of his palm. Its underside was light gray and green. Its eyes were startling: one eye opened wide, its stare fixed in death, and the other eye squeezed shut tight. Both eyes bulged from its head. Its face crinkled up, frozen in death. Light greenish-gray spikes covered its body, from its forehead, down the center of its back, and along its tail. Its mouth was similar to a crocodile, long and bumpy, with rows of razor-sharp teeth. He glanced at the creature for only a moment, but the image became a permanent fixture in his mind.

Persicus climbed back up the limbs and retrieved the rope. Then he jumped down and examined the dagger sticking out of the dragon's chest. The dagger was special to him; he couldn't leave it behind.

Persicus studied the lodestone wall for a few minutes, thinking furiously. It seemed that the hum resonated from within the black wall. The hum waxed and waned. When the hum grew louder, the red vein-like fissures glowed brighter, and steam bellowed from the fissures. Remembering, when he first arrived with his weapons, how the magnetic force had increased without warning, he thought that just maybe, the magnetic pull grew stronger when the hum and glow increased. Which meant the pull would be less when the hum decreased. If he was right, maybe he could get his dagger back.

Persicus walked along the side of the cave towards the river. After examining the walls and crevices of the main chamber, he concluded that no openings to the outside existed, except for the inaccessible crater high above. Going down the river was his only viable option, but he had no idea where it would lead him. Staying here was no option; it would be certain death, since no one in their right mind would *ever* venture to these parts. Hakim wouldn't tell a soul what he had done. There would be no rescue.

He returned to the dead beast and gazed at all the long-dead soldiers who had become a part of the macabre cave for all eternity. Never had he felt this alone. He allowed himself only a moment of self-pity before he snapped out of it. He realized if he didn't find a way out soon, he would become a part of this morbid menagerie forever.

He devised a plan.

Persicus walked over to the bandit's skeleton, which had come to rest under the crater, where Hakim had thrown down the gold coins. Some of the coins had landed inside the skeleton.

Persicus gingerly reached through the ribcage and picked up the coins, trying not to touch the bones. One of the coins sat inside its open jaw. Persicus told himself that he had earned this as he plunged his hand inside the mouth and plucked out the last gold coin.

He knelt by the water and washed the coins, hoping it would wash away any bad luck or curse that clung to them. He put the money in a small leather pouch that he wore around his neck, under his tunic. He found his belt at the base of the wall of death. As it was made of bronze and silver, it wasn't magnetic, which confirmed his suspicion that the wall was lodestone.

Next, Persicus would need a raft of some sort. He examined all the debris before he settled on the ancient chariot. He dismantled the wood and wheels, and used one of the swords stuck on the wall to cut the rope into several equal lengths. He tied the pieces of ancient wood together, hoping the raft wouldn't fall apart in the water. When he was done, he dragged his makeshift raft over to the riverside, and wedged the raft behind a rock.

Persicus walked back to the creature and tied the last piece of rope to his dagger, still lodged deep in the dragon's chest. He tried to pull it out, but the invisible force was too great.

Persicus wound the rope around his arm and waited for the incessant hum to decrease. After five minutes, the red fissures' glow diminished and the hum gradually faded until all he could hear was the sound of the rushing river. He pulled on the rope with all his strength. It didn't want to come free. He yanked and tugged, jerking the rope from left to right until the dagger slid out of the dragon's chest in a wave of crimson blood. He backed up, the dagger floating midair, vigorously pulling towards the black wall. Persicus kept a firm grip on the rope and struggled towards the raft at a steady pace, one slow step at a time, until his foot hit the rock in front of the raft. He knelt and tied the rope to the raft.

When he secured his dagger, he thought about his sword stuck to the wall, but he had had enough trouble with the much smaller dagger. He was sad to leave it behind — he had had it for many years — but he could always get another sword.

He turned and looked at the bizarre scene for the last time, and then dragged his small makeshift raft into the water. He pushed off the sandy edge, starting his mysterious voyage down the river into the unknown. The raft groaned under his weight, but it held together.

The journey had begun.

As he drifted at a slow, easy pace downstream, Persicus thought of the brave men who had left their home to secure the route that he had taken many centuries later. They had never made it home. How did their families react when they heard of their loved ones disappearances? He wondered who, if anyone, would grieve for him if he didn't make it home.

The river carried him along, gentle waves rocking the raft. At length, the force of the magnetic wall lost its hold and the dagger fell into the water. The raft lurched forward, speed increasing with the current. Persicus grabbed the rope and fished the dagger out. He dried it off and sheathed it with a sigh.

After a while, he lay on his back and raised his oil lamp. The soft light illuminated the ceiling of the underground river. The sight of caves always amazed him, the remarkable work of nature — much more splendid than the qanats he had helped build — but he was in no mood to admire the unique beauty of this cave.

Minutes ticked by — slow, torturous minutes. He had no idea what time it was. There was no sun or moonlight to judge the time of day by, but he knew he had been drifting for hours. He grew tired. He tried to stay awake, but his eyes closed as he struggled to keep them open. The gentle sway of the river lulled him to sleep.

### 𒀭

Persicus woke with an excruciating pain on his stomach, he had no idea how long he had been asleep, or how far he had drifted down the river. His eyes flew open and he lifted his head to see what was causing the pain, but changed his mind, and lowered his head immediately when he saw a stalactite looming above him, scraping up his chest, coming towards his face. He pressed his head down, turned his head to the side, and sucked in his stomach as the sharp edge of the stalactite grazed up his chest, to his ear, and temple. He felt heat and a second later felt thick, hot blood trickle down his ear to his neck.

He raised his head again and groaned. The ceiling had dropped down, too close to the surface of the water. Scattered stalactites hung everywhere, decorating the ceiling with their long, serrated, sharp edges.

One by one, Persicus pushed on the stalactites with his foot, moving the raft out of the way as he approached them. He dodged them swiftly, back and forth, from one side of the river to the other. There were no longer any sandy banks, now the water stopped at the walls on either side. Smooth limestone formations covered the walls, reminding him of overlapping layers of beige silk, some surprisingly human looking. The serrated ceiling was dropping at a steady pace, closer and closer to the water, but Persicus, so focused on his legs, and moving out of the way of ceaseless stalactites, didn't notice the ceiling lowering until almost a moment too late.

He rolled over and bailed out of the raft, into the cold water. He flung his arm around one of the wheel's spokes as the ceiling lowered to only inches above the water. He paddled alongside the raft. The oil lamp fell over and he heard it screech as it scraped along the ceiling. By some miracle, the lamp stayed lit and secure on top of the raft.

He ducked his head under the water as another dagger-like spike appeared in front of him, giving him no time to move out of the way. When he came up for air, another stalactite appeared, bearing down on him. This one seemed to be submerged deep into the water. He threw himself to the side, pushing off against the raft, and swam around the spiked column. He heard the raft groan as it crashed into the stalactite, then slipped to the side, and continued with the current.

The ceiling shot up twenty feet. Persicus paddled in the water against the current and waited for the raft to catch up with him. He pulled himself out of the water onto the raft and collapsed on his back, shivering in violent jerks.

He lay there, cold, his thoughts drifting. He wondered if he would get out of here alive. If the river would consume the cave all the way to the ceiling, which they are known to sometimes do. What could possibly lie ahead? And finally, how he could escape this dark lost river and find Hakim. His anger grew with his frustration at his precarious situation, growing ever more furious at this deception—Hakim's perfidy would not be forgotten.

Persicus closed his eyes and concentrated on breathing, trying to get his mind off the fact that he was freezing, trying to calm his seething anger. He remembered something he had learned at the Buddhist village. He had come upon a room in their monastery, where rows and rows of monks sat upon cushions in a tranquil silence. Ashoka later explained that it was the Dhamma Hall, where the monks observed Noble Silence, and tried to quiet their wandering minds. This, Ashoka said, helps you to see and control your emotions from a detached point of view. Anger, he said, is the same as any strong emotion. To conquer it, you must sit back, realize that it is only temporary, and let it wash over you and retreat, the same way the raging waves crash down on the shore, and then calmly merge back into the ocean.

Persicus remembered this now. Taking deep and slow breaths, he closed his eyes, tried to quiet his mind, to let the anger wash over him, and recede as the ocean waves do. When he felt calm, he opened his eyes.

However, the calm didn't last. As the minutes ticked by, his anger returned, as if the raging wave crashing back upon the shore, in perpetuity, intensified with each minute, accumulating fierce power as each new wave crashed ashore. He couldn't believe this betrayal and he couldn't forgive it. No, he *wouldn't* forgive it. He swore that if he got out of this cave alive, he would have his vengeance.

The river moved on at a slow, steady pace. By now, the sight of the limestone formations almost sickened him. Veins of gold and bits of turquoise decorated the ceiling. His eyes lingered on them, but they held no interest for him. He only wanted to get out of here alive. He thought about the people up there, oblivious to the wealth below their feet. At this point, he would gladly trade places with them for any amount of gold.

He began singing to himself to pass the time. Old songs he had learned over the years. He sang until his throat turned raw and his voice grew raspy, but anything was better than the sound of the drifting water.

Something caught Persicus' eye downstream. He propped himself up on his elbows and stared into the darkness. His eyes widened in surprise and he sat up, alert. His heart leapt. Slivers of light shone through the fissures in the rock ceiling above. He realized the river was not too far removed from the land of the living. It might lead him straight out of here into the daylight, but then again, he had no way of getting to the ceiling from his crumbling raft, and there might be no way out.

Still deep in thought, he almost didn't pay attention to the ominous sound of crashing water.

"No! Not this! No more!" he said to himself, anxious and weary, getting to his knees, and raising his oil lamp.

Ahead, a short distance away, he saw a huge rock extending from the ceiling to beneath the flowing water, which created two divergent tunnels, and so two different rivers. To the right of the rock wall the river's flow became choppy and violent, turning the water white where it rushed over large boulders that stuck up out of the water, and seemed to disappear in a rapid downward slope. To the left of the rock wall, the river flowed gently.

After the seconds it took him for his brain to process this information, he lunged down on his stomach, and started paddling with his hands, pumping his arms into the water as fast and hard as he could, trying to redirect the raft towards the left tunnel.

The raft picked up speed with the rapid flow. Persicus had just made it into the middle of the river when the raft crashed into the dividing rock wall. He lunged towards the edge of the raft, grabbing onto a formation jutting out from the wall, the rapids of the right tunnel pulling hard at the raft. He struggled against the surge, straining, teeth gritted, water splashing into his face as he tried to pull the raft into the calmer tunnel.

Persicus cursed Hakim again. His situation became perilous. He would *not* die like this, here, in this cursed place. Summoning strength beyond his comprehension, he yelled as he shoved the rock one last time. The raft jerked free of the stronger current and slipped around to the calm tunnel.

Persicus collapsed onto his back, breathless and gasping. A half-hysterical laugh escaped his lips. Exhausted, he thought about seeing the beautiful blue sky again.

No sooner than his heart stopped pounding in his chest, than he heard the familiar, ominous roar of turbulent water again.

"Guardian of the Steppes," Persicus shouted. It was hopeless. He got back up onto his knees.

He thought he must be dreaming. That he only needed to wake up. Maybe he hadn't even come to meet Hakim yet at the Caravanserai. Yes, it was the night before he even left for this adventure, he told himself. Better yet, that he could go back in time and this time he knew exactly how he would respond to Hakim's offer of gold and misery.

However, he knew this was no dream as the currents speed picked up and the raft began pitching from side-to-side as it made its way over white rapids, splashing cold water onto his face, bringing him back to his despondent reality.

Persicus held up his oil lamp as high as he could, while gripping one of the spokes in the wheel so as not to be pitched over the edge of the small raft. There it was, up ahead — the absolute end of the line.

He prayed.

It looked as if the river ended at a solid rock wall. The river, picking up speed by the second, rushed him towards this fatal crash. As he got closer, the deafening roar of the crashing water grew louder as it hit the wall with immense pressure, shooting and spraying torrents of water and mist into the air before it disappeared into the concealed abyss below.

Persicus had precious short seconds to act or face certain death. No way would he survive smashing into the wall at this velocity, into God knows what down below.

He stood on the shuddering, gyrating raft, desperate for a way out. He looked to the left and right, but he could see no way out of this situation—solid rock walls on either side, smoothed over by years of running water. He had nowhere to go, near hysterical, he stared at his approaching death, now only a few feet away.

A voice screamed inside his head, *Lost dark river! No hope! Look up!*

He didn't hesitate, always trusting his instincts. With the raft rocking viciously under the rapid, crashing waves, he looked up, frantic, searching the near darkness above him.

*No hope,* he thought.

Then his eyes locked onto a rock ledge protruding from the wall, a few feet above him, and an arm's reach away.

Survival instincts took over. Desperate to escape death, he dropped the oil lamp, and with strength he didn't know he had left, he jumped straight up, and grabbed onto the slippery ledge.

The moment his feet left the raft and his hands connected with the ledge, he heard a bone-jarring crash as the raft collided into the wall. He looked down, but without his lamp, it was pitch-black. He imagined the raft had shattered into a thousand pieces and disappeared into some dark abyss.

He clung to the cold, wet, slick rock in total darkness, his body precariously dangling over the abyss. Cold sprays of water rushed by his feet, causing him to sway with the rage of the river. His freezing fingers turning numb with pain as he clung to the slime-covered rock with his last bit of strength.

*Even if I could manage to pull myself up onto the ledge, what then? What good does it do me? There's no way I could swim back. What could I possibly do once up there? Sit and wait to die! This is the river of no return and there's no way out.* Thoughts churned in his head, as rapid as the waves below. He felt hopeless, doomed, yet a few moments before something had told him to look up, and he had found this ledge.

All of a sudden, Vinzeh's—the sage he had met in the monastery when lost in the Hindu Kush Mountains—voice echoed through his head.

*"You will embark on a quest for something seemingly very valuable, but you will find something much more precious beyond the lost dark river. Do not*

*give up hope, even when it appears all hope is lost. Reach high and you will find a way."*

A chill ran down his spine and he felt on the verge of some higher understanding, if only he could make it through these next few moments. He had gone on a quest for something valuable and now here he was in a lost dark river, hanging on for his life. He wondered how Vinzeh could have foreseen this situation. He remembered Ashoka had told him to heed what Vinzeh said, as he had never been wrong. *If Vinzeh had foreseen this, he must have known I would make it out alive,* Persicus thought. *Otherwise, why would he tell me this, for it would only lead to false hope.*

Now convinced that there had to be a way out, his spirit and strength were reborn.

He dug his fingers into an indentation in the rock and pulled. His face contorted with the effort. His muscles screamed at him — they had been too tried and tested over the last few days. To his disbelief, he felt his elbows bend and his body rise up. He threw one arm over the ledge and pulled his body up. Gasping, on hands and knees, he rested a moment, not yet daring to move. Then he felt around in the dark, running his hand over the slick surface. To his surprise, he found that it was a sturdy shelf, wide enough for him to sit.

Persicus sat down, laughing. "Thank you, Vinzeh!" He realized that if he had never got lost in those mountains, long ago, he would have never met Vinzeh, and he might have given up when it appeared to be the end of the river. He would have to pay him a visit and give his thanks.

He rested a while, rubbing his hands together, trying to warm them. It seemed a futile attempt. He was shivering from head to toe and his teeth were chattering hard enough to crack a tooth. He sat with his legs hanging over the edge. When he stopped shivering, he pulled up his feet, raised his arms up overhead, meeting empty air. Cautious of the slick rock, he stood, pressing his back against the wall behind him for support, and found the space was high enough for him to stand.

As soon as he raised himself to his full height, he felt something cool, long, and hard against his cheek. He batted it away, almost losing his balance in the dark. A second later, it came back, slapping his cheek.

He reached a tentative hand into the darkness. Not knowing what it was, he grasped it, expecting to be bitten by a bat, spider, or snake. Nothing bit him. He wondered if it was some kind of snake, as it felt long and cool to the touch, but it offered no resistance. *Maybe a dead snake?* He brought it towards his face and smelled it.

It smelled earthy. He touched it with the tip of his tongue. He paused, thinking. He tasted it again. *Earthy, like soil, and bitter, very bitter, as the bark of a willow tree.*

"A root!" Persicus exclaimed, ecstatic. "A root, a tree root. There is a tree up there!"

He stared up into the darkness. He reached up again, got a firm grip on the root, and yanked down on it, hard, with both hands. *It is strong. It will probably hold my weight.*

He put his foot against the wall, wrapped his hands around the root, and started to climb. The higher he climbed, the thicker the root became. It had gnarled knots, which he used for footholds. He reached the ceiling, where the taproot emerged from the earth above. He smiled, clinging to the root. He reached one hand up and scraped at the soil above him. The damp earth crumbled around his head and shoulders as he dug around the root. He shut his eyes tight and breathed through his nose as wave after wave of damp dirt and clay shifted down onto his head.

With one arm and both legs wrapped around the taproot, he dug, inching his way higher. When overcome by exhaustion, his arms grew too heavy to hold overhead any longer, he clutched the root, his arms at chest level until the burning subsided, and then continued clawing at the dirt overhead some more. He refused to go back down. After an hour, he felt tiny, fine roots catching on his fingers. He was close to the surface. He tore at the feeder roots and pushed his hand through the soil.

There, he felt the most wondrous thing he had ever felt: a cool breeze brushing against his hand. He brought his hand down and peeked through the small hole he had created.

A broad, delighted smile spread across his face. Beyond the entangled roots of this ancient tree, he saw a lone, bright star twinkling in the darkened sky.

# THE BANDIT'S CAMP

A surge of joy overwhelmed Persicus. He couldn't believe he had made it—alive! He widened the hole in unbearable impatience and squeezed his body through the damp soil. He was soaked in sweat, exhausted, and ready to collapse, but freedom was only inches away. His head pushed through the narrow opening he had made with his arm. After a moment of blinking dirt out of his eyes, he looked around, surprised to see an orange glow coming from a fire, reflecting off a massive tree trunk a short distance away.

Persicus' head, hair, and face felt heavy with dark, damp soil, and clay clinging to him in thick globs. He turned his head to see the source of the glow, but as he turned, he felt a sharp object cut into his cheek, right below his eye. Warm blood trickled down to his chin, mingling with the mud covering his face. Instinctively, he pulled his head away from the familiar cold, sharp tip of a sword, but the sword tracked his movement, trapping him in an awkward position.

"Don't move!" a man's voice demanded, just out of sight. "Who—or *what*—the hell are you?"

"Please remove your sword, sir! I am completely defenseless." He was desperate to get his arms up, but feared moving until he was certain this man wouldn't kill him. He felt as though his strength could fail him at any moment.

"Defenseless? What sort of hell-born creature are you, who lurks beneath the earth, and crawls out of it in the middle of the night, when all good men are sleeping? And you claim to be defenseless?"

"What? I am a man, the same as you. Please, help me up, and I will explain everything." Persicus tried to maintain a calm voice while the end of the man's sword pressed into his flesh, but his heart pounded in his chest, and his voice held the edge of panic. *No, please, no,* he thought. *This can't be happening.*

"You stay put. Don't move. Don't do anything or I'll kill you as you are. Your fate will be up to the chief." The man turned his head and yelled, "Atta Bashi! Atta Bashi!"

There was a small commotion behind Persicus, followed by the unmistakable sound of several swords being drawn from leather sheaths: the sleeping men reacting to the night watchman's call.

Persicus stifled the urge to swear at this man as he slid down an inch in the narrow hole he had made, the dirt encasing his body giving way, little by little. He felt it falling down his legs in clumps.

"What the hell do you want? This had better be good! Waking up the entire camp at this ungodly hour," a voice yelled from a short distance away. Persicus presumed this was Atta Bashi, the chief.

"Oh, believe me. It's good, but you need to come, and see this one for yourself," the night watchman yelled back.

Persicus couldn't see what was happening, but he could hear a lot of people getting up, moaning and groaning about being woken up in the middle of the night after a hard day, and finally, footsteps getting closer.

A tall, muscular man holding a torch led a group of men towards the tree, where the night watchman stood guard over the small, brown lump of Persicus' head.

"All right, now, Ali Bashi. What's so urgent for me to see that you had to wake up the whole damn camp?" Atta Bashi asked, irritated.

"Look!" demanded Ali Bashi, pointing to the ground.

Atta Bashi's eyes trailed to where Ali Bashi, the night guard, was pointing. He lowered his torch at the same time, illuminating the ground.

"A head!" Atta Bashi gasped sarcastically. He then fixed Ali Bashi in his angry gaze. "Oh good, we can use it to play polo with tomorrow. And when we're done with this head, we'll use *yours* to finish the game."

This was the third time this week that Ali Bashi had woken the entire camp during the night after hearing something in the woods, or behind a rock, certain that it was some evil force. Atta Bashi knew that this was no doubt the result of their shaman's persistent forewarnings about evil lurking everywhere.

"But this is no ordinary head, Atta Bashi! It chewed its way out of the ground."

Atta Bashi laughed. "Is that so?" he asked the head, nudging it with his boot.

Persicus jerked his head away. "My apologies for disturbing your peace. I—"

Gasps and murmurs of astonishment rose from the crowd. Persicus felt more dirt shift underneath him. He held on.

"Quiet!" the chief ordered. He stared down at the head for a minute. Persicus opened his mouth to say something, but Atta Bashi pointed at him. "You too," he told Persicus. He turned to a tall, old man with a long, white beard. "What is the meaning of this, Uzgal Bashi?"

The old man stepped forward, hands clasped behind his back, and walked in a slow, wide circle around the head.

Persicus sighed when he saw the man who started talking. He looked like so many of the crazy old wise men he had seen, telling the future and much nonsense about jinns, genies, and monsters.

"It's not good, I'm afraid. I have heard about this phenomenon and read some about it in the *Ancient Book of the Dead and Partially Departed*." The old man paused, studying the gruesome looking head in the ground. He pointed to the mud covered, blood-streaked head. "But this is the first time that I have ever encountered anything so innately evil in person."

"Well, what is it?" Atta Bashi asked the shaman.

Persicus sighed and held his breath. He knew it wasn't good, being referred to as *it*.

"Clearly, this is a manifestation of Satan from the depths of the underworld under our own feet, disguised in a poor human form." The old man paused and stroked his beard. "Most likely, it heard a call from above and crawled to the surface—where it doesn't belong—to answer that call."

"What? Are you saying someone here, in this camp, conjured *that* up?" Atta Bashi asked.

"You know very well who did it," Uzgal Bashi said knowingly. His old wrinkled hand stroked his long, white beard. "I told you to get rid of her. She will only bring more misery upon our people. You cannot trust *her* kind."

Atta Bashi glanced over his shoulder towards the camp on the other side of the tree and then looked at his men, gathered in a circle around the head. "I see everyone is here. Are you all enjoying the show?"

They all looked around at each other, mumbling yes, and nodding.

Atta Bashi smiled. "Very good. Nothing like a good show ... but who the hell is watching the prisoner!" he yelled. "You two, go, bring her to me. Now!" He pointed at two of his men, who took off running towards the tents. "If she escapes in this moonless night we may never find her!"

"She conjured up this demon to distract us." Uzgal Bashi accused.

"You fools!" Atta Bashi's face turned red, fuming. He turned back to Uzgal Bashi. "How much power does it have right now?"

Uzgal Bashi stopped stroking his beard. He set his eyes on the demon's head and swayed side to side for a moment. "Ah, good news. It has no power right now."

Persicus gaped at him, speechless.

"None?" Atta Bashi asked, a big grin on his face, pleased with the answer.

"Yes, none. It has no power over us as long as he is down there and we are up here. We are safe."

Persicus listened in growing astonishment. He glanced around at the men. At least thirty men stood around him and not one of them would say anything against their shaman on a stranger's behalf, regardless of how crazy the shaman was. It was hopeless. Finally, when he could formulate a coherent thought, he could no longer hold his tongue. "Now, you wait just a minute! I am not the devil or a demon. I am a man, the same as you. Please, hear me out!"

"Very well, speak. Give me a good reason why you are crawling up out of the ground in the middle of the night."

Persicus gulped. "A few days ago, I was hired by a scoundrel, a dishonest—nay, a corrupt man—to help him find the lost treasure of the Silk Road. As soon as we found it in a cave in the Forbidden Land of Fire and Dragons, he double crossed me, trapped me in the cave by blocking the exit with a huge boulder, and left me to die. I followed an underground river, which brought me to the root of this tree. I climbed the root, dug out, and now here I am. Please, please have mercy on me! I have been through hell today! I am not a demon or devil. I *am a* human being."

One of the men chuckled. "Hell, huh? Home sweet home."

Uzgal Bashi shook his head. "Don't forget that the devil is crafty. He is an expert manipulator, experienced in preying on the emotions of human beings." He sneered and mimicked in a high-pitch, whiny voice, "Oh, please feel sorry for me. Look what I've been through." The shaman glared at Persicus, looking him straight in the eye with undisguised hatred. "The Land of Fire and Dragons, you say? I suppose there was a dragon in your story. I suppose you slew the dragon, too."

Exhausted, not thinking clearly, he said, "Oh, yes. The dragon was there and we killed it."

Uzgal Bashi turned back to his tribesmen and waved his hand in triumph. "You see? There, I have proven my point. So predictable, are the words of the devil."

Two men returned with the young prisoner between them. They

each had a firm grip on her upper arms. They pulled her none too gently along. She stumbled and straightened up, holding her head high. She clung to a thin layer of bravado, which was all that kept her from breaking down and begging for their mercy — mercy that would never come.

Persicus stopped breathing for a few seconds when he saw her. He felt a sinking feeling in his chest when he saw the beautiful young woman held captive by a band of insane bandits and realized he was in no position to help her. She was the most beautiful woman he had ever set eyes on.

She was dressed in Sogdian finery. Her waist length, rich brown hair fell in tangled waves over her shoulders. She wore a ripped and filthy close-fitting, aqua blue tunic, embroidered with delicate golden threads. Her loose silk pants, the color of fresh cream, tapered to her ankles. Both legs of her pants were torn at the knee. Her feet were covered in slippers, which looked as though they had been crafted by the best shoemaker, but were now caked with dried mud, and covered in scuffs and scratches.

A rosy-red blush tinged her fair complexion, no doubt from the extent of heavy exposure to the elements she had endured since they took her captive. She had large, almond-shaped eyes, a striking vivid shade of green — the shade of early spring leaves, when the leaves start turning from the budding color to something deeper, richer. They stood out in startling contrast to her dark hair. Thick, long, black eyelashes curled up over the crease of her eyelids, framing her eyes as if painted by a brilliant artist. Her eyebrows had a perfect arch, like a bow. She was tall and willowy, moving with uncommon grace and surety.

Her hands were tied in front of her. One of the men jerked her closer to the tree and handed the rope over to Atta Bashi, who pulled her roughly, stopping short of Persicus' head.

The young woman tried to assess the situation; although frightened by her abrupt awakening, she scanned the faces of her captors in the torchlight, trying to swallow her fear. She noticed almost all of them were staring down by her feet. She followed their line of sight and beheld the most gruesome, horrible, and terrifying thing she had ever seen: A blackened face, full of slimy bumps with bits of red streaks dripping down, and a pair of dark, shining eyes looking straight up at her. A cracked, horrific grin splayed across its face. The torch's fire cast orange reflections that danced on the glistening surface of the thing's face.

She lost her composure. She screamed and struggled to get away. Atta Bashi tightened his grip on her. Realizing she couldn't break free, she stopped struggling, and stood shaking, her eyes squeezed shut tight, willing it away, and praying it wouldn't touch her.

"Are you sure that she summoned the devil?" the chief asked, looking to the shaman. "Looks like she's more afraid of it than we are."

Uzgal Bashi shook his head, his hand running down his beard. "Games, only games my dear nephew. These are the devil's games. Only fools and heretics fall for these tricks." Uzgal Bashi knew his nephew well, knew that he despised heretics, and had nothing but contempt for fools. "Your father, on his death bed, may Allah keep his soul, asked me to protect you, and that is what I intend to do. This girl is a *Sogdian*. They are *heathens*. They worship the evil fires in their fire temples! Everyone knows fire is the very symbol of hell. This devil and all who worship him" — he stood over the prisoner, spitting out the words into her face with vehemence — "are forever doomed to burn alive in fiery Hell below the earth for all eternity." He turned to Atta Bashi. "If you help it escape to the land of the living, you will cause the demise of our people!"

This caused a moment of silence, followed by a loud murmuring from the surrounding men.

Atta Bashi held up his hand and the men fell quiet. "All right, all right. Not that I don't believe you, Uzgal Bashi, but for the sake of fairness … and entertainment, why don't we take an up or down vote."

Persicus didn't like the sound of that. "Wait just a second! What do you mean up or down?"

The night watchman, Ali Bashi, pressed the tip of his sword deeper into Persicus' cheek. "Silence!"

Atta Bashi took a step closer to Persicus, dragging the girl with him. He unsheathed his sword and raised it above his head. "Men, shall we help this thing up?"

The men remained silent. The only sounds were of crickets chirping, the distant campfire popping and sizzling, and Persicus' heavy breathing. He slid down a fraction of an inch as the dirt shifted and fell around him.

Atta Bashi looked at Persicus and smiled. He pointed his sword at Persicus, the tip less than an inch away from his nose. "Or shall we help this thing down?"

All at once, the men began stomping their feet and chanting in unison, "Down! Down! Down!"

With each stomp, Persicus could feel the earth shifting and crumbling around him. The hole widened, one clump of dirt at a time. Desperate, he clung to the taproot.

"Stop! Stop doing that!" Persicus shouted.

The men paid him no attention and kept on shouting and stomping, some clapping their hands and cheering. Persicus felt a large chunk of earth fall away from behind him. The taproot swayed.

Atta Bashi smiled. "Why should they? Are they not free men? See how pleased they are? It is not often that my men can enjoy themselves so thoroughly in our line of work."

"Pleased? You are going to get us all killed!" Persicus shook his head, pleading with the chief. "The ground you are all standing on is hollow below. It could collapse any second. You will be swallowed up by the earth! Below is a river that ends violently at a solid stone wall and flows down into some damned abyss!"

Atta Bashi ignored Persicus' warning. "The people have spoken!"

"Oh, Guardian of the Steppes!" Persicus cried out. He struggled to free one of his arms, tangled in thousands of feeder roots of the tree.

"Down you go!" Atta Bashi put his boot on top of Persicus' head, pushing him down.

Persicus stiffened his neck, resisting. He felt a terrible rumble from the earth around him. Atta Bashi kept pushing until his face was shoved into the dirt and he got a mouthful of it as he tried to scream. The rumble became audible, a loud cacophony, the ground shuddered and shook.

The men fell quiet as they felt the vibration travel from their feet all the way up to the top of their heads. One second they stood still, eyes shifting to one another, and the next second the ground dropped five inches, tilting down towards the tree. Fear was palpable in the air. The men grabbed onto each other's arms for support; no one dared to move, except Persicus.

Persicus knew the collapse was imminent. He wiggled his arm free and got one arm above the ground. "See! Help me out of here."

One of the men turned and ran in panic. The ground abruptly dropped a foot and tilted at a steep angle, thirty feet out, sloping down towards the tree. It began crumbling from the tree outward. The fleeing man fell to the ground and tumbled down the steep incline. The earth directly in front of Persicus opened up and the man fell screaming down into the abyss.

As the first man slid down into the abyss, the rest of the men broke into action, and tried to flee, screaming, but the incline was too steep. One by one, the bandits fell and slid into the raging abyss below, as the ground crumbled, and fell out from under them. For a heartbeat, their screams tore through the air over the sounds of the quaking earth.

As the ground started its downward plummet, Persicus held tight to the root. He felt the tree titling towards the abyss. He saw Atta Bashi's terror-stricken face as the ground fell out from under him, only inches away. Persicus closed his eyes as he thought he was to be swallowed whole.

A body slammed against Persicus' back. The falling weight stopped with a jolt as a pair of delicate, rope-bound hands caught around his neck, choking him. His eyes were still shut, but he knew it was the prisoner. He could smell her exotic perfume and feel the warmth of her body pressed against his back.

The last of the screams echoed up from down below for an instant. Then nothing. Only the sound of water smashing into the rock wall, masked by the sound of Persicus' blood pounding in his ears. He opened his eyes and gaped at the devastation. The collapse had stopped just short of the tree, where he clung to the root. He hung suspended over the abyss and could look straight down into the raging underground river.

The earth gave another violent shake. He held his breath as the tree shuddered and groaned, the mooring horizontal roots tearing from the ground on the opposite side of the ancient tree. The tree stilled, Persicus let out his breath, and looked down into the total darkness. Not even one man could have survived the fall. In a blink of an eye, the land had disappeared, along with every trace of the men. All their egos, hopes, and dreams, gone.

As quickly and gently as he could manage, he pulled himself up the base of the tree, and crawled onto the ground with the unconscious girl hanging limply on his back, her hands clasped firmly around his neck. He stood up on the unstable land, grabbing the girl's hands so as not to strangle himself, and walked away from the tree, stepping as lightly as he could. Behind him, he heard the tree groan again, louder this time, and he felt a familiar rumble under his feet.

He ran as fast as he could with the girl on his back. He heard the tree lose its anchor and crash down, thick branches snapping as if they were twigs. As quick as he was running, he *knew* the earth was collapsing behind him after each step, falling into the roaring subterranean river below, which seemed to be mocking him, beckoning him home.

He ran for the tents. The earth grew quiet behind him. He stopped, breathless and gasping, gripping the girl's arms around his neck. When he thought he was a safe distance away, he pulled the girl off his back, and sat down with the girl cradled in his arms, staring down at her.

In the tent farthest away from the unstable ground, where he felt confident it was solid underneath, Persicus laid her down in the darkness on a soft pallet. She moaned in her sleep as he unbound her hands. He pushed some of her hair from her face and saw a growing knot on her temple. Something had struck her hard enough for her to lose consciousness. A joyous relief filled him. Fate had saved her.

Exhausted, he lay down next to her. He propped his head up on his hand and gazed down at her in amazement. She was simply the most beautiful thing he had ever seen. He wondered who she was and how she had ended up in bondage with those bandits.

He thought about Vinzeh, remembering his words: *you will find something so much more precious beyond the lost dark river.* Moments later, he fell asleep with a protective arm around her waist.

# 9

# A MERCHANT'S DAUGHTER

A high-pitch scream tore Persicus from his dream. He shot straight up in an instant, reaching for the sword he no longer possessed. The soft, early dawn sunlight streamed into the tent. He looked around, trying to gain his bearings.

The young woman scrambled away from him, screaming. "Get away from me! Leave me alone." She huddled against the far side of the tent, hands up in front of her, warding off the demon she saw before her eyes.

Persicus turned and looked behind him. No one was there. Bewildered, he realized that she was screaming at him.

"Who, *me?*" he asked in disbelief.

"Yes, you! I heard the shaman. You are Ahriman. Ahura Mazda! Protect me!"

"Areea who?" Persicus asked.

"Ahriman! The God of Darkness!"

Persicus shook his head; he didn't understand why everyone thought he was a demon. "I swear to you that I am human."

She didn't look convinced.

Persicus sighed and sat down facing her. "Last night, those men said you were evil because you worship fire. And you believe what they said about me?"

She squinted her eyes in suspicion. "Then why do you look like that?"

"Like *what?*"

She scanned the tent for a mirror or a shiny surface and then her eyes settled back on him. She reached around her neck, removed a silver necklace with a shiny medallion, and threw it at him. "Look at yourself! What are you, if not a demon?"

Persicus caught the necklace and raised it to his face. He screamed, in mock horror, throwing the necklace up in air.

The girl shrieked and scrambled out of the tent, fear ripping through her. She tripped and fell just outside the tent. As she got to her feet, fully intending to run as fast as she could, she heard a deliriously happy laughter inside the tent. She hesitated, looking back over her shoulder. She took a step back, undecided. She turned to run, but the bubbling laughter pouring out of the tent perplexed her. It didn't sound evil in the      least. She gave in to her curiosity and peeked back in at him. He knelt on the ground, doubled over, slapping his knee, laughing.

Confused, wary, she watched him from the tent's entrance until she saw the dried clumps of clay crumbling from his face. "That is not funny!" she said indignantly.

Persicus picked up her necklace and walked towards her, still chuckling.

She backed away from him, still wary.

"I'm sorry. To be honest, my face did kind of scare me for a moment." He lowered his voice as he handed her the necklace. "I don't normally look quite this scary."

She snatched the necklace from his hand and stepped away from him.

Persicus scraped away at the thick layer of reddish-black clay that had dried and cracked upon his face. She watched him with obvious distrust. He managed to get enough off that he looked recognizable as a human, though still smudged and dirty.

"At least now I understand why everyone thought I was the devil." Persicus grinned at her. "Is that better?"

She said nothing, looking him up and down.

"Well?"

"I'm thinking," she said.

He frowned at her.

"Why were you buried up to you head?"

"I had to crawl through layers of clay and soil to make it out of that underground river."

She looked around. "Where is everyone? What happened last night? I can't remember a thing after ..." She reached up her hand, feeling the knot on her head.

"They have all gone to the world beyond."

"You mean they are all dead? But how did you ..."

"Yes, they are dead, but I did not kill them. The ground collapsed beneath their feet. They all fell into the underground river and perished."

The woman nodded, beginning to recall the events of the evening. "They were all stomping their feet. You told them to stop and then the ground shook. That's the last thing I remember. How did I survive? I should have been swallowed up, as well."

"Fate, my lady." Persicus explained what had happened. "If your hands hadn't been bound, you would have fallen through. Being tied up actually saved you when your hands landed around my neck. But you did almost strangle me to death."

She bowed her head, thinking. "Then I suppose I owe you thanks."

She turned and headed towards the scene, having to see it for herself. She stopped just beyond the collapsed area. Persicus hovered behind her, afraid the ground would collapse again. She leaned over the hole, gazing down.

She made an involuntary gasp when she saw the tumultuous river below. She could feel the roar of the rapids in her bones. The river crashed into a solid wall of rock and dropped straight down, creating an opaque mist that was impossible to see beyond.

"Please come back. This area is not safe." Persicus held out his hand to her.

"You were down there?" She took another small step forward and leaned over more. He suddenly grabbed her around the waist and picked her up. She screamed and fought his hands. He pulled her back as the ground where she had been standing crumbled and splashed into the water below.

He set her down, but grabbed her hand. "Yes, I was. This place is too dangerous. Let's get out of here."

He tried to pull her away, but she dug in her heels. "Let me go!" she demanded.

He stopped and turned towards her, releasing her hand. She saw at once that her tone stung him.

"I'm tired of being pulled and shoved around."

Persicus looked back down towards the gaping hole in the ground. "I'm sorry, but we need to get out of here. It's too dangerous and I want to get as far from this place as I can."

"I had never seen an underground river and I wanted to make sure those men are dead." She took a firm stance, hands on her hips. "Are you in a rush to get somewhere?"

Persicus looked up at the sky, exasperated. "I had a dream last night. I was so hot that I jumped in that damned hole to cool off. As soon as I jumped, I thought, what on earth are you doing, you imbecile."

Her face creased into a smile. "Then what happened?"

He looked at her, crossing his arms over his chest. "Then I woke up to your pretty face screaming at me. Tsk, tsk." He shook his head. "And after I crawled out of there with you on my back, strangling me, and carried you to safety."

"Well, if you don't want people screaming at you first thing in the morning, you should be more considerate about how you look." She turned on her heels and headed back towards the tents.

Persicus followed, an amused look on his face. He wondered about this young woman. When he caught up with her, she stood in the midst of the camp, turning in a complete circle. She didn't recognize a single hill or tree. She looked frightened again.

"What's the matter?" Persicus asked.

"I need to go home, but I have no idea where we are. Do you know how to get to Mishin from here?"

"You shouldn't be traveling by yourself. There are too many people who would try to hurt you out here. If you trust me, I could escort you back to Mishin."

"That's very kind of you, but how am I to know you aren't one of the dangerous people out here?"

Persicus rocked back on his heels. "If anything, I should be worried about you being a danger to me. I wasn't kidnapped by a band of bandits."

She looked hesitant, but since she didn't have any other choice, she nodded. "All right. My father will pay you for your time, of course."

"That is not necessary."

She studied him warily. "So, what is your name?"

"Persicus, of Abrisham."

"Nooshin."

Persicus smiled. "Nooshin, that's beautiful. It suits you." He turned around, looking at the horizon, and turned again, surveying the area. "I recognize this mountain range. There is a town in that direction." He pointed south. "It's not too far from here. I think we can get there by sundown if we hurry."

Nooshin looked relieved. "Thank goodness." She walked around the tents. "There were dozens of horses here yesterday. Where did they go?"

"They must have taken off when the ground started shaking. They could be miles away by now."

"How will we get home?"

"We have to walk."

"Walk!" she said. "All that way? On foot?"

Persicus smiled. She was acting as if she were a little princess who never had to walk a mile in the midday sun in her life.

"Only until we get to town. I'll get us some horses there. Who knows? Maybe we'll find the horses on the way." He tried to be optimistic for her sake, though he knew it was doubtful.

She sighed dramatically.

"May I ask how you came to be with those bandits?"

Nooshin looked away. Her voice sounded strained as she spoke, "Four days ago they started following our caravan as if they were a pack of hungry wolves. On the third day, they disappeared. I thought that maybe they left during the night to follow some other caravan. We made camp that evening. In the middle of the night I awoke to the screams and shouts of my … um …"

Persicus figured she was remembering the grisly details, perhaps too horrible to recount aloud.

"—the night watchman's screaming," she continued. "Those murderous bandits snuck up on us in the middle of the night. They murdered everyone. They had come to rob and kill us for our merchandise."

It was an old story that he had heard many times. "I am sorry that you had to experience that." His voice held both sympathy and anger.

"It was horrible."

"Well, let's see what we can find and then let's get out of here."

Persicus walked into one of the tents and started throwing stuff around. Not finding what he was looking for, he went on to ransack the second tent.

Nooshin curiously watched him go from one tent to the next. "What are you looking for?"

"Food, water, basic supplies," Persicus answered, shaking out a canvas sack.

"There won't be any in here."

"Oh, why not?" He stood in the middle of a tent, hands on his hips, eyes scanning the mess on the floor.

"Atta Bashi kept all the food outside of his tent. He wanted to make sure none of his men stole food during the night. It's the last tent, at the end of the camp."

The sun was still low in the sky when an eerie howl broke through the still morning air.

"What was that?" Nooshin asked, stepping closer to Persicus.

"Sounds like jackals and where there's one, there's bound to be more. Wait right here. Do not move from this tent." Persicus rushed out into the early dawn.

He ran past the tents, towards the sound of the growling animals, and stopped dead in his tracks. Two golden jackals were fighting by the tent Persicus assumed belonged to Atta Bashi. The jackals were only slightly smaller than the common wolf, but just as vicious. Persicus shouted at the animals, but they didn't even look up in his direction. They were in an intense fight over the last scrap of meat lying on the ground. Persicus could see the remnants of bones, breadcrumbs, and fruits scattered on the ground. Fang marks and globs of saliva covered the fruit, mixed with dirt that had been trampled under the paws of the jackals.

While the two jackals snipped, growled, and clawed at each other over the last morsel, a third jackal came into view. He licked his chops, calmly walked over, and picked up the piece of meat. He looked at the other two jackals over his shoulder and slunk away.

The first two jackals abruptly stopped snipping at each other. They searched the ground for their food and then looked up to see Persicus, thinking he had stolen their prize.

Persicus had hoped to find some food left untouched by the animals, but he soon saw that all was lost. All of a sudden, the jackals turned towards him, eyeing him hungrily.

They bared their teeth at Persicus and took two slow steps towards him. Trying to keep his eyes on the animals, he glanced around for some sort of weapon. He dared not make any sudden moves. A long piece of wood stood propped against the tent, only a foot away. The two jackals growled, a low, reverberating sound, deep in their throats. Persicus yelled again, a loud barbaric sound. They startled, but didn't back down.

The larger jackal crouched, his fangs bared, saliva dripping down in a foamy string from his mouth.

*Rabies,* Persicus thought. *Healthy jackals would have backed down, but not if they're rabid.* He reached out his hand, slow and steady, towards the piece of wood. He knew the jackal was going to pounce on him at any moment. His hand touched the hard wood.

The jackal leapt, growling deep and vicious, foam spraying from his mouth. Persicus swung his makeshift club as hard as he could. The wood connected with the beast's head with a sharp crack, splintering the wood down the middle. A quick whimper escaped his mouth and cut off as he fell to the ground.

The second jackal growled, a fierce and angry sound. He crept closer. Persicus held his club up, ready to swing at the creature. He lunged forward and swung, attempting to scare him off.

Nooshin yelled from somewhere behind him. "Watch out!"

Her voice startled him. As he turned to search for the unseen threat, another jackal came out of nowhere. The jackal launched himself at Persicus from the side. Persicus fell on his back with the jackal on top of him. He brought up his splintered club, holding it in front of his face, trying to avoid the powerful jaws and sharp fangs.

The jackal bit down on the wood and it snapped in two. Persicus dropped the sticks and wrapped his bare hands around its neck, digging his fingers deep into its fur, struggling to keep the rabid animal away from his face.

All of a sudden, the second jackal appeared, ready to attack Persicus while the third jackal kept his hands occupied. It darted in and towered above Persicus, lowering his muzzle to tear into his neck.

A rock sailed through the air, hitting the jackal by Persicus' head. Another rock streamed by hitting the jackal again. The angry animal snarled at the rock. Nooshin threw rocks, one after another, raining them down on the rabid animals and Persicus as well. The jackals took off together, their bushy tails between their legs, leaving Persicus on the ground, protecting his head from the flying rocks.

Nooshin hurried over to Persicus. He looked up at her, still lying on his back. "I thought I told you to stay inside, where it would be safe."

"I was getting worried. And it's a good thing too, because I am much better with a rock than you are with a stick."

"You were worried about me?" he asked with an amused lilt to his voice, getting to his feet.

"Yes, well, if you had been injured, how would I get home?" she said efficaciously. When she saw the confused look on his face, she smirked, the corner of her mouth twitching upward.

Persicus hoped she was teasing, though he couldn't tell for certain.

"Well, the jackals devoured everything in sight." He heaved a heavy sigh.

"You mean we have nothing? Not even water?"

Persicus shook his head. "The water pouches are punctured. We will have to make do until we get to town. Let's get moving. The sooner we leave, the sooner we will get there."

Nooshin was exhausted from the previous days' journey, as well as the emotional distress she'd suffered from being held captive, and it showed clearly on her face. Persicus tried to console her, but she shrugged him off, annoyed by his attempt. "I do not need your sympathy. Tired as I am, I can make do, as you said. We will make it to civilization by this evening and that will have to do."

Persicus shrugged. "As you wish. I am at your aid, regardless, you just have to ask."

Persicus and Nooshin followed a path along a foothill towards the town. For an hour, they walked side by side, not knowing what to say to each other. The silence grew uncomfortable, filled with periodic, uneasy glances at each other.

The sun rose, slow and steady, glaring down on them. Nooshin's face turned red with the heat of the day. Persicus watched her out of the corner of his eye, trying to think of something to say.

"It's too hot. I'm thirsty." She stopped in the middle of the path, pouting.

"There's a small spring about a mile from here. We'll stop there and take a rest."

She looked miserable and Persicus wished he could do something about it. He stopped and unwound his waist shawl.

"What are you doing?" she asked in astonishment as he removed his garment.

"Relax." He wrapped his shawl loosely around her head, blocking some of the sun. "This is an old trick. What do you think we wear these for?"

"This is most inappropriate."

"Well if you don't want it—"

"Of course, I want it!" she exclaimed. "But ... just don't think you can take anything else off."

Persicus blinked at her. "Of course not. I think I can control myself."

A mile later, Persicus veered off the main path towards the sound of running water. They stood before a spring filled with sparkling blue water, edged with shady trees, boulders, and tall grass.

Nooshin knelt down at the edge of the spring and dipped her hands into the water, sipping it from her cupped hands. After she drank, she gently dabbed the cool water on her forehead and neck.

Persicus stuck his face into the water and guzzled down a great quantity. He waded into the middle of the spring, the water waist high. "If you don't mind, I want to wash out my clothes. I'm covered in dried mud and jackal drool."

"Don't worry about me. I can control myself."

She sat on a low boulder at the edge of the spring. She had taken off her shoes and dipped her feet into the cold water. She took out a handkerchief and dipped it into the water, squeezed out the excess, and patted her forehead and neck with the cold cloth.

Persicus took off his torn, filthy tunic and rinsed it in the water. He scrubbed his face and hair clean of all the remnants of clay and dirt. He wrung out his tunic and put it back on, delightfully shivering at the cold cloth clinging to his skin. Washed and cool, he felt revitalized.

Nooshin watched him in the water in concealed fascination. Her face was still flushed with heat and she continuously patted her face with the wet handkerchief in a futile attempt to cool down. "Oh, that is much better. You could almost pass for human now." She kicked her foot out of the water.

The water sprinkled down on Persicus. Amused, he watched her sitting there, attempting to cool off while maintaining her proper lady-like decorum. "Why don't you join me and cool off?" He waded up to the boulder where she sat.

She turned her nose up and away from him. "I am not an animal, to bathe in a spring."

A mischievous smile played across his face as he stared down at her.

She tensed as he bent down towards her. "Don't you dare!"

"Don't what?" he asked, feigning confusion as he reached around her to his boots that sat beside the boulder.

Nooshin relaxed when she saw him reaching for his boots. He turned to face her with a roguish grin, hands clasping his boots.

"What?" she asked, squirming on top of the rock.

He dropped his boots and he snatched her up around the waist. She squealed and tried to protest, but before she could say anything, he threw her into the water. He turned, hopped out of the water, sat on the boulder, and slipped on his boots as if nothing had happened.

She sat in the icy-cold water, stunned and speechless, watching as he nonchalantly took her place on the boulder, and slipped on his boots. Her mouth hung open. She looked down at her soaking wet clothes, stupefied.

He leaned back on his hands and looked beyond Nooshin to the mountains, enjoying the view. She detected a faint smile playing on his lips.

"How dare you!" she fumed, getting to her feet. The water felt wonderful, but her indignity remained stronger.

"Oh, it was quite easy, I assure you. And satisfying, wouldn't you say?"

"No! Now I am all wet and—"

"And cool." Persicus held out his hand to help her out of the water.

She ignored his hand and huffed out of the spring, wiping the water from her face.

Persicus let his hand drop back to his side. "Anyway, you look much better now and I'm sure you feel better, too."

She glared at him. "How I feel is no concern of yours."

"It is if I have to carry you after you faint from the heat."

"I never faint. You just get me home and don't worry about how I feel." She sat on the boulder and put her shoes back on. "I'll make sure you are paid well for your inconvenience."

"Well, you certainly aren't making it hard for me to care about how you feel. I guess I don't have to behave like a gentleman." He grabbed her arm and pulled her to her feet. "Let's get moving. I want to get to town before dark."

"Get your filthy paws off me!" She shrugged him off and pushed him away from her. He took a step back and his foot hit the boulder. He lost his balance and fell backwards into the water, his head going under, feet sticking up.

She looked stunned for a moment, unwilling to believe she had shoved him into the water. He sat up, glowering at her.

She burst out in triumphant laughter. "Serves you right!"

Having rested, they headed back to the path. Nooshin felt much better. With her clothes damp, the heat was no longer unbearable. However, now all her discomfort was in her feet, where blisters had formed from walking in her improper, fancy slippers. She had fought against the pain all morning, but now her pace gradually slowed, and she began limping after only a mile. Persicus saw that she was in pain, though she concealed a great deal of it. He decided he did care and tried to take her mind off it.

"When I was in Antioch, I met this Roman aristocrat. He told me he was once on a sea voyage when a horrible storm fell upon them," Persicus said, as they walked down the path at a slow pace. "The storm tossed the vessel mercilessly, almost capsizing. He saw his slaves crying in terror and trying to console them, he said, 'Don't worry, I have freed you all in my will.'"

Nooshin's lips curved into a small frown. "But wait, if he dies, won't they all die, too?"

Persicus laughed. "It's a joke."

"What's a joke?" She asked, her face curious.

He glanced at her dubiously. *Could she really have never heard a joke before?* he wondered. "A joke is a bit of nonsense, which its only purpose is to make you laugh."

"Oh, good! That's wonderful. Tell me another joke." She laughed.

Persicus wondered if she was pulling his leg. He fell quiet for a moment while he thought of another joke. "Well, once I was walking through a small village early one winter morning. All of a sudden, a pack of dogs surrounded me, snarling, and baring their fangs menacingly at me. I reached down to pick up a rock to throw at them, but it was frozen solid to the ground. I yelled, 'What kind of place is this? The dogs are loose and the rocks are tied down'."

Nooshin looked at him, her face impassive. "That's not funny.

Those dogs could have torn you to bits while you were playing around with some silly rocks."

Persicus gaped at her, but still, he couldn't tell if she was serious or not.

She smiled. "You made that up."

"Oh no, this really happened. It's not a joke. The village elders thought I was funny and invited me inside to warm up."

"Well, how come you didn't pick up a rock today when the jackals began attacking you? They weren't tied down, now were they?"

He chuckled. "I didn't want to take a chance this time. Bad experience. Besides, I had a perfectly good stick near at hand."

"Hmm. You know, you never did tell me how you managed to come up out of the earth looking like a demon."

He looked at her sideways. "Well, that's a long story."

Nooshin shrugged. "We have all day."

He sighed and thought of where to begin. At the beginning, he decided. He told her of how he had met Hakim at the caravanserai in Abrisham, of the horrible journey with the nomads trying to ambush them, the mountain path that had collapsed, and how they almost died in the sandstorm. Then he told her about how they had made it to the Forbidden Land, found the treasure, and slayed the dragon. And finally, about how his partner betrayed him and how he ended up going down the nightmarish underground river, which led him to the root that he had climbed.

She stopped in her tracks when he finished his tale. "Is this another one of your funny jokes?"

"No, of course not. There's nothing funny about what I've told you."

"You can't be serious? I mean, that's the most ludicrous thing I have ever heard!"

His shoulders sagged. He wouldn't believe this story if someone else had told it to him, either. "I know it is."

He pulled out the gold coins and showed them to her.

She took the ancient coins in her hand, studied them for a moment, and then raised her eyes to his. "You're serious about this story? I mean, all of it? You actually went in search of the lost treasure of the Silk Road and found it? It's a bedtime story for children. I wouldn't have ever believed it was a true story. And the dragon? There's no such thing as dragons. It's a myth, a fairytale."

"I don't know what that thing was. It looked like a dragon. It stood at least ten feet tall, had a huge, spiky tail, scales and—" he shuddered, remembering how he stuck his arm down into that things mouth, "— razor sharp teeth. I don't know. If it wasn't a dragon, I can't think of any other known creature that would fit its description."

"Hmm. What about the Komodo dragon?"

"Isn't that a dragon?" he asked sardonically.

She laughed. "No, not really. It's a giant lizard."

"I don't know anything about these Komodo dragons that are lizards. No lizard could be that big. It looked like a dragon."

"Well, I've heard tales of a gargantuan lizard, called the Komodo dragon. They're found off the coast of China, on an isolated island. They are often mistaken for dragons. They grow about ten feet long. Could that not be your dragon?"

He glanced at her, skeptical. "I don't know. I never heard of such a lizard."

"The poor mule," she said.

"What?"

"If your story is true, then your mule did fall to his death. The poor little guy."

"After all that I have told you, you are sorry for the mule!" Persicus couldn't believe it.

"Yes, well, *you're* still alive. Besides, I love mules."

Persicus noticed her limp getting worse. She would stop for a minute every few hundred feet in sheer pain. He led her to the shade of a tree to rest a while and wished he had food and water to give her.

Nooshin slipped off her shoes. Persicus glanced up to the sky and guessed it was about three in the afternoon. They still had a long way to walk to get to town. He knew they wouldn't make it by sunset at the pace they were going. He looked back down and saw red, swollen blisters covering her feet. Some were rubbed raw and bleeding.

"Those shoes were not meant for walking any distance," he said. "I will need to carry you the rest of the way."

"I can walk barefoot, *thank you*." She stood, grimacing, trying to ignore the pain, and walked back to the path.

Persicus couldn't help but smile. She was stubborn, proud.

Persicus watched as Nooshin slowly picked her way on tiptoe around the jagged rocks that littered the ground, carrying her battered slippers in one hand. Persicus shook his head, wondering how far she would go before she asked for his help. But she didn't ask; she continued tiptoeing her way uncertainly through the rugged terrain.

Persicus got to his feet and caught up with her.

As he came up behind her, she spun around, her mouth opening to say something, when his waist shawl tore loose from the wind, and wrapped around her face. She stepped backwards, batting at the shawl, and stepped on a jagged rock. She yelped and lost her balance, falling forward.

Persicus swooped in to catch her before she hit the ground. "That's enough of that!" He picked her up as if she weighed nothing and flung her over his shoulder, her head and upper body hanging down over his back.

She tore the waist shawl away from her face, crawling up his back with her hands until she was upright. "Put me down this instant!" she demanded. "I am not an invalid!"

"You will be if you continue to walk to town barefoot. Those silly shoes are useless here."

"I said, *put me down!*" Panic crept into her usual commanding voice.

"Are you always this stubborn? I have carried much bigger people than you on my journeys." But he set her down on her feet and knelt before her, offering her his sturdy back. "Put your arms around my neck and hold on tight. We will be there in no time."

"I will not ride on you as if I'm a child." She looked away with an obstinate expression, her arms crossed over her chest.

"No? Fine, but we won't make it to town before sundown with you tiptoeing around every rock. It doesn't get any better down the road; on the contrary, some of these roads are wretched. In that case we might as well set up camp, here and now, so I have time to gather some wood, and we'd be lucky if I can find some food and water before sundown." He rose to his feet and dusted the dirt off his knees. "And we can only pray that no bandits or wild animals find us during the night."

She stood there saying nothing for so long that Persicus threw up his arms in defeat. He was about to say that he was going to look for wood when, as if on cue, a long, mournful howl droned through the air behind them, answered by another howl, coming from another direction.

She jumped, looking around her surroundings.

"All right! If only to be in your barbaric presence one night less."

He smiled, shaking his head as he knelt again. "Barbarian. The Devil. Areea-something, the God of Darkness. Anything else?"

"All right, maybe you're not a barbarian."

"Thank you."

"You're the devil. And you are trying to trick me into trusting you." Nooshin teased, placing her arms around his neck. He stood, hitching her up higher on his back.

"Well, fate chose this devil to save you, but if you aren't nicer, maybe it will change its mind, and I'll have to leave you to the wolves."

"Do you truly believe in fate?" she asked, her voice low.

"Yes, I do."

"And destiny?"

"Yes. Of course. Some things are just meant to happen. Sometimes it seems that we have no choice in the matter."

100

"But that is saying that the outcome, regardless of the outcome, or where one ends up, is fate or destiny. That is like saying no matter what, it is fate. There's no way to prove it otherwise."

"You are right and wrong." Persicus said after considering.

"How so?" she asked.

"Well, say if someone foretold a certain set of circumstances and through no fault of your own, and no knowledge of what is about to happen, you fall into that exact circumstance. That is destiny."

"But knowing that destiny beforehand could have contributed to the circumstances of completing that which was foretold."

Persicus smiled. She was smart and he could see her logic. *So, she's not just a pretty merchant's daughter*, he thought. He remembered sitting in the caravanserai, talking with Hakim, he had felt the impulse to go on this journey even though he was uneasy about Hakim. He wondered if — in the back of his mind — he had remembered what Vinzeh had told him and wondered if this was that journey. He didn't think so, but he couldn't discount the possibility.

"Yes, I suppose you could be right."

Persicus wondered if Vinzeh had never told him of this journey, would he have even considered going with Hakim. If he hadn't, the bandits would never have fallen into the underground river and Nooshin would still be at their mercy.

She started to relax against him, little by little. After a while — and much internal debate — she leaned against his broad back, resting her cheek against his shoulder. She felt immensely embarrassed about him carrying her in such a way and she refused to admit that some small part of her enjoyed it. She had never been this close to any man before, other than her father.

Persicus spoke in a low, soothing voice, trying to ease away any discomfort she might feel. "We will arrive to town soon. We can find something to eat and get cleaned up. I'll get you some proper traveling clothes and shoes. It will be better if we dress you as a young man, if you don't mind. That way we'll have less trouble traveling to Mishin. We'll spend the night in town and purchase some horses and supplies before we head out tomorrow."

"That might be fun. I've never dressed as a man before."

Persicus could hear the excitement in her voice. It was first time he heard her express anything with enthusiasm. He was grateful for the heavy pouch around his neck, containing the gold coins Hakim had thrown down to him. Otherwise, they would have been stuck with no horses or supplies.

Nooshin listened to his soothing voice. The vibrations from his voice became strangely comforting. He kept talking in a soft, relaxing tone all the way to town.

He couldn't know that she was thinking that he seemed a noble man. Even after all her protests, he had treated her with kindness and he had behaved amicably. Not to mention, she was enthralled by this kind, handsome man — though he had an odd sense of humor — she found him funny and refreshing after her recent dealings, even as she tried to deny it.

# *10*

## THE BATHHOUSE

The sun was low on the horizon and darkness was creeping in when they approached the modest, unguarded entry gate to the town. The town was small, with the caravanserai the main support of its inhabitants. A mudbrick structure with arched alcoves wrapped around the square courtyard. The shops, housed in individual alcoves, were all closed by this hour, except for the inn and chaikhana. A round fountain sat low to the ground in the middle. A dividing wall separated the caravanserai from the modest homes beyond the courtyard.

It had been a long, hot day and they were famished. Persicus set Nooshin down outside the gate and they made their way to the chaikhana. She followed him inside the little tea house and they settled down at an empty table in the corner of the room. A low murmur flooded the room from the merchants who sat, talking quietly at almost every table.

She gazed longingly around the small room, her eyes wide in unconcealed fascination.

Persicus studied her curiously. "What's with you?"

"I've never seen a place like this before," she said, cupping her chin in her hand, eyes lingering on the walls.

Each wall had an old painting, telling stories of times long past. Worn Persian rugs were strewn across the floor, their edges fraying. The tables were old and scarred, but thick and sturdy. It was not one of the nicer teahouses in the region.

"You've never seen a chaikhana? There are a dozen in Mishin."

She turned to face Persicus, placing her hands in her lap. "I meant I've never seen one like this." In an instant, her expression changed from fascination to commanding and proud when the innkeeper came out of the kitchen, and made his way to their table.

The innkeeper, an old, weathered man with a short beard, and greasy white hair came to their table with a look of annoyance, eyeing the couple with unconcealed suspicion, noting their disheveled and torn clothing. His face looked drawn and tired. "What do you want?"

Persicus mouth was watering from the rich, savory aroma of the tea and food cooking in the kitchen. "Food! We need food. I can't remember the last time we ate. Bring us whatever you have already prepared. And bring us a pot of tea and water," he added.

The innkeeper shook his head. "We can't afford to give charity here. There is a temple in town where you two can eat for free."

Nooshin's face turned red, her entire body went rigid. "Charity! We don't—"

Persicus kicked her softly under the table. She glared at him. He wanted good food and he didn't want to be kicked out because they looked as haggard as beggars.

Persicus gave him a sheepish smile. "Sir, I am sorry about our appearance. We lost our horses two days ago and we've been through quite an ordeal, but we are not looking for charity. I will pay for our order."

The innkeeper stood, observing Persicus with obvious doubt. The town's beggars were dressed better than this man. Persicus gazed back at him, perplexed. The innkeeper cleared his throat sharply. Persicus glanced down and saw he had his hand out, waiting for payment.

"Ah." Persicus reached under his shirt and withdrew a gold coin from the pouch. He tossed the coin on the table. "I think this should more than cover our food and lodging for tonight, as well as some food to take with us tomorrow."

The innkeeper picked up the gold coin and bit down on it, testing to see if it was real gold. He spit into his hand and after a moment of rubbing off a layer of dirt, he examined the gold piece. He smiled wide, showing a row of rotting teeth. "Well now. This is the second old coin I have seen this week." He looked at Persicus with deference. "Interesting. Has some old treasure recently been found?"

Persicus ignored the question, narrowing his eyes. "Was the other man who gave you the gold coin missing an arm?"

"Yes, yes he was. Nice man. Paid the gold coin for the meal. Said I was in luck as he was feeling generous." The innkeeper laughed as he turned to go back to the kitchen, flipping the coin in the air, and catching it with gleeful jubilance.

"Wait, was he alone?" Persicus asked.

The innkeeper turned back to the table. "No, no." He scratched his head, trying to draw up his memory. "I recall two other men accompanied him. One was short and hefty, and the other was tall and skinny."

"Small world." Persicus mumbled to himself. This information didn't help much, but at least he knew Hakim had come this way. "How long ago was this man here?"

"A few nights ago and left early the next morning. I don't recall the exact day. I'll bring you some tea first and your food will be ready soon."

"By any chance, did he say where he was heading?"

The innkeeper eyes narrowed. "No, I don't suppose he did. He ate, slept, and left in the morning, same as everyone."

The innkeeper disappeared behind a thick wood door.

When Persicus turned back to Nooshin, he saw she had her head down, rubbing her wrist. She winced in pain. Persicus asked to see and she held out her hands. Red, angry welts and rope burns covered her small wrists. He placed his hands around hers. "Does it hurt much?"

She nodded, taking back her hand, and cradling her sore wrists in her lap.

The innkeeper came back out a moment later with a tray of tea and crystallized sugar, and placed it in the center of the table.

"Ah, thank you, sir. Do you have anything for cuts and bruises?" Persicus nodded towards Nooshin.

The innkeeper leaned over, inspecting her wounds. "That doesn't look too good. I think I have something for it." He patted Nooshin on the shoulder and disappeared back into the kitchen.

Nooshin looked up to meet Persicus' eyes. Her face was guileless. "So, those men you were asking about. Friends of yours?"

He gave her a wry grin as he poured the tea into two cups and slid one across the table to her. "Hardly. I presume it was Hakim and his two brothers. After they trapped me in the cave and left me for dead, they came here feeling generous." He grunted in disgust. "Oh, but he threw me a few coins for my trouble, to assuage his guilt about using me, and setting me up to die."

Nooshin gave him a sad smile. "Well, at least we survived. Everyone in my caravan was murdered." She sighed. "We should thank Ahura Mazda that we are alive." She picked up her tea and savored the rich aroma before she took a sip of the hot liquid.

Persicus knew she was right, but he couldn't quell his anger towards Hakim.

The innkeeper came back to the table with another small tray. "May

I see you wrists?" he asked Nooshin, as he picked up a bowl from the tray. Nooshin pushed up her sleeves and held out her arms. The innkeeper spread a greasy, yellow substance around the red welts, raw skin, and scratches on her wrists. After that, he wrapped her wrists in clean strips of soft, white cloth.

Nooshin grimaced at the feel of the cold, greasy substance. "What is this?" she asked, trying to conceal her disgust.

The innkeeper smiled and patted her hand. "Good stuff. Pounded turmeric and butter. By tomorrow, your wrists will feel much better."

"Could you leave the bowl?" Persicus asked.

"Of course." The innkeeper handed her something about the size of a lentil—brown and firm, but soft.

"And what is this?" she asked, taking the brown substance.

"Also good stuff. The nectar of the Poppy flower. Cooked in a slow heat to perfection. If the pain keeps you up tonight, eat this, and you will rest well. After all, we say nothing heals as good as a full night of sleep." He left, laughing to himself.

A moment later, a young boy brought out a tray full of food and set it on the table.

"Do you have a bathhouse here?" Persicus asked, as the boy set the table.

The boy gave him a dubious glance. "Yes, of course we have a bathhouse. It is behind the inn. Left for men, right for the ladies. Fresh water is heated every morning by sunrise." He leaned in close and whispered, "I would recommend waiting until morning, when the water is fresh."

Persicus nodded in understanding. "How about a tailor?"

"Two doors down. Isaac, he's the best tailor east of Amu Darya."

Persicus thanked the boy and turned to the food. He didn't know how long he had been in the underground river, but knew it had been at least two days since he had eaten. His mouth watered as he looked at the platter: a heaping mound of rice with saffron, lamb, roasted vegetables, and a pitcher of cold water. Persicus doled out the food onto two plates. He feverishly devoured the food and guzzled the cold water.

Nooshin ate half her plate before she slowed down. Her feet stung, a searing pain, and she couldn't enjoy the food. She picked up the little brown pill and bit down on it. Her face instantly registered a foul taste.

Persicus laughed, handing her the cup of water. "Drink it, don't chew it."

Fifteen minutes later, finished with their meal, they lingered at the table, sipping on the hot tea. Nooshin's eyes fluttered and a sigh escaped her lips.

"Feeling better?" Persicus asked, an amused expression spreading across his face.

"Mmm ... yes." A relaxing feeling overcame her, washing the pain away.

As Persicus silently studied her, his curiosity grew. She did not behave as most young women did. She wore fine Sogdian clothes, shoes that were not meant for traveling. She was in a caravan, so it was probable that she was a merchant's daughter, but it seemed that she had not traveled much.

"You never mentioned where you were heading when the bandits attacked your caravan."

She looked up, startled. She remained quiet for a long moment.

"You seem like a good and honest man," Nooshin said. "Can I trust you?"

This was not the response Persicus had expected. "Of course you can trust me."

She stared down into her lap with a wary expression for so long that Persicus almost asked her what was wrong. She looked up and met his unwavering gaze. "I am the daughter of King Ormozd, of Mishin."

Persicus' mouth dropped open. He gaped at her, speechless, for the third time in as many days.

"I didn't know if I could trust you at first. That is why I didn't tell you." She leaned across the table, her voice low and urgent. "But after all you have done for me and after getting to know you ... well, I feel bad about not telling you. But you can understand why I didn't, can't you?"

Persicus sat in shocked silence. He leaned back in his chair, his arms crossed, staring at her. His brain slowly processed the information, reluctant to accept it. After he closed his gaping mouth, he said, "Of course you are. That makes perfect sense."

Her eyebrows rose halfway up her forehead. "What do you mean by *that*?"

"Uh ... well, the expensive clothes, the impractical shoes, and ... it's obvious that you are well educated, and haven't travelled much."

She let out the breath she had been holding.

All of a sudden, Persicus felt uncomfortable in her noble presence. Did he call her Princess? *Of course I do*, he thought. Persicus didn't know what to say now. After a long moment, he asked the first question again. "So, where was it that you were traveling to, Princess?"

"Don't. I've liked just being Nooshin. Don't call me Princess," she whispered.

He smiled. "All right, Nooshin." He got the feeling she was trying to avoid answering the question. "Well?"

She let out a heavy sigh. "Turan. I was heading to Turan."

Persicus' eyes widened in surprise. "Turan! That is no place for you to be going! It's dangerous there."

"Yes, I know." Sadness overcame her and she looked lost.

"Why were you going there?"

Nooshin wasn't sure she should answer. He had saved her and she felt uncommonly safe with this man, but he was practically a stranger. How much truth did she owe him?

After a long hesitation, she answered, her voice full of contempt. "I am betrothed to King Salman. I was en route to his home in Turan."

"Salman!" Persicus said in a loud, surprised voice. His heart sank when she said she was betrothed, but then he realized that she was a Princess, and now well beyond his reach.

"Shh. Keep your voice down." Nooshin looked around to see if anyone was paying attention to them. "I take it you have heard of him."

"Yes, I have," he said with unveiled disdain.

She gave him an expectant look. "*Anything* good?"

"No, nothing that I know of him is good." He wondered what he should say about the man—the King—that she was going to marry. "He is infamous for the conquest and destruction of any small city unfortunate enough to lie in his path. He stops at nothing to get what he wants."

Her face crumpled. "Yes, I know. I know." Tears sprang up in her pure green eyes and she looked away.

"If you know all this, why marry him? It doesn't seem that you are happy about this marriage."

"I have no choice. I have to marry him."

Persicus could hear the pain in her voice. "I have only heard good things about King Ormozd, surely if you pleaded with your father—"

"No. It isn't my father's doing. I decided to marry him."

Persicus eyebrows shot up. "What? Why?"

"I overheard *King* Salman threaten my father—very tactfully, of course. I decided to marry him to prevent the destruction of Mishin and the loss of so many lives." The tears quivered in her eyes, but she stayed stoic, not allowing them to spill.

Persicus took her hand in his. "I don't know what to say. I wish I could do something to save you from this."

"Thank you, but there is nothing anyone can do. It is my duty to protect my people," she said, lifting her head up proudly. "No matter what I have to do, I can't let that man destroy my home, and kill everyone I care for. If my marrying him will prevent that, then that is what I will do."

Persicus gave her hand a gentle squeeze. She looked so young, maybe only nineteen, yet she felt it was her responsibility to save her city from the whims of a madman. It was unfair. "You are very noble and selfless, but those are horrible choices. Isn't there any other option besides marriage?"

Nooshin shook her head. "No. Salman made his intent clear. I saw my father worry for days, worry for the people of Mishin, until I told my father I wanted to marry Salman."

"And then the bandits attacked you and killed everyone in the caravan?"

Nooshin nodded, turning her cup of tea around in her hands. "My servants and guards, friends really, not just a caravan. I grew up with one of the servants, Negin. She was my constant companion and best friend." Again, the tears threatened to spill, but she willed herself not to cry. "When I heard the screams of my guards, Negin ran to me, terrified and covered in blood. She told me we needed to escape without being seen. She said that the bandits had surrounded us and were killing everyone on sight; all the guards were dead. We ran out of the tent together. Atta Bashi was standing there, smiling.

"Negin shoved me away and told me to run, and then she ran towards him, to give me a chance to get away." Nooshin took a quivering breath. "He killed her. He struck her through with his sword. She fell to the ground and I ran.

"Another man stepped out in front of me, out of nowhere. He grabbed me and carried me back to Atta Bashi. He pushed me to the ground in front of their leader. Atta Bashi tore off the tiara from my head and demand I tell them who I was.

"I told them and I told them I was en route to Turan to be married to King Salman. Atta Bashi paled when he heard King Salman's name. They became distressed when they realized what they had done. If anyone found out that they had kidnapped me, well, they feared Salman's revenge. They decided to retreat and leave the country. They would have sold me as a slave had they made it.

"A couple days later, Uzgal Bashi, that imbecile, figured out that I was Zoroastrian, and set to work trying to convince Atta Bashi that I was an evil fire worshipper. He wanted them to kill me and flee for their lives. He said they wouldn't be caught if they killed and buried me. They had talked about it all evening; Atta Bashi said he would decide in the morning. He said the answer would come to him in his dreams." She looked up at Persicus. "And then *you* popped up looking like a demon." A half-hysterical laugh escaped her lips. "I thought that was going to be my last night on earth."

Nooshin looked weary to the bone and Persicus felt the same, as the last few days caught up with him all at once. He helped her up and she swayed when she stood.

He wrapped an arm around her. "You all right?"

"Hmm, yes. That poppy, I think." She stumbled and leaned against Persicus, her head lulled backwards on his shoulder. She stared up at him with a beatific smile. "I feel fine now. Thank you, Perkoset."

Persicus grinned. The poppy had started working. *She will sleep well. She needs it,* he thought. *We have a long journey ahead of us.* He led her to the large communal room, where he found two empty beds in the corner.

The beds were essentially two narrow, wooden platforms covered with carpet, raised up about two feet off the ground. The innkeeper had placed two cotton-stuffed pillows and two rough felt blankets on each platform. The sleeping accommodations left a lot to be desired, but it was better than sleeping out in the elements without so much as a blanket.

Persicus helped her into bed, covering her with the blanket, and flopped down onto his own bed, exhausted.

He lay awake brooding over what she had said until his eyes grew heavy and sleep overtook him.

𒁹𒁹𒁹

The next morning, Nooshin awoke early feeling well rested. She had slept deeply, and her wrist and feet felt much better. However, not use to feeling so grimy, she couldn't wait to get to the bathhouse, but this was the first real rest Persicus had had in days, and he resisted her efforts to wake him up before dawn. Finally, she shook him awake and he got up with reluctance.

They had breakfast at the chaikhana, outside under the shade of a Willow tree. When they finished their breakfast and tea, they walked two doors down to the tailor. The tailor had not yet opened. Ten minutes later, Isaac opened his door and ushered them inside.

Isaac piled up various colorful women's clothes in front of Nooshin. She turned them down and asked for men's clothes. The tailor looked at her with a disapproving frown.

"Are you sure about that? I have many more fine clothes in back if these are not to your taste," Isaac pressed.

Persicus stepped in and asked for simple clothes for traveling.

"Nomadic clothing," Nooshin exclaimed, as if she had just had a brilliant idea.

"What?" Persicus said.

"I want to be a young nomad for this journey."

110

Isaac looked to Persicus, expecting him to protest.

"You heard the lady. Nomadic clothes."

Isaac took their measurements. Nooshin picked out a long, tan tunic, baggy pants, a khaki jacket, and a wool hat, under which she could hide her hair. She was ecstatic, acting as if she was a child on her first trip to the bazaar. Persicus reminded himself that this was probably something she had never done for herself. He hoped the baggy clothes would help hide her curves. It would be much easier to travel without attracting too much attention if she could pass for a boy.

Persicus selected similar clothing for himself, paid the tailor, and asked where they could find a shoemaker.

"Three doors down, across the courtyard," Isaac answered, staring at the gold coin.

They went straight to the shoemaker, where Persicus bought two pairs of boots, several pairs of thick socks, and the shoemaker gave Nooshin some lamb's wool to cushion her sore feet.

They arrived at the bathhouse around eight thirty. People trickled in, filling up the brick structure. Persicus led Nooshin to the woman's entrance.

"I'll meet you back here in about an hour." Persicus went around the building to the men's side.

Nooshin hesitated just outside the entrance. She peeked inside. She was on her own and nervous. She had never bathed herself and she didn't know what to expect. She had always been bathed by her servants, in her private bath.

A matron stood at the entrance, welcoming her in, taking in her once fine clothes, now caked in dirt.

The bathhouse was beautiful. A tile mosaic in deep blue, gold, and purple adorned the walls. Each glazed tile was done in exquisite detail, creating a geometric pattern which repeated within itself — the patterns getting smaller and smaller. The tall, arched ceiling rose up, creating a large dome inside the main room. A cool breeze blew in from the open-air windows, set high up on the walls. A plaster lattice weaved through the windows in an intricate floral design. The sun poured in through the lattice covered windows, light and shadows playing on the mosaic walls, giving the tiles more depth.

The matron wondered what the story of this beautiful young woman was. They all had stories, but this one seemed more interesting than most, as she was dressed in expensive Sogdian finery, but had obviously been through quite an ordeal.

The matron led Nooshin through the structure. The room reminded Nooshin of a honeycomb, with little arched tile niches hidden throughout. The matron stopped at an empty niche and gestured to

Nooshin. Nooshin stepped over to the niche and looked back at her. The matron handed her a clean towel and waited, gazing straight ahead, and then glancing back at Nooshin.

Nooshin just stood there, waiting, staring back at the matron.

"Well?" the matron said, placing her hand on her hip. "Are you just going to stand there or are you going to bathe with your clothes on?"

"Oh!" In the Palace, her servant always helped her out of her clothes. She stripped off her dirty clothes and put them in the niche. She looked at the matron.

The matron sighed, rolling her eyes. She took the towel and wrapped it around Nooshin, "Come on."

Nooshin followed the woman to a huge, square pool filled with steaming water and half dozen women of various ages. They sat facing each other, submerged up to their shoulders in the water, talking and laughing. A young woman smiled and nodded hello to Nooshin.

Nooshin looked at these women with uncertain anticipation. She could be free of royal treatment here and be treated as a normal woman. Her eyes nervously shifted over her surroundings.

Nooshin slipped into the water, wincing as the hot water found her blistered feet. She found a place in the bath, not intruding on the others' space, but close enough that she could hear them talk.

Two young female attendants waited on the women in the bath, bringing them various fragrant potions to wash their hair and bodies. Two other bath attendants stood on a platform off to the side. They each held a rough cloth, which they used to scrub the bathers until their skin turned soft and pink.

Nooshin tried to relax into the water, studying the room. On the far wall, another tile mosaic shimmered with candlelight. In the center of the mosaic, a half-nude woman with a large clay jug of water in her hands stood by a lake. The jug was tilted in such a way that from where Nooshin sat, it looked as though the woman was pouring water into the bath. Below the mosaic, a long narrow basin of water, sitting a little higher than the top of the bath, stretched across the length of the wall. Small Chinese candles sat in trays, floating in the water, casting golden reflections that danced on the walls and water.

One of the attendants offered Nooshin a tray with a selection of soaps and oils: rich olive oil, sesame oil, and potions infused with fragrant smelling flowers. "Which one you want?" the attendant asked.

Nooshin studied the selection, smelling the different types of oils. She smelled the rose, lavender, myrrh, and something she did not recognize. She picked up the unfamiliar scent.

The attendant smiled. "This is new, from Serendib. It's called cinnamon. Amazing, isn't it?"

"Yes, I don't know if I would rather eat it or bathe with it," Nooshin said, delighted.

Nooshin was about to pick the cinnamon when an old woman intervened. "Go with the rose. A young lady should always smell of roses."

Nooshin nodded, picking the rose for her body, and the cinnamon for her hair.

The old lady shook her head, disapproving. "You should have gone with the rose for your hair, too."

A young woman came running into the room. She threw off her clothes and jumped into the water. "Did you hear the news this morning?" she asked the other women.

"No," they all answered.

"The daughter of the King of Mishin in Sogdiana has gone missing!"

"What!"

"How?"

"What happened?"

"Her caravan was found slaughtered on their way to Turan. She was on her way to marry King Salman. Her body wasn't found amongst the dead."

The women gasped in astonishment and shook their heads. Nooshin sank into the water, listening intently. Her heart pounded hard and for a moment, she couldn't hear anything, but a roaring in her ears. She prayed none of these women would recognize her.

"Do they know what happened to her?"

"Was there a ransom?"

"No! Nothing yet. King Salman is livid. He has offered a large reward for anyone with information and has sworn vengeance. King Ormozd has sent off his troops in search for her. So far, they haven't found a trace of her, but they did find a camp some fifty miles from where they found her caravan. The camp was deserted, but they found her tiara there. The tents were empty, everything was intact, but no horses, and no people. Not even a foot print leading away, nothing. It's as if they disappeared into the air itself."

"The poor girl. She must be so frightened."

"Maybe the Princess escaped and is hiding."

Nooshin held her breath. She listened on, worried.

"What? Why would she hide?"

"So she wouldn't have to marry King Salman, of course!"

"Yes, that's what I would do," said a young woman, nodding in agreement.

"Anything would be better than marrying him," another agreed.

"Oh, the poor girl. Having to go from marrying Salman to being abducted."

"What would you do if you had to marry a tyrant like Salman?"

"I would rather be kidnapped!"

"It doesn't matter. If she is found, she will still be married to him."

"I can't see why anyone, especially King Ormozd, would have agreed to such a thing."

Nooshin listened with ever-growing anxiety. These women would rather be abducted than marry King Salman. She couldn't agree more. It dawned on her quite suddenly that since everyone thought she was missing, she could go on being missing, and never have to marry King Salman. Surely, he wouldn't go to war with Mishin if he thought she might return to marry him. This could buy her some time until she could figure out what to do. The idea grew in her mind. But she couldn't do that to her father—let him go on wondering what had happened to her—however, if she could somehow get word to her father that she was safe …

Nooshin was deep in thought when one of the women turned to her and asked, "What do you think?"

Nooshin felt all eyes turn to her. She swallowed her panic. "I … I don't know. Who is this you are talking about? I am not from around here."

"You haven't heard of the Princess of Mishin?"

Nooshin shook her head. She thought her heart would explode. She was sure she was going to be discovered. They would turn her over to King Salman, just when she thought that she could somehow manage to escape the marriage.

"She is well-known throughout the region. The daughter of King Ormozd. She was supposed to marry King Salman. You know King Salman, of course?"

"Yes. I have heard of him. The King of Turan? Yes?" Nooshin said, trying to sound uncertain.

The women nodded.

"I must say, I do not know much about him," Nooshin said.

"Oh, he is horrible!"

"He's a tyrant. He invades and conquers every city in his path. And that big pot of his!" The woman shook her head in disgust.

"The poor girl. And she is supposed to marry him?" Nooshin asked.

"Yes."

"I can't understand why she agreed to such a marriage."

"She lost a lot of respect from me! She could have married anyone! And she had a choice," an older woman declared.

"Well, maybe she is trying to avoid a war. You said King Salman fights and conquers every city in his path, maybe this is just another city he wants, and she is trying to save the lives of her people," Nooshin said with trepidation, turning away, not trusting the look on her face. Her eyes met with the matron's, who still stood by the entrance, staring back at her with a faint smile on her lips. Nooshin startled and turned back around.

"I would have fought!" said the young woman.

"Me, too. Mishin is one of the most tolerant cities. People come from all over to live there, so they can worship, and live as they please. If King Salman takes over, it will no longer be a desirable place to live. I am sure the people of Mishin would rather fight, than give in, and let that man take over," said the older woman.

All the women agreed.

The women went on talking and the topic eventually changed. Only then did Nooshin relax. The attendant washed her hair and scrubbed her body clean.

Another attendant came over and asked her if she wanted a massage. She got out of the bath, and the attendant handed her a fresh towel. She followed the attendant to another room, where she laid down on her stomach. The attendant started the massage, using rose oil.

"Why, you are so tense!" the attendant exclaimed, rubbing harder at her shoulders.

Nooshin lost all track of time. When the attendant said she was done, Nooshin got up with a smile on her face stretching her arms overhead. She looked up at an opening in the ceiling and saw the sun had risen high in the sky.

Nooshin panicked. Persicus told her to meet him out front at nine thirty. "Oh my! What time is it?"

She rushed back to the niche where she had left her clothes. The matron lingered by her niche, picking up the used towels. "Well, you look much better now. Over in that corner are the cosmetics. You go on over there and the attendant will make you up like a real princess," said the matron with a wink.

Startled, Nooshin dropped her clothes. She looked down so fast she was dizzy for a second. Steadying herself against the wall, she bent to pick up her new clothing.

The matron walked back to the entrance laughing to herself. Nooshin got dressed in a hurry, put on the new boots, testing to see if she could walk around in them. She walked around her niche and decided they were more comfortable than she had thought they would be, and much more comfortable than her own shoes. She shoved all her long hair up under her hat and went over to the cosmetics table to inspect herself in the mirror.

Persicus, waiting outside, paced back and forth in front of the bathhouse, having finished hours ago. *What could she possibly be doing in there for so long?* he wondered. It was almost noon; he walked over to the woman's entrance, and approached the matron. "Do you know what happened to the young lady I brought here this morning? She hasn't come out yet."

The matron smiled, nodding her head. "A lovely young thing, to be sure, but she was an awful mess. She looked like she'd been abducted by bandits. They finished up with a massage a few minutes ago. Don't you worry none, we fix her up real good for you," she replied with a wink. "You are paying for her?"

Persicus blushed at the thought of the Princess being prepared for him. "Ah ... a ... yes. I will take care of her ... It. I'll take care of it." Persicus stammered, reaching for the pouch around his neck. The matron gave him a knowing smile. Persicus hurried back to his spot and resumed pacing.

Nooshin looked over the assortment of cosmetics: sormeh, to outline the eyes; henna, to decorate her hands; qazeh, a red rouge; and vasmeh, to darken her eyebrows. She wanted to look good for Persicus, though she would not admit that, even to herself. Instead, she reminded herself that she was to be dressed as a young male nomad. After she inspected herself in the mirror, she snuck out quietly.

Nooshin came out of the bathhouse, refreshed and smiling. The matron stopped her at the door. "Goodness! Those clothes and that face!" the matron said, astonished.

"I ... um," Nooshin stammered, not sure what to say.

"That will never do as a disguise," the matron whispered. "Princess."

Nooshin felt the blood draining from her face; her mouth dropped open. "I don't know what you're — "

The matron peeked outside. "Come with me." She grabbed Nooshin's hand and pulled her into a small, unoccupied room. "Wait right here. I'll be right back with a better disguise."

Nooshin looked nervous and scared.

"Oh, don't worry; your secret is safe with me." The matron smiled and left the small room.

Nooshin wondered if she should sneak out, but the matron returned before she could decide.

116

Persicus still paced back and forth, a worried expression painted across his face. Nooshin came out of the side entrance of the bathhouse and headed towards him. Persicus glanced up at her, scarcely recognizing her. He stopped his incessant pacing mid-step and stared at her, astonished. A slow smile spread across his face and he laughed.

She posed for him, turning around in her new male attire, complete with dark stubble covering her chin and cheeks. She looked radiant, glowing with delight. "What do you think? Do I make a decent nomad?"

"Indeed." Persicus couldn't help but laugh. She looked great, even with a day's worth a beard. "I was a little worried that the clothes wouldn't hide your" — he hesitated, searching for a word that wouldn't offend her delicate sensibilities — "your, uh … curves. But the beard is perfect."

She smiled. "I think I will pass nicely."

He shook his head. "What on earth were you doing in there? You were supposed to be out in an hour. It's now almost noon."

She sighed and tried to look sorry, but she couldn't pull it off. "I got carried away. I've never been to a common bathhouse before and I wanted to experience everything."

He looked down and mumbled, "Apparently royal women are no better at telling time. At least you made use of the gold piece, I guess."

He stepped closer to her and tucked a stray strand of hair behind her ear. He leaned in close and took a deep breath. He gave her a mixed look of satisfaction and uneasiness. "Nooshin, we have done all we can to change your appearance and it may work well for the casual observer from a distance, if you keep your hair tucked into the hat, and keep your head down, but you are not going to fool anyone smelling so" — he leaned close again, taking another deep whiff — "so rosy, and well, edible."

"Don't you like it?" Nooshin asked.

"Well, yes, but — "

"Should I have gone with the lavender?"

"No. No, you smell wonderful." He took another deep breath of her intoxicating scent and thought, *Mmm, cinnamon.* "But that is the problem."

She looked uncomprehending and faintly disappointed.

"Please, Nooshin, you must keep in mind that, though we were lucky to escape Atta Bashi and his band, there may be others that would harm you if they found out who you are. Not to mention those who would harm you because you are a beautiful, young woman. Stay close enough to me that you are never out of my sight, but when I am speaking to any man, try not to stand too close, lest they smell you, or get a good look at you. We don't want anyone to recognize you until I get you back to Mishin."

Persicus' anxiety increased as a man walked by. He didn't know if they could reach Mishin without her attracting attention. He saw a bright red blush creep up her cheeks. He frowned at her, raising a questioning eyebrow.

She sighed and told him about the conversation in the bathhouse, and that the matron had recognized her, but promised not to say anything.

"Come on, let's go buy some horses, and get out of here before anyone else recognizes you."

They entered the stable and Persicus gestured over to a bale of hay in the corner. Nooshin went to sit out of the way and watched while Persicus haggled for two horses and saddles.

The proprietor — a stout, round faced man — brought out two horses that he proudly claimed were legendary Caspian horses.

Nooshin heard Persicus laugh. "They are much too small to be Caspian. They look like Mongolian ponies. Allow me to look around for some horses more suitable for my needs."

The proprietor became red in the face and shifted his weight from leg to leg. "Look all you want. But these are the only two that are for sale."

Persicus ignored him and scanned the stable for a horse that caught his fancy. His eyes fell upon two majestic Ferghana horses: One a glossy black and the other a beautiful, chestnut brown with a blond mane. These magnificent horses were known as *Heavenly horses*. They were highly prized and rumored to sweat blood when galloping. Persicus knew he would not leave without these horses.

"Those will do," Persicus said, nodding to the horses in question, as if he expected no argument.

"Those-are-not-for-sale."

Persicus turned to face him, a stern look on his face. "My good man, there is nothing in this world that is not for sale, given you have to means to purchase it."

The man shifted his weight again, his eyes sliding to his prized animals. With that look, Persicus knew he had him and so he began the ancient art of haggling.

Nooshin watched with great interest at first, but lost interest after a few minutes, and wandered over to the Heavenly horses, rubbing them affectionately.

The proprietor kept shaking his head. Persicus was trying to get the horses with two saddles and bags in with the price. Persicus took out his pouch, withdrew one of the ancient coins, and showed it to the proprietor.

"What is that supposed to be?" the proprietor asked.

"This coin alone is worth three regular horses."

"May I examine it?"

Persicus tossed the coin to him. The proprietor bit down on it and held it up to the light. Persicus handed him a few more coins and the proprietor nodded. "We have an accord," he said. "Pick out any saddles and two bags you want." He rushed out of the stable with his ancient gold.

Persicus smiled as he saddled his beautiful new Heavenly horses. He thought these magnificent creatures were worth their weight in gold. He grabbed some saddlebags and filled them with the dried food and supplies he had bought while Nooshin was in the bath. He led the horses out of the stable. Nooshin followed close behind.

Persicus looked over to Nooshin. "Can you ride?" he asked, eyebrow cocked.

She didn't answer. She just smiled, mounted the chestnut horse effortlessly, and nudged the horse hard with her new boots. The horse took off at a gallop out of the gate of the small city.

# *11*

## THE SEARCH PARTY

Persicus smiled as he watched Nooshin galloping away. She was proud. He liked that, a lot. He mounted the silky black horse and caught up with her. Once they were a good distance away from town, they slowed to a steady trot.

Persicus could see Nooshin was deep in thought. She had been brooding in silence for almost an hour.

Finally, she looked over at him and spoke tentatively. "I've been thinking ..."

"About?"

"About what the women in town said and ... maybe I can turn this situation to my advantage."

Persicus glanced over at her. "How do you mean?"

"Well, being that everyone thinks I am missing, abducted, maybe I can" — she hesitated, her face scrunched up, trying to find a way to explain her thoughts. She would have to present her idea in such a way that Persicus wouldn't worry about it being too dangerous. She would need his help. King Salman's entire army was probably out searching for her, as well as her father's men; plus every farmer and merchant within a hundred miles had no doubt heard about her disappearance, and would be on the lookout for her.

"The situation is this: When I didn't arrive in Turan, they sent out the cavalry to search for my caravan. They found every body at the site, but mine. They will continue to search for me for a long time, but since all the culprits were swallowed up by the earth, the search will be in vain. And we are the only two who know the truth."

"Well, you, me, and the matron," Persicus said.

"Yes, but she won't tell anyone."

"Go on."

"Sooner or later, the cavalry will return to Mishin empty handed. They will report to my father and Salman that they have searched everywhere, and I am nowhere to be found. To them, there would only be three logical options. That I was killed and buried somewhere, that I was taken to a foreign land to be sold as a slave, or lastly, that I am being held for ransom." She looked over at Persicus to see if he was following her train of thought. "They would pin their hopes on the latter two. If they think that I may eventually be found, I could buy my father some time."

"And Salman will not be so quick to attack Mishin if he thinks that you may resurface at some point. But what about your father? He will be grief-stricken."

"Not if I could send him a message, tell him I am safe, and I am in hiding. If you could help me do this, that is?"

Persicus nodded. He would be happy, even eager, to go along with any plan as long as he could spend more time with her, and help her escape her marriage to Salman. "Yes, of course. I'll do anything I can to help you; you know that. I think it's a good idea, but what you need to think about is, what do you need time for? The problem will still be the same once you do go home. If you are thinking about not marrying Salman, then you will have a war on your hands, because I don't see your father handing over Mishin to Salman."

Nooshin nodded. She hadn't really thought far beyond buying some time.

Persicus continued. "But what if Salman doesn't care about you going missing and you were only a convenient bonus. Then even now, Salman may be planning to attack Mishin. Your staying missing won't change that. Maybe we should go to Mishin and find out what's going on. If Salman is busy searching for you, you can send word to your father, and we can go into hiding. That would mean your father would need to start preparing for war without Salman getting wind of it."

Nooshin looked relieved to have a plan. "All right, sounds like a good idea to me."

By late afternoon, they were riding across a rocky terrain. Tall, imposing rock-covered mountains lined the path on the either side. The path became narrow, sloping up and down hill, with hard, compacted dirt between the rocks and boulders. The horses navigated around the large rocks that littered the ground.

"There is a small spring up ahead." Persicus called back to Nooshin, who was riding behind him. "We'll stop there for a rest. We should make it to the next town shortly after dark."

"After dark? Should we be traveling after dark? Isn't it dangerous?" Nooshin asked.

Persicus laughed. "No, not with me it's not."

"Says the man who couldn't handle a couple of jackals."

"I was ambushed. And it was three jackals."

The path opened up. The ground was strewn with small rocks and pebbles. After another mile, Persicus turned off the main path and followed a short trail to the mountain spring. They dismounted their horses and took their goatskin water pouches to the spring's bank.

Tall trees shaded the area, including a magnificent Persian Parrotia, overflowing with its reddish-purple flowers, sprouting along the hundreds of interweaving, layered branches. A gentle breeze fluttered through the leaves. The lush, green grass and wild flowers danced in the breeze. To their right, a steady flow of water trickled down from the mountain, filling the spring with fresh water. On the opposite side of the spring, large boulders had fallen from the mountaintop, ages ago, and settled at the bottom.

The water was ice-cold and delicious. Nooshin sat on a rock by the water, dipping her hands and feet into the spring while Persicus splashed water on his face. He turned to face her with a mischievous grin.

Her eyes narrowed. "Don't-you-dare!"

"Don't worry. I wouldn't want to ruin your beard."

Persicus unloaded the food from the saddlebag, handing Nooshin a portion of fruit and bread. After they finished their snack, Nooshin took off her hat, set it on the rock beside her, and leaned back on her hands, enjoying the shade.

"How are your feet?"

"Better."

"Are you really considering not marrying Salman?" Persicus asked.

Nooshin thought for a moment. "Yes. I don't know. When I heard those women ... They said they had lost all respect for me. Moreover, Mishin wouldn't be the same after I married Salman; it would be no better than any of the other cities he has taken over. I think I had this idea that if I married him, he'd leave my father in charge of Mishin, and nothing would really change there."

Persicus shook his head. "No, I doubt that. He would tax Mishin the same as all the other cities. He would bleed it dry. Your father wouldn't be King anymore; he'd be a satrap, answering to Salman, following Salman's rules. Salman has his spies that he sends to live in every city he takes over; they make sure everyone is living by his laws. Even some of the city's own citizens have been known to report on their neighbors and friends." Persicus sighed. "It's tragic. They are only hurting themselves by helping Salman."

Nooshin nodded, staring at the horizon. "I know. I can see all that now. I guess I just wanted to believe that everything would be all right."

Persicus jumped to his feet so fast he startled Nooshin. He stared at the main road, eyes searching for movement.

"What is it?" Nooshin asked.

Persicus frowned. "I hear horses. A lot of them."

"What is wrong with that?"

"They are moving fast. Caravans and merchants don't usually gallop." He spotted a dust cloud in the distance, moving in their direction.

"The army!" Nooshin exclaimed, jumping to her feet.

"Maybe. Take your horse and go hide behind those boulders." Persicus pointed to the other side of the spring. "Make sure your horse stays quiet and don't show yourself—no matter what happens—until I call for you."

"Why don't you hide with me?"

"No. They will see the hoofprints on the path to the spring. Besides, I might be able to get some information from them. Now, go."

Nooshin grabbed her horse, ran around the spring, and disappeared behind the boulders. Persicus spent a moment getting rid of her smaller footprints on the small patches of dirt around the area. Then he sat, waiting, watching a large group of men on horseback getting closer.

The man in the lead pointed in Persicus' direction with a whip in hand. Moments later, a cavalry of twenty soldiers approached from the main road.

The General of the regiment rode forward and stopped only feet in front of Persicus. Persicus stood, dusting off his hands. The General stared down at him, from his height atop his horse, with an air of authority.

Persicus felt hostility emanating from the group. "Good afternoon," Persicus said in a pleasant voice. "Hot day out. The water is cool. Help yourself."

"Who are you? And where are you coming from?" the General asked in an aggressive tone.

"My name is Persicus, of Abrisham. What can I do for you?"

"I am General Ghulam; General of the First Regiment of the Army of Turan. I am here on the official authority of King Salman, the

Magnificent. We are in search of information leading to the whereabouts of the Princess of Mishin, betrothed to King Salman. Do you know anything about it?"

Persicus' started to sweat. He cleared his throat. "Yes. I heard about it yesterday in the caravanserai. It is very unfortunate, but I am afraid I cannot help you. I know nothing of her disappearance."

"Where are you heading?" the General asked. He held his horsewhip in his right hand and began tapping it against his thigh.

"I am going home," Persicus answered.

"Are you traveling alone?"

"Yes, I am."

General Ghulam continued tapping his thigh with the whip. His eyes narrowed and he leaned forward. "When we were riding up here, I noticed two sets of hoofprints before the path was overcome with rocks." He looked from Persicus to his black horse. "But you have only one horse."

Frantic thoughts flowed through Persicus' head. *What would Hakim, that lying maggot, say?* "Ah, well, this morning I left the inn at the same time as a nice Chinese man. We were heading the same way, so we rode together most of the day." Persicus smiled, as if he were remembering. "He was a funny man, good company, but alas, I needed to stop to rest and refill my water, and he was in a hurry, so we parted ways."

"Hmm," the General said thoughtfully, continuing his incessant tapping with his whip. "How long ago was this?"

Persicus rolled his eyes up as if he were thinking. "Maybe about an hour ago."

"An hour? You have been here for an hour."

Persicus nodded, trying to give himself time to think of a response. "Yes, well, I didn't get much sleep last night. One of the men was snoring loudly at the inn and it kept me up. I am a light sleeper. I was so tired that I dozed off for a little while." Persicus shrugged and gave him a sheepish smile.

General Ghulam looked over Persicus' shoulder. His eyes fixed on Nooshin's nomadic hat, still sitting on the rock. Persicus turned, following the General's gaze. He silently cursed himself.

"A nomadic hat? Is it yours?" the General asked.

"Well, I found it lying there when I got here. I used it to block out the daylight while I slept." Persicus was getting used to lying quickly. *Not good,* he thought.

"Are you leaving now?" Ghulam asked, tapping his leg.

"No, I'm in no hurry. I thought I would have something to eat first."

"Aren't you eager to get home?"

Persicus laughed; it sounded forced even to himself. "If you knew

124

my wife, you wouldn't ask that."

The General nodded, smiling. "Men, ten minutes. Go refill your water." General Ghulam dismounted his horse.

The regiment dismounted and half of them went to the spring to refill their water pouches. The rest of the men stood, stretching and talking in hushed voices to one another, waiting for first group to finish filling their pouches so they could make their way to the spring.

Persicus stepped back over to the rock where Nooshin had sat. He was suddenly nervous. His horse gave a loud neigh and a nicker. His pulse sped up and he held his breath, waiting for Nooshin's horse to return the call.

The men lingered by the spring, washing their faces, and enjoying the shade. Persicus waited. Sweat trickled down his chin. Several of the regiment's horses stomped their feet and blew: a heavy sound blown through their noses. Persicus fished out a piece of bread and nibbled on it, chewing each piece until the bread disintegrated in his mouth. His mouth was dry and he found it hard to swallow. He watched the men covertly. The second group of men made their way to the spring. They drank some water, splashing water on their faces before filling their pouches. Seconds ticked by. Every moment was a chance of discovery. Persicus swallowed another piece of bread. He felt it slide down his throat as if it were a rock. He wasn't hungry, but he felt that if he wasn't doing something, they would read his deceit all over his face.

After what seemed an eternity, General Ghulam called out to his men to finish up and head out. "I want to catch up with the Chinaman," he declared "Hurry up! Mount your horses." Ghulam looked down at Persicus. "Do you know which way the Chinaman is heading?"

"Yes, he said he was headed to Golmud," Persicus said, sending them in the opposite direction of Mishin. A great idea sprang into his head. He scratched his chin. "You know, General, come to think of it, he was acting kind of funny. He kept looking over his shoulder until we were miles from town." He paused for a second and shrugged. "It may be nothing, but who knows? I thought I should mention it."

Ghulam nodded and his face lit up with the prospect of a lead, it was obvious that it was the first lead he had had. "Great! If you hear anything else, contact Mishin or Turan right away. There is a reward for any information that leads to the Princess' whereabouts. Good day." He tapped his leg twice and then he rode out at a gallop.

The rumble of hooves followed them, echoing off the mountain walls.

Persicus waited until the sound grew distant. When they were out of sight, he called out to Nooshin.

She came out from behind the rocks and came around the spring to

Persicus' side. Persicus saw she was trembling. He wrapped his arms around her and she all but collapsed against him.

"I'll never make it. They are going to find me." Her voice quaked and trembled with fear.

Persicus held her tighter, rubbing her back in soothing circles. "We'll make it. They are gone."

She pulled away from him and took a deep breath. "I didn't know you could lie so well. Golmud?"

Persicus smiled. "I learnt from the best. We should wait a while before we head out. I sent them in a different direction, but we should get some distance between us and them."

Nooshin nodded and sat on the low rock by the spring.

Persicus and Nooshin left thirty minutes later and reached the outskirts of town in record time, shortly before sundown. Nooshin had been worried about being out on the open road. As soon as they passed the rugged mountain range and the road smoothed out, she drove her horse hard, only slowing to give the horse a short rest every few miles. Sweat poured down her face and she wiped at it until there was nothing left of her beard, but a couple dark smudges. At last, Persicus warned her to slow down lest the horses get worn out. "We are only about two miles from town," he had said. With obvious reluctance, she slowed to a trot after he reassured her for the fifth time that the cavalry had gone in a different direction, after the imaginary Chinese man.

As they drew near the town, the sun was low in the sky, and the temperature was steadily dropping. A dark cloud cover was moving in from the north.

As they entered the caravanserai, the sky turned an ominous dark grey. A storm was brewing and the wind began blowing in heavy gusts, tearing at their clothes. Beyond the gate stood a small courtyard, with a fountain towards the rear. All the shops had closed. The inn stood straight ahead, appearing almost deserted.

Persicus looked around for a stable, but didn't see one. They dismounted their horses and tethered them to an iron ring protruding from the ground.

"This is the last civilization before we get to Mishin and that is a full day's ride from here," Persicus said.

Three horses were tethered to another set of rusty iron rings in front of the inn. A dim flickering light shone through the inn's solitary window. It was a haphazard building, made of flaking, dried mud bricks, and a wood roof. They heard a roar of drunken laughter as they approached the inn's heavy, splintered door.

Lightning struck the hill somewhere behind the inn, illuminating the sky. A deafening clatter of thunder followed an instant later. The sky opened up and hail began to pummel the ground. They covered their heads and Persicus pulled open the heavy wood door. It gave a loud groan as Persicus struggled to push it against the sudden gust of strong wind that blew against it. They rushed inside.

They stopped on the threshold of the door. Their arrival was met by an oppressive silence. Persicus surveyed the nearly empty room. Nooshin stepped closer to him, placing her hand on his arm, her eyes wide.

Three men sat at a table in the middle of the room with their hands clasped around their glazed clay mugs. A small stone fireplace cast an orange glow behind them, leaving their faces in shadows. All three men stared boorishly at the new arrivals.

Nooshin felt a sinking feeling deep in her gut as they sized up Persicus. When the men's eyes shifted to her, an icy shiver ran up her spine. She had never seen such a savage look. She shivered again and took a small step behind Persicus.

An old man with a long, graying beard stood at the kitchen entrance with a towel draped over his shoulder. His wife stood behind him, peeking over his shoulder, much as Nooshin was doing. The old man caught Persicus' gaze and nervously shifted his eyes towards the three men, trying to warn Persicus about the obvious danger. Persicus ignored the warning and greeted the innkeeper in a confident tone, as if there weren't three men biding their time until they tried to slit his throat.

"Good evening. We need a couple of bunks for the night," Persicus said.

The innkeeper pointed to an open doorway leading into a neighboring room. "Through that door. Take your pick."

Persicus nodded to the innkeeper. He grabbed Nooshin's hand and led her towards the bunks in the next room. They could feel all six eyes following them as they moved. Nooshin slid an apprehensive glance to Persicus. The look clearly said: *are you crazy?* However, they had nowhere else to stay tonight and they couldn't go back out into the hailstorm.

The three men were not the average merchants you would meet along the trade route. They were cutthroat bandits and made no effort to hide it. A pugnacious air surrounded them like a barrier. Wearing filthy sheepskin coats, greasy felt hats, and muddy boots, they appeared to belong in the wild, running with the predators, rather than at a civilized inn.

One of the men had a massive girth, with a thick, vicious, red scar that started above his left eye, extended across his nose, to the tip of his right jaw. Scar-face's disturbing grin slashed across his face, exposing his foul, rotten teeth.

The second man was tall, lean, and wiry. Ghastly pock scars covered his face and neck. He sat staring, rhythmically drumming a double-edged dagger against the wooden table, scoring it with each strike. His dark eyes blazed as he looked Nooshin up and down, his eyes lingering.

Persicus had seen this type of lethal dagger before, carried by the tribesmen of the Northern Himalayas. They caused massive damage and anyone stabbed with it most often died within a few hours.

The third man was tall and muscle bound. He sat motionless, with an arrogant, yet angry expression, his arms crossed over his massive chest. His cold, lifeless eyes tracked Persicus and Nooshin as a starving snake would track its prey.

Persicus stopped and turned to look out the window. Walnut-size hail pummeled down, driving into his precious horses, striking the building with devastating force, sounding as if an avalanche was barreling down upon the place. He couldn't take Nooshin back out into the hail and he couldn't leave the horses out there.

"Where are the stables?" Persicus asked.

"Behind the inn," the innkeeper said, still standing by the kitchen door.

Persicus put his arm around Nooshin's shoulder, guiding her to a chair. He sat her down in the main room, across from the men. He hoped to put out the message, by placing her here, in front of them, that he was not afraid of them. This tactic had often worked for him in the past and he hoped that it would work this time. "Sit down here. I will be right back. I have to get the horses out of this hail storm."

She gulped and met his eyes. "Why don't I go with you?"

Persicus shook his head. He gave her a brave, stern look, trying to tell her not to act scared. She nodded as if she understood, raised her chin an inch, and scanned the room moving only her eyes.

Persicus turned and walked casually towards the door. He felt all six eyes boring into the back of his head. He glanced their way out of the corner of his eye as he pushed open the door and calmly walked through it.

As soon as the door closed behind him, he sprinted to the horses, skidded to a stop, and untethered them, with the hail pounding down painfully on his head and shoulders. He ran with the horses around the building, stumbling and sliding along the hail-covered ground. He put each horse into a stall in the stable and ran back to the inn. He had been gone less than three minutes. He felt her panic as he reached for the door. He pulled the door open, the wind fighting against him. His heart sank to his stomach as his eyes fell upon the bandit's empty table.

# *12*

# THE DAGGER

Nooshin was in danger. The three men were up and out of their chairs the second the door closed behind Persicus. They began circling her like sharks. She sat on the edge of her chair, trying desperately to stay stoic. She closed her eyes for a second, taking in a deep, trembling breath, steeling herself.

The men roared with laughter: a loud, sinister sound.

The innkeeper hurried over to Nooshin's side. "I don't want no trouble here."

"Mind your own business and there won't be no trouble," Scar-face said, as he reached around the innkeeper and yanked Nooshin's wool hat off with his thick hands. Her hair fell down over her shoulders. She gripped the seat of her chair and glared at Scar-face. A fine tremble shook her body, from her legs to her arms.

"Where d'you get dese clothes," Pock-face sneered. "You ain't fooling anyone, dearie."

The muscular man with the cold, snake-like eyes stepped between Nooshin and the innkeeper, pushing the old man out of his way. Scar-face messed his hand through her hair. Nooshin jumped out of her seat, the chair falling over behind her, and she shoved Scar-face away. Pock-face shoved his pitted face in her neck from behind, smelling the lingering scent of cinnamon in her hair, his arm slithering around her waist, holding her in place. "He sure don't smell like a sheep herder, do he?"

Snake-eyes came up to stand in front of her. He smiled, leering, his breath sour, and his teeth yellowed. He grabbed her arms while Pock-face held her from behind.

Being as quiet as possible, Persicus crept into the room. Thunder and lightning ripped through the sky, masking his light footsteps. Two of the men had their attention on Nooshin, while the third one had his back to Persicus, and had pushed the innkeeper against the wall. Persicus grabbed the nearest heavy wooden chair, raised it overhead, and smashed it across Snake-eyes' enormous back. Wood and bones cracked simultaneously. The man cried out in agony as he fell in a heap onto the floor. The innkeeper scurried out of the way. As Snake-eyes tried to get up, Persicus raised the chair over his head, and slammed it down against the back of his head. Snake-eyes fell forward, his eyes fluttered and rolled back in his head, and he lost consciousness. With the biggest man down, Persicus felt the odds were much better.

Pock-face looked down at his fallen friend and then up at Persicus with an amused grin on his face. He pushed Nooshin aside. She tried to run, but Scar-face reached out and grabbed her, holding her firm against his chest. Pock-face withdrew his dagger as he held Persicus in his steady, amused gaze. With astounding speed, Pock-face lunged forward with a hateful cry, rapidly thrusting the double-edged dagger left and right. Persicus artfully dodged the blade, jumping back and to the side, turning to face the crazed man at the same time. Pock-face lunged again, swinging the dagger back and forth, as quick as a viper.

Persicus anticipated it would be the same rapid attack. He moved to the side and into the attack, grabbing the wrist that was holding the dagger. Persicus turned his body into Pock-face's body, yanking his arm forward. Pock-face lost his balance and Persicus drove his knee up into his gut. Pock-face fell to his knees, the wind knocked out of him. Persicus kept hold of his wrist, twisting his whole arm at a painful angle, almost to the breaking point.

From the corner of his eye, Persicus saw Scar-face charging him with a heavy chair raised over his head. Persicus glanced around the room for Nooshin and saw she was standing by the innkeeper. Looking back to the charging man, Persicus kept a firm grip on Pock-face's arm as the other man closed in on him, roaring like an angry beast.

Nooshin ran to the kitchen doorway. The innkeeper put a protective arm around her shoulders, pulling her behind him, close to his wife. She watched in terror, her heart pounding painfully. Her eyes were wide, breathing in short, hiccupping gasps with her hands over her mouth. She saw the man with the horrible scar look around for a weapon and pick up a heavy chair. He raised it over his head and charged Persicus. She looked at Persicus and saw he had his hands full. She fought her instinct to close her eyes so she wouldn't see Persicus being killed. She realized at that moment that she would really mourn his loss. She closed her eyes.

꠸꠸꠸

Scar-face's big gut was exposed under his filthy sheepskin coat, heaving and bouncing side to side, as he barreled towards Persicus with the chair raised over his head.

Everything slowed down. Persicus waited until the bear of a man was within striking distance. He swiftly raised his leg and kicked out at a right angle.

Scar-face's eyes widened in surprise at the last second, realizing that he wouldn't be able to stop in time to avoid the kick. He barreled into the kick with a meaty thud, bouncing backwards a few feet. Winded, he struggled to inhale, the air knocked out of him. He tried to throw the chair, but it fell from his stunned hands, and crashed down on top of his head. He swayed for a split second — dazed, breathless, and dizzy — and fell to the floor.

With two down, Persicus turned his attention back to trying to relieve Pock-face of the double-edged dagger. He tightened his grip.

"Drop the dagger!"

The man resisted, gritting his teeth, holding fast to the weapon. Persicus applied more pressure to his wrist.

"Drop it!"

The man stubbornly refused to let go. "Curse you!" Pock-face yelled, trying to get up to his knees.

Persicus twisted his wrist harder and harder, until the man cried out in pain. The dagger fell to the floor. Persicus was so focused on the man's face, it took him a moment to realize the man had dropped the dagger, but he didn't let go of his wrist. He was furious that these men had touched Nooshin, that they meant to harm her. He was outraged. He wanted to hurt them. As soon as Persicus realized that he just wanted to hurt him, he heard the man's agonizing screams.

"Stop! In the name of Allah! Stop! Please! It's broken! You've broken my arm!"

"Persicus! Watch out!" Nooshin yelled.

Persicus let go of his wrist. He looked around for the other two injured men. They weren't lying on the floor where he had left them. He looked up and saw the two men charging him. There was no useful weapon within reach. The chairs within reach were all broken. The table, too large. Dagger on the floor. His own dagger under his tunic, but he didn't want to kill them, not yet.

He was out of time.

Persicus bent down and grabbed the man at his feet, whose wrist was broken and shoulder dislocated, and was mewling in pain on the floor. Persicus grabbed him by the collar of his sheepskin coat and by the waist of his pants. He lifted the man, letting out a loud grunt as he hoisted him chest level, and threw him into the two charging men. Pock-face let out a cry as his body slammed into his two friends. They all fell into a pile, with Pock-face on top.

Persicus knelt and picked up the double-edged dagger. Pock-face rolled off the larger man. He sat up, but his legs were still over Scar-face's chest.

Snake-eyes was bleeding from his head. He sat up, looking at his blood on his fingertips as if he didn't know what it was.

Scar-face was pushing Pock-face off him. As Pock-face scooted over, Scar-face sat up, and saw Persicus standing over him with the double-edged dagger pointed at his neck.

Persicus wanted to slash his other cheek. He had acted in anger, not necessity, when he broke the man's wrist. He knew it was wrong. He had always tried so hard to control his temper. He looked up at Nooshin and found the reason why he had lost his temper. She was still shaking; tears had welled up in her eyes. His anger swelled again.

Persicus pressed the dagger to the man's neck, lightly, not drawing blood.

The man swallowed, careful of the dagger. He spoke, trying not to move. "Don't ... Don't kill me. We will leave, all of us, right now."

A satisfied snicker sounded from behind Persicus. Persicus stepped back, nodding to the innkeeper.

The innkeeper stepped forward. "Get the hell out of here. I never want to see your ugly faces here again." The old man gripped the back of a chair, his wrinkled knuckles turning white, his face lined in anger.

𝌆

Limping and huddled around their injuries, the three men left. Persicus leaned his hands on a table, his head hanging down. Nooshin stood by the kitchen door, uncertain. Persicus looked up at her, his eyes held sorrow for an instant, and then it vanished under his usual calm mien. He sank into a chair, setting the dagger on the table. Nooshin came over to him, resting her hand on his shoulder.

"Thank Ahura Mazda that you are all right." She sat down beside him, trembling.

Persicus leaned over and picked up Nooshin's hat from the floor. He dusted it off and tugged it on her head, tucking her hair behind her ear. He gave her a wan smile.

"Thank you for getting rid of those vermin," the old man said to Persicus. "We had a full house earlier, but everyone left after those cutthroats showed up."

"Don't mention it."

"Nonsense. Your stay here is on the house. You are my guests." The innkeeper turned to his wife. "Annahita, bring us all some of your famous vegetable stew and bread."

Annahita nodded and disappeared through the kitchen door. "I need to go lock the gate and make sure those swine stay out. Then how would you like some of my special homemade wine." He leaned in close. "It rivals even the *best* wine of Shiraz."

"That would be most welcome. Thank you," Persicus said, his voice devoid of emotion.

The innkeeper left through the front door.

"Are you all right?" Persicus asked Nooshin once they were alone.

She nodded slowly. "Are you?"

"Of course."

"I thought they were going to kill you."

The corner of Persicus' lips curved into a crooked smile. "They thought so, too. I've been in worse situations."

Annahita emerged from the kitchen carrying a tray with a large pot of stew, a basket of bread, and four bowls. The food smelled wonderful to the weary travelers. She placed the tray on the table, distributed the dishes, and spooned out the stew.

The innkeeper came back in shivering and shaking off the hail from his clothes. He stomped his feet on the floor, threw some more wood into the fire, and then disappeared into the kitchen. After a few minutes, he emerged with a blue glazed jug of red wine and four matching cups in hand. "This is a real treat!" He declared proudly as he came to the table and poured the wine.

The innkeeper and his wife sat at the table, opposite Persicus and Nooshin.

Persicus took a small sip. He nodded in agreement. "Not bad. As good as any Shiraz I have ever had."

Annahita laughed, her head tilted back. "Did he give you that old line? Don't let the old man fool you. That *is* Shiraz wine. His ancestors came from Shiraz and they brought their precious vines with them."

"Ah, don't listen to her," the innkeeper said, waving his hand at his wife in a dismissive gesture. "She doesn't know wine from vinegar."

Nooshin took a small sip, letting the rich liquid roll over her tongue, and down her throat. She laughed. "Sorry, but it does taste a little like Shiraz."

"Ah, but when a vine grows in a different land, it takes on a different flavor, given by its new environment," the innkeeper said, pointing his index finger up in the air. "That means it is no longer Shiraz!" he finished, tapping his finger firmly on the table.

"Why did your ancestors leave such a beautiful land?" Persicus asked.

"His ancestors were wimps!" Annahita taunted, smiling at her guests.

The innkeeper gave his wife a look that said she was trying his patience. "They were no wimps. They were amongst the first wave of refugees that left during the great barbarian invasion. They were proud Zoroastrians, who refused to repudiate their noble religion for the barbarian's ways."

"Wimps!" declared Annahita. She turned to her guests. "I hope you enjoy the stew. We follow the Avesta strictly and never kill our four legged friends for food, so it's all vegetable."

"It's excellent. I must know the recipe." Nooshin poured herself another glass of wine.

"When would you ever have to cook?" Persicus asked under his breath, taking a spoon full of the stew.

Nooshin gave him a dirty look, narrowing her eyes.

"Aha! I knew you were a woman. No man would have ever asked for the recipe," the innkeeper teased.

Nooshin gave the old man a beguiling smile.

"Where are you two heading?" Annahita asked.

"Mishin City," Persicus answered.

Annahita gasped, picking up her wineglass. "Oh dear, I don't know if I would be going there right now. I assume you have heard about the Princess going missing. Salman and his band of hired cutthroats are bound to be heading that way."

The innkeeper shook his head. "The poor girl, I've prayed every day for her safe return. And poor King Ormozd must be beside himself with worry." The old man raised up his wine glass. "To the safe return of the Princess. May Ahura Mazda keep Mishin safe."

Annahita sighed. "It's tragic. They are the last of the Sassanians in this land. All the others fled after the barbarian invasions. If Mishin falls to Salman, it will be the end of their noble linage."

Persicus and Nooshin shared a long glance. These were her people, Nooshin thought. True, they didn't live in Mishin, but they followed the

Avesta. That meant they were her people. She looked at Persicus and nodded.

Persicus turned to the innkeeper with a serious expression. "My good man, what is your name?"

"Oh, my goodness, I have not told you. Ardelan. My name is Ardelan and this is my wife, Annahita."

"Ardelan, Annahita. I am Persicus, of Abrisham, and this is Nooshin, the Princess of Mishin." The old couple set down the cups and spoons, staring from Persicus to Nooshin. "I happened to rescue her from the bandits that attacked her caravan and she has given me the honor of seeing her safely home."

After a brief shocked silence, Ardelan and Annahita both smiled and bowed their heads. "My noble Princess, daughter of King Ormozd. You have brightened our little caravanserai. We are honored to have as our guest a direct descendent of noble lineage from the Sassanian Dynasty, of our ancient land of Arya Vata."

"Thank you, my friends. But you must not tell a soul that you have seen me, I am trying to find a way out of the marriage to Salman. As soon as I get to Mishin, we are going to send word to my father that I am safe."

"You have our word."

They spent the next hour in the pleasurable company of Annahita and Ardelan. After dinner, when the wine was gone, Ardelan got up from the table, and fetched them plenty of blankets to pad the hard beds of the inn.

Persicus got up and laid the bandits expensive double-edged dagger on the table.

"Please, take this dagger, and use it to pay for the repairs."

"No, no, no." Ardelan shook his head. "You are my guest and you are not responsible for the damages."

"Please, I insist. It is the cutthroat's dagger, and they *are* responsible for the damage."

"Very well. Thank you, Persicus." Ardelan bowed his head and accepted the expensive double-edged dagger.

With that, the innkeeper and his wife bid them goodnight. Persicus and Nooshin went into the neighboring room and collapsed on top of two well-padded beds.

The next morning, Annahita prepared an extravagant breakfast. The inn was filling up with the morning rush. After breakfast, Nooshin and Persicus headed to the stable, where the Ardelan and Annahita were waiting, smiles plastered across their faces. They gave Persicus a large bag full of provisions for the day trip.

"I know it is a short journey to Mishin, but you never know what could happen. These items may come in handy. May the God of Goodness, Ahura Mazda, protect you both." Ardelan turned to Persicus. "And if you should ever come by this way again and need a place to stay, you are always welcome here as our guest."

Persicus shook his hand. "Thank you, my good man. I will not forget your kindness."

Nooshin and Persicus mounted their horses and galloped away as the old couple waved them goodbye.

It was early in the morning and Nooshin drove her horse hard, eager to see her home, only a day's journey away. The land was flat with tall grass lining the road and large, shady trees scattered across the plain. A tall mountain range lay in the distance. They slowed down after an hour, settling into a quick trot.

Persicus pointed ahead. "Mishin is on the other side of those mountains."

"Oh, good! I can't wait to get home and see my father," she said excitedly.

"We talked about this, Nooshin. We need to find out what is going on before you go to the Palace."

"Yes. Yes. I know." She sighed and whispered, "I just want to go home and for all this to be over."

"Well, it is up to you. If this is too much for you, I can deliver you to your father, and hopefully you can find another way out of war or marriage," Persicus said, knowing what her reply would be.

"What? Are you backing out on me? Just when I was thinking you really were brave and strong."

Persicus smiled. "All right, as long as you can handle it, we'll go check out what is happening in Mishin, and if Salman isn't planning anything, we'll go hide you away."

"That's better," she said and kicked her horse. The horse took off at a gallop.

Persicus called out to her to stay by his side as he raced his horse to catch up with her.

After an hour of hard riding, they stopped under the shade of an ancient Chenar tree.

Persicus spread a blanket on the ground. He sorted through the sack Ardelan had given them, finding fresh bread, cheese, basil, and walnuts. He set the food and water on the blanket, and plopped down across from Nooshin.

"We have a special treat for lunch."

"I'll say." Nooshin put the cheese and basil on the bread, topped with a couple walnuts.

As they ate, Nooshin kept glancing up at Persicus. She was growing fond of him. She traced the lines of his face with her eyes. Persicus chewed his food intently, trying not to pay attention to her. Her eyes followed the lines of three faint scars across his face. One scar started above his left eyebrow and cut through it, creating a pale line through the fine hairs of his brow, and three scars continued, cutting across his right cheek. Nooshin wondered if he got the scars during some great battle. She wondered if he was a warrior; that would explain his great fighting skills. As she traced the lines with her eyes, she didn't think the scars marred his face, but added to his considerable character.

Persicus felt her staring at him as he looked beyond her. He stole a quick glance at her and let his gaze settle on the distant horizon while he finished he sandwich.

"Wolf!" Persicus said, his voice abrupt in the silence.

Nooshin jumped, startled. "What?"

"Wolf. The scars are from a wolf, not a battle."

For a moment she sat, stunned, staring at him, her mouth dropped open wide. Persicus kept his eyes fixed onto the horizon, but he saw her reaction out of the corner of his eye as he took a long swig of water.

"How did you know what I was thinking?"

Persicus faced her and grinned.

She crossed her arms and narrowed her eyes at him. "What happened?"

"It's a long story."

She raised her eyebrows at him. "Oh? I see, you are good at fighting men, but when it comes to wolves or jackals, you are worthless."

"I was a boy when I got these scars," Persicus said, his voice held a defensive tone.

"Well? Are you going to tell me what happened?"

"Not right now."

"Why not? I know almost nothing about you."

He stood, packed up the food and goatskin pouch, and then tried to pick up the blanket that she was still sitting on. He tugged on it, but she didn't budge. She just sat there, blinking up at him with her vibrant green eyes.

He sighed. He could force her up, or he could give in. He gave in. "All right, I will tell you on the way, but we should get moving along."

She smiled and got up, dusting her hands. He packed up the

blanket and they headed towards the mountain.

"When I was a young boy," Persicus began, "about eight, I went on my first trip to China. We were following the caravan on foot. It was a frigid, windy day. A blinding, white snow began to fall. It made it difficult to see even the people only a few feet in front of me. Without warning, a huge, wooly creature jumped on me and knocked me to the ground. I could not move; its weight bore down on me, so heavy I could do nothing, but scream. I thought no sound would escape my lips, as when you have those horrible dreams where you stand frozen, unable to move or scream."

He remembered seeing sharp, yellow fangs bared inches from his face and felt the warm, stinking breath on his cheek. In the terror of it, he wasn't sure if it was his fangs or his claws that struck him, but he felt the blow as if a red-hot sword had struck him, and then felt the immediate sting of the cold seeping into the open wounds. He screamed until his throat hurt, fearing the wind would mask his screams, and with the blinding snow, no one would see him being eaten alive by the wolf.

"Then I heard a sickening thud over the roar of the wind. I realized my uncle was standing over me. He swung his club with all his might and sent the wolf flying into the air, as if he had struck a polo ball. It yelped when it fell into a mound of snow. It got up, wheezing and dazed, and limped away."

"That is why you didn't fight off the jackals well. You were frightened from your childhood experience," Nooshin said after a brief silence.

He frowned. "I was not frightened. I would have scared them off, even if you hadn't come throwing rocks," Persicus said indignantly.

"That's possible." Nooshin grinned. She knew better than to be too insightful or point out a man's weakness; they never took it well. Besides, he had been brave confronting the jackals and never showed his fear. She would let him believe what he liked.

Nooshin heard a faint hiss and her horse, suddenly spooked, reared, squealing. She hung on, leaning forward as her horse frantically bucked and kicked.

A poisonous viper was in a striking posture on the ground by the chestnut horse's hooves, hissing and dancing in amazing grace. Desperate to hold on, Nooshin clung to the reins. In a hysterical panic, her horse reared, bucked, and reared again. She lost her grip on the horse and went sailing through the air. Within an instant, she hit the ground, hard, landing on her stomach. Pushing herself up onto her hands, she saw the snake only inches away, its thin whip-like tongue darting out, hissing, staring straight into her terror-filled eyes. She froze, holding her breath, too scared to move.

Persicus turned around when he heard Nooshin's horse panic. His eyes locked onto the snake and the next instant, Nooshin was on the ground, the snake was inches away from her face.

Persicus lifted up his caftan, drew his dagger, aimed, and threw it.

Staring into the blank, lifeless eyes of the cold-blooded viper, Nooshin saw the snake rear back to strike.

Then a dagger pierced the snake, severing its body from the base of its head.

Nooshin froze, staring, hardly breathing. Although it was dead, the snake's body still twisted and curled upon itself, as though in agony. Her eyes moved from the snake to the dagger.

Persicus jumped down from his horse and ran to Nooshin. He knelt down beside her. She got up to her knees, pushing away from him. She reached out to the dagger, her hand hesitant, stopping just short of it, eyes shifting to the snake.

"What is this?" she whispered.

"Nooshin, are you all right? What's wrong? It didn't bite you, did—"

She got to her feet and stood over Persicus, looking from him to the dagger. "Why do you have my father's dagger? What is going on? Who are you really?" Nooshin demanded. Thoughts whirled through her head, but none of them made any sense.

Persicus gaped at her, not understanding. Expressions danced across her face, contorting her delicate features, looks he never expected to see directed at him—outrage, confusion, bewilderment.

"Your father's dagger? What are you talking about?"

"Yes! My Father's dagger! The Royal Dagger! Why do you have it?"

Persicus reached for his dagger, but she reached down, and grabbed it before he did, not at all hesitant now. The snake's head lolled side to side, coming to a rest with its eyes staring up.

"It is not your father's dagger. You *must* be mistaken. It was a gift from my uncle to me, years ago." He stood and stepped towards her.

She took a step back, shaking her head. "No, that is a lie! This is the Royal Dagger. It bares the Royal Symbol!" She yelled, furious, and held out the dagger to show him.

Of course, he knew every detail of the dagger by heart. His face held soft sadness; her anger at him was palpable. *How can she think it is her father's?*

140

Persicus' dagger was a beautiful masterpiece. It was old, but sturdy, and he kept it sharp enough that it cut as if it were new. The blade was straight, made with the strongest steel, and was as long as his forearm. The handle was made of pounded silver. The guard consisted of two lions, one on each side. Their heads were turned, looking back over their shoulders, their mouths' parted, fangs' bared. They each had a thick mane made of gold surrounding their perfectly carved heads. Both lion's front, right legs reached up, claws holding a golden rosette between them, at the tip of the handle. Their left, front legs reached straight across, claws wrapped around the top of the handle. The rear claws wrapped around the bottom of the handle, right above the hilt. The lions' tails crossed in the middle, at the base of the blade, creating the hilt. A star was stamped into the steel blade, right under the hilt.

She looked closer, inspecting the dagger. She turned it around in her hand, noticing the subtle differences. Her face changed; she now looked amazed and even more confused. On her father's dagger, the tails were bushier at the ends, where it created the hilt. And the lions' mouths were closed on her father's. There was also a slightly different design in the inlaid gold of the handle.

"How on earth?" Her voice was so soft, Persicus scarcely heard her. She flopped down on the dirt road and looked up at Persicus. "Where did you get this?"

Persicus knelt on the ground beside her. "What's wrong? Why did you think this was your father's?"

She shook her head. "Tell me how you came to possess this dagger."

In her eyes, he saw a fierce determination that he had never seen before. This is the royal blood in her, such relentless determination, just in her eyes.

"I told you, it was a gift from my uncle for my twelfth birthday. It is very special to me," he said, holding his hand out for the dagger. "It is all I have left from the man who raised me as if he was my father."

She held the dagger against her chest, as if she would never let it go. "Where did your uncle get it? Did he tell you?"

"Yes, I was there when he got it."

"Well?" she demanded. "Tell me."

Persicus stared down at her for a moment. He knew she would not let the topic go and he wouldn't force her to give it back to him. He sighed. "All right. My uncle and I were at the port of Alexandria, selling goods we had brought from China, when a Bedouin came to us, asking for a certain medicine from China. He said his son was deathly ill. We happened to have the medicine he was seeking, but he had no money. He offered my uncle the dagger in exchange for the medicine."

141

"Where did the Bedouin get the dagger from? Did he say?"

"Why is this so important to you?" Persicus asked.

"Please, tell me. Then I'll explain."

"My uncle thought the dagger might have been stolen because, as you can see, it looks very valuable. So yes, he did ask the Bedouin where he got it. The man said he had found it in the Valley of Skulls in the western Egyptian desert." Persicus tried to remember the name of the city "I think he said it was near El Kharga."

Nooshin held the dagger in her lap, both hands firmly gripping the handle. She appeared deep in thought.

Persicus knelt across from her. "Well? Will you tell me what this is all about?"

She nodded, still staring down at the dagger in her lap. "*That's where they died.*"

"Who died?" Persicus asked.

"You don't even know what this is that you have in your possession? Don't know the story of this dagger?" Nooshin asked fervently.

Persicus blinked, perplexed. "No. It's just a nice, gold-laced dagger."

Nooshin shook her head. "King Cyrus had a beautiful, well-made dagger. It was a gift from a Jewish blacksmith whom he had freed from slavery from Babylonia. He had it until the day of his death, about fifteen hundred years ago. The dagger was passed down to Cambyses II, his son and heir. Cambyses went with his army into Egypt, but they never returned. They seemed to have disappeared into thin air. They must have died in El Kharga. After Cambyses' death, Darius, who became the next Persian King, was supposed to inherit the dagger, but it was gone. Darius had been Cambyses' personal lancer and had seen the dagger often. Darius commissioned a replica from his memory. It was said that Darius thought that the dagger was the mark of Kingship.

"Today, my father wears that dagger—the replica. And he will pass it on to the next King. But there is supposed to be only one replica—and my father has it. This may be the real one. It is almost identical to my father's. It bares the Royal Symbols. You see, the lions and the rosette represent the Persian Kingdom."

Nooshin handed him back his dagger. "Here, I guess it is yours now, but would it be all right if I showed it to my father when we get back? He would love to see it."

Persicus nodded, taking his dagger. Nooshin got to her feet.

They stood, face to face for a moment, reflecting on what had happened. Persicus turned, taking a step back, and sheathed his dagger under his caftan. He walked over to his horse, suddenly angry.

"By the way, you are welcome," Persicus said, his voice slightly cold.

"Welcome? For what."

"For saving your life. That snake was about to bite you, instead of thanking me, you yelled at me."

"And I had every right to yell at you. Here you are, all along walking around with my family's dagger — a *Royal* dagger." She jump up on her horse and began riding down the road.

Insulted, Persicus' jaw dropped open.

After ten minutes of silence, she sighed, a loud, dramatic sound. "Fine. Thank you for saving my life ... again," she said begrudgingly.

"You are welcome." He frowned, furrowing his eyebrows. "But you should work on sounding sincere when you say thank you."

# 13

## MISHIN CITY

By four in the afternoon, they were riding up a steep mountain path. The enormous mountain reached up into the flocculent, white clouds. Sedimentary rocks lined the sheer, steep mountainside, with a sprinkle of scattered trees climbing along the winding path.

Nooshin had never seen beyond this mountain range and now she looked over the vast valley below. Miles and miles of drastically changing landscapes, stretching out to the distant horizon: treacherous, rocky terrains; green, rolling valleys with long grass and tall trees; and in the distance, a pale, hot, barren desert. However, it was a different world up here. The mountain was a multitude of colors. Patches of crisp-white snow still covered the shaded areas high above. The trees were blooming with pink, purple, white, and red flowers alongside new offshoots of bright green leaves. The brown rocks came in a multitude of shades, tinted with grey, black, and red, as if the sands of each time had changed, century by century, and every layer of mountain formed by those different colors would be forever exposed, visible to all in the crumbling rocks that tumbled down the mountain, so one could count the ages, and see the colors of times past. The thin air was crisp and it felt as if she was standing at the top of the world.

Nooshin's mood had steadily improved the higher they climbed, as she was looking forward to seeing Mishin. When she had left Mishin, she felt doomed, and was uncertain if she would ever see her home again. Now, though the situation was far from perfect, she felt hopeful, but she noticed Persicus' mood had drastically changed. He had ridden in almost complete silence ever since the incident with the dagger. It was a strained, uncomfortable silence.

Persicus was upset and was unable to hide it. He had suddenly had enough of this entire journey. Everything that had happened since he left Abrisham had gone wrong, with the exception of saving Nooshin. He was tired and wanted nothing more than to hand the Princess over to the Royal Guards on the other side of the mountain and be done with it.

They were a little over halfway up the mountain path when Persicus stopped his horse, his head tilted skyward. Above, a thick layer of fog was rolling over the top of the mountain and cascading down towards them.

Persicus turned towards Nooshin. "We cannot continue through that cloud."

"But Mishin City is just over the mountain. We are almost there."

Persicus shook his head.

"Why not? It may be fun. Like walking through the clouds," Nooshin said.

"It is too dangerous. When you are in its midst, you cannot see where you are putting your feet. Sometimes you can't even see your own hand in front of your face. It would be easy to end up at the bottom of the mountain. We will have to settle here until the fog clears."

"How long until it clears?"

Persicus sighed. "There is no way to know for certain. It could last for hours, or it could stay until tomorrow after sunrise."

"Tomorrow! You mean to spend the rest of the day and *night* up here?"

"Unfortunately. Even if it lifts in a couple hours, we won't be able to make it down the mountain before dark falls, and we can't ride in the dark." Persicus' voice sounded tired and angry. "By tomorrow, I hope I will get you home. Besides, there is nothing else we can do."

Nooshin heard what he said, but didn't know if she was interpreting it wrong. *Would he leave me in the city tomorrow, as soon as we get there?* She pushed the thought out of her head and concentrated on what was happening now. "There must be something we can do. I can't spend the night up here."

He glanced at her, trying to calm his frustration. "Unless you have a direct connection to God running through your Royal Veins ..."

Nooshin heaved a loud sigh and rolled her eyes. Looking down the mountain, she could scarcely make out the tiny green figures of trees that stood hundreds of feet below.

Persicus saw fear in her eyes, but he held on to his anger. After all he had done for her, she all but accused him of stealing, and if there was one thing he had never done in his life, it was to steal. Raised first by his parents and later by his uncle, they had both instilled in him a deep morality. Once, when he was a boy traveling with his uncle, they had been forced to make camp somewhere in the desert of the Beqaa Valley, in Phoenicia, as they did not make it to any inn that night due to delays. During the night, thieves had come in overwhelming numbers and stolen all of their merchandise, as well as their horses. It had all but ruined his uncle. He only had a few gold coins on him, hidden in a sewn up pocket, and they had gone hungry as they used what money they had to buy an old, sick horse, which was all they could afford. He would never, ever steal from anyone, not for any reason. That Nooshin had so misjudged him hurt him deeply, especially after all they had been through together these last few days.

However, that was only the surface of it. He was reluctant to acknowledge the real reason for his anger. Still, it floated somewhere in the back of his mind where he refused to pull it forward. It was what she had said after realizing that the dagger was not her father's, that it was the original—supposedly the dagger of Cyrus, the Great. Here he was, all along, walking around with her family's dagger—The Royal Dagger. As if he were not worthy to possess this dagger—*his own dagger*—and therefore, he was not worthy of her. She needed him for now. He was good enough to protect her in her time of need, but that was all. This was the cause of his anger that he refused to acknowledge, because he already knew this, and had known it from the moment she confessed that she was a princess. So now, he tried to convince himself that she was like all Royalty. Cruel and cold to those beneath them, thinking all peasants were thieves, even though he knew it wasn't true, even though he knew she hadn't meant what she said, at least not to be taken seriously. Nevertheless, her words had cut deep.

Nooshin desperately wanted to be home. She had always wanted more freedom. To travel and roam about the world without a royal escort, to be able to live as most people do, but after the last few days, she wanted her own bed, with her own servants assisting her, with her own food, with people she knew and trusted. She was so close, but as she watched the fog roll down the mountain, she knew that as close as she was, even when she made it over the mountain and through the city gates, she would still have to hide in the midst of everyone looking for her.

As the fog cascaded down the jagged slopes, Persicus worked as fast as he could, tethering the horses to a sturdy branch of a tree, so they wouldn't wander off, and fall off the edge of the mountain. He set up camp, pulling out the blankets, food and water, and then collected enough wood to keep the fire going through the night. Just as he started the fire, the fog descended upon them, swallowing their world in a thick white, opaque mist.

"Looks like the old man knew what he was talking about. You never know what's going to happen. Thankfully, he packed us extra food and blankets." Persicus settled down by Nooshin as he poked at the fire to get it going. He tossed Nooshin a blanket.

"The old man? Do not tell me you have forgotten his name?" Nooshin could scarcely see him now, only a foot away.

"Me? Forget? Never."

"Then what is his name?"

Persicus gave her an irritated glance. "I see what you are up to. You have forgotten his name and are trying to trick me into saying it first. It's not going to work."

"I remember. Ardelan." Nooshin still felt he was upset with her. He was being brusque. She was not use to apologizing to anyone, but she was determined to win him back over. "It was the name of a noble King from ancient times. It is a shame that people have forgotten the old names and our ancient ways."

"I forget nothing."

"Ardelan. It is a good name, don't you think?" Nooshin said in a soft voice.

"Yes."

"When I have a son, that is what I will name him: Ardelan."

A small laugh escaped Persicus' lips. "I had the same thought while we were eating dinner with him. Funny thought. Two sons named after the same person, but they would be worlds apart."

"Maybe not," Nooshin whispered. She yawned, tucking herself into the blanket, and inching closer to the small fire.

"What?" Persicus asked.

"Why were you traveling with your uncle to China when you were a boy?" Nooshin asked, changing the subject.

Persicus tried to read her face through the fog. "Well, I traveled all over with him. He was a merchant."

"When I was young, I always wanted to travel the world. As it is, I hardly leave the city."

"And when you did leave, look what happened." Persicus leaned back against a boulder, glad she couldn't see the tight grin on his face.

Nooshin ignored the comment. "Where were your parents?"

The memory came flooding back to him. He tried to repress it.

"I don't want to talk about it."

Nooshin paused, surprised by his terse, cold tone. She guessed there had to be some tragedy to put such a tone in his voice.

"My mother died during my birth. I never knew her, but my father told me so much about her, that I feel like I knew her."

She told him about her mother's beauty and kindness, and her deep devotion to the people of Mishin. His anger subsided as he listened to her speak, with such devoted fondness, of the mother she had never known. He simply couldn't hold onto that anger any longer.

"When I was little, every night my father would tell me a story about her. He told me about how she dedicated her time to making sure no one in Mishin went hungry. She gave out sweet breads, preserves, almond cookies, candied pomegranates and oranges. She could make just about everything. After she died, my father had the cooks continue bringing food to the sick and poor, but he didn't have them baking the sweets. So when I was ten, I started spending the afternoons in the kitchen while the staff cooked. I learned how to bake and make sweets, the same as my mother. Every Sunday and Wednesday, I make sweets for the sick, the poor, and the children, as my mother used to do."

Persicus was amazed by her. Her mother's good traits had passed down to her, regardless of her mother's absence; she tried to make her mother proud. He knew that she wasn't bragging. He could tell by her voice, which held no pride as she recounted her family's good deeds, and thought perhaps that she missed her home, and telling him about it made her feel better. He could feel her sitting only a foot away. He wondered if she was trying to make up to him, but didn't quite know how to. She was a princess after all and it was probable that she had never had to apologize to anyone. As Persicus listened to her soft voice ruminating about the good deeds she and her family do for their city, a deep respect for her grew in his mind. He knew she was smart, but that she was kind and genuinely cared for her citizens was rare for people of Royalty. His anger had vanished, washed away by the pain, and love in her voice.

"So you never had a mother. Who raised you? Your father must have been busy ruling the city and the rest of the Sogdiana."

"A woman named Tahmineh. She was a servant in the Palace before I was born and she started taking care of me after my mother died. She had come to my father after her husband and her parents were killed in one of the barbarian invasions. She had nowhere to go, no children, and no skills outside of keeping a household. She knew of Mishin and thought this was the safest place she could go. My father took her in and gave her a room in the Palace.

"My father says I was a terrible baby, I fussed and cried all night, and most of the day. My father says it was because I knew my mother wasn't there. Tahmineh came in one morning when I was two weeks old, I was crying, and as soon as she picked me up, I grew quiet. After that, my father moved her into a bedchamber next to my own. She became the mother I didn't have and I the daughter she never had. I love her dearly, though she will never replace my real mother, she is my mother that is here."

When Nooshin fell quiet, Persicus finally opened up to her, to answer the question she had asked before. It was something he always dreaded thinking about, but which had haunted him since his childhood, and shaped the course of his life. He hated thinking about it, because to think about it was to relive it.

He remembered every detail; it played out through his mind as if he was back in that moment in time. He heard his mother's voice calling him from his childhood friend's home. She wanted him to fetch the watermelon from the river, where they had let it sit, wedged between two rocks, in the icy water to cool.

"My friend and I ran down to the riverside to get the watermelon. My mother would always serve it cold, with a glazing of rosewater, on a little table in our yard on hot days. We took our time, playing in the water, kicking, and splashing each other. Then I grabbed the watermelon and headed back to my house. We had just made it to the top of the riverbank when it happened. I heard a deafening, thunderous roar, as if a thousand wild horses were running through the steppes. The sound echoed off the mountains, the ground shook and swayed with such a violent force. It seemed to last forever. I fell to the ground. My friend had also fallen and was trying to stand back up, but it was useless. The ground was shaking so hard we couldn't get to our feet until the shaking subsided. It was the worst earthquake I have ever experienced. It not only was shaking side to side, but also heaving and jumping up and down. Leaves and hard nuts fell from the trees onto our heads and arms. The melon had fallen to the ground and splattered, thick and red, all over the grass. I didn't realize I had fallen on it until it was all over and saw I was covered in bright red juices.

"When the quake came to a stop and the dust settled enough for us to see past the brown haze, the devastation was so great, I fell back onto my knees. The whole village lay in ruins. In those few eternal, traumatic seconds, the whole landscape, every familiar building had been devastated. Most of the homes and shops had collapsed in heaps of rubble. I heard cries for help from almost every pile of mud bricks and stones, from every corner of the village. But the heap of stones where my home had once stood was all too silent. No cry for help issued from the rubble. That is how I lost my family. My mother, father, and young sister all gone, taken from me. And that was how I came to travel with my uncle. He was on his way home when the quake destroyed my home, my family. He arrived the next day. He was my only surviving relative. He took me in and I traveled with him on all his long, arduous journeys."

149

SAEED & SHIRIN DERAKHSHANI

Persicus fell quiet. What he didn't say, but always thought about, was the guilt—that he was responsible for their deaths. If he hadn't selfishly played in the water with his friend, his mother, father, and sister would have been sitting outside, enjoying the watermelon when the quake struck. Instead, they were crushed to death by the weight of falling bricks.

He had not eaten a watermelon since.

She sensed there was more to the story, but she was sorry she had asked and didn't press. "I am so sorry, Persicus."

"Thank you, but it is all right. It was a long time ago. And I grew very close to my uncle."

"Is that what you do now? Are you still a merchant?"

Persicus hadn't wanted to tell her he was a qanat engineer—many people equated that to a hole digger, regardless of the danger and skills required—but since he learned she was a princess and well out of his league, it just didn't seem to matter to him anymore. He knew that she only needed him to protect her while she figured out what she was going to do. Therefore, he had been trying, since she had confessed to him who she was, to put the idea out of his mind, and act in accordance. After tomorrow, he might never see her again. He would have to accept that.

"I did that for a while, but after my uncle passed away, I bought an apple orchard. I also became a qanat engineer."

Nooshin smiled. *A man of many talents.* "So a merchant, a farmer, an engineer, and you know how to defend yourself. Is there anything I left out?"

Persicus gave an abrupt, nervous laugh. "Uh, no. Nothing that I can think of right now."

"We have a lot of fruit trees in the palace garden, but no apples. I would love to see your apple orchard sometime. How far from Mishin do you live?"

"It's in Abrisham. Not too far."

"What do you want to do next?"

"Well, in the morning, hopefully the fog will have cleared. We'll head over this mountain and see what's happening in Mishin."

"I meant with your life. You have accomplished so much already. What's next?"

Persicus didn't know what was next. It seemed to him that he had endured many vicissitudes throughout his life, but without any substantial accomplishments.

"Do you ever want to get married?" Nooshin asked.

"I suppose that is what I will do next," he answered. "There is a good family in Abrisham. They have offered their daughter to me in marriage. She is a sweet young girl. I am told she is a wonderful cook.

150

But it doesn't feel right."

Nooshin let out the breath she had been holding. "So you will not marry her?"

"I don't know yet. I am in no rush," he said. "But it would be nice to eat a decent meal every day. I'm getting tired of apples."

This was not the answer Nooshin had hoped for. She remained silent.

"What are you thinking? You just became terribly quiet?" Persicus asked.

"What would you do if you were King and Salman was threatening you?"

Persicus paused. He had not expected a question such as this. *What would I do?* he wondered. "That's difficult to answer, as I'm not in that situation. You can never really know what you would do, until it happens. I assume you never would have thought you'd be here with me, hiding from Salman's army, in hopes of escaping the marriage you had agreed to."

"True. But what do you *think* you would do?"

"Well, I am not violence prone. I am a pacifist when I can be. I don't like killing. But if I was King …" he paused, thinking. "The conversation you told me about in the bathhouse … I think those women were right. The people of Mishin like Mishin the way it is. They don't want someone else coming in and taking over, especially not Salman. In this case, I think I would fight. I would call every able body to defeat Salman. He is a tyrant and he will go on killing, destroying, and conquering until someone stops him. He could end up ruling all the land from Turan to China if someone doesn't intervene."

"There are many stories of the things he has done, people are terrified."

"Yes, they are, but unless someone stands up against him, all he has to do is threaten, and people roll over for him. You asked me what I would do. I would come up with a plan to defeat him. I would not roll over and surrender my land or people to him."

Nooshin thought about it. She had been thinking about it ever since she left the bathhouse, but ideas began to form and take shape in her head. They could fight. They could come up with some plan to defeat him and be free of him. This could work. It *had* to work.

The sound of a hawk calling overhead woke Persicus. His eyes still closed, he felt Nooshin tucked in beside him. She must have gotten cold during the night and crept closer to him for warmth. He didn't move, as he didn't want to wake her yet. He opened his eyes to narrow slits. The fog had cleared. The morning air was crisp and clean. He looked at Nooshin as she slept cradled in the bend of his arm. His arm was asleep and numb. He smiled and closed his eyes.

As if she sensed him looking at her, she gave a sigh of contentment and snuggled closer. "I don't want to get up yet. I'm warm and comfortable," she mumbled.

Persicus couldn't keep a wide grin from spreading ear to ear. He made a sound in agreement and held her while she slept for another hour.

The next time she awoke, she was a different person.

"What are you doing? This is most improper!" She pulled herself off his arm, wrapping the blanket over her shoulders.

"What am *I* doing?" he asked, startled by her sudden outburst.

"Yes. What are *you* doing? When I fell to sleep, you were over *there*." She pointed a few feet away.

Persicus' eyes widened and he gave her an exasperated look. "You came over to me while I was sleeping. If anything, I should be complaining. My arm is completely numb."

"I did no such thing," she insisted, turning her head away from him.

It was pointless to argue. He could see it in her eyes that she knew she had come to him and he also saw that she had no intention of admitting it.

The mountain pass was for the most part clear, with a few lingering ghost-like patches of clouds still clinging to the mountainsides. Persicus packed up, amused, and smiling to himself. Then they mounted their horses and made their way up the mountain with ease.

The path was well-worn, hard compact dirt and stone, smoothed over time by years of wear. They made it to the top of the mountain by noon, where they stopped. Persicus stood at the edge of a cliff, staring down at one of the most beautiful views he had seen in a long time. He was completely enchanted by this beautiful land. Nooshin felt a wave of relief; she had made it home. She was overcome by a rich gratitude that she had never felt before about her homeland.

Mishin Valley was green for as far as the eye could see. Majestic mountains flanked the valley on two sides: one on which they stood and the other in the distance, across the valley from them. A crystal blue river snaked along the entire valley, running through the center, alongside the exterior western wall of Mishin. Vast, fertile, lush farms and verdant orchards surrounded the city for miles in all directions.

The Royal Palace was perched on a hill in the center of the city, clearly visible from afar in all directions. It stood, bathed in the golden sunlight, shimmering as a beacon of hope, drawing people of different faiths to this tolerant and prosperous city.

Persicus had not been this way since his youth, during his travels with his uncle. As he stood above the vast, beautiful city, he at last understood the depth of the problem that Nooshin had been carrying on her shoulders. Though he did not think them trivial or insignificant before, he now remembered what a wonderful place this was, and the importance of keeping this land a safe haven for all who wanted to live a life of freedom and prosperity. He understood the magnitude of how many lives would be affected if Salman waged a war on this city, or married Nooshin, and gained control over it. This was no small village, as Salman was known to attack, but an ancient, prosperous, wealthy city, which included the surrounding valleys, and all the farmers who supplied the food for this entire enclave.

Nooshin spoke, not taking her eyes off her home, "The Palace is known as Sangin Shahr, because it was carved into a solid limestone rock. My ancestors hired the best of the Indian sculptors to carve it. It's impenetrable; many have tried to breech these walls over the centuries."

She looked at Persicus, fervid eyes burning. He saw in her a resolute determination to save her home. No other option would suffice now. The seed that had been planted in her mind back at the bathhouse had grown into a fierce, formidable forest.

Persicus nodded to her, letting her know that he understood, without words, and that he would do anything to help save her and her home. He didn't need to tell her this. She saw it in his eyes. She thought about what might happen to Mishin if she failed, if Salman attacked. So many thoughts and emotions painted across her face from one second to the next, until she gave him a sad smile, and looked away. This despondent smile almost caused a physical ache deep within Persicus' chest.

It took them all day to get down the mountain. They had stopped in a shady spot, where the path had widened, and trees grew out of cracks in the rocks. The sun was hot overhead. The cool, gentle, sporadic breezes felt wonderful as it stirred their hair, blowing against their flushed skin. They had a quick lunch, while letting the horses graze on random vegetation. Nooshin, eager to get home, didn't let him rest long. They ate and then got up to go.

By evening, they made it to the bottom of the mountain. Veering off the main road, to the riverside, they filled their water pouches, and Persicus insisted they give the horses a break for half an hour. They sat in the grass by a Willow tree whose branches flowed to the ground.

"Besides, we don't want to make it to town when the sun is still bright. It would be better if it's dark, people would be less likely to recognize you."

Persicus saw her becoming anxious. Her nerves seemed on edge. Every little sound made her jump. She crossed her arms, trying to appear at ease, but he saw her fingernails biting into the flesh of her arms. He tried to take her mind off her nervousness by talking. Searching for something to say that would take her mind off her problems, staring at the Willow tree, nostalgic memories came rushing back to him.

"My sister was a year younger than me. She would play outside in a little fortress I would make for her with the branches of a Willow tree, similar to this one. She would pretend she was a princess and the fortress was magical. While she was in the magical fortress, she could have her every wish, and turn anything into anything. Often it was me— she pretended I was her servant or her horse—and she'd turn me into a rock if I wasn't playing along, if I didn't let her ride on my back. I was a rock a lot."

Nooshin smiled. "When I was a child, I wanted to be rescued from the Palace. Sometimes I would pretend that a farmer would come and whisk me away, we would live on a small farm, with lots and lots of animals, dogs, cows, horses, goats, and birds everywhere."

This surprised him and he laughed. Every little girl wished to grow up to be a princess, so why shouldn't a princess want to be a farmer's wife.

"Why a farmer?" Persicus asked.

Nooshin thought for a moment. "I suppose it was because Tahmineh always told me stories about the farm she grew up on. She married very young and moved to the city. I think she longed for her childhood life and would tell me stories as a way to relive her past. But then again, I always wanted to travel, too. To sail across the sea."

"You're what, eighteen? Nineteen? I am surprised that you haven't married anyone by now."

Nooshin smiled. "Yes, I know. Foreign princes and kings have been popping up since I was twelve. They all want the same thing—a stronger alliance with Mishin, or control of Mishin."

"Why haven't you married one of them? They must be better than Salman."

"The Sogdian people are different from most. Our women are free to marry whomever they wish, that includes Royalty. When these noblemen came, offering gold, land, or power, if my father would give me to them, my father always told them that it was my choice, if they wished to marry me, I would have to accept, not him. He was always

154

cordial, he would tell them if they really were seeking a stronger alliance with Mishin, then they could discuss it, but it would have nothing to do with me."

Nooshin had always listened from a private, hidden room, whenever her father gave this speech to her would-be suitors. She always smiled when they acted offended. One King, she didn't even care to remember his name, or where he was from, had been outraged. He had brought his son, in hopes of his son becoming King of Mishin one day. Nooshin had no doubt in her mind that *one day* would be very soon indeed, for it would not be convenient to the Prince if her father was to live another ten, or thirty years. In return for the arrangement, he had promised a percentage of the taxes from his territory to be given to her father. When her father had told him no, in the exact same way he told them all, he had seen it as an insult. She remembered his outraged voice, filled with uncomprehending anger. 'To let a *woman* decide whom she marries. That is ridiculous! They are *women!*' Right away, she knew she would not accept, as she would never be a second-class citizen in her own home. Whomever she chose, they would rule together, or he would not be King.

By sunset, they reached the cobblestone road leading to the city gate.

Persicus looked over at Nooshin, inspecting her. "When we get to the gate, keep your head down, and stay a few feet behind me. Let me do the talking. If the gatekeeper asks you anything, don't answer. I'll tell him you are deaf and mute. Make sure all your hair is hidden."

Nooshin nodded. Her anxiety steadily rose the closer they came to the gate.

"What do we do if he becomes suspicious?" Nooshin asked.

After a slight hesitation, Persicus answered. "We'll be all right. They won't be looking for two men. They'll be looking for bandits, and of course, you."

A wide cobblestone bridge, with tall stone arches at each end, led to the gate, just beyond the end of the bridge. A colossal limestone wall wrapped around the city. The tall, thick wooden doors of the gate were open and a gatekeeper, who had been leaning casually against the stone wall, quickened to attention at their approach.

Persicus took the lead. Nooshin, a few paces behind, had made sure her hair was secure, tucked and hidden under her hat. She stared at the ground, trying to keep her gaze steady, but her eyes wandered up. Nooshin inhaled sharply, noticing the gatekeeper was not a gatekeeper at all. He was one of the Royal Guards. First noticing his uniform and

SAEED & SHIRIN DERAKHSHANI

then peeking up at his face, she recognized him.

The Royal Guards in Mishin all wore the same uniform: a light armor, which covered their chests and arms, and fell inches above their knees. The armor, designed to be flexible, was made with small, overlapping metal plates, resembling fish scales. Helmets protected their heads with thick, solid metal, with a similar flexible metal mesh hanging down over their shoulders, allowing more comfort, and range of movement for the soldiers in battle.

"Good evening, travelers," the guard said in a monotone voice, as though it was something he repeated day after day, even though Nooshin knew that was not so. "Welcome to Mishin. What is the purpose of your visit?"

"We are just passing through. We need a place to eat and sleep tonight," Persicus said, trying to sound weary and hungry. It wasn't hard.

The guard's eyes slid past Persicus to Nooshin. She kept her face diverted, staring down at the mane of her horse.

The guard looked back to Persicus. "We are inquiring to all who pass here if they know anything at all about the disappearance of Princess Nooshin, of Mishin."

Persicus put on a suitable grievous look. "I heard about it a couple days ago, but I'm afraid I know nothing of the matter. May the Guardian of the Steppes keep her safe."

The guard looked past Persicus again and settled on Nooshin. His gaze was fixed and searching, squinting his eyes to see better.

Persicus' heart sped up. Perspiration beaded on his hairline and trickled down his back. He fought to breathe, smooth and even.

"You there," the guard said to Nooshin. "Have you heard anything at all about our Princess?"

Nooshin didn't move. She kept staring at the mane of her horse, as Persicus had told her to do. Her heart was pounding hard, so loud that she feared the guard would hear it, and then he would *know*. He would surely recognize her. She thought she was discovered, certain of it. She would be taken to the Palace, where King Salman would come claim his prize. She shivered.

"He has not heard anything, either," Persicus said.

"Oh? And how do you know that? Let the boy tell me whether he has or has not heard anything that could benefit our search. Come now, speak up young man."

Nooshin felt his eyes boring into her.

"The boy is deaf and mute. He could not have heard anything."

The guard's eyes widened in surprise. "I've never seen a deaf, mute. Is he a eunuch, too? He does seem rather frail for a man."

156

"No, but he is still young. He is my brother, my mother had him too late in her life, he was born early—very small, deaf, and mute."

"Hmmm ..." He scrutinized the deaf, mute, underdeveloped boy, looking Nooshin up and down, and then gestured for them to pass. "The caravanserai is just inside the gate, to your right. You will find everything you need there."

As they eased past the guard, Nooshin held her breath. They rode through the gate, slow and steady, trying not to attract attention. The guard watched Nooshin with intense interest. Her heart sped up more than she thought she could stand. She wanted to race her horse past him, but she kept her easy, slow pace. When they were well out of the guard's unwavering gaze, Nooshin let out her breath, and gave a half-hysterical, half-laughing sob. Persicus almost collapsed on top of his horse. He picked himself up and looked at Nooshin.

"I thought it was over." She placed her hand over her heart, as if her firm touch could slow its rapid beating.

The caravanserai was just inside, as the guard had said. It was much larger and busier than the caravanserai in Abrisham. Although Nooshin had spent almost every moment of her life in Mishin, she had never once walked amongst the travelers in the caravanserai. The energetic atmosphere seemed almost overwhelming to her, with all the shops, and people hustling around. She tried to hide her excitement, though it was difficult. She was surprised at herself that this was a part of the city, which her father ruled, and someday she would rule, which she knew existed, but have never seen until now. Her father never wanted her to go into this part of the city, though it was usually safe, this area was full of strangers from all over the continent, and there was always the risk of danger.

The caravanserai was shaped in a large rectangle. Shops of every kind, stables, multiple chaikhanas, anything anyone could need, or want, were enclosed within this caravanserai, within the two-story structure that encompassed the courtyard. A large square fountain stood in the middle, fed by the river outside the walls of the city.

They left their horses in a stable, washed their hands and faces in the cool water from the fountain. Nooshin took care not to show her hair, keeping her hat secure on her head.

They made their way through the crowd. Nooshin stayed close to Persicus' side, nervous, excited. They found an inn where they could eat and sleep for the night.

The idea of sleeping in the Mishin caravanserai seemed crazy to Nooshin, but Persicus had told her that everyone in the caravanserai were travelers and merchants. None of them would know how she looked, even if they paid attention, and looked past her loose, male clothing. On the contrary, this was probably the safest place they could be, as no one would be looking for her in her own city. As crazy as it sounded, it made sense to her.

The inn was packed. They found an empty table next to the wall. Nooshin practically collapsed into her chair, her adrenaline levels plummeting, leaving her hands shaking, and legs trembling.

The innkeeper came ten minutes later, took their order, and disappeared into the kitchen. Their food came moments later and they dug into a platter of rice, fish, and steamed vegetables.

The tea came and they sat across from each other, both leaning arms on the table, talking in quiet voices, finally relaxed.

# 14

# THE SAGA OF THE CHICKENBONE AND THE MIDNIGHT MURDER AT THE INN

Y ou *imbeciles!* How could you lose it!" Hakim exclaimed.

Hakim sat at a table in an inn with his two brothers and a large man known as Aboli. Hakim hired Aboli from time to time, when their paths crossed, and when he was needed for his unnatural strength, or killing skills. Though *skill* might not be the word anyone would think of when they saw Aboli. He was abnormally muscular, brutal, completely without remorse, and—most important— he didn't ask questions. All qualities that Hakim valued in his hired help. Added to that, he was the largest man Hakim had ever laid eyes on; he seemed invincible, impervious to injury.

Aboli stood at six foot, eight inches. He had a large, square-shaped head, which he shaved bald. He hadn't shaved his face in days, so his cheeks and jaw were covered in thick, dark stubble. Thick, black eyebrows, extending well past his eyes, reaching almost to his temples, sat above his small, brown, eyes. He wore a tan tunic, brown caftan, dark brown pants, with muddy, scratched leather boots. His arms were covered in scars from his many sword fights and one large, rough burn scar. His face was scar free, as no one could ever reach it. He sat at the

159

table with Hakim, Asif, and Hamzeh, devouring a heaping plate of food.

Asif glared at Hakim, who he thought was as much to blame for the loss as himself. "Never mind about that. Let's just figure out how we are going to get it back."

Annoyed, Hakim looked from Asif to Hamzeh. "You let me deal with that. Did you get the rope and pick?"

Hamzeh took a long swig of wine. "Yeah, we got them. They're with the horses."

"But I don't see why we need this guy." Asif jerked his thumb at the big man sitting next to him.

"We need him because I said we need him. Don't worry about it. I'll fix everything, because that is what I do." Hakim glared at his brothers. "Since I can't trust you two to do anything right, you needn't worry your pretty little heads about it."

"Ah. But I am worried about it." Asif turned to the big man. "What can you possibly do to help us? What would you do if *they* showed up while we are there?"

Aboli was concentrating on sucking a chicken bone into oblivion, hardly paying attention to what these little, pathetic, weak men were saying. Noticing all three of them staring at him, he withdrew the bone out of his mouth. "What? I like chicken bones."

"Have you heard anything we said?" Asif asked, irritated.

"I don't talk business while I'm eating," Aboli said, not taking his eyes off his bone. He resumed devouring the remaining bits of flesh from the bone, scraping away at it with his front teeth. He didn't like talking at all, but really hated being disturbed, or watched while eating.

"You see? He's useless!" Asif banged his fist down on the table, facing Hakim.

A rich, light-hearted laughter flittered through the room from a couple tables behind Hakim. An eerie prickle of alarm rose over him, the little hairs on the back of his neck and his arms rose on end. He thought he must have been hearing things. Then he heard, as clear as day, a familiar phrase. "Guardian of the Steppes!" that laughing, familiar voice said.

Hakim froze, sucking in his breath. His hand gripped the table, turning his thin, knobby knuckles white. He shivered with a sudden chill and wiped his damp hand on his pants. His brothers continued their usual bickering, but he couldn't hear them anymore. All he could hear was the low, roaring rush of his pulse in his ears. His heart pounded up into his throat. He turned around in his chair, slowly, a horror-stricken expression slashed across his pale face.

Hakim's mouth dropped open, his eyes bugged out in disbelief, and he jerked back around. His eye twitched; he knocked over his cup of wine, spilling it all over Aboli's arm. His face turned as white as cotton.

Aboli looked down at his wet arm, seeming to comprehend after a long moment, that it was wine, and returned his attention to consuming his chicken bone.

"What's wrong with you?" Hamzeh asked. "You look like you've seen a ghost."

Hakim gulped and nodded. A hoarse, stuttering, whisper escaped his lips. "Ga-ga-ghost."

"What?" Asif asked, narrowing his eyes, leaning towards Hakim.

"What's wrong with you?" Hamzeh asked again.

Hakim leaned across the table. His eye twitched. Frustrated, he smacked the palm of his hand over his fluttering eye. "Three tables behind me, what do you see there?"

"What are you talking about?" Hamzeh asked, thinking his brother may, at last, be going crazy.

Asif looked past Hakim, peering over the heads of the merchants until he picked out the table in question. His face fell and his jaw dropped when he saw Persicus sitting there, grinning, and laughing with his companion. "Oh, Mighty Allah! How on earth ..."

Hamzeh turned in his seat to see what was so disturbing to his brothers. "No! He should be dead!"

"Thank Allah." Hakim was relieved.

"Thank Allah?" Asif repeated in astonishment. "Why would you say that? Are you crazy? He could ruin everything!"

"Because if you see him, too, then no, I'm not crazy, and I'm not being haunted by a ghost."

"It's not possible." Hamzeh turned back around, wide-eyed.

"Maybe he has a twin brother ..."

Hakim shook his head. "No. That is him all right. I recognize the scars on his face."

Asif looked from Hakim to Hamzeh, his hand in a tight fist. "But how on earth did he get out of his tomb? He was trapped. There's no way he could have moved that rock by himself."

Hakim peeked over his shoulder. "I *told you* not to underestimate him. Remember, I chose him because he knew how to navigate the underworld. There had to be another way out. A tunnel or another exit." His respect for Persicus' skills grew a little and he hated it. The man should be dead, or dying. Then, respect would be due. He always respected the dead.

"*You* warned us?" Asif said through gritted teeth.

Hamzeh drained his cup of wine and banged it down onto the table. "But we went around the entire god-forsaken hill. There was *no* way out. He should still be in there, damn it."

161

"But he's not." Asif narrowed his eyes at Hakim.

"Well, this wouldn't have happened if you two had just killed him, as we had originally planned, instead of trapping him, " Hakim whispered in a harsh, accusatory tone.

Hamzeh's mouth dropped open an inch and he gaped at Hakim, speechless.

"*Us* kill him." Asif clenched his jaws together, resisting his urge to scream at Hakim. "*You* are *the one* who didn't want to kill him. *You* wanted to trap him in the cave and pay him with our gold, so that on your judgment day—"

"Never mind," Hakim snapped. "That's not important. What's important is: what is he doing here and what are we going to do about him? We can't let him walk away again. He could ruin everything if he talked."

The three brothers huddled around the table to discuss how to dispatch Persicus once and for all.

"Why don't me and Hamzeh wait outside the city, we'll follow him until he stops for water, and kill him there."

Hakim shook his head. "There are several things wrong with that idea—"

"What's wrong with it?"

Hakim looked at Asif as if he were stupid. "First, there are two exits to the city. You can't be at both, unless you split up. Second, you don't know why he's here. He could be here for days and we can't wait that long. Third, he's smart and resourceful. He would know he's being followed and he'd kill you both."

After a short debate, Hakim turned towards Aboli with an expectant look.

Oblivious to their conversation, Aboli was still busy, noisily sucking his chicken bone clean. His eyes were closed in feverish concentration, scraping the bone clean of the last remnants of cartilage. He opened his eyes to the sudden silence, glancing from Hakim to the other brothers.

"What now? Can't I eat without you goons staring at me?"

"Eat your bone," Hakim placated. He didn't want to anger the big, dumb oaf.

"I can't eat when you people are staring at me," Aboli replied, annoyed, gripping his bone in his fist.

"Never mind your damn bone." Hakim leaned towards Aboli. "I've got another quick and easy job for you. Do you see that man sitting behind me, three tables back, next to the wall? The man with the scarred face who's talking to the young man in nomadic clothes."

Aboli set his bone down on his plate. He looked over Hakim's head, counted three tables back, and picked out the man with the scarred face.

He gripped his bone, ready to start gnawing on it again, unhappy about the interruption. "Yeah, Boss."

"Tonight, after everyone has gone to sleep, you will come here and"—he put his index finger to his throat and swiped it across in a cutting motion. "There will be ten gold coins in it for you."

"Twenty," Aboli countered, resuming nibbling on his bone.

Hakim fought his aggravation. "All right, you win. Fifteen."

"Twenty," Aboli replied in the same dry tone.

"Seventeen."

"Twenty." The imposing man set down his bone and looked Hakim in the eye. Aboli didn't have to do anything to be intimidating; an air of violence fell off him in waves.

Hakim conceded with a wave of his hand. "Fine! Twenty. But you must be very quiet and quick. No mistakes."

Aboli smiled, a cold-blooded, killer smile, lips glistening with grease. A look that said he could rip the head off a small horse with his bare hands and whistle while doing it. He sat back in his chair and crossed his massive arms. "I don't make mistakes." His voice, as always, was calm, lifeless, monotone.

Even though Aboli's voice was flat, giving no implications, Hakim felt scrutinized. It was there in Aboli's eyes. A look that said, above all else, that Hakim was a complete screw up. Hakim hated all that that look implied, especially from his hired help, but Aboli was necessary should the worst happen. He could put up with him, for now.

Hamzeh was more unnerved that nothing about Aboli's expression matched each other. The look in his eyes, the smile, and the voice, all said different things, simultaneously.

Hakim scowled. "Good." He glanced back over his shoulder. "Let's get out of here before he sees us." Hakim grunted. "Merciful Allah, I feel indigestion coming from this awful food." As he stood, a loud, burning belch escaped his lips.

Half the room turned to look at Hakim. Panicked, his eye twitched, and he winced, certain Persicus would be staring straight at him, as well. He looked across the room to where Persicus sat and found him still immersed in conversation with the boy at his table. Hakim sighed with relief.

The foursome headed towards the door, trying not to draw attention to themselves.

As fast as they vacated their chairs, the innkeeper descended upon the empty table to collect the dishes, and make room for the next guest.

Aboli suddenly stopped, halfway to the door. Asif almost ran into his broad back. "Hey, wait a second." Aboli turned and he rushed back to the table.

The innkeeper had stacked the dishes in a pile and was just turning to head back to the kitchen when he saw a huge man rushing towards him.

Aboli loomed over the innkeeper and snatched a chicken bone from the plate on top of the pile, startling the innkeeper, and knocking the armful of dishes to the floor. Aboli turned on his heels and stormed off with his precious bone firm in his grip.

Hakim and his brothers fled when the dishes fell with a loud clatter.

Dumbfounded, the innkeeper stared from the fleeing man to the mess on the floor at his feet.

Persicus heard a loud commotion and turned in time to see a giant of a man — the biggest man he had ever seen — storm out of the inn. The innkeeper stood in the middle of the room in a daze. After Persicus was certain the event had nothing to do with him, or Nooshin, he turned back to continue his conversation.

After they had eaten a delicious meal, they lingered over several glasses of wine, enjoying the relaxed atmosphere. Finding wine in inns was becoming increasingly difficult, but Mishin was one of the few places that proudly poured the beverage. They talked, taking their minds off their dilemma. They talked of everything, but King Salman, King Ormozd, or anything in connection to Royalty, which could be overheard in the crowded inn. First thing tomorrow, they would focus on gathering information, but tonight, they needed a pleasant, relaxing evening after their long, hard journey.

Persicus told her of his many dangerous and daring escapades into the earth, building the qanats, and traveling to different lands. He told her about the unusual and beautiful customs of foreign cultures. She was jealous of him and his travels, and told him so. Shocked that a princess could be jealous of him, he laughed — a loud, heartfelt laugh, smacking his leg, and using his favorite phrase. She told him of the places she wished to see, many of which he had been to, and described to her in detail. She had an excellent education and knew about many lands and kingdoms, but knowing of them was not the same as seeing them. Forgetting themselves in the wine, they began making plans to travel, Persicus offering to take her on a guided tour of the entire known world. Nooshin laughed with delight, she would love to travel the world with him. But by the time they headed for their rented beds, reality sunk home for Nooshin. It was nice, for a while, to forget who she was, and make plans for a life that was not hers.

Persicus could now see her clearly, as though before today, he'd seen her through a veil of facades. She was continuously surprising him. He saw her letting down her guard more and more each day, she grew more comfortable with him; it pleased him a great deal. He thought that perhaps her being in her home city also put her at ease. The more he listened to her talk of her hopes and dreams, the fonder he grew of her.

Later that night, while they lay on their uncomfortable, lumpy platform beds, the somber reality crept in upon them in the quiet stillness of the night.

For Nooshin, regret of her imagined life of adventure with Persicus drifted away on the verge of sleep to plague her dreams.

Persicus lay awake for a while, playing out the preposterous idea of what life could be, for the twentieth time. He grunted and tried, also for the twentieth time, to put all the ridiculous, impossible ideas out of his mind, and get some sleep.

The travelers and merchants were all in bed, several men snoring loudly, in different rhythms, creating a melody with each unique sound. The crickets and toads outside mingling their own song to the mixture.

Most of the weary souls had traveled long and far, had fallen sound asleep despite the racket. But to Persicus, the annoying rhythmic symphony was close to driving him mad. After a long while, he fell asleep, dreaming of frogs with nasally noses, honking and cooing.

𒁹

A little after two in the morning, the door to the inn screeched open. Aboli paused in the open doorway, scanning the room, assuring himself no one was awake. He crept into the hall, an oil lamp held out in front of him to light his way. Not knowing which bed his victim slept in, he would have to look upon each man, one by one, until he found his prey.

The room was large and rectangular. There were five rows of bed, with six beds per row. The beds were crammed together, head to foot, with less than three feet between one row and the next, to allow for maximum occupancy in the provided space.

He bent over the first bed and studied the man lying there. *Not the man with the scars.* His brain worked at a slow, but methodical pace. His footsteps light and hushed. He went to the next bed and the next, making his way down the first isle, studying each man for a moment.

At the end of the first isle, he found a man that had his entire face covered by a blanket. The hair color was right. He wasn't supposed to make a mistake. He could kill this man quietly and then see if it was the right man. If not, he could continue his search through the room for the right man. *That would not be a mistake,* Aboli thought, *but I am only being paid for one killing. No way am I going to kill two men for the price of one.* He

165

looked back down at the sleeping man. He could always come back to him if he didn't find the man with the scars in any other bed. He moved on.

*Poor stupid weak man. Doesn't know how close he came to death in his sleep.*

Aboli hated weakness. All his life he had been large and strong. When he was young, the other boys had made fun of him. *Well, they aren't laughing anymore*, he thought. Nevertheless, sometimes, he still dreamt of being surrounded by a circle of boys, chanting 'Aboli koon bolboli' or 'Aboli koon koloft darya-ee'. Since then, he had wanted to rid the world of the weak, the people who would stare at him for being strong, as though something was wrong with him. He had learnt control at a young age and now, wouldn't exert himself unless he was paid. Any other reason and he would have to admit to himself that something *was* wrong with him. Besides, there were always weak people, who were too weak to kill other weak people, whom they had their own problems with, which had nothing to do with weakness. The weak would always need him, no matter how much he despised them, though he took certain satisfaction from taking their money to kill, beat, or maim. Hakim was all right—for a weak, old cripple—only because his corrupt machinations made up for his puny, pathetic, deformed shell. But he could do without Hakim's two idiot brothers, though Hakim would have to pay him handsomely for it.

At the last row, two beds in, he stood over the man who he thought was the right one. He looked for Persicus' young, weak companion for confirmation and saw the incredibly weak sapling lying in bed across from his target. *This boy could pass for a weak little girl if you changed his clothes.* Aboli shook his head in disgust. At least he was now certain that he had the right man.

*I should kill the boy, too, for being so abhorrently bantam and weak,* he thought, standing over Nooshin, imaging the kill. *I could kill him with one hand, blindfolded.* He wanted to try, but again, he was not being paid for it. Anyway, without Persicus to protect him, the boy was sure to be mugged and killed as soon as he leaves the caravanserai. It would be a much more horrible death. He decided to leave the disgustingly small boy to die another day. He set his lamp down.

Aboli reached for a long silk scarf that hung over his shoulder. He wrapped each end around his thick, massive hands and stretched it taunt a couple of times as he prepared for the feat. He stepped onto the raised platform, which the beds sat on, and positioned himself beside the head of the bed. He would have preferred to be dead center at the head of the bed, but the beds were flush against each other, so this would have to do.

He glanced around one more time, assured himself that no one was awake, and then stared down at Persicus with a feverish intensity, anticipating the rush he would feel when the life slowly drained out of the man.

He kneed Persicus in the shoulder, hard enough to startle him awake.

Persicus, unaware of the eminent danger, bolted straight up, thinking some drunk had stumbled into him in pursuit of a bed.

At the precise moment Persicus sat up in bed, Aboli wrapped the scarf around his neck from behind, yanking him out of bed, and as easy as lifting a child, pulled him in one swift motion into the air, holding him over the floor as he stood on the platform.

Persicus hung two feet off the floor, the scarf wrapped tightly around his neck, embedding painfully into his flesh. Persicus knew he was in a bad situation. He thought it must be the giant man he had seen early in the evening, as it would be too much of a coincidence for there to be two men close to seven feet tall in town. He didn't know why he was being attacked and at that moment it didn't matter, because he seemed at a loss to stop himself from being strangled to death. He was always able to defend himself, to come up with some idea to get him out of whatever situation he was in, but now, nothing came to mind. He hung there, unable to breathe. He tried to yell, but couldn't make more than a shallow gurgling sound through his mouth. Unable to reach anything, unable to knock anything over in hopes of awakening the oblivious people sleeping soundly, who were unaware of the psychopath in the room, he hung there, mind racing, desperate, panicked. All he could do was pathetically pull at the scarf digging into his throat and try to postpone his death. He tried to wiggle a finger between the scarf and his neck.

The giant tightened his grip, the chokehold turning lethal. Persicus couldn't even manage to squeeze a finger in between his neck and the scarf now. In desperate need of air, frantic, Persicus kicked out with his legs, and found his feet came in contact with the killer's legs. The killer must have brought Persicus closer to his body, perhaps to better feel the moment when Persicus' life slipped away. He tried to brace himself by bearing his weight, pushing his feet against the killer's legs, but his stocking-covered feet offered no friction, and his feet just slid uselessly down the killer's legs. He flailed, with arms and legs. He kicked the giant in the legs and knees as hard as he could, one blow after another, hoping this would in some way disable him, or at least give him some chance, if only a second.

Aboli grunted when a kick landed on his knee, but he didn't let go. *Damned pest!* He needed to hold him farther away from his body to avoid the blows, but he didn't have much room to maneuver. Persicus connected another blow, too close to his groin for comfort. Aboli stumbled forward, almost off the platform, while Persicus went wild. He heard a thump of Persicus connecting another kick with some piece of furniture. Aboli straightened up, secured his footing on the platform, and turned so Persicus couldn't reach anything with his legs. He made it seem effortless.

Persicus felt the psychopath stumble backward, but he could not see; his vision was going blurry, darkness encroaching around the edges. He kicked out again, but his leg only passed through empty air. His arms and legs grew too heavy to lift. He felt the blood pounding in his temples, trapped, trying to flow past his neck. His head felt as if it was going to explode. His strength faded as his vision went in and out of darkness. He could not believe the strength of this man.

Nooshin awoke abruptly when someone jostled her bed. She looked up to see an enormous man standing with his back to her within arm's reach. Alarmed, she sat up, peering around him to find Persicus' bed empty. She crawled to the edge of her bed, suddenly afraid.

Hearing the rustling of bedclothes behind him, Aboli turned his head, and saw the boy crawling out of bed. He would have to deal with him in a moment, after this man was unconscious. He took a couple steps back towards the head of the bed so he could keep the boy in his view.

As the enormous man turned and looked at her, Nooshin saw Persicus, held up in the air, being strangled, his face well past red, turning purple. She screamed for help.

The merchants and travelers awoke with a start. The weary men sat up on their bunks, blinking and rubbing their eyes, some bewildered and confused. She looked around for help, but no one moved from their bunks.

Nooshin ran to the man in the bed in front of hers.

"Help him!" she pleaded.

The man just stared at her as if she were crazy and looked back at the macabre scene. She looked to the next closest man, who was also watching, but also unwilling to help. She looked from one man to the next. Some, upon seeing her pleading look, shook their heads with an almost audible, emphatic *No* before returning their gaze back to the murder in progress, while others completely ignored her. It only took her a couple seconds to scan the faces and realize that no one wanted to get involved.

She looked at Persicus again. His eyes glazed over and rolled into the back of his head. Seeing all white in his eyes terrified her. She would have to save him. *But how?* she thought, scanning the room for some sort of weapon, her heart pounding fast and hard, desperate to find something — anything.

Her eyes locked onto a huge cast iron pan sitting on a table next to the entrance. A large bowl sat in the pan. The pan was used to keep the bowl of water warm while people washed their hands and faces before going to bed, the cast iron retaining heat far better than any bowl would. The pan stood on three short, cast iron legs, so it could be placed in the hearth, sitting above the coals and flames, and had a long handle. She jumped over a man lying in his bed, ran to the table, knocking aside the bowl, splashing filthy water to the floor, and pulled the pan off the table. The pan fell to the floor with a meaty clunk, its weight much more than she had anticipated. She lifted it with both hands and ran to the killer.

A skinny man was lying in his bed, at the head of Persicus' bed, comfortably watching the struggle for life, with his head propped up on the palm of his hand, enjoying the free entertainment.

Nooshin knew she couldn't hit the killer in the head from her height and that was what she needed to do, and this other man was in her way.

"Move!" she yelled at the lounging man. He glanced at her, waving her off as if she were an annoying fly buzzing around his head. She dropped the pan and grabbed his feet, yanking him off the bed with strength she didn't know she possessed. He fell with a solid thump, cursing her in an unfamiliar tongue.

The rest of the men in the room laughed.

She climbed onto the raised platform bed, behind the giant, hoisting the cast iron pan over her head, but again, she underestimated the weight, her strength, and gravity.

As soon as she had it over her head, the momentum and gravity took over, pulling her backwards, pan first, off the bed, and onto the man she had displaced, who was struggling to get to his feet in a tangle of blankets. The man cursed her again, pushing at her as he scrambled to his knees.

The audience sighed an "Ahhh," of disappointment in unison, at her brave, but futile efforts.

Undeterred, she got up again, lifting the pan with her, and scrambled back onto the bed.

Persicus was dying. His body was going limp as she watched — he had stopped struggling and just hung there. His eyes were bulging from their sockets. His face a dark purple, his lips black. Her heart ached. She had to save him and only had one more chance to do it. Having a feel for the heavy pan, knowing her limits, she knew she wouldn't be able to raise it over her head. This time she swung the pan sideways, putting every ounce of her strength into the swing, praying that it would be enough.

Nooshin heard a sickening thud as the pan connected, hitting high up on his back. The momentum of the pan pulled Nooshin around in a full circle and rather than fighting to stop the heavy pan, she spun like a Sogdian whirling dancer.

The giant staggered, hunching over from the impact and pain, but he still held Persicus firm in his grip. Persicus' feet hung limp, touching the ground, but still the giant kept strangling him. Nooshin didn't hesitate. She had seconds before the man might decide to drop Persicus and attack her. Still hunched over, she knew she could nail him in the head. She used this advantage before he could straighten himself. She swung with everything she had left. The pan struck his head. She felt the vibration of it flow from the pan up into her arms and down her spine, reverberating in her bones.

Persicus immediately felt the scarf loosen and he fell to the ground, on the verge of unconsciousness. With a horrible, rasping wheeze, he drew his first painful breath.

Aboli felt a terrible pain in his head. He staggered again and dropped Persicus, as his hands were not working anymore. They felt *weak*. He turned, dazed from the blow, to face that weak maggot who had hit him with a cast iron pan. He couldn't believe that a weakling, such a scrawny excuse for human existence, was trying to fight him. He raised his hands menacingly towards her.

𒀭

Nooshin froze, in utter shock that he could still be standing. She thought he was going to hit her, and that would be it for her.

A thick drop of blood dripped to the ground. He took a step forward, his mouth opened and closed, trying to say something incomprehensible. His eyes rolled back in his head. As if his brain was slow registering the damage, he finally fell, slumped over in a heap, smashing into a small bedside table, wood shattering into pieces.

Nooshin let out her breath in a whoosh of air, exhilarated that she had nailed him.

The crowd gave a mixture of boos for the aborted show and cheers for the winners.

Ignoring them, Nooshin scrambled down from the bed and knelt at Persicus' side, smiling in relief as she saw he was alive, struggling to breathe.

"Are you all right? Can you breathe?" she asked, both exhausted and thrilled. Oddly, she felt more alive than ever.

Persicus was still wheezing, trying to get air. He studied her, with his breath rattling in his chest, relieved that she had not been harmed. He hadn't seen her brave heroics and did not realize she had saved him.

After a moment, Persicus got a full breath down and grabbed her hand. "Are you all right?"

Nooshin nodded. She saw he had a deep, red welt around his neck.

Persicus looked at the giant, who lay in a heap on top of the broken table.

"What happened? Who knocked him out?"

"I did," she said with conflicted emotions, both anxious and proud. "Do you think I killed him?"

Persicus eyebrows shot up in surprise. His face turning back to its normal color. "You?" His voice was doubtful.

Nooshin ignored the tone in his voice. She grabbed his other hand and helped him to his knees.

"Do you know him?" Persicus rasped.

"Me? Why would I know him?"

"I thought maybe he was … somebody after you."

"I've never seen him before."

Persicus crawled over to the giant and pushed him over so he could see his face. Something fell out of his pocket and rolled next to Persicus' knees.

"What's that?" Nooshin asked, squatting down next to him.

Persicus cleared his throat again, giving a sharp, painful cough. "Disgusting." He bent over to get a better look. "It's a chewed up chicken bone."

"A chicken bone?" Nooshin repeated.

"A chicken bone!" A man in the next bed said. "Was that what you idiots were fighting about? In the middle of the night for God sake!"

Nooshin and Persicus glanced at the man dubiously.

The innkeeper, awakened by the ruckus from all the cheering and heckling, had dressed in a hurry, and rushed into the room, overhearing the last comment. "Chicken bone! What's this about fighting over a chicken bone?"

Persicus and Nooshin stood, stepping away from the unconscious man sprawled on the floor.

The innkeeper approached to assess the situation. He bent down, studying the man on the floor. "Hmmm. This man was here earlier, eating dinner. He scared the hell out of me when he came barreling towards me as if he wanted to kill me. He grabbed that bone from the stack of plates. Broke six dishes."

"You want the bone back?" Nooshin asked.

Persicus coughed back a small laugh.

The innkeeper frowned.

"Is he all right?" Nooshin asked. She had never hurt anyone before, much less bashed someone's head in with a cast iron pan.

The innkeeper knelt down, holding his oil lamp over the man. The man's eyes stared back at him, blank and unseeing. He held his hand in front of his mouth and felt for a breath. After a moment, he stood, and went back to the kitchen, his face holding an edge of concern. He came back with a small mirror in hand. He held the mirror over the man's mouth for thirty seconds, and then got to his feet, shaking his head. "I am afraid he is dead."

Nooshin gasped. "Dead!"

"Is he a friend of yours?" the innkeeper asked solemnly.

"No. We have never seen him before. We were asleep when he snuck in and began choking me with that scarf."

"What happened next?" the innkeeper inquired.

"I woke up when he bumped into my bed. I yelled for help. All of these people" — Nooshin gestured to the entire room — "woke up and saw the whole thing, but no one would help me."

At this, all the guests — almost in unison — turned their backs to her, pulled their covers over their heads, and acted as though they had been asleep all along.

"Never mind these cowards. You did good." The innkeeper pat Nooshin on her back, hard, as a man would do to another man.

"I killed him," Nooshin uttered the words out loud, but it still wasn't sinking in. She couldn't believe it, or accept it.

"You saved me," Persicus said, hugging her one armed. He couldn't console her here, too risky.

"The first one is always hard. You'll get better. If you intend to stay on the road, young man, you had better get used to the idea of killing. Listen," the innkeeper motioned them over to the doorway, "he was with three well-dressed men. I overheard some of their conversation. I think they may be related to a very influential family. It won't matter if it was self-defense, not with these people. They will see you hanged or worse. If I were you, I would get out of here as soon as the gates to the city open at dawn."

Nooshin started to protest, but Persicus grabbed her hand, and squeezed it. Prickles of alarm were fluttering around in his stomach. Something warned him that he was missing some crucial piece of information that was essential to their survival. A thought came to him.

"You mentioned three men. Could you describe them?"

"Ah, yes." The innkeeper recalled the three men, bringing them before his eyes from his memory. "Yes, there was a tall man, though not as tall as that man"—he pointed to the dead man lying between the bunks—"but slim in build, you know ... eh, what is the word? Lanky. He was lanky. The second man was of medium height and muscular. He was bald, not naturally, but shaved. And the last man was older, maybe in his sixties. He looked as though he may have been the lanky one's father. They looked alike, though he had thinning, white hair, and a pinched face, like one of those little reptiles. What are they called ...?"

"A lizard?" Persicus offered.

"Yes! A lizard. I hate those vermin. The man got on my nerves just looking at him. You know the kind?"

"Yes," Persicus agreed. He knew more than he would admit, but needed one more crucial piece of information. "Was there anything else, besides his face, that stood out as unusual? Anything at all you can remember?"

Nooshin stood beside him in silence. She knew what Persicus was thinking. That was all they needed to add to their problems. The horrible one-armed Hakim making trouble for them while they needed to be gathering information about what was happening in the Palace and in the search for her.

"Yes, well, he was missing an arm. The left one I believe. I take it you know these men?"

Persicus nodded, his displeasure about knowing these men was clear on his face.

"I think it is prudent you take my advice and leave with haste at the

173

break of day. Try to get some sleep until then. I'll report the death to the officials in the morning."

Persicus agreed. Persicus and the innkeeper moved the heavy body to the back of the room and covered it with a blanket.

After the innkeeper went back to bed, Persicus motioned Nooshin back into the doorway, where they could speak in semi-privacy.

"Maybe we should talk to your father," Persicus suggested.

Nooshin looked panicked. "We have come all this way. If we go to my father now, King Salman is sure to find out, and all our efforts will have been for nothing."

"Couldn't we sneak into the Palace? Don't you know a way inside—"

"No. It won't work. We have suspected for some time that there may be spies in our land, but my father doesn't yet know who it is. The spy could be in the Palace, a part of the army. I don't know. But we can't risk going there. If Salman found out, he might think I disappeared on purpose to avoid him, and have more reason to kill my father." Her face was fervent as she tried to explain, tried to get Persicus to understand.

"Well then, we need to leave. I had no idea Hakim was of any importance to any affluent family." Another thought occurred to him. "He's not—"

"No. No way," she said, reading his mind. "He's not in any way related to my family."

Persicus sighed in relief. "What do you want to do? We can't stay here now. If the innkeeper is right, they will be searching for us in the morning, after he reports the death. Hakim will probably make up some plausible story. It was bad enough before, but now ..."

"All right. We'll leave tomorrow, first thing in the morning when they open the gate. There is a monastery up in the mountains nearby. Father Theodore will help us. He is a good friend of my father. He will hide us there while he figures out a way to get the message to my father in secret."

"And you trust this Father Theodore implicitly?"

Nooshin nodded. "I do. He is noble and honorable. I trust him with my life."

Persicus nodded in acceptance. "Let's try to get a couple hours sleep before dawn.

They went back to bed, stretched out on their bunks, and tried to sleep. However, neither could quiet their assiduously troubled, restless minds. Persicus lay wake, one thought chasing the next, playing out every eventuality. Nooshin was fearfully imagining being caught by King Salman himself, outside of Mishin, where she had no ability to reach her father. He would be cruel and would kill her for her betrayal to him; she had no doubt about that. He may think that she had never been kidnapped and had set up the massacre of her entourage to avoid marrying him.

Meanwhile, Hakim and his brothers waited for Aboli's return. As hour after hour passed, Hakim became worried that the idiot had indeed made a mistake. He was probably dead. Persicus was sure to have killed him, since he is a crafty, manipulative *Tajik*. Hakim was in a state. He should never have entrusted this duty to that idiot. Aboli was great at killing, but he should have known better than to send him after Persicus, that *Tajik!* No, that's not right. Aboli was the best. He found it impossible to believe that Persicus could have killed him.

At dawn, knowing Aboli should have been back hours ago, Hakim conceded to Asif's and Hamzeh's non-stop assault on his idiocy for hiring Aboli to dispatch Persicus. Hakim knew that Aboli's delay certainly meant that he had failed. They set to work on their next plan of action, to get rid of that damned Tajik for the third and last time.

# *15*

## TRAPPED

By morning, Mishin City was abuzz with the news of the midnight murder at the inn. The rumor, swiftly exaggerated to the point of ridiculousness, told that a fight had broken out at the caravanserai inn over a chicken bone—no doubt the work of the man in the next bed. It was said that two muscular men had beaten and clubbed to death a poor, unfortunate, deformed man over a scrap of bone with a cooking ladle. Thus, within hours, it became known as the "Chicken Bone Murder" which made people chuckle when they heard it.

Hakim and his brothers waited in the Palace Hearing Room for an audience with the King of Mishin, King Ormozd, to hear out their grievance.

The room was large and ornate, decorated with centuries of rich history from the people of Mishin. Beautiful and elaborate sculptures, paintings, and tapestries lined the walls, and colorful silk carpets were strewn across floor.

When King Ormozd entered the court and took his seat upon his throne, his bailiff approached him, and explained that three men were here to seek justice for the murder of their beloved servant. King Ormozd inspected the three men standing before him. Instinct told him to be wary of them, but he always judged each case as unbiased as he could, coming to a fair conclusion based on the two sides of the story. Albeit, he always gave his intuition and instinct the proper consideration that they required. He trusted his judgment.

King Ormozd was wise beyond his fifty years. His dedication to his land was second only to his daughter, whom he adored more than life, wealth, and royalty. He would be happy in a small mud-brick home on a small farm, anywhere, as long as his daughter was with him, and happy. The weight of worrying for the last week had surpassed any problem he had had as King in his entire life. His anxiety for his daughter's wellbeing had kept him up, tossing and turning during every long, sleepless night, since he had received word of his beloved daughter's abduction. Somehow, he sensed, deep down, that she was still alive, but that didn't stop his incessant, paralyzing, gut-wrenching anxiety—this unabated, unbearable time spent waiting. He had little patience of late to deal with his day-to-day duties.

Everyone in Mishin loved King Ormozd, as he truly cared for his people, ensuring everyone was treated with respect and equality, and all who lived there were as happy with their city as they could be.

At five feet, ten, he wore modest royal clothing, a rich, deep blue silk tunic with white embroidery, worn over soft, black cotton pants. His noble mien was all anyone needed to know he was King, though he did wear his crown when he needed to, during formal occasions, such as during court or when meeting with other princes or kings, but he never wore it otherwise.

The Royal Crown was made from solid gold. The ancient symbol of the sun rose an inch higher than the rest of the crown, in between two large rubies on the globed top. Engraved to the side of each ruby was the great lion, the symbol of strength. Smaller turquois stones ran around the rest of the crown on the top and bottom.

King Ormozd had fair skin. His deep-set eyes were dark brown with an amber halo around the iris. His usual intelligent, determined eyes were now filled with sorrow. His long shoulder length hair used to be black, but over the years had given way to more and more white, mostly concentrated at his temples. He wore a trimmed, full beard, stopping just below his chin. His once fit and muscular body had softened over the last few years, and was now more portly, since he no longer had time to go on his long, joyous walks around the Palace Garden, or the city, as he always had too many pressing matters that required his personal attention.

King Ormozd waved the three men forward. "Introduce yourselves."

Hakim stepped forward. "My name is Hakim. These men are my associates, Asif and Hamzeh."

"And you are here because your servant has been killed?" King Ormozd asked, his deep voice filling the room.

"Yes, Your Majesty. This fiend, Persicus—I mean, the murderer— has been stalking and harassing us for the past week. I hired him for a simple task and paid him in full for three days labor. These two men are my witnesses." Hakim gestured to his brothers. "Yesterday, we saw him again at the inn in the caravanserai. He sat there, staring us down. He was very menacing and he made me quite nervous. I asked my late, beloved servant, may Allah bless his soul, to talk to him, and ask why he had been following us." As Hakim uttered these words, his voice started to tremble. Asif stepped forward and handed him a handkerchief. Hakim dabbed the tears from his eyes, sniffling, his expression solemn. "Excuse me." Hakim's act was perfect. His voice choked, as if speaking of his late servant was too much for him.

"So what is this nonsense about the fight being over a chicken bone?" King Ormozd voiced a great deal of skepticism.

The courtiers and the bailiff snickered, coughing their laugh into their hands. The King shifted his eyes to his snickering court personnel, who fell silent under his watchful gaze.

"Oh, no!" Hakim exclaimed with distaste. "My servant was an honorable man, Your Highness. He would never fight over a bone. This must be a god-awful rumor. I have known my servant since childhood. He held everyone with the utmost respect due to all, as I have taught him since he was a boy. No, some people, without honor and respect of human kind, have no remorse for the pain they may inflict on other's good name by starting such revolting rumors. It appalls me." Hakim brought on his tears again, digging his fingernails deep into his stump.

"Hmm. I am sorry for your loss in this matter. It is unfortunate timing, as you probably have heard, my daughter, Princess Nooshin is still missing, and most of the cavalry is out in search of her. I can only send three palace guards with you to apprehend this man. He will be brought here when found, so I can get his side of the story, and we'll get to the bottom of this." The King paused, looking from Hakim to the assistants, noting a familial resemblance. "Your story does surprise me. This is a peaceful city. We haven't had a murder here in almost a century."

"Your Highness, I do thank you. But I feel I must caution you as well. This is a very dangerous man. After I hired him, I soon realized that he was beyond my control, and I could not trust him. As you can see" — Hakim held up his missing arm — "I am quite helpless in regards to defending myself. Aboli was not only my faithful servant, but also my guard when traveling. He was as good as any of your guards. No, I think this man, this murderer, is far too dangerous to be taken into custody, and brought here, before you. I fear it would put you in grave danger. I could not abide it if something were to happen to you, Your Majesty. I think it would be wise to kill this man on sight."

King Ormozd was surprised by the suggestion. "Thank you for

your concern, but that is not the way we do things here. Anyone accused of *anything* has the opportunity to give his version of the events. Trust me when I say my guards are more than capable of bringing in one man and I of getting to the truth. I have heard your version of events, but I also know that you were not present during the murder. It happened late at night according to the innkeeper. I find that most suspicious."

"Your Majesty, I think the innkeeper *must* have been deceived. I sent my servant to the inn after dinner. The murderer must have hidden the body until the middle of the night, to cast doubt upon the victim, and make it appear suspicious."

"Well, I will get to the bottom of this matter. In the meantime, I will send three guards with you. That is all I can spare at this time, but I think it should be enough,"

"Thank you! Thank you, Your Majesty! Three guards are more than generous. I am sure we will find this evil man."

After an eventful and restless night, Persicus and Nooshin woke up hours after dawn. They were shocked that they had overslept with all the morning noise of the inn, filled with people getting up, and getting on with their day. They rushed out into the caravanserai courtyard, saddled their horses in haste, and headed straight for the southern gate.

They fought their way through the overcrowded alleys, bypassing the main square. The alleys were packed with horses, carts, mules, vendors, and people walking on foot.

Persicus was berating himself as they made their way towards the gate. "I can't believe I overslept," he said for the sixth time. His irritation increased as they crept along the alley.

"Well, so did I, but you don't see me beating myself up over it," Nooshin said.

"Yes, but I am used to waking up at dawn. You probably sleep as late as you want every day. So you don't need to beat yourself up about it. It's normal for you."

"You're being too hard on yourself. We'll make it. Besides, I get up early every morning with my father. Therefore, based on your logic, I'm as much to blame as you. So, unless you want to admonish me ..."

"You're right," he said with a sigh.

Nooshin thought that would be the end of it. They stopped to allow a man leading his mule to cross in front of them.

Persicus looked over at her. "I can't believe you let us oversleep."

Nooshin startled, looking over at him, then saw he was smiling. She wasn't use to him joking with her. Other than the two jokes he told her that first day about frozen stones and slave ships—which she had thought hilarious when she was younger—he hadn't been particularly flippant or facetious with her. She smiled back at him now, not only at his sudden humor, but also at the memory of his reaction when she had pretended not to know what a joke was.

They turned the last corner that would lead them to the main road and out of the city.

As they approached the gate, Persicus came to an abrupt stop. He reached over and grabbed Nooshin's reins, pulling her close.

"What's wrong?" Nooshin whispered.

"We are too late. They are at the gate."

"Who?"

"Hakim, his brothers, and some guards."

"Are you sure? There is always a gatekeeper at each gate." Nooshin tried to see past the crowd of people congesting the exit.

"Yes, I'm sure. There's Hakim over there, the one in the expensive clothes who's waving his arm at the gatekeeper. They must have gone to see your father first thing in the morning. God knows what lie he told them to get the guards out to search for me. He's probably giving the gatekeeper my description to keep an eye out for us."

"We can use the northern gate. It is eight-thirty now and my father doesn't start his hearings until eight in the morning. They must have been the first case; I doubt they've had time to inform the other gatekeeper yet. I know a way through the city that will avoid the crowds; we will get there before they do.

"All right, let's go. You lead the way."

They struggled through the crowded road, to an alley with small houses on either side. It was virtually empty at this hour. They trotted at an easy, but quick pace, as not to appear suspicious, through the narrow alley that was barely wide enough to pass through side by side on horseback. They made good time crossing the city.

The northern gate stood a couple hundred feet ahead. Nooshin tugged her hat down and lowered her face. As they were about to turn off the small residential street to the main road, it seemed as though the gates to hell opened up. The streets were flooded with an almost solid mass—swarms of shoppers, merchants, vendors, horses, mules, and carts wandering aimlessly about—thwarting their progress, and clogging the road. As Persicus and Nooshin tried to navigate through this teeming mass, it seemed to them that everyone was motivated with a single purpose: to slow their forward progress to a crawl. Some people flat out stopped right in front of them, while others enveloped them on their sides while they admired the wares being sold on one cart or another, trapping the fleeing couple, oblivious to their dire desperation.

They were within a stone's throw of the gate when Persicus and Nooshin came to a simultaneous stop. They watched in helpless horror as pandemonium unfolded before them.

At the gate, twelve long shiny lances, divided into two rows, wavered above the heads of the crowd, as a fearsome cavalry violently forced their way through the gate into the street.

Nooshin knew the cavalry did not belong to Mishin by their attire and aggression. This cavalry had no qualms about injuring the citizens as they trampled through the crowd. All of a sudden, people were screaming and panic reigned as they struggled to get out of danger's way. People scrambled, trying to run left and right, pushing and shoving others who were blocking their escape. Horses caught in the mix reared up in fright and aggravation, throwing their riders into the crowd. Merchandise splattered into the air, raining down on the peoples heads', and then fell to the ground, causing people to trip and fall. Men cursed the cavalry. Women screamed, some frozen in terror, some calling out for their children, lost in the frenzy, and the children cried and shrieked, a heart-wrenching sound, as people surged against them, pushing them further apart from their beloved mothers.

Shouts from the cavalry could be dimly heard over the panic-stricken, screaming crowd.

"Clear the way!"

"Move!"

"Out of the way, swine!" the soldiers shouted, along with other obscenities.

The chaos continued as the regiment cleared the road, forcing everyone aside, smashing hordes of people against the outer walls, a few lucky ones escaping into the narrow alleys.

When the main road was clear, the cavalry stopped, falling into their designated places amongst each other. Persicus and Nooshin now had a clear view of the Turanian Cavalry, on horseback, wearing thick leathers and shields, their lances pointed up in the air over their horse's heads.

Trumpets bellowed, followed by the resonant gong echoing off the walls, and reverberating in bystander's ears.

Nooshin watched the spectacle in outraged astonishment. Never had she seen such devastation, never would her father approve of the way these men man cleared the street in preparation for *his* arrival.

"His Royal Majesty, King Salman, the Magnificent. King of Kings. Master of the Silk Road and the Lands Near and Far! The Light of Your Eyes! The Blessed Shadow of the Almighty Allah on Earth, will honor this pathway by crossing it. Bow all heads down in respect and gratitude for His Majesty, His Magnificence, and may all evil eyes go blind!"

Persicus and Nooshin sat on horseback, gapping. Persicus bowed his head, but Nooshin would never bow her head to Salman ... Never. She watched, seething with hatred so hot that she was certain that Salman should have felt the heat from her hate-filled gaze singeing the coarse hairs covering his putrid body.

The announcer, scanning the crowd for any upturned heads, locked eyes with a Chinese man, who was unfortunate enough not to understand a word the announcer had said. He stood looking at the announcer with a curious expression.

"I said, bow your head!" the angry announcer yelled, drawing his sword half way out of his sheath.

The Chinese man cocked his head to the side, oblivious to the imminent danger; he turned, confused, looking at the sea of downcast heads. The announcer stalked over to the ignorant man just as a hand emerged from the sea of bowed heads and mercifully pushed the Chinese man's head down, patting his head twice, a non-verbal message to stay put.

Satisfied, the announcer went back to scanning the crowd.

Persicus glanced over to Nooshin, shocked that she stared at announcer with a stern, furious defiance. "Bow," he whispered with urgency.

"Never," she said through gritted teeth

He grabbed her arm. "For all your people, to stay hidden, please, lower you head."

She looked pained, but she bowed her head.

The twelve cavalrymen, divided into two rows, pushed forward. King Salman, the Magnificent came into view. He sat upon a plushy upholstered litter, carried by ten muscular porters of similar height.

King Salman was tall, wiry, and oddly muscular in his thin frame. His face was long and narrow, festooned with piercing, mucky-brown eyes that sat sunken deep under his bushy brow, and an unfortunate, wide, and bulbous nose overshadowing his thin lips. A thin, patchy beard accompanied by a long mustache, which began at the outer edges of his wide mouth and ended below his angular jawbone, hung from his face. He looked absurd, but for all his unfortunate looks, his clothes tried to make up the difference. He wore the finest embroidered gold silk from China, which shimmered in the morning sunlight. A gold and jewel encrusted crown sat atop his head — the largest Nooshin had ever seen — taking up most of the space between Salman's head and the litter cover. Black hair peeked out from under the crown, framing his face.

King Salman was flanked by four armed horsemen and followed by another twelve cavalrymen behind his litter.

Nooshin made a sound of disgust as Salman made his way through the parted crowd. "There he is," her voice was hoarse and thick with derision, "my betrothed."

"After seeing that, I can appreciate why you would rather pretend to have vanished off the face of the earth, than marry him."

The raucous procession passed and the crowd, shocked and angry, emerged from the alleys and roadside to consume the road again. Persicus and Nooshin pushed on towards the gate.

"This is impossible," Nooshin said, crestfallen. "We're not going to make it."

"We're going to make it."

"No, we are not."

Twenty feet from the gate, they stopped dead in their tracks. Straight ahead, Persicus saw Hakim and his entourage walking up to the gatekeeper.

"Guardian of the Steppes! Help us out here!" Persicus muttered in disbelief.

Nooshin was resigned. "We didn't make it."

They looked at each other for a moment; motionless, in silence, and then they turned and retreated into the alleys. Both gates were now out of the question.

"There isn't a third gate, is there?" he asked doubtfully.

"No ... no."

"Well, what do you want to do?"

"Let me think." Nooshin bit her nails while she tried to think. Her mind was numb and racing down blind roads of panic, and each road led her to an unwanted marriage and a destroyed city. She couldn't think of anything else, much less come up with a plan to get them out of Mishin.

"Let's go to the Palace, get a hold of your father, and —"

Nooshin grabbed Persicus' arm, her face alight. "No! Wait ... There is a third way out!"

"Great! Which way?"

"We can't go now. We would be discovered. We'll have to wait for the cover of darkness. And it might be dangerous. We have to be careful."

"Define dangerous," Persicus said, full of skepticism.

"Through one of the water canals. We have to ... I mean, you will have to lift a very heavy gate, and then we can swim out of the canal, to the river on the other side of the wall."

Persicus' eyes widened, his eyebrows shooting straight up. "Water canals?"

"Yes, we can escape by the water canals. Come on, I'll show you." Nooshin led him through the alley towards the outer wall. They stopped by a pool of water, which flowed from an archway at the bottom of the wall. Within the archway, a thick, solid, metal grate prevented access in or out.

"See those little arches in the wall? They are connected to the river. When my ancestors had this city built, they incorporated these archways into the walls of the city, so that if we were ever under siege, we could never be cut off from our water supply. The river feeds directly through these archways."

"That means we have to let the horses go." Persicus' voice held a mild regret. His beautiful Heavenly horses. "But where can we hide until dark?"

Nooshin thought about it. "The grain storage building. It is not far from one of the water canals. And I'll buy you new horses. The same kind. Don't worry." She pet her magnificent chestnut horse's mane. She had grown fond of these animals, too.

"Sounds good, but first, we need to get another goatskin."

"What for?" Nooshin asked.

"Trick of the trade. If the water is rough, or too deep, you can drown. Fill the goatskin up with air and it helps keep you afloat."

"We have a skin."

"We need two. One for each of us, in case we get separated."

"Clever. Where did you learn that trick?"

"From the nomads. They cross raging rivers, with all their animals and belongings, by making wooden rafts with inflated skins tied all around the rafts. They are a very resourceful and ingenious people when it comes to survival. Those skins have saved me from drowning in the qanats on more than one occasion.

They crossed the city to the caravanserai, where they purchased an extra goatskin, some leather strips to tie the goatskins, and a length of rope. Then they went two doors down and purchased food for the night. This almost exhausted Persicus' gold he had received from Hakim.

The grain storage was a single, large room hidden in what appeared to be an ordinary house from the outside. Wooden shelves lined one of the walls. Across from the shelves, barrels stacked three high sat in organized rows, neatly labeled with fresh white paint, filled with oats, wheat, barley, and a variety of vegetable seeds. To the right, hay waited for winter in a huge mound. Other supplies filled the shelves in clay jars and wood containers.

They had left the horses in the caravanserai stable and carried a bag of food, goatskins, rope, and two blankets back to the storage house.

They spread the blankets on the floor, padded by hay, on the far side from the door, and stretched out to wait the day away, hidden from sight. Exhausted from the lack of sleep the night before, Nooshin fell asleep within an hour, while Persicus tried to stay alert.

Persicus awoke to the sounds of multiple horses and clacking armor close by. He held his breath, listening.

A search party had been sent out. He knew it by the sound of the horses' quick trot, the abrupt stop, and then pounding on the doors of the neighboring homes. Muffled voices carried through the walls. He heard people complaining about the banging on their doors and soldiers calming the people, asking them questions about the wanted man.

It was evening and deep shadows had since claimed the room while they slept. Persicus woke Nooshin by placing his hand over her mouth so she wouldn't cry out when he touched her. Her eyes flew wide open and he leaned above her, putting a finger to his lips.

"What's happening?" she whispered.

"A search party," Persicus whispered back.

Moving with quiet caution, he stood, and crept over to the door to hear better. He heard pounding on another door, a little closer. They were going door to door. He hurried back behind the mound of hay.

He told Nooshin and she squelched a sob, biting down on her hand, staring at the mound of hay that blocked their view of the door as if she could see through it.

"We should hide," Nooshin whispered.

Persicus quietly covered a blanket with a thick layer of hay, shoving their bags under the mound. If they came in, they could slip under the blanket, and hopefully go undetected.

The search party passed and a moment later, they heard banging on the door farther down the road. They continued to wait and listen, not daring to move. A few minutes later, the clatter of hooves returned and came to a stop outside. Muffled voices carried through the wooden walls, getting louder.

Persicus grabbed Nooshin, motioning for her to lie down. He lifted the blanket, careful not to let any of the hay fall or slide off, and he slipped under the cover beside her, folding the edge of the blanket with him so it wouldn't be visible.

Nooshin's breathing came out heavy, panicked. Persicus heard the door open and heard the clink-clank of the guards' uniform as they walked in. Persicus put his hand over Nooshin's mouth, trying to quiet her breathing.

"He won't be in here," one of the soldiers remarked, his voice coming from the doorway. "Only the locals would know about this place and this guy isn't from around here. Besides, it looks like a house from the outside."

"Well, we had to go to each house," the second soldier said. "Anyway, when the boss asks if we looked everywhere, I want to be able to tell him we did."

Persicus heard movement further into the room. The guard walked, clinked, and clanked around the barrels.

The air was suffocating under the hay-covered blanket. The smell of must, dirt, and dried grass filled the tight space. Persicus held Nooshin under the blanket, making sure she didn't move.

They heard the clink-clink-clank of the solider moving towards the mound.

Clink-clink-clink. He walked behind the mound. Then a sudden silence. Persicus and Nooshin froze, holding their breath.

"Satisfied?" the voice from the doorway said.

There was a pause. Persicus could almost see the man straining his senses, seeing through the hay, tasting them on the air.

Finally, the man replied. "Yeah. Let's get out of here. This place is giving me the creeps, like someone's watching me."

The other guard laughed. The footsteps retreated and a moment later, the door closed.

They waited until they heard the soldiers mount their horses and head down the road.

"You can breathe now," Persicus said, letting out his own breath in a heavy sigh.

Nooshin let out her breath in a rush and gasped for the air that she had deprived herself. They crawled out from under the hay-covered blanket and sat in a dumbfounded silence, uncertain of their safety.

Unable to sleep again for fear of not hearing the guards in case they made a second visit, they huddled together under the blanket in the cool, dark storage building, waiting for the veil of darkness to cloak the city, and aid their escape.

# *16*

# THE UNWELCOME GUEST

King Salman and his two generals were shown into the reception hall, overlooking the garden. The rest of his entourage was waiting outside the Palace. King Salman was asked to wait for King Ormozd, who would be with them shortly.

The reception hall was a large room adorned with beautiful, carved, wooden chairs softened with thick decorative cushions on the seats and backs. The chairs sat facing each other in a semi-circle in front of a large stone fireplace. A low table, with a bowl of fruit and nuts, was placed between the chairs and fireplace. Colorful, elaborate paintings and tapestries decorated the walls. Thick, woven Persian carpets softened the tiled floors. Flowers of all kinds filled the corners of the room, sitting upon pedestals in beautiful glass vases.

King Salman examined the room with unveiled distaste and disregard. His two generals followed his example, turning their noses up in repulsion at the artwork and flowers.

The Generals, Mahmood and Ahmad, were brothers originally from central Persia. They were both exiled from their province after committing repeated unspeakable acts, including perversions and corruptions against their fellow villagers. Thus, they appealed to King Salman, suiting his needs nicely.

Mahmood and Ahmad were both tall, well built, and muscular. They both shared features from their shared father: close-set, beady eyes; large noses; dark olive skin; and full lips. From their father, both had inherited a morbid fascination for pain. Ahmad was several years younger, born from his father's favorite wife, and from her he had inherited a refined sense of taste. Ahmad had a full head of dark brown hair, streaked with gray at the peak, while Mahmood had a receding hairline, with salt and pepper hair. Both wore their beards in the same fashion: thick, coarse hair falling past their chins; their mustaches, long and curving around their lips to blend with their beards. Both clad themselves in the same clothing, distinguishing themselves in their pristine uniforms as high generals in King Salman, the Magnificent's army.

The Generals would do anything for their King, as he allowed them to come up with the most proficient and thrilling ways of extracting information or otherwise torturing, stealing, and humiliating people beneath them. And everyone was beneath them, with the exception of King Salman himself. Their alliance with King Salman worked well for both the King—who had use for such ruthless men as these—and the brothers—who were able to do as they wished, being rewarded and praised for their crimes, rather than suffer exile or execution. They worshipped King Salman as they worshiped the great Allah himself.

ᵣᵣᵣ

King Ormozd was still in the hearing room, settling disputes. He held court three times a week, sometimes less when possible. He was in the middle of hearing a disagreement between two merchants when his personal guard entered the court from the side entrance and made eye contact with him. Anoush never did this unless something urgent came up that required the King's immediate attention.

"One moment please," Ormozd said to the merchants, waving his guard forward.

"What is it?" Ormozd asked.

Anoush leaned forward and whispered in Ormozd's ear.

King Ormozd rolled his eyes skyward. "Here?"

Anoush nodded and whispered again.

"Now?" Ormozd said, surprised. *Salman, here again*, Ormozd thought. *That's just what I need, as if enough hasn't gone wrong.* "What does he want?"

Anoush shrugged. "I don't know. He didn't say what the purpose of his visit is. He made a devastating scene at the city entrance. I've had several reports of people injured by his cavalry, who trampled their way through to the main square."

"*Damn* him. Any severe injuries?"

"Several. No one died, thank Ahura Mazda."

"You said he is in the reception room?"

188

"Yes."

"All right. Stand guard outside of the reception room. If he leaves that room, come tell me immediately. I'll be there after I settle this dispute."

Anoush nodded and hurried out of the room.

King Ormozd returned his attention to the two men standing before him.

"Luan, it is clear to me that you have defaulted on your loan. You agreed to pay back Braham twenty-four silver coins within forty days. What have you to give Braham to settle this debt?"

"I have three daughters, ages eight, ten, and fifteen. He can take his pick. I think that would more than settle my debt."

King Ormozd face turned red with anger. Braham slid a sideways glace to Luan, uncomfortable with the offer.

Ormozd fixed his searing eyes on Luan. "How long have you been living in Mishin, Luan?"

Luan shuffled his feet, glancing down. "About five years, Your Majesty."

"That is long enough for you to know that we do not trade humans here." Ormozd turned to the other party. "Braham, is there a guarantor on this loan?"

Braham cleared his throat. "No, Your Majesty. Luan is my friend. I trusted him to repay me."

King Ormozd tapped his fingers on the arm of his throne, thinking of a fair decision. "My ruling in this matter is: Luan, you shall pay Braham his twenty-four silver coins, plus two more in interest every week from today. You have forty days from today to come up with this. I want both of you to return to court in forty-one days. If the debt has not been repaid, Braham may take either fifty percent of your silk business for six months, up to fifty silver coins, or the value of fifty silver coins in merchandise. That will be up to Braham which he chooses at the end of forty days, if the debt has not been paid." He turned to his clerk. "Did you get all of that?"

The clerk nodded.

"Good. Show them where to make their marks for understanding these terms, then we will sign as witnesses."

The two men moved to the side of the room, where the clerk was waiting.

King Ormozd stood and addressed the remaining people waiting to have their cases heard. "I am sorry, but I have some urgent matters to attend to right now. We will recess for the midday meal. Rest assured, I will hear the rest of your cases by the end of the day."

King Ormozd slipped through the door behind his throne, into his private chamber. He removed his crown, rubbing his temples with his fingertips. He needed to prepare himself for dealing with the ruthless and ambitious King Salman.

The small room was filled with documents of his rulings, organized by date, and by what needed follow up. Old, smaller dispute contracts were eventually burned, only preserving the select, more serious offenses for reference and records of crimes. For the most part, all serious crimes happened in the caravanserai. The people of Mishin were generally peaceful. He sat in his comfortable chair, leaning his elbows on the table, trying to clear his head, rubbing his throbbing eyes. He wondered why King Salman had come back, unannounced. He was certain it would have to do with his daughter and he prayed Salman wouldn't wage a war, so soon after Nooshin's disappearance.

Ormozd thought of Luan offering one of his daughters for payment of his debt and he felt disgust with himself. He was certain Nooshin, his beloved daughter, had no desire to marry Salman. She sacrificed herself to save him from the travesty of war and he had allowed it. He couldn't believe he had allowed it. It had all happened so fast. One minute she was there, offering herself to Salman, the next she was gone, as if stolen from him, that very day. He didn't even have time to think it through. If he ever saw her again, he would tell her she needn't marry King Salman, that he would prefer to die than have her suffer for the rest of her life as a willing prisoner of that man. He felt no better than Luan—and all the rest of those ignorant people who valued women as no more than property, commodity, or one-third of a man's value—who would trade his daughter to get out of a bad situation.

Steeling himself for the confrontation, he stood, replaced the crown upon his head, and exited through another door that opened to the main hallway. He walked briskly through the large corridor into the reception room, with a sudden eagerness to get the preliminaries over with.

"My dear King Salman, what an unexpected surprise." King Ormozd succeeded in keeping his voice neutral.

King Salman turned to face King Ormozd with his generals flanking him on both sides. Salman nodded a greeting "Ormozd."

King Ormozd stopped halfway into the room. He understood the insult implied by leaving out his title. He frowned. King Ormozd was born of Royal Blood, unlike Salman, who had fought his way to self-titled King. Salman equated respect with fear and fear with power.

Ormozd covered his frown by his next question. "I suppose you have heard about my dear Nooshin?"

Salman smiled, nodding his head. He turned, pretending to inspect the room as he spoke. "News of the tragedy reached me on my way to meet her, no doubt before the news reached you." When Salman's eyes fell back on King Ormozd, they were filled with unconcealed rage. "I cannot believe that anyone who knew better would dare attack *my betrothed*. The King of Turan's wife! I promise you, whatever lowly, ignorant peasant is responsible for this delay shall come to a very unpleasant and painful end. We have started searching the nearby villages today. I will get to the bottom of this."

King Ormozd winced at the thought of all the innocent people in the nearby villages being searched by Salman's cruel army. He had injured several people just making his entrance into the city. Who knows what the local villagers are enduring at this moment? King Ormozd made a note to have Anoush send a few guards to check into what devastation may have befallen the surrounding villages.

"What makes you think my daughter has been taken by any of the local villagers? It appears that this was no small group of petty bandits or any peasants. I think Nooshin was attacked by a large, organized group of criminals." *No doubt, like your organization,* Ormozd thought. "My cavalry recovered the bodies of her guards and servants, they were found closer to Turan than Mishin. Over thirty good men and women were slaughtered. It is a great tragedy, but I am thankful there was no sign of her at the site. All indications point to her being taken alive. No one in Mishin, or the villages nearby have any large group of organized bandits, and that is what would have been necessary to successfully implement a full-blown attack on her heavily guarded caravan."

Anger flared in Salman's face at the insinuation that his search plan lacked intelligence and was doomed to fail.

"Searching the local villages is a waste of your valuable resources," Ormozd added to try to pacify him.

Salman waved his hand dismissively, flopping into a chair with an air of ownership. "My men are much better at searching and gathering intelligence than your men." Salman laughed, short, loud, and contemptuous. "You haven't had a battle here in ages. My men are most competent and utterly professional, which is why the wisest thing you have ever done is to become my ally. I am the only man who can ensure the survival of Mishin." Salman leaned his arm across the back of his chair, crossed feet propped on the low table. "Since I have ordered a thorough search, I *will* find the bandits that have taken my Queen.

Besides the villages, my men have searched the mountains, the valleys, and caves between Turan and Mishin. So far, we have found no trace of her, but wherever she is, I will find her. I will leave no stone unturned. I have sent messages to all of the surrounding Khanates, friend or foe, and put out a hefty reward for any information that can help us find her assailants."

"Thank you. That's very thoughtful of you," King Ormozd said, trying to sound pleased. He didn't want Salman to see that his belittling comments were laughable to him, nor did he want to insult him, and have his wrath upon the city, but it took more will than it should have to be cordial. Ormozd cleared his throat. "I was not expecting company today and have not prepared for a guest, so if you will excuse me, I will make sure the kitchen staff prepares something suitable for you. I am sure that you are hungry. I have some other important duties that I must attend to. A room will be prepared for you, where you will be comfortable until I return."

Salman looked Ormozd up and down, moving just his eyes. "Yes, do so. Then we must have a long chat about this situation. But first, I need some wine to relax—make sure it is the good wine you keep for yourself." Salman turned away, dismissing King Ormozd.

King Ormozd spoke from the doorway. "Here in Mishin, we have many different varieties of wine. They are all good. I will have them bring you a few carafes and you can choose your preference." He walked out of the room, shutting the door firmly behind him. He breathed a sigh of relief.

Anoush was waiting in the hallway. Ormozd gave him orders to have the servants tend to Salman's needs and then returned to his private chambers, where he would have a small lunch, and then finish his hearings.

King Salman walked to the window and looked out at the unimpressive view of the garden, to the city, and valley beyond.

"Beautiful garden, isn't it?" General Mahmood asked, standing beside Salman.

Salman waved his hand in a dismissive gesture. "Eh. I could have done much better than this garden, if I was not so occupied with all my campaigns," he said, referring to his non-existent garden. "When I have time, mine will be the best garden in the world."

"No doubt," Ahmad agreed, staring out the large window.

"Do you believe that nonsense he was saying?" Salman asked.

Mahmood shrugged. "I don't know much about wine, they all are the same to me."

"I wasn't talking about the wine, you moron," Salman said, his voice full of impatience.

"Beg your pardon. What were you referring to?"

"The sudden disappearance of the Princess!"

"Oh, well … ah …" Mahmood turned to his brother unsure what to say. Ahmad stared back at his brother, hollow eyed.

"Don't you two see what is going on here? When I first came to see Ormozd, with the intent of taking over, of course, Ormozd kept trying to delay me by saying he would consider my offer, and let me know. Since I had other campaigns going on, this was perfect for me as I made my way conquering villages west of Mishin. The next time I met with Ormozd, I also met his daughter. I gave Ormozd the deal of his life. I offered to allow him to retain his position here in Mishin as my governor, collecting taxes for me, as long as he gave his daughter to me. She jumped at the opportunity to marry me, but on the other hand, Ormozd showed no enthusiasm about his daughter's marriage. Any other king would have been elated at the prospect of their daughter marrying me and saving themselves in the process."

Mahmood nodded. "That is odd."

"No, it is not. These Sogdians are not as stupid as they pretend to be. All they have to do is look at a map of the region to see that they are the last enclave between my lands and the main trade route, where all the wealth of our world travels through. To take the trade route, I need to take Mishin. As you know, no one stands against me anymore, but Mishin is much larger than the smaller cities we have conquered so far. They may have chosen to fight us, but with Nooshin as my wife, I could get rid of this obstacle without bloodshed, and save my army for Persia, the biggest prize to the west." Salman paused, looking from Ahmad to Mahmood. "But now, with the Princess' *disappearance*, it seems that maybe, *just maybe*, they have chosen obliteration, rather than the safety of my protection. If that is so, it will create a delay for my campaign against Persia."

"You will be fighting the Caliphates. The Persian Empire is dead and its inhabitants are no more than slaves now," Mahmood reminded him.

"Yes, yes, I know. It's amazing that they were taken over by such an insignificant, barbaric tribe, but that just shows that it can be done. However, first, I must rule Mishin and the main trade route. Marrying Nooshin is the first step towards our westward expansion. Lucky for me, she is also beautiful, young, and healthy. She is the perfect specimen to give me many good sons to carry on the great tasks of building my empire."

"But you think something fishy is going on?" Ahmad asked.

There was a firm rap on the door.

Salman gave his generals a warning glance to keep quiet. "Enter."

Two men walked in carrying four glass carafes of wine and three glass cups. They set them on the table and poured a small amount of wine into one of the glasses.

"Your Majesty. By order of King Ormozd, I present you with these wines. Please, try them and see which you prefer."

"My preference is no concern to you. Leave them all and be gone with you."

The servants hesitated, not use to being spoken in such a harsh tone.

"I said, leave," Salman growled.

"As you wish," one of the men replied, pulling the other out the door with him.

Ahmad began to speak, but Salman cut him off, holding out his hand in request for silence. When the servants' footsteps faded, he turned, and filled the glasses with a wine the color of rubies. He handed a glass to Ahmad and Mahmood, and picked up the last one for himself.

"Now, where was I? Oh, yes. This business with the Princess' sudden disappearance. It is convenient that it was on her way to Turan for our marriage, don't you think? If we are to believe Ormozd, abducted by a large group of marauding, highly organized bandits, that no one has seen, no one has heard of, and who could attack without leaving a miniscule trace of evidence, or trail to follow." Salman sat in one of the chairs.

Ahmad came to stand to beside Salman. "It sounds suspicious to me."

"Damn right, it sounds suspicious." Salman slammed his cup down on the table, the wine splashing out of the glass, dribbling down, staining the Persian carpet.

"Not to worry," Mahmood said, his voice flowing with confidence. "I ordered fifty horsemen to keep watch on the outskirts of Mishin and the neighboring villages. Any suspicious activity will be brought to our attention right away."

"And if Ormozd is hiding his daughter outside of this Palace, we will find her," Ahmad added. "Someone will see her. The reward is too great for any peasant to pass up."

"And if she is hiding right here, in this palace?"

Ahmad looked Salman straight in the eye. "We will find her. Our spy has been asking his neighbor, who is a Palace Guard, about the Princess' whereabouts. She is not here."

Mahmood nodded. "Our spy is good friends with this guard. He hides nothing from him."

"Good," King Salman said, refilling his wine. He took a tentative sip. "Now, what do you think of this wine?"

"Excellent!" Mahmood said, twirling the wine in his glass.

"Very strong." Ahmad took a sip, slushing it around his mouth. "Rich, tart."

"I can make better wine than this." Salman proclaimed, taking another sip. "I simply do not have the time."

"Of course, Your Magnificence." Mahmood replied sympathetically. "You will someday soon."

King Salman leaned back in the comfortable chair, feeling sad and alone. He raised his now empty glass in the air and Mahmood refilled it.

# *17*

## THE MOONLIT ESCAPE

The sun had set, but the minutes ticked on slowly as Persicus and Nooshin waited for the neighborhood to fall asleep. Darkness enveloped the city as clouds covered the subtle moon and star light, deepening the night's gloom. Across from the Palace, the Fire Temple sat on a hill, its domed top rose above the narrow, arched windows. The light from the Sacred Fire flowed out of those narrow windows, not quite bright enough to illuminate the surrounding hill with its soft golden glow. The Sacred Fire within was eternal and had never been extinguished, not for hundreds of years, maybe a thousand, and hopefully it would stay lit for a thousand more.

Nooshin couldn't see the temple from where they were hiding, but she could see its comforting light reflected against the darkened clouds above the temple. Her anxiety eased when she could see that comforting light still burning, letting her know life continued on in the city. All was not lost. Not yet.

The night waned on. When all was quiet outside, when the neighboring houses had extinguished their lamps hours before, Persicus cracked open the door, and peeked out into the small, deserted alley. Nooshin waited behind him, pacing nervously.

"All right, it looks clear." Persicus opened the door wide, turning to Nooshin. "Which way?"

She slid out in front of him. "Follow me. It's not far."

They walked down the alley, keeping close to the shadowed walls, their footsteps light and hushed. At the end of the alley, they turned a corner, and followed the road until they came upon the pool, streaming in through the city's outer wall.

"This is it. These canals are located every three blocks, all along this side of the city."

Persicus stood, inspecting the pool of water. He couldn't see anything past the arched opening, where ink-black darkness pooled. "The grate is inside there, right?"

"Yes. And it's a heavy one; thick, solid metal. It always takes two strong men to lift it."

"All right." Persicus wondered if he would be able to lift it by himself. "Where do we lift it from?"

Nooshin pointed at the wall to their left. When Persicus peered at the wall, he almost missed the staircase protruding out from the stones, flush against the wall. The narrow staircase shot straight up at a steep angle, leading to a stone landing and a wooden door, halfway up the wall.

"This way." Nooshin led him up the stairs.

At the landing, high above the canal, Nooshin knelt beside Persicus, pressing on stones in the wall to the left of the door.

"It should be one of these." Nooshin grew frustrated as she pushed on stone after stone, uncertain if she was remembering correctly. She felt a stone shift. "This one. Pull this one out. There's a lever behind it that will open the door.

Persicus stepped around Nooshin in the small space. He grabbed the edge of the stone with his fingertips and tried to pull it out. Unable to get a good grip on the stone, he shifted it back and forth, wiggling it out from its housing.

Nooshin stood, dancing in place, pleading with him to hurry, feeling far too exposed.

Persicus set the stone down on the landing. He reached into the hole, wrapped his hand around the lever, and pulled. It was stiff, resisting, and then shifted down with a thud. A high-pitch squeak issued from the door as it eased open an inch.

The door groaned as Persicus pushed it open, rusty hinges creaking and squealing. They peered into the absolute darkness of the windowless room within the inner battlements of the city wall.

A small dog began barking nearby. It triggered a chorus of other dogs in various pitches around the neighborhood.

Persicus and Nooshin jumped inside the darkened room. Voices came from several directions, yelling at their dogs, grumpy at being awakened in the middle of the night by their incessant yapping. They held their breath and peered outside, down into the street, until they were certain no one had seen them.

Inside the hollow room, noises echoed from every direction. After a moment, the dogs settled down, a few stragglers giving half-hearted barks until everything fell quiet. Nooshin and Persicus turned back to the darkness for the task at hand.

"I don't think anyone has opened this door in years," Persicus whispered.

"The last time it was opened, I was ten years old. I watched with my father while they were making repairs. There should be an oil lamp hanging on the wall by the door."

Persicus ran his hands over the cold, damp stones and found the lamp. He dug his flint out of his pocket and lit the old, rancid oil. A small flame flickered up to reveal a small, square, dusty room. The air was thick with humidity, must, and mildew. The walls glistened. In the center of the room stood an apparatus comprised of a thick wooden pole suspended by two sturdy posts over a square hole. A large wheel with spokes and handles was attached to the post on the right. A heavy, rusted chain wrapped around the pole and descended into the dark hole below, where it attached to the grate in the canal below.

Persicus stood over the hole, staring down into fathomless darkness. His hands grew clammy and he felt the suffocating darkness rushing up to meet him. All of a sudden, he was hanging over the abyss in the underground river, hanging onto the ledge, the rapids surging below, waves catching his legs, trying to pull him down into the despairing depths of —

"Persicus? Persicus, are you all right?" Nooshin touched his arm.

Persicus took a deep breath, coming back to himself. He shook his head, ridding himself of the lingering feeling of desperation he had felt, clinging for his life over the dark abyss in the underground river. "I'm fine."

"Did you hear what I said?"

Still, Persicus stared down into the darkness as if mesmerized. "What?"

"Are you sure you are all right?" Nooshin asked, concern creeping into her voice.

Persicus shook his head. "Yes. Sorry, I got distracted, but I'm fine. What did you say?"

She eyed him, worriedly. "The chain is attached to the grate in the water down below. When you turn the wheel, the gate lifts up. We go downstairs, slip under it, swim through the canal, and get out of here."

Persicus studied the wheel. "Once I turn the wheel, how do we lock it into place?"

"That metal rod over there slides into these two openings and will hold it open. It should be secure." Nooshin pointed to the rod mounted on the wall. "The hard part is turning the wheel. The grate is heavy."

Persicus walked closer to the wheel, shying away from the hole. He gripped the wheel in his hands, getting a feel for it. He pushed, hard. The wheel was rusted and didn't budge an inch. He tried again, pushing harder, straining.

Nothing. Not even an inch.

"This is going to be tough. I am going to try to turn it by pushing with my feet, with my back against the wall. Can you lift the rod?"

She picked up the rod. It was heavy, but no heavier than the huge cast iron pan. "Got it," she said.

"Good. Put it in place when I tell you. I won't be able to do both."

"Well, what am I paying you for then?" she said, her face impassive.

Persicus' eyebrows shot up. "Paying me?"

He saw the corner of her mouth twitch, which, he had come to realize, was her restrained smile. He grunted, rolling his eyes at her. He pushed his back against the wall and propped his feet against the wheel.

"Ready?" he asked her.

Nooshin nodded.

Persicus began pushing with his legs, his back digging into the stone wall. His knees, bent. It wouldn't budge. He pressed harder and harder, grunting with the effort. The wheel moaned in protest and shifted an inch. Two inches.

As he inched the wheel forward, his legs straightened out until his body stretched parallel to the ground. When he could go no further, he grunted out, "Now! Now!"

Nooshin rammed the rod in and the wheel locked into place. Persicus collapsed to the ground, his muscles aching with the strain.

She knelt down beside him. "Tired?"

He looked up at her, rubbing his leg, hoping he hadn't pulled a muscle.

"Well, come on then, Hercules; we need to hurry." Nooshin's tone was sarcastic, though she was secretly impressed, she would never admit it.

Persicus stayed seated, rubbing his aching thighs. "Hercules? Like the Greek God? If you are going to compare me to anyone, I would prefer Rostam."

Nooshin gave a soft laugh. "Oh, no. Rostam was only human. Hercules was the son of a god and a human. So he was much stronger."

Persicus smiled as he got to his feet. "Exactly. Hercules was half-god, so his achievements are not as impressive as Rostam, who was completely human, with no divine aid."

"So, you would rather be compared to a man who killed his son, rather than an extraordinary demigod. All right, but either way, Rostam would not have been tired after lifting one grate."

Persicus shook his head, rolling his eyes skyward at the absurdity of the conversation. "I'm breaking out of Mishin through a water canal, with a missing princess, with the Royal Guard searching for us both, whispering about Hercules and Rostam. Where did I go wrong?"

"I think it was when you killed the man at the inn last night."

"*You* killed him."

"And you never even *thanked* me."

Persicus shook his head again. *Why do I even try?*

"Do you think the grate is lifted high enough or should I prove to you I am better than any dead man and lift it some more?"

Nooshin sighed and got to her feet. She had enjoyed the amiable banter. Persicus had a way of taking her mind off her anxiety, even if only for a brief moment, it was welcome.

"I think it should be enough. Let's try not to wear you out. We still have a long way to go on foot. We can always come back up, if we need to."

They extinguished the lamp, closed the door, replaced the stone into the wall, and rushed down the stone steps.

Standing over the pool of water, staring at the archway, into the canal, Persicus tried to see the grate, but could see nothing but darkness.

"I'll go check if it's open enough. Stay here. I'll be right back." He eased himself into the water. "How wide would you say this wall is?"

"Oh, I don't know … maybe fifteen feet."

Persicus took a couple deep breaths, slid quietly into the cold, dark water, and disappeared from view.

Nooshin stood at the water's edge, staring into the inky blackness. Time seemed to stretch out eternally while she waited for him to resurface. She felt extremely exposed. Exposed and defenseless without Persicus at her side. Her hands ached for a weapon—a dagger, a sword, *a cast iron pan*. She suddenly *knew* Salman was watching her. She felt him standing behind her, reaching out his disgusting hand to grab her. She spun around on her toes, arms up to ward off the evil menace. But there was nothing there. Her eyes searched the alley. *There's no one there*, she reassured herself, not quite willing to believe. Her anxiety was clawing up her throat, threatening to spill out of her in a piercing shriek.

Nooshin turned back to the black water and dropped to her knees, pleading for Persicus to hurry. Another thought seized her and she was now certain something terrible had happened to Persicus. Maybe his clothing had caught on something down there and he was drowning, while she sat up here waiting … doing nothing.

She squelched a sob as the surface of the water broke and Persicus emerged from the canal.

"It's wide open. I got clear to the other side," he said, breathless. "The water is freezing and it's very dark down there. The water level reaches up to the bottom of the wall. That means you have to hold your breath all the way through to the surface on the other side. It can get disorienting in the complete darkness underwater. Do you think you can do it?"

Nooshin nodded. Due to her panic, she felt dizzy and disoriented already. She took a deep breath. It was only nerves, she thought, until she realized she was terrified. She hated swimming, she was terrible at it, and here she was about to jump into a canal, in the middle of the night, in the freezing water, into a flowing river, and worse yet, it was her own idea.

Persicus took the rope he'd bought earlier that day, tying it around Nooshin's slender waist, tying the other end around his own waist. "The current is pretty strong on the other side. The rope will keep us tethered to each other. Try to stay close to me, but if you can't, don't worry, we won't be separated by much. Whatever happens, don't call out my name. We don't want to alert anyone that we are here. If you're in trouble, tug hard on the rope, and I'll come get you."

Nooshin nodded again.

"Are you ready?" he asked.

"Yes." The single word trembled from her lips.

Persicus helped her down into the water. She winced as the freezing water enveloped her body. In an instant, her teeth began chattering and her breathing turned rapid.

Persicus eased down into the water after her. "Control your breathing. Take a few deep breaths."

She slowed her breathing, trying to get down a full breath.

"On the count of three. One … two … three."

They ducked into the water.

It was pitch-black. Nooshin couldn't see the faintest form or figure or shimmer of reflected light, not even Persicus, who must have been only a foot away. She swam straight ahead. At first, she was sure of her direction, but within moments, she became confused. Her hands reached out slowly in the opaque water, trying to feel her way. She felt a tug on the rope and then Persicus' hand gripping her arm, pulling her forward.

The surface of the stone wall danced against her back; she used it to guide herself through the tunnel. She knew it was only a short distance, but panic gripped her, clutching at her chest, making it hard to hold in her breath.

She kicked out with her feet, until, with great relief, she felt the rough current of open water pushing against her, and knew she had made it through. She surfaced.

She took a deep, gasping breath as the cold night air stung her face. She clung to the side of the wall to avoid the heavy current.

Treading water, she looked around for Persicus, and felt a pull on the rope. He was reeling her towards him from five feet away.

They had made it to the other side of the wall, but they still needed to cross the river.

Above, the moon peeked out from the charcoal clouds, filling the night with its silvery light.

Nooshin reached out to Persicus, splashing a little water with her arms. Persicus grabbed her around the waist with one arm, his other hand clinging to the slick, flat surface of the wall.

Footsteps echoed down from the battlements. Two guards, making their rounds in the battlements at the top of the wall, stopped.

Persicus and Nooshin froze in the icy water.

Voices floated down.

"Shh! Did you hear that?"

"No. What did you hear this time?"

"I thought I heard something down there."

The two guards peered down into the river. Their silhouettes in clear contrast against the moonlit sky.

"I heard something down there. I'm sure of it."

"You're *always* sure of it."

"I'm serious this time."

"Really?"

"Yes! Listen ..."

Persicus hand was slipping. He treaded water with his legs, as softly as he could, worried that they might hear more than the gentle lapping of water from the current. He kept telling himself they couldn't hear anything over the running water, but one of them had heard them. Nooshin was trembling in his arms, he wasn't sure if it was from the cold or fear. Either way, if they didn't get out of this water soon, it would be too late.

"There's nothing there."

"I heard it all right," the guard said. "My father used to warn me about the river monster, Mamali. It lives north of here, in Cattula Land. It has razor-sharp teeth and the body of a giant snake, with fins as sharp as claws. Every night, under the cover of darkness, it swims south to Mishin River, and beyond. And if you are down there, or even standing next to the river, he will jump out, grab your leg, and bite it off in one pass."

"That's ridiculous. Your father made it up to scare you."

"No way. It's absolute truth. My baba would never lie to me."

"Oh, yes he would. That's what parents do, they tell you stories about monsters for their own sick amusement, but then they get frustrated when you believe in the monsters, and get scared in the dark, and they tell you you're acting like a baby for believing in monsters. I tell you, if they hadn't screwed you up to begin with, you would've never been afraid in the first place."

"Oh, really? What about Old Man Farhad?"

"What about him?"

"He lost his leg to Mamali!"

"You idiot. He lost his leg when he was a boy. He was thrown off his horse and a merchant's mule pulling a cart ran over his leg. An unfortunate accident. Let me tell you what my father would tell me to scare me lifeless. Do you remember the old abandoned cemetery outside the eastern wall?"

"Yes. All the children were afraid of that place. Damn, I'm even still scared of that place."

"Of course you are. But my sick, sadistic father beats your Mamali. He would tell me about the night he lost his bowels in his pants, when he saw a pair of red glowing eyes staring at him from under a cracked gravestone one evening, as he ..."

At last, their voices faded. Turning numb in the water, they waited until the sentries footsteps faded away as well.

"Did you know about this creature?" Persicus whispered, his tone accusing.

"Yes, but don't tell me you believe what he was saying?"

Persicus shook his head. "I don't know anymore. Last week, I didn't believe in dragons protecting lost treasures and it was almost the death of me."

"It wasn't a dragon. It was a Komodo dragon," she insisted through chattering teeth.

"Exactly. It was a dragon." Persicus looked downstream. "Well, we have made it this far and there is no turning back now. I can only hope Mamali is still home in Cattula Land and he won't be biting off our legs tonight."

Nooshin held onto a thin crevice in the wall, while Persicus grabbed one of the goatskins tied around his waist, and began filling it with his breath. Persicus hadn't anticipated being in the water so long waiting for the guards to depart. Now, too cold to fill both goatskins, unable to draw a full breath, teeth chattering violently, the cold squeezing his chest and lungs, he struggled to fill one completely for Nooshin. He tied the inflated goatskin around Nooshin's chest with the same length of rope

203

that tethered her to him.

They moved away from the wall and began swimming across the river, trying not to splash water or make much noise. As they navigated across the river, their limbs spasmed in jerky strokes. The closer they got to the center, the stronger the current became. Struggling to stay side by side, the river surged, sweeping them downstream, farther and farther away from each other, until the rope stretched taut between them.

Nooshin was worn out from struggling against the heavy current. Exhausted and numb, she finally relied on the goatskin to keep her afloat and the rope to keep her tethered to Persicus, while she made feeble attempts to paddle herself towards the riverbank. Small waves slapped at her face, causing her to choke, spitting up water. The current picked up, rapids surging downstream. Persicus was lost from view when Nooshin passed under the stone bridge. They had just passed the city gate, but it felt much further than that.

The current picked up speed again and the river swiftly became rough rapids, caused by the scattered boulders submerged deep underneath the surface of the water.

Persicus had lost control of his forward progress across the river. He knew from experience he couldn't fight the current and could only wait as the river carried him downstream for the opportune moment to get across, when the current calmed. He was silently cursing himself for not instructing Nooshin more before descending into the water, but in the deceptive darkness, the river had seemed calm when they had ridden by the night before. He knew better than to expend his energy struggling against the current when he would need it later. He knew, but he was hoping Nooshin would realize it as well.

Nooshin struggled against the rapid current, trying to get across the river, while the current rushed on, straight ahead. It was a losing battle. The freezing water—melted snow from the mountains—robbed her of most of her strength. She found it increasingly hard to move, much less swim. A sudden strong current pulled her under. She gasped, sucking in water as the undertow dragged her down. She tried to kick out her legs, but she found it near impossible to move in the paralyzing, numbing cold. Desperate, she clutched the goatskin to her chest with one arm, terrified that it would be ripped away from her. The goatskin pulled her up, sputtering, to the surface. Her breath expelled in shallow huffs, coughing, white mist exuding from her lips like smoke.

Another rapid gripped her and she went under with the current again. Another torrent ripped the goatskin's leather cinch away. With terrifying clarity, she felt it decompress, no longer aiding her, but dragging her down under its weight. She held her breath as she ordered her fingers to work, to untie the rope that held the goatskin to her, which tethered her to Persicus.

Persicus had tied the knot tight. Too tight. She managed to get one numb finger through the knot and started tugging herself free. The goatskin slipped away and she fought her way to the surface, thrashing and writhing, managing to hold onto the rope with one hand. She reached the open air, but her strength was failing her. She wouldn't have the strength to keep herself afloat for long. Her limbs felt impossibly heavy.

"Persicus!" she cried out, but her voice was weak and choked, and she was certain that he could not hear her plea for help.

She kept going under, waves crashing down on her head, and then pulling her back to the surface. Each time she went under, she wondered if it would be the last. If the current would hold her down this time.

She cried out again. "Persicus!"

She went under for the last time, the deluging power of the water forcing her down, as if the river had a consciousness, and it wished for her death. She held her breath, screaming for her arms to move, her feet to kick, but they just thrashed around with the undertow, until she was yanked up again. She felt something solid behind her and twisted around, craning her neck she found Persicus at her back, holding her tight.

*Ahura Mazda! Thank you!* she thought. A wave a relief flooded her.

"I've got you," Persicus yelled over the tumbling rapids.

"Don't let me go!" she said in a weak voice, clinging to his arms. "My goatskin is gone."

"I've got you," he assured her. "I won't let you go."

She felt his arms like a firm anchor around her stomach. It was the best thing she had ever felt. She relaxed into his secure embrace.

"How do we get out?" she asked, spitting water, teeth chattering, and shivering.

"Don't fight against the river. We just have to go with the flow. When it calms, we can get to the riverbank."

They continued down the river. They must have been two or three miles from Mishin by the time the water calmed enough to escape its cold grasp. Persicus swam sideways to the riverbank, holding Nooshin with one arm. He felt the precious ground under his feet and picked Nooshin up in his arms as he carried her out of the river.

Persicus slid on the slick surface and fell onto the muddy riverbank, with Nooshin still in his arms. Nooshin fell face first into the mud with Persicus landing on top of her. She turned her head to the side, wheezing out short, rapid gasps. They lay on the muddy bank until they caught their breath.

Persicus rolled over onto his back.

Nooshin got up on all four, staring down at her ruined, mud-covered clothes, her hands buried deep in muck. Her hair hung down in wet muddy globs. Her arms looked black in the darkness. "I used to be a Princess," she said dryly.

Persicus turned his head to look at her and smiled. She was caked in mud, which would dry like baked bricks in the heat of the fire. Tomorrow, she would look the same as Persicus did when he had first seen her. When she screamed at him, thinking he was a demon. He suppressed a laugh, thinking that maybe he should wake her up in the morning by screaming at her.

Then he saw the first tear glittering down her cheek, reflected in the moonlight. Her lips quivered, but not from the cold. She fought to maintain her composure.

"It's going to be all right. It's just a little mud, it'll wash off." Persicus took her in his arms, hugging her to his chest.

She was shaking her head. A sound escaped her lips and that sound seemed to break the thin control she was holding onto. She cried, clinging to him. "I can't do this. I'm a Princess. I belong in the Palace, not here ... covered in mud. I can't do this anymore. I almost drowned in the river, fell in mud, I was kidnapped, dragged across the country, walked for miles. I watched my best friend get killed! I'm dressed as a man. I *killed* a man! Killed him! Ahura Mazda!" she wailed, weeping. "This isn't fun. I can't do this. I'm not made for this life."

Through her hysterics, Persicus held her tight, rubbing her back in slow circles, comforting her as best he could. He wanted to promise her that everything would be all right, but he couldn't make that promise. So many things could go wrong and thanks to Hakim, had already gone wrong. He had wanted revenge, but now, holding Nooshin, he just wanted Hakim to go away so he could keep Nooshin safe. If Hakim interfered again, he would gladly kill him, and it wouldn't be for revenge for trapping him, and stealing the gold.

Her tears slowed, he held her until she lay quiet in his arms. She pushed away from him. "Sorry." She had to do better than this. "I'm all right now. I think almost drowning and falling in the mud was just too much." She looked down at herself and laughed, a short abrupt sound, almost a sob. "I look like you when you crawled up out of the ground."

"Yes, I was going to scream at you when I woke up in the morning, but I think you've had enough excitement."

Persicus needed to start a fire and quick. He was tired and he could have fallen asleep right there, in the mud. He contemplated heading farther away from Mishin before stopping to make a fire, but they had gone down the river quite a way. They were also off the main road, by the riverside, so he figured they should be safe. Regardless, if they continued on in wet clothes, in the cold, damp night, they wouldn't get far.

"I need to go find some wood," Persicus said between convulsions. He got to his feet on the slippery slope of the riverbank and held out his hand to help Nooshin to her feet.

After they gathered enough wood, they huddled next to each other by the warmth of the fire. Persicus emptied the small sack of essentials he had brought with him. He reattached his dagger, set their hats by the fire to dry, and pocketed his flint.

Nooshin scraped away at her face, attempted to wring the mud from her hair, and scrubbed at her clothes, only managing to smear the mud more completely over herself. Persicus watched in amusement.

"What?" she asked, looking over at him, her muddy hands tangled in her muddy hair.

Persicus shook his head and laughed. He scooted closer to her and wrapped himself around her, blocking the cold wind, and lay down with her facing the warm fire. "You're still a Princess," he whispered.

She didn't protest when he wrapped his arms around her. She turned into him with a contented sigh and wrapped her arms around his back. Exhausted, she cuddled into the bend of his arms. They lay shivering, until they fell fast asleep, entwined under the sporadic moonlight.

As the sun rose over Mishin Valley the next morning, a small twenty-man regiment of the Turanian Army was returning to Mishin City from their interrogations of several small villages on the outskirts of the valley. They were to report to King Salman in the Palace for further instructions.

The General held up his hand, signaling his men to stop. He stared intently off to his left at a cloud of white smoke rising in a lazy stream into the sky near the river.

"Abdul Kabir, Abd Al-Ala, Abisali, and eh ... Rami," the General called out to his troops.

The four mounted men crept forward. "Go check out who is down there and report back to me. If there's anything suspicious about them, bring them back to me."

"Ya wanna us ta see if they has any information about the Princess?" Abd Al-Ala asked.

General Ghulam winced at his cousin's language. The man couldn't speak properly if his life depended on it.

Abdul Kabir and Abd Al-Ala were twins, though one got the brains and the strong body, while the other was small, weak, and stupid. Though family is family, he could not show favoritism to one twin and not the other. They were a package deal. Ghulam knew this. Abisali was his sister's husband. Nepotism ran high in his regiment, although no one else was related to him in his regiment, his kin was his right hand.

The four men headed towards the smoke, through the brush, to the riverside.

They found two men snuggled next to each other, fast asleep by a dwindling fire. The two men looked terrible, wearing filthy, torn clothing.

Abdul Kabir jumped down from his horse and stood over the sleeping pair, a smile playing at his lips.

"Well, ain't that sweet!" Rami said, with a broad smile, leaning forward on his horse.

Abisali snickered. "That doesn't look sweet to me. Looks like a one-way ride to the blazing fires of the seventh gate of Hell."

"Now, now," Abdul Kabir said. "Maybe they are related."

Rami eyed Abdul Kabir suspiciously, wondering if the twins slept arm-in-arm.

"Don't look like they's related to me," Abd Al-Ala said.

"Come on; let's get out of here and leave these two love birds alone. They are nothing to us." Abisali said.

One of the sleeping men stirred, raising his surprised face up at the voices.

Persicus awoke and immediately saw that four soldiers surrounded them. He gulped and shook Nooshin awake. With as much nonchalance as he could muster, he said, "We've got company."

Nooshin woke up, bleary eyed. Propping herself up on her elbow, she looked around at the cavalry. She tried to keep the shock and fear off her face. She was relieved that she had woken during the night, cold, and put her hat back on, hiding her hair.

"What are you two doing here?" the lead guard asked, with obvious amusement.

"Us ... we ... uh," Persicus tried to clear his mind of sleep so he could come up with a good lie. He rubbed his eyes, stalling. "We ... We lost our way last night and decided to camp here." He didn't think these men were after him—the murderer—but figured they were out patrolling the area, looking for Nooshin.

"Were you in the river last night? You two look like hell," the same man asked, still amused.

"Yes. We crossed the river, but the current was strong, and we were swept away. That's how we lost our way." Persicus was relieved he gave a plausible story.

The four men burst out in laughter.

"Well, no wonder you look like hell. What kind of idiot would try to cross a river as big as this one at night?"

"Ah! I know. You're a Tajik, aren't you?"

"How dare you!" Nooshin burst out. "Under whose authority are you harassing us? I—"

Persicus' mouth dropped open. He grabbed her arm, hard.

The soldiers fell quiet, surprised by the sudden outburst from the effeminate young man. Their faces turned serious, their laughing smiles wiped away.

Persicus needed to defuse the situation.

Persicus moved protectively between the soldiers and the Princess. "Oh, Sirs! You must forgive my little brother. You know how it is with teenagers. We have all been through it. At that age, they think they are the center of the universe, and nothing can convince them otherwise."

"Maybe you can't, but I think I can," one of the soldiers said. "Gentleman, the young *man* here asked us a question … and he deserves an answer." The largest of the guards jumped off his horse and firmly pushed Persicus to the side. He looked down at Nooshin, with one hand on the hilt of his sword, and the other hand in a fist on his hip.

Nooshin lowered her face, staring at the ground, hoping he would back away.

"Please, sir. I am really very—" Persicus began, but the soldier pushed on as if he had not spoken.

"You want to know *whose* authority we are speaking under. Well, I will tell you. We are the First Regiment of the Great, the Undefeated Turanian Army; Serving the Greatest King of the Silk Road, and All Cities Between Turan and Cattula: King Salman, the *Magnificent*!"

Nooshin kept her eyes diverted, staring at the ground, acting as though she were a sulking teenager.

"I am sure you have heard of him? Haven't you? *Haven't you!*" he yelled the last.

"Of course, of course, all know of his Magnificence." Persicus reinserted himself between Nooshin and the soldier. "King Salman. The light of our eyes and the blessed shadow of the Almighty, of the earthly and insignificant creatures called men. Isn't that so, my young brother?"

Nooshin nodded, face hidden, eyes still cast at the ground as the man loomed above her. She crossed her arms in defiance and took a couple steps back.

Persicus wrapped a protective arm around her, his face set in discipline mode, as though he was chastising her for her defiant, adolescent behavior.

"You two wait here." The soldier turned and walked a few steps back to the other men to converse.

"Now is not a good time for a royal outburst," Persicus whispered into her ear.

"I am sorry. But I cannot abide these presumptuous foreigners questioning and insulting us in my own country." Her voice was outraged and her eyes seethed with anger. "They come with swords, hiding behind religion, ordering us around as if they own the land, demanding we follow their ridiculous laws! Pretending like *they* are the civilizing force of the world, when they are nothing but brutal, tent-dwelling barbarians!"

"Be quiet over there. I don't want you two talking behind our backs," one of the soldiers yelled and turned back to his men. He nodded in agreement with another soldier and walked with a quick stride back over to Persicus and Nooshin.

"You two have to come with us," he said with a pleased smirk.

"Come with you? For what? To where?"

"We have orders to bring any suspicious characters in for questioning. You two are definitely suspicious."

"But we were just on our way home to our mother … We need to get home to —"

The soldier held up his hand. "I am sure they will let you go after questioning, *if* they find you are not guilty of something."

"But —"

The soldier drew his sword and pointed it at Persicus. "Quiet! I don't want to hear anymore. Follow us and be quiet. Mishin City is just up the road and that's where you can plead your innocence to King Salman."

Persicus weighed his odds against the four armed men. There was nothing he could do. As good as he was, with only his dagger, he could probably handle two of them, it was not enough. Two guards moved in behind Persicus and Nooshin and the other two flanked their sides. The men escorted their captives up to the main road, to the General.

ᛏᛏᛏ

"Well, what have you found, Abdul Kabir?" General Ghulam asked, tapping his horsewhip on his leg.

"Two suspicious men." Abdul Kabir pushed Persicus forward in front of the General.

General Ghulam looked down at Persicus. He leaned forward on

210

his horse, squinting his eyes, thinking this man looked familiar. He tapped his whip on his leg. "What do you have to say for yourself?"

Persicus had his head down, but he saw the General tapping his leg with a horsewhip. *No, it can't be.* "I was ..."

"Look at me when I am speaking to you," Ghulam said, his voice raising.

Persicus rolled his eyes upward, keeping his face down.

General Ghulam froze, his eyes widening in surprise. "You!" he yelled, angry, pointing an accusing finger at Persicus.

"Me?" Persicus said, feigning confusion.

"You! You sent me to Golmud on a mad camel chase! I never found any Chinaman on the road *or* in the city!"

"I ... I ... I was sure he was going there. That is what he told me. Maybe he lied to me," Persicus stammered.

The General's eyes shifted to the other young man. He looked him up and down and settled on Nooshin's hat.

"That hat!" General Ghulam pointed with his whip in hand. "That ugly nomadic hat! You said you found that hat by that stream, but I see the hat belongs to someone after all."

Persicus was cursing himself silently. *How could this have happened?* Desperate to think of something, anything, he began rambling. "Yes ... eh ... well. I did find that hat. I met this young man later on and he needed a hat, so I gave it to him."

Nooshin scrunched her eyes, seeing his mistake.

Abdul Kabir broke in. "Wait a minute. Wait a minute. You told me this was your little brother!"

Persicus looked from one man to the other. It became apparent to him that he really wasn't a good liar. He had screwed everything up and Nooshin would pay dearly for it. He hung his head down while he tried to think of a way to salvage the situation.

"Wait just a second!" Nooshin said, stepping forward.

Persicus startled and gave her a warning glance.

Nooshin ignored him and plowed on. "He is not lying. I am his little brother and we met up two days go as we had planned, to go home to our mother's bedside. He came to get me from our father's home to bring me to my mother's sick bed. He did find that hat and gave it to me as a present."

Ghulam didn't believe a word of it. "Oh," he said leaning forward on his horse, tapping his horsewhip. "And your mother and father do not live together?"

Nooshin gulped, thinking. "Yes, they do. But my father has been unable to take care of her during her illness, so she went to stay with her parents."

SAEED & SHIRIN DERAKHSHANI

"That is good. That is very good. But I don't believe a word of it. He lied and you are covering up for him. You two are not related. Abdul Kabir, Abd Al-Ala. Tie them up. Let's bring them to King Salman and see what he has to say about all of this."

Abdul Kabir and Abd Al-Ala closed in on Persicus and Nooshin with please smiles plastered across their faces.

"No!" Nooshin and Persicus cried out together. "You can't do this."

"I can! And I will. I think King Salman will be quite upset when he learns why we wasted a day searching in Golmud for a mysterious Chinaman." He caught Persicus' eye. "But he will be very pleased that we have found the cause of our delay and I will look forward to watching King Salman come up with a suitable punishment for you. Both of you!"

"Hand over you weapons," Abdul Kabir ordered.

Persicus hesitated.

"We can do this the easy way, or we can kill you, take your weapons and money, and leave you here as food for the beasts of the night."

Persicus spread open his caftan and withdrew his dagger. "This is the only weapon we have." He handed the dagger over to them, hilt first.

"You," Abdul Kabir pointed at Nooshin, "open your caftan. Let us see for ourselves that you have no weapon."

She spread the ends of her caftan open. General Ghulam nodded in satisfaction.

Abdul Kabir handed the dagger to General Ghulam. Ghulam weighed it in his hand, inspecting the expensive blade and handle. "Well, well, well," Ghulam said, "who did you steal this from?"

"It is not stolen," Persicus answered with his own growing anger.

"I expect you will give this dagger back, when you realize the grievous error you have made," Nooshin said.

"King Salman will decide if and when he gets this dagger back." General Ghulam tucked the dagger under his uniform.

212

# THE TRUTH UNRAVELS

King Ormozd strode down the hallway from his bedchamber the morning after King Salman's surprise visit. Anoush nodded to his King from his post and fell into step beside him.

"Report?" King Ormozd asked, as they walked down the long hall.

"Salman and his generals woke up less than an hour ago. They wondered why their breakfast was not waiting for them when they awoke. Salman issued forth a volley of obscenities and threatened our staff. I came in when I heard the yelling and told them breakfast is always served in the garden at seven. I escorted them there and they are impatiently waiting."

"Good grief. Are the staff all right?"

"Yes. They were a little shaken. I told them they may go to their chambers to collect themselves for a few minutes … They deserved the extra break after dealing with the three tyrants."

"Good. Good. Let all the staff know I will include a bonus with their pay this week, in light of the extra work our guests are creating."

"I am sure they will appreciate that." Anoush hesitated as if he wanted to say more, but was unsure how to proceed.

King Ormozd sensed his reluctance. "What's wrong?"

"Uh … Do you know how you said to make sure Salman was comfortable and had everything he needed?"

"Yes."

"Yes, well, Salman and his generals went through ten bottles of wine last night."

"Oh? Well, that is all right. We have plenty more."

"Well … uh" — Anoush cleared his throat — "in the middle of the night, one of the kitchen staff was finishing up his chores when he heard a loud crash and went to investigate. He found one of Salman's generals had raided the cellar, we think to get more wine. The General passed out, collapsing into a wine rack. The rack then crashed into the second rack and so on. Broke every bottle. We had to call on the physician to come bandage him up in the middle of the night. The physician cut his own hand trying to pry a broken bottle from the Generals hands."

King Ormozd tried to put on a suitable facade of concern, but broke out into laughter instead.

Anoush felt a wave of relief that he wasn't going to be held responsible for not watching over them better, not that Ormozd had ever treated him unfairly.

"Don't worry, Anoush. The wine is replaceable. I think it is worth the embarrassment of the General, don't you?

"Yes, sir."

"Can you send out for some more wine right away? And was someone assigned to the clean up?"

"Yes and yes. The cellar is being repaired and cleaned. But I'm afraid there is more."

King Ormozd stopped and turned to face Anoush. "Oh?"

Anoush grimaced. This was the news that Anoush dreaded delivering. "This morning one of the maids came to me. She said that she had found two sealed amphorae of wine in King Salman's room. She said they were sitting in his traveling chest under his dirty clothes, which she had gone to collect and wash."

King Ormozd eyes widened in surprise. "Oh. Who am I kidding. I am not surprised. So he has stolen the last two bottles of wine. Let him have it. He can't get wine anywhere else, as he has forbidden it in all his land."

Nervous, Anoush wrung his hands. "It was the two amphorae of your three hundred year old Shiraz. From your library. The maid recognized them."

King Ormozd stood at the door to the garden. His face flushed red. Those two bottles of wine had been a gift from one of the first vineyards in Shiraz, given to his forefather, almost three hundred years ago.

The amphora — still commonly used in the rest of the world, however Mishin now sold their wine in bottles and decanters — were made of clay, with a long body, a narrow neck, and a flared opening at the top. A curved handle was mounted on both sides, starting under the flared lip, and ending at the top of the base.

These two amphorae had almost identical images painted along the base of the body. One featured a scene of traditional Shirazi woman raising a cup of wine in a toast, her eyelids half-closed as if in utter contentment. She lounged on a carpet, yellow mountains cresting a background of sea-blue sky. Pomegranate trees and flowering vines crawled in the foreground. The other amphora had a traditional Shirazi man lounging on a carpet in a similar position. A stamp marred the clay, identifying the wine as Shiraz and the kind of grape used to make the wine as Vitis Vinifera. It was one of the best wines that came out of Shiraz or the known world. No date or vineyard name was listed, so no one could say where these bottles of wine came from, or when they were made. This was to protect the vintner from repercussions of their oppressors.

A hundred years before the vintner of Shiraz gave these amphorae to Ormozd's ancestors, the barefoot barbarians had invaded the region, spreading their fanatical religious-based laws like a plague throughout the East. Now, four hundred years later, with most of inhabitants forcefully converted, enclaves like Mishin still fought against this fast-growing plague that had taken the citizens of Persia from an advanced and modern age, back into the plights of superstitious, ignorant darkness of centuries past.

The wine amphorae were a symbol of the strength of the people of Shiraz: their refusal to capitulate, their refusal to worship a foreign god, and their refusal to give up what had always been a part of their heritage and tradition—their wine.

For generations, the amphorae had sat in the King's private library, which remained off limits to anyone who did not reside in the Palace. Only the Royal Family and their staff were allowed admittance into this room. This was one of Ormozd's favorite refuges. The amphorae had sat mounted above a large fireplace, a reminder to never submit to tyranny.

To this day, the people of Shiraz couldn't openly make their precious, highly praised, and in demand wine. They still made it, but in less quantity, in hiding, and at a great risk.

And now the very man who had banished wine in his own territory, the man who was threatening Mishin's freedom and sovereignty, had stolen the precious wine, and with it, all that it stood for.

Ormozd lowered his voice. "Never mind. Go get that wine, right now. Salman can't object about it being missing, because he stole it. But if he

215

does, we don't know anything about it, and we suggest that his general probably drank it before sneaking out of his quarters, and destroying our cellar."

Anoush nodded and headed down the hall. He stopped after a couple of steps and turned back to his King. "Besides, if he opened those amphorae, the wine would be rancid. I don't think Shiraz used Terebinth tree resin for preservatives back then."

As Ormozd watched Anoush turn the corner at the far end of the hall, he thought about why Salman would venture into the library. Ormozd was certain that Salman never read — he doubted he even could read — so he was not looking for a good history book in his drunken stupor. Ormozd concluded that Salman, in all likelihood, had inspected the Palace, learning the ins and outs, preparing himself for when it would be his own. When he saw the amphorae, he thought that it was Ormozd's personal wine. He remembered Salman's demand to bring him wine. *Make sure it is the good wine that you keep for yourself*, he had said. Ormozd suspected that Salman had snooped elsewhere in the Palace. He would need to send someone room-to-room to check on other possible damages and thefts.

King Ormozd turned towards the garden, still standing at the door, and gazed at the immaculate paradise. It was almost seven and breakfast would soon be served. He took a few slow, deep breaths, calming himself down before going out into the garden to face Salman.

The garden surpassed the beauty of any garden that had ever existed. In the Avesta, gardens are known as pairidaēza — a walled paradise, which was true of this garden. King Ormozd and Nooshin had had breakfast every morning in the garden, until the day she left for Turan. And every day since then, when he stepped into the garden, his heart constricted as if being squeezed of life. As a child, Ormozd had played with his father in this garden; in turn, he had played with Nooshin here during her childhood, amongst the peach, cherry, and pomegranate trees that surrounded the garden. Mature trees yielding their delicious fruits while shading this paradise year after year. They were all in bloom, filling the air with their sweet fragrance, their scents mingling with the Persian jasmines, narcissus, and hyacinths that lined the stone paths. The paths wound through the garden, leading to a large rectangular reflecting pool in the center of the garden. Ever-beautiful Parrotia and Mulberry trees dotted the garden. Nooshin would often choose a path and sit under the shade of a vine-laden trellis, where she could sit for hours, contemplating why the bees, butterflies, and humming birds favored the Guliabrisham so much. Was it the pink, silky, thread-like flowers that exploded from their limbs, or was it simply the succulent nectar that they favored? Nooshin called them, her silk flowers, because each flower blossom had hundreds of thin pink thread, each as soft as spun silk.

Spring was Nooshin's favorite season and she spent much of her time in the garden with its beauty in full bloom. She always loved to watch all the small, colorful birds splashing in and out of the shallow pool. She had spent hours simply watching the birds.

Just past the reflecting pool stood a raised square garden platform, encompassed by a low wooden wall with intricate carvings of delicate birds perched on tree branches, covered in small leaves and flowers. Four stone steps led up to the platform on either side. Thick Persians carpets covered the platform floor, intricately woven with the same theme of garden trees, flowers, and colorful birds, woven in such detail that it looked as if the garden extended onto the platform floor, as if the birds could jump out and fly away. Bright colored, thick, silk cushions were strewn across the platform floor, around a low wooden table in the middle of the garden platform.

Salman and his generals, Mahmood and Ahmed, sat on the cushions around the table. The sacred garden platform, where Ormozd had so many fond memories, enjoying blissful mornings with his daughter. He couldn't stand the thought of Salman invading this precious space, his precious memories.

King Ormozd heard footsteps behind him. He turned and saw three servants carrying breakfast on trays. He raised his hand, stopping them. "Would you please take the trays to the Dining Hall. We will have breakfast there until Salman and his men leave."

The servants nodded and turned back down the hallway without a word.

King Ormozd walked out into the garden. "Good morning, Salman. We will be having breakfast in the Dining Hall this morning. I think it might rain today."

"Rain! There's not a cloud in the sky," Salman responded.

"Well, I don't know, maybe you're right, but one of my sentries said he saw a flock of birds leaving the area. They always flee when rain is coming. Breakfast is ready and waiting inside."

Ormozd didn't mind lying to Salman. Salman was a dishonorable man who had done nothing but lie and give subtle threats to Ormozd since the day he set foot in Mishin.

"Why the hell did your servant tell us to wait out here? The idiot. I will not tolerate such incompetence. He needs to know he cannot waste my time. I will have to have a stern *talk* with him," Salman said, getting to his feet.

"Now, now. It was my idea to have breakfast inside. He was following my usual daily routine. He is my personal guard and he is very good in this duty. He will not be reprimanded."

"You need to learn how to rule people and be King, Ormozd. Fairness has no place in ruling a city. People must *fear* you, or they will not respect you."

"I hope you all had a good night's rest." King Ormozd changed the subject.

Salman came down the platform steps and his generals followed. Ormozd casually examined the Generals. General Ahmad had a white cloth bandage wrapped around his head. A little patch of red had seeped through at his temple. Several small cuts were visible on his hands. King Ormozd lip twitched as he restrained a pleased grin. All three of them had bloodshot, glassy eyes. Ahmad looked pale and nauseated.

"Yes. It was a very good night indeed. After months on the road, sleeping in tents, I had forgotten how good it is to sleep in a room with solid walls and a soft bed." Salman's tone indicated that his life of hardship had been forced upon him.

"It must be hard," Ormozd said with feigned sympathy. He led them down the garden path, through the door, and into the hall.

Salman waved, grunting as though it was only a small nuisance. "It is nothing. The end justifies my suffering."

King Ormozd stopped outside the Dining Hall and turned to face Salman. "When will you settle down Salman? Are you not getting tired of all of these little campaigns? Life is too short."

Salman smiled, a slow spreading of lips and bared teeth. "I am almost done with my campaigns. I will have Nooshin awaiting me in Turan when I return — once I find her, of course — and then I will settle down. She will give me many sons, who will grow up to continue my life's work. And, of course, you will be here running things for me and all will be well."

Anoush came around the corner, leading Hakim, Asif, and Hamzeh down the hall.

"Good morning," Hakim said, his voice cheerful, a bright phony smile spread across his face.

King Salman's eyes widened in surprise. "What the devil are you three doing here?"

"I came to see King Ormozd in court. We have some follow-up business that needs some attention. I did not know you were here, though we heard about the tragedy. It is a horrible thing that has happened. I don't know what is happening to this world. It seems you can't trust anyone anymore: murderers, kidnappers, and thieving bandits. All over. It sickens me." Hakim shook his head in disgust.

Wearing solemn faces, Asif and Hamzeh nodded in agreement.

Ormozd frowned, looking from Hakim to Salman. "I am sorry …

Do you know each other?"

Salman narrowed his eyes at Hakim. "Yes. Unfortunately, my Aunt Fatima gave birth to these three spoiled brats," King Salman said in a bored voice, gesturing to his cousins: Hakim, Asif, and Hamzeh.

King Ormozd nodded, his eyes shifting back to Hakim, who just smiled. His suspicions about Hakim were now founded. Hakim was related to Salman and the other two were no associates — they were Hakim's brothers. He would have to look at this murder case in a different light.

"I am afraid there is no news yet about the man you suspect in the death of your servant."

"Servant? Death?" Salman inquired, leaning towards Hakim.

Hakim's eye gave a single twitch as he looked down.

King Salman smiled. "Anything I should know about?"

Hakim smiled back with a small shake of his head.

"Oh, you haven't heard? Well, you have a lot on your plate, I am sure it is difficult to keep track of everything. Your cousins here came to my court yesterday, regarding their beloved, long time servant." Ormozd watched their expressions while he talked. "Apparently, two drifters killed him over a chicken bone — according to a few witnesses we interviewed. So far, the alleged killers have eluded us, but we will find them. Speaking of court, if you will excuse me, I have a couple of disputes to follow up with today. I am sure you and your cousins have a lot of catching up to do. Please enjoy your breakfast." King Ormozd excused himself, signaling for Anoush to follow. He had lost his appetite. It happened a lot since the day Nooshin left.

Hakim, Asif, and Hamzeh bowed their heads as King Ormozd turned and walked down the hall. Salman and his generals watched him leave. Neither of Salman's Generals made a move to bow, as was customary when a king enters or leaves.

Salman walked into the Dining Hall with his generals at his heels. Hakim, Asif, and Hamzeh followed close behind.

ᵞᵞᵞ

The room was large and rectangular with a spacious banquet table standing in the center of the room. Candelabras hung from the raised ceiling, bronze candleholders with gold tips suspended in the air by silver chains, hung above the table. A tile mosaic covered one wall, depicting the eternal Sacred Fire, glowing with red, orange, and yellow flames, rising up from within a purple urn with inlaid gold. Hovering above the urn, two brilliant-yellow rosettes, accented with brown and white, were set against a turquoise-blue sky. Two majestic golden lions flanked the urn, guarding the Sacred Fire and the rosettes — the symbol of the sun.

Intricate silver platters were displayed in cabinets against one wall. A huge fireplace with a marble hearth sat across from the motif, loaded with wood, and ready to be lit. A gold Faravahar — the Zoroastrian symbol — was mounted on the wall above the fireplace. Bouquets of silk flowers, lilies, and roses stood in vases on pedestals in the corners. Another beautiful woven Persian carpet covered the stone floor, echoing the colors of the mosaic, with a scene of a feast in the center, and grapes vines edging the borders.

Three vases with fresh-cut roses stood on the table: one in the center and one at each end. The table was laden with a platter of fresh baked breads; bowls of cut fruits, vegetables, and herbs; a small plate of soft cheese; and a pot of hot tea, with a silver bowl of crystalized sugar.

Seated at the head of the table with his generals to his left, King Salman began loading his plate with food.

Hakim, Asif, and Hamzeh sat across from the Generals. The table had been set with four plates, four cups of water, and four teacups.

"Hungry?" Salman asked, piling up cheese, herbs, and slices of small cucumbers onto a piece of flat bread.

"Yes." Hakim eyed the feast, mouth salivating. "That food at the inn gives me indigestion. Can hardly eat any of it."

"Well, by all means, help yourself."

Hakim ignored his sarcastic tone and reached across the table. "Thanks."

Asif and Hamzeh began picking out the food, eating it over the table with no plates. They dumped the cups filled with water back into the pitcher and filled them with hot tea, sucking on chunks of sugar.

After Salman scarfed down his food, he stood, and walked up behind Hakim. He bent over and whispered in his ear. "Do you want to tell me something, eh?"

Hakim tore off another chunk of bread while scanning the expansive platters of food. "What's that, my dear cousin?"

"Well, *dear* Hakim, how about telling me what's new?" Still whispering into his ear, he placed his hands on Hakim's shoulders, tightening his grip. "For example, why would you have a servant? Or, better yet, why do you have a dead servant?"

Irritated, Hakim looked up, staring straight ahead. "I wish I knew. When we find the bastard that killed him, we will find out, won't we."

"And what about your servant dying over a bone?" Salman walked back around the table to face Hakim. "That doesn't make any sense. That has *Hakim* written all over it."

"Vicious rumor." Hakim bit into a slice of pear, juice dribbled down his chin.

Salman straightened out his clothes, tugging on his sleeves. He sat, intense gaze fixed on Hakim for a long, uncomfortable moment. When Hakim continued eating, paying no mind to Salman, he leaned back in his chair, inspecting his nails. "Hakim, have you ever seen the Caspian Sea?"

"No, cousin."

"Well, I have." Salman polished his nails on his tunic.

"Really?"

"Yes, really. Why would I lie to you?" Salman crossed his arms over his chest. "It is one of the most beautiful places I have ever seen and I have seen a lot of places. It's especially beautiful when you are coming over the mountains at sunset and see, for the first time, the amazing turquoise body of water against the dark green mountains capped with pink and purple clouds. Yes, it is beautiful." Salman paused his recounting for a moment, when he continued, his voice dropped to a low growl. "Until you get to the shore."

Hakim stopped chewing and set his food on the table. He swallowed, took a sip of tea, and leaned back, crossing his arms. "What's wrong with the shore?"

"Do you really want to know?" Salman chided.

"Yes, of course," Hakim answered, growing impatient.

All of a sudden, Salman was on his feet, leaning over the table, and banging his fist on the tabletop, hard and angry. "It stinks! It stinks of rotting fish! Just as the story you are telling me stinks!"

Dishes jumped and crashed back onto the table, teacups tipped over, spilling across the table.

An oppressive silence descended around the table.

A maid, who was walking into the room with clean plates and fresh hot tea, stopped mid-step, frightened by the sudden outburst. After a long strained moment, she turned and fled back to the kitchen, with the tray still in hand.

Salman straightened up and adjusted his disheveled clothes in abrupt, jerky motions. He sat back down into his chair, rigid, and staring at Hakim, pursed lips pressed together in a tight slash of a line.

Hakim and his brothers sat in a stony silence, not daring to move, eyes diverted, avoiding Salman's blazing gaze.

"Knowing you, I suspect something valuable is involved ... diamonds?" Salman paused, reading his cousins' reactions, shifting his eyes from Hakim, to Asif, to Hamzeh. They continued staring at the table. "A gold mine?" Again, Salman looked from one brother to the next. Still, no reaction. "Or maybe another long lost, forgotten treasure?"

Asif's expression changed, his eyebrows shot up, panic etched lines across his face. Hamzeh raised his head at last. Asif and Hamzeh turned, looking at each other, and then looking to Hakim, who would surely know what to say.

"Ah. Something at last. A treasure." Salman was confident in gauging his cousins' reactions, as their thoughts were written all over their faces. A greedy, satisfied smile spread across Salman's face. "So, my *dear* Hakim, you have been holding out on me." His tone was no longer pleasant.

Hakim bolted upright in his chair. "No ... No, Your Greatness," Hakim said sarcastically. "Of course, I was going to tell you, when you could donate some of your attention, but with all that has been happening, with the Princess disappearing, and all your campaigns, I thought now was not a good time."

"A good time? Now is a *very* good time. I *always* have time to make money." Salman's voice dropped down to a raspy whisper. "Do not try to deceive me with your excuses."

"Sorry. I just assumed ... that uh ..." Hakim stalled, his mind racing.

"So, entertain me! What have you come up with?"

"You mean now?" Anxious about losing his gold, Hakim fidgeted with his empty teacup. "Maybe—"

"Now! Yes, now. This very moment! Now! Now! Now!" Salman roared, slamming his fist against the table. Saliva sprayed from his mouth in thick drops, raining on the table.

Hakim hesitated, a nervous spasm twinged his left eye. He looked to his brothers for help, but realized that they are useless in these situations. "Well. Eh ..."

"Get on with it."

Hakim relented with a sigh. "Do you remember the story our grandfather told us, while we were sitting by the fire on the eve of winter solstice?"

"It was the longest night of the year; he told dozens of stories."

"The one about our great ancestor, Oghlu Beik, who confronted the Persian Cavalry and went missing, along with the bags of gold."

"Of course, I remember. He was collecting our taxes from the merchants crossing our land and they called it a robbery."

"Yes, that is the one."

"You are trying my patience. What about the story?"

"Well, the most amazing thing happened when we were riding through Astana a few weeks ago. We found a man calling for help. You see, he had been thrown from his horse and broke his leg. His horse took off and—"

"What has this to do with the story?"

222

"Patience! Now, where was I? Oh, yes. So, this man promised us gold if we helped him get to the Land of Fire and Dragons. Of course, we didn't want anything to do with that place, so he finally came out, and told us the reason he wanted to go there. He told us of a long lost treasure there, as it turned out, it was our own ancestor's gold. So, Hamzeh here killed him with his staff, we found his map, and then we … we … found the gold. In the Land of Fire of Dragons. One big bag of pure ancient gold coins."

Salman laughed, a hyena sound. Hakim jumped.

"The great legend of Oghlu Beik was true after all."

"Yes, it was. He was still holding onto the bags after all these years. When I saw him, I swear he was smiling at me, as if after waiting so long, he was happy that we got what was due to us, at last."

"What? His skeleton?"

"Yes."

Hakim did not mention his panic when the skeleton had grabbed ahold of him, his terror when the claw-like skeletal hand hooked into his tunic. He had convinced himself that it never happened.

"The dead have ways of communicating with the living, you know. Oghlu chose me to find the gold and led me to the treasure." Hakim decided he needed to try to stake his claim, or Salman would take it all.

Salman paused for a moment, narrow eyes studying Hakim. "Yes." He tugged at the sleeves of his tunic, leaned back in his chair, his hands clasped behind his head, and a wide, amused grin spreading across his face. "Of course he chose you to find my treasure, since he knows that I am a very, very busy man."

Salman let that sit for a moment. Hakim's faces flushed red with anger and his eye twitched again.

"Now, where are my *bags* of gold?"

"I … Uh, did you say bags?"

Salman gave one short, abrupt nod.

"No … No. There was only the one bag."

"Dear Hakim, you would not try to rob your own cousin! I know there's more than one bag. If you do not lie to me, I may be more generous than I should be with you."

"Two. All right, there were two bags. One in each hand. One for you and one for me."

"The legend grandfather told us, if I recall correctly, was four bags. Four bags of ancient gold coins.

"Ah, I wish it was four bags. But you know how these stories get exaggerated over time. Two become three, three become four, four become eight." Hakim shrugged. "It's just the way people are. They exaggerate. They lie."

"You now accuse my grandfather of lying! The Great Demirkan of Turan! No one in my family would dare lie to each other, not until your mother, Fatima, married my uncle, and gave birth to you."

Hakim ignored the insult. "I didn't mean to say that he lied. Just that he wanted to make it a good story. What have people started to call it? A little white lie."

Salman waved the thought away. He would have to keep a close watch on Hakim to make sure he didn't make off with any of his gold.

"I hope you have not squandered much on women and wine, as the rest of your worthless side of the family would have." Salman again watched all three's reactions, but received blank looks. He turned to General Mahmood. "Speaking of wine, I have a wonderful bottle of Shiraz in my quarters, worthy of only a King like myself, but I will share it with my family, and of course, my beloved Generals. Why don't you go fetch that for us. We need to celebrate the return of my long lost fortune."

General Mahmood jumped up. "Yes, Your Magnificence!" he said, with more than his usual enthusiasm. Still glassy-eyed, he swayed as he stood, and stepping forward, he bumped into the table. After regaining his balance, he made for the door, squinting and shielding the bright sunlight with his hand.

Mahmood, eager for more wine, rushed down the bright corridors. Wine, he thought, would help his aching head and persistent hangover.

Salman turned back to Hakim. "Now, where were we? Oh, yes. Where is my gold?"

"His gold?" Hakim mumbled under his breath.

"I asked you a question. Where-is-it?" Salman enunciated each word with precision.

"Oh, well, I don't have it. Isn't it a bit early for wine?"

"And what do you mean by that?"

"Well, it's only eight in the morning and I don't drink this—"

"What do you mean by 'I don't have it'? The gold. Where are my bags of gold?"

"Oh. I thought you were talking about the *wine*," Hakim said, quite deliberately angering his cousin. It was probably not wise to do, but he did enjoy it.

Salman leaned across the table, his voice soft, threatening. "I will not ask you again. Where is my gold?"

Hakim waved the stump of his arm in a frivolous gesture. "Well, if you'll be quiet for a second, I can finish explaining." He gave Salman a tight smile. "What I meant to say was that we misplaced them, but we have them."

Salman frowned. "What the hell does that mean? How can you

misplace them and still have them? By God, you are driving me crazy!" Salman gripped a fist full of his own hair and pulled, relishing in the pain as it calmed him. He took a deep breath. "All right. Now, tell me, do you know where the bags are?"

"Yes."

"And where are they?"

"They are safe," Hakim assured with a satisfied smirk.

"I didn't ask if they were safe. I asked you where they were," Salman growled. He was used to these games with his cousin Hakim, but had grown tired of them years ago. Getting information out of Hakim was worse than pulling eyeballs out of sockets when the person had their eyelids squeezed shut tight.

Hakim gritted his teeth. He didn't want to give up his gold to Salman, but to lie to him could be disastrous. Hakim sometimes worried that Salman would put aside familial sentimentalities, if Salman would cook him in a slow boil, and serve him to his brothers at his own funeral. "They are sitting on a ledge of a deep pit, beyond the reach of man. I think they call it *The Bottomless Pit*." Hakim shrugged. "See? They are safe."

Salman's face took on a grim look. "Go on."

"Where?"

"What bottomless pit? How did it get there?" Salman asked, playing along with this long-standing game.

"Well, on our way to the Silk Road, we took a shortcut through Cattula Land."

"My goodness, what brave men you are," Salman interjected sarcastically. He leaned forward, smoothing down his sleeves, and combing back his hair with his fingers.

"Oh, we didn't realize that the route we had chosen would take us through the Cattula Land. That was accidental."

"My dear Hakim, you are wearing my patience thinner than the cord that attaches the eyeball to the brain. I no longer have time to play these games with you. Would you mind telling me what happened to my gold, or shall I look the other way while Ahmad pries the information out of you, my *dear cousin*?"

Ahmad leaned forward with a dreamy smile, chin resting in the palm of his hand as he gazed at Hakim.

"*His* gold?" Hamzeh mumbled, disgusted.

"What was that?" Salman snapped, whipping his head around to Hamzeh.

Hamzeh shook his head, holding his hands up. "Nothing."

"How about you?" Salman turned to Asif. "Do you have anything to add?"

Asif's eyes widened and he shook his head. "No … No, nothing."

Satisfied, Salman turned back to Hakim. The other two were insignificant to Salman. Just two more worthless cousins who followed Hakim's every word. Although they would do as Hakim told them in all things, they would never ever say or do anything to disrespect Salman; they wouldn't even argue with him if he said the sky was green. If they did disagree with something, it was left for Hakim to argue. Their cowardice sickened him as much as Hakim's disregard for his authority sickened him. "I am all out of patience. Go on, now."

"Well, eh. Where was I?" Hakim raised his stump to his temple and scratched his head. He didn't believe Salman's threat was at all serious. If Salman were going to kill him, he would do it himself; he wouldn't have his generals do it. Family obligation.

Impatient, Salman waited, drumming his fingers on the table.

"Oh, yes! She told us that we were tres—"

"Wait a second. Who is 'she'? Where did 'she' come from?"

Hakim leaned forward, feigning confusion. "I told you about … Oh, silly me. I jumped ahead of myself there, didn't I?" He laughed, watching Salman through his squinted eyes. Salman's face turned bright red and a vein bulged down the center of his forehead. Hakim figured he had pushed him as far as he should. "I remember now. I was saying that it was late and we had to find a safe place to camp for the night. We found this nice flat rock next to the river, where we could keep an eye on our surroundings. Not long after, we saw *them*."

"Who?" Still drumming his fingers, he eyes narrowed down to slits as his cousin kept trying his patience.

"The Cattulas, of course. Five of them, galloping towards us. I had to think real fast, which I am very good at. I saw a crevice in the flat rock, so I cut some rope to tie the bags to, and lowered them into the crevice until they landed on what I thought to be the bottom. I gave the ends of the ropes to these two numbskulls, told them to stand by the crevice, and hold the ropes behind them, while I, of course, did the talking and handled—"

"Would you mind getting to the point? *What happened to my gold?*"

"Patience. All will be revealed," Hakim said, shaking his head as if Salman's behavior disappointed and shamed the entire family. "As I was saying, I had given the ropes to my brothers and told them to stand behind me while I did the talking. As they got closer, I realized that they were very short in stature! Why, their heads didn't even reach up to my navel."

Just then, Mahmood returned to the table. "Your Magnificence?"

Salman raised his hand to stop him from speaking; he kept his eyes fixed on Hakim. Mahmood went around the table and sat beside

Ahmad.

Suspicious, Ahmad asked, "Were they riding ponies?"

Hakim shook his head. "No. They rode regular size horses."

"Well, how on earth did they mount their horses if they are so short?" Ahmad asked, finding the tale a little on the tall side.

"Ah, they are indeed very clever. They had stirrups made of solid gold — quite impressive, if I might say so — and the stirrups had little ladders, made of chains on the sides, and little gold rods for steps. They untied them from the side of their saddles and the ladders rolled down. As simple as walking down stairs, they stepped down the ladder. Ingenious. I wouldn't mind having a ladder attached to my saddle. It would be useful, especially for children and women."

"Get to the point," Salman said, sounding bored now.

"Well, there were two men and three women. One of the women asked who we were. I told her that we were travelers who had lost our way on our way back to the trade route.

"She said that we were trespassing on Cattula Land, but since it was a new moon — which is when their ancestors look down upon them — she would grant us permission to spend the night there, though she forbade us to hunt or fish, and she made it clear that we must leave at sunrise, and never return — *or else.*

"When I agreed to her terms, she turned to Asif and Hamzeh and said, 'Why are you two standing there like stiffs with your hands behind your backs? What are you hiding?'

"I said to her, with my quick thinking, that they are not hiding anything, and that is the way they always stand due to problems with their backs.

" 'Let me see your hands!' she demanded.

"That is when my two genius brothers raised their hands and held them out in front of them … dropping the ropes."

Salman covered his face with his hands, shaking his head.

Hakim continued. "The Cattulas laughed manically! When the leader of their pack got control of herself, she said, 'If you dropped something down that crevice, I hope it wasn't valuable.'

" 'Why do you say that?' I asked.

"She replied, 'That crevice is directly above the infamous Bottomless Pit. Haven't you ever heard of it?' I must have given her a dubious look, because she added, 'If you do not believe me, go walk down to the riverbank, and find the opening to the cave that is under the rock that you are standing on. When you go inside, look down, and there you will see the entrance to Hell, where the Great Goddess Kali resides.'

"They all laughed, a horrible heckling sound, climbed back up onto their horses, and galloped away. When they were out of sight, we hurried down to the river, found the cave, and sure enough, there was a pit, the blackest pit I have ever seen. But lucky for us, Oghlu Beik was still watching over my gold, as the bags had landed on a small ledge protruding from the side of the pit. Unfortunately, they were on the opposite side of the pit from us. We had no way to get them, so we came back here, and hired that big, dumb idiot to help us retrieve the gold. He was the one who was killed at the inn."

"Who are these interesting little Cattula people?" Ahmad asked.

"Believe me, you don't want to know," Salman answered without taking his eyes off Hakim, weighing the story he had been told. "It would be best if we left them alone."

"Ha!" Ahmad said. "You are the Great, the Magnificent King Salman. These, you say, are a very small people. How can we not conquer them? What's to be afraid of? I have single handedly struck down many warriors three times their size."

Salman glanced over at Ahmad, giving him a look that suggested he was very naïve. "It doesn't matter if you have struck down a hundred men, ten times their size. You don't want to mess with them. They have powers beyond our comprehension. Powers that are not natural. If you cross them for any reason, you had better never fall asleep again."

"What is that supposed to mean?" Ahmad asked.

"According to legend, when you fall asleep, you are in the realm of twilight. Somewhere between life and death, both and neither, where you have no control over your thoughts, body, or soul. Those who have seen the victims of the Cattula's witchcraft warn of what will happen if you anger them." As he spoke, Salman stared unblinking at Hakim, his intense voice promising the horrors of which he spoke. "They say if you run afoul of a Cattula, they will put their worst curse on you. The next night, around the midnight hour, after you have fallen asleep, your eyes open wide, and you stare out into the vast darkness above you—a darkness that absorbs and consumes and nothing more. A horrible pitch-black made up of nothing known on earth. Your body begins shaking as if a jinn has possessed you and you start screaming and screaming and screaming. One breath after another, as fast and as loud as you can. No one knows why you are screaming. No one knows what you are seeing, or hearing, or feeling, and no one, nothing can help you. They only know that you won't or maybe can't stop screaming.

"You can't tell anyone what is wrong because you are rendered incapable of speech. They say your tear-filled eyes bulge from their sockets and they start to bleed, gushing blood like tears. Thick foam pours from your mouth. And after hours of this, if not days, your mouth dries up, your screams turn into a pitiful wheezing sound. Then, a sudden silence."

Hakim shivered at the thought of upsetting a Cattula. He turned his head to examine the eternal fire painted on the wall.

"Silence? It just stops? What then?" Ahmad asked. He had listened, raptured by the tale.

"Your heart bursts and you die," Hakim said, his voice monotone.

"That's horrible!" Mahmood said.

"What a way to die." Ahmad wiped a cold sweat off his forehead, wincing as he touched the bandage wrapped around his head. "Do you think we could learn to do all that?"

Salman gave Ahmad a withering look. "Yes, horrible indeed. Many times, I have imagined annexing Cattula Land; its fertile, golden valley is tempting. But I dared not attempt it for this very reason." Salman turned his attention to Hakim, who sat staring at the Faravahar above the fireplace. "Tell me about this man who killed your so-called servant."

"Oh, it is nothing important. He is some Tajik I hired to help me get to the Land of Fire and Dragon. I paid him well for his time, but when he got wind of what I hired him for, he followed us here. I was worried that he would try to ambush us and steal the gold, so I sent the servant to have a little talk with him, to convince him to leave us alone. The next morning we found out that the Tajik had murdered my servant at the inn in the caravanserai. The Tajik and his friend were long gone by morning."

"At least we have the gold and it is in a safe place until you can retrieve it for me. At last, I have collected the taxes that are due to my family, after centuries of our dynasty being unfairly maligned. The gold will be returned to Turan where it belongs." Salman leaned back in his chair, crossing his arms over his chest with a wide, delighted smile.

# *19*

## THE CONFRONTATION

General Ghulam rapt firmly on the Palace door. A palace guard opened the door wide and looked out at a pompous man wearing a Turanian uniform.

General Ghulam stepped forward. "I am General Ghulam, First Regiment of the Turanian Army, serving under the authority of King Salman, the Magnificent. These are my men. I must see King Salman at once."

The Palace Guard looked out at the twenty or so rough-looking men. "You may come inside, but the rest of your men will wait in the town square."

"I have two prisoners with me. I will need a few men with me to escort them."

The Palace Guard hesitated, then nodded his approval. "Salman is in the Dining Hall having breakfast. It's down the main corridor on the right. Follow the corridor all the way down and make a left at the end. It's the fourth doorway."

The Palace, built as an enormous fortress, was located on top of the highest hill in the center of the city. Solid, sharp, jagged rocks formed the surface of the hill, making it a dangerous climb if anyone were to try to enter by means other than the front. At the bottom of the hill, two guarded staircases rose up to the Palace. Each staircase opened to the main road, one pointing towards the city's northern gate, and the other pointing towards the southern gate. They rose halfway up the hill, converging at a broad landing, where a single staircase continued, leading up to a beautiful, carved archway, encompassed by a jasmine-covered trellis at the top of the hill. The stairs opened up to the courtyard, with a stone pathway leading to the Palace.

The Palace door opened to a large, charming foyer. Carpets, paintings, and fresh-cut, fragrant flowers filled the room. Two main corridors, to the left and right of the foyer, ran through the Palace, leading to other halls and rooms. The two main corridors wrapped around the interior of the Palace to meet in the very back, where they led to the Palace Garden.

While the Dining Hall was located down the right corridor, the Hearing Room, where King Ormozd settled civil disputes, was located off the left corridor, on the opposite end of the Palace.

General Ghulam stepped through the doorway and gestured for his men to follow. Abdul Kabir and Abd Al-Ala stepped in after him, followed by Persicus and Nooshin, with Abisali and Rami bringing up the rear. The rest of the men retreated down the stairs to the town square.

Bound together with a thick length of rope, hands tied behind their backs, Persicus and Nooshin walked into the foyer, ushered by Abdul Kabir, holding the end of the rope, pulling them along, while Abisali and Rami poked them from behind with their maces. General Ghulam led the way down the corridor, following the directions the guard had given him.

When Persicus heard the General ask for King Salman, he leaned over, and whispered in Nooshin's ear. "Whatever happens, don't say anything until we can get alone with your father. I don't think anyone will recognize you, being as dirty—"

"No talking you two." The soldier ordered from behind, poking Persicus in his back with his mace.

Nooshin understood. The riverbank mud had dried to a crust all over, caked on her face, clumped in her hair, she was a mess—no one would recognize her. Not even Salman, who had only seen her twice. If they could get past Salman, to her father, maybe they could still head off the confrontation with Salman, and though a long shot, maybe their plan could still work out. She could remain hidden, right under Salman's nose. However, the idea of being a prisoner in her own Palace ate at her. On the other hand, if Salman recognized her, here and now, and she refused to marry him, it would not have a good outcome. They would need time to prepare for war. Time that Salman would not give them if he discovered her here today.

Exiting the Dining Hall, Hakim and his brothers stepped into the corridor, just as General Ghulam turned the corner at the opposite end of the corridor. Immersed in their conversation, Asif and Hamzeh talked in low voices, complaining about why Hakim didn't stand up to Salman, and how they would now have to split two bags of gold, because no doubt Salman will take the two he knew about.

ꀭꀭ

Persicus hesitated mid-step as he recognized Hakim. He nudged Nooshin with his elbow. She looked up at him. Persicus shifted his eyes towards Hakim and lowered his face, hoping she would understand. Nooshin followed his gaze. She saw three men walking towards them, registering with shock the man with the missing arm. *Hakim!* She lowered her face. As she stared at the ground, she wondered what on earth he was doing here, in her home.

As Hakim and his brothers passed the soldiers of the First Regiment, he casually glanced at the prisoners, taking in their filthy clothes, but nothing else. A sudden nagging feeling overwhelmed him, but he couldn't quite put his finger on it. He took a couple hesitant steps, until he succumbed to the nagging urge to stop, and turned around.

"Hey! Hold it there!" Hakim rushed towards the prisoners.

Abisali and Rami stopped and turned around. Persicus and Nooshin kept walking, along with Ghulam and the other two soldiers in the front.

Asif and Hamzeh stopped in confusion.

"Stop those prisoners!" Hakim ordered the soldiers.

Abisali caught up with Persicus and Nooshin, yanking on the rope that hung between them. "Stop, you two."

"What's going on back there?" General Ghulam asked, making his way to the back of the line.

Hakim stopped in front of Persicus.

"You!" Hakim yelled, pointing his finger at him. "Raise your head when I am talking to you."

Persicus raised his head, revealing fierce, predatory eyes, boiling with such rage that Hakim shrunk back.

Hakim steeled himself. "I knew it! I knew it was you!" He raised his hand high in the air as he stepped forward, slapping Persicus square across his left cheek.

With a mace digging into the small of his back and his hands bound, Persicus could do nothing to protect himself from the slap. Nonetheless, he lunged forward, intending to knock Hakim out with his head. Nooshin jerked forward with him, the rope stretching taut.

232

Panicked, Hakim stumbled back, raising his arm protectively in front of his face, and ducked behind Abisali. Before Persicus could connect, Abdul Kabir and Abd Al-Ala jerked him back, subduing him.

"Murderer!" Hakim cried out. "I don't know how you got out of that pit of death, but you will regret it! You don't know who you are dealing with. After my cousin, King Salman, is done with you, you will wish you had died in that cave where I left you!"

Persicus ceased struggling, shocked. *Salman? Hakim's cousin? Surely not. Life couldn't be that cruel.*

"All right, Hakim, calm down." General Ghulam came to Hakim's side. "We are taking him to King Salman now."

Hakim stepped out from behind Abisali, confidence returning. "Good! He is a menace. He should be killed, slow and painfully."

"Cut the rope between them. I don't want them together. Abd Al-Ala and Abdul Kabir, you take the boy. Rami, Abisali, take the other one."

Abisali cut the rope between the two and handed Nooshin over to Abdul Kabir.

"All right. Hakim, lead the way to Salman," General Ghulam said.

The soldiers separated Persicus and Nooshin, walking between the two prisoners, shoving and pushing them down the hall.

Nooshin was so close to revealing herself, so she could turn on them, get her father down here, and then ... she didn't know what then. Never in her life had she been treated this way. She slowed her breathing in an attempt to calm her raging heart, but she was furious. *Stick with the plan. Persicus knows what he is doing,* she thought. *He has made it this far, helping me ... except for at the inn, where I had to save him, and then there were the jackals ...* A sudden doubt plagued her mind. They would fail in everything now. Everything had led up to this point, the unfolding events rapidly leading to the exact opposite of their plan — her worst fear. None of their suffering and hiding had mattered at all. They had ended up here anyway, with Salman and *Hakim.* She struggled to believe Persicus could get them out of this situation. She wanted to believe, but the doubt was beyond overwhelming. It was suffocating.

Her home was filled with strangers. *What has been happening here while I've been away?*

King Salman was still sitting in the Dining Hall. He was fuming. Mahmood had just told him that he found no wine in his room. He needed a drink. His head ached as if sharp knives mercilessly scraped along the inside of his skull and his wine had been stolen from him.

Probably by one of the damn peasants Ormozd kept around as his staff. *The damn thieves. All of them.* It was the main reason he forbade wine in his territory. No wine, less crime. There were other aspects to his prohibition against wine, but that was the key reason. He didn't want anyone stealing from him. He didn't want the peasant's money spent on wine, when it could be spent on taxes. Wine was an unnecessary distraction for peasants. They can't be allowed to be distracted. They needed to work hard. They had to provide for their country and Salman owned their country. In return, Salman gave them his protection. It was hard work, protecting so many peasants. Because it was such hard work — harder than any peasant could comprehend — he allowed himself, his Generals, and Cavalry to drink. They needed it to relax after all the hard work, the difficult campaigns. It was necessary for their wellbeing, to cope with their harsh lifestyle. This self-inflicted harsh life they suffered *for* the people. Besides, Salman and his men did not get distracted by the wine. They were disciplined, professionals. They understood the fine line between using wine to relax and being a drunkard. The peasants would not have their self-control. They would be drunk all the time. Their products and farms would suffer. Their income would diminish. Then Salman's *income* would suffer. If his income suffered, he would not be able to protect them. He would not be able to afford his campaigns, to strengthen his empire. All because of wine. The simple solution, forbid it. Problem solved.

However, *his* wine had been stolen. He would have to do something. Something terrible so they will *know* never to steal from him again.

Salman's thoughts were interrupted by a loud commotion in the hall. A moment later, Hakim returned, followed by Hakim's brothers, General Ghulam, members of his regiment, and two people he did not know. Prisoners by the look of it. Salman smiled. His day was looking up. Maybe he would be able to vent some of his seething anger after all.

Hakim stood with a wide, sanguine grin on his smug face.

"King Salman, the Magnificent!" General Ghulam greeted, bowing his head. The rest of the soldiers followed suit.

"Well, well, well. What do we have here?" Salman eyed the two disheveled prisoners.

Hakim cleared his throat and opened his mouth to announce the presence of the murderer, but General Ghulam stepped in front of Hakim, bumping his shoulder in the process, and began speaking first.

"Your Magnificence. We were returning from searching a nearby village when I spotted smoke from a campfire down by the river. I sent my men to investigate and they brought back these two. This man" — he pointed at Persicus — "was the man who sent us on the mad camel chase

234

to Golmud after the imaginary Chinaman! I recognized him right away. He wasted days of our time, when we could have been searching for the Princess."

Hakim cleared his throat to speak, but General Ghulam cut him off again before he could begin.

"Also, when I brought these prisoners here, your cousin recognized him. Said that he had murdered someone."

"Is that a fact?" Salman said pleasantly.

"Yes." Hakim pointed his finger at Persicus. "He is the murderer. This is the man I hired and paid for his service. He followed me around, harassed me, and killed my beloved servant. The murderer! He deserves to die!"

"That is a complete lie! It was self-defense," Persicus said, trying to remain calm. "Where is King Ormozd? This is Mishin and I want to see King Ormozd."

"It is no lie! You —" Hakim began, but Salman held out his hand for silence.

"Ormozd is not in charge here. You are not a citizen of Mishin and you have killed my dear cousin's servant. You answer to me and me alone."

"Your Magnificence, we also confiscated this dagger from the prisoner. It is obvious that is stolen." General Ghulam handed Persicus' dagger to Salman.

Nooshin stood statue-still, staring at the floor, peeking out through her mangled hair, looking from Persicus to Salman, forcing herself to stand still, not to tremble with both fear and anger.

Salman held the dagger to the light. He ran his finger up the edge, stopping at the tip. A dot of crimson blood blossomed on his thumb. He smiled. "A fine dagger indeed. Worthy of a king." He tapped the dagger against the palm of his hand while he walked towards Persicus, stalking around him in a tight circle. "What are we going to do with you?" Salman asked, seemingly to himself, subconsciously tugging at his tunic.

"Salman, you must kill this man! He must die for his crime against the Royal Family of Turan!"

"You bastard!" Persicus yelled. "How dare you! You have tried to kill me twice and you failed both times! You used me to get that treasure, after all I did to get you there, after saving your worthless life time and again, after I had carried all the bags of gold out to you, you —"

"Shut up!" Hakim yelled. "Shut up! You are crazy! I paid you fair for the work you did! We are square! I have two witnesses! And what do you do? You stalk me and murdered my servant!"

Persicus mouth dropped open, stunned by Hakim's version of events.

Salman turned to Hakim. "Hakim. Calm down. Let me ask the questions." He turned to Persicus. "Now, what is your name?"

Persicus swallowed hard and met King Salman's eyes, raising his head up high. "I am Persicus, of Abrisham."

"And you say you helped Hakim find the gold, Persicus, of Abrisham?"

"Yes. He came to me with a deal. He said we would split the treasure fifty-fifty if I got him there. After I carried the gold out, he had his brothers ambush me. They trapped me in the cave and left me to die."

"That's a lie," Hakim yelled.

Salman stepped closer to Persicus. "And how many bags of gold did you carry out of the cave?"

Hakim paled.

Persicus saw Hakim's eye twitch, he looked Salman straight in the eye. "Ten. There were ten huge bags of gold. Five were to be mine. More gold than you've ever seen in your life."

"You lie!" Hakim shrieked.

"Silence!" Salman shouted at Hakim.

"And what is his part in all of this?" Salman asked Hakim, nodding to Nooshin.

"I don't know the boy, but being an associate of this Tajik, he must be as evil as him. You should execute him, too."

General Ghulam cleared his throat. "Persicus told my men that this was his younger brother. I do not see a resemblance. I know Persicus lied. The boy was insolent and deceitful, as well."

"He has nothing to do with this," Persicus insisted.

Salman stepped closer to Persicus, close enough that their clothes brushed each other when they inhaled. Persicus felt the heat from his sour breath polluting his face.

"I deem that you have been paid in full for the work you did for my cousin. As for you killing his servant, you are sentenced to death. Ahmad!"

Persicus cried out. "No! You can't do this! It was self-defense! He was sent to kill me!" Ahmad went to grab Persicus, but he jerked away, yelling, making as much noise as possible. "Where is King Ormozd? Ormozd!"

Nooshin opened her mouth to yell. Persicus saw her tense and take a step forward. He shook his head.

*Not yet*, he was saying.

A Palace Guard had been making his rounds around the south side of the Palace. Anoush, King Ormozd's personal guard and the head of the Palace Guards, had instructed him to keep a watchful eye on their guests. As he approached the Dining Hall, he heard loud voices rising and falling inside the room. He stopped just beyond the door. He froze, listening to the voices. What he heard was not good. Something about gold and murder. He pressed himself to the side of the wall and inched his way to the door. With his ear against the door, he strained to listen.

King Salman's voice came through loud and clear. He gasped, taking a deep breath, and backed away from the door. *Execution. They are going to kill someone!*

The guard turned and ran down one hall, turned, skidding on the floor, and raced down the next hall.

Ahmad and Mahmood grabbed Persicus. Struggling, his hands bound behind his back, Persicus twisted, turned, and jerked, hands and body, making it difficult for the Generals to get a good grip on him.

"Help them," General Ghulam said to his men.

Abisali and Rami moved in and together, between the four of them, got Persicus under control. Ahmad gripped his tied hands and pulled them upward at a painful angle, his elbows threatening to snap. Rami had him by his hair, pulling his neck back at a sharp angle. Mahmood held his right shoulder and Abisali had his left shoulder.

Persicus stopped struggling. It wouldn't do any good if his arms were broken. He was severely outnumbered. He could not win a fight, unarmed, against this many armed men. His head hung down in defeat.

Hakim smiled, walked up to Persicus, and whispered, "Now, you die. You should have known better than to try to mess with me." He turned to Salman. "What of the other one? Shall we kill him, as well? Make it a lesson to anyone who dares stand with an enemy of Turan?"

Nooshin shook, radiating with anger.

Salman smiled and nodded. "I like your thinking, dear cousin." He made a gesture with his hand. Abdul Kabir and Abd Al-Ala moved in on Nooshin, grabbing her arms, and twisting them behind her back.

He ran until his lungs burned. The Palace Guard came to the last stretch of hallway before he reached the court. He burst through the door, into the room where King Ormozd was hearing his morning cases. The door slammed open, banging against the stone wall.

Everyone froze, staring at the out of breath guard. Two men stood before the throne, mouths open.

The guard ran up to Anoush, who stood beside the King. In his rush, he forewent bowing, addressing Ormozd and Anoush in a panicked, gasping voice. "King Ormozd, Anoush. You had better come quick! Salman — you have to stop him! He has ordered the death of two men, one no more than a boy. It sounds fishy! All of it! I believe they are innocent."

King Ormozd face fell. He snapped into action.

"Round up all the Palace Guards and bring them to … Where are they?" Ormozd asked the guard.

"The Dining Hall."

"Bring them all there!" Ormozd yelled to the court as he ran to the door. "Everyone will have to come back tomorrow."

The Palace Guard rushed out after them, to round up all the guards from their various stations.

King Ormozd and Anoush raced down one long hall after another. They came up to the Dining Hall and yanked the door open. The room was empty.

"Dammit!" King Ormozd yelled. He could not abide it if they killed some innocent because he didn't get there in time. "Where would they go?" Ormozd asked Anoush, as they rushed down the hall, listening for voices.

Manacled, Persicus stood between General Mahmood and General Ahmad. The Generals stood at attention, their swords drawn, ready for the execution order from their King. Ten feet away, Salman faced Persicus, watching with pleasure. General Ghulam flanked Salman on the left, with Rami and Abisali at his side. To Salman's right, Hakim, Asif, and Hamzeh huddled together, casting eager, hateful glances at Persicus. Held captive by Abdul Kabir and Abd Al-Ala, Nooshin struggled to see Persicus, who stood to her left.

Taking their time, savoring the moment, Mahmood and Ahmad shoved Persicus to his knees. Waiting, eager for the moment when fear would bleed into his eyes, waiting for him to fathom his imminent, inevitable doom.

The Generals had mocked his pleading for King Ormozd as they pulled him from the Dining Hall to the garden, whispering and hissing into his ears, so soft no one else could hear what torments they envisioned. Telling him they would bathe in his blood like rain after they cut off his head. They would carve out his heart while it still beat inside his chest and feast on it. They would make him beg for death long before they gave it to him.

As King Ormozd ran down the hallway, catching glimpses of empty rooms as they flashed by, frantic thoughts streaming through his mind. He couldn't let Salman kill someone innocent. And even if they were not innocent, execution was rare in Mishin. King Ormozd had never ordered an execution, nor had his father. As long as he'd been alive, his beautiful Mishin had been a peaceful place, a place where people came for *protection* against persecution.

*Damn Salman!* he thought.

Ormozd already knew he would fight Salman someday soon, but he might be forced to stand against him much sooner than he had anticipated. He couldn't let them execute someone in his Kingdom.

They came across a shaken, almost hysterical maid in the foyer.

"Your Majesty!"

"Salman. Did you see him? Where is he?" he said, coming to a stop and grabbing her by her shoulders.

"They are going to kill someone," she cried.

"Where?"

"The garden. Out in the garden."

They turned to head for the garden.

"You, to your quarters." Anoush yelled over his shoulder. "Tell all the staff to go to their quarters."

Nooshin prayed that her father would come soon. He had to. A terrifying thought crossed her mind, *If Salman thinks I'm dead, he might have killed my father. That's why there are no Palace Guards around. That's why there is only his family and army here.* She prayed for her father to appear. She pleaded silently to the silent God. Every minute her throat grew tighter, her stomach rolled with nausea, and she fought the screaming urge to reveal herself before she had to — though her bones ached to scream at them — but every time Persicus caught her eyes, he gave her a barely perceivable shake of the head. *Not yet.* She thought he would be saying that as they killed him. She couldn't bear it. Her heart pounded in her chest, up her throat, roaring like drums in her ears. She looked away, further into the garden. The platform where she had breakfast every morning with her father. The fountain, the beautiful birds, the flowers, and trees where she had played as a child, hiding from her father behind or in the trees, until he finally caught her, squealing with delight. *So many good memories here. Ahura Mazda, don't let this pairidaēza be destroyed by evil!*

Ahmad and Mahmood continued whispering vicious promises in Persicus' ear. Nooshin couldn't hear what they said, but she watched Persicus' reactions. His anger seemed to be increasing, but he didn't look scared.

Salman held up his hand. "All right Ahmad, Mahmood, enough. Let's get this done so we can get on with our lives."

"Salman!" Nooshin's father's voice. "Let that man go!"

Nooshin whipped around to the voice and saw her father. Her knees grew weak; she would have fallen if the soldiers weren't holding tight to the rope, forcing her arms up at a painful angle.

King Salman turned towards King Ormozd. "Ormozd, this does not concern you. These men have killed my cousin's servant and now they must pay for their crimes." Salman turned back to his Generals and nodded.

The Generals smiled, raising their swords.

"Ahmad, Mahmood. Stop until we get to the bottom of this." Ormozd approached Salman, his generals, and his soldiers. "This is not the way we do thing here in Mishin, Salman. No one is executed without my knowledge and approval."

"These men are not citizens of Mishin. They have killed a servant of my Royal Family. They've been deemed an enemy of Turan by their hostile actions. They are cold-blooded murderers."

"King Ormozd?" Persicus called out in a firm voice.

"Silence!" Mahmood hissed in his ear, jerking him backwards.

Nooshin hid behind her hat, her face down, peeking up at her father. She desperately wanted to run to him and hug him fiercely, but that would ruin everything. All that mattered was that her father was here. Their plan could still work.

King Ormozd stopped a few yards away from Salman. "I will not have it any other way, Salman. If I agree with you that they are murderers, you may proceed. But not until I have questioned them."

"What do you think you are going to do here, Ormozd? I have already ordered the execution. All that is left is for my order to be carried out." Salman turned back to his men. "General Mahmood, proceed. They *must* be slain. That is my order. I have spoken! And I am King!"

General Mahmood raised his sword. He looked at King Ormozd and smirked.

"Mahmood! Don't you dare!" Ormozd yelled, his voice booming with authority.

Mahmood hesitated; he glanced from Ormozd to his King.

"Don't look at me! Just do it!" Salman ordered.

King Ormozd couldn't do anything. He was outnumbered.

"No!" Persicus yelled, finally struggling, realizing that Ormozd couldn't help him.

Nooshin knew she couldn't wait any longer. Her father was unable to stop the execution. Salman ignored and disregarded her father. They were going to kill Persicus. "No! Wait! I did it! I killed him!" Nooshin yelled, in a deep, strangled voice, so as not to be recognized.

Mahmood lowered his sword to his side and looked at the boy.

Salman turned towards Nooshin. "You?"

"That's not possible!" Hakim yelled. "Aboli was the biggest, strongest man within a hundred miles. No way could that boy kill him. It was Persicus!"

Salman laughed at Nooshin. "You couldn't hurt a camel flea!" He turned back to Mahmood. "Continue."

General Mahmood raised his sword again. Ahmad gripped Persicus' tied hands with one hand and his grabbed his hair with the other hand, extending his neck for the blow. Mahmood froze for a moment, his sword held high above his head, savoring the moment while he concentrated on Persicus' exposed neck. He glanced at Ormozd with a sinister grin and began his downward stroke with his scimitar sword—curved, sharp, and lethal.

"Mahmood, no!" Ormozd yelled.

Persicus struggled to look up at Nooshin, to tell her 'Now!' but he couldn't raise his head from the grip holding him down.

Nooshin watched as Mahmood raised his sword. She saw Persicus begin to struggle, realizing Persicus was trying to raise his head to her, trying to tell her. It all happened too fast; Nooshin hesitated only for an instant, frozen in fear as the scimitar rose above Mahmood's head. As the sword reached its apex, Nooshin yelled, lunging urgently forward. "No, wait, I am—"

In an instant, Abdul Kabir was on her, jerking her by the rope back towards him. He grabbed her from behind, his hand covering her mouth, his other arm grabbing her around the stomach, lifting her off the ground, kicking, and trying to scream.

She struggled against his bruising grip. She *had* to tell them. Had to *save* him. She bit down on her captor's hand, the fleshy inside of his palm, tasting blood. Abdul Kabir screamed and Abd Al-Ala hit her, hard, across her face. Her head snapped to the side with the impact. Black and white starburst consumed her vision.

Mahmood's sword was halfway down, less than two feet from the decapitating blow to Persicus' neck.

Ormozd was yelling.

Hakim watched, eager. Hand clasped in a fist around his arm.

Ahmad's face glistened with sweat as he watched, anticipating the spray of blood that would cover his face.

Salman stood, watching Ormozd, pleased to have more power than Ormozd, in Ormozd's own Palace.

A low whistling sound breezed by in a rush, quick and invisible. A sharp sound of steel against steel came an instant later. Mahmood cried out, his sword flying from his hand, and striking the ground two feet from Persicus.

A heavy silence descended on the garden. Everyone froze, staring, uncomprehending.

Ormozd turned, letting out his breath as ten Palace Guards poured into the garden. The first guard had his bow in one hand, his other hand reaching for a second arrow.

Salman turned, seeing the guards flowing into the garden.

"Mahmood, Ahmad, let him go!" Ormozd ordered. He walked closer to Persicus. "Release him. Now."

The Generals let go of Persicus, but stood their ground.

"Back up," Ormozd ordered.

Mahmood and Ahmad took a step back, but grabbed the rope that bound Persicus' hands.

Still kneeling, Persicus raised his head, his eyes wide, peeking out through his long hair, covering his face. He got to his feet, his eyes jumping from King Ormozd to Nooshin. She was held in the firm grip of one of the soldiers.

"Did you kill the man they accuse you of killing?" King Ormozd asked.

"Yes, Your Majesty, but it was in self-defense," Persicus answered with obvious relief.

"Why did he attack you?"

"This is ridiculous!" Hakim interrupted, approaching Ormozd. "He killed my servant! After I paid him for his work! Now you want me to listen to his lies! While I am still grieving—"

"I have heard your side of the story, Hakim. Now it is his turn.

242

Please, be quiet."

Hakim crossed his arm across his left stub, appearing offended. He stalked back to his brothers.

"Now, why did he attack you?" Ormozd asked Persicus.

"I couldn't tell you, Your Majesty. Perhaps you can persuade one of these three brothers to clarify that for all of us. All I can tell you is that I was asleep at the inn when a giant of a man pulled me out of bed by my neck and started strangling me." Persicus lifted his chin up. Ormozd saw a necklace of bruises and red, inflamed welts around his neck. Persicus continued, "I had never seen the man before that night. I *suspect* Hakim hired that man to kill me after he found out I survived his first attempt to kill me."

"This is outrageous! He is crazy. *Crazy!*" Hakim said defiantly.

"I have heard enough." King Ormozd looked at the generals, still holding Persicus by the rope. "Release this man."

Mahmood and Ahmad gripped the rope tighter, looking to King Salman.

King Ormozd glanced to his guards and back to the generals. "Now!"

The Palace Guards raised their bows and arrows in unison, steadily aiming at Salman's men.

General Ghulam gestured with his hand and drew his sword. Abd Al-Ala, Abisali, and Rami raised their swords as well. Ahmad drew his sword, not quite pointing at King Ormozd.

Mahmood did a quick count of Ormozd's men, noticing they were about even. He considered going through with the execution, he could use Persicus as a shield. He couldn't be backed down by a weak, pathetic Sogdian like Ormozd. He knew Salman would agree. Then he noticed another troop of Palace Guards waiting just inside the door to the Palace and realized they were well outnumbered. He dropped the rope and Ahmad followed, lowering their swords to their sides.

Everyone fell quiet.

Persicus hung his head in relief. Nooshin sagged in her captor's arms, but she knew things were looking up for the first time since she had set foot in Mishin City two days before. She heaved a heavy sigh. Now they just needed to speak to her father — alone.

When Salman saw the Palace Guards with their arrows at the ready and another troop waiting inside, he motioned his men to lower their swords. As he tugged at his sleeves, the anger in his face unbosomed the mask he always wore, revealing a deep loathing, repugnance, a malignant malevolence, just for an instant, then his face flowed back to its normal arrogant countenance. "Well, now Ormozd. Let's not have an unfortunate accident here. There is no need for hasty actions. Besides, I am feeling rather generous today." Salman walked over to Persicus, his head held high.

Hakim's face grew incredulous. "Salman, you don't mean to let them go?"

"Yes. Yes, Hakim. As I said, I am feeling generous. I believe they have learnt their lesson—*never* to harm a Turanian. I give them as a gift to Ormozd here, to try and punish as he pleases." Salman grabbed Persicus by the hair and his bound hands, pulling him up forcefully, and then threw him to the ground by King Ormozd's feet.

Persicus fell to his knees. Anoush helped him to his feet, but did not move to untie his hands until King Ormozd told him to do so.

King Ormozd had a slight smile on his lips. "How very gracious of you, King Salman." He knew Salman was trying to save face in front of his men. It was humorous, as everyone, including Salman himself, knew he had no choice in the matter. However, if his guards had not shown up at that moment, Ormozd didn't even want to think about what would have happened. The blood of an innocent man would have been on his hands.

Hakim couldn't stand it and he couldn't keep quiet. "Salman, you can't let them go! You can't—"

"Enough from you Hakim," Salman barked, seething anger seeping out as he stormed over to the next prisoner: Nooshin.

Hakim followed at his heels, whispering urgently. "No ... No ... You can't ... He is a killer. And this one is, too. You can't let them go. *He'll try for our gold!*"

Salman turned on him and whispered back. "Well, you'll have to deal with that and figure something out. Because Allah help you if I don't get nine bags of gold. And I mean *nine!* For all the trouble you have caused me, I should take all ten, one is more than you deserve. Now get away from me before I change my mind." Salman reeled around, grabbed Nooshin, jerking her forward. "Here, Ormozd. Here is the other one." He shoved her towards King Ormozd. She propelled forward, landing on her knees at her father's feet.

She looked up at her father, her eyes wide with surprise.

"Nooshin?" Her father whispered in a hoarse voice. "Nooshin!" he cried louder, ecstatic and shocked. He reached down, grabbing her by her shoulders, pulling her to her feet, and embracing her, holding her tight, rocking gently side to side.

Nooshin couldn't say anything for a full minute. Her throat tightened until she couldn't breathe. She swallowed the lump in her throat, choking back a sob, her voice came out as an abused whisper, "Yes, father, father. I'm home." She began trembling in his arms. With her hands still bound behind her back, she could not hug him back, but she buried her face against his chest.

After a shocked silence from everyone but the King and his daughter's soft whisperings, Salman realized this prisoner was no murderous peasant. "What is the meaning of this? Why are you pretending to be a filthy peasant?"

Nooshin didn't respond. She pulled back to look at her father. Brown streaks of dirty tears rolled down her cheeks. She felt the rope slice free. She turned to see Anoush on his knee at her side.

"Nooshin dear, are you all right? Did that man hurt you?" Ormozd asked, indicating Persicus. He held Nooshin's face cupped in his hands, brushing the muddy tears off her cheeks with his thumbs.

"No, no father. He saved me … several times. He risked his life to bring me home." She turned to point at Hakim. "And that man tried to have Persicus and I killed while he was escorting me back here," she said it loud enough for her voice to carry across to where Hakim stood, thirty feet away.

King Ormozd face flared red with anger. He shifted glaring eyes to Hakim.

Hakim stood with his brothers, far from Salman, not wanting to risk his anger. "That is a lie!" Hakim half shouted. His eye began twitching to the rhythm of his pounding heart.

"You dare call my daughter a liar?" Ormozd's voice squeezed down tight, his face filled with rage at the thought of this man, whom he had let into his Palace, eating his food, who had tried to kill his daughter.

Hakim looked down at the ground. "I didn't send Aboli to kill anyone. He was only trying to find out why —"

"Enough!" King Ormozd yelled. "Enough of your lies."

"My lies?"

Salman shoved Hakim aside, moving in towards Nooshin and King Ormozd. "I want to know what is going on. Is he the bandit that kidnapped you?" Salman pointed at Persicus.

Ormozd stroked Nooshin's hair. "Yes, Nooshin. What has happened? Where have you been? Oh, I have been worried sick about you, dear. Thank Mazda that you are safe."

"Father, it is a long story. Persicus saved my life from certain death at the hands of the bandits. And he escorted me all the way here. I killed that man in the caravanserai as he was strangling Persicus. It was unintentional. I was only trying to stop him from killing Persicus. I hit him on the head with an iron pan and then he didn't get up. I was worried for Persicus' safety. We were warned that we had killed a man connected to someone powerful, who, they said, would seek vengeance. Fearing for his life, not knowing if I could reach the Palace before they would find us and kill us, we fled." She would have to give her father the more complete version of events when they were alone.

Hearing this, one of the guards slit the rope that bound Persicus' hands.

"Don't you worry about that worthless servant," Salman soothed. "The important thing is that you are here now and safe. I will escort you to Turan myself this time. I should have done so the first time, but I was returning to a campaign. I will see to it that nothing like this ever happens again. Rest assured, Nooshin, I will never let you out of my sight again. We will leave right away." He glanced down at her, taking in her dried-mud covered hair, face, clothes. She was filthy. "Well, after you have bathed." He placed an arm on her shoulder, leading her away from her father.

Nooshin abruptly shrugged off his arm and stepped closer to Persicus. She shook her head, slow, fear creeping down her throat, coiling in her stomach. "No."

"No? What do you mean 'No'?" Salman asked, his voice dropping to a low growl.

"No, I am not going with you. No, I am not going to marry you."

Salman was quiet for a second, shocked, and then laughed. The sound slithered across Nooshin like writhing snakes. She hated the sound of his laugh.

"*No?*" he said with derision. "Well, my dear child. I am afraid you have no choice in the matter. You are to be my queen. The Queen of Turan." He leaned in close to her, whispering into her ear. She still held onto Persicus. Salman knew the Tajik could hear, but didn't care. "Your father has given you to me. To save his own life, he gave you to me. It is not really up to you, but I thank you for telling me your true feelings in this matter, Princess. I would have given you anything, but now you *will* do as *I* say. You will be my slave. You will learn when to speak and when to sit and be quiet, as a good woman should. You will learn to walk in my shadow and never, ever object to me."

Hearing his voice, so cold, abhorrent, and evil, Nooshin trembled. She looked away from Salman, to Persicus. Salman grabbed her chin and turned her face back to him. She jerked away and backed up, plastering her body against Persicus.

Persicus wrapped his arms protectively around her, glaring at Salman as he backed away from him, towards Ormozd.

When King Ormozd saw her terrified face, he came to stand between her and Salman. "Father, I do not wish to marry him."

King Ormozd nodded. "I know, dear —"

"Ormozd, tell your daughter. Tell her that it is not her choice. You, her father, have the right to give her to anyone you choose, and you chose me. Tell her so that she knows, though she is Princess, she is still a woman, and therefore in the eyes of Allah, she is only worth one-third of a man."

King Ormozd turned towards Salman, scorn in his eyes. "Our Prophet, Zarathustra, taught that man and woman are equal. He deemed every woman is free to choose a husband for herself. I have never deviated from that principle for my citizens or my family. She chose to marry you, Salman. I never even asked her to. And if she wishes to change her mind, she has the freedom to do so."

Salman's face burned, a deep wine-red. He clenched his hands into tight fists. "You forget it is by my sufferance that you remain on your throne. You forget the deal I made with you, Ormozd. You do not want to become my enemy. You do not want to experience my wrath."

"I forget nothing. Beware you do not insult me. I have been kind to you thus far. But need I remind you, you are in my Palace." The threat was subtle, but the Palace Guards knew what he meant. Several of them raised their arrows and pointed them at Salman's chest, making the threat clear.

"You dare to threaten me! I am King Salman, the Magnificent. You are nothing but another weak city sitting in my path to ruling the entire region." He took a step closer to Ormozd. "My friends benefit from my generosity, but you have forsaken it. Now, know that you are my enemy and you will suffer. Mishin will suffer. You will all feel the sharp edge of our sword of justice." He turned to Nooshin. "When your father is dead and there's no one left to protect you, when no one alive remembers your name, I shall have you as my slave, girl. All you have done is ruin your city and kill your father."

"Guards, escort this low-life bandit out of Mishin." Ormozd ordered.

Salman straightened out his clothes. He looked up at the Palace Guards moving in on him and his men. He began walking towards the door to the Palace.

Anoush stepped in front of Salman, stopping him with a raised hand. "You leave through the garden exit. I will send a Guard for your things."

"Wait." Persicus called out. "You have my dagger." He nodded to his dagger stuck in Salman's waist shawl.

"What dagger? I have only my dagger."

"Anoush, the dagger belongs to Persicus. Please, get it." Nooshin stared at Salman with a satisfied smile.

Salman glared at Nooshin. He pulled out the dagger and threw it to

247

the ground before Anoush could reach him. "Take it. I will get it back later."

Anoush picked up the dagger, his eyes widening when he saw the design, so similar to King Ormozd's Royal Dagger.

When Salman and his men were out of sight, Nooshin turned to her father. "Father, are you mad at me?"

Ormozd embraced his lovely daughter. "No, Nooshin dear. You know, you are just like your mother. She would not have tolerated that arrogant, scheming jackal either. I am so relieved that you are home. Do not worry dear; we will survive this ordeal. The thought of you being at his mercy made my heart ache and made me ill since the day you left."

Nooshin smiled.

Ormozd released Nooshin and walked over to Persicus. Persicus looked down at the ground, nervous. "I wish to give you a thousand thanks for bringing my daughter back to me. You shall be greatly compensated for your time and dedication to seeing Nooshin safely home. You are welcome to stay here as long as you wish. I will send someone out for fresh clothing for you. Then you both can tell me, in detail, what has happened during these last two weeks."

Persicus bowed his head. "Thank you, Your Majesty."

Anoush walked over to Persicus with the dagger in hand.

"This is yours?" Anoush held the dagger, displayed on the palms of his hands.

Persicus nodded. "Yes, it is." He glanced at Nooshin, who gave him a private, breathtaking smile.

"Ahura Mazda!" King Ormozd stared wide-eyed at the dagger.

# 20

# THE SHABESTAN EXCHANGE

After Persicus bathed and shaved, he dressed in fine silk clothing that someone had set out for him. Not use to wearing such expensive clothing, the silk felt odd, yet smooth and cool against his skin.

Anoush led him back to the garden, where Ormozd awaited for a detailed accounting of events. Ormozd lounged on a cushion in the garden platform before an elaborate display of fruits, nuts, herbs, cheese, and breads spread across the low table, along with a bottle of wine and a steaming pot of tea.

"Persicus, come," King Ormozd called.

Persicus crossed the lawn, feeling panic bubbling up from his belly. As he walked up the steps, Ormozd stood, and he couldn't quite read the King's expression. With each step, his feet felt heavier and heavier until they felt like lead. He stood before King Ormozd and bowed. "Your Majesty."

"Please, call me Ormozd."

Persicus nodded. "Ormozd. How may I be of service?"

"Please, be seated."

Persicus sat on a blue and gold silk cushion, across from Ormozd.

"I understand that you are from Tajikistan."

"Yes, Your … uh … Ormozd. I am, but I live in a town called Abrisham. It's not too far from here," Persicus said, trying not to ramble. He realized how nervous he was and wiped his sweating palms on his silk pants, realizing too late that it left damp marks on thighs.

SAEED & SHIRIN DERAKHSHANI

"I have been through Abrisham. A nice little town. What do you do there?"

"I have an apple orchard. I also fix the qanats for our town and other nearby villages. I'm the only one around who knows how to work in the qanat," Persicus said by way of an apology, feeling embarrassed about having such a job.

King Ormozd sensed his embarrassment. "My. The qanats? Really? That is such a dangerous job. You must be incredibly brave or plain crazy."

Persicus laughed, a surprised burst of a sound. The King restrained his own smile, happy his comment put Persicus at ease.

"Yes, well. Most people think it's brave, but I'd go more with crazy. Every time I crawl through those tunnels, I swear it's the last time, yet year after year, I keep doing it."

Ormozd picked up Persicus' dagger from the table. He held it in his hands, examining it. Once Ormozd had seen it, he had asked Persicus' permission to examine it further, being so similar to his own dagger. He called on the city's historian, who had archived the inventory of books and ancient artifacts within the Palace.

The historian, Nersis, had once been a Nestorian Monk from the nearby monastery, where he studied and translated ancient texts until the day his elder died. The new elder who took his place decided to change the interpretations of the New Testament of Christ and other important documents, which was an affront to the Nestorian ways. Nersis left the monastery shortly after, coming to Mishin, where Ormozd gave him a job studying the ancient books and art within the Palace. Father Theodore—Ormozd's and Nooshin's close friend—had stuck it out in the monastery, trying to preserve the Nestorian ways, though it was a losing battle. However, Nersis once again had the freedom to interpret documents and books without the restrictions of an elder who wished to interpret findings to his own advantage—for power and control. In return for being allowed full access to Mishin's greatest treasures, he taught Ormozd, Nooshin, and countless others who were interested, ancient languages, history written in lost languages, and whatever other marvels he discovered.

The dagger had excited Nersis, though at first wary of its authenticity, he had spent a good hour comparing the two daggers. In fact, Ormozd had never seen his quiet scholar so excited. Ormozd trusted Nersis implicitly.

The King withdrew his own dagger and laid them side by side in front of Persicus.

Persicus reached towards Ormozd's dagger. He stopped mid-motion. "May I?"

Ormozd nodded once.

Persicus picked up the dagger, running his fingers over the lion's mane, slipping his hand through the guard, gripping the handle. It even felt the same in his hand. Now he could understand some of Nooshin's reaction a little better.

"Where did you come by this dagger?" Ormozd asked, laying his hand on the handle Persicus' dagger.

Persicus told the story of how his uncle came into possession of the dagger, in return for medication, and where the Bedouin had found it, in the Valley of Skulls.

Ormozd fell quiet for a moment, pondering the implications. "Do you know the story behind it?"

"Some. Nooshin told me about a Royal Dagger, which belonged to King Cyrus," Persicus answered, setting Ormozd's dagger back on the table.

"I had a historian examine your dagger. I hope you do not mind. It is ironic that this dagger has made it here."

"You don't mean that this is really Cyrus' dagger?"

Ormozd smiled and leaned forward. "Yes, it is." He held up Persicus' dagger, pointing to the base of the blade. "Do you see this?"

Persicus leaned forward, squinting his eyes, and saw the tiny, strange mark at the base of the blade. He had always figured whoever had made the dagger had left his mark. "Yes. It's only the maker's mark, isn't it?"

Ormozd shook his head, his eyebrows arched up in question, and a slight smile played on his lips. "So you never learnt what this says?"

Persicus frowned and shook his head.

"Do not frown so. I didn't know either, until the historian, Nersis, examined it. It is an ancient language called Cuneiform — the first written language." Ormozd paused, letting the anticipation mount. "And those are Cyrus' initials."

Persicus' jaw fell open. Ormozd laughed at his surprised expression.

"You're serious?" Persicus asked, thunderstruck.

Ormozd smiled. "Quite serious. What do you know of King Cyrus?"

Persicus closed his gaping jaw. "Well, it was a long time ago. I know he freed the Jewish slaves from Babylon and he ruled Media, Persia, Lydia, and Babylon, maybe more."

"Yes, he did and much more. To this day, people refer to him as Cyrus the Great because of how he led his people. He ruled, but did not dictate. Tax money was invested back into the communities, *for* the people. He gave people freedom to keep their customs and religions —

but it also allowed people, in all the lands under his control, to openly worship whomever they wished, when previously they might have been killed for their apostasy. His priorities were establishing human rights, an organized government, and an advanced military. I try to rule Mishin after Cyrus' example."

"He sounds admirable, especially for a king." Persicus winced, forgetting for a moment that Ormozd was a king.

Ormozd laughed. "Don't worry. You are absolutely right. Many kings are like Salman, who take from the people, but never take care of the people. To me, they are not kings at all, but leeches who feed off the citizens. Speaking of leeches, why was Hakim trying to get rid of you. What happened these past weeks? Nooshin is in her bath, so we have some time."

Persicus smiled. "Yes, I took her to a bathhouse, told her to meet me out front in an hour, and I didn't see her again for almost four hours."

Ormozd sighed and shook his head. "Her mother was much the same. I don't know what they do in there. So, tell me what happened, since we have a while."

It was a long story. He began at the caravanserai after he had returned from the qanat. He told Ormozd of meeting Hakim there, the bargain they had struck, finding the cave in the Land of Fire and Dragon, killing the dragon, and finding the gold.

"Dragon?" Ormozd interrupted, with a look of pure skepticism. "Are you aware of a creature, mistaken for centuries as a dragon, which is actually called a Komodo dragon?"

Persicus furrowed his eyebrows, giving the King a cynical look. "You know, now I see the resemblance between you and Nooshin."

Ormozd laughed. A deep, hardy sound. "Well, she looks like her mother, but her personality definitely came from me. I take it she already told you this."

"Again and again. And I asked her, 'Why would they call it a Komodo *dragon*, if it is not a dragon?'"

"Yes, I see your point. Several years ago, we had a visiting prince from some island near China who told us tales about these dangerous, vicious creatures. The Komodo dragon, a giant lizard, which is native to that island. Apparently, years ago, some hopeful fools tried to tame these creatures and brought them by boat to the mainland. It did not take long for these creatures to eat through their ropes and escape. Maybe you found and killed one of these lizards."

Persicus shrugged. "I don't know. I can tell you it was huge, had sharp teeth, a long spiky tail." Persicus shivered. "And really bad breath."

"Well, never mind all that, go on with your story."

Persicus continued. He explained how after he carried out the gold, Hakim had betrayed him and trapped him in the cave. The long, miserable voyage down the underground river, the abyss, climbing the root, and then crawling up out of the earth right into the bandit's camp, where by mere luck alone, he came upon the bandits who had kidnapped Nooshin. When he told Ormozd about the bandits stomping on the unstable, hollow ground and how every last one of them fell screaming into the abyss as the ground crumbled around him, with Nooshin surviving only because her bound hands caught around his neck, Ormozd's stricken face paled.

"Ahura Mazda. Thank goodness you both made it out of there alive." After a moment's pause, he said, "No wonder we never found a trace of them. They vanished completely off the face of the earth." Ormozd shook his head at the incredible tale.

Persicus stopped at the point when King Ormozd came into the garden, saving him from execution.

Ormozd sat in silence for a full minute, tapping his thumb against the table.

"Well, you and my daughter have been through quite an ordeal together. I am speechless." Ormozd fell quiet again, then he shook his head. "I swear there were moments when I felt her fear and panic, I know that sounds crazy, but it is true."

"I believe you."

"I am so relieved that you are both here and safe."

"Safe, but for how long? How much time do you think we have before Salman attacks?"

"Sooner than I would have liked. I need to start preparing. This city has been most impenetrable for centuries, but knowing Salman, he will find a way. I'm sure he has prepared for every eventuality."

"Nooshin … Uh, I am sorry, Your Majesty. Princess Nooshin said the grates in the canals cannot be opened from the outside, but with enough force, couldn't Salman's men gain entry through there?"

Ormozd considered him for a moment. "No. They are secure. The lever behind the stone you pulled also releases a latch that unlocks the grate, allowing it to be lifted by turning the wheel. The latch is up inside the wall, above the grate. There's no way to open it, unless you're in that room. The entire city was designed to keep out the worst enemies imaginable." Ormozd smiled. "And please, you are my honored guest, call me Ormozd. And I am certain you have not been calling Nooshin 'Princess' during your journey here."

Persicus gulped and nodded, wanting to steer the topic back to something safer. "Mishin does seem far more secure than most other cities I have visited. Your ancestors who built this place must have had some formidable enemies."

"The majority of people here in Mishin are Sogdians, descendants of the people from my homeland. My ancestors built this fortress after the most ruthless adversaries had invaded our motherland. Mishin is a haven to keep all our people, along with anyone who wishes to live here in peace, safe from such savages, past and present. I will die defending us before I let anyone invade us again." King Ormozd voice was resolute, his hand in a tight fist.

"Salman is bad news; he will be trouble. People speak of his atrocities as far away as China."

"Salman is bad, yes, but we have faced much worse throughout the centuries."

Persicus gave him a quizzical look. "Worse than Salman? What happened to your ancestors?"

Ormozd picked up a carafe of wine. "Do you drink wine, or would you prefer tea?"

"Wine. Thank you."

Ormozd poured two cups of ruby-red wine, handing Persicus the cup, and savoring a small sip. He held his cup in his hand, twirling the dark liquid inside; he seemed lost in thought as he watched the spiraling fluid. "According to the Gathas of Zarathustra, my ancestors lived in a land called Airyanem Vaējah—the Land of Aryans. It was described as a land of tall mountains, waterfalls, and beautiful horses—the first of sixteen good lands. Our people lived there in peace and amity for centuries. They cultivated the land, bred horses, and built beautiful monuments and Fire Temples. That is, until the day when an army of desert dwelling savages decided to disrupt our way of life forever, making these proud, noble, and peaceful people their slaves. They came like a dark cloud of locusts that spread over fields of golden wheat, destroying everything they touched. They demolished everything in their path. Our buildings, architecture surpassing anything we have now, masterminded by brilliant engineers, reduced to ruins. They destroyed our monuments, our temples, took axes and torches to our beautiful art, and they burned our books. We had never known such violence before they descended upon us."

"Who were they? What did they want?" Persicus asked.

"My father called them 'The Barefoot Barbarians from the Desert Beyond'. A savage people. Those who would slaughter us all just for our way of life. They turned our men into slaves and hid our women away as though they were third-rate citizens in their own land. They did worse than kill my ancestors—*they stole their identity*.

"Salman is bad, yes, and maybe just as ruthless. But the difference between men like Salman and men like the barbarians is just different flavors of insanity. The barbarians would kill and destroy to spread the word of their God, while Salman would do the same for profit. I am beyond relieved that Nooshin has changed her mind. I am glad we both realized that her marrying him would not have saved Mishin. We need to fight."

Persicus recalled his friend, Ashoka, from the Monastery. "A friend of mine, a Buddhist monk, told me the exact same story, that the barefoot barbarians invaded his home, killed his family, and destroyed their temples."

"Yes," Ormozd said. "They were busy on their iconoclastic crusade. They tried to conquer many lands and have succeeded all too often. Who could have ever imagined that the great Persian Empire would fall to the barbarians?"

"What happened to your ancestors? What did they do?"

"Well, after they destroyed Airyanem Vaējah, our people split up. King Yazdgerd, along with the Royal Family, and the survivors of his loyal army headed north to China, where his daughter had lived since her marriage to the Emperor. He intended to gather an army and return to Airyanem Vaējah to save his land and people, but somewhere near the Pamir Mountains, the barefoot barbarians caught up with them. To save his family, King Yazdgerd had to make a tough final decision—he sent his wife and children off ahead, over the snow-capped mountains, while he and his army stayed behind. King Yazdgerd and his men attacked the advancing barbarians to stall them, while his wife and children got away. They were severely outnumbered, but they held them off long enough. Their sacrifice paid off. Prince Pirooz, who was six, witnessed the barbaric beheading of his father from the mountaintop. Later, when he grew up, he carried out thirty-three successful campaigns against the barbarians.

"Another group of people from Airyanem Vaējah headed east, looking for a peaceful place to settle, a place where they would be accepted, and be able to live and worship as they wished. Many kingdoms refused them or demanded too many restrictions. Then they found India, where they settled amongst the peaceful and civilized people of that land.

"After the initial slaughter and pillaging, those who stayed in Airyanem Vaējah continued to suffer under their occupiers. The barbarians tried to force them to give up their homes and live in tents, as they did. They forced them to change their names, speak their language, and worship their God. Those who refused suffered further, either impoverished by heavy taxes that the barbarians levied upon them, sold as slaves, or killed. There were vast differences between the barbarian's customs and our own. Their religion permitted, even encouraged, men to have many wives, whereas ours believes in the sacred union between a couple. They said if we wanted to continue living, we must give up our 'inferior' and 'infidel ways' and live and worship as they did. In time, after a few generations, the people changed. They never knew or learned the truth of their past. The barbarians fed them lies about their history. The truth, destroyed, forgotten, lost to them. They lost their identity."

"My ancestors came north and settled here, along with hundreds of Sogdians who fled with us—after all, this place was the second of the good lands that Ahura Mazda created. And knowing the necessity of a good defense, they made this fortress, first and foremost.

"Well, not long after our fortress was completed, the savages showed up at our gates with their gift of misery. However, this time we knew the nature of the beast and we were better prepared. We were victorious and they retreated in defeat." King Ormozd shook his head, sadness in his eyes. "But the poor souls who remained in their homeland of Persia, it saddens me to think of their proud heritage, *who they are*, it was all stolen from them. As usual, history was rewritten by the victors, claiming they civilized them, educated them, and were kind to them. In reality, our Golden Era of Knowledge became the Dark Era of Ignorance. The Barbarian's false version of history spread to all the known lands. They will remain in darkness for years, if not decades, centuries even, unless they can remember who they are and *fight back*."

Persicus listened, both fascinated and despondent. When Ormozd sat back, sipping his wine, Persicus was deep in thought. Then Ormozd stood. It abruptly awoke Persicus from his ruminations. "Follow me to the Shabestan. I will show you something really amazing that we discovered."

Persicus followed Ormozd into the Palace, through a long hallway, and down a stone staircase. Deep beneath the main floor, was a large Shabestan—a summer room. The large room was adorned with ornate, sculpted columns, supporting the ceiling, spaced evenly throughout the room. Blue, tan, and gold tiles covered the support beams in a traditional pattern. A rectangular fountain sat in the center of the room with a cushioned bench bordering its edge. Smokey sunlight trickled in through thick glass windows near the ceiling.

The Shabestans were built with the qanat tunnels running underneath them, creating a cooling system. Cool air travels up from the qanats into the shabestans by way of vertical airshafts. In Mishin's case, the river water flows into an underground tunnel, to the shabestans. During the hot summer days, royalty, merchants, farmers, and peasants alike, venture down into the Shabestans to enjoy the refreshing, cool air.

Ormozd walked to the opposite side of the room, to one of three closed doors. After opening one of the doors, he motioned Persicus through.

Shelves upon shelves of ancient books lined the walls. Tables filled with clay tablets and crumbling scrolls with fading writing. Old vellum and papyrus sitting in stacks. Statues of all sizes filled the rest of the large space, along with artifacts of bygone eras, the likes of which Persicus had never seen in all his travels.

Persicus followed Ormozd through the maze of antiques to another door, almost hidden at the rear of the room. Persicus had been struggling with his discomfort, battling the overwhelming feeling of inferiority of being in this immaculate Palace with the Sogdian King, but Ormozd's amicable decorum kept putting him back at ease. Nonetheless, servile thoughts kept popping up in his head. Certainly, the King of Mishin had better things to do than exchange garrulous pleasantries with him.

Ormozd held the door for Persicus, smiled chidingly, giving him a fatherly pat on his shoulder, almost as if he could hear Persicus struggling with his thoughts.

*What does he want to show me?* Persicus wondered. As he stepped into the next room, he pictured a dungeon, a waiting hell for those unworthy, those who had dared look at the Princess the wrong way. He came to an abrupt stop just inside the doorway, gazing in awe at the wall in front of him. His mouth dropped open in surprise, all submissive and inferior thoughts torn from his mind.

The most beautiful and horrible thing he had ever seen stood before him, against the far wall. An enormous mosaic stretched across the length of the room. Each tile made and placed with exquisite attention to detail. It portrayed an intense, fierce, and deadly battle scene. The image blazed against the wall, having more depth than the room itself, as though he could step beyond the wall, and fight side by side with those brave soldiers. The mosaic, divided into two scenes, from two different moments of the same battle, exploded with color, unscathed by time. His eyes followed the flowing limbs and wind-blown hair, picking up the smallest details, though there was too much to see at once. The flow of a warrior's beard as he galloped on horseback—his beard black and gray, splashed with glistening-red droplets as though it had rained blood. Another warrior held an intricately designed shield, with only his terrified eyes peeking over the top. Pupils small as pinpoints, the brown iris flecked with amber. Reflected in the shine of his eyes, an arrow plummeted down upon him. Persicus followed the scene, not trying to see all the small details now, but the whole picture, until he reached the top of the mosaic, where the emblem of the Kingdom hovered over the entire battle: a proud, male lion stood, one leg a step in front of the other. A brilliant sun shone over the lion's back, golden rays shooting up into the heavens.

Ormozd gestured to the mosaic. "This is what I wanted to show you. In these rooms are the few things my ancestors were able to save from the destruction caused by the invaders. This was the most invaluable artwork they were able to salvage from the devastation. So much more was destroyed."

"I see what you mean by they live in the Dark Era now. Such beautiful art, replaced by what?"

"Nothing. Absolutely nothing. The Barbarian's religion forbids everything aesthetically pleasing or educational: art, literature, monuments, temples. Anything that is not about their God is evil. So they fill their lives with religion, while seeking to destroy everything else in God's name—as if any God finds joy in destruction."

"What battle is this?" Persicus asked.

"The Battle of Carrhae. Have you heard of it?"

"I've heard mention of it while I was passing through Syria, but I must admit I do not know much about it."

"Earlier, I told you about two types of insanity. Two forces of evil. The men who destroyed Airyanem Vaējah were crazy enough to kill and maim to force their beliefs on others. The man who started this battle was the other kind of crazy—the same as Salman—Marcus Crassus."

"Isn't he the one who defeated Spartacus, the slave rebel, around the time of Caesar?"

"Yes," Ormozd confirmed, "but do you know anything else of him?"

Persicus shook his head. "No, I can't say I do."

"He was a vile man. Truly vile, the sort driven by greed, pride, and envy. At that time, in Rome, they had an abhorrent law called Proscriptions. It not only allowed them to kill their enemies, but to take their fortunes, and forbid the widows of their enemies to remarry, ensuring poverty for the wives and children. As Crassus' wealth grew from proscriptions, he developed a second source of income—his firemen. He dispatched his firemen when any house caught fire. They would arrive on the scene, but they would only put out the fire once the owner sold Crassus the property at an absurd price. He would then fix it up and resell it for a large profit, often right back to the people from whom he had bought it. Once he became the wealthiest man in Rome, he saw another way to further his vast ownership of land and property—politics. He was quoted as saying, 'You are not rich enough, until you can buy an army' and that's just what he did. When he became Censor to Syria, he decided he could stretch his greedy paws to his eastern neighbors — the Parthians. Crassus ignored Rome's treaty with Parthia and led his army across the Euphrates.

"The Battle of Carrhae." Ormozd gestured to the mosaic. He stood in front of the wall-size mosaic, recalling the adroit way this terrible battle was fought and won. "General Surena, of Parthia was sent to intercept the Roman army. Surena had with him only ten thousand men, while Crassus had bought himself an army of thirty-five thousand men." Ormozd looked back at Persicus, who stared at the mosaic as if transfixed. Ormozd pointed to the horsemen in the first scene. "The element of surprise is key here. You see these horsemen here, these were Parthian Cataphracts. They wore armor unlike anything the Romans had ever seen."

The mosaic showed the Cataphracts wearing thick armor that covered their entire bodies, head to toe. They held long, sturdy lances. A thick, solid armor also covered their horses, protecting their heads, chests, sides, and legs from the enemy's swords, arrows, and lances, allowing the Cataphracts to keep their horse, which put them at a greater advantage. Their horses were a special breed, bred to be large and strong with extraordinary speed and strength.

The first scene portrayed the beginning of the battle and the second scene portrayed the end of the battle.

In the first scene, the Romans stood in their famous turtle formation — row after row of men, forming a large square. Those on the outer edges held their shields in front of themselves, while those on the inside held their shields above their heads, so they would be protected from all directions.

Ormozd continued. "While approaching, the Parthian Cataphracts covered their armor and their horses' armor with sheepskins and blankets. Not until the last moment before they charged the Romans did they throw off their coverings and let the Romans see, for the first time, what they were truly up against."

Ormozd's voice held reverence as he described the battle to Persicus. "The Cataphracts charged the Romans, but they were unable to penetrate their turtle formation. The Parthians began to retreat. At this point, I'm certain the Romans believed they would be victorious, as their enemy was on the run. However, they were in for a grave surprise. The Cataphracts' retreat was only a ruse." Ormozd walked to the other end of the wall to stand before the second scene.

Persicus followed.

"The Parthian Light Cavalry came out of nowhere as the Cataphracts retreated. They rode in from all directions, circling the Romans. Just like that, they were surrounded."

The second scene showed the Romans still in their defensive

formation, the image capturing them as they tried to move forward. The Parthian Light Cavalry had them surrounded, riding in a wide circle around their square formation.

"Surrounded and under constant attack," Ormozd said, pointing to the Parthian Light Cavalry. "The Light Cavalry were expert archers. They were strapped onto their horses so they could ride with no need of holding onto the reins, freeing their hands for their weapons."

The archers shot a bevy of arrows from all directions. With their hands free, they could shoot with precision. Amazed, Persicus saw a group of the archers riding away from the Romans, shooting backwards, turned halfway around on their horses.

"That is incredible. They could really shoot backwards, while riding away?" Persicus asked.

Ormozd smiled. "Yes. It's called the Parthian Shot. They were well known for it. Turning and giving a last parting shot before they circled back again. I'm sure you have heard the phrase *a parting shot*. But, that was not the most surprising thing the Romans discovered right before their demise."

"What was?"

"The Parthians' arrows. They had armor-piercing arrows. The Roman's shields were useless. They had never even heard of such a thing. The Light Cavalry never gave them the slightest reprieve. Crassus ordered his men to stand their ground, thinking that eventually the Parthians would have to run out of arrows."

"But they didn't?" Persicus said, guessing what was coming.

"No. Surena had thousands of camels carrying food, water, and weapons. When an archer ran out of arrows, he would go refill his quiver, and another archer would take his place. The same would happen if someone was injured. This was why they became known as the Immortals, because there was always the same amount of men fighting, no matter how many were injured or killed, their numbers never dwindled. The poor Roman Foot Soldiers could only watch, as one by one, they were shot down despite their shields and breastplates."

Ormozd turned to Persicus. "Salman is the Crassus of our time. He is as crazy, as greedy, and as evil as Crassus. Crassus outnumbered Surena three to one, but Surena won the battle because he adroitly planned it with sagacious foresight. He knew what the Romans would do and he was prepared to strike back. He surprised the enemy with his advanced skills and weaponry." Ormozd sighed. "This is what I will need to defeat Salman. I need to do something that Salman won't expect, something that will leave him defenseless."

Persicus had an idea, but he felt foolish offering his thoughts to help the King strategize a war. He kept his thoughts to himself for the time being. Maybe he would speak to Nooshin about it.

"The Parthians had a standing army—men trained and waiting to fight if the need arose—with supplies, an armory, and plenty of horses, while the rest of the world hired peasants and noblemen to fight, however, only the noblemen could afford horses and good weapons. The rest of the men made do on foot, with crude or cheap swords. My ancestors built this Kingdom after the example of the Parthians. We have an armory and a standing army. We have plenty of horses. Salman has an army of hired bandits, but their numbers are daunting, and they are merciless cutthroats. All I need is a plan to defeat him, however he may attack."

Ormozd turned, walking towards the door. Persicus followed.

"That is what I wanted to show you. So you could see the parallels between then and now. Not much has changed in a thousand years."

Persicus stopped in the corner of the room, where a large, gold statue of a man sat on a pedestal. The man's long hair fell over his broad, muscular shoulders. He wore pants and a tunic, and held the handle of a sword, sheathed at his waist.

Ormozd smiled as Persicus stared, perplexed with growing awe.

"Is this solid gold?" Persicus asked, looking from the sculpture to Ormozd, who stood a few feet away.

"No, but it is supposed to look that way. They called it gold plating."

"Wow." Persicus felt elated, as he realized the King had taken him under his wing, and shown him the Kingdom's most precious treasures. "This is amazing."

"This is a Parthian nobleman, it may be General Surena, no one is certain, but it was made around the same time as the battle."

"How did they make it? What is under it if it is not solid gold?"

Ormozd turned and made his way through the maze of history, back into the Shabestan "It was a technology developed by a Parthian alchemist, centuries ago. We know very little of how they accomplished this. All we know for sure is that they used big vats of some sort of acid. All we knew of this and much more knowledge was lost when the savages burned our books."

"What about the people who made them? Did they not teach anyone else how to create these kinds of sculptures?"

Ormozd shook his head. "Sadly, they were all killed by the barbarians—all the alchemists, astronomers, mathematicians, and writers. A horrible tragedy."

"That's crazy. Why kill the smartest people? The inventors and writers? The essence of progress?"

Ormozd laughed. "Any *rational* person would ask that question.

However, these were not rational people. You want to know what they would say? 'We have one book, which makes all these infidel books obsolete.' They believe all the knowledge you will ever need can be found in their one holy book." Ormozd scoffed. "They actually compared it to an onion. When you peel off the first layer, you find more knowledge under the next layer. It's a tragedy. Some cultures evolve while others regress. Those that regress like to take everyone else with them. It's not enough for them to believe whatever they want, they must force everyone else to believe it too, or else they call them infidels whom are not worthy of life, who they are duty-bound to kill." Ormozd looked despondent.

They made their way back into the garden, expecting to see Nooshin. Anoush reported that she was still with her maids in the bath.

King Ormozd poured more wine and they sat on a bench overlooking the city.

"Tell me about Salman. What do you expect him to do?"

"Eh, Salman. King Salman, the Magnificent," Ormozd said, voice filled with disdain, waving of his hand, splashing wine down into the grass.

"Master of the Silk Road!" Persicus mocked.

"The King of Kings!"

"The Blessed Shadow of the Almighty Allah on Land!"

"The Light of Your Eyes."

"Yeah, that guy." Persicus confirmed with a laugh.

Ormozd took a deep breath. "That rodent was no more than a highway robber. A common thief, who was wanted and had a price on his head, who came from a long line of thieves. His ancestors fled from their province because of their crimes and settled in some mountain caves near the trade route, where no one knew them. Then they began 'taxing' the merchants who had travelled that route for generations. Whenever the army came, they fled back into the treacherous mountains, where they hid within a network of caves. This went on for generations, but since their thefts were usually small and random, it didn't warrant a thorough search of the dangerous mountains, where no doubt the army could be easily ambushed and killed — they were well sheltered in those caves. Then Salman came along. He gathered a small band of cutthroats and harassed merchants along the Silk Road worse than his ancestors ever did. People began avoiding what he claimed as his territory, taking alternate routes, even if it took a week longer. When he realized the merchants avoided coming his way and he was no longer making enough money, he changed his tactic. He began attacking small, defenseless communities and villages along the trade route. He made them pay a ransom. He called it protection money, but it was protection against himself. Those who resisted him had their towns leveled and burned. The survivors, he took and sold as slaves. He made rounds on all 'his' towns, collecting money from them until many were impoverished, and fled the area. Many of those people came here.

"His cruelties became well known. He began raking in money. He prospered. He was still only a low-life bandit, but then several nomadic tribes, with no loyalty to land or people, sought him out, and joined with him. Now he had himself a small army and he began to take over larger towns along the trade route. More cutthroats, bandits, and nomads came flocking to him. For criminals, Salman is a way for them to steal and kill, and get away with it, with no threat of being captured and put to death, so long as Salman is feared. Now, he has a good size army, who are as ruthless as he is. They moved out of the caves, built a fortress at the base of the mountain, and named it Turan. With their help, he made himself an empire and named himself King." Ormozd paused. "I've often wondered if he named it Turan after the mythological Turan in the Avesta—though I doubt it. I don't think he realizes Turan means *those with a dark mind*."

"I don't think he is the reading type."

"But now you can see how a small problem can become a big one. I should have dealt with him years ago."

"But if you defeat him, maybe others will also stand against him."

"Most towns along the trade route are too small to stand against him. Unless, Ahura Mazda forgive me, I kill him. Without Salman to hide behind, what's left of his army will go back to their tribes or become simple highway robbers once more." Ormozd sighed. "Just like a game of chess, I need to anticipate what he is going to do, so I can take him out."

"Chess? I am not familiar with it."

"You have never played chess before?" Ormozd said, delighted at the prospect of a new opponent.

"No. What kind of game is it?"

"It is a game of strategy. A battle played on a board with kings, viziers, elephants, horses, and soldiers. I will teach you and maybe I can come up with a plan to defeat Salman while we play."

Anoush sent a servant to retrieve the chessboard.

# 21

## THE SECRET WEAPON

Persicus awoke half an hour before dawn. Unable to clear the thoughts of the previous day from his mind, he had lain awake most of the night with the memory of Ahmad and Mahmood, the sword above his neck, Salman's promises to Nooshin, the look on her face, all playing out again and again, every time he closed his eyes. Having slept no more than three hours, he rolled out of bed, dressed, and made his way out to the garden.

The air was chilled and crisp. He took a deep, cleansing breath and exhaled a warm plume of white mist. At the edge of the garden, he stood and looked down upon the darkened city. A strong feeling of déjà vu overcame him, like an obscure, ominous premonition. Chills ran down his spine and he looked up, almost as if expecting something to swoop down upon him. A rustling sound came from the gloom to his right. Startled, he jerked around, eyes searching for movement in the near pitch-black jumble of trees.

"Are you always such an early riser Persicus?" Ormozd asked, coming to stand beside him.

Persicus' heart knocked against his chest. He let out a shaky breath. "No, not usually, but sleep eluded me last night."

"Yes, me too. This business with Salman, I've been thinking about it all night."

"If only it were as easy as a game of chess."

Ormozd laughed. "You are a fast leaner. You checkmated me twice last night. You are the first person ever to beat me." Ormozd leaned in and whispered in a confidential tone. "Are you sure that you have never played before?"

Persicus smiled. "I'm positive. I'm certain that I only beat you because you had your mind on more important matters. Thank you for teaching me, though. My uncle always promised to teach me board games as a child, but he never got around to it."

"Chess is a great game for distractions. Sometimes, if you can get your mind off your troubles, the solution comes to you, right out of the blue sky." Ormozd sighed and leaned against the stone garden wall. "Unfortunately, it did not work for me last night. These walls have withstood many armies, but I fear Salman is a beast of a different nature. He is unpredictable, who knows what he may have hidden up his sleeve. Another day is upon us and now I must prepare for war. We must be ready for anything." Ormozd leaned his hands against the wall, scanning the plains beyond the city for a hint of glowing campfire that might signify Salman's men lurking in the darkness. "Every plan I've come up with feels inadequate."

A streak of radiant orange crested the eastern mountains. The midnight blue sky lightened in increments.

"And you still need a surprise," Persicus said, cautious, still reluctant to offer his idea to the King.

"Yes. Something that *he* won't be prepared for." Ormozd's voice was strident.

The sun slipped out from behind the jagged pinnacle of the eastern mountain range, casting the first rays of golden light into the retreating darkness, and sparkling slivers of red and orange upon the river.

As Persicus watched the sunrise, he decided he was being foolish, Ormozd would approve of his idea, and even if he didn't, he wouldn't lambast him.

"May I propose an idea?" Persicus asked.

Ormozd glanced sideways at him. "Yes. I am open to suggestions."

Persicus paused, trying to think of a way to sound believable and legitimate. Finally, he said, "Well, I have an idea, but I will have to explain what I saw first.

"When I was in China I witnessed an amazing battle between their military and the nomads of the northern territory. They fought with a new weapon that I have heard nothing of since my departure from China. It is called Fei Huo."

"Fei Huo? What is it? What does it mean?" Ormozd asked.

"Flying Fire. It means flying fire." Persicus watched Ormozd's eyes narrow, no doubt wondering what flying fire was, and why Persicus felt inclined to waste his time with it.

"Go on," Ormozd said, skepticism clear in his voice.

265

Persicus continued with a smile that bid Ormozd's patience. "This is a weapon that you set on fire and it erupts like a volcano, spewing red-hot metal and flaming black smoke. It makes a tremendous bang, like a roaring clap of thunder, and the force of it shakes the earth. It all happens in an instant. As it kills and maims your enemies, it will strike unspeakable terror in their hearts. I am confident Salman has never seen anything as horrific as this."

Ormozd nodded. He sat on the bench, gripping his bearded chin between his index finger and thumb, his other arm resting across his stomach. "How does it work?"

"The secret lies in a black powder the Chinese invented. They have taken great measures to keep this invention and its formula secret, the way they tried to keep their silk production secret. This is why I am sure Salman will not know of it."

As Persicus spoke, Ormozd's expression changed from skeptical to thoughtful to frustrated. "This sounds interesting, but if the formula is *secret*, what good does it do us?"

Persicus gave him a meek smile. "I may have overheard the formula by accident."

"Overheard it? How did you overhear it?"

Persicus' associate, Ng, had ordered a large load of sulfur from Persia, to be brought to him with utmost discretion. He gave Persicus specific instructions to follow, including which routes to take, to arrive in the evening, under the cover of darkness, and to give the gatekeeper the password 'gǎu' — which he must not forget. Due to unforeseen delays, he arrived late that night, the gatekeeper told him to go directly to the inn, not to stop for anything else, which was fine with Persicus, since he was exhausted. When he opened the door to the inn, he paused at the threshold, surprised to see row after row of empty beds and tables, and the innkeeper looked equally surprised to see him. Over a late dinner, the innkeeper explained that the city had been closed to travelers, as they were expecting a war within the next few days. This explained a lot for Persicus — the password and the specific instructions — but that he had been allowed into the city at all perplexed him most of all.

"I was taking a load of sulfur to the capital city in China — Cháng'ān. No one else slept at the inn because of the upcoming battle. I tried to sleep, but a terrible storm blew in, and all the thunder kept waking me. While lying in my bunk, almost asleep, the door to the inn banged open, and two men came struggling in. At first, I thought they were drunk, so I tried to ignore them.

"One of the men kept saying, 'You're going to be all right … you're going to be all right,' but the second man said that he knew he was gravely injured, and that he wouldn't make it through the night. He told his friend that he had perfected the formula and asked him to write it down and take it to the Emperor, at once. The first one said that they were not alone and suggested they go somewhere else, but the injured man insisted he could go no further. Then I heard footsteps walking towards me. I heard him say that I was sleeping, but not to worry, because I was one of those big-nosed people from the West, and that I couldn't pronounce 'ni hao' if my life depended on it, let alone understand Chinese."

Persicus remembered feeling his nose under the blanket. He had never thought of himself as having a big nose before, but he supposed that to people with flat noses, it would seem big.

"The injured man recited the formula in Chinese. He was dead by morning. I saw his face, black and scorched with severe burns."

"But he recited the formula in Chinese?"

Persicus nodded. "I understand Chinese."

Ormozd's eyes widened in surprise and he gave Persicus an appraising look, as if seeing him for the first time. This supposed simple man became more intriguing by the minute.

Persicus laughed. "My uncle was a merchant and I traveled everywhere with him, but we spent a great deal of time in China. One of his partners was a Chinese man, named Ng, who had two sons about my age. I learnt Chinese so I could play with the only companions my own age," Persicus said, by way of an explanation.

"In the morning, I found Ng and delivered the sulfur to a large building, which smelled acrid and smoky, as if charred wood had been burning inside for days. While Ng spoke in a low voice to the stuffy, angry man in charge, I looked through an open door, and saw a puzzling sight, so I slipped into the room where dozens of men worked feverishly, cutting stalks of bamboo, inspecting it, and carving holes into the wood."

Persicus watched in fascination until the stuffy, angry Chinese man found him, grabbing his arm, and yanking him out of the room, yelling at him for being nosey, and sneaking off, asking what he was looking for, anyway. Was he snooping or spying? Persicus thought the outburst was way out of proportion for simply watching the men work, so he played dumb, while Ng covered for him. Ng paid him with a bag of gold coins and hurried him out the door. Later that night, he dined with Ng, who spoke of everything but what was going on in that building—even when Persicus pressed him, Ng changed the subject. Ng had never been a secretive type; indeed, he had always been gregarious and chatty. Two days later, Persicus left the city with a load of Chinese medicinal herbs.

Ormozd nodded for him to proceed with his story.

"Later, as I was leaving the city, I witnessed the battle. The Chinese fought with this amazing new weapon. At that point, when I saw the weapons in use, I connected everything. This was why they allowed me into the city, this was the reason for everyone's secrecy, and unwittingly, I had heard the perfected formula, saw them making the weapon, and saw what it did during battle."

Ormozd gave him a dubious look. "But it burned his face and killed him!"

"Yes, he explained to his friend that they would need a longer fuse. That was the only problem. He had run out and used a short one. He said it was his own mistake, he should have known better, but foolishly, he rushed the test, so excited he was that the formula was perfected, at last."

"What is a fuse?"

"It's what sets the black power on fire and causes it to erupt."

Persicus and Ormozd turned towards the sound of clanking metal. A man clad in light armor stepped into the garden from the Palace.

"Ah, here is the man I've been waiting for," Ormozd said.

The man bowed. "At your service, Your Majesty."

"Gerisha, meet the man who saved my daughter."

Gerisha gave Persicus an appraising look as he stepped forward to shake his hand.

"Persicus, this is General Gerisha, Commander of my army."

Persicus nodded hello as they shook hands. Gerisha squeezed Persicus' hand, showing off his strength. Persicus gave him a pleasant smile. He had never felt the need to show his strength in a handshake, it seemed prudent to let people underestimate him, as you could never know who would turn out like Hakim.

Gerisha released his hand with a spirited smile. "May I speak for the entire army when I say we are all immensely grateful you found our dear Princess Nooshin and brought her home to us, safe and unharmed."

General Gerisha stood at five feet ten, with medium but muscular build hidden under his armor. Sleek, straight black hair, the shade of the night sky, sprinkled with a touch of grey, hung to his shoulders. A thick, full, black beard framed his lips, neatly clipped. His piercing brown eyes held intelligence and a hint of gleaming mischief.

"It was my honor," Persicus replied, already growing to like Gerisha.

"General Gerisha is a great warrior who came from the land of Armenia. He left after a change of dynasty. Their loss was a great gain to me." Ormozd's voice held a certain pride usually reserved for fathers speaking of their son's achievements.

Gerisha gave his King a gracious smile, bowing his head. "Thank you, Your Majesty. It is my honor to serve and protect a King worthy of the title. We were almost to the border of Cattula Land when your messenger arrived with the blessed news about Princess Nooshin's return."

"Looks as though your worries about entering Cattula Land were unnecessary."

Gerisha gave a small, nervous laugh, shaking his head. "Yes. Thank God. You know I would have gone to the ends of the earth for the Princess, but that is one place I don't ever want to go. All is well, then."

"Yes and no." Ormozd clasped Gerisha's shoulder and leaned in close to him, speaking in a low voice. "Now we face another serious problem. Salman's wrath will soon be upon us. Nooshin has rescinded her offer to marry him and told him so to his face." Ormozd paused as he saw Gerisha's face crease in concern, but he also detected a wave of relief. It pleased Ormozd that Gerisha reacted as he did. He knew he had made a wise decision in choosing Gerisha as his General. "He did not receive the rejection well and left with threats of war. We must start preparing, right away."

"Where is he now?" Gerisha asked, speaking of Salman.

"He's gone, thank goodness. I had him escorted out of the city. I am sure he is heading back to Turan to gather his army. We don't have much time to prepare. The farmers need to harvest whatever they can. We must be ready for a long siege, as it may come down to that. We need to check all the city walls and water canals. Persicus and Nooshin escaped through one of the canals." Ormozd tapped his lower lip with his finger, reviewing everything that needed immediate attention.

"Escaped?" Gerisha looked from Ormozd to Persicus.

"Oh, never mind that, I was thinking aloud. It is a long story and not relevant. Persicus can tell us which canal is open. We need to close it and check on all the others, as well."

Gerisha eyed Persicus, curious, wondering why the Princess escaped through the water canal. He began making his mental list of things to do as well.

Ormozd stood with his arms crossed, rubbing his chin. He looked at Persicus and seemed to be trying to decide on something. Gerisha waited, he knew Ormozd would speak when he was ready, after thorough consideration.

"Gerisha, Persicus just finished telling me about a weapon the Chinese have invented. He has seen it used in battle and claims it works well." Ormozd turned to Persicus. "If you could fill in Gerisha about this weapon."

After Persicus finished explaining, Gerisha nodded, squinting his eyes thoughtfully, thinking he may have to revise his initial opinion of this man, who appeared utterly uncomfortable in his silk clothes.

"It's worth looking into. If we can make it quickly and it works, great. If not, we won't waste any more time on it." Gerisha looked at Persicus. "What is needed for this weapon? What are the components?"

Persicus hesitated and faced Ormozd. "With all due respect, first, I'd like to make sure this weapon can never fall into just anyone's hands. After all the Chinese's secrecy, I don't want to be responsible for making this known to the world. The consequences of this weapon can be truly devastating, especially if men like Salman ever got hold of it. I am aware that you suspect there may be a spy within the army or Palace staff. Can we agree to keep the components of this just between us?"

"Yes, of course, but we must include Anoush, who you met earlier. And for the record, yes, there may be a spy, but I'm convinced he will not be found amongst the Palace Guard."

Persicus nodded in agreement. "It is a mixture of three substances: coal, sulfur, and a certain mineral that can found in stables and some caves. I'm sure you have seen it in stables. It's white and looks powdery, formed by the byproduct of horse waste. It's called saltpeter. You soak it in water for a day, dry it, and ground it into a powder."

"And then what do you do with these three substances?" Gerisha asked.

"You mix it together in the correct proportions and it becomes inflammable. I saw the Chinese military use this weapon in two different ways. They fill up little cuts of bamboo with this mixture and attach the bamboo to their arrows. Right before they shoot the arrow, they set it afire. When the arrow hits the target, it bursts into many fiery pieces, causing grave injury. The other way they use it was much more efficient, frightening, and lethal. Using the thick section of the bamboo, they fill it with the black powder, followed by a handful of small metal balls, then they set it on fire through a small hole at the end, using a fuse. When the fuse reaches the powder, it erupts in a burst of flames, shooting out the hot metal with destructive speed and force. When the smoke clears, all that is left of your enemy is a pile of injured and dead. A truly horrible sight, but the most effective weapon I have ever seen." Persicus said the last in a grave tone.

Persicus looked at Gerisha and Ormozd, expectant, waiting for their reaction. Ormozd now sat on the bench facing the city at the edge of the garden, while Gerisha stood at his side. After a silent moment, Gerisha nodded in approval and Persicus breathed a little easier.

"I will be interested to see what this weapon can do," Gerisha said.

"This sounds good. Maybe just what we need." Ormozd stood. "Persicus, I have no right to ask this of you, you have already gone out of your way, and risked your life for my daughter, but will you stay, and help us make these weapons? I don't think we can put this together without you. Mazda willing, this could put an end to Salman's reign of terror once and for all."

Persicus smiled and bowed his head. "Of course. It would be an honor."

"Thank you, Persicus."

"You are most generous with your time, Persicus. I thank you." Gerisha looked to Ormozd. "Are you certain that this war is inevitable? Salman has never taken on a city of this size, with a fortress such as ours."

"Yes, I am afraid it is. Now that Nooshin has refused him—in front of his men no less—he has to. Mishin is his last obstacle between his growing empire and the main trade route." Ormozd stood and looked down upon the city, to the trade route, where caravans were already traveling along this well-worn, busy road. "Everyone that passes through this part of the Silk Road can do so without fear of bandits and taxes. We have never collected taxes from the traveling merchants. They come willing and eager, spending their money in our caravanserai, and our people make a good profit, and all benefit. The merchants and our citizens.

"Salman would annex our Kingdom, tax us and the merchants to make himself richer, and expand his empire. If he could have done so by marrying Nooshin, he would have done so without violence, but now he has no other choice but war, if he wishes to continue expanding his rule, his land, and his profit. He would take Mishin, take the trade route, and tax all who pass through, as he has done to his own territory. The merchants would grow wise and find alternate routes to avoid being robbed, and all the people here who rely on the business of merchants would suffer, and become impoverished. So, we must fight and fight well."

Anoush came into the garden, he nodded hello to Persicus and General Gerisha. "Your Majesty, the army has gathered at the square and they are awaiting your command."

Ormozd thought for a moment. "Make sure everyone is prepared for battle, their armor fits well, and their swords are sharpened. In light of our new plan, there is nothing else for them to do today, so they can rest tonight. Tomorrow, we will begin preparing the men for war. We will need some men to collect the materials needed for Persicus' weapon. Select a handful of your most trusted men from the Palace Guard to assist Persicus." Ormozd turned to Gerisha. "We will keep this as quiet as we can. Only the Palace Guard will collect the materials, but do not tell them what it is for until we are ready. We will instruct the army right before the battle. Gerisha, you and Persicus will be in charge of it."

Anoush and Gerisha both nodded.

"I know of numerous mountains nearby with plenty of sulfur.

Maybe we can find that saltpeter in the caves around there as well," Gerisha said.

"That is all for now."

Gerisha and Anoush both bowed and took their leave. Persicus looked uncertain, unsure if he should follow them.

"Ah, breakfast is being served, come Persicus, let's eat."

The servants set the table in the garden platform. As the servants filed back inside, Persicus followed Ormozd up the platform steps, and they settled onto the cushions around the table.

Persicus wondered where Nooshin was. He had not seen her since she left the garden the afternoon before, for her so-called quick bath.

Just then, Nooshin walked into the garden, looking pristine, in crisp, vibrant, silken clothing. Her clean, shiny, dark brown hair fell in a thick braid down her back. She wore new, uncomfortable looking slippers. Completely refreshed, her bright-green eyes shined in the morning sun.

Persicus stared at her, amazed by her radiant beauty, as she walked through the garden. He smiled when she sat across from him, remembering the first day he had met her. "Nice shoes, but I don't think you will be able to walk far in them."

She frowned at him, smirked, and then laughed. "I will be just fine, *thank* you."

Persicus filled her cup with tea.

"I suppose you will be leaving us soon, Persicus. I'm sure you are eager to get home to your orchard." Nooshin said studiously, picking up a piece of flatbread. She avoided Persicus' steady gaze. "Father, I promised him payment and to replace his horse in return for bringing me home."

"And of course we will, but he is not leaving yet. This young man has turned out to be quite resourceful. He has agreed to stay and help us with our war efforts. He is going to be building a new weapon for us. He and Gerisha are in charge of it." Ormozd took a sip of the hot, savory tea. "And of course, I will compensate you for your time."

Nooshin's mouth dropped slightly in surprise. She looked over at Persicus who had a wide grin, pleased by her reaction. "I told you no compensation is necessary. I won't accept a feather's weight in gold. I am no longer seeking gold." Persicus recalled what the Buddhist teacher, Vinzeh, had told him. "Sometimes, you find things that are much more precious than gold." He realized that he had said the last part aloud and hadn't meant to, and now he avoided Nooshin's gaze. Flustered, he changed the subject. "I ... I wonder if our Heavenly Horses are still at the stable. I should go look for them."

"Magnificent creatures!" Ormozd said. "I had one a long time ago.

You left your horses in town?"

"Yes, father. We had to leave them when Hakim and some guards came looking for us, we couldn't leave through the gates. And then Salman also showed up." Nooshin looked down at her plate. "I will accompany you into town, Persicus. I want my horse back, as well. He is a beauty. And of course, we will repay you for them."

Persicus opened his mouth to protest, but Nooshin spoke first. "And what have you found that is more precious than gold?"

Persicus startled. "Well, I — "

Just then, Gerisha came clanking back into the garden, walking purposefully as though on a matter of great importance, drawing everyone's attention, saving Persicus from having to respond.

Gerisha stopped in front of King Ormozd. "Your Majesty, sorry to interrupt your breakfast, but I have important news."

"Yes? What is it?"

"We assumed that Salman had gone back to Turan to collect his army, but we were wrong. Two of our men spied them at Twelve Wolf Creek, where Salman and his men have made an encampment."

"I see." Ormozd rubbed his temples with his fingertips.

"I'm afraid there is more," Gerisha said.

Ormozd looked up. "Go on."

"They are cutting down trees and building some sort of structure."

"What could they be making?" Persicus asked.

"As I said before, Salman always has something up his sleeve."

Persicus leaned back, crossing his arms. "When Gerisha and I search the caves for the minerals, we can stop by, and check out his encampment. Maybe we can figure out what he is up to."

Tahmineh watched disapprovingly as Persicus walked ahead of her, side by side with Nooshin.

After Nooshin's mother died, Tahmineh had raised Nooshin as her own daughter. Although Ormozd could have taken great care of his daughter by himself, he wanted Nooshin to have a mother figure, so he had assigned her to be a surrogate mother, which had delighted Tahmineh. Now, she watched Nooshin's happy face as she spoke with this man, this Tajik.

Tahmineh was about fifty years old. She weighted over three hundred pounds and always said that was how a woman should be. She kept her hair chopped short, so she never had to fuss with it. She wore no make-up. Thin wrinkles lined her plump lips, testament to her constant pucker-lipped frown.

273

With a censorious frown, she shook her head again, for the thirtieth time since they had left the Palace. "Nooshin!"

Nooshin turned towards Tahmineh with a look of angelic innocence. "Yes, Tahmineh?"

Tahmineh hobbled up to her. She leaned in close and groused in her ear. "This is most improper. Do not walk so close to this man. He is a stranger and a commoner. Have some self-respect or Mazda knows what these people might think and for goodness sake, stand up straight lest the entire city thinks your father raised a barbarian."

Nooshin rolled her eyes and smiled at her. She always said 'Yes, Tahmineh' to all of her motherly bickering. However, now she said, "This man *saved* me, Tahmineh. I have been with him for the past week and he has always been a perfect gentleman. Besides, I am not doing anything improper. We are simply going to find our horses." Nooshin turned and rejoined Persicus.

"She is something, isn't she?" Persicus whispered to Nooshin as he watched Tahmineh give him the evil eye again. He smiled at her and gave a little wave, and she scowled back.

Nooshin smiled up at him. "She is making sure you don't kidnap me and run off to the barbarians."

"Hmm," he said thoughtfully.

It was still early and the sounds from the bazaar echoed from every direction. They strolled at a casual pace along the main road, watching as the merchants opened their shops, one by one, breaking out into song, advertising their wares and foods.

Persicus couldn't help but laugh at the delightful, noisy spectacle. As they headed towards the stables, he admired the great variety of offerings. Vegetables, dried and fresh fruits, nuts, seeds, and colorful cloth bags filled with spices and herbs from around the world. The aromas mingled in the air, creating an exotic perfume.

Princess Nooshin frequented the city often enough, delivering her sweets and food to the sick and the poor, that she was recognized by the men and women who walked by, bowing to her and, thanking Ahura Mazda for her safe return.

Some vendors had permanent shops in little shallow niches along the wall. Their tables overflowing with goods, spilling onto the floor. Others set up shop between the niches, along the walls, under canvas canopies that shaded their small display tables and goods. Some sold their goods in street, from a cart pulled by their horse, donkey, or from a rough cloth bag slung over their mule's back.

They passed the dairy stalls without incident and by the smell alone, Persicus knew the next shop was the bakery. The smell of fresh-baked bread infused the air with an intoxicating aroma. Persicus' mouth watered, even though he was replete from a king's breakfast. Next, they passed the metalworkers, pounding away on copper pots in hypnotic harmony, creating a loud cacophony, which could either grate on the nerves, or be soothing, depending on the mood. At the moment, Persicus and Nooshin found the sound pleasant, while Tahmineh was developing a headache; her mouth transformed from her usual pucker to a teeth-gritting grimace. The finished pots hung from hooks in the ceiling above the metalworkers' heads. The more expensive items with elaborate designs, engraved silver, and gold platters sat propped on the tabletops behind them.

They reached the last intersection before they came to the stable. They waited for a donkey pulling a heavy cart to pass. Another horse-drawn cart clattered along from the opposite direction, followed by a throng of people. As they struggled through the intersection, Persicus glimpsed a chestnut-colored horse beside a solid-black horse, and an old, stooped man leading them out of the stable by their reins. Their Heavenly Horses.

"He's taking our horses!" Persicus said, trying to push through the procession of people.

"Who is?" Nooshin hollered from a few steps behind.

"Stay here. I'll take care of it." Persicus surged through the crowd as fast as possible. He ran over to the man, yelling at him to stop.

The old, stooped man with white, willowy hair sprouting from the sides of his head stopped and looked up at Persicus. He paused and then continued on his way. The old man walked with a limp, holding the reins in one hand, and a long walking stick in the other. The stick was smooth with age and wear, but still a solid piece of wood.

Persicus jogged up to the old man and kept pace alongside him. "Hey there, those are my horses."

The man kept walking, his eyes fixed straight ahead. The walking stick striking the ground with a heavy thud every other step.

Persicus jump in front of him. He saw the old man had a death grip on the reins. "I said these are my horses," Persicus repeated a little louder.

The old man stopped and stood up straight, narrowing his eyes at Persicus. "Who are you to tell me these are your horses?"

"I am their owner."

"Owner? Ha! Ownership means responsibility. Responsibility means feeding your horses. Neglect means to throw away, as you have done to these poor creatures. This is their third day here, with not so much as a thought from you. You have forfeited your right to ownership. Get out of my way!" The man shook his stick at Persicus.

Persicus stood his ground, crossing his arms, and frowning down at the old man. "Listen, I don't have to explain anything to you. They are mine. I left them here. I can take them out of your hand or you can do the right thing and give them to me."

"What? You would steal from an old, crippled man? Ha! Do you know what they do to horse thieves here in Mishin? King Ormozd would have your head!"

Several people stopped, staring with amusement.

Persicus was dumbfounded. How could he get his horses back without hurting an old man? Moreover, what would the people here think if he did? He decided to stand his ground, the only thing he could do without abusing an old cripple.

"Go on. Go now. Out of my way, before I call a guard!" The old man swung his stick sideways, hitting Persicus on his shin.

Persicus shook his head and stared down at the old man. Though the stick was solid and sturdy, the weak blow wouldn't even leave a bruise. "I am not going to move. Please hand over —"

The man suddenly bowed, as much as he could. Persicus watched him, perplexed.

"Hello, Aviham." Nooshin's voice came from right behind him. He turned and saw her and Tahmineh. "I see you have found our horses."

"Yes, yes. I was just returning them to this man here." The old man handed the reins to Persicus.

Nooshin smiled at him. "Thank you. How very thoughtful of you to bring them out to us."

"Oh, it was no trouble at all." Aviham looked at Persicus as if he was a grandfather chastising a stubborn child. "And I told you, I don't want any money for taking care of them." He turned to Nooshin. "And I am elated about your safe return, Princess." He bowed again and continued down the road, horseless.

Persicus stared after him, speechless.

Nooshin turned towards Persicus, her smile still plastered across her face. He cocked an eyebrow. "A friend of yours?"

Nooshin shrugged. "He is a citizen of Mishin."

"He was trying to steal our horses."

"Not steal, take care of." Nooshin laughed. "*You* weren't taking care of them."

"I take it he has done this before." Persicus looked back to Tahmineh. His eyes met hers and she turned her face away from him.

"Yes. He comes from another land. He believes that if something is left unattended, it has been discarded. My father has heard many cases against him. But he is harmless." Nooshin pet her chestnut horse's mane, the horse nudged her shoulder.

"We had better get back and get these neglected horses some food."

Persicus reached around Nooshin to pet the horse. Nooshin turned around, bumping right into his arm. Startled, she lost her balance and stumbled forward into his chest. Persicus caught her and helped her right herself.

Tahmineh let out a quiet shriek and rushed forward, grabbing Persicus by the arm, and jerking him backwards. Her strength surprised him. She put her arms around Nooshin and inched her away from him, trying to protect her from the fiend.

"Are you all right, dear? You keep your hands off her. Gentleman you say? Certainly not, just another barbarian. You can't trust a one of them, Nooshin dear. "

"It's all right, Tahmineh. I tripped. It wasn't his fault."

"Don't you tell me you tripped. I saw it all." Tahmineh leaned in and whispered, "He was grabbing for you. Don't you be fooled." She straightened up and looked around. "Look now. We are creating a scene. Let's get you back to the Palace at once."

Persicus looked around and saw everyone milling about, on their errands, and minding their own business. He grinned at Tahmineh, shaking his head in disbelief. Persicus turned and headed back to the Palace, leading the horses. Nooshin fell into step beside him.

"If we hopped on the horses and headed back without her, what would she do?"

Nooshin smiled. "She'd probably grab the closest horse and catch you. I think she'd lock you up in the dungeon herself. But don't worry about her. She really is a sweet woman. Besides, she likes you. I can tell."

Persicus gave a short bark of laughter. "I'd hate to see what she would do to someone she didn't like."

"Me, too. Too bad she never met Salman."

"You know this wouldn't have happened if you were still wearing those boots instead of these silly shoes."

# 22

## TWELVE WOLF CREEK

I t was afternoon by the time Gerisha and Persicus rode out in search of the caves to collect the materials for the new weapon. The sun-drenched spring afternoon was warm, nearly perfect, if not for the impending threat of doom that hovered over the citizens of Mishin. They left the city, traveling alongside the Mishin River.

"Where are they encamped?" Persicus asked.

Gerisha pointed down the road. "Behind that hill over there. A place called Twelve Wolf Creek. There's a small rivulet flowing off the main river, which feeds the creek. There's a good size pine forest around it. It's the perfect place for them to hide."

"Why is that?"

"No one ever goes there."

Persicus waited for an explanation, but none came. "Why? What's wrong with it?"

Gerisha turned and looked at him. "You just had to go and ask, didn't you?" He sighed. "Many years ago, we had an infestation of wolves there. Twelve big, vicious wolves to be exact. They would venture out at night and hunt the farmer's livestock. Having a hard time with the loss of so many animals, the farmers appealed to the King for help. Not King Ormozd, this was long before his time, but his great-great grandfather, I think. Heeding their desperate pleas, the King sent two of the best hunters in the land to track down, and kill the wolves." Gerisha paused for effect. "Those two men were never heard from or seen again. The wolves continued wreaking havoc on the local farms for months, until one day a small boy went missing. All the farmers knew the wolves had killed him, as they had found a small caftan, torn and bloody, at the edge of the forest. After that, the farmers were fed up. They hired a band of hunters who descended into the forest, heavily armed with the finest weapons and traps—all but one vanished. Twelve Wolf Creek became a forbidden land.

"The one man who survived hadn't a clue as to what happened to the others. He said they were chasing the wolves and all of a sudden, he was alone. He called out to the others, but no one answered his calls. As he turned to flee back to safety, he heard a little boy's voice calling for help, and screaming in agony. The hunter searched for hours, the voice kept retreating from him, leading him deeper into the wood. He never found the boy. It is said that the spirit of the boy who disappeared is still there and he can be heard from the road from time to time, still calling for help. No one has been there since. The farmers, on the brink of ruin, called on an old wise man from a nearby village. He said the Cattulas had put a curse upon the pine forest. The wolves would rule that land and any man who dares set foot there would die, trapping their spirits within the boundaries of the forest, until Kali, the Goddess of Wrath and Vengeance, is cast out of their land. Well … nobody has set foot near Twelve Wolf Creek ever since."

After a moment's silence, Persicus said, "That doesn't make sense. Why would the Cattulas curse a pine forest in the middle of nowhere? Not to mention, the wolves should still be out there, killing the livestock, and if no one has been there since, how did someone see Salman's army there? And for that matter, why isn't Salman's army dead?"

Gerisha's somber face cracked into a grin. Persicus realized he had been had; he shook his head, laughing.

"No one goes there, because there are much nicer parts of the river, where you don't have to climb a rocky hill, and fight your way through the thick brush of the pine forest. That is a tale we tell to the children when they want to know why it is called Twelve Wolf Creek."

As they approached the hill, the distant sounds of sawing, falling trees, and hammering grew louder, the sound echoing off the hills.

They both fell silent, straining to hear. Gerisha motioned Persicus to follow him into the woods. They dismounted, tethered their reins to a branch, and walked the rest of the way up a steep, thickly wooded hill to the top.

Gerisha stopped and held up his hand to Persicus. He pointed to a Turanian watchman, sitting straight ahead, leaning against a trunk of a tree. The watchman had a high vantage point and surely could see them walking up the hill, but he just sat there, staring straight at them. They stood motionless, holding their breath, waiting for him to start yelling, and announcing their presence. Then they heard a faint snort. They both let out their breath in a sigh of relief.

They tiptoed around him, climbed the hill, and crouched by a bush as they peered down the hill. They had a clear view of the men working below. A group of men was chopping down the tall pine trees. Another group measured and cut the wood into smaller pieces. They used thick ropes to heave the timber to the top of the half-completed structure, where the carpenters selected a piece of wood, placed them in the appropriate place, and hammered them in. They worked with quick efficiency.

King Salman stood, bare-chested, in the middle of the clearing, waving his sword around, and barking out orders and insults. His voice carried to them over the sounds of the hard working men. "Not there, you worthless idiot! Pull it farther up! Can't you see where it has to go, you imbecile?"

Gerisha tapped Persicus on the shoulder and nodded his head to leave. Gerisha had seen all he needed to see and he was not pleased at all. They descended the hill as quietly as possible, keeping a wary eye on the sleeping watchman. The guard was in a deep sleep, snoring loudly as they crept past him and untied their horses. Halfway down the hill, they mounted their horses and sped away.

When they reached the main road, certain that no one had seen them, they slowed, and settled into an easy pace.

Persicus noticed Gerisha's grim expression. "What are they building?"

Gerisha shook his head. "It's not good, that's for sure. It's called a Heliopolis—a siege tower. It is an effective way to overtake our fortress walls."

Persicus frowned, remembering Ormozd saying that Salman always has something up his sleeve. He was certainly right.

They checked several caves in the nearby mountains for saltpeter. As the daylight faded into dusk, they had only found one cave with a substance that might be saltpeter. It fit the description, but he couldn't be sure until they tested it. He took a large sample with him. Before returning to the city, they rode out to the nearby sleeping volcano, collecting a large amount of sulfur.

They arrived in Mishin well after dark. Gerisha had proved to be both pleasant company and intelligent, with considerable knowledge of war and strategy. He described many battles to Persicus, both his victories and losses. He said failing was as important as winning, from an educational point of view, as he learned much more from the battles he had lost. He described how the enemy had shown up with a siege tower, the failed attempts they had made to defend themselves against it, and how they had finally won that battle.

Gerisha escorted Persicus back to the Palace and bid him goodnight. They agreed to meet the next day to discuss plans for the new weapon.

# 23

# W.M.D:
# WEAPON FOR MISHIN'S
# DEFENSE

The citizens of Mishin had been notified that King Ormozd would make an announcement in the town square an hour after sunrise. Concerned men and women began filling the town square at the foot of the stairs leading to the Palace, eager to hear the coming announcement. The citizens all knew about the King of Turan's intentions. King Ormozd hadn't hidden the news from them; he had informed them long ago about the gravity of the situation. Months of anticipation had mounted up to this day, when their fate would be revealed to them.

King Ormozd, General Gerisha, and Anoush descended the steps. Behind them, Persicus and Nooshin followed at their heels. They stopped on the landing above the town square. King Ormozd raised his hand, quieting the rising murmurs that their appearance had caused. The crowd gave off an intrepid energy as they waited for the King to speak, stealing glances at the unknown man standing behind Ormozd with the Princess.

Ormozd waited until the crowd had calmed, taking the moment to gather his thoughts. "Citizens of Mishin, I thank you all for coming at this early hour. I am sorry that I cannot deliver better news. By now, I am sure that you are all aware of the evil cloud of hostility that has descended upon us. Soon, our prosperous city will be enveloped by it.

But we are familiar with the devil that we will be facing. He needs no introduction.

"Our wise ancestors built our impenetrable fortress in this beautiful, fertile valley, blessed by the life-giving Mishin River. Because of their foresight, as long as our river still flows, we have an endless supply of water through our aqueducts, and we have enough food to last us two years, if it became necessary — which I doubt it will.

"Our ancestors have successfully defended Mishin from all intruders since we settled in this peaceful land and so shall we. Our army is well prepared and we will be ready. When the time comes, we will instruct you on what to do to protect yourselves and your loved ones. For now, you may return to work or your homes as any other day. We have our sentries upon the walls, who will sound the gong when the time comes. Do not fear, Ahura Mazda has always protected this great city.

"Thank you all for coming this morning. May our victory come quickly."

Ormozd held out his hand and waved his citizens goodbye. The crowd gave an ebullient applause and then dispersed back to their everyday lives.

Gerisha stepped forward and addressed the gathered army. "Division Commanders, please follow me to the Palace. The rest of the troops, please wait here until further instructions."

Five men stepped forward, walked up the steps, and followed Gerisha to the King's inner sanctum.

Inside a large room with sparse furnishings stood a long, rectangular table surrounded by large comfortable chairs. The five Division Commanders stood at attention at one end of the table. Gerisha asked them to be seated. As if bred of the same ilk, they all sat in one smooth, fluid motion. Ormozd took his seat at the head of the table, with Gerisha and Persicus to his right, and Anoush to his left. A few raised their eyebrows, silently questioning the stranger seated next to their General and their King.

Gerisha looked at King Ormozd, who nodded at him to begin.

"Gentleman, thank you all for coming," Gerisha said. "I would like to introduce to you a good friend of Mishin, the man who saved our beloved Princess from the hands of the murderous cutthroats. Persicus, of Abrisham."

Persicus bowed his head in greeting.

"Persicus brings us news of a new secret weapon the Chinese have invented and we will be helping him recreate it. If all goes according to plan, we will use it in our fight against the Turanians." Gerisha nodded to Persicus and sat down.

The men's attention sparked at the mention of a new weapon. Several of them leaned forward with interested.

Persicus stood. "Greetings to you all. We need to prepare as fast as we can and I will need all of your help to gather the elements we need. First, we need to harvest all the bamboo canes from the riverside. The older and bigger the better. We need the strongest ones. They cannot have cracks or weak spots on their walls. Those will not work, don't bother cutting them down. Next, we need wood for charcoal, lots of it. Last of all, we need small pieces of lead or iron. They have to be small enough to fit inside the bamboo stalks. Any bigger and we cannot use them." Persicus took a deep breath and looked back at Gerisha.

"You are in charge of the procurement of these materials." Gerisha looked each man in the eye. "Do not tell *anyone* what these materials are for. This includes your troops. We suspect that Salman may have spies here, possibly someone who lives here, and we can't disregard the possibility that the spy is a member of our army. Know that we have complete trust in you and most of our men. However, word of mouth can travel fast. So, have your men collect the materials and tell them it will all be explained when we are ready, but tell them *nothing* about this weapon."

To get everything done in time, Ormozd, Gerisha, and Persicus had all agreed the army could collect certain materials, while Persicus, Anoush, and Gerisha collected the key ingredients, and the Palace Guards helped assemble the weapons. If the new weapon worked, they would begin instructing the soldiers before the battle, but if it did not work or if they chose not to use it, the army would never know about the weapon, and the information would go no further than King Ormozd's most trusted Palace Guards.

Gerisha dismissed the Division Commanders and they returned to the town square to delegate the tasks to their men.

"What have you to report on Salman's activities? Did you see the structure he is building?" Ormozd asked Gerisha when all the commanders had filed out.

"Yes, Your Majesty. I fear it is bad news. They are building a siege tower."

Ormozd leaned back in his chair, drumming his fingers against the table. "I've heard of these structures, but I've never seen one. Please, describe it?"

"It is a simple wooden tower, on wheels, built high enough to overcome our tall fortress walls. It works very well. I saw it used when I was a boy, but I remember the day as if it happened last week." Gerisha's eyes glazed over and took on a haunted look. His monotone voice gave no indication of any strong emotion, but it was clear to Ormozd that the horror of what he spoke was all too vivid in his memory.

"The Roman soldiers hid inside the structure as they pushed it up against our wall, under the cover of darkness. Inside, they were well protected from our sentries' arrows. The tower itself stood taller than our fortress, designed so their archers could stand on top of the tower, on a platform protected by a barrier—similar to our parapet on the fortress wall—and rain down arrows on our exposed sentries. The Romans defeated our sentries in the battlements a short time later.

"After they disabled the sentries, a portion of the structure dropped down like a bridge over the top of our fortress wall. A steady stream of their men poured into our fortress, like an army of ants that found a hole in a bag of sugar."

"I see." Ormozd thought for a moment. "They are making the tower out of pine wood. Can't we set it on fire with some flaming arrows?"

"A good thought, Your Majesty, but the Romans covered their tower in armor and thick leather. I am sure Salman has the same plan."

Ormozd's voice lost some its surety. "Well, what did your people do with the Roman's siege tower? How did you fight them?"

"We were losing. My father, General Armen, had come up with a plan that, thank goodness, worked. He poured a vessel of naft down over the wall. Then he shot a flaming arrow at the ground below the structure. The fire spread all along the ground and up under the tower. Within minutes, flames engulfed the entire structure. The Romans who had lined up, waiting behind the tower ran for cover, and never came back. The poor men who were already inside, well ..." Gerisha took a deep breath and looked up at the ceiling. "Their agonizing screams haunted my youth. After it went up in flames, the tower groaned, and collapsed into a massive fiery heap. That's how we saved our city from the Romans."

"Naft? That is that thick, black liquid, correct? Can we get it here?" Ormozd asked, optimist once more.

"It's plentiful by the Caspian shore, it oozes from the ground there, but I have not seen any around here. It would take at least a week to get it. Salman will probably attack within a few days."

"How about digging ditches around the wall?"

Gerisha shook his head. "It would only delay them until they refilled the holes."

This was what Ormozd liked about Gerisha. He could foresee what the enemy would do. Almost every eventuality. But he was growing grim now. Once, the walls of Mishin were impenetrable, but the siege tower was a beast of a different nature, leaving the city at risk. It would be as if there was no wall there at all. The enemy could just stand on their tower, protected, and rain down arrows on his men. Then, as easy as anything, walk across a bridge, and into the city. And there seemed nothing they could do about it. It was unacceptable.

Ormozd's face flushed red with anger. "Well, what do you propose? We just open the gates and let them march right in? Is there nothing we can do? For goodness sake! Think of something!" Ormozd stood abruptly, sending his chair crashing to the floor.

Everyone sat in silence, surprised by the outburst. Ormozd turned away from them, facing the wall, and took a deep breath, his face tilted up to the ceiling. He stood like that until he regained his composure and his panic subsided, then he turned back around to face Gerisha.

"I apologize for yelling, Gerisha, but you have to come up with a defense plan. The lives of everyone in our city depend on it, on you. Mazda forbid, he defeats us, Salman will end up ruling the entire region. We must stop him." Ormozd turned and left the room.

𒅗

While the army went to collect the materials Persicus had requested, Anoush and Persicus went off cave hunting in hopes to find more saltpeter. Gerisha stayed behind, trying to come up with a plan to defend the city. Persicus and Anoush traveled to the mountains on the east side of the valley, opposite the way he and Gerisha had travelled the day before. A couple of horses loaded with plenty of leather bags to haul the materials followed.

Persicus had told Anoush that he could go alone, as he was certain that Anoush was needed at the Palace. Anoush had said it was no trouble to accompany him. After a short protest from Persicus, Anoush finally raised his hand, shaking his head.

"Listen, Persicus. You brought this new weapon to the King's attention. He wants to know if it works. To test it, he needs you, as only you know the formula, how to make it, and use it. This means he wants you protected at all times. King Ormozd has made that painfully clear to me. Ahura Mazda forbid you fall and twist your ankle without someone there to catch you." Anoush shook his head again. "I like my job, so be careful."

Persicus smiled and almost laughed. He had his own guard — the King's personal guard.

Anoush smiled as well. "Look, I know you don't need protecting. You proved yourself to me by bringing Nooshin back unharmed, against all odds." He shrugged, as if to say, he's only following orders.

Once they reached the caves, they found plenty of saltpeter. They spent the day collecting materials and hurried back to the Palace as evening fell.

That evening, Persicus was again brought to the table to dine with the Royal Family. Persicus didn't have time to clean up after his day of spelunking; a fine layer of golden dust still covered his hair and clothing. The maid who had called on him to join the King in the Dining Hall had insisted he hurry, not to worry about his clothing. She waited impatiently when he insisted he had to wash his filthy hands, telling him the King did not like to be kept waiting for his dinner guests.

Nooshin sat at the table in the Dining Hall with her father. She smiled at his appearance as he sat down across from her. "Caving again?"

Persicus looked down at his clothes. "Yes, I didn't have time to change. I could go — "

"Nonsense, Persicus. Sit down and eat. You have been out all day," Ormozd said.

"You come across another dragon in this cave?" Nooshin asked, her face guileless.

Before Persicus could answer, the servants brought in several large trays food, setting them on the table. A young, male servant served the food from the platters to their individual dishes.

Nooshin gave Persicus a questioning look.

"No, no dragons," Persicus answered, matching her guileless expression, "though I did see few lizards. The size of a lizard, you know, about a foot long."

As they dug into their meals, Gerisha came through the opened doorway. He stopped a few feet from the table. He looked exhausted and stressed. Everyone turned to look at him.

"You sent for me, Your Majesty."

"Yes, Gerisha. Any progress?"

"I have been considering several ideas. I am going over the layout of the city and trying to determine which is the best course of action, Your Majesty."

"Can you give me any details about these plans of yours?" Ormozd asked, taking a sip of wine.

Gerisha swallowed and stole a quick glance at Persicus. "Yes, Your Majesty ... uh ..."

Persicus could tell Gerisha didn't have much. He had been thinking about the situation all day. Ormozd had made one comment that had stayed with Persicus and formed into an idea. An either genius plan or a possible utter disaster.

"Yes … Well, several of the plans are not quite finished yet. I would not want to give you any incomplete information, Your Majesty."

"That is all right, Gerisha. Please, tell me what you have so far."

Gerisha looked pained. "Yes, Your Majesty …"

"May I propose an idea?" Persicus interjected.

Ormozd turned to Persicus and he felt the weight of the Kings eyes. They clearly said, *This had better be good.* Persicus glanced at Gerisha and saw he was visibly relieved.

"We can trick them into not using their tower," Persicus said.

Ever the skeptic, Ormozd raised an eyebrow. "How?"

"Chess."

"Chess! What does a game have to do with anything?"

Nooshin winced and her hand went to her mouth, surprised by her father's outburst.

"Well, uh …" All of a sudden, Persicus felt unsure of his genius plan. "Something you said earlier struck me and has been formulating into an idea all day. If I could explain?"

Nooshin kicked him under the table, trying to warn him not to anger her father. Not to say whatever he was going to say. She glanced at her father, who, at that moment, bore no resemblance to the kind, calm, and patient man she had always known. She feared for Persicus.

Persicus glanced at her and locked eyes with Ormozd again. "If you remember the first game of chess we played, you put one of your foot soldiers within my horseman's strike zone. I thought to myself, Oh, what a bad move. Looks as if he already forgot the rules of the game." Persicus smiled. "I thought it must be your age," he said jokingly, trying to lighten the mood.

Ormozd's eyes widen. He gave Gerisha a pleading glance. Gerisha shrugged, as if to say, Don't ask me, he's your man.

"I apologize for that assumption, but the point is, I got greedy, and didn't look at the whole picture."

Nooshin couldn't believe what she was hearing. She cleared her throat, hoping to catch his attention, and get him to stop.

"Yes, I remember."

Persicus could tell by Ormozd's tone alone that he wasn't happy with where the conversation was heading.

Ormozd tapped his fingers rhythmically against the table. "Go on," he said, with an unspoken *if you dare.*

Persicus ignored the silent threat and plowed on. "By not looking at the consequences of my actions, I took your soldier out, leaving my king exposed to your elephant, and you checkmated me."

Gerisha sat down between Persicus and the King. "What does this have to do with our current situation?"

Persicus smiled. "If we set the scene with a situation that is too good for Salman to pass up, he won't be looking beyond the first move. He'll jump into action without thinking about the possible consequences."

Everyone, Nooshin included, stared back at him with identical puzzled, frowning faces.

Persicus leaned in close to Gerisha and Ormozd, whispering.

Nooshin could not hear what he said, which irritated her, but she tried to gauge how much of a fool Persicus was making of himself by her father's and Gerisha's reactions. She took a bite of chicken.

Her father sat up straight, hands splayed flat on the table. "What!" he said, outraged. "Are you crazy!"

Gerisha looked at Persicus with pity, shaking his head side to side in disbelief.

Nooshin buried her face into her hands. *He is making a fool of himself.* She had tried to stop him, but he had plunged blindly ahead with whatever crazy idea he had in his head. She wanted to yell at him to stop. To just let the professional, Gerisha, handle it. It was one thing to beat some bandits on the road, but planning a war takes experience. Now, much too late to stop him, she could only wait, hoping her father didn't kick him — and all his plans — out of the city for good, for whatever absurdities he was now spewing. Not that her father had ever done such a thing before, but there could always be a first time, and Nooshin feared now would be that time, given the stress of the situation, and her father's apparent new short temper.

Nooshin heaved a heavy sigh and flopped back in her chair. She didn't want Persicus gone.

Persicus was standing now, pantomiming, she thought, with his imaginary bamboo weapon flung over his shoulder. Finally, she heard a portion of the conversation.

"Maybe I should present this as a game of chess," Persicus said.

"Maybe you should," Ormozd retorted.

Persicus looked down at Nooshin's dinner. "May I?" He grabbed the fork from her hand before she had a chance to respond.

Nooshin sat, stunned, her mouth dropped open as she watched Persicus rearranged the entire table to demonstrate his plan. She glanced at her father, who sat observing her, smiling at her surprised, silent objection.

By the time Persicus finished with his demonstration, the plates, silverware, cups, and trays were spread across the table in disarray. Not having paid attention to what he grabbed from where, he struggled to set it back in order. "Uh? Who had the chicken?" Persicus asked, plate in hand.

"Me!" Nooshin answered, snatching the plate back from him.

He gave her a sheepish grin.

"Then the fish must be yours, Your Majesty." He placed the cold dish down in front of Ormozd, who still held his fork and knife in hand, and resumed eating without a word.

In fact, no one said a word.

Impatient, Persicus waited for a reaction to what he thought of as an ingenious plan. He glanced from Ormozd to Gerisha. "Well?"

King Ormozd set his fork and knife down, giving Persicus a long look. "I honestly don't know, Persicus. You seem to be a bright young fellow and I do hope this new weapon of yours works well, but I am not sure you are qualified in the aspects of war. It does *seem* like a good idea, *if* everything goes as you described it, but war is a chaotic thing." Ormozd turned to Gerisha. "Do you have any thoughts on this proposal?"

Leaning back in his chair, Gerisha made a tsking sound as he thought. He stood and paced around the room. Finally, he turned to Ormozd. "Well … Of course, I have not yet seen this weapon in action. If it works as Persicus describes it … well … this crazy plan may just actually work."

Ormozd looked down at his half-eaten fish. He glanced back at Persicus. "Maybe you're right. I shouldn't dismiss this idea outright. First, let us see this weapon in action. I want a demonstration by noon tomorrow. You have everything you need?"

"The men have procured the bamboo and wood for the charcoal, and we collected the sulfur yesterday." Gerisha reported, pleased to be able to give some good news.

"Anoush and I found more saltpeter today. It should be enough for the battle," Persicus added.

"Good. Now, what are you waiting for, a royal decree? Go make this weapon. And Gerisha, just in case, do come up with a good defense plan."

Persicus and Gerisha jumped up and left the King and his daughter to finish their cold dinner.

The next day was more productive than the previous. By dawn, the town square was buzzing with activity, people racing back and forth, setting up their workstations. A hill of bamboo and mounds of wood for charcoal sat in piles in the center of the square. A row of men pounded and ground the saltpeter and sulfur in large mortars with their pestles. Another group of men sorted through the bamboo with flaws, passing the whole pieces down the line, to the men who measured, and cut it into the length that Persicus had specified.

As Persicus walked through the town square first thing in the morning, he noticed that no one had set the wood on fire to make the charcoal. He brought it to General Gerisha's attention and Gerisha called over one of the Palace Guards.

"Don't your people know how to make charcoal?"

"Of course they know how, but they won't do it because fire is sacred to Sogdians. To extinguish it is forbidden. We always just let it burn itself out."

"Well, what if your house is on fire?" Persicus asked facetiously.

The guard laughed. "It does present a bit of a problem, doesn't it?"

Those nearby laughed and another guard shouted, "Zoroastrianism isn't for sissies, son!"

Gerisha shouted, "Are there any Palace Guards here that are not Zoroastrian?"

Three men raised their hands.

"Wonderful. Step forward. You are now the official charcoal makers."

"All right, after you make the coal, it needs to be ground into a fine powder. No lumps. It should be as thin as the sands from deep within the Gobi desert."

With all the materials ready, it was now up to Persicus to recreate the weapon he had seen in China. He selected a thick section of bamboo and sawed a clean cut just behind the second joint. He cut the last joint clean off, resulting in a narrow cylinder with one end closed and the other open. Next, he burned a small hole in the top, near the closed end, with a red-hot iron rod he had the blacksmith make the day before.

In a small bowl, he mixed the charcoal, sulfur, and saltpeter according to the formula's proportions. He poured a small amount of black powder into the bamboo. With the end of a thick stick, which he had wrapped in leather, he packed the black power into the bamboo. Then he inserted five small pieces of metal.

At last, he was done. He hoped he had remembered everything correctly. The moment had come. He wiped the cold sweat from his brow with a trembling hand. He didn't think he had ever been so nervous.

Gerisha walked over to him. When he examined the finished

product, he appeared faintly disappointed and unimpressed. "Are we ready?"

Persicus stared down at the meek looking weapon in his hands. "As ready as I am ever going to be. I hope this works."

"What do you mean 'hope'? You know how to make it and use it, right?

Persicus looked him square in the eye. "You just had to go and ask, didn't you?"

Gerisha gave a bark of laughter.

"I'm pretty sure it's right. My memory has never failed me; it would be a hell of a time for it to fail me now."

Gerisha gazed towards the Palace. "I don't even want to *think* about it not working. I still haven't any good ideas about defending us against the siege tower. It just creates so many problems."

Persicus gave him a weak smile, almost a grimace. "Maybe with the Guardians help, it will work, and save us both." He hesitated and looked up at the sky. The sun loomed overhead as if the eye of the Guardian was watching him, ready to laugh uproariously at his failure. He swallowed past the knot in his throat. "Better send for the King." His knees felt weak. He flopped down onto the ground, waiting for the King.

𒐖

King Ormozd and Nooshin descended the stairs to the town square. Nooshin settled on a bench under the shade of a giant oak tree, ready to watch the show. She silently prayed Persicus would succeed and not make a fool of himself today. If the weapon didn't work, she feared she would never see him again. Her father was putting a lot of faith in a man he had only known for a few days.

"Are we ready, Persicus?" Ormozd asked expectantly.

Persicus nodded. "I have one weapon completed, to the best of my knowledge and memory."

Ormozd narrowed his eyes. This was not what he wanted to hear. Persicus had sounded very sure of himself when he told him about the weapon, but now he detected a definite uncertainty in his voice.

"Explain what we have here," Ormozd ordered.

Persicus laid his hand on the weapon, which he had propped on a makeshift worktable. "This section of the bamboo has been filled with the black powder and five pieces of metal." Persicus pointed as he explained the individual compartments and components of the weapon. "This string on top has been coated with fat, as well as a small amount of black powder. Gerisha will set the end of it on fire and jump away." He pointed to the middle of the square, where five water-filled goatskins hung from a makeshift scaffold. "Those represent the enemy, of course."

Persicus looked at King Ormozd, who nodded for him to proceed. He turned to Gerisha and gave him a nod. It was time to test the weapon.

Persicus knelt on one knee with the weapon perched on his right shoulder. He had placed a leather pad under the bamboo for protection from the heat. He held tight to the bamboo with both hands: one by his shoulder and one supporting the front end. He took a deep breath. "All right, Gerisha. Ready."

Gerisha stepped in close, holding a slim piece of wood with the end ablaze. With visible tentativeness, he touched it to the fuse, and jumped back when the fuse caught, scintillating, popping, and hissing as the fire progressed down the fuse, towards the hole in the bamboo stalk.

Ormozd watched the fuse—eager, hopeful, and fighting the resignation of possible failure.

Nooshin closed her eyes at first, not wanting to see, and then wanting to see. Summoning her courage and steeling her nerves, she opened her eyes wide, and watched, her gaze fixed on the small fuse.

The Palace Guards stood all around, silent, holding their breath, eyes wide open, not daring to blink, and miss it.

Persicus stood as Gerisha stepped away, holding tight to the bamboo with sweating palms. The sparkling fire disappeared into the hole, followed by an eternal second of eerie, heart-clenching quiet.

All eyes were fixed on the hole the spark had disappeared through. The guards pressing in closer. Nooshin stared with an almost panicked expression, her fists clenched around the seat of the bench, knuckles turning white. Ormozd held his breath, hoping, praying it worked, that it would save his Kingdom.

Gerisha looked at Persicus, worried, wondering if—

Persicus and Gerisha heard a faint sizzle and then a thunderous explosion burst from the weapon, shattering the silence. Scorching fire lashed out of the bamboo stalk. An invisible wave of force knocked Persicus off his feet, sprawling to the ground. A plume of foul black smoke enveloped the shocked and panicked spectators.

Several guards cried out in terror, falling, diving to the ground.

As the acrid smoke dispersed, while the guards scrambled to their feet, rubbing their ringing ears, Persicus lay sprawled on ground with a joyous smile plastered across his soot-covered face, the weapon splayed across his chest. He began laughing uproariously.

Nooshin rose to her feet, jumping up and down, ecstatic that it had worked.

The guards cheered.

Gerisha was suddenly standing over Persicus with a delightful smile that stretched ear to ear, offering his hand to help him to his feet. Persicus accepted the help and stood, wiping some soot from his eyes, he said, "I may have put too much powder in there."

"Wonderful!" Ormozd rushed over to Persicus. "Absolutely wonderful. A hell of a demonstration."

"Let's see the results. I've never seen anything like this. This is amazing."

Ormozd, Gerisha, and Persicus walked towards the goatskins. The Palace Guards followed, fanning out behind them.

Three goatskins had circular, jagged holes torn through their skin, water gushing from the holes. Small flames ate at the wood scaffolding and two skins hung still intact and untouched.

"Amazing," Gerisha said.

"One of our men with this weapon can take out three of the enemy at once," Ormozd said, his voice bursting with elation. He turned to Persicus and put a hand on his shoulder, giving it a firm squeeze.

Persicus couldn't read all that he saw in the King's eyes. He felt relief like a retreating ocean wave that had held him down to the point of exhaustion.

"Yes, but this is only a part of it," Persicus said. "This will create a fear unlike anything they have ever known. This is the impact of only one weapon. Imagine when we have row upon row of soldiers, armed, and ready. Can you imagine what one hundred bamboo weapons would do when discharged in unison." Persicus shook his head at the thought. "As destructive as an erupting volcano, maiming and killing all in its path."

"Forgive me, Persicus. I had my doubts. I was putting a lot of faith in this, in you, with no real reason or substantiating evidence. By God, now I am convinced. Ahura Mazda—the God of Light and Righteousness—has sent you not only to save Nooshin, but to save Mishin, as well. Tonight, we shall celebrate. I will send for the famous Sogdian Whirling Dancers and we will drink to our survival, and to our honored guest, Persicus."

Persicus bowed his head. "Thank you, Your Majesty. I think we all can use some relaxation after all the misery that Salman and his family have caused us."

Ormozd turned to Anoush and Gerisha. "We will definitely need more security from the Palace Guards to make sure this is kept secret and none of Salman's spies get wind of it. What steps can we take to further ensure our secrecy?"

Gerisha looked around at the surrounding men. Every one of them a trusted Palace Guard. "The rumor of war spreads like fire. The merchants are now avoiding this area, taking a detour through the southern pass. I received a report that the inns in the caravanserai are now empty. Anyone who tries to come this way is either deaf or a spy. Our guards at the gates are rerouting them to the next town. Only citizens have access to the city. We have four men at each gate that who will only allow our citizens to enter. And of course, the town square is off limits to everyone, including the army."

"Good. Good," Ormozd said. "I am glad to hear that. I will see you both tonight at the festivities. Come Nooshin, we have much to plan for tonight." Ormozd turned and walked back to the Palace, with Nooshin following, glancing back over her shoulder at Persicus.

"About how many weapons would you say we need?" Gerisha asked.

"How many men in your army?" Persicus replied.

Gerisha smiled and nodded. "I doubt we'll need that many. We'll figure it out later. All the materials are ready. We just need to put it all together."

# 24

## THE FEAST

As the sun disappeared behind the western peaks, the servants rushed about the Palace garden, preparing for the evening celebration.

Two young servants built up a pile of wood for the bonfire that would burn throughout the night. Others scurried around, bringing out the tables, chairs, and torches. They strung Chinese paper lanterns from the limbs of trees, and hung colorful silks from the Palace walls and the lower branches of the trees, flowing in the gentle breeze. Candles were lit all around the garden, flames flickering and glowing in the fading light.

The full kitchen staff had been working since one in the afternoon, preparing the sumptuous feast. As the sun set, they hurriedly added their finishing touches to the menu, which included steaming platters of roasted lamb, wild boar, fish, chicken, and duck. They heaped trays full of saffron rice, mixed with slivers of roasted almonds, and candied orange peels, which was Nooshin's absolute favorite rice dish.

They loaded the tables with fresh baked breads, eggplant and walnut dip, cucumber salad, yogurt, nuts. Fresh fruits and delicious, sweet pastries would be served after dinner.

Inside the Palace, the famous troupe of Sogdian Whirling Dancers had arrived and were preparing for their performance. Twelve female and six male dancers were putting on their costumes and makeup.

The highly prized Sogdian Whirling Dancers were most often employed in the courts of Kings. The Emperor of China collected them as if they were expensive souvenirs, along with the famous Ferghana horses. This troupe of dancers, best known for their mesmerizing beauty and their enthralling, fluid movements, were a favorite in Mishin.

The musicians who played with them were also of the highest order.

The musicians filtered in, one by one, and took their seats in the corner of the garden, close to where the guest tables had been set up. As their performance approached, each musician took turns fine-tuning their instruments. First, the heart of the ensemble — ten dap players, with their large tambourine-like instruments, beat out an intense, complex rhythm. The sound of the dap alone often caused the audience to become entranced in its thrumming beat, entering into a heightened spiritual state of ecstasy. They not only played their instruments, but also put on a fantastic show, tossing their daps spinning into the air, in unison, between beats. It was an awe-inspiring display, a feast for the ears, eyes, and soul.

Next to the dap players, four young women tucked the end of their neys under their upper lips, breathing into the instrument. The ney elicited a haunting, heart wrenching sound from the simple looking instrument. The tambour and setar players strummed and plucked out their parts of the boisterous melody, sitting beside the four ney players. The last of the group, a young woman playing a santur, hammered on the strings of the dulcimer-like instrument.

Even while warming up, the uplifting music that emitted through the garden from their instruments instilled a sense of wellbeing as the Palace personnel worked feverishly setting up the garden.

ᛁᛁᛁ

Nooshin sat relaxing in a large bath filled with enough rose oil to fill the room with fragrance. She could hear the heavy beat of the musicians as they practiced. It filled her with an anxious anticipation. She couldn't wait for the festivities to begin, as she was looking forward to seeing Persicus again, when he was not distracted by her father or battle plans.

Persicus had paid her little attention over the last few days. He had remained a perfect gentleman on their long journey, but she felt certain that he had feelings for her. She was determined that tonight would be the night that he declared his love, or at least his intentions for her. Tonight, she would give him every opportunity to say what needed to be said.

She sighed and stepped out of the bath, dripping with water. Nadira, one of her maids, wrapped a thick towel around her as she stepped out of the tub. Nooshin stood, lost in thought, absently staring into a large oval mirror as Nadira dried her off. Next, Nadira started working on her hair. When it was dried and brushed, she began styling it. The end result pleased Nooshin. Her hair shone through a string of fresh water pearls that Nadira had woven through it, with tiny fragrant jasmine flowers on both sides, wound in with the pearls. The rest of her thick mane of hair flowed in waves over her shoulders and down her back.

Nadira stepped back and nodded in approval at her work. "This will do nicely. Now, we just need the prefect dress." She disappeared into Nooshin's wardrobe.

Nadira was twenty-three years old and had been working as Nooshin's handmaid since she was sixteen. Nooshin thought of her as her closest companion. Negin, her maid that had been accompanying her to Turan, who had been slaughtered by the bandits, had been Nadira's older sister. Nooshin felt both relieved and grateful that Nadira had stayed behind, or else both of them would have been killed. That would have been unbearable.

Nadira had long raven-black hair, dark brown eyes, and a delicate triangular face. She wore simple, but elegant silk clothing. Nooshin made sure Nadira had everything she could ever want or need. Since the death of her sister, Nadira had a weariness about her that saddened Nooshin. Nooshin had described to her how brave her sister had been when she attacked the bandit in order to give her a chance to escape. Nooshin, Nadira, and Negin had always been close; the death of Negin had only strengthened their bond. Nadira knew that if Nooshin could have saved her sister, she would have, and she also knew that Negin would have risked her life for her Princess again and again.

Nadira emerged from the closet with a beautiful pale-gold gown. Nooshin shook her head adamantly. "No, I can't wear that."

Nooshin had received the gown as a gift from a tailor in town, but she had never had the courage to wear it because the bodice dipped scandalously low.

Nadira held up the dress in front of Nooshin. "Oh, yes you can. It is beautiful. You will be stunning in this."

"What will people think? They will think that I am throwing myself at him."

Nadira threw her hands in the air, exasperated. "And where has your modesty gotten you. You love this man. You have spent many nights with him, in the middle of nowhere, and he hasn't made a single move on you, or said a thing about his feelings for you. This is a war of wills and you, my dear, are losing." She spread out the dress again. "This will help. This dress is *your* secret weapon."

"He hasn't made a move on me because he respects me. And, I think he is too humble to say anything like that to me. But he won't respect me anymore if I sit next to him spilling out of this tiny bit of fabric you call a dress."

"My dear, he won't know what hit him. Trust me, he will still respect you, you're the Princess, for goodness sake. But he won't be able to hide what he thinks of you if you wear this."

Nooshin looked at the dress, somewhat wary and curious.

"Now, put it on. That's an order."

Nooshin sighed and assented.

She slipped into the gown, watching her reflection as Nadira tightened the bodice, and laced the dress up along the back.

Nadira stepped back and examining Nooshin, hands on hip. "Poor bastard. He doesn't stand a chance."

There was a knock on the door. It opened and Tahmineh walked into the room. She took one look at Nooshin and gasped. "Nooshin! What in God's name are you wearing? You are *not* going out in that dress."

Nooshin looked down at herself. She grabbed a thin silk shawl and ran to the door before Tahmineh could get halfway across the room.

"It's all right Tahmineh. I'll wear this over it." She was out the door, listening to Nadira's laughter, and Tahmineh's grumbling.

Nooshin joined her father in the hall. His eyes widened as he took in the dress, but then he smiled. "You look lovely, dear."

Nooshin blushed, wrapping the lavender silk shawl around her shoulders and they walked out into the garden, arm in arm.

There was a loud crash when a young servant dropped the bottle of wine he had just opened. He stood staring at Nooshin with wide eyes and a gaping mouth.

Everyone in the garden turned when they heard the sound of breaking glass, searching for the source. A silence fell over the garden — all eyes watched Nooshin with amused shock.

A maid grabbed the arm of the young server who had dropped the wine bottle, trying to get his attention off of the Princess, and back on his work.

Persicus stood by the garden wall talking with General Gerisha in a low voice when he saw Nooshin walk out with her father. Persicus' jaw dropped as he got an eye full of his usually modest Nooshin. He stood routed to the spot, unable to move, or think. Always beautiful, but this evening she was ravishing.

Gerisha looked at Persicus perplexed, as he had stopped mid-sentence, staring like a fool. He even thought he had stopped breathing.

He followed Persicus' gaze and saw that all the men in the garden had froze, staring as Nooshin walked out from the Palace.

"Down boy," Gerisha advised. "Don't make a fool of yourself. She is way out of your league."

Persicus closed his mouth and tore his eyes away from her. He didn't say a word as he walked to the tables, which were placed end to end, creating three sides of a huge square. The layout of the tables allowed all the guest to have an unobstructed view of the entertainers.

Nooshin walked over to Persicus, gave him a saccharine smile, batting her eyes at him. "Hello, Persicus."

Persicus fumbled a chair out from under the table for her. She sat, scooting her chair in, and pat the seat next to her, telling him to sit, which he immediately obliged.

The musicians began playing without delay. Guests had been trickling in until the garden was full of people listening in silence, riveted by the music.

Persicus was enraptured by Nooshin and he didn't notice the music. He couldn't stop himself from looking down at her. She sat beside him, pretending not to notice, glowing, and radiating an energy that made his heart race.

The music paused and the dap players took up a solo, pounding out a heavy beat. The female Sogdian Whirling Dancers emerged from behind the garden gate, one by one, with their arms raised to the heavens above, and their full skirts splayed out as they whirled with artful skill and grace, winding their way around the flowerbed, the shrubs, and trees. They moved with fluid elegance, an altogether mesmerizing display. As they danced into the open space between the tables, the other instruments began to swell. The male dancers joined the females, adding the masculine element to the spectacle.

Now, Persicus watched with unveiled fascination.

A full-grown dwarf emerged from out of nowhere and started following the dancers, clumsily imitating their every move.

The audience erupted into laughter. For a moment, the dancers did not know what to make of the laugher. Their performance had never inspired that kind of happiness. The dwarf kept dodging out of their sight, always just behind them, until after a couple minutes, one of the male dancers spotted him, pointing out the little nuisance to the others.

Still dancing, spinning in rapid circles, they tried to corner him, but he was quick, and they couldn't catch the little devil. He kept darting between them at the last moment before they caught him. The dancers locked arms and circled him, certain that they would catch him this time. At last, they had him surrounded. He dropped to his knees and scurried between one of the female dancers legs, disappearing under her skirt.

The dancers lost sight of him, but the audience had not. A roar of laughter went up from the audience as the dwarf mimicked the dancer's frustrations.

The Sogdian Whirling Dancers were professionals and they had been humiliated by the little imp. The dancers all stopped. Embarrassed, almost furious, one of the men threw up his arms, about to storm off, when another dancer grabbed his arm, and turned towards the audience. They realized that everyone, including the King, was laughing heartily. One of the female dancers held out her hand to the little imp and invited him to join them. They laughed as he tried to learn their moves, acting out their dancing in clumsy pantomime. At the end of the song, they pronounced him an honorary Sogdian Dancer for the day, and the crowd applauded.

Nooshin blotted the tears of laughter from her eyes. Persicus leaned into her. "Who is that man?"

"That is my friend and companion, Zorka. Isn't he hilarious?" she said, before she fell into another fit of laughter at Zorka's antics.

Persicus stared down at her in amazement. He had never seen her this happy before. She looked radiant. It warmed his heart and made him see, for the first time, how young she was. Some tension around her eyes had suddenly disappeared.

"What is it?" Nooshin asked when she saw the serious look on his face. "Do you not think he is funny?"

"No, it's not that." He shrugged. "It's just, this is the first time I have seen you really happy and laughing."

Nooshin leaned into him, whispering into his ear, trying to compete with the music. "Well, he has always been spontaneous and filled with good humor. That in and of itself is a miracle considering his past." Nooshin's voice changed and Persicus detected the familiar sadness returning. "My father found him by chance on a wild boar hunting expedition. They stumbled upon a nomadic village that had just been burnt to the ground. All of the inhabitants lay slain. My father sent for more men to help bury the dead and found this small child alive amongst all the dead. Zorka was the sole survivor. His mother had hidden him under her body, shielding him from the murderer's sword. Zorka was only three. He had stayed under his mother's body, too scared to move. My father brought him back to the Palace. He is several years younger than I am, but we have been close friends since. He grew up here with me and I think of him as my brother."

"I'm sorry. Now you're sad again."

Nooshin sighed and cradled her chin in her hand. "I am just sick to death of all the unnecessary suffering. You know, the savagery inflicted on Zorka's tribe had all the telltale signs of King Salman's work and if *fate* had not intervened, I would now be married to him." She shuddered.

Zorka had been watching Nooshin from the open area where the dancers continued their performance. The man had keen senses and now sensed sadness from his beloved Princess. He approached the lead musician, who leaned down to hear what he was saying. They discussed something back and forth for a minute. The musician turned to the rest of his group and had a brief discussion.

A moment later, a dirge-like song began, low and mournful, with a heavy beat, the ney standing out above the rest, sounding as lonely as the desert wind.

Zorka smeared some charcoal on his upper lip, managing to make it look like King Salman's mustache, and place a child's toy crown upon his head. He strode towards Nooshin. He had the crowd's full attention. When he reached the table, he snapped his fingers, and pointed to a server, who stepped forward, and leaned into Zorka on bended knee. Zorka said something briefly to the server. The server smiled and made his hands into a step. Zorka climbed up and stepped onto the table, deftly stepping around plates and serving trays.

Zorka stopped in front of Nooshin and began dancing again, but this time, he made a parody of a drunken dance, his limbs loose and flailing. He danced around the table, always missing the dishes, until he spotted a bottle of wine. He grabbed for it and chugged it straight from the bottle. He hugged it to his chest, looking guiltily over his shoulder as he snuck back to the other side of the table where Nooshin sat.

His parody was clear to everyone who had heard about Salman's antics with the wine and the destruction his general had caused in the wine cellar. The crowd laughed, slapping the table, hysterically. Zorka grabbed another bottle of wine from one of the servers, dancing as a drunkard across the table, shaking his finger at others as they sipped their own wine.

King Ormozd roared with delight. "If only Salman could see you!"

Zorka turned towards King Ormozd and stalked towards him, holding the bottle in the bend of his arm. He pretended to trip and landed on his elbows over the platter of roasted chicken.

The audience erupted again, pounding on the table in applause.

King Ormozd, trying to catch his breath, motioned the servants to come pick Zorka up, and take him away.

Two men stepped forward and grabbed Zorka's little arms and legs as he wrapped his arms around the chicken.

"Take the roasted bird with him! I am glad he fell on it; the meat was a bit tough today. That will be his dinner!" The King proclaimed.

Zorka rose up on his arms and looked at the tray underneath him.

"Wait, did I fall over the chicken? No, no. I meant to fall over the boar!"

"Too late," Ormozd said. "Take them both away. And don't forget Sal's crown." He tossed the painted wooden crown and it landed on Zorka's behind.

The two servants reached in again and lifted the platter with Zorka spread eagle, trying in vain to get up.

"Wait a minute. Put me down, I say. You don't understand, I was supposed to fall on the boar. I am ordering you to ..."

The music swelled, drowning out his voice as the dancing resumed.

𒌋𒌋

King Salman and General Mahmood rode to the outer Wall of Mishin City to survey the area. Five men bearing torches accompanied them, lighting their way.

They stopped several hundred feet away from the wall. Mahmood dismounted and inspected the ground.

"This road is fine. Nice and level. We shouldn't have any problem rolling the siege tower here. I say we push it up against the wall over there." Mahmood pointed to an area a quarter of a mile down from the gate.

"Good. That's settled." Salman turned to Mahmood. "Now, tell me where we stand with the copper pots."

"I received word that they will be here tomorrow or the day after."

They all turned to the distant sound of laughter and a burst of music coming from the top of the hill within the center of the city. The music echoed through the great valley. They backed up and saw the reddish-orange glow of an enormous fire.

One of the soldiers began whistling with the music. Everyone turned to look at him. In the torchlight, the whistler saw Salman's face take on a red hue. His whistle died off and he cleared his throat. "Sorry, it's catchy."

"What the hell! What is going on in there? Why are they celebrating?" Salman fumed, enraged. He looked to Mahmood for an answer.

"I don't know. Maybe it is somebody's birthday."

"Celebrating? They are celebrating! They should be mourning their dismal future! Those idiots! Damn Sogdians. These people are morons." Furious, he tried to calm down, yanking at his sleeves. "All right. All right. Who do we have inside? Can anyone find out what is going on?"

Mahmood looked grim. "The last two people I sent to the city returned back to camp. They have closed the gates to the city to all

303

merchants."

Salman's rage returned.

Late that night, one hundred men slipped out of the southern gate. They carried numerous supplies with them. They worked in shifts for three hours and then another group of men came to relieve them. Sentries kept watch from the battlements, looking for any torchlight that might signify Salman or his men returning to the gate. They estimated they only had two nights to finish their work before the battle would begin.

# 25

## THE MARCH TO WAR

Persicus stood with General Gerisha early the next morning, overseeing the army practicing with the bamboo weapons for the first time, in the town square. Barricades had been set up around the square, blocking the view from the citizens. Here, Persicus instructed the army on how to use the new weapon. Speed and precision timing were of the utmost importance for the success of the battle. He tried to stay focused, but his thoughts kept drifting back to Nooshin until he groaned, and told himself to get a grip.

Gerisha glanced at him, raising a questioning eyebrow.

They drilled non-stop, hour after hour. They practiced their formations, timing, and reloading their weapons. Persicus and Gerisha smiled, pleased with the progress.

Meanwhile, in the Turanian encampment, the soldiers were growing restless. The work was almost done, but a few men still worked on the siege tower. The rest of the men milled about, trying to entertain themselves under the rising, hot sun. Some men practiced with their swords, lances, and maces; some men wrestled and fought hand to hand; and others sat around, staying in the shade as much as possible.

King Salman was happy with the progress, but he couldn't wait for the action. They had built the siege tower in record time. It left a lot to be desired, as far as siege towers go, but it would get the job done, and that's all that mattered. The builders had begun fitting the siege tower in armor early that morning and by noon, they had worked their way up to the railings, fitting armor around the top of the tower. Salman had rushed the builders; he couldn't wait to show Ormozd and his blasted jezebel of a daughter who was in charge. He couldn't comprehend how they could have shown him so little respect. Him—King Salman.

Hakim, Asif, and Hamzeh, arrived at the encampment, returning from Turan with the great, terror-inducing copper pot. Hakim ordered some men to set the pot outside of Salman's tent and went inside.

Inside the tent, Salman stood, looking down at a map spread out over a table. Without turning or looking up, he said, "Grandfather would have been very proud of you. At last, you three have done something good for our country."

Hakim crossed his arms and took a deep breath before he spoke. It had been a long journey and he was getting much too old for this nonsense. "Greetings to you too, dear cousin. That is what we wanted to talk to you about." Hakim stepped forward, ahead of his brothers. "The copper pot is here."

"I know," Salman replied absently, not taking his eyes off the map, leaning against the table with his hands on either side of the map.

"Eh, well, about the gold that we ... misplaced—"

"What about it?" Salman snapped. He turned and looked down at Hakim.

"Well, we are not warriors. Not really trained for battle in any way. We will be of no use to you in this battle. We do want to help you in any way that we can, but if we stayed here, we would only get in the way." Hakim tried to persuade Salman by using his ever-so-reasonable tone. "That is why I think—with your permission, of course—that the three of us should go back, and retrieve the gold before someone else stumbles upon it."

Salman smiled, not fooled by Hakim's false sincerity. "I appreciate your concern about my treasure, Hakim, I really do," Salman said, mimicking Hakim's sincerity. "But as you can see, I am not sweating over it at the moment. I have a war to manage and people to see punished—people who have done me wrong. Tomorrow morning, we shall attack and this irritation will likely be done with before the day is at its end. Then we can all go down to this alleged bottomless pit and collect my gold. When I have my gold, we shall march back to our beloved Turan, victorious and rich, with our heads held high." Salman smirked as he watched Hakim try to hide his annoyance. Neither Asif nor Hamzeh could hide their anger. "Don't you worry about it, Hakim. I am, after all, a fair man. I will compensate you for finding my gold."

Hakim's eye twitched once. "Yes, but—"

As Hakim tried to object, General Ahmad entered the tent. "Your Magnificence?"

"Ah, yes. Ahmad. I am glad you are back. What have you found out?" Salman turned away from Hakim dismissively.

"All the activities around Mishin have been normal, with the exception of one thing. They have harvested a great quantity of bamboo from the riverbank and I also spotted a caravan of mules carrying a heavy load that entered the city."

Ahmad had been stationed on a hilltop with a group of men, watching the activity of the city. He had seen a lot of men going to the riverbank, but was unable to investigate what they were up to until last night, when all the Sogdians had left the riverbank.

Salman coiled his fingers through his fast-growing beard. "Where is Mahmood?"

Ahmad stuck his head out of the tent and yelled, "Mahmood! Get over here!"

"Your Magnificence?" Mahmood said, entering the tent.

"Didn't you say they are diverting all caravans to a nearby town?" Salman asked.

"Yes. They are."

"Why did they let this caravan through?"

Ahmad answered, "It was brought in under the protection of their army."

"So, what were the mules carrying?"

Ahmad bowed his head. "I could not say, Your Magnificence."

Salman looked to Mahmood, who didn't know anything about the mules. He shrugged his shoulders.

"You can't say? Fine. Anything else?"

"No, Your Magnificence."

"It's probable that all the mules were carrying were the bamboo sticks. Maybe those stupid Sogdians are intending to throw bamboo spears at our mighty warriors."

Mahmood and Ahmad snickered.

"The siege tower will be finished today. Tonight, we move it into position and tomorrow morning, they will have a nice wake up call. I will teach them about having a celebration. What nerve! Who do they think they are dealing with?" Salman grew furious at the thought of them celebrating, when they should have been cowering and running for cover. "They are nothing! Nothing, but dead wood. A termite infested tree that I have to burn down, so that the forest — my empire — will flourish!"

"Those simpletons cannot imagine what's waiting for them just beyond their precious river," Hakim said, with a broad smile.

"They will get what's coming to them, don't you worry, Salman." Mahmood consoled.

"Indeed." Salman smoothed his hands down his chest. "Indeed. I will have that girl, the little *Princess*, one way or another. I offered her the privilege to be my Queen, a real Queen — the Queen of Turan. I tried to be nice, tried to spare her precious city and her incompetent father. But no, she betrayed my generosity. She rejected me. Me!"

ꕥ

At noon, Persicus interrupted the training for lunch. He sat with Ormozd in the garden as the servants set the table. After they ate, King Ormozd and Persicus sat, discussing the army's progress.

Ormozd studied Persicus for a moment. "The day of reckoning is closing in. How is everything going?"

"Everything is going well. The troops are all proficient with the weapon. I think everything will be ready to go. We will continue practicing today and tomorrow."

Ormozd gave him a stern look. "What do you think is going to happen?"

Persicus considered the question for a moment, leaning back. "I think Salman is depending entirely on their siege tower. They think they have the element of surprise. I think they will be devastated when they realize how much they have underestimated the King of Mishin."

Ormozd smiled. "You're trying to flatter me. You have an excellent mind for war. I do not. It has never been necessary for me and I couldn't have done this without you."

"Thank you. I am not fond of violence, either. I now see that my whole life, all the hardships I have gone through, prepared me for this moment. This time and place."

"You say that as if you are surprised."

Persicus thought for a moment. "I guess I am. After more than a decade on the road, all I wanted to do was settle down, grow a few apples, and help keep the water flowing from the qanat."

"But you have a great calling, I believe, that will take you far beyond the simple life of a farmer. I think you were, in fact, called here."

"It was my own greed that called — that, and a one armed man and his two crooked brothers."

"Who also happened to be Salman's cousins, a striking coincidence, but I disagree with you. It was not your greed or any corrupt, one-armed man." Ormozd spoke with such conviction that Persicus looked up and met the King's eyes.

"What was it?"

Ormozd nodded towards the edge of the garden, where Nooshin stood watching the city. "She called you. If it wasn't for you, my daughter wouldn't be standing there today. And if it wasn't for her, you wouldn't be standing here today, and Mishin would be in a precarious situation."

Persicus watched her standing there, staring off into the distance. A gentle breeze fluttered her hair and her loose tunic. When he thought about what could have happened to her, a lump formed in his throat, and he got a sick feeling in his stomach.

"Why don't you go talk to her while I find Gerisha."

Nooshin heard footsteps coming from behind her. She turned and saw Persicus. She glanced at him. "Oh, it is you." She turned back to the city.

Persicus paused, surprised by the disappointment in her voice. "I was just talking with your father."

"I saw you. I assumed you were talking about the upcoming battle. I didn't want to disturb you."

"Yes, we did talk about the battle, but we ended up talking about you."

"What about me?" she asked, finally looking at him.

"Nothing in particular. We discussed how everything that happened led me here to Mishin. How something I saw a long time ago could help us defeat Salman."

"Oh," she said, the disappointment crept back into her voice. "If we win the battle, what do you plan on doing after?"

"There is no *if* about it. We are going to win. But I haven't really thought about what I will do after. It seems an eternity away from now. I suppose I should go home, though there doesn't seem to be much there for me anymore."

"Do you not like Mishin? Most people who come here decide to stay," Nooshin said, staring straight out to the distant eastern mountains.

"I have grown very fond of Mishin."

"My father could certainly use a man as clever as you, if you decide to stay."

Persicus glanced down at her. "I don't think I want to spend my life planning battles."

"What do you want to spend your life doing?"

Persicus paused. "I don't know. I had planned to settle down on my apple orchard. Grow apples, sell them." Persicus shrugged.

"And now? What are your plans? Don't you want to get married? A wife and children?"

Persicus sighed. Yes, he did, but he could not say this to the Princess. As Gerisha had said, she was well out of his league.

Nooshin's frustration grew the more she talked to him. She did not understand his new aloof attitude towards her. She decided to change the subject. "I haven't forgotten the promise I made to you."

"What promise?"

"About the gold. I promised you gold if you brought me home, remember?"

"Oh … well, remember I said there are more important things than gold."

She smiled up at him coyly. Now she had him on track.

At the feast, Nooshin had been disappointed when she couldn't get him to say what she wanted. Then the man sitting beside her had talked to her nonstop all night and Gerisha had come, and sat next to Persicus, monopolizing his attention. By the time she went to bed, she felt like screaming. The man sitting next to her had been nice, an old friend of her father's, but he kept rambling about his son wanting to see her again. They had not seen each other in years, since they were children, and he had come to play with her. He had been a bully, who on numerous occasions had pulled her hair, pushed her to the ground, and was overall obnoxious to her, and downright cruel to Zorka, whom she adored. At last, she had agreed to have them over for dinner when everything had settled down. She hoped not to have to keep her promise.

Now she had Persicus' full attention. "And what could be more important than gold? We trade with it, we wear it, and some people even kill for it."

Gerisha came back into the garden and waved to Persicus.

"You," Persicus said, distracted by Gerisha, not realizing he had said it aloud.

"What?" Nooshin asked, feigning confusion.

"Persicus, have you seen the King?" Gerisha called from across the garden. "We have some new developments."

"He went to look for you," Persicus called back.

"Well, come on then. We have to find him and have a quick meeting."

"Wait a minute." Nooshin grabbed his arm. "What did you just say? What do you mean by me?" Her frustration grew, breaking though her practiced calm mien.

Gerisha waited, staring from across the garden. Persicus looked down at Nooshin, surprised. Not sure of what he had said or what to say.

"You … uh … you must be hungry. You didn't have any lunch. You should go eat while we figure out what's going on," he sputtered.

Relieved, he turned and walked towards General Gerisha, while Nooshin stood, angry, and clenching her fist together. She stifled a scream.

ʏʏʏ

Persicus and Gerisha found King Ormozd and Anoush coming down the hall.

"Gerisha, has something happened?" Ormozd asked.

"Yes, Your Majesty. The siege tower has been completed. I think they will be moving this evening."

"When can we expect them at the gate?" Ormozd asked.

"I think they plan to attack in the morning. They will stop somewhere for a rest tonight and move into place early, around dawn."

"I'm afraid we won't have an extra day of practice for our men."

Nooshin came into the hallway and stopped to listen to the latest developments.

"How many men?"

"We estimate close to thirty thousand men."

"Thirty thousand!" Ormozd gasped.

"The majority of them are not Turanian. They are mercenaries that he has collected from all over the Asian steppes. They speak many different tongues and may have little loyalty to Salman when things get tough. They are looking for a payday, not a life or death fight."

Nooshin thought about that and said, "Well, we have more than thirty thousand."

"No, Nooshin, dear. We only have ten thousand eternal guards," Ormozd told her patiently.

Nooshin shook her head. "No, I mean our citizens. We have plenty of capable men and women. We can all fight them. We can assist the eternal guards in any way. Simply tell us what needs to be done."

They fell quiet for a moment after Nooshin's suggestion. Neither Gerisha nor Anoush would dare say it was a bad idea.

Ormozd took his daughter's hand. "They are civilians, Nooshin. I cannot ask them to fight. My job is to protect them, just as when you are Queen, you will protect our people, not endanger them."

Persicus cleared his throat. "If this battle goes according to plan, there will be no need to risk the lives of civilians."

"Yes, yes, you are right. It shouldn't matter how many men they have," Ormozd said.

"It is time to assemble the army and go over the plans, and to answer any questions that still might be unanswered," Gerisha said.

The men turned and went down the hall to go over their plans,

311

leaving Nooshin standing in the hall by herself.

General Gerisha and Persicus stood on the landing of the Palace steps. The army stood below in ranks, with the Division Commanders at the head of each group. They had gone over the plan one last time, in detail, explaining exactly who would be where and what each person was to do.

"You all know what to do," Persicus yelled. "Remember, timing is essential in this plan. Remember to wait for the sound of the gong."

"Does anyone have any questions?" Gerisha asked.

A low murmur eased through the crowd, but no one spoke up to ask a question.

The noise subsided when Ormozd made his appearance at the top of the stairs, with Anoush at his side. He walked down, and stood with Gerisha and Persicus.

Ormozd scanned the familiar faces of his men, standing in ranks. "Over three hundred years ago, our ancestors fled our motherland, Airyanem Vaējah, after the brutal invasion of the cruel desert dwelling tribes. Since then, we have defeated all who have attempted to take over and destroy what we have built here. Mishin has always been, and always will be, a haven for all the oppressed people who have found their way to this land. May Ahura Mazda protect each and every one of you, and give you the strength and courage to rise to the task before you, as he has done for our ancestors." He paused a moment. "Long live the free and noble citizens of Mishin!" he yelled, his fist held high overhead. He placed his right hand over his heart and bowed to his men.

The crowd roared, applauding their King.

Ormozd and Anoush turned and ascended the steps, elated and overwhelmed by the reaction of their men.

Gerisha raised his hands to get the men's attention. "Men, go home. I want you all well fed and rested. Report back at the southern gate an hour before sundown."

By sunset, the army had gathered with their weapons by the southern gate. They waited with an anxious alacrity. A mixture of nervousness and excited energy radiated off the men. Their anticipation mounted as adrenaline surged through their veins.

While the men waited, the sun had set behind the western mountains. A small group of Turanian Vanguards emerged out from the

312

darkness, attempting to get close to the city wall. A barrage of arrows rained down around them, sending them scampering back into the safety of the dark.

The Turanian Vanguards could hear a loud commotion, laughter and heckling, in the distance, but they could not see where the noise came from in the thick darkness. They dared not attempt to venture closer again until the rest of their army arrived.

The moon was a small sliver in the sky. The stars shone as bright as a billion scattered jewels twinkling in a sea of black, casting down their subtle scintillating light. The Mishin Army was able to slip out of the gate and get into their assigned positions unobserved. They settled down in the dark, with their blankets and weapons to await dawn.

# 26

## THE SECRET RECIPE

In the middle of the night, a sentry paced back and forth in the battlements, shivering in the cold, damp, heavy, fog that had enveloped the valley. He stopped in his tracks, listening intently as he heard the sound of approaching horses galloping towards the gate. He was tired and sore from standing and pacing for hours in the cramped space on top of the fortress wall. The cold, damp air tightened his muscles into a constant, dull ache.

He could not see beyond the fog, but he knew two people were down below on horseback. "Who goes there?" he bellowed.

"It is us," a voice said. "Let us in."

"Who is us?" the sentry asked.

"Rustam and Dastun. Let us in!"

The sentry smiled. He knew them well. "What is the password?"

"Arshya, you know damn well who we are. Open the gate!"

"I need the password to open the gate, Rustam."

"I can't believe this idiot!" Rustam whispered to his father. "We've been wall-to-wall neighbors all our lives."

Dastun rolled his eyes and sighed. Tired and cold, he just wanted to go inside and get warm. "All right, all right. Just wait until I get inside, Arshya, and tell your wife what a pain you are being."

"Waiting ..." Arshya said in singsong.

Rustam grunted and recited, "May Mithra, the Goddess of kindness and light, enlighten the dark hearts of the desert dwelling savages."

Arshya smiled in satisfaction. "They are good. Open the gate," he called to the gatekeeper below, who stood at the gate, straining not to laugh, and finally falling into a fit a laughter along with the other sentries.

As one of the massive wooden doors creaked open, Rustam said, "Next time, he's going out there and I'm picking the password. I'll make him recite an entire poem."

"Na, make it a story from Shahrazad," Dastun suggested.

"All the stories in Thousand and One Nights."

They slipped through the gate and jumped down from their horses, handing the reins to the gatekeeper.

"Where are they?" Dastun asked.

The gatekeeper looked up, nodding towards the staircase that led to the battlements. "They've been up all night. I don't know how they are going to fight come morning."

Father and son climbed the steps of the fortress wall, leading to the inner battlement, and came upon eight men huddled next to a smoldering fire, sound asleep.

Persicus and Gerisha sat, leaning their backs against the parapet—a barrier wall that surrounds the battlement. They both wore light armor suits, their helmets sitting in their laps. The sound of approaching footsteps woke them from their light sleep.

"Are they here?" Gerisha asked, groggy, sitting up straight.

"Soon. My guess is they will be here soon, before dawn," Dastun answered.

"Did you see them?"

"Yes."

Gerisha waited for more information and Dastun cast his eyes down to the floor. He looked from Dastun to Rustam and fixed his eyes on the younger man.

Rustam shuffled his feet, nervous. "We were waiting for them a couple miles down the road. We thought they would be waking up about now, but they were already on the move. But ... uh ... they emerged from out of nowhere in the thick fog and almost marched right over us. We scrambled to our horses and got away. They heard us. A few of them followed, but we lost them in the fog."

Gerisha weighed what the young guard said. "I see. So what you are saying is that you fell asleep and almost got caught."

Rustam bowed his head, ashamed. His father gave him a stern look out of the corner of his eye. His son had a lot to learn about giving information and giving too much information.

Persicus felt sorry for them. He glanced at Gerisha, clearing his throat. Gerisha looked at Persicus, reading his mind, he narrowed his eyes at him as if to say, *don't you dare.*

Persicus ignored the look. "You did fine, Rustam. You both escaped and were able to warn us in time. To tell you the truth" — Persicus smiled at Gerisha — "we dozed off, too. It's been an exceptionally long day. It's only natural."

Gerisha shook his head at Persicus. "If you're done pacifying my men. Don't let it happen again. It is not from my anger that I say this. You two could have been killed. I don't want to have to tell your wife and your mother that her husband and son are both dead."

Rustam sighed and Dastun nodded.

"All right, let's forget about it. You two go get some sleep. We have a long day ahead of us and I want you at your best."

"We'll rest, but I doubt we'll sleep." Dastun gripped Rustam's shoulder. "Let's go, son."

Persicus, Gerisha, and fifty sentries kept watch in shifts, peering through the crenels from various spots along the southern battlements. Persicus sat next to Gerisha, nervous, knees drawn up, tending to a small fire.

They waited.

A young sentry called out, "They are coming! They are coming! Look, look … over there."

Persicus and Gerisha jumped up and ran over to the anxious sentry.

At first, all they could see was the ink-black darkness. Their eyes ached as they tried to penetrate through the fog-wrapped night air. At the same instant, Persicus and Gerisha saw a faint orange glow through the dense fog, flickering in the distance, becoming sharper and brighter as the seconds ticked on. The flaming torch progressed at a slow and steady pace. They held their breath, watching, straining to hear. Seconds later, the sound of a faint hum shattered the silence of the night. They both recognized the unmistakable sound of a large army approaching.

Gerisha whispered, "Sound the alarm."

A Sogdian trumpeter blew his horn. A couple hundred yards away, another trumpeter blew his horn, long and keening. Somewhere close by, a gong sounded. Three loud, reverberating strokes rang out. The first horn set off a chain reaction that stretched across the city. The eternal guards awoke with a start, both those stationed outside the city gates, and those inside sat up, suddenly alert, wide awake in the early, pre-dawn hour. All the dread and anticipation that they had all been feeling, that had been simmering just below the surface, boiled over, and spilled out. Uncertainty and anxiety filled them. Their future would be determined within the next few hours. Persicus and Gerisha were fervid to begin, if only to quell their screaming nerves and the mounting fearful, uncertain tension, and get it over with.

Within minutes, those closest to the south side of the city began to hear the low, ferocious roar of the Turanian invaders' pre-battle cadence. They pounded their swords against their shields, three quick strikes in a raucous rhythm, chanting 'Allahu Akbar' in deep, loud voices. Except for their glowing torches, the enemy still lay hidden behind the impenetrable early morning fog, but the menacing pre-battle cry could now be heard throughout the city.

Within the city, the soldiers donned their armor, and made their way to their assigned positions. The rest of the able-bodied men rushed to get dressed, prepared to defend their homes and families should the enemy break through Mishin's defense. They clad themselves in their thickest leathers and armors, gathering what weapons they could find. They would not hide away while their city, their families, their homes were attacked and destroyed.

Persicus, General Gerisha, and his five Division Commanders stood, watching from the battlements when Ormozd and Nooshin rode in from the Palace. Ormozd jumped down from his horse, while a guard assisted Nooshin off her beautiful, large Heavenly Horse. Ormozd had tried to convince his daughter to stay put, safe in the Palace, but she refused, and he hadn't the time to argue with her. They hurried up the steps and joined Persicus and Gerisha to assess the situation.

An unusual gust of heavy, cold wind came in from the east and swept the low laying fog away. As if by magic, the Turanian army became visible. They stared at the spectacle down below them for a minute, speechless. A sea of armor spread out across Mishin Valley. From their perch, they saw the Turanian Army advancing towards them as a single, solid, insurmountable unit, chanting and pounding on their shields in unison. All of a sudden, the odds didn't seem all that good. Ormozd's mouth went dry and Nooshin trembled as she watched.

The enemy's advancement came to an abrupt halt a safe distance away. The siege tower stood prominently in front. Not far from the tower, four oxen pulled a gigantic copper pot. Curious, they watched from the battlements as Salman's men propped the copper pot up upon three large rocks and then stuffed wood beneath it for a fire.

"That's odd," Persicus thought aloud.

"Maybe they are hungry after marching all night." As Nooshin said this, she recalled something one of the women in the bathhouse had said. *And that big pot of his*, but she didn't remember them saying what they used the pot for.

"Yes. That must be it," Ormozd said, rubbing Nooshin's back in slow circles. He knew that was not the case.

Gerisha raised his eyebrows at Ormozd, who gave him a slight shake of his head. She did not need to know.

King Salman came forward on horseback, with Generals Ahmad

317

and Mahmood flanking him. They rode halfway to the gate and stopped.

"So far, so good." Persicus turned to Gerisha and Ormozd. "Think he wants to negotiate the surrender before we even start."

Ormozd gave a sad smile. "That would be wonderful if it were true."

Gerisha turned to King Ormozd, "With your permission, I will go see what his demands are."

Ormozd nodded. "Be careful. Remember the Caracalla massacre of the Parthian Princess and her wedding party. I don't want anything happening to you down there. Sentries, have your arrows ready in case something goes wrong."

The archers stepped forward to the parapet. They drew their arrows, ready to shoot. They stood behind the merlons, which would protect them in case the enemy shot arrows at them, and peeked out through the crenels to aim and keep watch.

Gerisha turned to leave.

"Wait," Persicus said. "I'm going with you."

Gerisha turned to stop Persicus with a hand on his shoulder. "No, you should wait here."

Persicus stared him in the eyes with stubborn defiance. Gerisha could see that Persicus did not intend to wait behind the wall, safe and sound, while he went to speak before Salman and the entire Turanian army. But Persicus did not know the purpose of the giant copper pot. If things went wrong down there, he would find out.

Gerisha acquiesced after seeing the determined look in Persicus' eyes. It was the same determination he had had in his own eyes fifteen years earlier, before he fought his first battle.

The Turanians' chanting cadence continued, growing louder, as though it were reaching its apex. Three clanging strikes against their shields and the 'Allahu Akbar!' Each verse louder than the last.

When they reached the bottom of the steps, Gerisha turned to face Persicus.

"Wait. I didn't want to say anything in front of Princess Nooshin. Before we go any further, I thought you should know the purpose of the pot is not for any," he paused, searching for the right word, his hand waving in circles, "conventional cooking."

"I can only imagine. But I will not allow you to go in harm's way alone. I am with you all the way. And with the two of us, they are less likely to try anything before the battle begins. I presume Salman has some honor in that respect. He's not going to try to kill us during negotiations?"

"I wouldn't be certain of that." Gerisha sighed. "Come on, let's go get this over with."

They walked down to the gate. The gatekeeper brought out two horses, handing them the reins. They put on their helmets and mounted.

A flat cart waited by the gate. Zorka appeared and hopped on the cart. He smiled as he was handed his miniature crown, which he placed firmly on his head.

Gerisha smiled down at Zorka. "Are you ready for your mission?"

"Of course. I can't wait. Let me at him," Zorka said feistily.

Gerisha turned to Persicus and whispered, "That little man is crazy."

Persicus couldn't help but laugh.

The gate eased open and they galloped out towards Salman.

Persicus and Gerisha stopped a few yards from Salman. Salman sat on horseback with his Generals on either side. Salman raised his hand and his men fell silent. The sudden stop in the chanting and banging was startling.

"Well, well, well." Salman leaned forward on his horse, leading his crossed over the animal's neck. "What do we have here? A homeless Armenian and a wandering peasant Tajik will speak on behalf of the Nobles of the Sogdian People." He chuckled. "Or is it that the Sogdians have no men left, so they have to import real men?"

"Or is it that our great King is not required to speak to low life bandits," Persicus said.

Gerisha smiled, not taking his eyes off Salman. He was pleased and surprised to hear Persicus call Ormozd 'our' King.

"We have come under the decree of King Ormozd. We are to see if we can persuade you to stop this madness and go home while you still have a chance," Gerisha said. "His Majesty doesn't wish for you to lose face in front of your army. He wishes to work out a bargain. You leave Mishin alone and never set foot here again, and we will allow you to live. Barring that, if you decline his most generous offer, we are to ask your demands."

Salman and his Generals laughed. A loud, surprised sound.

"Did I hear you right?" Salman turned to Mahmood. "I must've heard wrong, because I am certain he didn't just threaten me."

Mahmood smirked. "Indeed, it does seem that he did threaten you, Your Magnificence."

Salman's face changed. The laughing smile wiped clean away. The light in his eyes dulled and his lips became a thin slash across his face. "Now, you listen here *peasants*. You must be blind. You and those damn fire worshiping, infidel Sogdians do not understand the gravity of the situation that you are in—"

Persicus and Gerisha both put on a bored expression. Gerisha leaned into Persicus and whispered in his ear. Persicus nodded. He lifted his hand, as if examining his fingernails.

"Look at me when I am speaking to you!" Salman fumed. "Look at the reality of your dismal situation. Do you see what is behind me?"

Persicus looked up then. "Yes. I see a poorly constructed heap of kindling in front of a bunch of soon to be dead men."

"Do you believe this insolence?" Salman pointed at the wooden structure. "That there is a siege tower. I know no Tajik would know what it is, but maybe your Armenian friend here can educate you on that matter. I hear he's had firsthand experience with one."

The siege tower stood several stories high, tall enough to breach the fortress wall. A ladder ran up to the top, through the center of the tower. There were several landings inside the structure; each landing would hold twenty men at a time. At the top, a drawbridge stood upright and a thick, pinewood railing ran around the square structure. Metal and animal skins encased the railing on the front and sides. They had soaked the animal skins in vinegar to prevent being set afire. Narrow machicolations were spotted along the walls of each landing, allowing the soldiers inside to shoot their arrows through the small openings. Gerisha noticed it had no battering ram or other accessories that a well-built siege tower would have. They had built it in a hurry. Overall, the design of the structure was rather poor, but once pushed up against the fortress, it would get the job done.

The siege tower that had almost destroyed Gerisha's home as a child was altogether a much more sophisticated piece of equipment. Gerisha put on an impassive face. He willed his voice to be neutral, burying the horrors of his youth under his impenetrable self-control. "If I recall, my father destroyed their siege tower with some black liquid from the earth and a couple flaming arrows," he said, inferring that he had acquired the naft. "And that was a real siege tower. Not this ill-constructed structure you have here."

Salman smirked. "There is no black liquid within a three day journey from here. There is no way you could have found it and come back. Now, if you are done bluffing, here is something for you that is not a bluff. Do you see that pot sitting near the tower?"

Persicus and Gerisha looked over at the pot. Five men stood by tending to the fire. The pot was huge, larger than anything Persicus had ever seen. It looked about six feet deep and ten feet wide. Water and oil boiled and steamed up out of the pot. Persicus and Gerisha looked back to Salman.

"Good. This is what we call 'The Bowl of Soup for the Defeated

Nation'."

"That was smart thinking. We certainly were not planning to feed you and your men after your loss," Gerisha said.

Ahmad chuckled.

"I am afraid you simply do not understand." Salman tugged on the sleeves of his caftan. He was not wearing armor and he held no shield. He had only a sword at his waist. He felt confident enough to believe that no one would dare try to attack him during negotiations.

"Don't understand what?" Persicus asked Gerisha.

Gerisha shrugged, still managing to appear bored. "Don't know, but I doubt it's important."

"Oh, it is important. It concerns you personally. Ahmad, would you like to explain our tradition?" Salman asked, smiling, lips slashed across his face.

Ahmad grinned. "Yes, thank you, Your Magnificence." He leaned forward on his horse, eager, cracking his knuckles. "What happens to you after your city is captured, you may wonder?"

"I'm not wondering," Persicus said to Gerisha.

"Me either, but I don't suppose he'll stop."

"Crazy people never do."

Ahmad continued, speaking over them as if they hadn't spoken. "If you do not resist, we will not put the pot to any use and you needn't worry yourself any longer. But if you do resist—which I am really, really looking forward to—we will tear the eyes out of all the able men. I would say between the ages of eleven and sixty-five, though if we find some troublesome youngster fighting us, we do make an exception for them. To my delight, there are always some pesky children, throwing rocks or some such nonsense, who will be reduced to tearless crying when we snatch them up. Young eyes are so much more tender and chewy. What do we do with all these eyeballs? No, it is not only to punish those who resist. We add all the eyes to that copper pot and cook them down until it has a nice brownish tint, and it is nice and smooth. But of course, it can never really get completely smooth." His voice dropped lower. "Then, we invite the survivors of the defeated city for a bowl of soup."

"And what happens if the survivors refuse to eat this soup?" Mahmood prompted with a wide grin.

"They *have* to eat the soup. There is no real choice in the matter," Salman said. "But Ahmad will explain in further detail."

Gerisha could see that these two men were truly sick. They seemed to take great pleasure in talking about cannibalism.

"It is a simple solution. If you don't eat your share of the soup, then *you*—and I mean the whole body—will be added to the soup stock. This is something that makes everyone else extremely unhappy since it is they that will have to eat you and your share."

"Well, isn't that barbaric and disgusting," Persicus said, disgusted. He wondered if they were serious or if they only used it as a threat. Staring into Ahmad's eager face, he was almost certain they were not bluffing. He couldn't keep the revulsion off his face.

Ahmad laughed.

"Disgusting, yes. Barbaric, no. We do this as a humanitarian gesture, so that the next city won't follow the footsteps of the previous one who tried to resist our superior army. In this way, we have saved countless lives." It seemed that Salman's belief in his obscene humanitarian efforts was genuine.

"With your permission, Your Magnificence," Ahmad said, "I must object to this notion that eyeball soup is disgusting. On the contrary, it is actually quite good. Tart, as a certain kind of wine that has been left too long in the sun. It is also nutritious and you don't need to add salt. Black pepper is sometimes good with it, especially for blue eyes; they are a tad bit bland."

Blue-eyed Persicus stared opened mouthed and Gerisha grimaced. Mahmood had a considering look on his face.

Salman laughed. "There you have it—the official opinion from our connoisseur chef. He is in charge of the cooking by the way, but don't ask, he never divulges his secret recipe."

"All right, enough grandstanding. If you won't accept our King's generous offer, let us hear your demands. I'm growing more eager to be done with this war, the more I listen to your Generals here talk."

Salman stared at them a moment with a wide grin. "Yes, enough, though your attempted bravery is entertaining. Hand over the King and his daughter, open the gate, and we will march in. If there is no resistance, I may show mercy upon the citizens by allowing them the honor of being a part of the Turanian Empire. They would enjoy all the rights, benefits, and privileges that the rest of the cities of my empire are enjoying. That includes protection from all external enemies. I could even use the two of you to be in charge of collecting the taxes here. Neither of you are Sogdian. Your loyalties, therefore, are flexible. Tax collecting is a lucrative business. What do you say about that?"

Gerisha nodded. "I will take the message to King Ormozd and we will see what he says about that."

"You do that. But remember, my time is valuable, therefore I am not a patient man. I need an answer soon, or I will assume you choose to be added to the soup. I still have another city to conquer on my agenda for the week, so make it quick."

They turned and galloped back towards the gate, trusting the sentries in the battlements to watch their back. The gate opened and they went inside.

# 27

## THE BATTLE

The Turanians cheered, hooted, and applauded as King Salman and the Generals rode back towards the army. Salman wore a fierce, arrogant smile, pleased with the way the negotiations had ended.

They had just dismounted when General Mahmood pointed back towards the city. "Look, they are opening the gate."

Salman turned, looking back at the gate. "That was faster than I expected."

The gate opened halfway. A cart pulled by two men emerged from the city. A Sogdian drummer marched beside the cart, pounding out a fast, cheerful beat. The men pulling the cart stopped twenty feet outside the gate and ran back inside.

Zorka stood alone on the cart, cloaked in a blanket that covered him from head to foot. He threw off the blanket, sending it floating to the ground, and began dancing to the fast beat of the drum. As before, he made it a mockery of a dance, shaking himself to the left and to the right, stumbling and spinning. He moved from one side of the cart to the other, dancing as he had at the feast. He stopped at the edge of the cart, pulled down his pants, and bent over, mooning the Turanian Army.

An aspiring Sogdian artist had painted Salman's face on Zorka rear, covering both his small, plump cheeks. Salman's mustache, painted in exaggeration, curved around Zorka's hips.

Zorka shook his behind back and forth at Salman and his men. He grabbed his wooden crown, bent over, and placed it on the small of his back, so it appeared to be sitting on Salman's head.

The drummer knocked the wooden crown off Zorka's back, sending it tumbling into the dirt.

A roaring laughter and cheers erupted from the men in the battlements of the city.

### ̄TTT

Mahmood frowned. This was not supposed to happen. He looked to his King.

Salman watched through the crystal lens of his spyglass. "I don't believe this! Are they trying to make a mockery of me?" Salman yelled furiously, his face turning the color of a ripe beet. "Kill him! Kill him, now!" Salman roared at the archers, pointing his finger at the dwarf.

Five men ran up to the front of the line. They reached for their quivers, strapped to their backs, and pulled out their arrows. They took aim.

### ̄TTT

Persicus had a clear view from the battlements. He had been concerned about this idea and instead of having a fit of laughter, bent over at the waist, as the rest of the men were doing, he watched with apprehension. They had come up with the idea at the feast, after several glasses of wine, with the thought that it would infuriate Salman, and may make him act on impulse, which is what they wished for him to do. The next morning, after the wine had left their blood, Persicus and Gerisha changed their minds, thinking it not only churlish, but also dangerous, but Zorka had insisted. He had spent half the day having an artist paint his rear and the rest of the night on his stomach, waiting for the paint to dry. He wanted to do his part, since he could not fight.

"You better come in and I mean now!" Persicus yelled down to Zorka and the drummer.

The drummer heard Persicus' warning and squinted into the distance. He saw the archers taking aim. He dropped his drum and shouted to Zorka as he sprinted back to the gate, but Zorka, immersed in his performance, did not hear the shouted warning.

The first barrage of arrows came raining down, hitting the cart all around him. Hearing the buzzing sound and feeling something thump against the cart, Zorka bolted upright, stunned. He froze, seeing several sharp arrows imbedded in the wood, the closest only inches from his foot.

Another arrow sailed past him.

He yelped and jumped down from the cart. He tried to run, but his pants sagged around his ankles, and he fell flat on his stomach. A second barrage of arrows came showering down. As he rose up on his hands and knees, an arrow struck him, penetrating his flesh, deep into his left buttock, right through the image of Salman's eye. Zorka screamed and collapsed. He tried to get up again, but moving his left side hurt too much, and he knew he wouldn't be able to stand, much less walk. He crawled, tears of pain rolled down his cheeks as his face turned red and hot, his breathing rapid.

The drummer had reached the gate and turned around in time to see Zorka fall to the ground. An instant later, the arrow struck Zorka. The drummer's heart constricted and he felt a sharp ache in his chest. *Zorka!* He raced back out to Zorka, picked him up, slung him over his shoulder, and disappeared through the gate. The gatekeeper began closing the gate as a third round of arrows struck.

"Ahmad!" Salman yelled.

"Yes, Your Magnificence."

"Take the Third Regiment and march towards the gate on the north side. You know what to do."

"Right away, Your Magnificence," Ahmad said, eager eyes alight. He could not wait to begin.

Ahmad hurried over to the Third Regiment. "Abdul Afuw, we are marching to the north gate."

"Mahmood, take the Second Regiment and pull the tower towards the fortress. Have the archers cover the tower."

"Yes, Your Magnificence." Mahmood signaled the Second Regiment to the tower.

Ten oxen had pulled the tower all the way from Twelve Wolf Creek. Mahmood shouted out orders, waving his sword around. The men whipped the oxen; they gave a bellowing grunt and began pulling the tower at a slow, steady pace. Twenty men walked alongside and between the oxen with their shields held up to protect the animals.

All of a sudden, Mahmood stopped and stared. Unable to believe his eyes, he blinked, looked away, and focused again, his attention fixed on the fortress, where he noticed an unusual amount of frantic activity by the gate.

"Salman! Your Magnificence!" Mahmood shouted, running back over to Salman. "Your Magnificence!"

"What?"

"Look!" Mahmood gripped Salman's shoulder and spun him around to face the city.

"What the ... I'll be damned. Their gate."

"Looks like they are having some problems closing the gate."

"Yes, yes. I see it. The great Allah is with us. Stop the siege tower. I don't think we are going to need it. Prepare the cavalry."

General Ghulam of the First Regiment walked over.

"Do you see this?" Salman chuckled. "Stupid Sogdians! We're going in."

Ghulam watched the activity around the gate, where several men pushed and pulled, trying to get it closed. Another two men stood, tools in hand, doing something at the hinges of the gate, but he couldn't make out the details in the distance. "Hmm ... wait a second, Your Magnificence. I don't think we should go rushing in. We might do something we will regret."

Mahmood, always irascible with General Ghulam, narrowed his eyes, glaring at him. "I've always told Salman you are weak, a coward."

A loud crash came from the vicinity of the gate. Salman and Mahmood looked on, grinning. Ghulam watched, frowning, disconcerted.

The gate had fallen down to the ground, coming off its hinges. The Sogdians ran around, frantic, throwing their hands up in the air, trying to lift the gate.

Salman and Mahmood burst into laughter. "Of all the times to have your gate fall off." Salman smacked his hand against his thigh.

"It is simply too perfect."

Ghulam shook his head.

Mahmood gave Ghulam a smile that was anything, but friendly. A smile that promised pain and violence, hot, and yet somehow cold and dispassionate.

Salman grinned at Ghulam — an unnerving grin, though not nearly as disturbing as Mahmood's. "Do you honestly have *any* doubt that our cavalry can't annihilate of a bunch of Sogdians? They were cutting bamboo for their weapons, as the primitive tribes used to do."

"Yes, I understand that, but I don't think we have the full picture. This, however convenient, is just *too* convenient."

"As you can see, their gate just fell off. Allah is working for us here. They are in an utter panic, running around like chickens with their heads chopped off. *That's* your full picture."

"I can't believe my eyes," Mahmood said. "This will be our easiest conquest yet."

"Forget the tower. I want the cavalry mounted and ready in two minutes."

Mahmood nodded. "Stop the tower!"

"This is wrong," General Ghulam whispered to himself. Nervous, he rapped his leg with his horsewhip.

"Ghulam! Get your men moving!" Salman shouted. "Cavalry, lances! Archers!"

"Cavalry... mount! Arms!"

The men slowed the oxen as they neared the huge copper pot. Several men stood by the pot, tending to the fire. The tower came to a halt, precariously perched near the bottom of a small incline, leaning at a slight angle, several yards from the pot. The men abandoned the tower and ran back over to the rest of the troops to prepare for the charge.

The ranks of men took a moment to check and secure their weapons: lances, swords, scimitars, daggers, bows and arrows, and an assortment of other lethal items. The cavalry headed to the front of the line, the foot soldiers waited behind them, and the archers stood with their arrows propped in their bowstrings, ready to aim and shoot, to provide cover for the cavalry when they charge. Thirty thousand men waited.

Mahmood made a quick decision. Based on the narrowness of the road leading to the gate and the slight incline of the hill on either side of the road, he divided each regiment into groups of forty. Eight rows, with five men per row in each group. He figured that would be the most that could make it through the narrow gate together, side by side, with little room to spare. They would overwhelm the Sogdians with the initial slaughter.

The first two groups, comprised of General Ghulam and his First Regiment, would be the vanguards of the cavalry—the first to charge into battle. Of course, the vanguards, being the first into battle, are often killed in the first few minutes. However, as far as Mahmood was concerned, this was a pleasant bonus. A two for one, or in this case, killing Ghulam and his inept family, while making way for the cavalry. Though he wished he could kill him himself, but this was nearly as good.

Mahmood anticipated half their army would be more than enough to bring Mishin to its knees. Fifty groups sat atop their horses, ready for the first assault—two thousand men altogether. They will crush the initial resistance with their charge, causing chaos and massive casualties, so that the rest of the military can come in and quell any remaining Sogdian soldiers or civilian resistance.

Salman and Mahmood rode in front of the troops, waiting for everyone to fall into place.

"Men of the undefeated Turanian Army. This will be an easy conquest," Salman yelled. "The Sogdians have little weapons and virtually no army. That they chose to fight us does come as a surprise. We will crush them and any feeble attempt they make to thwart the plans for my great empire will be dealt with swiftly. By this evening, we will make our Sogdian Stew. You all know what you need to do. Allah be praised!"

The men roared, banging their swords against their shields. The noise grew wild and boisterous.

"Cavalry! Ready!" Mahmood shouted. "Up in arms!"

All at once, the Turanian Cavalry raised their lances, a loud whoosh whistled through the silence. A thick, quiet lull filled the air, anticipation mounting as they awaited the order to charge.

King Salman raised his sword. "No mercy! Charge!"

The cavalry took off at a full gallop, riding in a frenetic fury towards the open gate. The earth trembled with the force of the horse's hooves, stirring up a cloud of golden dust into the air.

General Gerisha and Persicus stood side by side in the battlements. Their eyes widened as they saw about two thousand men charging the gate that had fallen down only minutes before. Gerisha looked at Persicus, anxiety filling his eyes. Persicus gave him a feeble grimace and tried to quell his own anxiety. They peeked through the crenel, looking down at their men working at the gate. Persicus turned to King Ormozd, who stood by the far wall, arguing with Nooshin, trying to get her to go home.

Nooshin stubbornly kept shaking her head, her arms crossed across her chest. Ormozd glanced up and saw Persicus' face, and knew that he had to get her out of here. The enemy would soon be upon them. With the worried look from Persicus, he could now hear the unmistakable sound of a vast army approaching. He never should have allowed her to stay this long, or come at all. He knew the safest place she could be was in her vast rooms in the Palace, under the watchful eye of the Palace Guards. He said a quick prayer.

Ormozd turned to watch the approaching army. The Turanians were closing in, fast.

Persicus gave a signal.

As the vanguards neared the gate, the dust grew thick as heavy fog. The men in the frontlines heard the faint sound of a gong over the rumble of hooves pounding against the road. They charged on, paying no heed to the sound. Before them, they could see inside of the city. The gate had completely come off its hinges and lay useless on the ground to the left of the entrance.

General Ghulam rode in the front row. He drove his horse hard. He began thinking Salman may be right. They were going to make it into the city, no problem.

Just as that thought came to mind, as the last sounds of the gong reverberated off the city's walls, something happened that for the life of him he couldn't understand. The ground to the right of the gate rose up, as if a wave came crashing up out of the land itself. *Impossible*, he thought. It gave the illusion that earthquakes sometimes give, deceiving the eye, as if the land itself was rising and falling at the same time.

Persicus had given the signal and the gong sounded.

Ormozd walked over to Persicus and Gerisha. "Is everything going according to plan?" he asked, having to raise his voice to be heard over the sound of the Turanians' horses and the fading sound of the gong.

Persicus nodded. "The men are ready. They know what to do. Here ... Watch." He pointed down below.

When the Turanian vanguards were two hundred yards from the gate, Persicus gave the second signal, and the gong rang out again. The Sogdian Army threw off their dirt-covered blankets that hid the trenches in which they had been hiding in since midnight.

Four large trenches stretched out alongside the fortress, at a slight angle from gate. Each trench held one hundred men armed with the new secret weapon — the flying fire.

*Earthquake*, General Ghulam thought, but he kept charging, along with the rest of his men. The earth rose up to the right of the gate and in the next instant, from the corner of his eye, he saw something again that he thought couldn't be true. A scene resembling the end of times ensued. *Impossible*, he thought again, as hundreds of men rose up out of the earth, as if the dead were coming back to life, crawling up from a mass grave. From his point of view, he could see hundreds of men, still half buried in a pit of death, staring out from the earth with darkened eyes. Every one of them obscured by the clinging soil that covered them, adding to the menacing illusion of the dead, moving and animated.

No sooner had he taken all of that in than the sound of a volcano erupting came from the pit of death. Ghulam didn't have time to react.

In the same instant, a blast of fire came out of nowhere, sparking and flaring brighter than fresh pine in a campfire; thick, black, choking smoke enveloped the road; and almost simultaneously a shocking, agonizing pain. Ghulam felt as though a scorching, sharp tree limb had hit him across his chest. He gasped, pain tearing through his chest and lungs, but couldn't expel the air from his lungs. Never in his life had he felt such a terrible, excruciating pain, deep inside his chest. He fell from his horse, slowly, as if time ceased to move at its normal pace. All he could hear as he fell was the rapid thud of his own blood pumping through his veins, roaring into his head, pounding like a drum beating in his ears, thick, fast, and implausibly loud. Blinded by smoke and dust, he couldn't see anything happening around him. As he hit the ground, a cacophony of agonizing screams erupted in a chorus around him and with a sudden jolt, he realized that he was screaming in the same piteous way, and he hadn't been aware of it until this moment. His hearing came back, everything sounded crystal clear, and intolerably loud.

Another explosion blasted overhead. Ghulam could feel the ground rumble with the force of it. He reached for his chest and knew something was terribly wrong. He shouldn't have been able to feel what he was touching. Wet, soaking wet with his own blood, though no arrow had penetrated him. Nothing stuck out of his chest. *How?* His finger caressed something warm, slick, almost like silk, inside his chest. *Inside! I'm feeling inside my chest!* The shock of that realization became too much for him to comprehend or cope with. He screamed — shrieked. Something trampled on top of him, he felt someone fall. A hand landed on his chest, fingers digging into his wound, followed by a body — much too heavy to be human — which landed on his head, smothering him. *The pain!* A hoof kicked him in the leg and he felt his shinbone snap. He couldn't move. He couldn't breathe. He felt the weight shift on top of him, becoming heavier. Then, with a suddenness that scared him, he felt nothing. *This is it,* he thought, a calm acceptance enveloping him. A moment later, blissful death.

The first group of forty men were down, dead or dying, all of them.

The second group of vanguards charged a hundred feet behind the first group, oblivious to the dead a short distance ahead of them. They rode on, lost in a cloud of golden dust, when quite suddenly, the dust turned to black smoke, and the smell of something unusual and acrid filled the air. Something loud rang out over the sounds of the hooves, but they continued at the same fast pace. With each step closer, it became more difficult to see what lay ahead through the thick, choking smoke.

By the time they came up upon the corpses of their fellow soldiers, it was too late. The first row of vanguards saw the blood-splattered bodies sprawled across the road; the few men that remained alive, though gravely injured, struggled to clear off the road, moaning and screaming.

The shock of seeing the utter devastation of the regiment right in front of them stunned them beyond their comprehension. Everyone had said this would be an easy conquest. They had all been wrong. They saw the faces of the deceased through the hazy smoke, faces frozen in fear, in death, covered in a black soot and blood. Screams rang out from every direction.

Abisali glimpsed a familiar face, lying face-up in a heap. He stared down as he drew near and saw Abdul Kabir, half his face, just gone. Under Abdul Kabir and his horse, a familiar hand, still clutching his horsewhip — General Ghulam — completely buried, except for that hand.

The second group couldn't slow down in time and they trampled over their fellow warriors, friends, and family. In the midst of the smoke and scattered dead, they came upon a writhing heap of bodies — equine and human. Their horses attempted to jump over the obscene mound, but couldn't clear the obstacle. Some fell, landing on top of the dead and wounded, some flew into the air, thrown from their horses, and others landed with their legs pinned under the great weight of their own horses. As they struggled to get to their feet, they were hit from behind by the next row of cavalry.

Then they heard the discernible sound of a gong.

A loud explosion came an instant after the gong rang out and the blast came like a phantom out of the smoke. They felt a scorching heat and something hard biting into their flesh. The next few rows of incoming cavalry fell from their horses, hit by the flaming, flying fragments of metal, adding to the growing pile of screaming bodies.

The Sogdians in the second trench stood up and took aim. From where they stood, they could only see a faint outline of the enemy as they continued to charge forward in an endless stream. They all seemed to be falling around the same spot, about two hundred yards away, where their horses trampled over the mass of thrashing bodies. It was there that they aimed. They didn't really need to see their targets. The Turanians rode in a cluster on the narrow road, as Persicus and General Gerisha hoped they would. The new weapons worked better than they ever expected. They kept firing, certain that every shot from their simple-looking weapons would hit someone, if not in the front of the line, it would hit one of the hundreds of men following close behind.

The men in the second trench fired. The ground rumbled with the force of a hundred weapons discharging at the same moment. As they sat down, the third row of men behind them stood, ready to shoot while the previous row reloaded their weapons.

The blockage on the road up ahead forced the fourth and fifth groups of Turanians to slow down. They heard the sound of the gong and a series of explosions—one … two … three … four—in a rapid succession. Their forward progress came to an abrupt stop. Chaos lay twenty yards ahead, wrapped in an impenetrable abyss of suffocating smoke. The gong rang out again. Another series of explosions jarred the air. They felt the vibration of it from where they waited, stalled. More agonizing screams followed. As they waited, anxious to move forward, wondering what was happening beyond the smoke, several men from the third group came running back, shouting at the top of their lungs. They caught a few words about hell and fire. The men from the third group surged past the men behind them, yelling at them to retreat.

"What in the world is wrong with them?" a cavalryman of the fourth group asked.

"I don't know," another replied. "Cowards!"

Several more men came running by them on foot. The leader of the fourth group tried to stop one of the fleeing men. He had room to move forward now, but he hesitated. He grabbed the shoulder of a man rushing by. The man's arm looked burnt and singed. Blood poured down his face from a long gash at his temple.

"There's no order to retreat. What's happening up there?"

"Death," the man yelled. Under the mask of blood, his face appeared pale. "Fire! Fire! Death!" he sputtered, jerking his arm free, and taking off at a run.

"This is ridiculous. Come on, men."

The front row started forward, at a quick pace. A few men hesitated, but the men behind them nudged them forward, and they trotted to catch up. The air turned pitch-black and they choked on the acrid smoke. A foul smell clung to the back of their throats. As they approached, a vague outline of something large appeared, squirming in middle of the road like a hoard of snakes.

"What is that?" a young cavalryman asked, his voice quivering.

They could hear the sound of men in agony a few yards ahead.

Then, the sound of a gong rang out, loud and resonant.

### ᛏᛉᛏ

Meanwhile, General Ahmad rode around to the north side with the Third Regiment. The Third Regiment, comprised of cavalry, archers, and infantry, totaled one hundred men. Two men rode ahead to scout the area. They came back to report to Ahmad a few minutes later.

The north side of city was similar in structure to the south side, though the gate remained functioning and locked on this side. A smooth, straight road led to the gate in the center of the fortress. Hillocks stretched out for miles on either side of the road, with a few small, scattered, wooded areas. On the west side of the fortress, the Mishin River ran flush against the city's wall.

Ahmad and his men hid behind a cluster of trees. He knew the west side would be the most difficult side to try to enter the city by and therefore, the least guarded spot. He chose the northeast corner.

The regiment gathered around Ahmad when he signaled them, awaiting their orders.

"All right, men. There are at least twenty Sogdian men up in the battlements on the north side that we can see." He knelt down in the dirt and drew his plan with his fingertip. "We have to assume there are more, but since the action is taking place on the south side, there shouldn't be too many sentries up there."

Ahmad looked up and pointed to the first designated group. "You ten will go to the northeast corner and scale the wall with the grappling lines. Try to go undetected as long as possible. If you get spotted, the archers will move up and cover you. Archers, I want you back here in the cover of these trees. Infantry, you will shield the archers until it is time for you to attack. I want you in a line, in front of the archers. The rest of you, stay back here in your ranks until it is time to go." He looked up at his men. "Any questions?"

### ᛏᛉᛏ

"No, no, no! What is going on down there?" Salman yelled when he saw about fifty men retreating, fleeing the battle to safety.

The Turanian Army waiting at the encampment grew apprehensive and puzzled. They watched, clueless to the unfolding events on the road to the gate, though they all realized it was anything, but ordinary.

Salman had set up a table and chairs fifty yards from the big copper pot, where he watched the scene before him, disbelieving. General Mahmood stood beside him, concerned, his lips pressed together in a tight line, turning white. Never in his life had he seen Salman this angry, on the verge of an apoplectic, frenzied outburst.

"What is that sound? What is on fire? Where is that *blasted smoke* coming from? What are the most *fearless* men in the land *fleeing* from? *Dammit!* Why? Mahmood! Go bring those men to me."

"Yes, Your Magnificence."

Salman could hear the agonizing screams between the clangor of the gong that kept repeating about every thirty seconds.

Hakim, Asif, and Hamzeh ran to the siege tower. They climbed the ladder, hoping to get a better view, and see what had happened beyond the cloud of black smoke. When they reached the top, they ran to the railing, where several other infantrymen stood gazing at the spectacle, wide-eyed. They could hear the terrified, pitiful screams of the injured, but they couldn't see a thing through the heavy smoke. Then they saw several men retreating, running out from the cloud of smoke, covered in some dark substance. One of the men ran in a blind panic, completely hysterical, shrieking about black magic, hell, the devil, and fire.

Hakim saw the face of the hysterical soldier as he ran past the siege tower. Wide, terror-filled eyes, showing mostly white, bulged from their sockets. Blackened skin. His hair stuck out in little tuffs from his scorched and blistered skull. Hakim looked back to the city, straining to see, but he could only make out faint outlines of people, glimpsed through the shifting smoke.

"Can you see anything?" Hakim asked.

Asif shook his head. "Nothing, but shadows."

Mahmood grabbed one of the fleeing soldiers and dragged him to King Salman. Salman turned in a rage to glare down at the frightened man. The man breathed in heavy, gasping gulps, swallowing down the air as if it fought him.

"What happened?" Salman demanded, glaring down at the soldier with complete distain and contempt.

The soldier stood trembling, eyes wild. Little streams of sooty sweat trickled down the soldier's forehead, dripping into his eyes. "They are … a … a … army of devils … from hell." He swiped his hand across his blistered forehead and winced. "They came up f-f-f … from the b-b-beneath the earth. Fire … fire …" He seemed lost for a moment, lost in the moment of the explosion.

"What about fire?" Salman asked, impatient, resisting the urge to shake the man.

The soldier looked up, the fearful look in his eyes retreated, and a moment of clarity came, as if just now realizing he had made it back to the encampment, safe, alive. "Fire came like lightning from nowhere, like magic. Invisible things came flying through the air, killing our men. The fire ... Look"—he touched his red, scorched face—"my face ... my face, burning." He started trembling uncontrollably and his babbling became incoherent again.

Mahmood shook the soldier by the shoulders, but he fell to his knees, his face cupped in his hands. Mahmood pushed him to the ground, annoyed and disgusted.

"Never mind this coward. It's obvious he's crazy. Magic, my ass!"

"What did he mean by things flying through the air, killing my men?" Salman asked.

Mahmood shook his head and shrugged.

"Get rid of him," Salman said.

Mahmood drew his sword and drove it downward.

"No! Don't!" the terrified soldier cried out, raising one arm up, the other hand going for his sword.

Mahmood stabbed him through the heart before the scorched soldier touched his hilt.

The man looked at the sword in his chest in disbelief. A sigh rattled out from his lips and he died.

Mahmood put his boot to the man's head, yanked the sword from his chest, and knelt down to wipe the blood off his sword using the dead man's sleeve. "We'll add him to the pot." Mahmood stood and sheathed his sword. "Its blood will make a good stock for the soup."

Salman rolled his eyes. "I meant, take him away, but whatever, he's better off, now."

Salman gazed out into the distance, surveying the battle. "Mahmood, get the rest of the cavalry and infantrymen ready. The infantry will follow the cavalry."

"Cavalry! Infantry! Ready to charge in one minute," Mahmood yelled.

$$\text{𒐉}$$

General Ahmad watched as Regiment Leader Abdul Afuw led nine men to the northeast corner of the fortress. Ahmad stood behind a barricade of his infantrymen's' shields. The fifteen archers stood with him, also protected by the shields. The archers had their arrows ready to shoot. To his left, the cavalry waited with their lances in hand and swords sheathed at their sides, ready to charge towards the fortress when

Ahmad gave the order.

Ahmad had his main objective, which he, Salman, Mahmood, and a few other men knew about. His main objective didn't actually need the Third Regiment to scale the wall or make it into the city. He didn't need them to reach the battlements and fight the Sogdians. His true mission required only few of his men to make it into the city, sneak into the Palace, grab the Princess, and bring her back to King Salman. The Sogdian King would also need to be found and executed, but they would bring him to King Salman himself, for a special death, after they won the war. At this time, Ahmad's only concern and goal was the Princess — and this, none of the Third Regiment knew about.

An eternal guard up in the battlements saw a small group of Turanians advancing from the northeast. As he turned to call out a warning to his men, an arrow pierced his throat. He grabbed his throat, choking on his blood, trying to swallow, and with a sudden horror, he realized he couldn't breathe. He was going to suffocate on his own blood as it gushed in a thick, hot flood down his throat and into his lungs. He fell to his knees.

Five grappling hooks sailed through the air and landed at the top of the wall, wedging into the parapet. Abdul Afuw and his men tugged at the ropes to make sure they were secure. They began climbing hand over hand, the ropes wound around their legs. Two men on each rope, while one man stood below to hold the ropes steady.

Ahmad watched with detachment as the Sogdians stuck their arms out of the narrow windows — the machicolations — and dropped heavy stones on the men scaling the wall. Knowing Mishin's fortress wall had been built with defense as a top priority, knowing that the limestone merlons and corbels around the machicolations would protect the men in the battlements from getting shot from almost any angle — including the angle where Ahmad had chosen to set up his post — he watched as his archers shot a steady stream of arrows. A slight smile crept in, pulling at the edge of his lips as he watched the arrows bounce harmlessly off the corbels, while the Sogdians dropped their stones, and his men fell to their deaths, and he didn't care. He had sent them to die and now he was ready to send more.

"Second group! Go!" Ahmad yelled.

The second group of ten charged, running to the grappling lines.

Ahmad had sent another five men to the west side of the city. These men dying here were merely a diversion. He had set up his post in a visible spot, though he remained safe behind the row of shields.

The five men on the west side would wait until all the Sogdians were tending to the men trying to scale the northeast corner wall. They would swiftly gain access to the city by the same method and sneak into the Palace to get the Princess. It was a genius plan and he prided himself on it.

"Sir! They are all dying! Why don't we send in all the men at once and overwhelm them?"

"No," was all Ahmad said.

"But sir! There are only twenty Sogdians up there. All our men will die if you only send ten at a time."

"I am in charge here." Ahmad stepped up to the man and stood inches from his face. He spoke in an eerily calm voice. "If you think you are a better general than me, go make a complaint to Salman." Ahmad turned his attention back to the fortress.

Two of his men had made it to the top. They began to fight, but they would lose.

"Third group!" Ahmad yelled.

The five men on their mission to get the Princess waited until the battlements on the west side appeared deserted.

Their blacksmith had designed a lightweight grappling hook, which he attached to the wooden shaft of an arrow. They stood at the edge of the river and shot their grappling hook towards the parapet. They missed on the first two attempts, having to adjust their aim for the weight of the hook. The hook lodged in on the third shot. They each had a dry change of villager's clothing, wrapped in a goatskin, which would stay relativity dry as they swam across the river.

It had not rained in days. The current felt light and the water was not too high at this spot, though it remained icy cold. Once across the river, they grabbed the grappling line, which floated in the gentle current. Their hands turned numb by the time they reached the fortress wall. The five men climbed, pulling themselves up with their hands, and pushing with their legs against the wall.

They scaled the wall unnoticed. They reached the battlements and took a quick look in both directions. All the Sogdian sentries were on the other side, tending to the men who were trying to invade in plain sight.

They changed into their dry clothes and threw their wet clothes over the wall, into the river. They moved the grappling hook to the inner wall and descended down to the ground, still undetected. In all, from the time they shot the arrow across the river, to the time they set foot down on the ground inside Mishin City, less than seven minutes had passed.

It was a brilliant plan. Distraction at its best. They had Salman's Army on the south and north side, and they had used the city's own defense against them. Nobody worried about the west side; the Sogdians believed the river to be foolproof, though it was only a hindrance. Nothing is foolproof. There is always a flaw in every defense system. No matter how secure they tried to make it, or how much planning had been put into its design.

They walked briskly down an alley towards the center of the city, so as not to arouse suspicion.

The streets appeared deserted. All the houses had their widows shut and curtains drawn. They made it to the center of the city in little time. They slowed their pace as they neared the Palace and stole a discreet glance at the Palace Guards.

Palace Guards stood everywhere.

Four guards stood at attention at the bottom of the limestone steps on the north side and another four guards stood on the south side. At the broad landing, where the two stairways converged, five guards stood, keeping a watchful eye on the road and buildings.

The Turanians couldn't see anything beyond the landing, but assumed more guards milled about above. As they walked down the main road, a guard standing on the landing followed the five men with his eyes. He perceived them as villagers, though suspicious that anyone should be out right now, he watched until they disappeared around a corner.

The Turanians took a side road to an alley to discuss the plan.

For this utmost secretive mission, Ahmad had selected five of his most capable men. Ahmad placed Safwat in charge of the operation. Abbass, Dhul Fiqar, Qurban and his younger brother, Usman, comprised the rest of the unit.

Once they reached the alley, Safwat turned to his men. "All right, here is what we are going to do. Pay attention. We can't make it in from the front, by the stairs. There are too many guards"—he looked at Usman, who was concentrating on chewing his fingernails into tiny stubs—"Hey! Pay attention, this is important."

Qurban smacked his brother on the back of his head. "What's that for?" Usman asked, rubbing his head.

"You gotta listen."

Usman glared at his brother. He gave his attention to Safwat, making his reluctance obvious. He really didn't know this man, whom High General Ahmad had placed in charge. He didn't like following orders from a stranger. He would have preferred his cousin, General Ghulam, to be here with him on this mission. Ghulam, he could trust, but Qurban and Usman had been reassigned to the Third Regiment after they had an argument with their other cousins, Abdul Kabir and his retarded brother, Abd Al-Ala, which had ended in blows. After that, Ghulam split them up into different regiments.

"All right, as I said, we can't go in the front. We are going to need to go around to the back. There is a garden back there that we can get through, but it is a steep and rocky cliff. The Palace is well-protected by guards at the front; the cliff around back should have minimal guards."

"Why don't one of us run up to one of the guards by the stairs and say a bunch of Turanians have come through the gate. We'll send them running in search of the intruders. When they're gone, we go up, grab the Princess, and make a run for it."

Safwat shook his head. "No. They would never leave their post. They are in charge of protecting the Palace and the Royal Family. The people out there fighting are the ones they would send." He stared up at the sky with his head tilted back while he thought.

*General Ghulam would never have taken this long making a decision,* Usman thought, watching Safwat charily.

Safwat shook his head. "No, we don't have a choice. We have to climb the cliff. We'll use the ropes. Dhul Fiqar, you're the best archer, you will stay at the bottom of the hill, as a look out. We will be exposed while climbing. Whistle if anyone is coming. If we hear that signal, stop moving. We are less likely to be seen on the cliff if we are not moving. There are a lot of rocks and shrubbery to hide behind, if needed. Once up the cliff, if it's clear, we go into the Palace through the garden, and straight to the Princess' room. If we run into anyone, we kill them quickly, before they make a sound. If we are not close enough to kill them right away, act as if we are supposed to be there, walk down the hallways, confident, as if you own the place."

He went on in detail. Everyone agreed with the plan. Dhul Fiqar would stay at the bottom of the hill, ready with his bow and arrow should any passing guard try to sound the alarm.

The other four men began up the steep hill.

For the second time, Salman tried to order the army into formation, but the infantry and cavalry watched the parlous battle, as if transfixed by the tumultuous scene. They milled about, talking to one another in boisterous voices, heedless of King Salman's angry shouting.

"Cavalry, I said one minute till charge!" Salman yelled again.

Several men glanced at him as if he was a fly buzzing in their ears, but none of them moved to obey the order.

"What's going on down there?" one of the cavalrymen yelled the question everyone wanted an answer to.

"This is a battle! What do you think is going on down there?" Mahmood barked, his eyes scanning the crowd for the one who had spoken with such hostility to their King.

"You think this is an ordinary battle?" said another man.

Mahmood mounted his horse. "For God's sake! These are Sogdians we are talking about. Infidels. Fire worshippers damned to Hell! We are the Sword of Allah. The invincible. Come on, men!" Mahmood drew his sword and pointed it skyward. "We are the Turanian Army! Allahu Akbar!"

About half the men cheered, pounding on their shields.

"Charge!" Mahmood yelled and began galloping towards the gate.

About half the remaining cavalry charged with General Mahmood, galloping at full speed towards the city. All fifteen thousand of the infantry turned tail, waving their hands in disgust, and shaking their heads. They headed down the road, away from the city, in a long procession. The infantry, all on foot, had poor weapons and shields. They fought with Salman for the money, but they didn't want to endanger themselves. No one in a long time had decided to stand against Salman. These men had no loyalty to the Turanian King beyond their weekly pay for a show of force, and that pay didn't do them any good if they wound up dead.

"What the hell are you all doing?" Salman roared as the men began walking away. "You can't leave! I hired you for war! You damned cowards! You walk away and you're all finished!"

The men ignored him and continued down the road, en masse.

Mahmood and the charging cavalry were halfway to the city. Salman turned to watch. He heard Hakim's panic-stricken voice, yelling from above. He looked up to the siege tower and back down to the huge copper pot, where it sat alongside the siege tower. The water and oil boiling over the brim, and flames licking up the sides of the pot.

Hakim watched General Mahmood and his men charge towards the gate. The smoke had started to dissipate. At last, he had a clear view of what lay beyond. He saw hundreds of men, kneeling in trenches dug into the earth. They held bamboo sticks in their hands, but it didn't make sense to him. Bamboo couldn't cause the fear and devastation that was unfolding down below. He called down to Salman, to warn him of the men in the trenches, when the siege tower gave a loud groan, and shifted slightly to the right.

Hakim froze. He looked sideways to his brothers and saw they had also stopped moving. He reached out, grabbed the railing, and turned, slow and steady. When he had turned around, facing the exit, he lifted his foot to take a step towards the ladder. Something cracked, loudly. The siege tower shuddered and shifted to the right, giving another loud groan. He gasped and froze, holding his breath.

Studying the ground below, Hakim realized the men had abandoned the tower on uneven ground. The siege tower stood on an incline near the bottom of a small hillock; the ground under the tower's left wheels sat higher than the right side.

Hakim gulped and looked up. "Nobody move."

No sooner had he said this than he heard a crowd gathering down below and the sound of men climbing the ladder. The tower creaked and groaned under the weight of so many men. The tower shifted again, further to the right.

Hakim ran to the ladder, yelling emphatically at the men climbing the ladder. "Stop! For God's sake! Stop right there." His face distorted in panic and fear; sweat dripped down his neck and back, somehow managing to feel hot and cold at the same time.

"What? You're not in charge here," one soldier said, looking up at Hakim.

"Please, stop! You're going to get us all killed. The tower—"

Another man climbing the ladder cut him off, yelling in a furious, terrified voice. "My son was in the first assault! I have to see what's happening. Hurry up. Move! Get your ass up there."

"No!" Hakim yelled, but it was futile. "No, wait! Wait!"

The men clambered up the ladder. Petrified, Hakim backed up to the railing as he felt the tower shift again.

Hamzeh looked ashen. "What are we going to do?"

"Push them down. Don't let them up!" Hakim ordered.

Asif and Hamzeh ran over to the ladder, the first four men had made it up to the top and ran to the railing, hoping for a better view of the battle.

Hamzeh grabbed one of the soldier's swords from its sheath as the soldier climbed up onto the landing. Hamzeh started yelling, threatening the men trying to come up, but the men on the ladder push forward, determined to make it to the top.

"Get out of my way. Who do you think you are?"

"I need to find my brothers! I made it back from the fiery hell down there, but I couldn't find them! They didn't come back with me. Now, either you move out of my way or I will kill you myself! But one way or another I will find my brothers!"

"Kill them!" Hakim yelled.

Hamzeh looked down at the man. "Forgive me." He thrust the sword down at the soldier.

Meanwhile, on the north side, Ahmad sent the fourth group to attack. He smiled to himself as he watched the slaughter. The annoying man who had argued with him earlier began protesting again. Ahmad assured him that he knew what he was doing.

"No, you don't know what you are doing! You are purposefully getting our men killed, when we should have wiped the Sogdians out thirty minutes ago. I'm not going to stand around here and let you get me killed, too!"

"Then go."

The soldier mounted his horse. "If you all know what's best for you, you should leave with me." He looked at his friend, who stood conflicted by his horse, awaiting the order for the fifth group to charge. "Come on, Sadik. Don't stay here. He's going to get you killed."

Sadik stared his longtime friend in the eyes. He looked at Ahmad, who had a strange, satisfied grin on his face. He realized something was terribly wrong with General Ahmad. He nodded to his friend and mounted his horse. The two men headed back towards the encampment.

Ahmad turned back towards the fight, watching his men getting killed, falling from the wall, or slain once they reached the top by a quick blow from a sword.

"Fifth group, mount," he yelled. He had twenty more men, plus the fifteen archers, and fifteen men bearing the shields.

"General Ahmad!" one of the men yelled in an uncertain voice.

"What?"

"Look. What is that?" The man pointed towards the crenels of the battlement. He squinted into the distance and burst out in laughter.

"What is that, you ask. Bamboo! They are going to throw bamboo at us."

A few men laughed with Ahmad, but the rest didn't look too certain of that.

While the Turanians laughed, a loud, thunderous sound exploded from the bamboo, followed by thick smoke rising up from the battlements. Ahmad looked startled at first and then he dove behind the shields. He heard piteous screaming from his men—not the men dying up by the fortress, but the archers, right here, by his side. He looked up and saw about six men, writhing on the ground, bloody and screaming, and a few men sprawled on the ground, terribly silent.

A second explosion came from the battlements. The man in front of Ahmad, holding the shield which he huddled behind, fell over. He landed on his back and Ahmad saw a hole in his chest. Dark-red blood poured out of the wound in his chest in gushes. The shield was useless.

Horrified, Ahmad looked up to the battlements again, on his knees, now completely exposed. Another explosion blasted out from the bamboo. Ahmad felt something bash into his head, painful for only a spilt second, and then the odd sensation of something digging into his brain. The next instant, he felt nothing, no pain. He fell backwards, weightless, to the ground. His eyes staring wide. He couldn't blink. His face seemed frozen. He couldn't feel his body, but felt cold to the core. In the distance, the last thing his paralyzed eyes saw before the lights went out was the two men who had fled, looking back at him.

Persicus was standing behind the parapet in the battlements with General Gerisha when General Mahmood began charging the gate with what appeared to be five or six thousand cavalrymen. Gerisha pointed into the distance. Persicus followed his line of sight and saw the rest of Salman's men retreating down the road, away from the city, on foot.

"They are fleeing!" Persicus exclaimed.

Gerisha nodded, grinning. "Yes. The majority of them."

They looked back at the men charging.

"There are too many this time. I don't think they can get them all," Persicus said. "Better get the rest of the men ready."

Gerisha ran to the other side of the battlements, facing Mishin city, and his men below.

The rest of the Sogdian Army waited inside the gate, at their assigned positions. A tension ran through them as they saw their General appear up above them.

Persicus and Gerisha had planned on the bamboo weapons scaring and killing a good part of the Turanian Army, but their plans had included detailed instructions in case any of the enemy made it through the gate, which, it seemed, would happen within a few minutes.

Persicus, Gerisha, and Ormozd had decided on a plan that would put into place four different lines of defense. The first was the men with the bamboo weapons outside the city gate in the trenches. Next, more men with bamboo weapons inside the gate, positioned on each side of the gate, at a thirty-degree angle from the wall, with four rows of men on each side. They were positioned off to the side, so they would not be the first thing the enemy would see as they came through the gate. The first thing that they would see would be the third line of defense. The Sogdian Cavalry lined up in rows with their long lances and their full, but flexible, body armor. Behind the cavalry, the infantry stood, wearing a lighter armor, but just as protective and flexible—the last line of defense.

A total of one thousand men with the bamboo weapons waited inside the gate. Persicus had given them intensive instructions. They could only fire at the gate, or risk hitting their own men because of the angle, and being stationed across from one another. They couldn't follow their targets as they would with an arrow, but keep firing only at the gate where the enemy would be pouring in. This would also create an advantage of blocking the gate with bodies to make it difficult for the enemy to come through. Any Turanians who made it past the gate were no longer their concern. Their cavalry would take care of those men. They didn't anticipate many to make it past the cavalry. The cavalry stood nearly wall to wall and five deep.

Ormozd had fashioned his cavalry after the Parthian Cataphracts. They wore the same heavy, scaled, and plated armor sewn into thick leather undergarments. Their helmets were fitted to each man's head to prevent being knocked off. Their armor, an advanced steel that was impenetrable by their enemy's weapons, served as their shields, freeing their hands. Each man sat strapped into his saddle, so they needed no stirrups, giving them more maneuverability. Their lances, attached to their horses by a chain, hung within reach at their sides. With their swords at their waist and their bow and arrows strapped to their backs, their hands were virtually free to maneuver their horses, while still being able to quickly grab their weapons. Their Nisean horses were also fully armored and strong enough to move quickly carrying the fully-armored Sogdian men.

Gerisha yelled down to the waiting men. "Men, steady, they will be coming in a few moments. Remember, the gong is for those on the outside. The horn is for you on the inside."

Gerisha turned to Persicus. "Are you ready to do this?"

Persicus took a deep breath and nodded.

They watched Mahmood and his men approach.

Persicus waited. His eyes fixed on the fast approaching enemy. Then he gave the signal.

Mahmood turned and looked behind him. He saw thousands of his men fleeing, but about five thousand men followed. *Five thousand will be enough.* He kicked his horse to go faster and yelled as he approached the gate. The dust rose up around him in a thick cloud and he could hear the sounds of thousands of hooves trampling the dirt road right behind him. The smoke ahead had begun to clear. He thought he saw dark images beyond the soft-gray smoke.

This was the moment. This was what he longed for. He was ready to kill and maim. It had been a long time since anyone had dared defy Salman, which had resulted in him not being able to satisfy his urges. After all, he had joined with Salman because it exhilarated him to be able to kill without the hassle of being branded a bandit and wanted for murder. Yes, he was pleased with Salman, and the pay was great, but he had not killed enough people in the last few years, since everyone feared Salman and his Generals too much. A small downside, but fear was a kind of sustenance as well, which he could live off of for short periods of time.

He passed into dissipating grey smoke.

The gong sounded; a thick, trembling sound.

The booming explosion seemed much louder up here than it had seemed from afar. The ground trembled and he felt the vibrations of something hot and forceful on the putrid air. Mahmood saw movement to his left and turned his head in time to see a man fall from his horse, screaming. The next instant he was airborne. He landed with a solid thump on something soft and wet. Another explosion rocked the air and he felt heat rush by over his head.

The thick, black, rancid smoke rolled in, almost suffocating. Mahmood took a deep breath, coughing, and trying to stand. His foot slid against something and he realized what he had landed in as he felt hair, thick, slick blood, and bones protruding from torn flesh. He was familiar with these textures. He screamed with frustration and anger, and lunged himself forward.

Confident and feeling invincible, Safwat and his three men walked down the main corridor of the Palace. They had swiftly killed three Palace Guards and pushed them into various rooms along the way, and left one guard hidden in the garden behind some rose bushes. They had climbed the steep hill in less than six minutes and peeked over the garden wall. There, they saw one guard pacing back and forth in front of the entrance. Qurban shot the guard with an arrow through his heart and they dragged him out of sight.

Now, it was only a matter of finding the Princess; they assumed she would be in her bedchamber. General Ahmad had given them a detailed description of the Palace and the routines of the staff. On a normal day, all the staff would be in the staff quarters, or tending to their duties in the work areas—the kitchen or the laundry room. Being that they were at war, the staff, in all probability, would be hiding in their rooms, so they were not worried about running into maids or servants. The guards, however, prowled the hallways, doing a sweep of the entire Palace every fifteen minutes.

They walked down the corridor and turned down the hallway that led to the Royal Family's living quarters. They rushed by a large reception area, followed by an enormous, immaculate living area. Past that, they would come to another hallway that went off in either direction: one to the left that would lead to the King's chambers and one to the right that would lead to the Princess' chambers.

As they headed towards the living quarters, a door behind them opened. An old, male servant walked out, his eyes widened in surprise, and he reached for his sword.

Usman turned as he heard the door open. Qurban used Usman's broad shoulders to block himself from view. He grabbed an arrow from his quiver and knelt down on his knee to take aim.

Usman drew his sword and held it out in front of him, giving the old man an opportunity to charge him. As the servant opened his mouth to yell, Qurban shot his bow, and the arrow penetrated the servant's chest.

The servant stopped, looking down at the arrow in his chest, surprised. He grabbed the arrow as he fell to his knees. He looked up at the intruders in shock. A small amount of blood oozed out from his pale lips.

Usman took three striding steps over to the dying man. He grabbed the servant and jerked his head around, snapping his neck in one fluid movement.

Not knowing if any guards were in the room that the old man had come out of, Usman and Qurban picked him up, and carried him to the next room with an open door. They dumped him in the corner of the room and shut the door behind them.

They continued down the route they had previously plotted out, past the living quarters, and down the last hallway to the Princess' chambers.

They stopped outside the third door on the right. They listened for a moment and heard movement inside.

Abbass would stay outside the room, to be the look out. They planned to go in, grab the Princess, and leave as fast as they had come.

Safwat threw open the door. He, Qurban, and Usman charged into the room. They saw her sitting in a chair beside a large bed.

The Princess screamed and jump up out of her chair as the men charged her.

She ran towards the window, but they quickly surrounded and overwhelmed her. They grabbed her. Usman covered her mouth to silence her shrill, incessant screams.

She jerked her right arm free. Her hand reached out to the bedside table and grabbed a heavy hairbrush. She swung the brush at Qurban's head. He blocked her hands with little effort and grabbed her flailing arm.

Another woman came in from a door at the end of the room. She screamed and turned to run.

"The chamber maid. Grab her." Safwat jerked some sheets from the bed.

Qurban left the Princess with his brother and went after the chambermaid.

Safwat tore the sheet into strips and tied the Princess' hands. He shoved a silk cloth into her mouth and tied a strip of sheet around her head to hold it in place. Qurban came back into the room, holding the struggling chambermaid in his arms. They tied up the chambermaid in the same fashion. After they had them both bound, hands, Usman threw the Princess over his shoulder, and Qurban shoved the maid ahead of them, and headed back the way they came.

Hamzeh shoved his sword down at the soldier who was trying to climb up to the top of the siege tower.

The soldier saw the blow coming. "What the hell are—" He blocked the sword with his right arm, raised up over his head. The sword sliced down his arm, peeling off a huge chunk of flesh. He screamed.

Hamzeh reared back to strike again.

The soldier grabbed Hamzeh's leg and pulled it out from under him. Hamzeh fell backwards. The entire tower rattled with the impact. Hamzeh kicked out with his leg and connected with the soldier's face, crushing his nose. The soldier's head snapped back. He lost his grip on the ladder and shot backwards.

As he fell down the long shaft, his back hit a horizontal crossbeam, cracking the wood. He felt his left shoulder dislocate and howled in pain. The soldier tried to grab onto the beam with his injured right arm, but his hand slipped, slick with blood. He continued plummeting down the shaft. He landed on top of another man, his full weight landing on the other soldier's head. In an instant, the second soldier's head was compacted down to his own shoulders, his neck broken and shoved down into his chest cavity from the impact. They tumbled down together, hitting and cracking support beams along the way until they slammed into the ground with a solid whump. Both of them were dead before they hit the ground.

With the horizontal support beams cracked and broken, the top of the tower shifted even further to the right. Wood began falling from its fastenings in chunks. The top landing, where Hakim and his brothers stood, tilted to a thirty-degree angle.

Hakim screamed as he slid to the edge of the railing. He grabbed the railing with his one arm. Hamzeh held on to the entryway where the ladder came up to the top. Asif scrambled, trying to grab hold of something, anything. Asif hit the railing five feet from Hakim; the railing broke from his weight smashing into it. He grabbed the edge of the flooring and hung, suspended in the air.

"Hakim! Hakim! Help!" Asif yelled, terrified, his feet flailing in the air.

Hakim turned away from his brother's pleading and held onto the railing.

Other soldiers hung on where they could. One man kicked out his legs, trying to get a grip on the floorboards so he could scoot himself back towards the ladder.

Asif's hands became sweaty as he pleaded for help.

"Hakim! Hamzeh!" Asif screamed, his voice growing hoarse.

The weight shifted with the soldiers' movement and the tower shuddered.

Asif's hands slipped and he fell, screaming.

Hakim whipped his head around to watch his brother fall.

"Great Allah!" Hakim cried, horrified. He saw the giant pot beneath him. He watched, dismayed, as his brother's body plunged into the hot, boiling water and oil with a hiss of steam and a splash. His eye began twitching hard enough that it distorted his vision.

Hakim heard his cousin's angry voice yelling from down below.

"You idiots! Get down from there!" Salman cried out.

The soldier who had been trying to scoot backwards grabbed onto Hamzeh's leg and began pulling himself up.

"Let go of me!" Hamzeh yelled. "Let go!" His hand began slipping, still slick with the blood of the man he had stabbed. His arms shook with the effort to hold on. His bloody arm slipped and he flailed, trying to get his arm up again, but the soldier on his leg kept pulling him down, clinging to him, crawling up to his hip.

Hamzeh kicked out, frantic, desperate to get the man off him.

"Please! Don't!" the soldier cried, terror-stricken. "No ... no ..."

Hamzeh connected, kneeing the soldier in his stomach. The soldier grunted and lost his grip. Winded, he slid across the bare pinewood floor. Hamzeh let out a sigh of relief as the soldier released his leg.

The soldier crashed into the railing. He grabbed at a spindle; it cracked and broke as his weight bore down on it. Screaming, he plunged into the boiling pot.

The tower shuddered, groaning, and another man fell from the top of the tower, crashing into Hamzeh. Hamzeh lost his grip and started sliding down the wood flooring. He used his feet to slow his descent and managed to get a grip on the side railing, a foot away from Hakim, before he crashed through it.

Hakim held on, staring down at the copper pot, wide-eyed. Sweat tricked down his neck and arms. His hand dampened and began to slip.

"Hamzeh!" Hakim yelled.

Hamzeh began swinging his weight, kicking his leg up, trying to get his legs up on the pinewood floor.

The tower shifted even further, almost to a forty-degree angle. It rattled, shuddered, and creaked. They could hear bits and pieces of the wooden structure snapping and falling away.

"Hamzeh! Help! I can't hold on much longer! I'm slipping! I'm slipping!" Hakim's voice rose until it grew high-pitched. "Help me!"

Hamzeh swung harder. The tower swayed with his shifting weight. He threw his leg up and managed to get it on the solid wood, but kicked Hakim in the process.

Hakim grunted as his brother accidently kicked his hand. The kick jerked his hand away from the rail and he grabbed his brother's leg. He held on, clinging to his brother's leg with his one arm, the rest of his body hanging midair, over the boiling pot.

"Help! Pull me up! You idiot! Pull me up!" Hakim yelled. Hamzeh's pants began to sag, pulling down with Hakim's weight.

Hamzeh's face blossomed red, furious. Clarity came with a suddenness that startled him. He thought of his life, wasted doing his brother's biddings. All the stupid scams. All the chasing after treasures that he never saw. All the times he had helped and gave and gave to his brother, Hakim. Hakim. It was always all about Hakim. What *he* wanted. What *he* needed. Never about what was best for himself. What was best for Hamzeh. Hamzeh had forsaken his best friend for the sake of one of

Hakim's damned schemes, a scheme that didn't even pan out. Hakim, who had wasted and destroyed his life, and now, was going to drag him down to his death. "As you helped Asif?" Hamzeh yelled, straining to hold on. The blood on his hand had dried to a tacky, grainy coating.

"Help me, Hamzeh." Hakim's voice again.

Hamzeh felt his pants sliding down.

"Is it always about *you*?" Hamzeh yelled, angry, remorseful, and on the verge of deliriousness. Before he could think about what he was doing, he reached down with one hand and unbuckled his belt. His pants jerked down, off, and ripped away, along with Hakim.

Hakim screamed, shrill and piteous. He plunged into the boiling water as Hamzeh watched with grim satisfaction.

The tower groaned, louder. It gave one last final shudder before the whole structure collapsed, caving in on itself. The top of the tower tumbled down, with Hamzeh and the rest of the soldiers, into the gigantic copper pot, boiling over with a splash of red and pink, and darker things. Flesh boiled and scorched, floated in the putrid water.

$$\text{\Te-}\atop\text{YYY}$$

Persicus watched as the siege tower started to crumble. When he saw Hakim hanging from his brother's leg over the copper pot, he smiled, and drew an arrow, but just as he took aim at Hakim's remaining arm, Hamzeh completely shocked Persicus by unbuckling his belt, and depriving Persicus of his revenge. Nevertheless, as he watched Hakim plummet to his boiling death, he felt satisfied, as having Hakim's own brother betray and kill him was even better than shooting that arrow himself. Betrayal will always hurt more from family — even if only for a brief moment before death.

$$\text{\Te-}\atop\text{YYY}$$

Salman watched his cousins plummet, one by one, screaming, into the boiling liquid. He looked away, wincing. Which put him looking at the battle and that was definitely not an improvement. He turned the other way and saw his infantry walking away, down the road to safety. A rage was growing within him. This was going all wrong. He saw Mahmood in the distance, entering into the mysterious smoke, and then lost sight of him. He heard the gong sound again, a noise which was on the verge of driving him mad, and volcanic sounding explosions. One after another. Boom ... Boom ... Boom ... Boom. He couldn't see a damned thing. Salman screamed in frustration, loud and furious, gripping his hair in both hands.

Two men came galloping from around the corner of the city. They arrived at Salman's side within moments.

"General Ahmad is dead," one of the men said.

Salman's face flamed red; he looked to the second man.

The second man mumbled, "And so is the Third Regiment."

$$\overline{\text{ΥΥΥ}}$$

General Mahmood stumbled on the bodies, some moaned under his weight. He crawled out of the mess, got to his feet, and ran towards the gate, screaming. Heat washed over him. The explosions came, maddeningly repetitive. Something hot, sharp, and stinging grazed his arm. He stayed low to the ground in a crouch. Never in his life had he experienced a battle as exhilarating as this one.

"Go around!" he yelled to his men who were struggling, falling over the smoke-masked mound of bodies. He hoped some would hear him over the volcanic eruptions. "Go around! Get off the road and go around!"

Mahmood ran for the open gate. He stumbled out of the smoke and charged on foot, drawing his sword as he ran. Smoke stung his eyes and he blinked back the burning tears.

He saw the Sogdian Cataphracts straight ahead. He stopped, realizing none of his men had made it through the gate yet. He stood alone.

He clearly heard someone say, "You have got to be kidding," and another voice, "You take him."

He whipped around to his left. There, he saw several hundred men, standing with bamboo stalks over their shoulders. Mahmood frowned. Then one of the bamboo stalks exploded, spewing fire and black smoke. Something hit him, hard, sharp, and painful, an excruciating pain deep in his stomach and legs. He staggered backwards and fell to his knees, still gripping his sword. Looking down at his body, he saw blood pouring out, soaking him more completely than any man he had beheaded. He looked back at the Sogdians. He felt his sword slip from his hand. He fell forward, catching himself on the palm on his hand, and held out his hand to them, reaching, as if pleading for help.

They watched him, silent.

Mahmood collapsed, rolling onto his back.

A trumpet bellowed out, a long, shrill sound.

The Turanian Cavalry poured in through the gate, the majority of them on foot, though about twenty of them had managed to hold onto their horses. They charged forward, seeing only the Sogdian Cataphracts ahead.

The Sogdians with their bamboo weapons, off to the sides of the gate, fired their weapons in succession. They kept firing at the spot in front of the gate. The row in front knelt down on their knees and fired their weapons. The next row stood, fired, and then knelt down again. They took turns firing between the men on the left and the men on the right. This way, it was a constant force of firepower.

The cataphracts had their bows out and rained down arrows on the enemy. Not many of them made it more than thirty feet past the entrance to the city.

Persicus smiled and pat Gerisha on the back. They watched everything from the battlements. They had worked on this plan together and it couldn't have worked better. It was perfect. The smoke rose, building up around the gate, adding to the confusion. The pile of shrieking bodies, growing moment by moment, created another obstacle for the Turanians still trying to enter the city.

About five hundred injured and dead men of Salman's Army lay heaped in a pile just inside the gate, a few trying to crawl to safety. Persicus walked over to the outer wall of the battlement to see how many Turanians remained outside, still trying to get in through the gate. A few men were shoving, hysterical, trying to run, to get away. He couldn't be certain through the smoke, but the mass amount of bodies down below seemed to have grown. About three thousand men were still heading into the smoke, stalled, and trying to go around the smoke-concealed obstruction in the road. Shots rang out from both directions.

Gerisha walked over to Persicus and pointed out into the distance. Salman stood alone at his encampment, beside his gigantic pot. He seemed to be gazing skyward.

# 28

# THE ROAD TO HELL

All was lost now. Salman knew it with certainty. His remaining army lay in shambles. Ahmad was dead. Hakim, Asif, and Hamzeh were dead. He was almost certain Mahmood was dead, as well. The thunderous eruptions—whatever they were—were killing everyone. He looked up to the sky, wondering how everything had gone so terribly wrong.

But there was something that could still be right. The treasure. The lost treasure from the Silk Road. His ancestors' hard-earned gold. He turned, walked over to his horse, and mounted. He couldn't believe it. *How did this happen?* he asked himself.

He looked out into the distance. A trail of dust hung in the air, aftermath of his fleeing army. "God damn you all," he said aloud. *The cowards.* He had been good to them for years, but they abandoned him as soon as a difficult task came their way. He took one last, long lingering look at Mishin City. "I'll be back," he vowed. He turned and headed north.

After a couple hundred yards, Salman heard someone yelling his name. Pulling on his reins, he stopped his horse, and turned around.

Salman waited as one of his men, Safwat, caught up with him.

Safwat looked over his shoulder at Mishin. "What the hell happened?"

Salman shook his head. "I am surprised you are alive. Where is the rest of your unit?"

"When I came around from the west side I found Ahmad and the

Third Regiment dead. I saw a lot of smoke coming from the southern gate. I rode out through the trees, so I could spy on what was happening from a distance, but I couldn't see a damn thing. I sent my men to Twelve Wolf Creek to await you there. Then I saw you leaving."

"Await me for what! The whole damned cavalry is gone — dead. The rest of those damned cowards fled."

"Yes, Your Magnificence, I saw that, but you have power over Mishin City now."

Salman narrowed his eyes. "What are you talking about?"

"We have the Princess. She is on her way to the creek with my men."

Salman's lips spread into a wide grin, eyes glittering with both joy and relief. He laughed, almost hysterically. Tears of happiness trickled down his cheeks.

"Safwat, isn't it?" Salman asked.

Safwat's face lit up, pleased that the King knew his name.

"Yes."

"You have done very well. How would you like to be my new General?"

Safwat's eyes widened. "It would be the greatest honor."

"Excellent. The pay is good. Three times your current pay. Here is your first assignment. I am going to Cattula Land. I want you to go back to Twelve Wolf Creek, select one other man from the group, and bring the Princess to me in Cattula Land."

"Yes, Your Magnificence," Safwat, General Safwat said enthusiastically. "We also have a chambermaid."

Salman tugged at his sleeves, holding his head up high. "Good. Great work... General." After Salman gave Safwat directions, he rode off, laughing. His gold lay within reach, his Queen would soon be delivered to him, and then he would have power over Mishin, regardless of the battle.

Persicus watched from the battlements. He saw Salman mount his horse and head north.

"I am going after him." Persicus checked for his sword and dagger. He headed for the stairs.

"Take some men with you," Ormozd called down after him.

Nooshin came running up to her father, frantic and panicked.

"Where is Persicus?"

"He's heading down the stairs to go after Salman," Ormozd said. "What is the matter?"

SAEED & SHIRIN DERAKHSHANI

"Four men, Turanians. I saw them leaving from the west side only minutes ago. They rappelled down the wall, right into the river. They have Tahmineh and Nadira." Nooshin's voice sounded strangled with emotions. She spoke rapidly. "They were in my bedchamber, waiting for me to return. The Turanians have taken them!"

Ormozd paled. "We will find them, Nooshin. Don't worry." He ran over to the parapet and leaned over the edge. "Persicus!" he yelled, trying to be heard over the sound of the battle. "Persicus!"

Below, Persicus heard his name called over the havoc around him as he mounted his horse. Looking up, he saw Ormozd signaling him to wait.

Ormozd turned back towards Nooshin, but she was gone. His heart constricted and he looked over the edge again, straining to see his daughter. "Nooshin, no! It is not safe down there!" He saw her on the steps, heading down towards Persicus, the battle only several hundred feet away.

Nooshin stopped halfway down the stairs and looked back up at her father. "I will be with Persicus. I am safe with him." For a brief moment, she stared up into her father's worried face, the fear and concern clear in his eyes. She turned and fled down the stairs.

"Are you crazy? Get back up there, where it is safe!" Persicus said, running up to Nooshin.

"They took Tahmineh and Nadira!"

Persicus looked back towards the battle. "I will get them back. Tell me which way they went and then get back up there."

Nooshin grabbed the reins of the nearest horse and mounted.

"What do you think you are doing?" Persicus grappled the reins from her hands.

"I'm going with you."

"No! You are going back up to the battlements. This is no place for you." Persicus tried to keep the incredulity out of his voice.

Nooshin shook her head, hands on hips. "Listen here, Persicus. You do not get to order me around! They have taken my friends. After *everything* I've been through, do you honestly think I won't *be there* at *the end*? *We're* going to get Tahmineh and Nadira, and *we're* going after Salman. Besides, what if you need me? As you did when that giant was strangling you?"

Persicus shook his head and pleaded with her. "No. You have to go back. This isn't a conclusion. I don't even know where Salman is heading, or what his intentions are. This is too dangerous."

Nooshin glared at him with a look of utter, obstinate determination. "Salman thinks his men have kidnapped me. When he finds out that it's not me, he'll kill them. Now, let's go."

Persicus could see it was no use arguing with her. She wanted to come. She was no longer the compliant, docile Princess he had first met, who had wanted nothing more than to come home, and avoid conflict. He stared into her determined eyes, wondering if he should force her back up the stairs. How angry would she become with him if he did? How angry would the King be with him if he didn't? Finally, he nodded, and mounted his horse.

They left through the unobstructed northern gate.

"Which way did they go?" Persicus asked.

"South. Towards Twelve Wolf Creek, I imagine."

"Salman headed north, on the road to Cattula Land. I don't know if he continued that way."

"Why would he want to go there?" She wondered aloud.

"I don't know. First, let's go find your friends."

They rode alongside the river until they had gone a good distance from the city, crossed the river at a shallow point, and galloped alongside the riverbank, avoiding the main road, where they might be seen by the fleeing Turanians. In the distance, they could see smoke rising from the battle. Smoke obscured the gate, but they could still hear the distant sounds of the explosions and men screaming in terror and agony.

They slowed after a few minutes of galloping at full speed.

Persicus shook his head slowly. "I shouldn't have allowed you to come. You could get hurt."

"Are you trying to tell me, the Princess of Mishin, what to do?"

Persicus grinned. "Yes."

Nooshin gave him a flirtatious, yet smug look. "Only the King can tell me what to do. If only you were King."

Persicus chuckled. "Ormozd ordered you home and you still didn't listen."

"And if I had?" Nooshin sighed. "It should be me they have, not Tahmineh and Nadira."

"Nothing against your friends, but it would be much worse if they had you. Salman would try to control your father by threatening to hurt you."

Nooshin shook her head. "It's not right that they could get killed in my place. My father said it earlier. As onerous as it might be, it is our responsibility to protect our people, not endanger them."

"And you getting hurt by coming won't help your people either. If anything, you risk being captured and giving Salman control of Mishin, after everything we have done to fight him. If I am outnumbered ... Nooshin, I really don't want anything to happen to you. I shouldn't have let you ..." He paused, uncertain how to continue. "I mean, if anything happens to you, I would ..." He couldn't find the words.

"Persicus, what is it you are trying say?" she asked coquettishly, blinking up at him with big, innocent, green eyes.

Persicus stared down at her, trying to control his expression, and get a grip on himself.

"Ahai! Is that you, Persicus?" A voice called out from behind.

Persicus turned to see Gerisha and two Division Commanders galloping towards them at full speed.

"It's Gerisha." Persicus turned back to Nooshin with a look of relief.

Nooshin rolled her eyes. "Of course it is."

Persicus stopped to allow Gerisha to catch up with them.

Nooshin's face flushed red. She had always been fond of Gerisha, but he had formed a nasty habit of interrupting, always at the exact moment she had cornered Persicus into saying how he felt.

Gerisha had gone down to check on the black powder supplies. He figured they had to be running low by then. When he had come back, Ormozd had told him the latest developments, including the Princess running off into unknown danger with Persicus. He had hurried down the path alongside the river to catch up with them.

"I'm glad we caught up with you. The battle is over. We had to come out of the northern gate to get the men out of the trenches. The entire road to the southern gate is blocked off with bodies. You could see a cloud of dust from the remaining Turanian army, scattered in every direction, as they ran for their lives."

Persicus nodded, pleased with the news.

"We're going after Salman?" Gerisha asked.

"Yes, but first we need to find Tahmineh and Nadira. Hopefully, we can catch up with Salman after."

"Those men will have to meet up with Salman at some point," Nooshin said.

They fell into a steady, quick gallop. Persicus and Nooshin rode side by side. Gerisha rode on the other side of Nooshin, and the two division commanders flanked Persicus and Gerisha.

Nooshin, still determined, tried to resume her conversation with Persicus. "What was it that you wanted to tell me?"

"There is a path up ahead that will lead us right to Cattula Land," Gerisha said.

"I was speaking to Persicus."

Gerisha smiled, dipping his head in a bow. "My apologies, Princess."

Nooshin ignored him.

"I ... I can't imagine where he is heading. There is nothing north of here, other than Cattula Land," Persicus said.

"Well, we will find out soon enough," Gerisha replied.

Nooshin sighed, thoroughly annoyed. "That was not a satisfactory answer."

Newly appointed General Safwat selected Usman to join him on his journey to Cattula Land to meet King Salman. They had who they thought to be the Princess and chambermaid tied up on a couple of horses. To ensure they wouldn't jump off the horses in an attempt to escape, they also tied them to the saddles. They raced to meet Salman, taking a short cut across the valley to the northern road.

Persicus, Nooshin, Gerisha, and the Division Commanders stopped at a well-worn intersection. One way would lead them to Cattula Land and the other to Twelve Wolf Creek. They turned onto the path to Twelve Wolf Creek.

After about ten minutes, Gerisha held up his hand, signaling the others to stop. He listened intently, his head tilted. The road curved half of a mile ahead. After a moment, they all heard the sound of a horse whinnying in the distance.

Gerisha signaled them off the road into a dense copse of trees. They waited in silence, holding their breaths, while Gerisha climbed a tree to see how many men were coming beyond the curve in the road.

Gerisha hurried back down. "There are four of them," he whispered. "We can handle it."

Moments later, two men on horseback appeared in the distance and then two more followed, connected together by a long rope. Nooshin leaned forward and pointed, recognizing the two women's' forms. "That's them!" she whispered.

"Stay with Nooshin," Gerisha told Persicus, nodding for the Division Commanders to follow, and took off racing towards the Turanians.

"Let's go with them." Nooshin angled her horse forward.

"Oh, no, you don't." Persicus grabbed her reins, leading her further into the thicket of trees. "We'll wait there. There are only two of them. Gerisha can handle it." He wanted to go, but he didn't want Nooshin to get hurt, so he stayed, though it ate at something deep inside him not to be a part of the action. He had played a key role up until now and he wondered if Gerisha would try to keep him out of it now that the battle was over.

Nooshin gave him a suspicious look. "You want to go, but you don't want me to go. Why?"

"You're the Princess and you shouldn't be involved in —"

They heard shouts up ahead, someone screaming in pain, and then a woman's frantic cries.

Nooshin jerked her reins out of Persicus' hand while he was distracted and took off. Persicus muttered a curse and took off after her.

𝕋𝕋𝕋

Two men sat on the ground. One of them had an arrow in his upper chest. He coughed blood. Persicus knew the arrow had penetrated a lung. He would die in minutes and there was nothing anyone could do about it. The other man sat on the ground, with an arrow through his leg. Gerisha stood over him, sword in hand, pointed at the man's neck.

"Tahmineh! Nadira!" Nooshin jumped off her horse and ran to them.

The Division Commanders helped the two women down from their horses, cutting away the ropes and sheets that bound them.

"Oh! Nooshin, dear! Nooshin!" Tahmineh cried.

Nadira hugged the Princess, holding onto her for a full minute. Persicus could see the young girl trembling and that she had been crying. Her cheeks were red, and her eyes were pink and swollen. He felt miserable looking at them.

"Are you all right?" Nooshin asked, pulling back to see them, grabbing Tahmineh's hand. "Are you hurt?"

"The barbarians!" Tahmineh yelled. "They came into your room. They came right in there without warning and grabbed us!" Tahmineh turned like a storm on the wounded Turanian. She walked up to him and kicked him in the face before anyone realized what she was going to do.

Persicus and Gerisha gave a bark of laughter as the Division Commanders tried to pull Tahmineh away from the wounded man. She struggled against them, yelling. "Barbarians! No good, desert-dwelling savages! How dare you! Have you no scruples?"

The women appeared uninjured. Nooshin sighed in relief. They had not been hurt in her stead.

Gerisha looked down at the wounded man. "Where is Salman going?" he asked, sword still poised to his neck.

The man glared at Gerisha. He spit on the ground.

"What is your name?"

"I am High General Safwat of the Turanian Army!"

Gerisha squatted down by Safwat and looked him in the eye. He

360

spoke in a calm, confidential voice. "Safwat, I don't know if you know what happened back there in Mishin, but Turan no longer has an army. Salman is finished. Tell me where he is heading and I will see to it that your life is spared, your wound is tended to, and if you fully cooperate, I will speak to the King on your behalf."

Safwat glared at Gerisha. Gerisha gave him an earnest expression that all but said, don't be stupid, this is an easy choice. Safwat looked away in disgust.

"I will tell you nothing."

"Oh, for goodness sake!" Nooshin stomped over to Safwat.

Persicus trailed behind, not comfortable with her getting close to the enemy.

"Answer him. Where is Salman going?" Nooshin's tone said that he had better comply, or else.

The man glared at her. He spit again and it sprayed onto her shoes.

Nooshin reached down and grabbed the arrow that protruded through the man's leg. She jerked it, not causing more damage, but a lot of pain.

He screamed. One loud, ragged shriek. Pain like a red-hot brand seared through his leg, up to his head.

Persicus grimaced, looking away. *I've made a monster*, he thought.

Nooshin let go, but her hand hovered around the arrow. Safwat's breathing turned to short, loud gasps. His vacant eyes glazed with the pain. Gerisha knew the look; he was close to going into shock.

"Tell us where he went, or I will grab this arrow, and jerk it around!"

He hesitated. Nooshin closed her fist around the shaft, not yet moving it.

Safwat looked up at Gerisha, to Persicus, and back to Nooshin. He saw cold, dispassionate eyes looking back at him. She would do it. He knew she would. "At the bottomless pit! In Cattula. He told me to meet him there with the Princess. Don't, don't touch the arrow again! Please!"

Nooshin looked up at Persicus with a triumphant look.

Gerisha stared at Nooshin as if he had never seen her before. She used to be kind, innocent, and gentle, the epitome of the perfect daughter. He leaned close to Persicus. "When did she turn into the killer Princess?" he mumbled under his breath.

Persicus almost laughed, a wide grin spreading across his face. "I think it was the pan."

Gerisha gave Persicus a puzzled look.

Persicus waved the thought away. "Never mind."

Gerisha ordered the Division Commanders to escort the women back to Mishin. They tied Safwat up and loaded him onto his horse, and the Division Commanders led the women, and the prisoner, back to Mishin.

Nooshin had made a decision while the men cut Tahmineh and Nadira free from their bindings. Salman had to die. Whether Persicus and Gerisha approved was their own concern. Salman's reign of terror was over. Mishin would set the example for any tyrant who came along, thinking they could conquer, and make the citizens conform to their will. Forcing people to change their religion. Taxing citizens for being a different culture, or religion, turning them into little more than slaves in their own homes. They would become as Salman will become. She could not abide it any longer. Not in her lifetime. Not in her homeland. She thought of the dagger of King Cyrus, what she believed it stood for — the Jewish man who gave it to Cyrus for freeing them from slavery. She thought of Zoroaster, who taught fairness, kindness, equality, and the power of goodness. She thought of the Nestorian monks, trying to teach and learn from their messiah, Jesus, and the corrupt priests attempting to pollute the pureness of their church by pushing their own agendas. Salman, the barefoot barbarians, and corrupt priests — they were all the same. They all enforced the same things. Not to celebrate life, not to enjoy life, not to drink, or dance. Those people who say God wants you impoverished, servile, and to worship, and work hard, but nothing else, so He knows they love him and fear him. All of it was an agenda, to get people to work harder, to pay more taxes, to never step out of line, or question their authority, for fear of God's punishment, as if God would punish those who sing, when He gave them a voice; dancing, when He gave them grace; or drinking, when He gave them grapes. She thought of everything her father had taught her and realized that Salman must die. The only way to stop this kind of selfish evil was to destroy it. Crazy people like Mahmood and Ahmad would always support and enable that evil. They must be stopped. Only then could the people live in peace.

Nooshin stood and mounted her horse. "To Cattula Land. Salman is waiting for me."

Persicus heard a cold eagerness in her voice that scared him. He and Gerisha locked eyes.

Never in her life would she have thought she wanted to take another human life. Never in her life had she made a decision of such importance in a matter of moments and believed in that decision with her whole being. In the time it had taken for Nadira and Tahmineh to be cut free, she had decided. A calm came over her, a calm that she had not felt since Salman first showed up. Knowing that it was wrong, but also that it was right. Right for all the people Salman had enslaved and all those that would follow if she did nothing.

# 29

## THE BOTTOMLESS PIT

*This is it!* Salman thought, as he reined his horse to an abrupt stop. He dismounted and examined the huge, flat boulder before him. He smiled, now certain he had found the place his dearly departed cousin, Hakim, had described before his tragic death.

The air felt fresh and cool against his hot face. A gentle breeze stirred the trees. He tied his horse to a wiry, dead bush and surveyed the area. Taking in the serene landscape, he felt much better. No smoke rising up in the distance. No pathetic crying from dying men. No loud explosions that he could not understand. He put all that out of his mind and focused on finding his gold. Ten sacks of gold, hidden somewhere beneath this rock. And soon, Satric—or whatever his name was—would deliver the Princess to him. He would have her as his servant, his slave, until she grew too old to please him. Then, he figured he would sell the Sogdian Princess for a high price. This thought pleased him to the point of laughter and it spilled out from his lips. He laughed until he struggled to breathe. He had not lost.

When he regained control of himself, he climbed onto the flat boulder, and found the crevice where his cousins had dropped the sacks through to hide from the Cattulas. Lying flat on his stomach, he reached his arm down the crevice, and could feel nothing, but cool, damp air. He got to his feet and stared down at the small, dark hole.

"Idiots!"

Following Hakim's instructions, he walked down the path to the river. The boulder ran alongside the path, growing in height closer the river, and ending in the water. He searched around the riverbank, finding nothing. He cursed to himself as he eased into the frigid water, searching until he spotted the entrance to the underground cave. A nearly obscured opening into the boulder sat a couple feet above water level, about fifteen feet from the path, camouflaged by vines crawling over the hole.

Salman waded over to the cave's mouth.

The mouth of the cave was located in a shallow oxbow of the river, where the river's flow diverted and wound around the large, flat boulder. He had misestimated the height of the opening. Once standing in front of it, he realized it sat four feet above water level. The water came up to his hips. If he were any shorter, it would be difficult for him to make it. As it was, he stretched his arms up, and grabbed the bottom edge of the cave's mouth. He pulled himself up, got a foot on the edge, swung his other leg inside, and turned around so he was sitting in the opening. He looked down at a six-foot drop and jumped, landing on his feet in a crouch.

His cold, wet clothes clung to his skin. Inside the cave stayed damp, the air thick and humid, but the rock barrier kept the water out of the cave. Beyond the pale beam of sunlight filtering in past the overgrown vines around the entrance, an almost complete darkness permeated the enclosed space. Salman stood there, his eyes fixed to the deepest, darkest part of the cave, waiting for his eyes to adjust to the dim light. Once he could make out the slight difference between the rock walls and the ground, he continued forward. Towards the rear of the cave, a beam of light shone down from the ceiling. Since no other beams of sunlight penetrated the darkness, that had to be where his cousins had dropped the gold down the small hole. The gold had to be there.

The cool, damp air smelled musty. The air flowed regularly through the cave's mouth and the crevice, allowing the staleness usual to caves out, and fresh air in, but the smell of detritus still clung to the air—a smell that was unclean to Salman. A smell he associated with the poverty he experienced growing up in the vast cave system in the mountains above Turan. He had rejected that lifestyle, moved his family out of the caves, built a city, giving them legitimacy, after generations of being unfairly maligned—generations of being forced to *hide* and *live* in *caves*. He laughed at the irony of being back in a place like this, to collect the long lost gold, which was the cause of his family being forced into the caves. He felt as if, at long last, a curse was being lifted.

He wrinkled his nose.

The cave stretched about thirty-five feet long and eighteen feet wide. The ceiling rose ten feet high by the entrance and graded downward towards the back of the cave to just over six feet.

Eager to find his gold, Salman hurried through the cave, and almost didn't see the pit that opened up along the length of the wall below the crevice. He stopped and jumped back right before he took the last, fatal step. He looked down into a darkness so complete that it was no wonder why people called it, *The Bottomless Pit*. The pit ran along almost the entire length of the wall, thirty feet long, and eight feet wide. He looked up.

There they were. In the dim light trickling down from the crevice, he could make out the shapes of the sacks of gold. The gold for which his ancestors had given their lives. They sat right there, across from him, precariously perched on a small ledge above the pit. The ledge sat at ground level and ran the length of the pit. His eyes widened and he clenched his teeth, his fists tightening at his sides when he saw that only four sacks of gold sat there.

*Four!* His rage was instantaneous. More than half of his gold, he thought, had fallen down into the pit. Gone.

"Damned fools!" he yelled. *Ools ... ools ... ools,* echoed back at him like a fugal chorus.

As Hakim had told him, each sack had a rope tied around its neck, the ends trailing into the darkness of the pit, out of reach.

Salman bent down and picked up a fist-sized rock. He held it over the pit and dropped it. He waited. Time passed and he didn't hear a sound. No splash. No sound of rock hitting rock. Not even a little *tink*. Nothing.

Salman laughed to himself. A nervous laugh. "Looks like they were right. It is a bottomless pit. Straight to hell."

He stared up at the crevice, thinking. After a few minutes of coming up with and rejecting ideas, he grinned. He ran back to the entrance, climbed out, waded through the ice-cold water, ran along the path, and skidded to a stop in front of his horse. He grabbed a long rope from his saddlebag. He climbed up on the boulder. He could see where his cousins had made a fire, a few feet from the crevice, before the Cattulas confronted them, subsequently causing them to lose his gold. The black residue still looked fresh, but would soon fade, just as what little imprints Hakim's life had made on the world would fade.

Salman looked around for something to tie the rope to and noticed a large, cone-shaped rock protruding out of the boulder, only three feet from the crevice. He wound the rope around it three times, tied it, and pulled hard to ensure it would hold, and then threw the rest of the rope down the crevice.

Off to the side of the path stood a group of trees and bushes. He took his time selecting a tree limb that would suit his needs and hacked one off with his sword.

Salman continued back into the cave. Once inside, he approached the edge of the pit with more caution than before. The rope he had dropped through the crevice hung down into the black abyss. Using his sword, he cut the smaller branches and stems away, leaving one curved branch at the end of the tree limb. With the aid of his makeshift hook, he tried to snag the rope, and guide it to his hand. After several failed attempts, in which the rope slithered away, and slapped back against the wall, he snagged the rope. Grabbing the rope, he let go of the branch, and watched as it fell down the dark chasm without a sound.

Salman tossed his sword to the ground, out of his way, and wrapped the rope around his waist and tied it to his leather belt. He leaned back on the rope, testing its hold. He smiled. *This will do, nicely.*

He eyed the distance from the edge of the pit to the ledge where his gold sat—about eight feet. Gripping the rope, he stepped to the edge of the pit, and focused on the area to the right of the gold. The ledge was narrower on either side of the gold. By a stroke of blind luck, the sacks themselves had landed on the only spot wide enough to hold them. If he could land in the right spot, he could grab the gold. He would have to bend over to grab the ropes attached to the sacks, without losing his balance, and tie the ropes to his belt. Once he secured the gold, all he would have to do is swing back to the other side. *Simple,* he thought.

He took a deep breath.

Persicus, Gerisha, and Nooshin spotted Salman's horse tied to a dead bush, next to a large, flat boulder. They stopped on the main road, surveying the area. They did not see Salman, but knew he must be nearby.

"What do you think?" Persicus asked Gerisha.

Gerisha shook his head. "What the hell is he doing here?"

Nooshin giggled.

Persicus and Gerisha turned towards her with identical, concerned expressions. This was not the time for laughter, and perhaps—they both thought—the events of the day had been too much for her young and sheltered soul.

"I'm sorry," Nooshin said. "I just remembered something. Do you remember the stories from the unfortunate, lost travelers who ventured into this godforsaken land by accident? They spoke of a flat rock that shelters what they called, *The Gateway to Hell.*"

Gerisha nodded. "Yes, I've heard the stories."

"Zorka made up a song about it when we were little, based on a story one of the men told him in the caravanserai." She paused, trying to remember the words.

*"The gate to hell is near, my dear,*
*If that's your destiny, don't fear,*
*To the water then, you must,*
*Climb through the rock, to ancient dust,*
*Behold, below the gate to hell,*
*Where Kali waits and evil dwells,*
*She calling you to come on through,*
*Now, close your eyes and jump."*

Nooshin pointed to the end of the boulder, which protruded into the water. A cold breeze shuffled by. Nooshin and Persicus both shivered. Gerisha frowned.

"Into the water and behind the rock?" Gerisha thought aloud.

Persicus angled his horse towards the boulder. "Let's go have a closer look around. Stay close, Nooshin."

Before they reached Salman's horse, they dismounted, and quietly made their way towards the boulder on foot.

As they drew closer to the boulder, they spotted a rope tied to a rock, stretched taut through a small crevice. They stood on top the boulder, looking down at the crevice. Gerisha motioned them away from the crevice. They walked a couple feet away.

"What do you think?" Persicus whispered.

"General Sadr … uh … Safwat. Is that you?" Salman's voice called out from within the boulder.

They froze. There must be a good-size cave beneath them. Persicus had whispered soft enough that someone standing five feet away wouldn't have heard him. The small crevice must have amplified their voices in the cave.

Persicus answered in a gruff voice, trying to match Safwat's voice. "Who else."

"Good! You have the Princess?"

Nooshin put her hand over her mouth and made incoherent struggling sounds, loud enough to be sure her muffled voice carried.

Persicus smiled. "Yes, she's right here."

Nooshin muffled a scream and cursed again. Persicus and Gerisha suppressed the urge to laugh as she acted out her own detainment.

"Good, General. Tie her up and wait right there. I'll come for you soon."

Salman still stood on the edge, preparing to jump across, when he heard his new General outside. The sound of Nooshin's muffled cries delighted him. He wanted to see her beg and cry, but first, his gold.

He jumped and swung straight to the ledge. The instant he leapt off he knew he missed his target. As his feet hit the wall, he pushed off, springing back to land at the edge of the Bottomless Pit, where he had started. He adjusted his position and tried again. His feet left off the ground and he slammed into the wall. He reached out with one hand, grasping for handhold on the wall, as he planted his feet on the small ledge.

Standing on the balls of his feet, facing the wall, he soon realized his predicament. It wasn't possible to reach the sacks in this position, as he couldn't bend down without his knees hitting the wall and losing his balance. The gold sat by his feet, inches away. He decided to try anyway.

Salman gripped his rope with his left hand and began to bend his knees, while reaching down with his right arm. As expected, his knees hit the wall and he lost his balance. He cursed as he swung back a few feet and then forward, hitting the wall several feet from where he started. He scrunched his legs up, planted his feet against the wall, and pushed off, swinging back towards solid ground.

He landed and stood, irritated and angry. "Damn you, Hakim!"

*Am ... akim ... Am ... akim*, echoed through the cave. Salman felt his own echo mocking him, as if Hakim himself somehow managed to make his voice bounce off the walls, saying Hakim's name over and over, to remind him — no, to *blame* him — for his cousin's pitiful death.

The echo died away while Salman stood there, contemplating, fuming. How could he get the gold? Then he realized his mistake. Facing the wall, he couldn't bend his knees, facing the other way, he could.

Not wanting to slam into the wall backward, he turned around, putting his back to the pit. He then lifted up his feet and gently swung out over the pit, allowing the momentum to die down. When he hung suspended over the pit, in line with the gold, he began swinging back and forth, each swing bringing him closer to the ledge and his gold. At last, he felt his back touch the wall and on the next swing planted his feet on the small ledge, less than a foot away from his gold. For several minutes, he stared down into the pit, mesmerized. He felt its pull, as if the darkness itself had substance, a heavy weight, and it called to him, beckoning him home.

Something moved in the cave and it broke Salman out of his trance. He looked up, straight across the cave. Three figures stood there, lost in the shadows, silhouetted against the light from outside the cave's entrance.

*Safwat, Nooshin, and the other soldier*, Salman thought. "I told you to wait outside."

Salman noticed that they stood side by side, each about foot apart from each other. He could make out Nooshin's feminine figure. Her unbound hands hung free at her sides. No ropes or ties bound her, at all. There was no cloth or leather tied around her mouth. Salman frowned.

"Oh, but I couldn't wait to see you," Nooshin said.

The three dark figures took a couple steps closer, revealing themselves in the small beam of light from the crevice.

As Salman stared at them, he felt the blood drain from his face. These two were full of surprises today. They had tricked him, twice. Oh, but what fools to follow him here. His anger had been brewing to a rapid boil since the first explosions came, destroying his plans, his future. Now, at least he could unleash his fury on them, knowing that it would feel good, better than anything. He smiled. "Deadwood. You are all nothing, but deadwood."

Salman glanced at his sword, still on the ground, at their feet. Together, Gerisha and Persicus drew their swords.

"Now, now. Where is your honor? Surely, you will allow me to solid ground before trying to kill me. You wouldn't kill me here, unarmed and helpless?"

"You may cross back, but after that, we will not allow you to live," Gerisha said.

They stepped back, out of Salman's way.

Salman gave a bark of laughter. "And what does your King have to say about that? After he whined to me not to kill this one here, until he had heard his desperate plea?"

Gerisha gave a cold smile. "Yes, you are absolutely right. Come across, you can't stay there all day anyway. We will escort you back to Mishin, where King Ormozd will judge you. Whereupon, after he orders your execution—the first execution in Mishin in a hundred years will surely be a gala event—we will take you to the town square for a very public, humiliating death. Maybe we will execute you with our wonderful new weapon that your army experienced today."

"No, I don't think he's worthy of our new weapon, it would be too quick an end," Persicus said, grinning mischievously. "However, you and your men left in such a hurry that you left your copper pot. It's still sitting there, waiting. Wasn't the defeated nation supposed to partake in a pleasant bowl of soup? It's too bad Hakim won't be there to enjoy it with you, but he will be there all the same."

Salman smiled. "A wonderful speech, but I must decline your offer. You see, I have other plans."

"Then we fight you here, to your death."

Salman swung across. His feet connected with the ground. He rolled away from them and picked up his sword.

Gerisha began raising his sword, but Persicus stepped in front of him. "No, let me." Persicus got into a fighting stance.

Gerisha looked at Persicus and then Nooshin, who hesitated briefly before nodding her approval. "As you wish," Gerisha said, and led Nooshin to the back of the cave, out of harm's way, giving Persicus room to fight.

Salman stood facing Persicus, still tethered to the rope.

Persicus moved forward. His eyes locked onto Salman's body, waiting for the telltale sign of tension to play in his muscles. Salman tensed a moment before he lunged forward, swinging his sword from right to left, in a failed attempt to knock Persicus' sword out of the way. Persicus stepped swiftly aside, getting into a defensive stance.

Salman charged him. His face contorted in unfathomable rage and hatred. Again, Persicus moved smoothly out of the path of Salman's blade, stretching out his arm as he moved, and lashing out with the tip of his sword. Persicus' sword tore through Salman's sleeve, sliced down his right arm. Salman jerked away and grabbed his bleeding arm.

Salman glared at Persicus with malicious, seething fury emanating from the depths of his withered soul. Persicus smiled and gave a small bow of his head.

Persicus had trained in sword fighting all his youth, practicing wherever, and whenever he could. Dozens of different opponents and teachers over the years. Learning different techniques and styles from everywhere he travelled. In the end, he could draw from every style he had ever leant. He could switch from Japanese Kenjutsu to Indian Śastravidyā in the blink of an eye; he could incorporate any technique he had learned from Asia, Europe, and Egypt.

Salman smiled confidently. "Oh, you are going to be fun." He put on an amused face. The Tajik was a decent swordsman, though he moved with an odd form. Nothing that Salman could put his finger on. Nevertheless, Salman knew he himself excelled in the sword, trained by the best in Turan. He had competed with his friends and neighbors in sparring matches and almost always won. He pumped himself up with confidence, telling himself he had been trained by experts. *I am better than any damned Tajik. I am the best swordsman. I will win, no doubt. I know what I am doing. I am the best. I'll kill this Tajik and the Armenian, and make off with Nooshin and my gold.*

Persicus strode forward, slashing his sword in a rapid series of strikes. Salman stumbled back, trying to block the sharp blade that Persicus wielded with incredible speed. Persicus stabbed his sword from overhead, downward. Salman blocked the strike with the forte of his blade. Persicus drew his sword out and around in a circle, coming up from below, and slashed Salman's face. A two-inch gash, deep into his cheek.

Salman jumped back, breathing hard. He had felt the cold tip of steel across his right cheek. A moment later, he felt the pain, sharp and incessant, throbbing in tune with his own pounding heart. A warm gush of blood washed down his face.

Forgetting his training, Salman charged again; he wrapped both hands tight around the grip of his sword, swinging the blade in a flurry. Left, right, left, overhead, left again, backhanded. Thrusting outward and overhead in a stabbing motion. He swung from every angle possible, pushing Persicus back towards the pit. Salman didn't give Persicus a chance to strike back, and could only parry, block, and dodge Salman's frantic thrusts.

Persicus fended off strike after strike. Salman was terrible at swordplay. He swung frantically, without rhythm or reason, or any style that Persicus had ever seen or heard of, but he kept Persicus from doing anything, but deflecting the blows. To Persicus, it seemed as though Salman had never been in a true life or death swordfight. No calm reason to his technique. No practiced offensive style. Salman fought with raw, unpredictable rage. Madness had consumed him, leaving behind only the unhinged passion of animalistic instincts.

With the pit behind Persicus, which he knew had to be only a few more steps behind him, he couldn't risk backing up anymore. Between two of Salman's thrusts, he stepped to the side, and away from the pit, ducking at the same time as he blocked Salman's next strike with the forte of his sword. He took another quick step to the side as Salman raised his sword for the next blow, forcing Salman to step with him, so that now the pit ran parallel to them both. Persicus saw that Salman's rope, still tied tight around his waist, was now stretched taut, and Salman couldn't move any farther towards him. Persicus moved in for a counter thrust, halting Salman's flurry of assaults. He stepped back, out of Salman's range and watched his frustration with fascination.

Salman backed up a few steps, trying to draw Persicus to him, into an attack, since he could go no farther. He could have untied himself, but he planned to get the gold after he killed them. If he let go of the rope, it would swing back into the center of the pit, and Salman would have to waste more time to go out, and find another perfect branch to hook the rope. Better to leave it on. Especially since he figured time was of the essence. He doubted that the Tajik and the Armenian had come here alone. Others would soon follow. He needed to get his gold and be gone. If only the Tajik would rush him, he could step aside, give him a small shove, and let Persicus plummet to his death, maybe he could stab him on the way, adding sharp pain to his fatal plummet, but the deadwood just stood there, his concentration focused on Salman in the most uncanny way. Salman thrust his sword forward, aiming at a downward angle.

Persicus sprang forward and smashed his sword down on top of Salman's, forcing Salman's sword to towards the ground. As Salman tried to raise his arm, Persicus kept his sword in contact with Salman's, jerking his blade around in a circular motion, sending Salman's sword flying across the cave.

Salman stood there, glaring vacuously at Persicus. The Tajik had beaten him. *Him!* Salman, defeated by a *Tajik*.

Persicus kept his sword pointed steadily at Salman's chest. Salman took a small, uncertain step to the side, stealing a quick glance in the direction his sword had flown, searching for the silvery gleam of steel. His hand went to the rope around his waist, gripping the thick knot. He would have to untie it to go for the sword. He pulled at the hem of his tunic, shifted his weight from foot to foot, and stole another quick step towards his sword.

𒌋𒌋𒌋

Nooshin and Gerisha stood towards the back of the cave. Nooshin had seen Persicus fight before and knew he fought well, but she had never before seen Salman fight. She had only heard tales of how ferocious and ruthless he was. It dawned on her that before Salman had developed an army, he had only attacked small, defenseless communities. In all probability, he had never gone up against anyone even moderately prepared and trained himself. He had had his crazy Generals and his army for that. Now, the only word she could find to describe Salman fighting abilities, against a well-trained swordsman, was *pathetic*. She felt like laughing. It trickled out of her lips, even as she tried to suppress it. That someone such as Salman had managed to conquer land after land seemed unbelievable, absurd. Everyone had been too scared to fight. It was that simple. They had all heard the stories and even seen the burning buildings in the small, defenseless villages along the Silk Road. She was not worried in the least about Persicus' safety and felt a strange satisfaction that the Great King Salman, the Magnificent should come to his end at the hands of a man such as Persicus. A merchant, a farmer, and qanat engineer. She wondered if maybe she had been through too much in the past weeks. Maybe the mental strain and physical fatigue had taken its toll without her realizing it, resulting in the sudden giddiness she felt, or maybe it came from the realization that the whole ordeal would soon be at its end. Knowing all this, hearing her own laughter echoing through the cave, sounding almost hysterical, she still couldn't stop. She felt light, relieved, exuberant, and incredibly, joyously happy.

Persicus waited for Salman to make a move towards his sword, his own sword poised, ready to attack. He could hear Nooshin's stifled giggles from where she stood, somewhere behind Salman, but he only had eyes for the man in front of him, though he couldn't help wondering what could be making the Princess laugh in such a situation. *Maybe Salman's poor fighting skills?* Still, he worried about her. She had been through too much. The weight of the responsibility for her people, her decision not to marry Salman, the toll of lives lost in the battle, she would view it all as on her hands.

"Why did you come here?" Persicus asked suddenly.

Salman inadvertently glanced to the ledge above the pit, where his gold sat. Salman laughed, forced, fake, and loud. "I came here to get the Princess, of course. Thank you for delivering her to me."

Persicus flicked his eyes to where Salman had glanced and caught sight of the sacks on the small ledge. Then, he knew. He knew those sacks. "Those sacks!"

Salman smirked. "What about them?"

"Those sacks are the lost treasure, from the Land of Fire and Dragons. The ones I helped your cousin find. The gold your cousin betrayed me for."

Persicus saw something flicker in Salman's eyes. *Was it sorrow? Grief for the loss of his cousins? Or was it worry that he would now lose his precious gold?* Persicus decided to see if it was the former. If Salman was capable of love and sorrow. "My condolences for Hakim and his brothers' tragic passing. What a way to die. Did you see it? Them falling into your giant pot? The oil boiling and hissing? Boiling their flesh, cooking them alive. I can't imagine the pain they went through in their final moments."

Salman scoffed. "I despised those varmints. They were never of any use to me. Completely useless, incompetent. That part of the family bred nothing, but a bunch of lazy, good for nothing, thieving morons."

*So much for sorrow*, Persicus thought.

Salman took a step back. The peasant had him. *Unbelievable.* The Tajik had gotten lucky, that was all. Pure luck. Salman had never feared anyone. Nevertheless, this damned Tajik somehow managed to disarmed him and cut him, twice. In an unorthodox way of fencing, an undisciplined, mysterious style, the Tajik had taken the sword right out of his hands, with a swiftness that surprised him. He would die here, he thought, unless he came up with something, quick.

As fast as that thought came, it left him. There was nothing he could do. Persicus and Gerisha were both professional thugs and they outnumbered him, and that was the real truth. He was outnumbered. He couldn't take them both. One of them, yes, but not both. It wasn't fair — *two* against one. *They* were *unfair.* What had he ever done to hurt either of them that they should pursue him here, while he was minding his own business? He had left Mishin. He had allowed them to win that battle. Now, they came *here*! It wasn't enough that they had taken his Generals, his dear Ahmad and Mahmood, now they came for his blood, as well — after he had left them unharmed! They wanted to take his life!

With grim pleasure, he told himself that he wouldn't die alone. No, one of them would die with him — the one that had disgraced him the most.

Salman made a movement as though he were going for his sword, to throw Persicus off guard. Persicus moved to stand between Salman and his sword, but Salman spun around, and pounced three long steps back to where he had heard the Princess' soft laughter. Salman grabbed her, even as Gerisha threw himself at him. Salman threw himself out over the Bottomless Pit with Nooshin locked in his arms.

Nooshin screamed, beating at her captor. An instant later, she froze, terrified, as they flew through the darkness, the air whistling by. She knew that they hung suspended over the Bottomless Pit and only Salman's arms kept her safe.

Gerisha catapulted himself after Salman. His fingertips grazing Salman's back as he flew off the edge. Gerisha landed hard on the edge of the pit. He had missed them. He tried to stop, but his momentum kept going, and he tumbled over the edge of the pit. He grabbed onto the edge with both hands, his legs flailing against thin air. He looked over his shoulder, down into the opaque, impenetrable darkness. He turned away, dizziness overcoming him, and began pulling himself up.

Persicus ran for Gerisha. Conflicted, he looked up at Nooshin.

Nooshin screamed. Salman peeled her fingers off him, one by one. His arms no longer embraced her and now she clung desperately to him.

"Now you want me, you little tramp, but I don't want *you.*" Salman laughed. "I-don't-want-*you!*" He tormented her with the prospect of the fall. Pulling a finger at a time. Pulling her hair back, straining her neck. All the while, she clung to him, as she could do nothing else. His sinister, heckling laughter stabbed through her like an icy dagger.

"Get Nooshin," Gerisha yelled as Persicus knelt down to pull him up.

Persicus looked up at Nooshin. Her frantic cry cut through him painfully, but he would need Gerisha's help to save her. Persicus grabbed Gerisha's forearm and he pulled him to safety.

Gerisha stood next to Persicus, breathing in panicked gulps. They watched Nooshin's terror-filled face, helpless to save her.

Nooshin slid down six inches, grabbing Salman around his upper abdomen, her face pressed into his chest.

"Don't!" Persicus yelled. "Don't hurt her! We'll let you go. You can walk out of here, unharmed! Don't drop her."

"And I suppose you get the gold?" Salman asked, his arm snaking around Nooshin's back, hugging her to him, fondling her hair.

"Gold means nothing. You can have it. I don't care about gold," Persicus pleaded. "Just don't drop her."

"And the Princess? You give her to me, as well? Allow me to walk out of here with the gold and your Princess?" Salman asked, one hand running down her arm.

Nooshin felt his hand crawling up and down her arm, and felt repulsion creep in on top of the fear, but she could do nothing, but cling to him. She turned her face away from him and stared wide-eyed at Persicus.

Persicus wanted to promise him anything, *anything*, not to hurt her. He almost said it, but knew it was a trap. If he agreed that Salman could walk out of here with Nooshin, Salman would know he was lying. Then Salman might think he was lying about the gold, as well.

"No," Gerisha said.

"No," Persicus echoed. "You live. You get your gold, but you leave Nooshin and Mishin alone."

Salman threw his head back and laughed uproariously. The sound of it raised the hairs on Persicus' neck. Goosebumps ran up Nooshin's arms and down her back. Each time he laughed it sounded increasingly crazed, his sanity slipping, disintegrating.

"You see, I have all the power right now. I hold your dear Nooshin's life, quite literally, in my hands." Salman began to swing with the rope. He swung, not front to back, where Persicus or Gerisha could grab them, but side to side, towards the back wall, and along the length of the pit. Salman's intense gaze never wavered, he just stared intently at Persicus as he built momentum.

Salman blamed Persicus for everything that had happened. Nooshin, who had been on her way to marry him, had changed her mind while with *Persicus*. It was *Persicus* whom Hakim had hired to find the gold. *Persicus*, who had followed and pestered Hakim, and he knew without a doubt that somehow, *Persicus* was responsible for the gold being dropped down the Bottomless Pit. *Persicus*, who had murdered his cousin's servant, which had led to Nooshin's very public rejection of him — humiliating him! It had to have been *Persicus'* weapon that destroyed his army, his plans, his empire, his *life. Who killed Ahmad and Mahmood!* He knew without a doubt that if the Sogdians had such a weapon before Persicus' arrival, they would have used it long before now. It was *Persicus'* fault! That supercilious peasant *Tajik.*

"Do we have a deal?" Persicus shouted.

Salman's lips contorted into a savage smile. "No deal."

"Persicus!" Nooshin called out in a heart-wrenching scream. Nooshin's heart pounded painfully. She didn't know what to do other than hold on and hope Persicus could save her. Each swing brought her closer to the back wall.

As the momentum built, Salman swung harder and faster. The rock wall looked jagged with sharp points jutting out all over the surface.

Persicus realized, in horror, what Salman planned on doing. He was going to bash Nooshin into the wall, while they watched, unable to stop him. Desperate, Persicus looked around, trying to think of a way to save her. His pounding heart raced faster, shooting a fresh bout of adrenaline through his veins.

Nooshin's back hit the wall, softly the first time, but with the promise of sharp, excruciating pain to follow. She couldn't stay helpless in his arms, at his mercy. She had to do something. She wouldn't give Salman the satisfaction of dying, cowering in his arms. She began to fight. Clinging to him and hitting him at the same time. She managed to tear one hand away from him long enough to wrap around it the rope. Frantic, she kicked at him and hit him with one fisted hand. While she struggled, she glimpsed the knot tied to his belt. An idea formed in her mind. She tugged at the knot tied to his belt. She pulled at it, angrily beating his chest at the same time, hoping he wouldn't realize what she was doing. All the while, he laughed. Laughed as they swung back towards the jagged wall a second time.

Nooshin's back was to the wall and she couldn't tell when the exact moment of impact would be, but she knew it was coming, and soon. She stopped fighting and held on. Looking up, she saw Salman's eyes light up, his face feverish and eager as he stared down at her, awaiting her pain. She braced herself.

The next instant, she slammed into the wall for the second time. Salman's weight smashed against her. Her head flew back with the impact, hitting the wall hard. Darkness rolled over her in waves and her vision cleared as they soared the opposite direction. Somehow, she had managed to hang on.

They flew away from the wall, soaring towards the other side. Fortunately, the rope didn't reach the opposite end of the cave. She only had to worry about Salman crushing her against one rock wall.

Salman's crazed laughter slithered out from his lips. Nooshin began fighting him again, hoping to untie the knot, and make him fall, while she held on to the rope, but she worried he might realize what she was doing. She needed a distraction. They reached the apex and the momentum shifted, back towards the wall. Back towards terrible pain.

Nooshin saw the sacks of gold flash by as she swung past them, sitting on the ledge with their ropes trailing down into the pitch-black of the pit.

All of a sudden, she could hear Persicus and Gerisha frantically yelling and screaming at Salman to stop. Logically, she knew they had been yelling the whole time and she had not noticed. All of her focus had to remain on Salman and the wall she was about to be pounded into again. They offered him anything. *Anything*, if he would only stop. They could do nothing else to save her. Yet, they didn't understand him as she did. You couldn't offer him anything, not even things he wanted, such as gold and power. He had been humiliated. He had lost a battle he felt so certain he would win. Maybe he couldn't even bare to face his men — or what remained of his men. Now, the only thing that mattered was getting even. Hurting her. She knew this with every fiber of her being. To redeem himself, in his own twisted mind, he needed revenge. He needed to prove himself more powerful than them. He would kill her, but he wanted to torture her first. To show Persicus and Gerisha that he had control and they couldn't do anything to stop him. To show how powerless they all were against him.

Nooshin saw his eyes light up again, sucking in the darkness so that they appeared black. She stopped fighting and held on with both hands.

Nooshin crashed into the wall. The impact was harder this time and Salman's weight crushed against her, pushing all the air out of her lungs. Unable to breathe, she somehow managed to keep her head from hitting the wall too hard. She thanked Ahura Mazda that the waves of darkness didn't consume her vision this time, but she felt the sharp, jagged edge of a protruding rock stabbed through her skin on her lower back. Her back exploded into a massive ache. Sharp, excruciating pain tore through her, knocking the air out of her. When she could draw a breath again, she cried out from the pain. As they started their descent, soaring back towards the gold, she gritted her teeth, and tried to think past the pain. Her left hand shook when she let go of the rope. Reluctantly, she wrapped her legs around Salman to help herself hold on. She couldn't give up, not to Salman. She began beating at him. Punching him in the stomach and chest, and tugging at the knot at his waist. Her right hand maintained a death grip on rope above the knot. Glancing over at the ledge, she saw the sacks almost within reach.

Just a little further. She screamed as loud as she could, right into Salman's face as she reached out her left hand towards the sacks. She didn't think she could take another bashing against the wall. She would lose consciousness and fall to her death. She hoped, prayed, she didn't miss the rope. Her only chance, her only hope, was to distract him.

Her hand locked onto one of the sack's ropes. As they soared past, the sack pulled off the ledge, jerking her arm down with its great weight, but she held on to it. When they reached the apex, she used the shift in momentum to help swing the heavy sack up over her head and around. Every ounce of her strength went into that swing, as hard and fast as she could.

Salman began swinging harder, faster, wanting her to hurt. The last slam had almost made her lose her ferocious grip on the rope. She looked dazed and it filled Salman with a sense of power, unlike anything he had ever felt. As they cascaded back away from the wall, she suddenly screamed up into his face, and started beating at his chest again. Her punches surprised him and he laughed, she hit strong for a girl, but they didn't hurt him. When her small fist stopped beating at him, he turned to watch Persicus and Gerisha's reactions. He wanted to absorb as much of their horror and fear as he could. This next bash was sure to knock her off the rope. He wanted to watch their faces fall as she plummeted to her death. He wanted to see her falling beneath him, arms reaching for *him*. To hear her shrill scream echoing up from the pit below.

Out of nowhere, something slammed painfully into his head and face, disrupting his thoughts, so unexpected that he let go of the rope in surprise, and cried out in an automatic reaction. He turned his head in time to see that little wretch swing a heavy sack of gold at him again. Before he could get his arm up in defense, the sack crashed into the side of his face, and slid down his shoulder. He heard his nose crunch and he howled in horrible pain. One hand rose up to cup his nose as blood began to trickle down his chin.

"*My gold!*" Salman yelled, reaching out to grab the sack, but she already pulled it away from his reaching hands.

Gliding through the damp and musty air, they slammed into the rock wall, this time side by side. Nooshin took the impact on her left shoulder and Salman on his right side. They soared backwards again.

Nooshin's arm shook with the effort she had put into swinging the sack at him two times. Even with the help of the centrifugal force, it remained difficult. Salman's arm had padded some of the impact for her, but her left shoulder still throbbed with pain from multiple impacts. This needed to end.

She looked down at the sack and began shaking it, trying to get the cinches to loosen and open. She felt exhausted, her arms ached and trembled, and she couldn't lift the sack an inch. She waited until the momentum shifted again, so she could use it to help swing the sack. As they reached the apex, she helped get the sack into motion with the force from shifting direction aiding her.

Salman reached for the sack. "Give it to me! If you drop it, I'll kill you!"

### �ᛀ

Salman saw the sack coming again. He watched in horror as the sack's cinch started to come open as it rotated through the air above him.

"No ... No ... No ... No!" he yelled. Reaching for the sack, he stared with wide eyes as a few gold coins tumbled out, glinting into the darkness of the pit. Salman stretched his arm up higher, clenched his fist onto the sack's rope, and jerked it out from Nooshin's hand. He pulled the sack to his chest as it smacked into him. Relinquishing his hold on the rope, he cradled the sack with one arm, and pulled the cinch closed with the other.

### ᛀ

It was too good to be true. He grabbed the sack, more worried about losing the gold than his life. Exactly as she had hoped. Nooshin let him take the sack away from her. As he pulled the sack in to his chest, she reinforced her grip on the rope tied to Salman's belt with her right hand. With her left hand, she reached down, and jerked the knot around his waist, determined to get it to loosen and unravel.

Persicus and Gerisha had fallen quiet. No doubt, they saw what she was doing. She clawed at the knot, digging her finger into the loop. Salman, concerned only with closing the sack, paid no attention to her for the moment. One more tug and the knot came loose.

### ᛀ

Salman felt her beating at him again and he felt an odd tugging around his waist. After he tightened the cinch around the neck of the sack, he tied the leather cord into a knot, so it wouldn't come loose again. When he finished securing his gold, he looked down.

*Oh, great Allah!* he thought, as the rope around his waist unraveled. He began falling, still clutching his sack of gold to his chest.

He fell about eight feet before he managed to grabbed a hold of the rope with one hand, stopping his fall. Looking up at that blasted Sogdian, he cursed vehemently. He wouldn't be able to climb up the rope one handed and he couldn't— wouldn't—let go of his gold.

The swinging started to slow. Nooshin heard Salman's angry voice and looked down in horror to see Salman still clinging to the rope, as angry as she'd ever seen him, filth spewing from his mouth in a tide of venomous rage. Though he couldn't possibly grab her from eight feet below, she didn't doubt that he would start climbing, he could probably climb it while still holding onto his beloved gold. He would grab her and she would be right back where she started, at his mercy. She felt like screaming at him to just die already, but it would be useless.

She wrapped her legs around the rope, a great relief to her exhausted arms.

As the rope slowed to a gentle sway, she reached out, and grabbed the second sack. Her arm jerked down with the weight. She clutched the sack close to her body and aimed for Salman's head. She dropped the sack.

Seething with uncontainable fury, Salman glared up at her with fiery eyes, picturing her at his mercy, begging for her life as he wielded a sword above her lovely throat. He *needed* his vengeance. He closed his eyes for a moment, the better to see her death in his mind.

*They have ruined* everything. Nothing *has gone according to plan today*, he thought, as he opened his eyes. Again, he looked up at Nooshin, only to see another sack of gold barreling down at him. It crashed into his face and his already broken nose. He roared, as the sack started to slide down his chest. Quickly, he drew his knees up, just as the sack slid down his abdomen, and landed in his lap. Another heavy sack crashed down on him, hitting his already sore right shoulder. Furious, he roared, the pit amplifying the sound, monstrous echoes reverberating within the cave.

Nooshin choked back a sob. He was still down there. She reached out with a trembling arm and grabbed the last sack of gold. She *had* to get him off the rope and this was her last chance. Drawing up her knees, legs still coiled around the rope, she cradled the last sack, and pulled the cinch halfway open. She turned the sack upside-down and let it fall, the gold spilling out around the sack as it fell.

Gold spilled down on Salman and he looked up as his last sack of gold hit his shoulder. The shoulder of the arm holding onto the rope. His right arm that had already been cut by Persicus' sword. That had taken a beating against the wall. That had already been hit by another sack of gold, feeling as if a fifty-pound piece of limestone had fallen on him.

He felt his shoulder dislocate, felt it sliding out of socket. In an instant, he lost control of his arm. He stared at his useless hand, as the rope slid out from his grip, and he began his long plummet down into the unknown depths of *the Bottomless Pit*.

He couldn't believe it. This whole day seemed too outrageous to be true. He, King Salman, the Magnificent, couldn't be falling, with his ancestor's gold, down a bottomless pit. No way could a damned Sogdian Princess beat him. He felt he had to be dreaming.

*Yes, a dream,* Salman thought. *A pre-battle nightmare. Surely, there was no exploding fire. No damned Tajik. No murderous Princess.* Convinced that the entire day was a dream, he thought the whole thing was terribly hilarious. *A bottomless pit? Impossible!*

Salman's curses turned into laughter. An insane, hysterical, incessant, baying laughter.

Somewhere, in the depths of his crazed mind, a voice told him to drop the gold, and grab the rope, told him this was no dream, that he was losing his mind.

Nooshin glimpsed Salman's face as he began to fall down the Bottomless Pit, gold sparkling around him, clutching three sacks of gold to his chest. His tearful eyes bulged from their sockets. Grotesque veins protruded at his temples and down his forehead. Wiry tendons corded his neck, down to his collarbone. His face had turned a deep, bright red, the color of a pomegranate. Blood had dried to a maroon crust around his smashed nose, streaking down around his lips. The force of his endless laughter stretched his lips into a demonic snarl.

Persicus leaned over the edge, watching the darkness swallow Salman whole. Long after he disappeared from sight, Salman's laughter echoed up through the pit into the cave, now sounding as a wounded wolf, howling its plight to the moon.

Nooshin held onto the rope, blessedly alone. "Ahura Mazda, thank you. Thank you."

381

Salman's laughter faded. Distant and faint, the sound of a surprised yelp carried up to them, and at last, a terrified scream that cut off with startling abruptness.

Salman was dead.

Persicus and Gerisha let out a sigh of relief.

Persicus looked up at Nooshin. "Are you all right?"

Nooshin stared back at Persicus. She had a distant look in her eyes. "Yes." Her voice sounded hollow. She looked back down into the pit.

"All right. I want you to try swinging towards the edge here. We'll catch you."

"Okay," she said. She took a deep breath and tried to swing, but swinging the rope was much harder for her than it had been for Salman, since she wasn't tied into the rope, she couldn't lean back and forth to get the momentum going.

"Try kicking out with your feet," Gerisha instructed.

Nooshin followed Gerisha's instructions and the rope began to sway. As the momentum built, up above, through the crevice, the rope wrapped around the cone-shaped rock shifted, and unwound a little, the knot loosening from all the activity.

The rope dropped down three inches. Nooshin froze, holding her body stiff. The rope slowed and came to a stop.

Persicus' eyes widened in fear. The rope dropped another inch. Nooshin yelped. She began shaking uncontrollably.

"Persicus ..." she whispered.

Persicus turned to Gerisha, who stood stone-still, staring, disbelieving.

"Run out to the top and secure the rope," Persicus said, the worry and fear in his eyes betraying his voice, which he tried to keep from quaking.

Gerisha didn't waste a moment replying. He turned and ran faster than he had ever run in his life.

The rope dropped again, this time half a foot.

"Persicus?" Nooshin's voice trembled.

Persicus mind raced. *How to save her? What can I do? Not a damn thing. Oh, Guardian of the Steppes! Mother of Lightning! Father of Thunder!* He couldn't lose her. He couldn't watch her fall. He couldn't even bring the word *dead* to mind when he thought of her. No, he had to save her. *Had to.* Yet could think of nothing other than jumping across the pit, to the ledge, and grabbing her, or the rope, before she fell. *No, that's crazy. I'd never make it*, he thought. *There has to be some other way.* Panicked, he

382

looked around. *Nothing.* He didn't have any other choice. He took two steps back. Three steps.

It had been less than a minute. The rope dropped again.

Nooshin gasped. She saw Persicus backing up and knew what he would do. He couldn't make it; she couldn't watch him fall. "No. Persicus, no. Don't."

Persicus shook his head and backed up to the end of the cave. He had about ten feet to run, to give himself the lift off he needed to clear the eight-foot pit. He had to land on the small ledge that wasn't even a foot wide.

"Persicus, no!" she screamed it. "You'll never make it. Please, *please* don't die trying to save me."

"I can't let you die." The words fell from his mouth, so heavy that it almost dragged him to his knees in despair. He knew this was a one in ten chance. Maybe not even that. The small ledge saw to that. His feet felt heavy. He wanted to fall to his knees and scream so loud the Guardians would hear, and grant him this miracle.

The rope above unwound further and Nooshin dropped another foot.

She gasped and started praying. "Kêmnâ Mazdâ mavaitê pâyûm dadât, hyat mâ dregvå dîdareshatâ aênanghê, anyêm thwahmât âthrascâ mananghascâ, ýayå shyaothanâish ashem thraoshtâ ahurâ, tãm môi dâstvãm daênayâi frâvaocâ."

Persicus could hear her whispered prayer. He recognized it as a Zoroastrian prayer about protection from the wicked with Mazda's fire and good mind. Her murmured prayers echoed through the cave. Persicus could hear her voice, crystal-clear, and yet far away, as he focused on what he had to do. He took a deep breath and ran full out. His foot touched down at the edge of the pit and he leapt.

Nooshin screamed as the rope completely unraveled above and she started to plummet.

Persicus was midair when he heard her scream. A sound of pure terror that ripped through him, clutching, squeezing his heart. His hand hit the ledge and he grabbed it, and looked over in time to see the end of the rope slithering down from the crevice above.

He reached out and grabbed the rope with his other hand. When he felt the heavy weight down below, a wave of relief washed over him, even as his arm jerked with the pressure.

"Nooshin, are you all right?" Persicus asked through gritted teeth.

"Yes."

"Can you hold on?"

"Yes … What are you going to do?"

"Hang on." Persicus tried to lift himself one handed, up onto the ledge. He knew he could do it, if it hadn't been for Nooshin's additional weight pulling on his other arm. As it was, he struggled just to hang onto the ledge, and hold the rope at the same time.

"Nooshin, try to find a crevice for your foot. If you can put some of your weight against the wall, I can get up here, and pull you up."

Nooshin stretched her legs out in either direction, feeling around with her feet, but the rock wall of the pit felt smooth and unblemished everywhere she could reach. She couldn't find any bit of rock protruding or concaved in.

"There's nothing!" Nooshin sounded resigned to her fate. She looked up at Persicus, her eyes filled with unshed tears. "Persicus, there is nothing."

"Try!" he yelled. His arms burned with the strain. He couldn't hold on to both for long. He knew it.

"There's nothing! Persicus … you can't pull me up … I can't hold on much longer."

"Try! Please, Nooshin! Don't give up!" The muscles in his arm that gripped the rope felt as though they would tear at any moment. A sudden spasm jerked through his arm. The rope slipped through his fingers several inches before he forced his fingers to clench down and tightened his grip once more.

All of a sudden, Nooshin's weight was gone. Horrified, afraid to look, he froze. Air trapped deep inside him.

"I found one." Nooshin yelled. "Hurry!"

Persicus let out his breath in an expulsion of air. He couldn't believe that his failing strength—the rope slipping through his fingers a few inches—had dropped her just enough for her to find a foothold.

"Persicus!" Gerisha yelled from above, out of breath, gasping for air. The fear in his voice felt palpable.

"She's fine, but we'll need your help. Go grab a rope from the horses, secure it to the rock, and drop it through."

"Right." Gerisha ran for the horses.

"Hold on a little longer, Nooshin."

After Persicus carefully released some slack in the rope, he pulled himself up onto the ledge with one hand. Without having to struggle against Nooshin's additional weight, he only had his own to fight. His arm burned from exertion. He got his arm up first and then his leg. From there, he pulled the rest of his body up on the small ledge, stood, and gripped the rope with both hands.

"I'm going to pull you up now, hold on."

He started pulling the rope up, hand over hand, unable to bend at all, or he would end up losing his balance, and falling down the pit, taking Nooshin with him. He pulled, with his back as straight as possible, pressed up against the wall behind him, using only his arms, foot by foot. Nooshin's head came into view. His arms shook, but he kept pulling until she threw her arm over the small ledge. He squatted down and pulled her up onto the ledge. She fell against him, trembling, wrapping her arms around him. He held her as close as possible, standing in the only area of the small ledge that was remotely wider than six inches, where the sacks of gold had sat.

Gerisha lowered a rope to them, through the crevice. "It's secure. I'll stay up by the rope, just in case. Yell out when you make it to the other side."

"All right." Persicus took the rope as Gerisha lowered it in. He wrapped the rope around his waist and tied it. He looked down at Nooshin. "Are you ready?"

She nodded, unable to speak, staring up at him with haunted eyes.

Persicus picked her up and held her around her back and waist. Nooshin wrapped her arms around his neck. Then they were airborne. Her arms tightened around him.

Persicus landed on the other side and set Nooshin down. She collapsed to the ground and crawled away from the pit. Persicus untied the rope and crawled after her. He leaned back on his knees and tentatively touched Nooshin's shoulders.

She looked up at him, wide, green eyes welling with unshed tears. She fell against him and held him, her hands and arms gripping, clinging to him as if she still hung over the pit, holding on for her life. He hugged her back with the same fierceness.

"You're safe. You're safe. I've got you," he whispered to her, over and over, until her shaking subsided under the weight of Persicus' assuring arms, and comforting voice.

Nooshin pulled back and stared up into his eyes. He gazed down at her, arms still wrapped around her, not wanting to let her go, but knowing he had to. She felt truly amazed by this man. He had risked his life for her. Faced certain death without even the slightest hesitation. She moved her hands from around his neck, to his jawline, and leaned into him, certain that he wouldn't turn away. Certain that if he cared for her enough to risk his life, she could no longer hold onto her doubts, that he must love her.

Persicus watched her moving in towards him. He froze, panicked. He didn't know what to do. Was she going to hug him again? He didn't know, but it couldn't be what it seemed.

She hesitated inches from his face, staring at him, waiting for him to kiss her.

Gerisha called down from the crevice. "Persicus, Nooshin, did you make it across?"

Persicus turned his head away from Nooshin, towards the crevice. "Yes, we're fine. We're coming out."

Nooshin gaped at him, astonished, as he got to his feet. He held his hand out to her, to help her up. She stared at his hand, then up at him, seeing his face now completely closed off. She got to her feet, ignoring his hand, and turned away from him, hurt and indignant.

Persicus let his hand fall back to his side and watched, frowning, as she turned, and walked away.

# 30

## THE WHITE RAVEN

Once outside, Persicus took a deep breath of cleansing air. They sat down for a rest on top of the flat boulder. Nooshin sat with her back to Persicus. Gerisha left to fetch some water from the river.

The silence felt oppressive.

"Are you hurt?" Persicus asked.

Nooshin ignored him, staring straight ahead.

When Gerisha came back, he passed the goatskin around. They sat in silence. Gerisha sensed something wrong between Persicus and Nooshin.

After a while, a white raven flapped up from behind the boulder and fluttered to the ground. It got to its feet and flapped its wings, trying to fly, but only lifted a foot off the ground before it fell back down.

Nooshin got to her feet, intending to help the bird. Persicus jumped up and grabbed her wrist, stopping her before she touched the small creature. "Don't touch it. It's obviously sick."

"It's hurt."

"Look at it. It's not hurt. No broken wings, no blood. It's sick."

Nooshin jerked her hand free and stood conflicted, staring at the raven.

Gerisha stood and jumped off the boulder. "We had better get going. Your father is probably worried sick by now."

They mounted their horses and headed back to Mishin, traveling on a path that ran alongside the river.

Nooshin rode in silence, studiously ignoring Persicus. Persicus watched her, confused. He glanced over to Gerisha and raised his eyebrows in question. Gerisha shrugged.

They followed the path through a narrow canyon flanked by rugged mountains on both sides. Mounds of rocks and boulders sat at the base of the mountain, some scattered across the path, creating a dreadful maze through the narrow passage. Above, more rocks sat on the edge, waiting for their time to tumble down.

An eerie silence plagued this canyon. No sounds of any kind penetrated the stillness. The dulled clatter of their horses' hooves should have echoed off the mountain walls, but didn't.

Persicus couldn't stand the silence.

"I don't think I'll ever forget that laugh," Gerisha said, shaking his head, trying to get the sound of it out of his mind.

"I can't fathom why he continued laughing as he fell. It sounded crazed," Persicus said.

"That man was pure evil."

Persicus' eyes scanned over the mountains. "I swear I can still hear him laughing."

Gerisha and Nooshin both stopped.

"I thought I was remembering the sound of it," Gerisha said.

"Do you hear it, too?" Persicus asked Nooshin.

Nooshin gazed straight ahead. "Yes. It's faint. I thought I was imagining it."

Persicus tilted his head, trying to hear the sound better. "It can't be Salman. We all saw him fall. He's dead. It's only the wind blowing through the rocks of this canyon."

Gerisha shook his head. "No, it can't be. There is no breeze. The trees are still."

"And I feel something ominous." Nooshin rubbed her arms, fearful eyes trying to see behind the mounds of boulders.

"Look, we're all tired. It's been a long day and a longer week. After everything we've been through, it's no wonder we're getting spooked. Believe me, the bravest men can get spooked while traveling through these lonesome canyons."

The Sogdian Army was still out in the battlefield. The men had cleared the bodies from the southern gate and were busy burying the dead.

Persicus, Gerisha, and Nooshin arrived in Mishin late that evening. They entered through the southern gate and left their horses in the town square.

At the Palace steps, a Palace Guard motioned Gerisha over and whispered in his ear. Gerisha frowned. He waved Persicus and Nooshin over.

"Do you mind repeating what you said for them?" Gerisha asked the guard.

"Yes, Commander. We had an unexpected guest this afternoon."

"Who?" Nooshin asked, her eyes narrowed in concern. She had had enough unexpected visitors.

Gerisha grimaced and looked away.

"Sultan Morad Ali," the guard answered.

"Go on. Tell her what you told me."

"Everything?"

Gerisha nodded.

The Palace Guard looked uncomfortable. "Rumor has it that … Uh … Well, we think he is a suitor. He has come with gifts for King Ormozd."

"A suitor? What is a suitor?" Persicus asked, though he thought he knew.

"He's looking for a wife," Gerisha explained. "Most often, they are from a Royal Family and come seeking to marry another person of Royalty."

Nooshin glanced at Persicus and for the first time, she noticed an anguished look on his face. She felt vaguely pleased. "What's the matter Persicus? You look upset."

"Me? No, no. I'm just … tired. It's been a long day." Persicus tried to give her a smile, but he hadn't yet recovered from the news.

Nooshin frowned at him and turned to walk up the steps.

𝗧𝗧𝗧

Nooshin had a word in private with Gerisha before she bid them goodnight. Persicus and Gerisha went into one of the many sitting areas with a bottle of wine.

Persicus sat in silence, deep in thought, sipping his wine.

"What are your plans now that the battle is over?" Gerisha asked, taking a long swill of wine.

"I've been thinking about that. I guess I need to go home. I've been neglecting my orchard. Perhaps I should leave in the morning."

389

"Is that what you want to do? Go back to Abrisham?"

Persicus hesitated. He looked down into his glass and shrugged. "It is where I belong."

"What happened in the cave? Why is Nooshin upset with you? I mean, you had saved her only minutes before."

Persicus sighed and slid down lower in his seat. "I don't know."

"She is very fond of you," Gerisha said.

"What do you mean?" Persicus asked.

"You know what I mean." Gerisha hesitated and took another long swig of wine. "I told you before that she was out of your league, but now I have seen how she behaves around you. And you, my friend, keep acting as if you're a little boy who's gotten his first Mongolian pony and doesn't know what to do with it." Gerisha leaned forward in his chair. "She asked you what your feelings are towards her and you never answered. Why?"

Persicus sighed again and looked up at the ceiling. "You're right. I am acting childish. The truth is, I've never been in this situation before. If she was an ordinary woman, I don't think I would be nervous, but she isn't ordinary. She is a beautiful, Sogdian Princess. A descendant of the great Kings of the Sassanid Dynasty. What would she want with a commoner? She has Kings and Sultans coming to ask for her hand."

Gerisha nodded that he understood. "Your doubts hold you back and you will lose unless you reach out and grab what you want."

A sudden shiver overcame Persicus. He had a fleeting feeling of some importance that he couldn't put his finger on. He fell quiet for a long moment while he thought.

Gerisha watched him. "You've thought of something."

Persicus nodded. "Years ago, a Buddhist monk from India told me that I would be going on a great adventure for something valuable, but that I would find something much more precious along the way. He told me other things that have happened, just as he said it would, word for word. He said, 'Reach high and you will find a way.' When I was in that underground river, right before I found Nooshin, I had come to the end of the river, nowhere to go but down. I had to reach up to find a way out of the subterranean river and that river took me right to Nooshin."

Gerisha saw the connection that Persicus, maybe intentionally, was missing. 'Reach high' didn't just refer to his situation in the river, but in his life, as well. "Don't you see? There is no doubt in my mind that this is meant to be. And you are fighting it because you think you are unworthy. Now, because of your doubt, another man has come to challenge you for his claim of the Princess. He is a worthy competitor. I've heard much about his campaigns in the West."

Persicus sighed, dejected. "Thanks. That's encouraging. Maybe I should pack up tonight and leave early in the morning."

Gerisha gave him an angry look. "You're going to give up that easy? I thought you were a Tajik? I thought the Tajiks were brave, smart, and fierce warriors. The fearless horsemen of the rugged Steppes. When you leave, do you think Nooshin will want to marry another? That she would accept anyone else? Mishin cannot afford another war with another self-centered bastard from the deserts beyond. I have already lost my original country at the hands of foreign forces. Now, this is my country. And I will defend my King and Princess with my life, for the lives of all these people. But we may not survive another war." Gerisha paused and looked Persicus in the eye. "These are the noblest people I have ever known. It is a great honor to dine with the Royal Family, as you have done every day. It is a great blessing that Nooshin wants to marry *you*, not a king from another land, not someone of Royal blood, but someone who genuinely cares about her. Who risked his life for her. Who is smart, brave, and strong enough to protect Mishin."

Gerisha sat back in his chair. He was done. Nooshin had asked him to speak with Persicus. Gerisha had told her that he did not want to get involved, but she had persisted with her wounded eyes, filled with fear and anguish, so that he couldn't say no. He had reluctantly agreed. She was, after all, his Princess, and he was supposed to protect her from all pain.

Gerisha watched Persicus think about what he had said.

Persicus sat in silence for several minutes, deep in thought. He gulped down the last of his wine, set his cup down on a low table, stood, and stretched.

"I'll see you in the morning," Persicus said. "If you would join us in the garden for breakfast." He turned and left, going to his room.

# $3^I$

## THE SUITOR

Persicus awoke early the next morning. He had only slept for five hours, but couldn't get back to sleep. His thoughts churned in his mind, until he knew he had to do something, or risk going mad. He made his way down to the kitchen, intending to make Nooshin's favorite breakfast. The kitchen staff arrived a short time after and began brewing the tea. Persicus set out all the ingredients, telling them he wanted to prepare bread with cream, honey, and grapes. While they pounded out the dough for the bread, Persicus got the milk boiling. After it cooled, he carefully skimmed the cream off from the top.

When the bread was baking in the tanoor oven, Persicus left the final preparations to the staff, and went out into the garden. He sat by the fountain, watching the birds singing and splashing in the shallow water as the sun came up.

King Ormozd came out into the garden. He saw Persicus and sat beside him.

"Good morning, Your Majesty." Persicus greeted, as he stood and bowed.

"Good morning. A wonderful morning. I heard about Salman last night. I am sure only his mother will mourn his loss. Thank you for taking care of Nooshin, yet again."

"I think he would rather have died than let go of that gold. I am sorry that Nooshin got hurt. Gerisha and I both tried to stop Salman before he grabbed her."

"She's a bit banged up, but it's nothing serious, so Tahmineh has told me. Though I doubt she will let Nooshin out of her sight any time soon."

"Have you seen her this morning?" Persicus asked eagerly.

Ormozd restrained a smile, knowing full well how anxious Persicus felt. The kitchen staff had already informed him that Persicus was in the kitchen before them, preparing her favorite breakfast. "She is getting ready for the day. I would guess that Nadira is trying to cover her bruises with some of that face powder."

"I'm truly sorry. I wish I could have done something to save her from that pain. I should have killed Salman straight off."

"Don't blame yourself too much. You are all alive and that's what counts. She told me you jumped the Bottomless Pit, to a ledge only a foot wide. You did everything you could. You saved her and Salman is dead." Ormozd could see Persicus was beating himself up over it. At that moment, he knew that Persicus would see to Nooshin's safety. He would protect her with everything he had, every ounce of strength, to make sure she remained safe and happy. If only he could be pushed towards thinking himself worthy of her.

Ormozd always stayed out of Nooshin's decisions regarding her suitors and left it completely up to her, but Persicus was good for her. He approved. That Persicus remained insecure was his only fault. He could not rule, could not be King, if he remained insecure and humble. Ormozd knew Persicus' reluctance stemmed from his social status. In any other land, this would be an issue, but Ormozd's father had raised him to treat all people with equal respect and value, and he had raised Nooshin the same way. "We have another visitor. He arrived yesterday, after the battle." Ormozd studied Persicus' reaction.

Persicus stared straight ahead, but his eyes flinched. "Yes, I heard." He didn't sound pleased. "A suitor."

"Yes, well, when you have a beautiful daughter, you become popular amongst the other rulers, near and far. Someday, you'll know what I mean." Ormozd stood and looked out towards the trees and flowers in the garden. "Sultan Morad Ali is from Baghdad. He is related to the Caliph, who appointed him Viceroy of a province somewhere south of here. I'm not sure where exactly. They have changed their name since the invasion." He turned around and looked down at Persicus. "Tell me Persicus, what is your plan now?"

Persicus took a deep breath. "To be honest, I thought about going home last night, but Gerisha talked me out of it. Now, I don't know. I ..." He didn't know what to say. He wanted to say Nooshin didn't need a suitor. That he would marry her, but he couldn't say it, couldn't make a fool of himself. The King would laugh at him, telling him that he couldn't marry his daughter, because he didn't have an ounce of Royal

Blood.

King Ormozd put his hand on Persicus' shoulder. Persicus looked up to meet Ormozd's steady gaze, studying his face.

"We all like you, Persicus. Somehow, you are the son that I never had. You see, Nooshin's mother died in childbirth and I did not have any more children. Nooshin is wonderful; I love her more than anything in the world. She let me teach her archery and horsemanship, and she is quite good, but I always wanted a son, too. What I am saying is that it feels as if you are a part of the family. I think you would be wise to stay here. Of course, I don't know what the outcome will be with our guest, but you have my favor. I think you should talk to her."

Persicus couldn't believe his ears. Surely, the King of Mishin hadn't just told him it would be all right if he stayed here. That he favored Persicus over a Sultan. He sat there, speechless. After a long pause, he closed his gaping mouth, and tried to speak.

"Thank you, Your Majesty. Those are the kindest words I have heard in years."

Ormozd gave him a chiding look. "Ormozd."

Persicus nodded, grinning. "Ormozd."

They heard footsteps coming out into the garden. Persicus turned to see a slender man of about five foot seven, with unruly, curly, black hair, and a thick beard encroaching on a well-trimmed moustache, pointed at the ends. His eyes were piercing black and set deep under thick, dark eyebrows. A large, humped nose would have dominated his face, if not for the beard balancing his nose out. Most of his dark olive skin was covered in the long garbs worn by many of the nomadic tribes of his ancestral land, leaving only his face, hands, and feet visible. He wore a solid-black bishtor, a long cloak worn over the clothing; a white thowb, a long-sleeved gown that covers from the neck to the ankles; a shumagg, a shoulder-length scarf worn on the head, and kept in place by a black band called an ogal, that wrapped around the shumagg. He wore several gold necklaces and bracelets around his neck and wrists, and gold rings with rubies and emeralds on his fingers. An expensive, long, curved scimitar dagger hung at his side, as adorned with gold and jewels as his rings and bracelets.

He displayed his wealth from head to foot, flaunting it as though he needn't worry about the bandits who stalked the trade routes. He walked with a swagger that would have seemed feminine on anyone else. He seemed to dance his walk, smooth and elegant, placing one foot right in front of the other with each step, as if walking on a plank of wood over a cliff.

A tall, bald eunuch followed with his arms crossed over his chest and a sour look on his long face. He wore a white thowb and plain sandals. No hair grew from his face or head, he wore no jewelry, and he had a plain scimitar dagger half hidden in the folds of his gown.

"A very good morning to you." Sultan Morad Ali bowed to King Ormozd, touching his fingertips to his lips and forehead, by way of a formal greeting.

"Good morning, Sultan Morad Ali." King Ormozd turned to Persicus. "May I introduce Persicus, the man who saved our city from the perils of the Turanian siege."

Persicus stood and bowed. "Good morning."

"Ah, so this is the man everyone is talking about." Sultan Morad Ali glanced at Persicus and, as if dismissing him, turned to face King Ormozd as he stepped in front of Persicus to cut him out of the conversation. "You know, it is unfortunate that you didn't send a messenger to me. If you had, this man's services would have been unnecessary. I would have made certain the Turanians never dared set foot onto your territory. A battle would have been averted. We would have kicked them out of your territory for good and made it clear to them that you are an ally of the great Caliphate Em*bire*, but oh well, you have learned for next time. Tell me of this mysterious *bowder* you used against the Turanians. My *sbies* have seen it used by the Chinese military, an effective *weabon*, I must say, but they have ke*bt* its *bro*duction a great secret."

Morad Ali spoke with flamboyance and wild hand gestures, somehow making everything smooth and effeminate, but at the same time oddly masculine. The combination confused Persicus in an amusing way.

"Well, it is really Persicus' here weapon." King Ormozd said, as he stepped around to pat Persicus on the back in a fatherly manner. Ormozd did not like that the Sultan had dismissed Persicus as unimportant and ignored him. He also full well knew the formula for the secret weapon, but he would not be sharing this information, not with this man. He thought there might be some similarities between Morad Ali and Salman. They were both war hungry men, bent on conquering other lands, but that seemed to be where the similarities ended. While Salman was avaricious, he suspected the Sultan's wars were more religious, or so he wanted it to appear.

Persicus wondered how the Sultan could be such a great warrior and be this flamboyant. He realized that having never seen him in action, he couldn't possibly judge his capabilities. Most people underestimated him as well, but for different reasons. He also wondered, if not for the hundredth time, why Morad Ali or his people never could pronounce the sounds of the letter P.

Sultan Morad Ali looked at Persicus. "Well, Bersicus, tell me about this weabon."

"Well, uh ..." Persicus didn't think he should be giving out the formula to anyone, especially not to a man at war. A war, not for protection of his homeland, but to expand his own empire. He had given it to Mishin in their time of need, knowing they would use it to protect themselves, not for greed or power. He looked at King Ormozd. Ormozd gave a slight shake of his head behind Morad Ali's back.

"Well, Bersicus? You do sbeak, don't you? Come now, what about this new weabon? Where did you get this information?"

Persicus still hesitated, unsure of how to avoid answering. "I got it in China, but I don't have the ingredients on hand." He didn't want to lie and he had avoided it for now. Deceptive, but not an outright lie.

Sultan Morad Ali could see Persicus' distrust as clear as the midday sun in a cloudless sky, but that didn't matter. Morad Ali had long ago convinced himself that anything and everything was available to him, it was only a matter of finessing it out of Persicus, or if all else failed, gold and power speaks to all—louder than honor, or distrust ever could. No one would say no to an offer of ruling your own province. Since the Chinese had first invented this weapon, he had been determined to get his hands on the formula, thereby ensuring for himself an honorable distinction from his fellow sultans, so that the Caliph would take special notice of him. Once he had this new weapon, his conquests would be much more efficient. Indeed, he could see himself conquering land after land, with swiftness never before known to man. No one would dare resist his campaign once he had this weapon. Moreover, the Caliph would finally reward his hard work, granting him more territories, power, and wealth.

Morad Ali thought for a moment before changing his tactic. "You know, I could use a smart and ambitious man in the western front. I do need a man who can think fast and strategize as I do and from what I've heard, you seem to have these rather rare qualities. As you know, we are fighting the infidels. I need all the helb I can get from your beoble. For the glory of Allah, we could sbread the great word of the one true God much, much faster. You would be the key instrument of saving the eternal souls of the infidels. Allah himself would be sure to bless you and your children for your great service to Him and humanity." Morad Ali paused, glancing up to the heavens as if receiving approval from Allah himself. "All I need is the formula of this weabon and I could make this habben, and you would reab the rewards."

His accent and his pushy, pestilent behavior grated on Persicus' nerves. He took a couple deep breaths to calm himself. It didn't work.

"I am a man of peace, Your Highness. I do not believe"—Persicus began, but before he could finish, Sultan Morad Ali interrupted him with a dismissive wave of his hand, raising his voice to be heard over Persicus.

"Nonsense. I know a warrior when I see one. Berhabs I should also mention that there are a great many benefits available to you when you join my cambaign. Indeed, a whole new world will oben ub to you. Allah blesses those who fight for a worthy cause. You may even become a governor of a brovince, if you fall into the good grace of our magnificent Caliph; may Allah keeb him safe ubon his throne." Morad Ali saw Persicus' eyes glaze over and a cold look overtaking his warm demeanor. He turned back to King Ormozd, hoping to give Persicus the impression that his opportunity was slipping away. "And with your blessing, we could form a strong alliance with Mishin, if Nooshin becomes my wife. Between us, we could rule the entire region one fine day," he added, hoping to appeal to Ormozd's desire to expand his territory, though he did not know that Ormozd had no desire to rule anywhere, but Mishin.

"And a great blessing that would be," Ormozd placated, "but the ultimate decision will be made by my daughter, as that is the way we do things in Mishin."

"Truly? I have heard of such things about Mishin, but I assumed it was a vicious rumor. How odd. Well, I will deal with these things as they come ub. I had blanned to offer you a strong alliance and trays of the finest Arabian jewels and gold for the burchase of your daughter. Am I to assume you will not accebt these fine offerings?"

"A strong alliance is always welcome, for we want no enemies, but yes, I cannot accept your offer, for it is Nooshin you must convince to accept your hand, not I."

Persicus' anger flared. *Purchase!* Before he came to Mishin, he had never thought of arranged marriages as an odd thing, never thought of a dowry as a purchase, after all, it was all too common, but since he had met Nooshin, and been the guest of the Royal Family, their customs had imbedded deep into his own, as though he had lived in Mishin all his life. Now, the idea of an arranged marriage, in exchange for dowry, made him ill and angry. That this man would say he wants to purchase *Nooshin* made it all the worse. He completely did away with the pretense of arrangement for a dowry. Just a purchase, as if buying a mule in the caravanserai. The thought of her marrying the Sultan infuriated and repulsed him to the point of nausea. Recalling her words on the mountain above Mishin, he felt certain that she wouldn't marry the Sultan.

"I see. Well, I am certain she will be honored to be my wife. It is a *great* honor to be abart of my family, as the great Allah himself has blessed us, chosen us to lead as his vessel on earth. The Brincess will see it that way." Morad Ali turned to Persicus. "And I hobe you will accebt my offer. I am eager to hear of this Chinese weabon. I hobe I do not have to go elsewhere and give someone else, less worthy, the obbortunity to give this formula to me, and reab the benefits and rewards in your stead."

"I will keep that under consideration, Your Highness," Persicus said through gritted teeth.

"Yes. You do that."

Nooshin came into the garden wearing a radiant turquoise dress made of silk, embroidered with lavender flowers, their rich green leaves forming a mesmerizing geometric pattern. The neckline and hems were a deep violet fabric that looked soft to the touch, perfectly framing her neck and wrists. A golden sash wound around her waist and hips. A lavender ribbon pulled her hair back away from her face, but her long hair still fell over her shoulders in thick, silken waves. The dress covered her arms, so Persicus couldn't tell how bruised she was, but he could see a scratch and a bruise on her left cheek, which Nadira had almost succeeded in masking with powder.

"Good morning, Nooshin dear," her father said.

"Ahhh ..." Morad Ali walked up to Nooshin. He moved with that graceful dancing swagger. "The describtion of the Brincess given to me does her no justice." He raised one hand up, as if beseeching the heavens. "How can anyone describe the beauty of the full moon on the horizon, when the wind scattered clouds have kebt her illumination at bay, hidden under garbs of white and gray?" He looked back to Nooshin, placing one hand on her shoulder and his other under her chin, raising her face up towards him with a curled index finger. "How can you describe the beauty of a rose beddle, without seeing the vibrant red, without smelling the sweet, succulent scent, without feeling the smooth, silken texture?" His hand traced down from her shoulder, to her arm, to her hand. He lifted her hand to his lips and gave it a soft kiss.

Princess Nooshin gave him a saccharine smile. "You are trying to flatter me, Your Highness." She desperately wanted to see Persicus' reaction, but she dared not look. She would not give him the satisfaction.

Persicus turned away, trying to remain calm. "Your breakfast is ready, Your Majesty, Princess."

The servants finished setting the table. In honor of their guest, they had carried out a table large enough to accommodate everyone, with comfortable chairs instead of cushions.

"Where is the rest of your party?" Ormozd asked the Sultan.

"The guards? I sent them to the caravanserai for their breakfast. I have no need for them here. Excebt for my taster," he nodded towards the eunuch, "he stays with me at all times."

"I see," Ormozd said, noticing that Nooshin wouldn't even look at

Persicus. "Let's go eat. Persicus, I heard you were up early in the kitchen preparing a special meal."

"Yes. I thought in light of our victory yesterday, we should celebrate. We're having cream, honey, and grapes, with fresh bread."

"Oh! My favorite breakfast. Thank"—Nooshin caught herself, resuming an ambivalent attitude—"you, how thoughtful of you, Persicus."

Still, she wouldn't look at him.

"You're welcome."

At the table, Persicus pulled out a chair for Nooshin. She sat down and he pulled the chair next to her for himself. Before he could sit, Morad Ali slipped in and sat next to Nooshin.

"Thank you, Bersicus," the Sultan said.

"My name is *Persicus*."

"Yes, I know. King Ormozd said your name when he made my introduction to you." Morad Ali picked up a cloth napkin next to his plate, dabbed his forehead and cheeks, and placed the napkin in his lap.

The eunuch stepped up to Persicus, grunting. Persicus' hands still gripped the back of the chair, not wanting to relinquish it to the Sultan, but Morad Ali was already sitting in it, and talking pleasantly to Nooshin, while the eunuch made unrecognizable threatening noises behind them. Persicus let go of the chair with a sigh, walked around to the other side, and sat across from Nooshin.

As Persicus sat down, Morad Ali leaned in close to Nooshin, whispering into her ear. Nooshin tilted back her head and gave wonderful laugh. Persicus stared down at his empty plate, while he tried to control his countenance.

Gerisha walked out into the garden. "Good morning, everyone."

"A glorious morning. Come, Gerisha, there is a chair next to Persicus." Ormozd faced Morad Ali. "This is General Gerisha, our Military Commander. Don't know what I would do without him. Gerisha, this is Sultan Morad Ali."

The Sultan nodded hello and he resumed his conversation with Nooshin.

Gerisha sat next to Persicus. He glanced down and saw Persicus' fists clenched tight in his lap, under the table.

"What's the matter?" Gerisha whispered to Persicus, choking back a big grin.

"Nothing."

"Are you sure?"

"Positive," Persicus answered in an angry tone, glaring at Gerisha.

Ormozd called for everyone's attention. "All right, everyone is here. I want to take this opportunity to give my most grateful thanks to both

Persicus and Gerisha. You two worked together marvelously. Because of your great skills, quick thinking, and wise insights into the nature of battle and our enemy, we have not only won the battle, but also put an end to Salman's reign of tyranny. My dear daughter, Nooshin, and I, as well as our army, and every citizen of this great city will forever be grateful for everything you two have done. Thank you! Both of you. Now, let us eat."

Morad Ali scooped a large spoonful of thick cream onto his plate. "Cream for breakfast? I never would have thought of it." He plucked up a piece of bread.

The Eunuch reached down, picked up his master's plate from behind, swiped his finger into the cream, and sucked his finger clean.

Everyone froze and watched the eunuch.

"Mm ... Good." The eunuch nodded and set the plate back on the table.

"You must forgive my servant. He always tastes my food in case of an accidental boisoning. He is immune to many boisons."

Nooshin looked confused. Ormozd gave him a wary look. Several of the servants appeared startled. Gerisha coughed into his hand to hide his smile. Persicus thought a poisoning would be too good for the Sultan. He wanted to regret that thought, but couldn't muster enough admonitions to his conscience to feel truly contrite for his churlish thoughts. Instead, he focused his angry eyes on the eunuch, deciding it best to ignore the Sultan.

Morad Ali looked at the startled and confused faces around the table. "What is the matter? Of course, you have had beoble die as a result of boisoning in your little town. Whether intentional or accidental, it habbens all too often."

King Ormozd narrowed his eyes. "No, not that I've ever heard of. People here die of old age. Some die from an occasional accident or illness, but not poisonings."

"Really?" Morad Ali said as if he didn't believe it. "Well, death by boisoning is much different. I have seen it too often in Baghdad. The victim feels anguish, at first. This is followed by a variety of different symbtoms. You see, it debends on the boison itself—very fascinating, indeed, the many kinds of boisons. Nausea, headache, stomachache, dry mouth, malaise. There are also boisons that cause fever, delirium, difficulty breathing, or foaming from the mouth. Some may turn your skin green. Merciful death will follow these symbtoms and then you are in Allah's hands." He finished talking, leaning forward in his chair, his eyes lit up in excitement.

Everyone stopped eating, gaping, wide-eyed, and disgusted at Morad Ali. A silence descended around the table as Morad Ali grabbed another piece of bread and lopped another spoonful of cream onto it. He dropped a smudge on honey on the cream and added a single grape. He ripped off a small chunk, eating as if it would crumble in his hands like a delicate pastry, taking dainty bites, chewing each small bit of bread thoroughly. He dabbed his lips with his napkin and looked around the table.

Persicus broke the silence. "With your permission," he said to King Ormozd. "I ordered some wine for our breakfast celebration. I would have ordered it for dinner, but I had planned on leaving this morning."

Nooshin's head whipped around and she looked at Persicus for the first time. This was the first she had heard of him leaving.

Ormozd noticed his daughter's reaction. He knew that Persicus wouldn't leave this morning. Ormozd smiled. "Wine! An excellent idea, Persicus." He nodded to the servant, who hurried into the Palace to retrieve the wine.

"I don't drink wine," Morad Ali said. He paused for a moment, rolling his eyes skyward in thought. The corner of his lip twitched into a smile. "I'm not going to lie, may Allah strike me dead. I have tried wine, but only once. I did enjoy it. I really don't know why He" — he pointed to the sky — "has forbidden it, but I always follow His rules."

The servant returned with an amphora filled with a white wine. The servant poured a small amount into a cup for Ormozd. He took a sip and nodded his approval. The servant refilled his cup, Nooshin's, and then he reached over to fill Morad Ali's cup.

The Sultan put his hand over his cup. "No. No wine for me."

"I am no scholar in the matter of theology," King Ormozd said, "but what I would suppose God's intentions for us to be, is not to abuse wine. Did he not provide us with the grapes?"

The Sultan scrunched up in face thinking. The servant stood behind him, ostensibly waiting with endless patience, though no doubt waiting for the wine to be poured, and tasted.

"Yes, yes. I see your boint and a good boint it is. All right, I will have some wine, but I will *not* abuse it."

The servant filled his cup. The eunuch reached over Morad Ali's head and grabbed the wine out from his hand before he could raise it to his lips. The eunuch drank the contents of the glass in two long gulps. He wiped his mouth with the back of his hand and set the empty cup back on the table. "Mmm." He pounded his fist against his chest and burped.

The servant smiled as he refilled the Sultan's cup. The eunuch reached around to grab the wine again.

"Now, you stob that!" Morad Ali snapped, slapping the eunuch's hand. "You've already tasted. That is enough. This is not Baghdad. You don't need to taste everything. As you can see, that is unnecessary here."

The big man scowled at his master and grunted.

Ormozd looked at the servant holding the amphora of wine. "Mastan, pour some wine for the Sultan's ... uh, taster. Get him a plate, as well."

Mastan nodded. After he produced another plate and cup, he continued pouring the wine.

Morad Ali stood, raising his cup. "I would like to brobose a toast. To the most beautiful Brincess near and far, for whom I have journeyed a great distance to ask for her hand. Allah willing, she will accebt my brobosal, and become a member of the great Ben Khalid Family."

Persicus watched as Nooshin smiled up at the Sultan, reaching out her hand to him.

"No!" Persicus shouted, slamming his fist down on the table. "That cannot be!"

Another intense silence descended around the table. Everyone, including Persicus, froze, taken aback.

Nooshin stared down into her lap, trying to hide her relief. *Finally!* she thought.

Morad Ali held his head high, giving Persicus a look of utter disdain.

Astonished by his own outburst, Persicus sat with a gaping mouth, staring down, hands splayed flat on the tabletop. He didn't know what to say, or do. Never in his life would he have thought he could lose his temper and yell at a sultan. This was all he needed, to get on the wrong side of yet another ruler.

"What is it that cannot be, Bersicus?" Morad Ali asked in an icy-calm voice. He raised his hand to his mustache, twisting the ends with his fingertips.

"My name is *Persicus*," he said through gritted teeth.

"Yes, I know, Bersicus. You dare interrubt my brobosal with such a boorish outburst. Do you think that," Morad Ali paused for a second, twisting his mustache. "What was the name of your brofession ... you dig holes, yes?"

"A qanat engineer." Persicus flicked his eyes to Nooshin.

"Yes. A qanat digger. In all honesty, do you think that my good Brincess here would ever choose a hole digger for a husband, rather than Sultan Morad Ali?"

Persicus stood, rage boiling within him. The chair toppled over with a loud crash. He slammed his cup of wine on the table. "If you think I'm just going to sit here and watch—"

"Why, Bersicus, I thought you were a man of beace." Morad Ali stood, facing Persicus on the opposite side of the table.

402

"What? I don't even know what you are saying. What the hell is bee—"

"Never mind." The Sultan interrupted with a wave of his hand. "I asked you, if you thought my good Brincess would have difficulty choosing between a hole digger from a small village, in the middle of nowhere, or the Viceroy of the great Caliphate Embire, which by the grace of Allah has sway over this great land, from here to the rock of Gibraltar, and ever expanding westward?"

Ormozd didn't like where this conversation was heading. The threat of war hung heavy in the air and that was the last thing he needed.

"No. As a matter of fact, I don't think she will have any problems choosing." Persicus turned to the Princess. "Right?"

Nooshin looked away from him, unable to meet the desperate look in his eyes. "No, I won't have a problem choosing. You had your chance and you blew it. Don't act as though you like me now." She felt incredibly angry with Persicus today, after thinking and berating herself half of the night. She had all but thrown herself at him in the cave and he had acted as if she had the plague. All right, maybe it wasn't that bad, but his rejection had felt that way. She felt humiliated. Now, she wanted him to beg for her.

Morad Ali sat down again, smiling, leaning closer to Nooshin. He placed his hand over hers and wrapped a possessive arm around her shoulder.

Ormozd saw Persicus' face flush red, as did Nooshin. She withdrew her hand out from under the Sultan's and leaned forward, away from his arm.

Nooshin spoke, glancing up at Persicus, and then fixed her eyes on her cup of wine. "You need to sort this out amongst yourselves. You said you believe in fate, right? Maybe we should let fate decide."

Persicus' mouth dropped open. He had finally found the courage, finally believed she loved him, but now it might be too late. He might lose what could have been his. The air expelled out of him and he couldn't inhale it back in for a full minute.

Morad Ali's eyes flowed up and down Persicus, sizing him up. "A fight to the death. What will it be? Sword? Lance?" He stood, dropping his napkin onto the table. "I must warn you, I have seen many skilled swordsmen to their early graves."

Persicus stared at Nooshin, his lips pressed tight. Nooshin's comment had stabbed through him. He couldn't help wondering if he was wrong. Maybe she didn't want him, after all. *No*, he thought, *Gerisha wouldn't have told him all of that last night, wouldn't have given him false hope, unless he knew for sure.* She loved him. Now, he felt certain of it, but she was angry. She had been angry with him since they left the Bottomless Pit. Even now, she wouldn't look at him. It was his own fault and he deserved her anger. Nevertheless, he couldn't let this man come in and take Nooshin away from him, not after everything they had been through together. He couldn't see Nooshin marrying another war-hungry leader, a man who so obviously clashed with her own beliefs, and way of life.

"Plenty of ruthless men have tried to kill me and none of them have succeeded. I will fight you with whatever weapon you choose."

Ormozd needed to head off this fight. Somehow. He didn't care about the Sultan, though he couldn't help wondering if the Caliph would cause trouble if the Sultan died here in a duel, but he cared about Persicus. Persicus had saved them—all of them—and though Nooshin remained angry, her obliquitous attitude wouldn't last long, and she would never forgive herself if Persicus died fighting for her.

Ormozd shared a long glance with Gerisha. "I believe we have had enough bloodshed, don't you, Gerisha?" King Ormozd's inflection seemed to suggest something, but Persicus hadn't a clue as to what it might be.

Gerisha nodded. "Yes. I believe you are quite right, Your Majesty."

Ormozd sat forward in his chair and looked at Persicus. "If I may suggest an amicable way to sort out this situation. Not by sword, but a game to decide who is the most worthy."

"Game?" Persicus sat back down, looking at Ormozd, but he couldn't help glancing at Nooshin, who stared down into her hands, unwilling to lift her face and meet his eyes.

Gerisha caught on. "The ancient game of the people of the Steppes."

"What game?" Morad Ali asked, growing annoyed. He would have preferred to simply kill the peasant and be done with it.

"Buzkashi," King Ormozd said.

Morad Ali frowned. "Buzkashi? What is a buzkashi?"

"The game is simple," Gerisha answered. "Though it takes great strength and skill. We set the carcass of a large mountain goat in front of the King's throne. The object of the game is to pick up the goat and hold onto it."

"Which means you cannot tie it to yourself, your horse, or your saddle," Ormozd added.

Gerisha nodded. "Yes. You have to hold it with your hands and ride on horseback to the far corner of the field, around a marked rock, and come back towards the throne. You place the carcass back in the circle, in front of the throne. Whoever does this wins the game."

"That sounds simble enough," Morad Ali said. "Much easier than the games we play at home."

"The concept is simble, but in practice it is quite difficult." Gerisha stopped, looked at Persicus, and whispered, "Oh, God. Did I just say simble?"

Persicus gave a half-hearted smirk. "Yes."

"I still do not understand," Morad Ali said. "Where is the challenge? How is this difficult?"

"Persicus is your challenge." King Ormozd smiled and took a sip of wine. "And what a game it will be."

"Yes," Gerisha said. "In a normal game, there are twenty to thirty horsemen trying to get at the goat. In this instance, it will only be the two of you. Once one of you picks up the goat, you have to try to keep hold of it, while the other chases you, and tries to snatch the goat away from you. There are a few rules. You cannot hit each other with whips, fists, or any other weapon. You cannot hit, bite, or kick your opponent. You can use your horse to push your opponent off the path and you can grab the goat, but that is all."

"No sword or lance?" Morad Ali asked, surprised.

"That is correct. This is supposed to be a friendly game. Not life or death, though sometimes the riders can be mortally injured. This is a challenge to your physical strength, endurance, skill, and horsemanship."

Persicus looked at Morad Ali, who sat leaning his elbows on the table, pulling at the ends of his mustache.

Persicus nodded. "All right. Sounds good to me."

All eyes turned to Morad Ali. He ran his tongue over his teeth and made a sucking sound while he considered. He slid his eyes across the table to Persicus, once more sizing him up.

"I accebt this challenge." Morad Ali stood, getting ready to take his leave. "When will we have this tournament?"

"Well, you will have to get your horse ready. You'll need a few days to practice. We always hold this game on a flat plateau, north of the city. I'll have to go and check it out for erosion and make sure it is still safe." Gerisha stood and turned to Persicus. "Do you want to come with me Persicus? I think some fresh mountain air will do you good."

Persicus let out a sigh and stood. "I think you are right. With your permission, Your Majesty? Princess Nooshin?"

"Yes, of course. I think our good Gerisha is right. Make sure you inspect the side near the big Devil's Drop. We had a lot of snow up there last winter."

"Yes, Your Majesty."

They bowed and left the garden.

Persicus and Gerisha headed north on horseback, along a narrow path that meandered through a rocky terrain. Giant formations of jagged rocks protruded out from the ground and mountainside. The path graded up a slight incline and headed northeast to the mountain range, growing steeper the higher they climbed. Trees sprouted out from cracks and crevices in the rocky mountainside, lining the path on either side.

Persicus remained uncommonly quiet halfway up the mountain. Gerisha could only guess what thoughts and actions were playing out in his mind.

"Are you all right, Persicus?" Gerisha asked.

Persicus shook his head, disgusted with himself. "I don't know why I lost my temper."

"Especially when you're supposed to be a man of beace."

Persicus looked at him out of the corner of his eye. Gerisha laughed. "Laugh it up. Guess I deserve it."

"Well, it's not too late to win back what you've lost. You're at an advantage because the Sultan doesn't know anything about buzkashi."

Persicus shook his head. "It makes us even, because I don't know anything about it, either."

"What do you mean? You're from the Steppes and that's where this game originated. You've never played it?"

"No. Remember, I grew up traveling the Silk Road with my uncle. I left the Steppes at a very young age. I don't remember ever seeing the game, or even hearing about it."

Gerisha considered this as they neared the plateau. "I'm sorry. The King and I both assumed you knew this game well and would have an advantage, that's why we suggested it." Gerisha shook his head and sighed. "This game is won if the rider and the horse cooperate and are in tune with each other. The most important thing for the rider is to have the strength to hold onto the goat and be skilled and strong enough not to let anyone wrestle it out of his possession; however, the horse is more important. A well-trained horse watches his opponents and knows the game better than his rider. He knows when to stop, when to evade, or gallop as fast as an arrow shooting out from the arch of a bow."

"Do you know of such a horse?"

"Do I! Tomorrow, I will introduce you two. Maybe you should stay at my house tonight, anyway. You need a good night's sleep and some stress-free time before the game."

They rode side by side up the meandering path, along the side of the mountain, until they reached the center of the plateau, which stretched out about half a mile.

Persicus scanned the nearly level field.

"This is it." Gerisha said, gesturing around the plateau. "Where the hopes and dreams of many brave men have been shattered while fighting for the glory of victory. That is where the King will be." He pointed towards the northeast end of the plateau. "Do you see way over there, the largest boulder, shaped like an amphora?" He pointed to the southwest end. "That is where you will have to ride to and circle, while holding the goat. That's the big Devil's Drop, over there to the west. We call it that because the land is as deceptive as the Devil himself. The angle plays a trick on the eye. An outsider will not realize this until it is too late. The slope has a gradual descent, until all of a sudden, you pass a point of no return, especially while riding fast — the horse's weight and momentum will be no match for the Devil. The closer you get to that drop, the harder it will be to get back."

Persicus shaded his eyes from the sun, staring westward towards the Devil's Drop.

Gerisha turned to Persicus and gave him a light jab on the arm. "Come on, I'll show you."

Persicus followed Gerisha on foot towards the Devil's Drop. They stopped at the edge of the escarpment. From where they stood, they could see the entire valley below and the crystal-blue river that snaked through the land, glittering like jewels.

"The land is loose and soft here. The further down you go, the worse it becomes. That's the point of no return there, where the weight of the horse can pull you right over the edge." He turned towards Persicus and gave him a stern look. "*Many* have perished here when their horses got cornered and pushed over the edge. Avoid this area at *all* costs." Gerisha had tried to keep the instructions and conversation lighthearted, but the stakes were high. He knew Sultans and Kings — such as Sultan Morad Ali — who had never lost, had never been denied, nor would they tolerate losing to a commoner. He knew the honorable Persicus would play by the rules, however, every instinct told him the Sultan's integrity would vanish at the first opportunity, and that he would cheat if he felt he could get away with it. Gerisha didn't want Persicus anywhere near the Devil's Drop.

Persicus took a few steps forward. His feet sank into the soft, unstable earth. "This land cannot bear a man's weight, let alone a mounted horse." Persicus bent down and grabbed a handful of dirt, which crumbled in his hands.

"Yes, I know. Every year we lose more and more land because of the erosion. This is the only flatland nearby for games, but soon this place will be too dangerous, and we will have to find somewhere else, if we wish to continue to play."

Persicus studied the slope. It didn't look that steep from where he stood, but when he walked down a few steps, he realized how deceptive the illusion was. The soft ground was much steeper than it appeared a few yards back.

Gerisha looked up at the sun and saw it was past noon. "Why don't you ride the plateau for a while? Get to know the land's contours."

"Good idea."

They mounted their horses and rode throughout the plateau until afternoon. They raced along in a mock game, with Gerisha acting as his opponent.

When they finished, Persicus took a long swallow of water from the goatskin and passed it to Gerisha. Sweat dripped down from their temples. Gerisha soaked a handkerchief in water and wiped his face with it.

"You did well," Gerisha said.

"I need a lot more practice."

"We'll have enough time. I think you can win. You have everything to lose if you don't. I think you will be playing with much more enthusiasm than the Sultan." Gerisha gave the goatskin back to Persicus. "Come on, let's head back. You need your rest tonight. Tomorrow, you will practice with Tashtar and I'll teach you how to pick up the goat."

"Tashtar?" Persicus asked.

Gerisha smiled. "Tashtar, the horse you will be partnered with tomorrow. She is named after the God of the Rain, who came to earth as a white horse with golden hooves, who fought and defeated the demons that brought famine to these lands. My Tashtar is a brilliant, magnificent creature. She will help you fight and win this battle."

They headed back to the city. The sun had vanished behind the western mountains and dusk had crept up on them as they made their way through the city to Gerisha's home. The modest-sized house, overflowing with expensive silk carpets, glazed ceramics, and comfortable furniture, faced the town square, close to the Palace.

Persicus could look out the front window and see the Palace. An orange glow from a fire reflected off the trees in the Palace Garden. He wondered what Nooshin was doing. If she was with the Sultan? If he was stealing her away from him at this very moment? He thought of everything she had told him, about it being her decision whom she married. He wondered why she would let her fate be decided in this way. Would she really marry this other man if he lost?

Persicus sat in the front room, while Gerisha went to tell his wife they had a guest. Alone in the quiet, comfortable room, he felt he should be kicking himself. How had he let it come to this? How had this happened? Deep within, where he was reluctant to acknowledge, he knew. He had thought he had time. He had been unconditionally attracted to Nooshin ever since the first night he set eyes on her, bound and held captive by the ruthless bandits. He had tried to remain aloof with her. To protect her without showing his ridiculous feeling for her. He thought he was doing the right thing. Since the day she had told him that she was the Sogdian Princess, prudence dictated him to regard her as off limits. A ward to be escorted home and protected. Then, once they reached the Palace, she surprised him by repetitively asking him about his future. He couldn't acknowledge why she kept asking, because he couldn't believe he could have a future with her. Wary of angering her father, he had avoided answering her persistent questions. He knew he had nothing to offer her. He was no prince or sultan, nor did he have an ounce of royal blood. Besides, he had refused to believe that she cared for him any more than she cared for her servants or guards that protected her, until yesterday, in the Bottomless Pit, when he realized without doubt, that she did in fact love him. Moreover, today, King Ormozd had shocked him by giving him his approval. Persicus played the conversation in his head over again. *'I don't know what the outcome will be with our guest, but you have my favour. I think you should talk to her.'* It was unbelievable.

He still had a problem. He was not prepared for marriage. He had nothing to offer her right now. He knew that. He was a simple man from a small town. He thought he would have to prove himself financially worthy, at the very least. He would have to bring something into the marriage. He thought he would have time to sell his orchard and his home in Abrisham. He could work hard and make enough money to bring *something,* anything, into the marriage. He had thought he had time. Time to improve his image and his name. Time to try to make himself good enough for her. That was all he needed. Time.

Then Morad Ali had shown up and thrown all his plans—his entire future—into the wind. He grew angry again, ever more nervous. His stomach twisted in a knot. His breathing quickened. He felt panicked. He leaned forward and buried his face in his hands. The panic grew overwhelming. His pulse quickened; his face and hands began to sweat.

He felt something churning in his gut, trying to claw its way up his throat. He sat up, concentrating on his breathing, taking deep, calming breaths, until his pulse slowed, and the knot in his stomach eased.

Gerisha came into the room with a small olive-skinned woman. Her black hair fell below her shoulders in a wavy mess. Light brown eyes sparkled in her beautiful, round face. Gerisha introduced her as Araxis.

"Welcome to our home," she said. "I have heard much about you. I am glad I could finally meet you. I'm preparing dinner right now; it will be ready soon. We will talk then."

Persicus thanked her for her hospitality. She excused herself and went to finish cooking. The smell of rice, kabob, and vegetables floated in from the kitchen.

After they washed up outside in a rectangular pool in the courtyard, they had a nice, quiet evening with good food, pleasant talk, and a several glasses of wine.

Persicus went to bed early. He fell asleep within minutes.

# 32

## TASHTAR

The next morning, Persicus and Gerisha woke up well after dawn. It was the first full night of sleep that Persicus had had in a week. Refreshed and alert, he was eager to learn the game. After a light breakfast of beaten, fried eggs and chopped spring greens, they hurried out to the stable.

Inside the dark stable, surrounded by the comforting smell of horses and hay, Gerisha led Persicus down to the last stall, and opened the small, wooden gate. A beautiful, white horse with a long, thick, golden mane stuck her head out from the darkness and gave a delightful whinny.

"Here's my beauty," Gerisha opened his hand to reveal a lump of crystalized sugar. Tashtar nudged his shoulder and licked the sugar off his hand, crunching it into pieces. "She is a descendant of one of the great Nisean horses—a special breed of horses, often used in warfare for their speed and strength during the Sassanid dynasty. We still have a great many of them in our military, but we have to keep a close eye on them, as they are highly valued and envied. Wars have begun because other Kings wanted to own these animals."

Persicus approached the horse and gave her an affectionate rubbing. "Yes. I saw them during the battle and King Ormozd told me about them when he showed me the rooms behind the Shabestan. I saw them in the mosaic down there."

"Ah, so he has let you into his secret lair. Not many people are so privileged. Let's saddle her up. We'll use a goatskin filled with water for practice."

They left from the southern gate and stopped on a small stretch of level land, not far from Twelve Wolf Creek. Gerisha drew a large circle in the dirt with a stick and grabbed the water-filled goatskin.

"Now remember, the game begins as soon as the goat hits the ground. You have to pick it up without getting off your horse."

Persicus smiled sheepishly as he mounted Tashtar. "All right. No problem."

"Are you ready?"

Persicus nodded.

Gerisha stood on the line of the circle, across from Persicus. He counted to three and dropped the goatskin into the circle.

As soon as Gerisha dropped the goatskin, Tashtar moved into the circle and stopped beside the goatskin. Persicus leaned off the side of his horse, reaching down with his right arm. The goatskin remained well out of his reach. He stretched further, straining. As his fingertips brushed the top layer of the goat's fur, he lost his balance, and fell sideways off the horse, onto the goatskin.

Tashtar craned her neck to the side, watching Persicus.

"Not as easy as you thought, huh?" Gerisha laughed.

"Not on the first try. I'll get it this time." Persicus got to his feet, dusting off his hands, and remounted.

"Put all your weight on the stirrup and hold the saddle with one hand when you dive down. You'll get it."

Persicus tried again, putting his weight on the right stirrup as he leaned off that side. Straining his arm, trying to reach the goat, his fingertips brushed the fur again. He stretched further. *A little more*, he thought. Again, he toppled over, landing on his stomach with a loud *umph*.

Persicus sat back on his heels, looking up at Tashtar, who, he could swear, was grinning at him.

"Usually people start off on a smaller horse, but we don't have time for that, and she is the horse you will want during the game." Gerisha mounted his horse. "Watch me do it and maybe that will help."

Gerisha moved his horse into the circle. He leaned sideways off the right side of the horse, bending his right leg, and putting all his weight onto the right stirrup. He slid sideways with his left leg moving up and over the horse's back, until it straddled the top of the saddle, and his head hung near the ground. He reached out and grabbed the goatskin. Once he had a firm grip on the goatskin, he pulled himself upright, using his left arm to hold onto the saddle horn while holding the goatskin with his right arm, and he steadied himself with his left leg as he pushed himself back up with his right leg.

"There. That's how you do it." Gerisha dropped the goatskin back into the circle.

Persicus tried again, this time, following Gerisha's example, hanging off the side of his horse, his hair trailing down almost to the ground. He grabbed a hold of the goat's neck. He was almost upside down and he didn't realize how heavy the goatskin felt from this position. He strained with his whole body to lift it while trying to right himself. As soon as he lifted the goatskin two inches off the ground, Tashtar started galloping away. Persicus wasn't ready and slid off the side of the horse, headfirst to the ground. He landed on top of the goat, softening the impact.

Gerisha jumped down from his horse and ran over to Persicus. "Are you all right?"

Persicus got to his feet, dusting off his clothes. "Yeah, fine," Persicus said with the beginnings of frustration, finally realizing that this was much harder than he had thought. He felt the pain of a bruise forming on his shoulder and chest.

"I forgot to tell you, Tashtar is trained specifically for this game. She will take off at full speed as soon as you pick up the goat. And she can run at an incredible speed. She'll out run just about any horse."

Persicus sighed. "At least the horse knows what she's doing."

"You only need some practice. It's difficult at first, but you'll get the hang of it. It's the same as riding a camel; once you learn how, you can do it every time."

Persicus trained for the rest of the day. As soon as he got the hang of picking up the goat, they began practicing together. At first, Gerisha would get the goat away from Persicus each time, but by afternoon, Gerisha had taught him everything he needed to know about evading his opponent, playing aggressively, and maneuvering the horse as a weapon. By sunset, Gerisha felt pleased with Persicus' progress and believed he could win the game.

Persicus' confidence began to return, though he felt bruised and had several scrapes from his multiple falls, he began to come back to himself. He had never worried about losing before, as he never had fought for something so important. Never in his life had he felt so insecure, but when Morad Ali had shown up, when he saw Nooshin smiling, laughing, and whispering with him, all his confidence had washed away. He hadn't felt that way with Salman in the picture, because Nooshin despised him, but she didn't seem to despise Morad Ali, and that's what bothered him the most.

On their way back to Mishin, Gerisha insisted that Nooshin was playing with him. She was upset with him, yes, but that did not change her deeper feelings for him. Persicus hoped this was the case, but a seed of doubt still clung to him, planted within the depths of his consciousness. When he asked why, if she was playing with him, had they suggested a game to decide whom she will marry, Gerisha shrugged, and said they didn't need another war on their hands because of another leader with a wounded pride. They had suggested buzkashi, thinking Persicus knew the game well, and would win, thus saving the city from another potential war. If the Sultan lost the game, he couldn't blame anyone, but himself. That Persicus hadn't known anything about the game was unfortunate. The game was from his own homeland.

Meanwhile, while Persicus and Gerisha practiced, Sultan Morad Ali awaited word from the viceroy of a nearby province. He had sent an emissary with a letter requesting aid the previous day. The converted subjects of this province were most sympathetic to his cause and knowledgeable in the art of buzkashi.

The local viceroy sent their best buzkashi player, as well as his famous red horse, to train Morad Ali. Jahil arrived with Alhamra, the red horse, and they began training that day.

King Ormozd scheduled the game to begin at the end of one week, giving both men time to practice this unknown, difficult game.

Like a wild fire, word of the upcoming buzkashi game spread throughout the land. The morning before game day, the leaders and heads of many tribes, villages, and cities from across the region gathered in Mishin's town square, demanding an audience with King Ormozd. After an hour of waiting, the King, he granted their request. A Palace Guard escorted the group into the Grand Audience Hall.

During the hour Ormozd kept the visitors waiting, he sent a guard to fetch Persicus and Gerisha to attend the meeting. It was the first time Persicus had been back to the Palace since the morning after the battle.

The Grand Audience Hall had been arranged with rows of chairs facing the raised platform, where King Ormozd sat on his throne. Nooshin and Anoush sat on either side. Next to Anoush sat Persicus and Gerisha. Persicus, perplexed as to why he had been summoned, tried to appear relaxed, but the tightness in his chest felt nearly painful. Sultan Morad Ali, who had stayed at Nooshin's side at all times, whenever he wasn't practicing, sat at her side, with his eunuch standing close behind him.

The visitors filed in and hurried into the rows of chairs facing the throne. Several men squabbled over the seating, voices rising, each one of them thinking that they deserved to be in the front row, as they were the closest village to Mishin, or their town, or city was larger, and therefore more important. After a while, they all settled down.

King Ormozd acknowledged them with a slight nod of his head. "Good morning. Now, what brings all of our good neighbors to our humble city? If this is regarding our little war with Turan, that matter has been dealt with, and you have no need to worry yourselves over your welfare. There is no longer any threat from King Salman."

They had all already heard last week's news of Salman's demise and now had a more pressing matter that needed to be urgently addressed.

An elderly man with a long, white beard, wearing a brown tunic with a black caftan, and baggy pants, stood up, leaning on a thick, wooden walking stick. "If I may speak for all?"

"Who are you?" Anoush asked. "Please introduce yourself for all of us."

"My name is Mithridates, the Elder of Samangan."

King Ormozd nodded.

"You may speak," Anoush said.

"For centuries, there has been an unwritten law. Buzkashi is to be announced to all the people of the region. *All* the able-bodied men of this region should have the opportunity to participate in this game. That is how we know who the bravest and strongest man is. This is the way it has *always* been. It's tradition." The old man's voice rose as he spoke. "So why have we found out about this game through the tongue of an outsider by the name of Jahil?"

Jahil, who was standing in the corner of the room, stepped forward yelling. "I am no outsider, you infidel! Who do you think you are?"

A low mummer went through the room.

"Quiet!" Gerisha shouted. "Please, do not speak until you have been addressed by King Ormozd."

"I am well aware of our traditions," King Ormozd said, once they fell silent, "but this is a private matter, which only concerns three people: Persicus, the battered man you see standing here, Sultan Morad Ali, and my daughter, Princess Nooshin."

"Your daughter? I do not understand. What concern does your daughter have in this time-honored game? This game is to see who is the bravest and the strongest man. Women have nothing to do with it."

A few men in the crowd shouted in agreement.

King Ormozd raised his hand, calling for silence. "As I have said, it is a private matter."

Several visitors grumbled, ready to argue.

King Ormozd realized it couldn't be dealt with that easily; these people won't be satisfied without an explanation. "Being that I do not want to anger my good neighbors, I see no reason to keep it a secret, so I will tell you, and that will be the end of it. These two men have agreed to play a game of buzkashi in order to determine which my daughter will marry. They have both agreed to the terms."

A tall, dark man stood. "I am Abu Lahab, Elder of Vazirestan. Are you saying that this game is not for money or honor, but for the hand of your beautiful daughter here, for the purpose of marriage?"

"Yes," King Ormozd answered with a frown, thinking this man seemed much too enthusiastic.

"Well, Allah be praised! This is my son." Abu Lahab pulled a tall, lanky young man up by his arm. The young man had the beginnings of a coarse beard growing in patches on his narrow face. "His name is Abdulmajid Bin Abu Lahab. He will participate in this game for the hand of your daughter!" Abu Lahab's voice held undisguised zeal. A determined, pretentious smile spread across his face.

Abdulmajid Bin Abu Lahab, kept his head down, staring at the floor, but stole a quick glance up at the Princess, shifting only his eyes. His face flared red in embarrassment. He let his hair fall forward, covering his face, fidgeting with his waist shawl, hoping no one would see him blushing, and accuse him of having unclean thoughts about a woman.

However, no one paid attention to him. Everyone jumped to their feet, and began shouting over each other, waving their hands in dramatic gestures, attempting to get the attention of King Ormozd. Each wanting their son, grandson, or nephew to participate in the game. Their voices grew in an ever-rising chorus of shouts, pleas, and bargains.

Nooshin panicked. She had not expected this. Her eyes widened as she watched the unruly mob shouting, staring, and gesturing at her. She buried her face into her hands. She felt like a piece of gold on display in a bazaar, being fought over by hordes of eager, bickering men.

"Please be quiet! Quiet!" King Ormozd yelled. When that got no response, he lost his temper, stood, and shouted, "Silence! Everyone!"

The men grew quiet as the Palace Guards poured into the room, fanning out around the visitors.

"We are *not* going to do this! My daughter is a descendant of the Sassanid Dynasty. She is the Sogdian Princess. The future Queen of Mishin. She is *not* some trophy for *any one* of you to win. You will not inherit this ancient crown by playing a game!" Ormozd turned to Anoush. "Get them out of here before they make me sick!"

It wasn't until that moment that it really dawned on Persicus that if he married Nooshin, he wouldn't simply be marrying the woman he loved, but the future Queen, which meant that one day, he would be King. He knew, but he really hadn't comprehended it, until now, because he hadn't believed it was a possibility before.

The men protested as the guards herded them out before they could argue about entering the game. Anoush went with his guards as they pushed the visitors out of the Palace.

Persicus didn't dare move. The King's face was red with anger.

Morad Ali turned to Ormozd and shook his head. "Well, the nerve of those beoble. Such a shame. Is everything ready for tomorrow? I want to get this over with before we have any more of these disastrous confrontations with the locals. You understand, it is not good bolitics for my embire."

Ormozd swallowed the contemptuous glare he wanted to give the Sultan. "Everything will be ready," he replied, giving his daughter a frustrated and angry look. "Now, if you will excuse me, I have things I must tend to."

"Yes, and I must go bractice more with Jahil."

King Ormozd left the room in a growing storm of fury. Morad Ali bid Nooshin goodbye and left with his eunuch and his trainer.

Nooshin sat stone-still in her chair, staring at the empty seats. Gerisha slipped out of the room to wait for Persicus in the hallway. Persicus watched Nooshin for a moment before he stood to leave. She hadn't even looked at him. Hadn't spoken to him. He felt foolish. Tomorrow, he would fight for her and she wouldn't even acknowledge him. He turned and walked out of the room, conflicted.

Persicus had gone halfway down the hall before he heard Nooshin call his name. The tightness eased in his chest. He turned and saw her standing in the doorway of the Audience Hall, clutching the doorframe.

"Wait, wait a minute. I want to talk to you," she said.

Persicus stopped and waited as Nooshin walked sheepishly towards him.

Nooshin stopped a few feet away.

Gerisha continued down the hall and turned the corner, leaving them alone.

Persicus leaned against the wall, waiting for her to say something. She stood, gazing at the floor, avoiding his eyes.

"I don't know what to say. I didn't mean for it to turn out like this. Everything seems out of my control now."

"Yes, it is. I won't let you take all the blame, Princess. I guess I share some of the responsibility."

"Good, I'm glad you see it my way," she said, looking up at him, at last, with a small smile.

"Your way? No, I don't see it your way." He gave an abrupt, short, and unamused laugh, shaking his head. "You've made it so that you don't have any choice about who you marry."

Nooshin sighed. "I know. And I'm sorry. I didn't mean for this to happen. Trust me, I didn't. But you had to go and get mad, and insult a sultan, and then Gerisha suggested the game. And *then* it was out of my control. That wasn't my fault."

"If I hadn't said anything at breakfast, would you have married him?"

Nooshin froze. She knew the answer to that, but she'd be damned if she would tell him. "Never mind all that. I need to tell you something important about Morad Ali. You have to be careful of him. I had someone ask around about him. They found out he has a terrible temper. He can be nice and charming one minute and turn into a beast the next, especially if he doesn't get what he wants. He can turn out to be a very dangerous man if he feels that he is losing." Nooshin looked at him, full of concern.

"Why, Princess, you sound worried," Persicus said.

"Please don't kid around. If he wins, I'm stuck with him for the rest of my life!"

Now Persicus sighed. "How do you manage to attract all these sore losers to you? One right after the other. I'm only one man. I can't keep fighting indefinitely. I need a break."

"I wish I knew," Nooshin answered. She leaned forward and kissed him, a small peck on his cheek. "I'll see you tomorrow. Good luck."

Nooshin turned and fled down the hall.

# 33

## LET THE GAME BEGIN

The day of the buzkashi game arrived. Persicus had awoken at dawn, rested and restless. An hour later, he sat with Gerisha in his courtyard, drinking tea. After a brief murmured greeting, they both fell silent, contemplating the coming day.

Persicus clad himself in a cream-colored tunic; a thick, deep blue, wool caftan with short sleeves, embroidered with a verdant green design; and baggy, black, cotton pants tucked into his leather boots. His dagger hung at his side, under the caftan, hidden from view.

Over the past week, he had practiced day in and day out, and felt confident in his abilities to play—and more importantly—to win the game.

Persicus and the horse, Tashtar, bonded over the last few days. She was an excellent, intelligent horse who seemed to live for this game. When he looked into her eyes, he saw an energetic eagerness that reminded him of his own beloved horse, Tandiz, whom he had lost during his journey with Hakim in the sandstorm. He hoped that Tandiz had made it back to his home in Abrisham, and was waiting for his return, eating apples in the orchard.

Persicus and Gerisha left for the plateau at ten o'clock and arrived at noon. The game was set to begin at one. They found a spot on a large, flat boulder, where they could watch the people arriving.

Minutes later, servants from the Palace arrived and began setting up two thrones on top of a burgundy, silk carpet with a purple and black trim. In the center of the carpet, a horseman rode through a golden plateau, surrounded by flowering vines. Several rows of chairs, placed beside the thrones, sat on top of another beautiful carpet. Tables were set up and laden with nuts, sweet breads, a variety of fruits and vegetables, water, and wine.

People from the villages and towns began arriving in large groups. Persicus grew antsy watching all the people filing through the plateau, filling up the sidelines. He hadn't anticipated a large audience.

Tashtar stood nearby, watching the procession of people filling the area with ardent eyes, growing restless, knowing the game was moments away; she danced in place, raring to begin.

King Ormozd and Princess Nooshin arrived on horseback. They took their seats upon their thrones. Trying to be discrete, Nooshin searched the crowd for Persicus, moving only her eyes. Anoush stood on guard beside the King and Princess, warily scanning the large crowd for potential problems. Nadira and Tahmineh took their seats beside the Princess, excited, chatting amongst themselves.

Morad Ali appeared on the edge of the plateau with his faithful eunuch following close behind. Jahil, the trainer, rode beside the Sultan. Two other heavily armed men flanked them. The two men looked lean and muscular under their loose thowbs. Each wore identical sour expressions on their faces.

"His guards," Gerisha told Persicus, nodding towards the two men.

"Do they think they can protect him from losing?" Persicus asked.

"No, but they could just kill you if he loses. Then Nooshin couldn't marry you."

Persicus grimaced. "Thanks for that."

Gerisha laughed. They jumped down from the boulder and headed over to Ormozd and Nooshin.

"Greetings Gerisha, Persicus," King Ormozd said, when they approached.

Persicus and Gerisha bowed.

"Good day, Your Majesty," Gerisha said.

Ormozd looked at Persicus. "Are we all ready to begin?"

"Yes, I am, but I think my opponent is still consulting his trainer."

Ormozd glanced over and saw Morad Ali speaking in a hushed whisper with Jahil, nodding and gesticulating.

Persicus turned to Nooshin. "Good afternoon, Princess."

Nooshin wore another expensive Sogdian dress, made of blue-green silk with delicate yellow swirls. Her shoes matched the dress and had blue sapphires embedded into them. She wore a new, jeweled tiara on top of her head. Her hair fell down her back and over her shoulders in thick, silky waves. She had a beautiful emerald necklace around her neck. Her green eyes were striking against the blue-green of the silk dress. The bruise on her cheek had faded to a faint yellow. Her arms, exposed in this dress, still showed the battering she had taken—scratches, scrapes, and bruises that had turned light blue and green.

She smiled at Persicus. He had been on formal terms with her for the past week and he had to know that it bugged her. She wished he would call her by her first name. "Persicus," she said, dipping her head down in acknowledgment. She kept eye contact with him, refusing to show her discomfort or concern. Her life would be decided for her within the next hour. She didn't think her father would be happy with her if she chose Persicus after the game, if Morad Ali won. And neither would Morad Ali. He would be the kind of man who would want to extract his vengeance. She couldn't be responsible for another war. She would have to marry him.

Mithridates, of Samangan, the elder with the long, white hair from the previous day, stepped forward to address King Ormozd. "Your Majesty, if I may speak on behalf of my people?"

"Speak." King Ormozd had a tired look on his face that clearly said he wouldn't put up with any nonsense.

"First, I would be most grateful to you and especially to the young Princess here, if you would accept my apology. I didn't know the circumstances around this game that you had planned."

"Apology accepted," King Ormozd said, glancing at Nooshin, who nodded her head in agreement.

"Good, good, and thank you. Second, I have a simple request. I would be most grateful if you would bestow upon me the honor of dropping the goat between these two fine, young gentlemen here? When I was younger, I never lost a game. This game is a part of me; it is in my blood, however, since I am well into ripe old age, I wish to contribute to the game in the only way I can." Mithridates bowed his head, his walking stick clasped in hand.

Persicus almost smiled. The man couldn't walk without a stick and he wanted to throw the goat into the circle.

King Ormozd turned to Nooshin, asking her opinion with a glance.

"He seems to be a fair and honorable man. Why not?" Nooshin shrugged. It made no difference to her. "Let him initiate the game."

The old man smiled. "Thank you, Your Majesty, and thank you, Princess!" He bowed and walked towards the circle.

Abu Lahab, the dark-haired Elder of Vazirestan, stepped forward with his son, and several tribal elders following close behind. The elders bowed. Abu Lahab's son stood staring at Nooshin until his father pushed down his head.

"Permission to address His Majesty?" Abu Lahab asked, as he bowed.

"Granted," Ormozd said in a way that made it clear that he recognized the pushy elder from the previous day and was not pleased by his presence.

"All of these fine men standing here with me – the heads and elders of all the cities and tribes across this land – have come before you to ask that you reconsider your decision on this great matter. It would be a grievous error not to give serious consideration to this matter and to remedy this situation in all haste. As our good friend, Mithridates, mentioned yesterday, this game has a time-honored unwritten law, a tradition passed down, generations after generation, that we have all abided by for a thousand years, and we should continue to follow that tradition. If *you* change it once for one thing, it can be changed again and again, until the game becomes an empty husk of what it once stood for! *All* able-bodied men who can ride a horse have a God-given right to participate in this game. That is how we know, beyond any doubt, who is *the best* man among us. As King of Mishin, you should want your daughter to marry the best. Not the best out of *two*." Abu Lahab yanked his tall, lanky son forward. "Look here. This is my eldest son. As tall as a cypress tree and brave as the lions of Panjshir Valley. One of the best chapandaz around. He has the same right to play against any man in this competition. If you want your daughter to marry the best man, you will open up this competition, immediately! *My* son will *win* this game."

After he was done, all the elders gathered around, yelling in agreement. Shoving their sons, whom they wanted to participate in the game, and have the chance to marry the Sogdian Princess, forward. A roar went through the villagers who stood near enough to the throne to hear, protesting that the game only had two players.

"This is not how the game is played," one man yelled.

"It's an abomination!" yelled another.

King Ormozd stood up. "Enough!"

Anoush stood guard at his side, signaling for more guards to move forward.

"This is not the grand cloth bazaar of Kandahar where you can bargain. This is not a debate open for any kind of discussion. My daughter is not a trophy to be won or lost. As I said yesterday and will only say one more time, this game is a private matter between two men, and only two men. They have decided to settle their differences by winning or losing this game. Now, you are all trying my patience. Enough discussion. Step aside. You may watch the game, but none of you will participate in it!"

King Ormozd gestured to Anoush, who started pushing people back to the sideline.

The villagers were still objecting and arguing with wild hand gestures as the Palace Guards cleared the way. The protesters and the elders reluctantly moved off to the sidelines.

Morad Ali mounted his red horse and trotted the short distance to stand before the Royal Family.

King Ormozd nodded to the trumpeters and waved his hand. Five trumpeters raised the instruments to their lips, initiating the start of the game.

Anoush cleared his throat and spoke in a clear, loud voice. "The rules of the game are simple. You may not hit, kick, or otherwise use any weapon against each other. When the goat is dropped into the circle, the game has begun. You must each go around the amphora rock. Whoever brings the goat back here and drops it into the circle is the winner."

It was time. Persicus mounted his white horse and moved beside Morad Ali.

"Representing the great Bin Khalid Family, the brave Viceroy, conqueror of many lands, and its people, in which reciting them would be too great a task for our short introduction. A man whose deeds, past and future, will stand the test of time, and will be named in many great books. A legend in the making—Sultan Morad Ali!" Jahil announced, bowing with a flourishing wave of his arm in the Sultan's direction.

Morad Ali waved his hands in the air. The villagers cheered, hooting and praising him.

Gerisha came to stand at Persicus' side. He waited until the villagers quieted.

"Here is a brave and honorable man from Tajikistan. A great horseman from the Steppes. A sagacious man, whose keen insights, quick thinking, and fearless fortitude saved our beloved Princess from the hands of murderous bandits, and who went on to help save our glorious kingdom, and all the citizens of our great city. Persicus, of Abrisham!"

Cheers erupted from the citizens of Mishin, but the visitors remained silent. As Persicus approached the circle that had been drawn on the ground with white powder, his throat tightened, and his heart began pounding against his chest. He looked back over his shoulder at Nooshin, hoping to gain some insight into what she was thinking.

Nooshin sat stone-still, watching, her face blank, but her eyes took in every detail. Her heart constricted as she met Persicus' eyes.

Persicus stopped at the circle and turned to face Morad Ali.

Morad Ali smirked, looking Persicus up and down. "Why Bersicus? All those cuts and bruises. Having broblems with your horse? I could have given you a good horse, a real horse, had you asked, instead of whatever that thing is. This sad creature abbears to be an unfortunate mistake."

Persicus' lips twitched, almost curling into a smirk of his own. "The horse is fine. I've just been *bracticing*."

Morad Ali raised his hand to his lips and twirled his mustache between two fingers. "Bracticing, you say. It is good to bractice, but you're subbose to stay on tob of your horse, not fall on your face."

Persicus frowned when he noticed that Morad Ali didn't have a single bruise or scratch on him. "How come you are not bruised?"

"My simble friend, the wise man uses his head, not his muscle."

Persicus narrowed his eyes, his frown deepening. Before he could say anything else, the trumpets sounded again, a long, joyous tune.

Mithridates, mounted on a solid black horse, galloped towards a large bucket filled with salted ice water, which the goat carcass was soaking in. He reached down and extracted the waterlogged goat. Mithridates moved with agility that was rare for his age, managing to reach down and pull the goat up with little difficulty. With the goat held under one arm, he galloped towards the circle, water drizzling down behind him. He rode between Persicus and Morad Ali, dropping the goat into the center of the circle.

The game had begun. Persicus was ready.

The instant the goat touched the ground, Tashtar moved into the circle, alongside the goat. Persicus noticed that Morad Ali had not moved. He looked over at Morad Ali, who sat motionless on his horse; his eyes focused Persicus. Persicus didn't waste any time wondering why the Sultan made no move to get the goat. He reached down, putting all his weight on his right stirrup, leaned off the side of the horse until his hair trailed along the ground, and grabbed the goat by the ankle. As soon as he lifted it off the ground, Tashtar sprinted towards the amphora-shaped rock, accelerating with every step.

Persicus was trying to get back up on top of his horse when Morad Ali came up on his right side and grabbed the rear ankle of the goat. Morad Ali tried to pull the goat out of Persicus' arm, but Persicus had a firm grip on the goat, his arm wrapped around the goat's back, and his hand holding it under its front legs. Persicus tried to pull himself upright, but Morad Ali pulled the goat, angling his horse away from Persicus.

Persicus muttered a silent curse. He couldn't sit upright holding the goat the way he was and he couldn't ride hanging off the side of his horse for long, either. Each long, galloping step the horse took bounced him up and down, causing him to slide further down Tashtar's side. Eventually, he would fall. He took a chance and shifted the goat in his arm, so he could pull himself up.

Waiting for the right moment to yank the goat away, Morad Ali saw

Persicus maneuver the goat, while still struggling to sit upright in his saddle. Morad Ali yanked his reins, moving his horse into Persicus, and then away in the opposite direction, jerking the goat along with him.

The crowd roared.

Persicus was halfway up, his left leg reaching to get back onto the proper side, when Morad Ali suddenly pushed his horse towards him, brushing against him. He struggled to get out of the way, terrified that he was about to be crushed between the two horses, and then Morad Ali jerked the goat away from him. Persicus lost his footing on the stirrup, his right hand skidded along the ground, and he fell to the ground, rolling.

A mixture of cries came out from the crowd, cheering and jeering.

Persicus jumped up to his feet. Tashtar stopped the moment he fell and hurried to Persicus' side. Persicus mounted again and Tashtar took off at full speed after Morad Ali. Morad Ali had a good head start, but Tashtar was the faster horse. Tashtar galloped full out, trying to catch up with Alhamra, Morad Ali's horse.

"Come on, Tashtar! Go! Go!" Persicus yelled.

Morad Ali looked back over his shoulder and saw Persicus gaining on him. He kicked his horse with his heels, urging him to run faster. Persicus was coming up on his left side. Morad Ali directed his horse westward, towards the Devil's Drop. He raced along the edge of the incline, right where the solid land ended, and the eroded, unstable land began, and shifted the goat so that it hung halfway off his horse's right side. If Persicus wanted to grab the goat, he would have to risk riding into the loose and soft dirt that bordered the point of no return.

Persicus was on Morad Ali's tail. He saw Morad Ali switch directions, now riding alongside the Devil's Drop. Persicus dropped back a few feet while he tried to figure if he should risk it. No way would he let Morad Ali win. That wasn't an option.

"What do you think, Tashtar? Can you do it?"

Tashtar didn't wait for Persicus to make up his mind. She increased her speed again. Persicus directed Tashtar to come up on Morad Ali's right side, on the dangerous slope. Within seconds, Tashtar was neck and neck with Alhamra, her hooves sinking into the soft dirt, kicking up a cloud of dust.

Persicus leaned forward, focused on the land, the goat, and Morad

Ali's red horse. When Tashtar's nose passed Alhamra's by six inches, Persicus reached out his left hand, and grabbed the goat's leg, which hung off Alhambra's side.

Sultan Morad Ali held onto the goat, yanking it back, but Persicus was the stronger man, and without an advantage of some kind, he would lose his precious goat, unless the Tajik made some fatal error. Morad Ali tightened his grip, pulling with all his strength, but it wasn't enough. Persicus ripped the carcass from his hands.

*I have to get away from this slope.* Persicus looked over at Morad Ali, less than a foot away. He tugged on his reins, trying to force Morad Ali's horse over onto more stable land.

Morad Ali stubbornly held his ground. He grabbed a whip that he had been holding between his teeth and looked over his shoulder. The spectators seemed far enough away from them that he thought he could get away with breaking a rule—that shouldn't have even been a rule anyway, so he felt justified in what he was about to do.

The Sultan reached over and whipped Persicus' left hand—the hand holding onto the goat.

"Looks as if your cuts and bruises are healing. Allow me to refresh them for you!" Morad Ali taunted, whipping him again, harder.

At that moment, Persicus couldn't do anything to stop the Sultan. He couldn't go any further to his right or he would pass the point of no return. The horses galloped side by side, neck and neck, Tashtar's speed impeded by the soft, crumbling earth. His left hand still held the goat and his right held the reins. Persicus' gritted his teeth when the Sultan whipped him again. Red, swollen welts began springing up and blood flowed down his hand to drip on the pure, white coat of his horse.

"They say suffering builds character. What doesn't kill you makes you stronger!" Morad Ali whipped out his hand, repeatedly striking Persicus. "I'll make you strong. I'll give you character. Now, give me that goat, you insibid hole digger or I'll bush you over the edge."

"The only place this goat is going is to the throne—with *me.*"

The top of Persicus' hand was a bloody mess. Morad Ali began whipping his forearm; his tunic gave no protection against the pain. Persicus' face furrowed in concentration. He drove his horse harder.

For the second time in his life, Persicus wanted to hurt someone. He resisted the urge to drop the goat, reach out, yank the Sultan off his horse, and throw him over the edge of the Devil's Drop. *Nooshin was right,* Persicus thought, remembering the warning she had given him. Persicus' hand and forearm stung in one massive, sharp, throbbing pain. Still, he held onto the goat, more determined than ever. He switched the goat to his right side, away from the Sultan, and clenched his teeth, trying to ignore the pain.

Persicus and Gerisha had practiced and trained for every possible move Morad Ali could make. He leaned forward, nudging his horse with his boot. Tashtar knew what to do. "Now, Tashtar! Now!"

Morad Ali pulled his reins, angling Alhamra towards the Devil's Drop, pushing Persicus closer to the edge. Tashtar sped up, galloping as fast as she could through the soft, eroding terrain. As she passed a neck's length ahead of Alhamra, she cut across, in front of the Sultan and his horse.

Morad Ali cried out in startled panic. No horse would ever do what that big, dumb beast just did. Horses try to avoid collisions at all costs. Morad Ali tried to move away, but he didn't have any warning or time. They had been too close together when Persicus' stupid horse cut him off.

Alhamra collided with Tashtar's rear haunch and he panicked. Morad Ali could do nothing as his horse veered and took off at full speed back towards the throne, and away from Tashtar.

Relieved and bleeding, Persicus watched the Sultan head back towards the starting line. Persicus took full advantage of the short reprieve and headed for the amphora shaped rock.

The Sultan roared furiously. He redirected Alhamra back towards Persicus and kicked the horse in the gut to get him moving. Then he whipped his horse to get him to move faster. Alhamra began to bleed under the repetitive blows from the talon-like whip. Alhamra was already going as fast as he could, but the Sultan whipped him anyway, yelling at him to move faster.

Jahil, the trainer, had taught Morad Ali as much as he could about how to win at buzkashi—winning the game depended on physical strength. Persicus, because of his peasant lifestyle, was much stronger than he was. Morad Ali couldn't win by brute strength alone, so Jahil had taught him all the dirty tricks—that weren't exactly cheating—he would need to win. He had let Persicus pick up the goat. 'Why waste your energy trying to pick up the goat, when it is much easier to snatch the goat away from the Tajik when he is trying to right himself on the saddle,' Jahil had said. Jahil went on to teach him how to knock Persicus off his horse, also when he was trying to get back on top of the saddle. This would give him the lead, Jahil assured him, as the Tajik would have to run to his horse, who would continue on without him for a ways. Jahil also said that, if by chance Persicus did catch up with him, to ride on the edge of the Devil's Drop, and hold the goat on that side, so Persicus would not be able to grab it without risk that no half-way intelligent person would take. According to Jahil, if he did all of that, he would win.

Jahil had been wrong. Morad Ali was all out of sneaky maneuvers.

Jahil hadn't told him what to do if that damned Tajik out-maneuvered him on the Devil's Drop, got the goat from him, and sent Jahil's incompetent horse scampering away in the wrong direction. And now, Persicus was rounding the amphora rock. The Tajik couldn't be allowed to win. No way could he allow a peasant Tajik to beat him. He would sooner kill him than lose. He would have to go around the rock too, but if he did that now, he would never be able to catch up with Persicus. Instead, he charged Persicus, straight on.

Persicus saw Morad Ali heading directly towards him. He changed course, heading further east, towards the tree line, but Morad Ali changed course with him. They were headed straight for each other. Persicus held on tight to the goat, not knowing which side Morad Ali would pass on. At the last moment, Alhamra veered a foot to the left to avoid a collision. Morad Ali reached out and grabbed the goat's leg. They both held on tight, refusing to let go, to relinquish the goat to the other man.

As the horses passed each other, both men flew backwards off their horses, as neither of them let go of the goat. They landed on their backs with a solid *whump*, feet from each other; the goat sprawled in between them. The goat's rear leg had torn off in the Sultan's hand.

Tashtar stopped and galloped back to Persicus. Alhambra continued a couple hundred feet before he stopped and looked back at Morad Ali.

The impact had knocked the wind out of Persicus. For an eternal moment, he lay sprawled on the ground, dazed, trying to breathe. The air was thick with dust, stinging his eyes. As he choked down his first lungful of dust-laden air, he gave a painful cough, and got to his knees. He saw Morad Ali five feet away, also getting up on hands and knees. Persicus grabbed the goat and pulled it to himself.

"Oh, good. You have decided to suffer like everybody else," Persicus said snidely.

Morad Ali's eyes widened. *No one* had ever dared insult him before. "You know nothing of suffering. Just wait until I am done with you, you stubid, simble beasant. Now, give that to me!" Still clutching the goat's torn leg in his hand, he swung it as if it were a club, hitting Persicus across the face.

Persicus had his hands full and couldn't block the leg that smacked him across his left cheek. Morad Ali reared back and hit him again.

The spectators heckled and jeered, amazed by the scene playing out before them. Never had they seen a buzkashi game played in such a laughable way.

King Ormozd shook his head in disgrace. This was an embarrassment. He could hear Gerisha laughing and he turned to give him a stern, disapproving look, but then he heard his daughter laughing, along with her chambermaid, Nadira. Tahmineh, to his surprise, jumped up and down, chanting, "Persicus! Get up! Persicus! Go! Go!"

Anoush's face had turned red with suppressed laughter.

Still on his knees, Morad Ali lunged at the goat, grabbing the remaining rear leg.

Persicus pulled back on the goat, the Sultan jerked forward a foot, but did not let go. He could hear the crowd, laughing, cheering, heckling, and someone chanting his name, but it seemed distant. *I have to end this,* Persicus thought. He couldn't stand here, struggling over the goat until it was torn into ten different pieces. He remembered a Chinese wrestling technique his uncle had taught him as a child, when other little boys would try to steal things from him. They would tug and he would tug back. It could go on and on. Until his uncle had taught him this move, which he figured would work just as well for angry sultans as it did for bullying kids.

Persicus' left hand ached and when he clenched his fist around the front leg, a deep, stinging, pain tore through his hand, stabbing up into his arm. He yanked the goat as hard as he could.

Exhausted, Morad Ali resisted, using his last vestige of strength to throw himself backwards, his sweating palms holding tight to the goat's leg. He expected Persicus to resist and pull back, and wasn't prepared when Persicus propelled himself forward, shoving into him instead. Morad Ali stumbled backwards, falling, landing on his back, and hitting his head on the ground, furious, but still holding on tight in utter desperation.

Persicus landed on top of the Sultan and jumped to his feet. He stood over Morad Ali, put his boot to the Sultan's chest, intending to shove him back down. As he heaved the goat out from the Sultan's arms and onto his shoulder, Morad Ali swiftly produced a dagger from the folds of his loose thowb, and drove the blade up towards Persicus' leg.

Nooshin bolted up out of her throne, fear clenching her heart, when she saw Persicus standing over Morad Ali. She saw Morad Ali's hand disappear and an instant later, the gleam of metal, obscured by the distance, but she knew it was a knife of some sort. She turned to look at her father, who watched in horror. It was supposed to be a fair game of strength, *not murder.*

"No! He can't do that!" Tahmineh cried out.

Gerisha came to stand beside Ormozd, wondering whether he should do something. *If* he could do anything. They had never had to stop a game before, not due to someone cheating with a weapon. Ormozd shook his head, eyes still fixed upon the distant players. There was nothing they could do. The two men were in the middle of the large plateau, too far away for them to do anything, but watch. There wasn't time for anything else.

Nooshin felt something in the pit of her stomach tighten and a roll of nausea washed over her. This was it. Her fate was now sealed. She felt a horrible, suffocating panic. She couldn't breathe. She closed her eyes. She couldn't watch.

𒈫

The blade easily cut through his leather boot and bit into his flesh. He felt the blade slice into his shin and penetrate into the fleshy part of his left calf. Morad Ali tore the blade out and drew the dagger over his head to strike again. Persicus felt a flood of blood wash down his leg.

Persicus didn't scream, though he wanted to. He gritted his teeth and kicked out with his uninjured leg. The heel of his boot connected with the hilt of the blade as the dagger arched down for the second assault, sending the dagger flying through the air. The goat slipped off Persicus' shoulder. Morad Ali rolled forward onto his knees and lunged for the goat. Persicus jerked the goat away from Morad Ali, backing up with a limp. Morad Ali landed on the palms of his hands, still on his knees, glaring up at the infernal Tajik. As Persicus flung the goat over his shoulder, Morad Ali catapulted forward again, tackling Persicus, ramming his shoulder into Persicus' knees. Trying to maintain his balance, he flailed his arms, and the goat slid from his shoulder to the ground. He fell backwards. Morad Ali's hand disappeared for a second and when it reappeared, he wielded another knife—a much smaller, six inch blade—that he had kept hidden in a sheath under the sleeve of his left arm.

As Persicus landed on his back, Morad Ali drove the knife into Persicus' left foot. The same leg had already been stabbed.

This time, Persicus did scream, a scream that exuded furious outrage rather than pain. He felt the blade penetrate through the leather and into his foot, sliding between the bones that connected the big toe and the second toe, down into the sole of his boot.

Persicus, now seething with fury, hardly felt the pain. He couldn't believe the blatancy with which the Sultan had brandished his dagger.

430

He couldn't believe that Morad Ali thought he could get away with this, with everyone watching. The whipping, he could almost understand. No way could Ormozd or Nooshin have seen that. However, the audacity of it infuriated him more than the Sultan's actual cheating. It said, louder than words, that he thought of Persicus as such an insignificant nuisance that no one would care if he cheated to win; moreover, that everyone would be okay, if not pleased, with him cheating, because the Sultan *should* win over a paltry peasant, but Persicus refused to cheat. He wouldn't use a weapon. He would win Nooshin playing by the rules of the game. He would not risk losing her to this damned, dishonorable man, because of a weapon. Besides, he didn't *need* a weapon.

Persicus lay on his back, with Morad Ali on his knees by his feet. Before Morad Ali could yank the knife free, Persicus kicked out with his uninjured leg, a forceful blow that pounded into Morad Ali's lower jaw, forcing his lower teeth to bite through his own tongue before the blow rattled his senses, and sent him flying backwards to the ground.

Persicus sat up and looked at Morad Ali, lying dazed on the ground. He jerked the knife out of his foot and threw it as far as he could. Tashtar trotted up, stopping a few feet away. Persicus got to his feet. The goat lay mangled behind him.

Morad Ali struggled to sit up, glaring at Persicus through a red haze.

"If you get up, I will kill you. I won't need a knife to do it."

Morad Ali sank back onto his knees. He was out of weapons. He looked at his horse, Alhamra, twenty feet away, and turned back to Persicus. A look of uncomprehending defeat slowly crept into his face.

Persicus threw the goat over Tashtar's back and managed to mount the horse, leaving a smear of blood against her white coat.

"You don't want to do this. If I don't marry the Brincess, the Caliph will be very ubset. He will be angry with you for getting in my way. For ruining his blans," Morad Ali pleaded. "You don't want the Caliph angry with you. Give me the goat; I will save you and sbare your life."

Persicus stared down at Morad Ali. "This is the steppes of Sogdiana and I am the future King of Mishin. We don't give into threats. You can tell the Caliph, if he wants to fight, we will destroy him, the same as we destroyed Salman, and his army."

Persicus turned and galloped towards the circle.

Persicus felt both exhausted and elated. His arms resisted his efforts to hold onto the goat. Thick trails of blood ran down his leg, filling up his boot. As the adrenaline faded, an agonizing pain shot through his entire leg. The wounds on his hand and arm seemed minor in comparison, and the red, angry welts on his hand had already begun to scab over, but every flex of his fingers caused a searing pain to shoot up from his hand to his arm. Sweat mixed with dirt clung to his face.

The ride from the middle of the plateau to the finishing line seemed excruciatingly long. He stopped in the circle in front of King Ormozd.

𝗬𝗬𝗬

Abu Lahab watched the whole spectacle from the sideline, seething with anger at King Ormozd for not allowing his son to enter the game, which flew in the face of tradition. When Persicus rode away from the Sultan and the game seemed to be over, he approached the eunuch, a false visage of calm and friendship spread across his face.

"Hello, my good man. I am Abu Lahab, Elder of Vazirestan. Interesting show, I must say. If I may ask, Sultan Morad Ali is a relative of the Caliph, yes?"

The eunuch grunted yes, nodding his head while eyeing the elder with suspicion.

The smile widened, stretching across Abu Lahab's face. "The Great Allah always provides. Thank you, my good man. Peace be with you."

He hurried across the field to Morad Ali.

𝗬𝗬𝗬

Morad Ali glared at Persicus as he rode away. He got to his feet, spitting blood from his mouth. He ran his tongue over his teeth, making sure they were all still there. A front, upper tooth felt jagged. The damned Tajik had broken his tooth when he kicked him. He flicked his tongue across the chipped tooth and pain shot through his upper gum, straight up to his head. The tooth moved back and forth under his tongue. He pushed on the tooth until it detached from his gum. He spit it into his hand and stared down at the bloody, yellow tooth. He clutched his hand around the tooth in a tight fist, steaming with anger, and stared towards the throne again. Furious, he threw the tooth and plunged his tongue into the hole where his tooth had been, lapping up the blood, making wet sucking sounds. He turned to go search for his knife and dagger and nearly collided with a man rushing towards him.

"Greetings, Sultan Morad Ali," Abu Lahab said, bowing his head and introducing himself. "An unfortunate game. You cannot trust those Tajiks. Cheaters, all of them." He shook his head in disgust. "But alas, when all else fails, Allah is still watching out for us. When one door closes, another opens wide, and you must act quickly to seize the opportunity!"

"Oben wide, you say? I do not see it this way. Now, be kind and leave me alone, I must find my dagger."

"But my kind sir, being as you are still in need of a good wife, of noble blood, and my daughters are in need of a good husband, I thought I could be of assistance. Both of us would gain in the process. I have many, many beautiful daughters. All of age, between nine and sixteen."

The Sultan's eyebrows rose; the elder had his full attention now. He spotted his dagger, picked it up, and put it away in a sheath under his thowb, hidden from view once more.

"Many daughters? Who did you say you were again?" Morad Ali asked.

Abu Lahab put his arm around the Sultan's shoulders and they walked back to the sideline. "I am Abu Lahab, Elder of Vazirestan. I will allow you, and only you, to have your pick among my beautiful girls. I would not offer them to just anybody, but you are a brave and honorable man. It would be a grand union. You, a great Sultan of the Caliph Family and the daughter of the Elder of Vazirestan."

𝖸𝖸𝖸

Persicus stopped in the circle in front of the throne. He pushed the goat off the side of his horse and it flopped into the circle with a thud. After disposing of the goat, minus a rear leg, Persicus dismounted, careful of his injured leg, and limped over to the King.

"Your Majesty," he said, bowing. "I have come to claim my trophy."

Nooshin's mouth dropped open, offended. King Ormozd bowed his head, trying to conceal his smile.

Persicus turned and limped three paces over to Nooshin, where she sat beside her father, rigid and anxious.

Nooshin gave her father a bewildered, pleading look. "Father!" She gasped, terrified and indignant. *Trophy!* she thought. At the same time, she felt utter relief, because Persicus was alive and he had won.

Ormozd smiled at his daughter, knowing full well this was what she wanted, though she would never admit it. Nooshin stared straight ahead, past Persicus, a shocked look on her face, her green eyes wide.

Persicus tapped her on her shoulder. "Ahhhem."

She sat still, refusing to acknowledge him. He stepped in closer to her. Slowly, she turned to face him. She looked up into his grinning eyes. He looked downright pleased with himself.

Persicus gestured for Tahmineh and Nadira to move out of his way. They got up from their chairs and moved off to the side.

Tahmineh nodded at him, beaming with a brilliant smile. Persicus couldn't remember ever seeing her smile at him before. He only glanced at her for second before turning back to Nooshin.

He leaned over and whispered into her ear. "I won, my dear Princess. And you are my prize."

433

Nooshin clenched her fists; her cheeks burned and blushed bright red. Looking straight ahead, trying to quell her anger, she said, "I am the Princess of Mishin. How dare you come to me and say I am your prize!"

Persicus' lips twisted into a satisfied smirk. He bent down as if he was getting down onto his knee. *That's better,* Nooshin thought. Instead of bending down on his knee, Persicus leaned forward, snatched her from her seat, and threw her over his shoulder.

"What do you think you are doing?" She protested, hitting him half-heartedly. Persicus took a few steps, his leg protesting the weight.

"Father!" she yelled. "Help me! You can't let him do this!"

Ormozd watched Persicus limping away with his daughter. He felt pleased. "You are the one who told them to figure it out for themselves. The decision has been made. You're stuck with it."

Nooshin couldn't see her father, but she detected a hint of laughter in his voice.

Persicus carried Nooshin towards his horse.

"What are you doing? Put me down this instant! I'm not an invalid. I said, put me down! Who do you think you are?"

Persicus set her down by his horse, but kept his arms wrapped around the small of her back. "I am to be your husband. Soon to be the Prince of Mishin. And in the distant future, the King of Mishin. So, you had better behave."

She stared at him, opened mouthed, flabbergasted. He pulled her against him, craned his neck down, and kissed her. She froze and then made a feeble attempt to push him away. A moment passed and she stopped resisting. She leaned against him, wrapped her arms around his back, and stood on tiptoe, her head tilted up. She kissed him back. She felt safe and happy, at long last. He broke from the kiss and she rested her head against his chest trying to hide her glowing face and a treacherous smile. Persicus laid his cheek against the top of her head.

After a couple minutes, Persicus released her. She stood gazing up at him. Persicus knew he had the same goofy expression on his face as he had the first time his eyes fell upon her.

Persicus put his arm around her and they limped around Tashtar. He grabbed her around the waist and lifted her onto his horse. He jumped up behind her and took control of the reins, his arms still around her.

Persicus thought of how he had come all this way, on this long and treacherous journey. From his home—his *previous* home—in the small town of Abrisham, to the Land of Fire and Dragons in search of the mythical lost treasure of the Silk Road with the deceitful, old, one-armed man. By some odd chance or twist of fate, Hakim happened to be the cousin of King Salman, who was betrothed to Princess Nooshin. He thought of how he had been lost in the underground river, floating aimlessly until he came to the end of the river, certain that it was *his* end. He had crawled up out of the earth to find the precious, beautiful woman now in his arms, bound, held captive by murderous bandits. She had fallen into his arms—or around his neck—he had saved her. In turn, she had saved him from Hakim's hired killer. He had fought hard to bring her home. He had helped plot out the plan to save her city. After surviving the battle and the events at the Bottomless Pit, he had to fight to win her from the pompous, flamboyant Sultan.

He had won. The struggles, the fights were over. He would marry the woman he loved and she was going to give him a Kingdom. And what could he give her?

"Are you ready to go back to our Palace, in our city?" Persicus asked. Those words sounded strange to him, but he had to say them aloud.

"We'll see about that. Nothing is written in stone yet," Nooshin said, facing forward, her head held high.

Persicus smiled and angled the horse down the mountain pass.

ᛗ

Tashtar stopped in the middle of the path and whinnied, backing up as though in fear. They were halfway down the mountain pass and only an hour away from Mishin.

"Now what?" Persicus asked. Tashtar danced backwards, rearing and kicking out her legs.

Persicus looked around for a snake or something that would frighten the horse, but he saw no snakes, nor large lizards.

"There. Look, Persicus." Nooshin pointed to the side of the path. Rocks of all sizes lined the edge of the mountain path. On top of a large boulder, a white raven sat, watching them. It flapped its wings, trying to fly, and fell off the rock to the ground.

"Oh, the poor thing. It's hurt. You have to help him," Nooshin said.

"Help him? How?"

"Give him some water. He's probably thirsty. I think his wing is broken."

Persicus sighed and shook his head. He jumped down from the horse. A sharp twang of pain shot through his leg. He poured a small handful of water into his hand from his water pouch, limped over to the bird, and knelt down in front of it.

Nooshin watched him from behind.

Persicus put his hands down in front of the small white raven. The bird hobbled over and stuck its beak into his hand, sucking up the water. Persicus smiled, pleasantly surprised that the bird hadn't bolted in fear. It was a beautiful creature. He had never seen a white raven before and now he had seen two in a week. He felt it must be a sign of good luck, of troubles passing.

The bird finished drinking and looked up at Persicus, its small head cocked to the side. A disturbing feeling overcame him and suddenly he felt the bird wasn't good luck at all. Persicus sat back on his heels and examined the raven.

In its blood-red eyes he beheld something crazed, some semblance of fury and hatred. The wretched bird squawked—a piercing, manic sound—and beat its wings in a frenzy. It drove its beak down into Persicus' hand, pecked and bit him. Its talons dug into the flesh of his palm.

Persicus cried out. He jerked his hand back and stood, but the bird clung to him, its tiny claws speared into his flesh. The bird continued shrieking as it tore into his hand.

"What are you doing? Don't hurt him, Persicus!" Nooshin yelled from atop of their horse.

Persicus whipped his hand back and forth and flung the bird away. "Guardian of the Steppes! What on earth is wrong with that thing?" Persicus shouted, cradling his freshly bleeding hand.

The bird got to its feet, ten feet away, where it had landed. It hopped away from them, its blood-spattered head turned to watch Persicus. It squawked one more time and then hopped out of sight, behind a rock.

Persicus inspected his hands. One whipped and battered by the Sultan and one bleeding, pecked, and clawed by a damned bird. He dropped his hands to his sides and turned back towards Nooshin.

She watched him with anger in her eyes, her arms crossed over her chest.

"What did you do to that poor bird?" Nooshin asked, trying not to yell.

"The damned thing attacked me, as if possessed by demons," Persicus said in defense. He wiped his hands on a handkerchief and mounted his horse behind Nooshin.

Persicus saw King Ormozd, Anoush, and Gerisha had almost caught up to them. Behind them, the rest of the spectators and servants from the Palace followed in a line down the path almost a mile long.

Nooshin's indignant anger returned. He had hurt a bird. An innocent bird. She couldn't allow this kind of behavior. No, she would have to tell him that that was not going to be tolerated. It took a moment for her to realize that she wasn't angry about the bird. She was still angry that he had called her a trophy. *Well, maybe not angry,* she thought. *Offended. Embarrassed.* He should have bowed down before her and asked her to be his wife, her prince, with sincerity, respect and—for Ahura Mazda's sake—some romance. Instead, he had humiliated her in front of her father, the Sultan, her people, and people from the entire central region of Asia. He had thrown her over his shoulder — *again* — as though she were an invalid or a naughty child being carried off to some unknown punishment.

"All right, *Persicus*. We need to get a few things straight here."

"Yes?" Persicus said, sensing her mood had changed.

"If you want to be a part of my family and be the future King of Mishin, there are certain rules you will have to abide by."

Persicus restrained himself from laughing, though she could feel him shaking. "Of course."

Ormozd, Gerisha, and Anoush listened to them from behind, curious. They rode at a slow, leisurely pace. Ormozd chuckled. Gerisha shook his head.

"Rule number one: You don't hurt birds," Nooshin said.

"Yes, my dear."

"Rule number two: You can't go around screaming 'Guardian of the Steppes' anymore. We are Zoroastrian. We believe in Ahura Mazda. The people of the city can believe in whatever they want, but the Royal Bloodline has to remain Zoroastrian, as it has always been. So no more Guardian of the Steppes, or Father of Thunder, or Mother of Lightning."

"Yes, my dear."

Tashtar picked up her speed going downhill. Persicus held onto the reins, holding Nooshin at the same time, with his arms wrapped protectively around her.

"Rule number three: I am *no trophy!* I am a Sogdian Princess. You can't go picking me up and throwing me around … *ever again.*"

"Yes, my dear," Persicus said, happily accepting her rules.

"Rule number four: I am the future Queen …"

Gerisha laughed, watching Persicus and Nooshin as they rode ahead of them, the distance becoming greater until they could no longer hear the rules. Gerisha shook his head. "Poor fool. Doesn't know what he's gotten himself into."

Ormozd chuckled. "Heh heh heh. That's my girl."

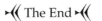 The End

*Or is it…*

# EPILOGUE

Sogdiana.

Twenty years later.

The sound of a gong sliced through the stillness of the night. A chorus of dogs barking and howling sprung up as the last reverberating sounds of the gong faded, spreading like a wildfire through the dark alleys and neighborhoods, forecasting the looming, ominous presence approaching from the south.

Persicus had lain awake through the night. He opened his eyes and stared up at the ceiling. *They are on time*, he thought, as the gong rang out a second time, echoing along the walls throughout the city.

It was two hours past midnight. He quietly rose from bed and slipped into a wool caftan. He grabbed a torch off the wall and walked out into the darkness of the night.

An unusual thick white fog enveloped the city. The luminous full moon cast down its subtle silvery light, mingling with the fog to create gruesome shapes of ghosts long gone.

Persicus held his torch high and walked to the edge of the garden, and tried to see past the dark and unyielding fog. He could hear the sound of footsteps as men rushed through the dark alleys below, followed by the sounds of doors and windows being slammed shut and locked.

Persicus looked up to the blackened sky. "Why does this keep happening?" he asked, his whisper muffled and hollow in the silvery fog.

We hope you've enjoyed Persicus' tale. As new authors, your thoughts are extremely valuable to us. Reviews are very much appreciated. Thank you for reading and helping spread the word about our first novel! You can tell us what you think on Amazon.com and Goodreads.com and come join us on Facebook. Again, thank you for reading and helping us spread the word about The Guardian of the Steppes. Continue on to read about King Yazdgerd on the following page.

# HOMAGE TO A FORGOTTEN KING

King Yazdgerd III was the last Persian King to descend from King Cyrus the Great, the founder of the Persian Empire.

In the early 7th century, the brutal Islamic crusaders—the ISIS of their time—invaded Persia, city by city, much as they are currently doing in Iraq and Syria. After several crushing losses of crucial cities, including the Persian capital, King Yazdgerd III retreated with his family, friends, and the remnants of his army.

Yazdgerd had intended to make his way to China, where his daughter was married to the Chinese Emperor, and return with enough men to oust the brutal invaders wreaking havoc through his land, killing innocent civilians, and destroying everything in their path.

Somewhere near the Pamir Mountains, en route to China, the Islamic crusaders caught up with Yazdgerd and his men. Realizing there was no escape, Yazdgerd and a few brave men took a futile stand against the barbarians, so that his family and the rest of the clan could escape safely over the snow-covered Pamir Mountains, and reach China, who had been their ally for centuries.

After his men were slaughter, Yazdgerd was captured, tortured, and beheaded. Prince Pirooz, Yazdgerd's son, bore witness from somewhere on the mountain, a safe distance away.

Prince Pirooz grew up in China, becoming a General in the Chinese Army. He fought many battles against the Islamic crusaders to avenge his father's death, to try to save what his ancestors had built. He was buried somewhere atop the Pamir Mountain Range, with his head facing his beloved home of Persia.

Prince Priooz' son, Nerseh, chronicled his father's life in a diary, which was recently found in China. It was written in an ancient aristocratic script. Only after the Chinese scholars translated the ancient text did they realize what it was that they had found.

The contents of the diary directly contradicts what all Iranians have been taught since the Islamic invasion—that King Yazdgerd III sought shelter in a windmill and a Christian miller murdered him and stole his clothes. Moreover, it contradicts the story that Yazdgerd's own daughter married a descendant of Mohammad, joining Yazdgerd's noble bloodline to theirs.

At the time of the invasion Omar Ibn-Khat-tab Caliph of Islam wrote a letter to King Yazdgerd III, demanding his surrender and Persia's submission and conversion is Islam.

King Yazdgerd responded to this demand, noting the ignorance of this Caliph's belief that Zoroastrians were polytheist. He pointed out the barbarity of forcing people to convert at the point of a sword, of forcing woman to marry, of killing people who refuse to convert. He also explains that the Persians had, for thousands of years, valued culture, art, kindness, amity, righteousness, and had laid the foundation of philanthropy. He admonishes the Caliph to stay in the desert from whence he came and not let loose this evil upon the Persian people.

*You can view both letters in their entirety at our website:*

www.TheLostTreasureOfTheSilkRoad.com
*Also, join us on Facebook for fascinating updates about Ancient Persia, Sogdians, and more.*

# ACKNOWLEDGMENTS

We would like to thank:
Dorothy Derakhshani—she wrote plenty of this book.
Nick Derakhshani, for reading and critiquing.
Derek Murphy, cover designer, thanks for the great advice.
Carolyn Gramlich, logo design.
Jennifer Fresnedi, GoodReads reviewer, thanks for the feedback.
Ann Bukowski, who proofread for us.
John D. Meyer.
Dr Frederick Ueland.
Casey Wright-Litch, because you read the story like he never will.
And Glee Palmer-Johnson, for running around, yelling "Guardian of the Steppes."

# ABOUT THE AUTHORS

I, Saeed, was born in Abadan, Iran in 1957. Abadan is an island located near the mouth of the Persian Gulf, where the muddy Arvand River flows gently into her turquoise water. My family descends from the clan of the Zand Dynasty, on my mother's side. Karim Kahn Zand referred to himself as *Vakil,* meaning Representative of the People. His reign from 1751-1779 was a period of peace and prosperity. When the Zand Dynasty fell, my ancestors fled in exile to India. My great-grandmother, who was born in Bombay, India, lived with us towards the end of her life. Recalling her many exotic tales of India, I jumped at an opportunity to attend a Parsi school there.

My adventures continued as I explored India, and then headed to Western Europe, living in England for several wonderful years. I came to the United States in 1979, at the height of the Iranian Revolution — known by some as the Second Arab Invasion.

I met my wife, Dorothy, at a Greek restaurant, where we were both working our way through school. We soon married and were blessed with a son and a daughter. We are now proud grandparents of a beautiful granddaughter.

I am a truck driver and an avid history buff. The tale of the Silk Road merchant Persicus and Zoroastrian Princess Nooshin was born in the cab of my 18-wheeler one frigid winter's night, during an intense snowstorm in Michigan's Upper Peninsula. It was ugly outside and my small television had recently died, so I picked up my yellow legal pad, and began to write, mostly to amuse myself and pass the night away. A couple of months later, I sheepishly admitted to my wife what I had been up to. Though it needed some work, she was very excited about the story she read. We refined it a bit and then asked Shirin, our daughter, to edit the book.

Shirin grew up in a remote area of Los Angeles County. With no cable or satellite, we rented and borrowed old movies classics, and she cultivated a love of great film. She eventually made her way to a prominent film school in Los Angeles where she focused her creative talents on editing and sound design. She worked briefly in Post Production before returning to more fulfilling work at a Hospital.

While visiting Saeed and Dorothy in the mid-west, her father asked her to edit his mistakes, since English is his second language. She agreed, and promptly proceeded to re-write the book. At first, stubborn as they are, Saeed and Dorothy objected, but soon they finally realized it was a vast improvement (I mean come on! You can't give away the ending at the very beginning! It drives me mad when authors do that) She took off with the book, adding much more detail to the characters, depth, humor, and intensified the action scenes.

Although she doesn't want credit, Dorothy did in fact work on this book as well, typing in the original from the legal pad, and adding in much detail.

444

Printed in Great Britain
by Amazon

13365014R00263